IN THE TIME BEFORE LIGHT

Ian MacMillan

LŌ'IHI PRESS
HONOLULU

FIRST EDITION

ISBN-13: 978-0-9822535-2-6

Author Photo: Susan Bates MacMillan
Cover Art: Carl F.K. Pao
Cover Design: Robert Barclay

Title fonts in Windlass and Bolton
Text in Adobe Garamond Pro
Drop Caps in Treasure Map Deadhand

Lōʻihi Press
735 Bishop Street, Suite 235
Honolulu, Hawaiʻi 96813
www.loihipress.com

PEER PRAISE FOR IAN MACMILLAN

I am a great admirer of Ian MacMillan's writing–what a careful, responsible craftsman he is!
> — Kurt Vonnegut Jr.

[Ian MacMillan's] stories are distinguished by their powerful sense of place and most of all for the grim humor of their humanity.
> — Paul Theroux

Ian MacMillan is an intense and wonderful writer.
> —Ron Carlson

Ian MacMillan's stories are invaluable and unforgettable.
> — Jonathan Penner

PREVIOUS CRITICAL PRAISE

Eloquently, MacMillan shows that the truth we can absolutely, factually know…is not the whole story.
> —*The New York Times Book Review*

…distinguished by unflinching fidelity to truth, unsparing immediacy and literary resonance.
> — *Publisher's Weekly*

…brings you eye to eye with life in Hawai'i–not the flowery, painted-over stuff but the real nitty gritty.
> — *Honolulu Advertiser*

Also by Ian MacMillan

Novels

Blakely's Ark (1981)
Proud Monster (1987)
Orbit of Darkness (1991)
The Red Wind (1998)
Village of a Million Spirits (1999)
The Braid (2005)
The Seven Orchids (2005)
The Bone Hook (2009)

Collections

Light and Power (1980)
Exiles from Time (1998)
Squid-Eye (1999)
Ullambana (2002)
Our People (2008)

Awards

The AWP Award for Short Fiction
The O. Henry Award
The Pushcart Prize
Best American Short Stories
NEA Fellowship
Hawai'i Award for Literature
PEN-USA-West Award for Fiction
Elliot Cades Award for Literature

TO OUR IMAGINATIONS

CONTENTS

1.

August 20, 1824

That first day I found myself walking alone in the port of Honolulu, ill with a fever and feeling hot and dazed, having committed the error of believing in the helpful effects of alcohol, urged upon me by a filthy sailor named Johnson, who said, "A cold 'ave ye? Why, sop it with grog, sir. It'll burn the fevers out, it will." In this reeling state, the plane of my vision unmoored into a dancing, bright picture as of some bad dream, I paused to lean against a building, at which my hand went through a thatched wall, nearly pulling my body behind it. Those who passed by, sailors and kanakas, appeared in a rapid, smiling animation, and although the port at that time was not a large place, I feared that I had become lost. I did not know that better buildings were just nearby, stores and the like. Where I walked, billows of red dust rose from between the low, ugly structures, and here and there before me, despite the heat and the arid, malodorous dryness of the place, muddy pools reflected the harsh, late-afternoon sunlight. The worst jest so far, I thought. The subject of many a sailor's and merchant's enthusiastic tales was indeed an ugly, wretched place, begrimed and coarse, smelling of rot and iniquity.

Among my pursuits in this place, I had at the time an interest in the military exploits of the natives of the islands, their feather-bedecked kings and ferocious armies, but no native I had yet seen seemed the stuff of a soldier—rather, all the men appeared indolent and mired in a kind of spiritual decrepitude, idling their time away.

A violent assault of mud-pool reflected sunlight on my eyes made me turn, deciding to make for *The Clarel* where a breeze might help. Associates of mine were at that moment making their way to the estate of a Mr. Marin, a longtime resident of this place, but I was in no state for social occasions, and the waning sun meant no more than a lonely evening nursing a fever which I feared would soon be associated with foul eruptions from my stomach or perhaps, if my deeper fears were to be realized, 'fever accompanied with a flux of blood, not proceeding from any external source.' It was my misfortune to have too recently studied the Medical Arts, my head therefore tumid with such terms as epistoxis, hemoptysis, and hemorrhois. What for the filthy sailor was 'a cold' was for me a complicated litany of the terminology of disease, rife with the suggestion of creeping fatality.

From where I stood, the dirt path ran to the port, and ended in an opening between the buildings revealing, farther out in the water, the mast-poles of ships. This reassuring picture put me back on course. The foul, acidic rumblings in my stomach abated, and I heard the laughter of sailors in that direction. Sunset was nigh, and the prospect of a cooling of the air had an illusory bracing effect, a trick of the mind but welcome.

Brought awake, I became aware of my surroundings, to wit: a line of dark mountains rising into clouds, clusters of trees in the crevices of cliffs folded as of a dark curtain—there was one of my goals, to draw and describe the flora of this remote place. I needed to rid myself of months of bodily filth, soothe chafed skin about the neck and loins, and get over this dizzying affliction. Johnson claimed that sea-bathing was cleansing—hadn't I seen the dark, healthy women doing so upon our arrival? Indeed I had. Nature's naked, unabashed children. Extraordinary, I had whispered to myself, seeing them dive headlong into the port water and then climb back up on the docks, water streaming down their bodies. The sight of these young women made my heart race.

I made my way back toward the wharf where I would find our cutter to take me to *The Clarel*, although this time I went by an alternate route, just east of the dirt path dividing those huts. There, not thirty feet from the lane, I beheld another lane, this narrower, fringed with dusty grasses and running along the backs of some of the grog shops. Recoiling at the thought of vermin but driven by a bleary curiosity about this ugly place, I walked on. To my left, toward the parched brown profile of Diamond Hill, I saw English-style houses, and beyond, a multitude of low thatched structures, homes of the savages of this land, I was told. To my right was the Russian fort, now of course no longer Russian, a square walled enclosure overlooking the water.

Between two of the decrepit huts I passed, I saw a man standing, staring at a flimsy wall of stained tent-material, before him on her knees a woman wearing nothing but a pair of filthy sailor's pantaloons. As the odd picture sharpened in my vision, I realized that the woman was holding in her right hand his large, half-flaccid member, by the root, while the other end vanished repeatedly into her mouth, her head bobbing forward and back. She was dark and full-bodied, the sailor older, perhaps in his fifties. I began to turn away in disgust, but was caught by an attack of prurient curiosity.

Then the sailor turned and looked at me, as did simultaneously the woman's face, but not enough to have that pale atrocity drop from her mouth. The sailor laughed. "Can ye believe it sah? She's an 'alf breed, and but tharteen year of age. Can ye believe it?"

I said nothing. Thirteen? I thought. Yes, she was indeed young, and understanding this, I realized at once the exotic depravity of this place, wherein no sin was prohibited. Indeed I wanted to leave, but because of my state, I found myself in an ugly, dreamlike swoon, staring at the girl, who kept on with her work while the sailor continued to smile at me. "Come now sah," he said, placing his hand on her head and moving dark, shiny hair around, "would ye like to put it in 'er? She'll do it for a coin, and it don't matter what coin, I'll tell ye. Can ye believe it?"

I removed myself, and felt a twinge of disgust at the recognition of my own dim arousal at this picture, my head full suddenly of images of fruits of the filthy beggar's invitation, an unwanted shudder of pleasure, so to speak.

Thus I made my way toward the port. The sun was setting, sending nearly horizontal planes of dusty orange light over the path ahead of me. Now, with the abomination I had just witnessed, I felt more awake, perhaps because of a dawning outrage, or at the least amazement, at what I had seen.

I came thereupon to a kind of crossroads, busier with activity than the place I had been. In the center was a mud hole large enough to make continuing toward the port a problem, the water dark now because of the waning sun. There on the other side, two sailors talked, one apparently angry with the other, the second gesturing with an obsequious defensiveness. I saw, too, across the right side of the pool, an old savage wearing sailor's clothes, sitting on a rotted log that went along the base of one of the huts, a bench as it were. He watched the sailors talk, then saw me, and smiled with a look of a challenging arrogance.

I began to make my way around the shallow pool of filthy water, and saw a white woman coming up the lane, well attired and carrying a parasol tipped to the faint orange light. I stopped, remembering the sailor and the young half-caste. Would the swine have discharged himself in her mouth by now, or were they in some other lewd position? I should warn the woman, I thought.

"Madam," I called.

But she had stopped to regard the muddy pool before her. I was about to go to escort her around, a bit of chivalry hastened upon as an escape from those images of the sailor and the wench behind me. But then came a brown child running from the cross-lane, a girl of perhaps eight or nine, wearing no more than a rough loincloth. She changed course with astonishing agility and danced around the pool, in her haste not noticing the white woman, whose dress she then soiled with a single splot of mud from her bare feet.

"Why you rude little fool!" the woman yelled, at which the child stopped and stood at a thunderstruck attention. "You dirty little animal!" the woman continued, shaking the parasol at her. "Look at what you've done!" She leaned over and then lifted the skirt a couple inches, studying the splot of mud.

The old savage looked at the woman and laughed. "An extraordinary display of petulance, my lady," he said. "Were you not once a child, or were you born in your finery?"

"I beg your pardon!" she said.

"That blot becomes you," he said. "An English poet wrote of his boredom with perfection—'a careless shoestring, in whose tie I see a wild civility; do more bewitch me—'"

The woman gasped. "I'll not have this!" she snapped. "You will stop that now."

The child took the opportunity during the lady's distraction to vanish, leaving her staring at the old man.

"You are presumptuous," she said, and turned away from him. Then she sighed and, pulling her parasol shut, went to her right to circumvent the mud hole. This left me staring at the old fellow. What, indeed, had I heard him say? And why did he say it with a perfectly modulated English accent? In fact, the dark, white-bearded old man had quoted the poet Herrick, a man of the cloth but possessed of a despicably indecent sense of humor, a thorn in the side of Puritans.

The muddled condition of my mind had indeed delayed full recognition. A savage who quoted English verse? Nonsense. My mind was playing tricks on me. I studied the dark pool of water, and then chose a direction around to the other side, toward the bench where the old man sat.

Had I gone the other way, this account would not exist. Such are the vagaries of chance. With an idle, somewhat arrogant bearing, for I bore myself generally with the arrogance of superiority in the presence of any native, I made my way around that pond, and in every respect I did not, that day or ever again, go the path I had originally planned.

I slipped as I made some space between myself and the old savage so as not to brush his knees, and riding on my boot-heels, I slid downward toward the mud hole, at which a hand firmly caught my wrist and pulled me aright.

"Aye Captain," he said. "I don't want those magnificent boots sullied by the water."

Upright on the dry dirt, I looked at him—he was as tall as I, lean yet with a physical aspect that appeared at once youthful and but for the mild visage, dark skinned and encircled by white hair and a beard, formidable, strong and quick. Quick enough, I thought, glancing once at the putrid water, to save me considerable embarrassment.

"My thanks to you," I said. "You've rescued some of a wretched day."

The man stared at me. In fact the stare was careful, thorough, if you will, and the only thing that prevented me from looking away or asking him why he stared so was the lingering inebriation that removed the ordinarily defensive propriety I was given to.

"Ah, you have a cold," he said.

"Indeed," I said. "A sailor told me to burn it out with grog."

It took some time for his face to come into focus. There were scars on his forehead, divisions in the white facial hair that no doubt hid scars beneath. His eyes were a deep brown, the whites a stark blue-white, and his teeth were all still there. The skin of his arms, at least the forearms emerging from the sleeves of his dull blue shirt, was hairless and mottled, finely wrinkled as of the neck of a turtle, his hands muscular and bony, fingernails clean, to the carefully trimmed off-white quarter moons of the ends.

"Grog, sir," he said, "is the agent of Morpheus, luring you to ignore your symptoms. You will lose water and end up fatigued and weary, numb and sicker than you would have been. You must drink water."

"Yes, I know that," I said.

He raised his shoulders and held his hands out, as if astonished at my stupidity. He irritated me just then—the idea of being advised by a savage on my condition made me square my shoulders and ready myself to leave.

"Come and sit, sir," he said, at which I did, still muddled and not sure of my balance. Thus placed on the log, I felt more in control of my faculties.

"Say," I said, "how is it that you speak English with—" I searched my mind for the words. "—with such facility?"

"I learned your language on a ship," he said.

"Ah, then you are a native of some other place?"

"I am kanaka maoli," he said. He looked around, toward the mountains, which were a fading blackish green, topped with clouds yet bathed in the remaining sunlight. "Of this place," he said. "Or the place this once was."

"But I am still curious," I said. "One does not learn of English verse on a ship, at the very least verse raised above the bawdy."

"It is a long story," he said.

I was curious, true, but not in the mood for long stories.

"Very well," I said. "I won't press the matter. But I remain interested. Were you here during the time of the great battles of the chiefs? Of Ta— Or is it Ka—the rest of which I have forgotten."

"Yes. Kamehameha, called 'The Great', I suppose not unlike Alexander. I saw him long ago, but was not here twenty-seven years ago at his last great battle." The man then stared at the mountains, thinking. He sighed.

"Up there, do you see it?" he asked. "In the gap between those two tallest mountains. They are Lanihuli on the left, and the taller one on the right is called Kōnāhuanui. There he carried out one of his greatest battles."

"Konahuanui."

"To be precise with the language, you must draw out the *o* and the first *a*, so that your voice holds those two letters longer. Ko-nah-huanui."

"What is up there?"

"A footpath that goes over a high pass, hundreds of feet high, beyond which is the northeast side of this island. I was in other battles, but all this was a long time ago."

I was nearly overcome with a guffaw. Beside me sat an old savage whose accent was impeccable, as perfectly modulated as that of an earl. Why did this seem such high humor? I suppose it was the filth and the ugliness of the place, the image of that sailor's pizzle in the mouth of a child, contrasted with the image of the elegant white woman with a splot of mud on the hem of her dress, all against the dirt, the rude structures, the depravity of the place.

I found, however, that I no longer wanted to return to *The Clarel*. So many months in the presence of dirty, half-articulate men, wretched, childish blighters they were, had left me thirsty for more intelligent social contact, what I might have had at Mr. Marin's house, meeting with businessmen and perhaps, I was told, a French adventurer who had lived here many years. Yet it was here, near this filthy puddle, that I had found just such contact. At length I laughed.

"Sir?" he said.

"My apologies," I said. "It is amusing to me to find someone so well-spoken in a setting such as this."

"I suggest that we change the setting then. Have you eaten?"

"Yes. Too much, I think. I've felt a bit shaky in the stomach."

"A walk will do you good," he said, rising from the log. "Perhaps the beach. It'll be cooler there."

I felt both foolish and uncertain walking shoulder to shoulder with the savage. What motive did he have with me? Would he take me to some dark place and hit me over the head, my money being the object? Or worse, wrap a rope around my neck? I had heard stories—cannibalism, infanticide, incest, brutal if not grotesquely exotic sacrificial practices. But I supposed also that these stories had been embellished over their journey from mouth to ear and imagination to imagination, that some medium of truth lay in the middle.

"By the way," I said, "I am Matthew Davis."

"I am Kaʻalokulokupono," he said. "Those who know me call me Pono."

"Pono," I said.

"And I shall call you Matthew then."

As we walked, I noted that he was leading me back toward the port, which reassured me somewhat. There, I saw oil lamps glinting through the window-holes of grog shops, shadows randomly blocking them, and near the water, where some sailors had built a small fire, we came upon an open area within the sound of water sloshing against rocks.

In a grassy area still in view of the sailors' fire, he stopped and said, "Here it is cooler, and we can sit and enjoy the evening."

I sat, my legs out toward the sound of the water, my hands flat on the ground, supporting my upper body. He sat down, cross-legged, and rested his right elbow on his thigh, his hand cupping his chin.

"Well then," I said. "*Battles*, you said earlier. Please, describe them to me."

He crossed his arms, thinking. "If you were hungry," he said, "would you attempt the consumption of an entire pig?" He shook his head. "I shall tell you of a battle that was small in comparison to the ones you've heard of."

"Good. As I said, or at least intimated, I am fascinated by the legendary ferocity of your warriors."

"My family were of the common class, called makaʻāinana, which is below the aliʻi class, as you probably know."

"I heard that, yes," I said.

"My father was bitter about this, and felt that fate had misplaced us, that an ancient curse had taken our true status from us. But this is another story. So, I will continue: we lived in a valley which was over a ridge from another valley, the two valleys joining just a thousand paces from the water. These valleys formed a V pointing at the path to the water. This path led to what we called Kānalua, or the place of the uncertain winds. It was a remote part of the island, sparsely populated because of the harsh weather. Part of the year our stream ran dry, and our land lay parched under hot sun and forceful winds. The winds present in areas have names, I should interject, and ours was varied: strong one day, weak another, wind here at the stream, no wind thirty paces away at the path. I should say also that we rarely, if ever, saw our highest born—they remained in more hospitable areas, separate from us, their priests and warriors with them. We could not approach their sacred area, and they did not sully themselves by coming to ours, except in cases where their priests collected offerings, at specific times during the year. I will forego the details of this, because it does not add to my account of the battle.

"Our valley was populated by people who came in large part from other places. Normally concentrations of people are related directly, in effect large families, but we were not. The valley next to ours, however, was populated by a group of people who were related, and they were greater in number, their living conditions, soil, access to water and so on, better than ours. They had an elder, or village chief one might say, who had more direct access to the high born than we could ever dream of.

"Then this chief died, and his oldest son, a strong and arrogant man of some twenty-five years, started his reign by claiming both valleys as his own. Hence, a form of tax—fish, foods, feathers and the like, normally shared with generosity amongst the families in our valley, would be collected by his 'warriors'. This information was received by the elders of our valley with dismissive waves of the hands. Nonsense, they said.

"Another claim came a short time later: should the new chief decide he wanted another wife, he would choose as he desired from among our women. Again, the announcement was received with snorts and groans of jocular puzzlement. I should say that behavior of this sort would normally be disapproved of by the king, or by district leaders, because this arrogant ākēkē, or puffer fish as we called those whom you might call 'blowhards', was acting as if he were ali'i, which of course he was not. But in this case I believe those who might have intervened on our behalf either thought this claim was just or simply did not care, because no intervention was forthcoming. We were left to fight it out amongst ourselves.

"Our elder by acclamation immediately prepared for a battle. To call it 'war' might amplify it beyond what it actually was, considering our numbers. In all, we had perhaps fifty men whom we could call 'warriors'. In all likelihood, a confrontation would take place where the two valleys met, at the footpath to the ocean, one I had as a boy walked hundreds of times as I learned the skills of fishing, learned from Kū'ulakai, The Red One of the Sea, the ability to see under the water."

"Excuse me," I said, "but what do you mean by that?"

"I am sorry," he said. "It has nothing to do with my story."

"But how do you see underwater?"

"This would be an improper digression."

"Very well," I said, beginning to think that this man was a liar, or perhaps unbalanced in some strange way. For a few moments he was silent. Voices drifted to us from the group of sailors around the fire, its light dully illuminating my new acquaintance's face a warm copper-brown. Pono, yes, that was his name.

"Well?" I said.

"I am gathering things in my head," he said. "That little error of mentioning seeing underwater has pulled me off my plotted course." He thought more and said, "Very well. As I said, the battle, should there be one, would take place at the opening to the footpath, from which one could see the entrance to the two valleys: dark, lush openings into terraced foothills and a stream for each valley becoming one. Running alongside the footpath were rocky hillsides, boulders of volcanic rock, and in flat areas, the lo'i, or kalo patches of our people. Kalo is a root that resembles your potato."

"Yes, poi," I said.

"Ah, you are aware of that," he said. Then he was silent, apparently righting his ship again. "Amid these patches were the thatched dwellings of the people. These groupings were arranged on each side of the stream, so that the dwellings of the people of the other valley were quite close, up the banks somewhat because of the tendency of this stream to flood." He paused. "I was fourteen years of age, my father perhaps forty. I had two sisters and a brother, all older than myself. Young men are trained from an early age in the fighting skills, and gradually come to favor a particular weapon."

"Ah," I said, "we're getting to the marrow of this."

"Yes," he said. Then he remained silent again, for long enough that I began to become vaguely irritated.

"A weapon," I said.

"Yes," he said. "I am sorry. The word 'marrow' took me to another area. The very mana of us. But like seeing under water, it is too complicated a digression." He shifted, then arched his back and took a deep breath. "A weapon, yes. The one I chose was the ihe lau ma-ke, a hardwood spear of about a man's height, with large barbs around the pointed end. I had two, one to throw and one to hold in combat. I was most envious of my brother, a strong boy and destined to be a koa, or warrior, perhaps for the ali'i. He had a leiomano, which is a short, thick, and spatulate club, not an arm's length, embedded on the edge sides with lines of shark's teeth. He held it in his right hand, a loop of strong cord woven out of my sisters' hair around his wrist, so that he might not lose it in battle. My father had a pololū, a finely wrought spear of perhaps five paces long. One did not throw this weapon—rather the warrior thrust with it, and made it difficult to grab from the other end by a coating of coconut oil." He thought now, as if carefully enumerating things in his mind.

"Our men also carried pahoa, hardwood daggers fashioned in various shapes, but sharp enough to cut a man's throat. Warriors carried clubs of various sizes, including war-axes called ko'i pahoa, all of which had wrist-cords of braided hair or coconut fiber. Cord was also used to make ka'ane, a strangling loop, and another implement called pikoi, or a long cord with a rock woven in one end, used to snag and trip the enemy around the ankles. Cord was used also for rock throwing slings, with which a warrior could loft a fist-sized rock some two hundred paces or more.

"Those are the basic implements of our warriors. As I said, each boy was trained in the use of a weapon. I chose an ihe because I also used mine for fishing. My father disapproved of my using the ihe to fish, but reasoned that because his spear was used to hang gourds, he had little basis to object.

"As I said, I envied my brother for the leiomano, but I would hold my spear trying to achieve a feeling of acceptance of it despite this envy, and whisper 'ihe kauila, ihe kauila' and over time the hard wood it was made of, kauila, became smoother, and took on the dull reflection of the polish of my own skin oil. Over time the little crevices around the heavy barbs became blackened by this oil, and the oil of the fish I killed with it.

"My father also trained us in fighting positions, crouched with left leg forward, the upward thrust, or the proper throwing techniques, using carved branches from other trees to represent the ihe. I was a frail child, sickly and weak in my early years. My father nevertheless encouraged me to compete with my brother. We practiced wrestling and other forms of physical competition, and my brother was, how shall I put this? A great athlete, legendary for his strength in the Makahiki games. Do you know what Makahiki is?"

"No," I said, now more irritated in his manner of telling.

"It is a festival-period of about a third of a year during which war is not allowed. In your English year it would be late fall to early spring."

"I see," I said. "But I wonder, Pono, about all this detail. I suppose I had expected some more efficient presentation."

He remained silent a moment. "Stories can be told in different ways," he said. "My way is to endeavor to put you there, to make you see, feel, and smell it."

"I see."

"However, if this is wasting your time, I can stop here."

"Oh no," I said. "Please continue. Put me there."

He looked somewhere next to my head, the dull firelight changing its illumination on the left side of his face. I waited.

"One can make a claim to rule over his neighbor," he said, "but achieving that right is another matter. The young chief made no move for many days, as if allowing us to prepare. And we did prepare. My father learned that their men had gathered to discuss various strategies, and the elders were questioned on the nature of their dreams and visions, on their readings of signs in the clouds, winds, the night sky.

"It seemed, then, that the young chief's claims were no more than the breaking of wind, or as is said of one who talks without action, the puffing of an ākēkē. Then the situation began to achieve a sort of definition, because of a series of small incidents at the joining of the two streams. One of the chief's warriors demanded the catch of a fisherman from our side of the stream. The fisherman, of course, gave up his fish, but this angered the elders of our valley, who sent warriors to the joining of the streams to take fish from the fishermen on the other side. One incident involved my sisters, who had very long hair. High-born women tended to keep their hair very short. Makaʻāinana women sometimes grew it long because it makes excellent cord. In any case my mother and my sisters were down the stream, having come from the ocean where they had done a monthly purification rite not relevant here. Up on a bluff was a warrior who called to them. You see, they were attractive—"

"Excuse my interruption," I said. My mind had again been invaded by the image of the beautifully endowed child whom I had seen on her knees before the sailor. "How did they dress? Were they matured?"

Pono stared. "How did they dress?" he asked. "Why, with a bark-cloth skirt we called 'paʻu' and sandals, and yes, they were matured."

"That is, naked above the waist," I said.

"Yes, and I am aware of how that shocks you English, or delights you, depending on your aims. Americans too. But I should say that they were attractive by standards of beauty of our world, and by standards of beauty of yours. They were tall and well-formed, with dark eyes and dusky skin."

He stared once again next to my head, and laughed. "I am sorry," he said. "I remembered games they played with me, and my time with them when I was a child. But that is another digression, one that would have me shielding my eyes from the sun before I finished."

He thought, again seeming to will himself into some recollective trance. "My mother and sisters were by the stream, and the warrior, dressed in his malo, or loincloth, grabbed his genitals and shook them, calling to them that he wanted my sisters' hair and would get it by taking them as wives, at which my sisters erupted with saucy, derisive laughter. Then they continued on their way, walking quite fast to reach the safety of the valley opening before the warrior could react.

"It was learned that this warrior was the younger brother of the new chief, who, upon hearing of the insult, was pushed toward action, and this is how the battle started. Being laughed at by comely, healthy girls like my sisters was a spear to the heart of their exalted illusions about themselves, and it required redress.

"My mother was angry at them, because she believed that the offering of hair and perhaps, in my older sister's case, some more alluring cordiality to that fool on the bluff, might have helped avoid what seemed inevitable. My sisters sneered at the very idea of letting that pompous idiot have either their hair or their good manners. The ridiculous display of grabbing and shaking his manhood at them had negated even the remotest possibility.

"My father took the story as a bad omen. He spoke in rueful whispers to his acquaintances, gazed down toward the opening of the valley, his face crossed with an expression of fatalistic repose, and he frequently stopped by the water and fruit gourds in our men's house to softly run his hand along the dully-glinting shaft of his pololū. Our elders sent two men to appeal to our district leader, but we learned that he was across the mountains at court.

"I began staring at the ihe, holding it, then practicing the moves of a warrior, feeling at the same time the melancholy desire to preserve the use I had thus far put it to—fishing. Was I to throw this now at a man? And would I get it back? Clearly not, for it was crafted for a single throw, or if not that, to be thrust and lodged in an enemy's body. The very idea made my hands shake and constricted my throat.

"My brother came down the valley from the area he was living in, with friends and close to women he was fond of. He carried with him a bundle of long sticks, and gathered around him the men of the stream basin, my father and myself included. He appeared to me magnificent, as if I could hardly believe he was that older boy I had once wrestled with and spent entire days throwing our play-spears, and practicing our thrusting motions to the sounds of our ferocious yells, all of this done much to my father's approval and nodding satisfaction. He was proud of my brother, who was taller than I, and stronger than any man we knew. It may be irrelevant here, but he was rumored also to have fathered a child by a woman from another valley, in fact a high-born woman, who, it was said, made herself miserable wanting him.

"In any case, my brother stood in the center of a circle of curious men, all of whom wanted to know if there would be a battle. Thus my brother addressed them, and I translate here, leaving out certain refinements of address that a properly rendered account would include: 'We are to meet two days from now a hundred paces down from where the two streams become one. Our elders have had favorable visions, and see a victory for us. The battle takes place when the rising sun brightens the water of the stream, a trick our enemy is using, because the sun will come up over their ridge and be in our eyes.' At this the men nodded, and spoke softly to one-another. 'But we have decided to allow them that bit of cowardice—we have tricks of our own.' He then looked down at the long sticks at his feet. 'Take these sticks and fashion ihe of them, color out their paleness with dirt, each ihe thrower making two.' The men regarded the sticks with confused skepticism, for they were of different woods, mostly soft and light. I reached down to pick one up—it was not the wood of war instruments. 'Yes,' he said. 'You can break it easily over your knee.' My brother then grinned at the men, and finally laughed loudly, showing his teeth.

"'Tell us,' one man said, 'what we are to do with these.'

"'You are to fashion ihe, as I said.'

"'And would you have us use 'ōhi'a 'ai as rocks, mai'a as knives?'

Pono then thought a moment. I shifted on the ground, to sit as he was sitting, crosslegged, a position I found quite uncomfortable.

"I must explain this," he said. "'Ōhi'a 'ai is a fruit not unlike an apple, and mai'a is banana. Do you see?"

"Yes," I said. "Clever."

"But my brother did no more than laugh once again. 'Do as I bid, and of course bring your ihe and pololū,' he said, and then he left. The men, my father included, were left staring at the pile of sticks. 'It is not even good for firewood,' one whispered. Others watched my brother making his way up the path, their faces showing confusion and growing anger. But my father intervened and said, 'He said that we have a trick of our own. We must do as we are ordered.'

"And so they each picked up two of the sticks and went away to do as they were told. I took my sticks to one of the boulders and began scraping them rapidly against the rough, porous stone, and indeed the wood was so insignificant that the task was easy.

"My mother loved all her children, I believe me particularly because my growing up and remaining alive, then finally becoming healthy, seemed a miracle, and the coming battle seemed a terrible waste of that miracle. She wept at times, my sisters consoled her, and when they looked at me, they seemed to be looking at someone they would not see again. My father never doubted the importance of the as yet unknown use of our poor imitations of ihe, and answered all queries from my mother with 'Be still,' or 'No.'"

"And the trick?" I asked. The change in the expression on Pono's face told me of the impropriety of my query. "Yes, yes," I said. "In due time."

He nodded. The firelight from the right of us illuminated his face more brightly than before, the last of the light having left the western sky.

"I thought, when I was alone, that I was in the last day of my life. My two useless spears now darkened by the red dirt of our valley floor were ready, dismal imitations of the ihe of a warrior. I looked up the ridge toward a place where I had a secret cave, realizing that I would never see it again. It seemed to me that I had lived a very long time, and when I walked from one place to another, I felt old, in fact hobbled feebly, my back bent and my knees shaking, as if I had actually aged far past the age of my father. My hands felt weak, and my heart thumped so that I could see in the foreshortened view of my own chest the movement, a drum pounding in a slow, mournful cadence. The fact that I had quickly become a large boy for my age, something that had seemed to me a gift and had allowed me a certain arrogance among other, smaller and thinner boys my age, seemed now to be a curse, for those boys were not preparing for battle. I would die and my bones would be passed among the enemy to make fishhooks.

"My father must have seen the fear in me because he drew me into the men's house and told me to think bravely, to trust in the visions and dreams of our elders, and to look to my brother as an example of the attitude and bearing I should adopt in the coming battle. He told me he was proud that I had emerged from my sickly childhood to become strong just in time to honor myself and the family in battle. He told me to trust also in the flimsy spears, for my brother was, in addition to being a strong and brilliant warrior, one whose ideas, whose imagination, was the envy of others. How else could a common boy rise to such a lofty reputation?

"I straightened myself up and promised to be brave, and walked to the bank of the stream and stared across, not to the place where the battle would take place but upstream where our land was. I imagined their warriors, and I held an imaginary ihe in my fists and practiced the advance: one step, then stamping my foot and whispering the ferocious cry that I hoped would come from my mouth the following morning.

"Long before dawn on the day of the battle, I was awake, irritated at the beating of my heart and fatigued because of lack of sleep. By that morning I had negotiated with myself an acceptance of my own death. I was saddened about being robbed of a future, and bitter that I had only one experience by this time with a woman. The memory of it swelled my ule, and made the sadness more severe, a sense of sweeping melancholy wetting my eyes and swelling my throat.

"I thought of using my hand to relieve myself and steal one last burst of pleasure from the doom I faced, but upon a very quiet, tentative beginning, I heard my father approach.

"He handed me a finely woven malo, made by my mother and sisters. I put it on, tightly securing my manhood in the pouch, the waist cord tied high above my hips. Thus girded, I sat with my father and ate fish and poi and then went outside where other men were gathering in groups of two and three.

"My father told me to wait for my sisters and mother, who were at that moment wrapping food in ti leaves and putting water in carrying gourds. They would wait near the site of the battle to feed us and give us water should the battle go on for a long time.

"At length they emerged out of the darkness, my mother and sisters carrying bowls. My mother wept. Despite the darkness I could see in my sisters' bearing the fear and the awe at what was happening. I could smell it, feel the heat of fear from their bodies.

"My father instructed them to cover us with coconut oil, and put none on our feet and none midway down our forearms to our hands. He told me not to touch myself after the oil was on, because it would make the ihe slick in my hands. This oil would make me as difficult to grab as an uhu, which is a fish that is particularly slippery. But my hands must remain dry. The oil, he said, would become even slicker when the heat of my body increased, as he said it surely would.

"It was then that we heard, coming from the other valley, gourds being slapped in a steady, slow rhythm. The warriors and elders were approaching. The faint but increasingly audible sound of some self-appointed kahuna calling a war-chant joined in the thumping of the gourds.

"By now the early light had come, making visible the glistening bodies of the men. As if to announce what was about to happen, the wind began to blow in its unpredictable way, first out of the valley, then from the ocean, the smell of sea-foam mixed now with the coconut oil.

"To condense the elaborate processes leading up to the positioning of our men, I will move ahead to when we could see clouds over the ocean, almost blinding in their beautiful, radiant whiteness. We were still in the half-light of the shadow created by the eastern ridge. It seemed to me that the sky over the water, hung with those clouds, possessed a brightness the intensity of which I had never seen, and I thought that they were showing themselves to me in this majesty because it was the last day of my life.

"Our elders arrived, followed by the younger men, my brother among them. As they made their way into position on the bank of the stream, facing the path from which would emerge the other army, the young men moved into our ranks, the leiomano bearers with those who carried the same weapon, the carriers of tripping and strangling cords gathered in another area.

"We were still in the muted light of the ridge-shadowed morning, and the sight of these men made me begin to shake again, I thought so visibly that I would suffer the humiliation of being allowed to go to my mother, up there somewhere behind a boulder in the tall grass, watching, along with other women who had come down the valley behind their men.

"I suppose it was a small bit of good fortune that the shapes of the men of the next valley emerged from the darkness where the path to that valley disappeared into the foliage, because I took the moment to slip behind a boulder, place my spears in the grass, and empty my bowels, holding the cord of the malo aside, my body trembling miserably. I then wiped myself with a handful of grass, and returned to stand with the men, feeling a deep shame at the defilement by my own excrement, the odor of it wafting up my chest like heavy smoke. My stomach felt empty and in a way like an air-space, and that sensation caused in me a strange feeling of sudden confidence, as if killing one of those men, or more, had surmounted self-preservation in importance.

The feeling faded quickly when I saw the opposing army—their number exceeded ours, as did the size and physical definition of their warriors, and this brought the fright back, and then I felt myself being bitten by ants, in the very spot I had wiped with the handful of grass. Their bites were worse deep in the cleft of my buttocks, and I ran my fingers in there to get rid of them, and got coconut oil on my fingers. Reasoning that because my fingers were already slick, I worked at digging them out, and pinching them until I felt no more than a sensation of itching that would have to be tolerated.

"My brother then appeared before the gathering of men. He looked up the ridge, his handsome face composed and thoughtful. 'Soon now,' he said. 'Gather the ihe warriors here.'

"Men turned to call other men into a circle around my brother, who raised the leiomano before him and gestured with it as he spoke. 'You have practiced throwing,' he said. He looked at me, and placed his hand on my shoulder. 'My brother can split a coconut at thirty paces.' I had never split a coconut. I had, instead, fought with it, being unable to get the spear-point out of the heavy husk. He lifted his hand from my shoulder and said, 'You are to place your real ihe at the water's edge, and move back four paces. From this position you are, upon my command, to loft your false spears, one after the other, and as quickly as you can, up, so that their flight describes a high arc, so that these spears will rain down upon them from the sky. Just as you loft your second false ihe, run to your ihe at the water's edge, pick one up and throw it straight at their bodies in a low arc, and prepare to advance holding the other.' The men looked at one another, the logic of this strategy still a mystery to them. 'Listen,' my brother said, 'the spears lofted first will rise in sunlight, but drop in darkness and appear to vanish for an instant—this will surprise them so that, this one time, they will be caught gazing upward, and will not think to deflect the genuine ihe as they come at them. Remember, this must be done only upon my command, and the real ihe thrown as fast as you can.'

"We all looked across the stream at the warriors gathering. We then went and placed our ihe at the stream's edge, all of them lined up in the tufts of grass. We looked up, now having to shield our eyes somewhat because soon the sun would appear over the ridge. Indeed, behind us it had already bathed the hills in light.

"This, as I said, was the place of the uncertain winds, and now it wafted gently at us from the sea, the smell of foam and seaweed gracing it, so that I again experienced a horrible dread, probably because this was the smell that earlier had drawn me to the water to fish. My brother must have seen something in my bearing, the shaking hands, the expression of fright and anguish on my face, because he stepped away from the bank of the stream and came to me, then drew me back behind the men. He said, 'Open your mouth,' which I did, and he spat directly in it so that the tangy saliva hit my tongue. 'E mana i ke akua,' he said, which means 'let it be mana from the gods.' I swallowed his spit. 'You will be brave,' he said. Then he went back to the stream, and I swallowed again, tasting the remains of that spit gratefully, for he had given me some of his own mana, which I felt radiating into my body.

"Three elders from the other side approached bearing their spears and began to thrust them above their heads and come out with explosive yells, at which two of ours did the same. One from our side threw a stone that clattered uselessly on the rocks rising above the running water. Then young men from their side came to the water's edge and advanced partway across, one swinging his leiomano, two more threatening to throw their ihe. The sun's first blinding point of light rose from the ridge. The shadow of the ridge was now but a few paces behind us, the shadows of the men farther from the stream already stretched out on the ground. And then, too quickly it seemed, the blinding yellow-white ball sat on the ridge, warming our faces and upper bodies, and I felt a line of sweat tickling my side, and wiped it, making my hand slick.

"Without taking my eyes off the warriors on the other side, I stooped down and rubbed my hand in the dirt, scraping the oil off. There was no wind where we stood, yet on the far bank the leaves of the trees waved, and then we beheld the magnificent cape of an ali'i waving, undulating with color. Men looked at one another. Some made as if to prostrate themselves on the ground. What was he doing there? My brother saw him too, and said, 'No. Do not acknowledge his presence. It is a bit of fun for him, this battle.' He looked once again at the figure, high on the bank away from the little army. Others were with him there, perhaps kahuna, or priests. They had come as spectators. 'Then we shall give them something to talk about when they go back to court,' my brother said.

"Then, at the time the sun advanced before us toward the water, we realized something else that perhaps even my brother had not anticipated. The dancing water went a blinding silver, the light playing off it in a manner that sent brilliant, nearly blinding flashes of reflected light into our eyes, and in the midst of our reacting to this, turning our faces slightly away and reducing our vision to bright, horizontal slits with those dizzying explosions of light still coming off the water, a rain of stones came down upon us, followed by a ferocious yell of exultation from the other side, and two men fell, others grabbed their legs or shoulders or heads. A man near me sat dazed, two lines of bright blood running down over his cheek. He produced a roar of rage, picked up a handful of dirt, jammed it on the wound, and then rose and reached for his false ihe. He raised it, his face contorted with anger, and I heard my brother's voice: 'No!' at which the man paused. More rocks came at us, and this time we were more prepared, watching as they flew and dodging them, then hearing them bounce off the rocks and dirt behind us.

"Now the majority of their warriors advanced toward the water, preparing to throw spears. The warriors of the cord weapons and pololū interspersed while others with clubs waited behind, and began to spread along the stream's bank.

"Voices behind us, the elders perhaps, yelled for us to be ready to advance, and then my brother's glistening form was before us, him standing at the water's edge, his leiomano in his right hand. He raised it, then shouted, 'Ready!' over his shoulder, and we drew back our false ihe. The warriors on the other side began to yell out a series of explosive shouts, all in unison, as they moved into the water, their ihe throwers just behind them. A man near me growled, 'Throw, throw—what are we waiting for?' But my brother held the leiomano up, carefully watching for rocks or spears. The chanted yells grew louder, and it was clear that the warriors were just at the threshold of attack, when the leiomano fell and we launched our false ihe, up toward the sun, which in that moment blinded us, then picked up our second false ihe and launched those too, as if we were trying to spear the sun itself. Other men were already ahead of me, rushing forward for their hardwood ihe as, in keeping with my brother's prediction, all the men on the other side looked up as the bright, sun-illuminated ihe reached their highest point and then fell, vanishing for a moment in the changed light, at which the men crouched, dodged sideways, parried the spears with their own, and when I threw my hardwood ihe, trying to make my eyes clearly see a target, I saw the other spears already crossing the stream in their low, fast arcs, the one that got there first as mine had just left my hand hitting a warrior in the shoulder, at which he turned away holding the shaft, and then other men screamed in pain as other ihe reached their marks, a stomach, a leg, a strange glimpse I had of one going through a man's hand as he raised it to fend the spear off. I lost sight of mine in flight. I do not know how many seconds passed, because it was as if each of us wanted to see exactly where our own spears had gone, and then were held in an awed captivation by what we saw: men unharmed advancing, other men, perhaps eight of them, addressing with shock and confusion the shafts they beheld vanishing into their trunks, or thighs, or, as I said, a hand.

"But a ferocious yell from he of the leiomano brought us back, and we each picked up our second ihe and walked into the water crouched, holding them low for the upward thrust. The slippery shoulder of a man slid over my arm, and my hip was banged by the forward part of a long pololū, perhaps my father's, I don't know, and ahead I saw the leiomano appear above the slick shoulder of an ihe bearer and then vanish downward to a cry of pain. I had fallen back, feared burying my ihe in one of our own men, but continued to advance, trying to hold my balance on the slippery stones in the stream.

"A strange thing then happened—we had moved under the sunlight, at which everything I saw became rich and dense in color, in its very lucidity, my own hands gripping the shaft of the ihe, the folds of skin, the brown wood and the tensed cords of my wrists, and below, the running water sweeping over my feet with patches of red that elongated and vanished like red smoke thinning out in the wind. With that came the smell of blood and viscera, and the sounds of things had become a din, a nightmare cacophony of yells and reports of wood clacking on wood, thuds, the thrashing of water as feet struggled for purchase on the stones. When I pushed myself forward, the slippery back of one of our warriors drove me back. Then we surged to the side, and I tripped and quickly righted myself on something elevated, but soft, and I looked down just as I put my weight on the stomach of a man whose throat had been cut, at which the sound of a wet, liquid flatulence bubbled from the wide gash in his neck. I fell back, felt a pololū shaft bang the side of my head, then slide along the hollow next to my neck.

"In this loud, jostling struggle, I had not yet seen the enemy's face. I saw for an instant, when there was a division between wet shoulders, the yellow, feathered cape of that ali'i up on the bluff, and then just paces away, clubs rise and fall, and directly before me the straining legs of our warriors, but encircled as I was, I had nothing at which to thrust my spear.

"Then, in what seemed to me magical speed, the point and shaft of a pololū shot from the lower back of the man in front of me and raced past my side, then pivoted in the man so sharply that it knocked me sideways. As magically as it had appeared, it raced back, the shaft and then the point vanishing into the man, at which it came out once again, a few inches from where it had first appeared. The man fell sideways, the long shaft again against my right side. I could not hold my balance, and went to my knees in the water, bracing my fall with the ihe still gripped in my hands so that I bruised my knuckles on the rocks in the streambed.

When I righted myself, pushing against the shaft, it raced away once again, sliding along my side, its point cutting, or scraping my skin. The man speared fell back on me, and I fought to hold myself up, pushing him aside with my ihe, at which there appeared a space, centered by the shaft of the pololū, and I crouched and saw the man bearing it lunging forward, almost as if to try to step on me, looking behind me as if for an instant I had become invisible, the other end of his spear too far ahead of him to use on me, and I rose up and thrust, my ihe running diagonally through the man's low belly, my hands feeling first the subtle vibration of the skin popping at its entry and then a rhythmic series of vibrations as the barbs passed the entry point, then a strange resistance as the spear sunk past its barbs to where the point rammed into bone. The man released his spear and grabbed the shaft of mine and fell back, his hands slipping, and I felt the ihe pulling me toward him and feared losing it. I planted my feet and lunged back, jerking the spear, at which the hole where it had vanished swelled up in a surging pout, followed by a burst of pink and grayish entrails which bloomed on his side, the sharp viscera odor mixed with the smell of excrement. I fell down, staring at the slick, veinous mass, the far side of which held what appeared to me as a large, dripping sweet potato.

"I tried to let go of the spear and found that my hands no longer functioned, as if with a will of their own they had decided to maintain the hard grip on the shaft. The man fell back, pulling the spear, more entrails leaving him. Just beyond that man a warrior was bringing his club down on the face of another, and in three powerful strikes caved the face into itself. I tried to open my hands, and then, recognizing that they had become fused thus because of the tense grip I had maintained, I went face down in the water, twisted the spear so that the now elongated mass of entrails turned in the water, and one by one began peeling my fingers off the shaft with my teeth. When my right hand was free, I used the numb fingers to peel the fingers of my left hand off, and engaged as I was at that task, did not at first see the two sturdy legs planted before me.

"He brought the war-axe down just as I rolled away, and the force of the blow on a rock shattered the blade, bits of it stinging my leg and side, and broke the shaft of the axe in half. I ran downstream, away from him, and unlike the situation earlier, where there was no room, where slick shoulders and spear shafts slid along my body, now there seemed to be altogether too much space, the bodies in the stream near my feet, some away, and when I turned, I saw a warrior twisting a piece of broken spear in a cord which encircled and was buried in the neck of a sitting man who clawed uselessly at it, the image strangely sedate, as if one were leaning over to whisper in the ear of the other.

"A wooden knife bounced along under the water to me, and I picked it out of the water, and stupidly studied the refinement of its fashioning. The handle was imbedded with a core of basalt rock, making it heavy. It was a good knife. Then, as if the inclination to do so had been denied me because of the close quarters of the struggle, I looked outward. There were two dozen dead in the stream, dead long enough that their blood no longer colored the water. The man with my spear connected to him by that mass of entrails was there. On the far side of the bank stood the ali'i, still in his red and yellow feather cloak, leaning on a spear and looking out over the streambed.

"I did not understand why he was doing that until I turned. On the banks of the stream on our side, perhaps twenty men on their feet were engaged in killing twenty men on the ground, while beyond them, warriors ran up the brushy hillside after our warriors, some of whom stopped to throw stones at them. I saw figures farther up on the bluffs, women and children, running. I stumbled downstream. It was as if I had become invisible, because no one seemed to note my presence, not even the relaxed, observant ali'i. Only fifteen paces away, a man bearing a spear prodded it up into the ribcage of a prone man apparently having no success finding his heart, for the man on the ground growled and kicked, his hands on the shaft. Beyond those two was a warrior hammering another warrior's head in, swinging his club as if trying, somewhat wearily, to crack a coconut, and with each blow a pink mist exploded away from the prone man's head.

"I did not see my brother or my father. I stood there in the water, the knife in my hand, benumbed with indecision. They were dead, I realized. Nearly all of us were dead, the largest concentration of bodies creating a small dam upstream of me. If I ran, I would be seen, or perhaps suddenly become worthy of killing. If captured, I might be devoured by some god-image at that ali'i's place of worship.

"I ran. Instinct told me to run toward the ocean, where, if I must die, I preferred drowning in that place I had always felt so spiritually at one with. So I ran diagonally, up the bluffs, around boulders, sprinting along familiar footpaths past lo'i, or kalo patches I knew, and once I reached the top of the bluff which afforded me a wide view of the ocean, I was astonished to discover that I was alone, the yells, clattering of stones, screams of agony, all far away and peculiarly remote, as if part of some odd dream, the sounds hollow and flat, the occasional echo of a yell coming from our valley, and below me, at the stream, the bodies of our warriors which would be pulled up the banks and left to rot, and just below the largest collection of bodies, the man I had speared, the pale line of entrails from the wound in his stomach ending at my ihe, which from that distance was a dark, insignificant twig.

"I turned, feeling airy and without substance, the knife still in my hand. There, as before, the clouds over the ocean remained as huge and brilliant as they had early that morning."

"Matthew?" Pono queried.

The sound of my name brought me back. Yes, I was sitting on the ground in the darkness, staring at the black sky over the water.

"Yes," I said.

"I'd thought you'd fallen asleep, difficult though it would be in that position."

"I'm sorry," I said. "I was not asleep. I was there."

He stared at me for a few moments. Then he arched his back and sighed. "Well, you requested a battle, and I have described one to you."

"A small one, you said. I wonder what a big one would have been like."

He laughed. "I would still be talking while shielding my eyes from the sun."

I sat there, my buttocks numb. I began to feel an irritation about this man, something about his—I wanted to think the word 'intelligence' but finally I thought 'intellectual arrogance,' which seemed more appropriate. He had paraded before me so impeccable a narrative that I could do aught but disbelieve him. His voice modulation, word selection, control over the complicated grammar of the language, had convinced me that the tale could not have been real, for how can one remember the tiny details that he had included? No, it was a fanciful concoction made up and then carefully rehearsed for any fool white man to be impressed by. And the irritation was also for the shameful fact that he did indeed put me there.

"Even in this light, with but half of your face visible," he said, "I detect skepticism."

"No," I said. "I am thinking." In the faint orange light from the fire, the passive gaze showed no calculation, no careful consideration of the 'effect' his story had had on me. He simply stared, white eyebrows raised. "Come now," I said, "one can't remember experience in such detail. Surely this is manufactured from whole cloth."

"Memory is of course an indefinite thing," he said. "But to the best of my recollection, that is what happened."

"But ants? The cords of your wrists?"

"What would be the reason for forgetting that?" he asked, arching his back again.

"Memory selects out the significant and ignores the trivial, is that not so?"

"Perhaps," he said. "But that would depend on how you define the word *trivial.*"

I laughed. Semantic games now, I thought. He was humoring me with his supposed knowledge. I had seen it before—one who has recently learned something cannot resist the impulse to find someone to flaunt it on, and it felt like an arrogant challenge, from one eager to match wits with me, I suppose to match wits with any white man who wanted to accept the challenge. I had always felt that I should treat all humans with a kind of equality, to include Englishmen, Americans even though I do not like them, and natives of any far-off place, but the clever presumptuousness of this man irritated me.

"I am curious, still," I said. "I would like to know how it is that you have mastered the language. It fascinates me that one whose native language is so relatively simple could gain a sense of a language which is, I suppose possibly excluding Chinese, the richest in the world."

"The first assumption," he said, "that my language is simple, is not correct. But I spent many years learning your language, that is, carefully studying its texts—"

"Texts?" I said. "Am I to assume, then, that you can read?"

"Of course."

"Extraordinary," I said, then realized the insult, as if I were accusing him of being a well-trained parrot, which I suppose I had thought he was. "Pardon that," I went on. "I simply mean that command of the language is one thing; command of its textual representation is quite another."

"True," he said. "When I first beheld a page, I was on a ship. I saw an oddly shaped object sitting on a raised platform suspended by a strangely wrought piece of wood, as of a series of fruits skewered through the middle forming a stack waist-high. On the top platform was an object, from the side shaped like the wings of a bird in flight. I walked to this object and looked at its top. There were two soft rectangular blots, each rectangle gently curved, two identical domes, but cut at right angles, top and bottom. The grayish square stains, upon closer inspection, were actually a series of fascinating, minuscule shapes, lines twisted around themselves as of tree roots just above ground level, and I could not believe the effort that had gone into lining up so many of them, so many that it would be difficult to count them. Then I beheld the gaps between these gatherings of tiny rounded-off or squared-off shapes, and thought that perhaps the one who had so painstakingly scratched or dyed these markings into the material, for I had never seen paper before, had suffered from some fatigue, and had moved ahead in frustration because of the very magnitude of the project.

"I saw marks that were larger than others, and whispered to myself interpretations of these—a house, a woman with child, an advancing warrior, a headless man, and so on. I should say that I was alone that first time, and stared at the odd arrangement of markings for some time before a puff of wind lifted this very thin square of material, very tightly woven, and revealed to me another two squares of markings. When I realized that what I was looking at was a very carefully fashioned pile of these squares, all joined on one side, and then opened out so that as many were on one side as the other, I was so astonished that I began laughing. There were more of these marks, I thought, than leaves on all the trees I had ever seen, or drops of rain.

"The first mate then came into the Captain's cabin and said, 'Aye Pono, what keeps you?' I pointed at the object and he said, 'Why, that's a book.'

"'Book,' I said. It seemed then that the first mate believed he had satisfied my curiosity simply by giving a name to the object I referred to. He left, and later I asked a sailor, 'What is a book?' to which he said, 'Bunch of bloody words on a bloody page it is—nothing for you to worry about. Nothing for me to worry about.'"

"An amusing story," I said. "It doesn't occur to one what an object may seem like to one who has never seen it."

"Yes," Pono said. "It was some time before I got my answer to the question, and it was the Captain who finally answered it. He drew me into his cabin and showed me a picture, oddly, of an elephant. You can surmise that if the lower case letter 'b' was to me 'pregnant woman,' then the picture of the elephant was many times more fascinating. Then he took a quill and drew a circle on his thumb, which he then placed on the top of a page, leaving that circle, three times, each successive circle fainter. This I could understand, because of how kapa cloth is made."

"When, may I ask, did this occur?"

"The year Seventeen and Eighty-six," he said. "Thirty-eight years past."

"Oh," I said. "That explains your facility with the language then. Your long experience with it has made you a master, I must say. And who was your Captain?"

"Thank you," he said. "I might not be a 'master' as you say, but I have worked quite diligently to become fluent." He paused, it seemed to me briefly lapsing into that recollective reverie. "My Captain was Roger Beckwith."

"Beckwith!" I said. I reached out and touched his knee. "And you are yet alive?"

He laughed. I recoiled somewhat at the idea that this man had sailed with Roger Beckwith. The name of his ship, *The Tiburon*, was a legend in sailors' lore, and carried with it tales of so despicable a nature—murder, piracy, cannibalism—that he, Beckwith, stood as an emblem of all that is degraded and immoral in the military and merchant trade. But by now his name had faded from the mouths of drunken sailors, receded into that indefinite region of myth, so that any story told about Roger Beckwith would have to be taken with much doubt. I stared a few moments at Pono, and said, "In England, in America too, there's a length of hemp awaiting that man," I said. "Is he alive? No, indeed he would either be dead by now or have reached three numerals in age."

"I have not seen him in many years," Pono said. "Perhaps twenty."

I calculated this out. "But that would mean that he lived into this century. I very much doubt that this could be true. Are you sure it wasn't thirty, or forty years?"

"No, twenty. It was in mid-April of Eighteen and Four."

So he was at it again. How on Earth could he fix the date that precisely when most of us remember something a decade ago by estimating the year? This put me back into an aggressively jocular mood. "So did you yourself eat anyone then?" I asked.

Pono smiled. "Is that one of the stories told about him?" he asked. He shook his head, and laughed softly. "No, perhaps a rumor started by some enemy of his."

I had little more to ask, then, because there seemed altogether too much to ask.

Pono sat, thinking. In that silence I was taken back again to that stream, and in my visualizing of it, of the battle, I felt the need to ask one question. "Would you explain briefly what happened after your escape?"

"It would depend on what you intend with the word 'brief'," he said.

"I withdraw the question," I said.

"Well, is your stay here brief?"

"No, *The Clarel* needs work. I'm stuck here for longer than I had planned, and I must oversee this work, because my family is part owner of the ship. I had planned to stay three months and study some of the flora here, particularly medicinal plants."

Pono looked up into the darkness to the left of my head. "I am familiar with many of them, if you would like some assistance."

"Perhaps," I said. "I must get over this condition first. It's fatiguing."

"Well," Pono said, "I fear I am keeping you from your recovery, then. Are you staying in one of the houses?"

"No, I'm in no condition to occupy anyone's bed. I shall sleep on the ship." I looked to my right. The sailors' fire had begun to die out, making slightly brighter the points of light at the docks. "And how long are you here?" I asked. "Or, may I ask you, what brought you back?"

"I've lost contact with all but a few old people here," he said. "I may stay for quite some time. Soon my sailing days will be over." He stared at some space next to my head. "I have, or had, family whom I think survived past some rather difficult times," he went on. "When I come here, I look for them, my wife and children."

"How old would your children be?"

"They would be in their forties. But I—" There he stopped. I detected some emotion in his expression, this memory obviously paining him. "They were small when I lost them," he said. "But I shall be here for the foreseeable future." He paused. "You are tired, sir," he said, slowly pulling himself up. I did so, too.

"Well, it's been fascinating talking to you," I said. He held his hand out, and I shook it. "Perhaps I'll hear the story of how you are able to see underwater?"

"If you wish," he said. "I'll be here tomorrow, on the same log in the late morning. I am entertained by the odd mixture of people who happen by."

"Very well," I said. "I'll look for you then."

"Then I bid you aloha," he said.

I left him standing there, and made my way back to *The Clarel*. Our little cutter and a half drunk sailor awaited any of us who wanted to be rowed out. There, what awaited me was a somewhat dirty bunk, but because the air had cooled somewhat, I believed I would rest comfortably.

I did not. I was awake far into the night. The tale he had told me was indeed just that—a tale, perhaps fiction, yet in the last faint echoes of that rum-induced inebriation, I kept visualizing the stream, and the battle, as if I had actually experienced it, and not as an outside observer, but rather from inside that glistening tangle of men, with its sights, smells, and sounds, the loud reports of wood against wood and wood against bone, the yells of agony, all of it.

George Swift, the Captain of *The Clarel*, had given me free use of his quarters for whatever work I might wish to do, and I got out of my bunk and went to his door. But it was locked. I suppose he therefore did not mean free use when he was not there. An imperious man in any case, Swift. Perhaps he didn't trust me. Thoughts occurred to me about my aim in coming here, but the invasion of Pono's story presented a new, rather unlikely idea to me.

I am not an anthropologist. That is, discourses on human nature do not greatly interest me. But the word anthropology, with what seemed to me an almost seductive sound, echoed to me another word, in fact two of them: anthropothysia, which is the practice of offering human sacrifices, and anthropophagy, the practice of eating human flesh, both of which were attributable to such places as my location. The notion that words are somehow seductive might seem preposterous, until you think about it. Pono was seduced by the word 'leiomano', in some odd mental affliction that imbues words with a certain power. Why does the word 'suction' both mean a concept and also sound like the very sound produced when the event takes place? The word I recalled is 'onomatopoeia', which has itself no capacity to seduce.

But then I guffawed at these musings—the notion of allowing Pono to continue any of his narrative would be in effect an admission that I believed him, or at least believed that one could have a memory that precise and lucid.

So I tried to sleep, to rid my head of that imagery, of oiled bodies and taut cords in the wrist, and found myself speculating again on that young wench on her knees before the sailor. That I had indeed seen, in fact had conjured images of her offering similar ministrations to me, to my shame, but the picture I retained had strangely faded, as if that which I had not seen had carried with it even more credibility as experience.

2.

*W*ith the bright light of morning cutting across the deck of *The Clarel*, the shadows of the mast and rigging sharp on the oiled planking, I looked out over the structures fronting the harbor, at the line of high mountains to the northeast, and mulled over my situation: indeed I had gone over in my mind many times the details of what Pono had told me, and I reasoned that if this tale was the account of a 'small battle,' what of the others he had been in? In addition, if he had sailed with the brigand Roger Beckwith, what tales could he tell in regards to him? Beckwith was a man to whom much in the way of crime had been attributed, these crimes mostly in that mysterious part of the world far west of where I stood, and although sailors' tale-spinning was known to exaggerate into fantasy and myth, Beckwith's 'attributions' had achieved a level of renown that had rendered him an equal to Attila the Hun or the Devil himself.

I had read, over the years, accounts of our explorations into distant lands, and had also felt the want of precisely the sort of vividness that Pono had provided. What if I were to try to record such narratives? Others had done it, some to their financial benefit, although having come from some wealth I needed none of that. Would England appreciate something more believable, something perhaps closer to the Truth than either the fantastical tale of an inebriated sailor or the somewhat vague, pompous rhetoric of the scholar? I returned to my cramped quarters, where I had some books and a small desk. Standing there, I stared at the desk and considered the idea.

But allowing this man to tell his tales still irritated me. I shook my head, gazing around at my quarters bathed in the dim lamplight, feeling the first shadow of an understanding about myself, that I could be subtly affected with envy in regards to him. No. He was no more than a savage who had somehow appropriated our language and manners, a thing about him that despite his warmth and apparent lack of ulterior motive (something I yet remained uneasy about), he had in a way stolen our language and manners, and it is this, I think, that irritated me most. To assign to a man like that the mantle of 'intelligence' seemed problematic—do we assign those of inferior culture with this feature? To use the idea of 'cleverness' or perhaps 'intellectual nimbleness' was acceptable, but beyond that I was not sure I was willing to go.

But the recognition of the very nature of my own musings in a way shamed me. Was my own self-image being somehow tested? Were my own doubts about this man's mental acuity simply a manifestation of doubts about my own? I thought, then, that I should be more accepting perhaps, more amenable to the idea that the world had many remarkable cultures and people of those cultures. The use of some sort of a record of the man's experiences was undeniable, for the very aim of exploration is to discover, and Cook had started this out for us, at least in these regions. Even if only to honor the great man's memory, perhaps carrying on with discovery was just, and useful. I should precede any decision with a series of queries: are you telling the truth? Is your facility with our language what I think it is, or rather, is it limited in terms of a very careful preparation of a single tale after which there would be no more, or at least no more of the quality of that tale? Would you be willing, then, to reveal more of your past experiences, if not all of them? At which, of course, I thought that perhaps we did not have a decade in order to complete the task. Could you be 'efficient' in your narrative? In addition, I would have to find someone nimble at writing. In a place like this, the likelihood was of course remote, but I thought I might try anyway. If not, then I might have to do it myself.

I had a few matters to attend to before going out to find him: the donning of clean clothes, not so much for presenting myself properly but because my clothes had gone quite filthy and uncomfortable; and some repast—the desire for which somewhat enlivened me with the conviction that perhaps my medical condition had improved.

Within an hour it was done, *The Clarel* having maintained eating quarters for the men assigned to remain aboard. The ship's cook was one of the filthiest beggars I had ever beheld, and in an amazing irony prepared food that seemed fit for a duke, in this case kippers, biscuits with jam, and tea. Even the hand that placed the plate and cup upon the long table was one not to be shaken, yet the food on the plate was immaculate.

I made my way out to the deck to request transport in, and once on land, walked in the direction of the mountains, observing as I went a rather vigorous movement of people, dock workers, merchants and many natives of the island in European dress going here and there, and a rather odd sight: a carriage drawn by four natives, followed by a small retinue of other natives, a figure of a native woman sitting inside, a large figure, jolly and smiling, and waving at the people who had stopped to observe her passing. When the fascinating parade passed, I asked a kanaka standing on the roadside who that was. "Da queen," he said, "on her way to church."

So, that was the Queen of the Sandwich Islands. Extraordinary, I thought.

I did not find Pono on the log. The large mud pool from the previous day had receded to the size of a drawing room rug, flies hovering over it. So I sat down on the log, and waited. As I did so, I again wondered about the use of this idea, and concluded that a man of some means as myself can do what he pleases, and although this did not 'please' me, it was nevertheless something I wanted to do.

After perhaps ten minutes I beheld the figure approaching on the cross-path to the same intersection of dirt paths. I found myself studying his gait, rather square-shouldered and youthful, with him appearing alert to his surroundings, almost as if he were looking for someone.

He saw me from a hundred feet, and held his hand up in greeting. "You are well today?" he asked, approaching. He sat down on the log next to me.

"Yes, I am feeling very much improved," I said. He nodded, and there was a somewhat awkward silence, which I broke as follows: "I would like to propose something to you." I went on to describe for him my aim, first complimenting him on the quality of the account he rendered for me the previous evening, an account, I told him, that I would like repeated. If he were to accept the task of giving account of his experiences, I would reward him amply in British Sterling. I noticed that as I explained this, his face gradually went dark, as if in some rueful contemplation of this idea.

"I would not require payment of any kind," he said. That metamorphosis I had witnessed in his facial expression, from a musing skepticism to a dawning of understanding and finally to a grave and haunted contemplation, caused me to wonder what doors this proposal had opened in his mind. "But surely you have other matters to pursue here."

"I'd rather do this," I said.

He stared toward the mountains, and seemed locked in that grave and haunted contemplation. "The entire story?" he asked.

"Yes, from the beginning."

"It would be impossible," he said.

"Why?" I asked, thinking that some whim had forced a change of mind.

"It must involve selection, for a complete account would exhaust a lifetime of talking," he said.

"But of course," I said. "You may summarize as you deem necessary."

He thought about this. "Yes," he said. "I suppose that would be possible, although any compression insults the experience summarized. Selection is a process that necessitates incompletion. We cannot call it 'complete'."

"Very well," I said. I fell back into that same series of suspicions about him that had occurred to me the previous evening. "I am still curious," I said, "about your apparent ability to remember things so clearly. How is that possible, I wonder?"

He looked at me, then said, "Please name for me your great-great grand-father, his dates of birth and death, and the names of his children."

"His name was Oliver Davis," I said. "But his dates I do not recall. If I needed such information, however, I could look it up."

"The information is in a document," he said. "We of these islands did not have the advantage of a written language. For this reason all such information resided in the po'o." Then he tapped his head. "What for one culture is an advantage has its own consequent shortcoming—you don't have to remember things, so therefore you don't." He thought a moment. "But we kanaka had to be able to keep information in our po'o, and I should point out that even in our daily lives we had much to remember. Cultivating a skill at recollection was central to making our way in the world. If you wish, I can name my forebears back for ten generations." He raised his eyebrows, then laughed. "I am sorry," he said. "The expression on your face told me just how frustrated you would have been had I proceeded. He raised his hands and brought them down on his knees. "Well then," he said, "how do we proceed?"

In sum, the task was executed as follows: we made our way to the grog shops. Although it was but ten a.m., men were already florid with drinking, jolly and stupid. There were at the time in the Port of Honolulu perhaps thirty-five of these shops, rude structures divided one third to two thirds by a bar of splintered planking, behind which were casks and flagons, and then lines of dull pewter or tin cups. Behind these planks was usually a proprietor, who might be a white man or an enterprising islander, and a large man bearing a heavy truncheon. The drinkers, mostly white men, were deserters, riffraff who had beached themselves here, perceiving a lifetime of revelry. They were of many nationalities, but they lacked money, and worked at temporary labor about the docks, and what money they had they wasted in these shops.

I functioned as no more than a bystander as Pono went from proprietor to proprietor enquiring as to the possibility that a man versed in short-hand might have washed up on these shores. I was fascinated at Pono's social skills. He made himself likeable to all in but ten seconds. Sailors who had jumped ship feared being apprehended by their injured employers, and Pono had to convince most he addressed that first, he was not "hunting" for anyone.

The candidate that surfaced for us, that morning, was one Ethan MacFarlane, who was pointed out by the barman, that man sitting over there against the wall reading. Indeed I experienced a flicker of optimism, the book he held seeming proof of his literacy. We approached the young man. He was sun-darkened and somewhat shabby, his clothes worn and his brown hair longer than seemed proper, making me wonder what life forms resided in it. His face seemed to me mild enough, however. Upon perceiving the two of us standing before him, he closed his book, and looked up.

Pono took the challenge of presenting to Mr. MacFarlane the details of our enterprise. The young man, or I should say, younger than I, perhaps thirty, listened carefully. Pono concluded his presentation and said, "What do you think sir? Would you be willing to accept this employment?"

"I reckon so," the young man said.

I believe my face must have lost some of its color there. He was an American, and considering the late war, and what I had heard about the competition for alliance here where we stood, between His Britannic Majesty and that American 'President' Monroe, who had planted an arrogant 'consul' named Jones here in Honolulu, I wondered whether or not I could tolerate the man's presence.

I tried to remain cordial. "So what brought you here?" I asked him.

"I came aboard a merchant ship. Stayed because the place pleases me."

"And what is that you're reading?" I asked.

He held the book up so that I could read the faded gold lettering on the back rib, a gesture only an American would use, for simply naming the book would have sufficed.

"More," I said. "*Utopia*. And I assume you've found it here?" I asked.

He smiled and opened the book, and read as follows: "'...nature herself prescribes a life of joy (that is, of pleasure) as the goal of life. This is what they mean by saying that virtue is living according to nature. And as nature bids us mutually to make our lives merry and delightful, so she also bids us again and again not to destroy or diminish other people's pleasure in seeking our own.'"

"Ah," Pono said. "A capital sentiment."

"And I assume that when you were informed that writing this down was part of the enterprise, your rather vague nod meant that you write nimbly enough to produce a readable text?"

"That there is what it meant," he said.

Why they either use gesture or vague implication in the place of simple language baffled me. Were all Americans like this?

Thus it was agreed upon—Mr. MacFarlane said that he could get a small anteroom attached to one of the shops, wherein we could conduct our business. In addition, he pointed out that he'd rather I tickled the palm of his hand at the end of each day, as opposed to paying him weekly.

MacFarlane ended by picking up More's *Utopia*, opening it, and looking at a page, then coming to as if he had forgotten something. "The only paper I've got is drawing paper, and the pens I use are for drawing."

"We'll find pen and paper," I said. "There are stores here that have it, I believe."

We chose ten a.m. as a starting time each day. Activity at that time is more the business of port-work, far enough from our thatched anteroom that all but a few sharp reports of metal on metal or the slap of fresh boards being dropped upon other boards remained barely within the range of our hearing, and occasionally we heard the cannon reports of ships coming in, followed by cannon reports from the fort.

MacFarlane was unkempt and somewhat clumsy, yet when he sat down before a blank ledger we procured at the port, he appeared at once to be efficient and studious, a line of quill pens and a bottle of ink next to the open ledger, bits of sunlight coming through the breeze-animated thatch dancing in little coin-sized circles on the desk.

That first day, as we placed ourselves on two chairs at MacFarlane's desk, there was a long moment of awkwardness, as if we had suddenly no idea of how to proceed. Just outside, an old man in a filthy smock, a daft beachcomber muttering over an open Bible, shuffled along the lane apparently looking for sailors sleeping off their inebriation so that he might have someone to preach to. He poked his bearded face through the door opening and stared at us. Pono bade him good day, and he said, "Ah, may the Lord bless you," and looked with watery-eyed confusion at his Bible, and went on.

At length MacFarlane picked up a quill and dipped it carefully in the ink, and wrote on the top of the first page the date: August 22, 1824. With the soft scratching sound of the quill, Pono looked at me with an uncertainty, as if not knowing exactly how to begin. MacFarlane looked up from the ledger, his eyebrows raised.

"Before we begin," Pono said, looking at the empty doorway, "I should tell you how I plan to go about this."

"Very well," I said.

"The story I told you two days ago involved an experience I had at the age of fourteen. I shall begin at the beginning and make my way to that day I described to you. As I said, it involves selection, and invites the criticism that many things have been left out. I can do nothing about that, unless you are prepared to sit here for a year."

"Very well," I said.

"Then shall we proceed?"

3.

My father believed that our family line was afflicted by a curse put upon us in the time before light. That time is called Pō, the limitless darkness, wherein the only inhabitants were the gods. They existed in a place called Kahiki ka-papa-lani, or the high sky. In time they decided that Pō was incomplete without ao, or day, and so they endeavored to change the darkness, first creating creatures to occupy the light of day. This was accomplished by the heavens rubbing the earth, Pō dividing itself into the male, or Kumulipo, and the female, Pō'ele, and the male force and the female force together made the creatures of the sea, then the winged creatures, the creatures of the earth and water at once, amphibians they would be called.

The gods then created the gods Kāne and Kanaloa at the same moment they created Ki'i, the first man, and La'ila'i, the first woman. It is here, in this creation, that the curse is said to have visited our line. Between Pō and ao, the latter the first day of light, the unborn Kāne was whispered to by a sorceress who before there was light predicted that his issue would be stolen from him by Ki'i. And indeed this happened, because Kāne the god slept first with La'ila'i, and then Ki'i slept with her, thus stealing Kāne's children from him. The sorceress goddess, anticipating this, cursed the line of generations of one of La'ila'i's children, decreeing that one male child would, at the whim of the gods, be stolen from the father, then the stolen child would turn upon him and force him to prostrate himself in humiliation at his son's feet.

The curse was seen in a dream dreamt forty-four generations ago by an ancient forebear, and passed down generation by generation to my father. The result was that each visitation by this curse displaced the father, from village chief to commoner, from commoner to kauwā, or outcast. My father told me once not to mention this curse, for it was an offense to some, and besides, the curse was based solely on someone's dream. Many claims are made on the basis of dreams. If a weak man dreams that he is strong, does he wake up strong?

When I began hearing of this, I was perhaps seven years old, a time in a boy's life when curiosity blooms in the po'o, a pleasant fever burning there that wants all questions answered. I would find him in the morning, sometimes making a fire near the men's house if the fire had gone out during the night. I would sit and watch as he picked up the fire stick and said, "This belongs to Kū as the coconut tree belongs to Kū." He would hold the stick out and say, "Male," and point to the block of wood centered by a smooth trench and say, "Female." He would commence the vigorous rubbing of the stick, which, burning rapidly in a tuft of dry fern root, would produce a thin line of smoke.

When it was cold in the mornings I would fight the impulse to run to the women's house to push against the soft, warm flesh of my mother, and as time passed, I reveled in a manly rejection of that warmth in favor of being with my father, cooking and tending the fire, exclusively the business of men.

I came to see my father as a man ensnared in a perpetual bitterness, so that all he did was done with a brown visage crossed by an expression of doubt and long buried anger, and I wanted to know where this anger came from.

As I grew older he told me. First he told me of the curse, how according to his forebear's dream, a jealous god was to be helped by a sorceress eager to taint the lives of men far into the future. But for more than thirty generations the kanaka maoli lived in peace, under the protection of their own gods and the great gods responsible for our very creation. The visitation of the curse had a force of import equal to the relative sedateness of life: a son would fall in love with the daughter of a powerful village chief, and once married he would return as a superior to his father, causing the sting of humiliation but no more. We must all grow old seeing those who were children rise up and insult us, he said. You, perhaps, will do this to me, but if you do, at the very least I will know why.

Ten to twelve generations prior to my father's generation, however, was the arrival of the new aliʻi, who made their way here from a far-off land they identified as Kahiki, and they proclaimed their divinity, telling the people of the land that they traced their line back to the gods, and in time they grew in power.

My father recited to me, more than once, a chant created by one of his forebears about their invasion into our peaceful world. Here is a part of it, which I offer translated into your language:

Then came a storm from the sea
The huge storm
And it blew down our houses
And ripped the kalo from the earth
The storm from the sea

With the harsh voice
And the storm threw us to our knees
The storm of the harsh, crackling voice
And the harsh-voiced storm
Took Kamaleʻeʻs wife
The storm plucked the feathers from the birds

Like many poems and chants, this is a conceit natural to our language as it is to yours. The people from afar are the storm from the sea. Because their language differs from ours, in that the *k* sound, which we render with the softer palate in the back of the mouth, is analogous to their *t* sound, which involves more the middle part of the palate, the chant identifies the 'harsh, crackling voice.'

The storm ripped the kalo from the earth means that these new aliʻi, with the help of their priests and warriors, took from the kanaka what they pleased, and proclaimed that, as they were close to the gods, in fact themselves close enough to be divine, it was our duty to serve them. The storm stripping the feathers from the birds is the aliʻi needing many birds to make their feather malo, their cloaks and bright kahili, which as I described to you earlier is a standard of sorts, on a long pole pointed at the bottom so it can be put in the ground.

The storm took Kamaleʻeʻs wife. This line narrows the chant's focus to my father's moʻo, or line. Kamaleʻe was my father's eighth generation forebear, whose wife was very beautiful. During her second pregnancy she was taken as a consort by one of the koa of the aliʻi, and Kamaleʻe was angered, then saddened by this. He loved her, and could do nothing to get her back. Years passed, Kamaleʻe going about his daily business with his face held in an expression of bitterness and doubt. He had his remaining son, who watched his father, I believe, just as I watched mine, speculating on the lined brow and sad eyes as he moved the fire stick in the tuft of dry fern root. Kamaleʻe knew that his lost son had entered the priesthood, and would become a high-ranking member of the king's closest associates. Boys who enter the priesthood are hidden away and educated in the matters of the spirit-world. They cannot cut their hair or their beards, and so priests appeared always as figures with tangled hair. Kamaleʻe knew that his wife was yet alive, and dreamed of her every night, to awaken each morning to his work, his face held in the expression of the perpetually dispossessed.

Eventually the aliʻi who had stolen his wife died, and that aliʻiʻs son became king of the district. Believing that the situation had changed in the absence of the aliʻi who had stolen the woman he loved, he endeavored to inquire after her during a ritual that takes place when a new king takes power.

Each village chief, each high-ranking member of a district, goes to the king to recite his lineage. Kamaleʻe was not considered ʻaliʻi by people of this family, and in effect endeavored to both see his wife and to commit to record his moʻo, all the way back to the gods. He believed that his wife, who still loved him, he was sure, would mitigate any doubt, or perhaps outrage, at the presence of this supposed makaʻāinana. Kamaleʻe himself would present the case for his family.

The risk he took was great, for by this time one could be put to death for breaking even a small kapu, or taboo as you might call it. It required only a priest to sanctify the punishment. Men had had their legs broken and heads crushed by clubs for the sin of fishing on a kapu day. Men had had their throats bound by cord for the sin of trespassing on the sacred ground of the aliʻiʻs living area. But Kamaleʻe was enflamed by hope, and also by bitterness, that perhaps a public account of his ancient forebear's dream might somehow result in his and his family's proper re-enfranchisement.

So came the day of the ritual. With his first son he made his way to the house of the king. Men gathered at the king's house, and one by one entered, on their knees, to rise and recite their families' lines. If the priests and king felt favorable toward the petitioner, perhaps more property would be awarded, property taken from those whose presentations did not please the king. Kamaleʻe looked at his eldest son and then entered, on his knees, and then with the formal announcement of his name, stood to recite his genealogical past. As he did so, he looked around at the feathered cloaks, the kahili, the priests listening, the koa positioned around, their ihe and koʻipahoa in hand, and rested his eyes on one priest, and there saw the eyes of his wife. This enlivened his spirit, for his son, the kahuna and apparent advisor to the king, stood close to where the king was seated. As the account of his family's past neared its end, Kamaleʻe felt his heart beat with joy, because his son did lean down and whisper into the ear of the king.

The following was witnessed by my forebear nine generations back. As men outside waited for their names to be called, koa emerged, then the priests, the king having remained inside the great house. Kamaleʻe was led out of the house and into an area not sacred, and there he was forced to the ground and his legs and arms broken by clubs, leaving him looking like the dull tan shell of a dead crab. Then did the king and his kahili bearers emerge from the great house and approach the prone, groaning figure. As the king passed, all fell to the ground and averted their eyes.

Kamaleʻe's eldest son, looking along the ground like a lizard, saw his father held down, after which the priests approached with the bright kahili. They then lifted them and lowered their points into Kamaleʻe's eyes and dug them out, the feather standards waving, and Kamaleʻeʻs son heard the sound of wood thudding the bone of his fatherʻs eye-sockets, and heard the vibration of the long shafts as the priests pivoted the points in their removal of Kamaleʻeʻs eyes. Thus Kamaleʻe was left by himself, to be offered to the gods later. He could not be touched now by any but a priest, because in his unclean state, he was defiled by his own blood, by the very mana of him leaking from the hollows of his broken bones.

So ends the tale of Kamaleʻe, victim of a curse visited upon his line by a sorceress intent upon mitigating a godʻs jealousy over the first woman, at the very end of the period of the endless darkness.

As you recall, I said that I heard these stories as a child, usually sitting with my father as he tended the fire, myself watching as he added each new sentence, he watching me so that he was sure I heard and understood, so that I might not forget, for the existence of a family depends upon an accurate account of its past, even though Makaʻāinana were forbidden to cultivate the arrogance of preserving anything but oneʻs makua, or parents, and ʻaumakua, departed forebears who live forever in the form of living creatures like the turtle, which is my ʻaumakua.

The bitterness my father carried as a lifelong burden was one that exerted little if any pressure on my back. Life itself seemed so much a marvelous gift that the curse was but a minor thing. As I grew older, I learned more about the reasons we lived the way we did. Our Kauhale, and I suppose the proper name in English would be *homestead,* was composed of five important structures on an excellent plot of land commanding a view of the ocean, and close to the base of a mountain so that sound itself had a rich, reverberative timbre, our property line a short walk up from a stream.

Of the five structures, one was for men, three for women, and the fifth was where the sexes joined. The same arrangement was the case with any prosperous family, and may yet be, I think, in some areas of our islands. The hale mua is the menʻs house, and the hale ʻaina is the womenʻs eating house. Each is forbidden to the other. The other two womenʻs houses are the hale keʻa, or menstrual hut, and the hale lua, where women make kapa and talk amongst themselves. The common house is the hale noa, or free house, where men and women may mix. One cannot eat or make fire in this house. Men may not eat with women, and so they eat in the hale mua.

I perceive that you begin to grow irritated with the elaborateness of this description. I shall simply move on, and then imply what the significance of this arrangement was, and I say 'was' because from what I have observed recently, these traditions are now nearly dead.

As a boy and son of an important man in our ʻiliʻāina, or area within our ahupuaʻa, or district section, I saw the world as a place of great beauty, endlessly fascinating, from the smallest creature on a plant or in the sand, to the immense, brilliant clouds, to the multitude of stars at night. I had also a fascination for females, the slight difference between myself and my sisters, whose bodies seemed to me softer of limb, and not as heavily boned as mine. The sexual difference was obvious to the point that at eight or nine years of age, it meant little. I was fascinated more by their closeness, perhaps because of the similarity of their ages—they could lie naked on the beach facing one another, their heads not a foot apart, and talk for hours with an earnestness that baffled me. And of course for them it was that soft cleft, for me it was the ule and huahua. My father told me that the first coconut tree brought from Kahiki had two coconuts, and that all trees were descended from that one, each an ule penetrating the ground, the huahua above, nestled in their hair. The tree belongs to Kū, as do all things straight in nature. I would study my sisters, thinking about this difference, and at others times, dismiss them and conclude that this was the way nature and the gods had arranged things. What did it matter that humans were divided into these two types?

But I enjoyed my sisters' company, for they were only one and two years older than I. The older was Laka, named after the goddess of the hula, and the younger was Kaʻahupāhau, which is a name drawn from a shark goddess. I should here insert my and my brother's names with an explanation: inoa, or names, form the bearer of the name. Mine is Kaʻalokulokupono, which means *fearless, with goodness*; that is, it suggests a fearless goodness, perhaps goodness that is without hesitation. My brother's name was ʻIolana, which means *soaring hawk,* which indeed he was, a powerful warrior.

When I was eight or nine, the world I knew had its own order. Men and women lived their largely separate lives, yet my contact with my sisters was familiar and without taint. We ran on the bluffs, wrestled, played games. Life for a child was very close, I suppose, to the brief statement read by Mr. MacFarlane from More's *Utopia.*

The ocean was the source of the greatest enjoyment. We played games of our own invention, involving such things as throwing stones made of wet sand at targets, or holding our breaths underwater, and the like. It was at this time that I began requesting permission from my father to fish, because other boys who were my friends were allowed sometimes to fish, and my weapon was a toy ihe I had made, with barbs at the point. My father was reluctant because certain fish were kapu, and fishing itself was kapu sometimes during the year. Fishing was the business of men. How could I know if a fish I caught belonged to the aliʻi and not the makaʻāinana? If I caught a kūmū, did I know that it was not to be touched by women? Did I know which fish were noa, or 'free'?

I sensed in his explanation a sort of ill-concealed jocularity—he assumed that I could never catch a fish, but continued anyway, like a man trying, despite his knowledge of the uselessness of the enterprise, to explain the lunar calendar to a pig. I believe that he finally allowed me to play at fishing because he was first convinced that the gods' wrath was no real danger to me, because youth meant ineptitude.

I had by this time used sharp stones to fashion an ihe, dreaming of great achievement in battle. The stick was of a strong wood, and I scraped at it with stones and ran it against the rocks at the stream's edge, until my arms wearied with fatigue, and the skin of my fingers grew blisters. I used pieces of coral to rub around the barbs. I showed my spear to my father one day, and as he held it in his hands, thinking, I asked, "Is today noa?" and he said, "Yes, today is noa," and shook the spear. He touched one of the barbs and said, "Maika'i," which means *excellent.* I understood the look of doubt on his face, because what he held was not a stick. It was carefully fashioned, straight, and I believe he was trying to determine exactly how it was that I had made the barbs.

So when my father released me from my job of pulling weeds that were trying to choke the 'uala, or sweet potato plants, and picking tiny insects off the leaves, I took my spear and went down the path to the ocean. I saw boys out in the water, floating in the waves that broke over the reef some distance from the shore, and went into the water thinking that their play was merely wasting time, and that I was educating myself to become a great fisherman.

But the problem was obvious once I opened my eyes to what I already knew, that one cannot see under the water—the vague, shifting wash of colors, which I had been familiar with for years as I had worked my way through it to find my sisters' legs while we played, now became an obstacle I knew would never be overcome.

I dove down, and brought my eyes close to the bottom, at which things clarified somewhat, but I was looking at pebbles. Then, recalling the games I played with my sisters, I moved into slightly deeper water and blew the air from my lungs, at which I sank slowly to the bottom, once again to stare at pebbles. Perhaps I could find a hole and probe with the spear and catch a he'e, or what you call an octopus, but I knew that men had already perfected methods of doing that, either by walking through the water and looking down into it, or by using hooks decorated with bright shells to lure them from their holes and jerk them out of the water when they pounced.

After floating around for some time, I gave up in despair, miserable because I had not gone out to roll in the surf with the other boys. That night, lying in the radiated warmth of my mother's and sisters' bodies, I had a dream in which I saw underwater, and moved in the heavy medium like a fish, and a voice told me that I should not release myself from the hope of seeing under the water. I told the voice that I would go on without fulfilling that dream, and then I felt a series of punches on my shoulder—Ka'ahupāhau told me that I was snoring, and I rolled off my back and went to sleep.

Two more days I tried. Both days I saw only that brilliant, vague wash of colors. Perhaps the dream was a joke at my expense, I thought, carrying my spear home and shivering, my eyes stinging. At night that same voice, speaking very softly to me, urged me to return, after which I received several slaps on my head from my mother, who ordered me to turn over on my stomach and then sighed in exasperation.

Perhaps seeing under the water was not seeing as I knew it, but some other way of seeing. I would go in the water, assuming that the trick was to imagine a fish, and then thrust. Perhaps this was the method advised in riddles by the soothing, encouraging dream-voice. I felt sure that the secret lay there. I swam out to a place where reef comes close to breaking the water's surface, and assumed that small caves and hiding places were down at the bases of these dull greenish formations.

I thought, *now I will see under the water,* and dove down with my spear. I saw appear in that vague plane of color a dark spot, and I thrust my spear. It hit the reef with a clacking sound, and I surfaced and stared at the blunted point. I tried again and again. Near the time when the chills were making me stupid, I decided on one more dive, after which I would go home and abandon this nonsense forever. I dove down and thrust at a dark spot, and because the spear met nothing, I surfaced without it. It was caught in that dark hole, and I felt the water moving me away from it. So, I had lost the spear, my ihe—the ocean's final humiliation, and proof that my arrogance was unjustified.

I put my face in the water. Somewhere down there was the spear I had fashioned with my own hands. I allowed all the air to leave my lungs as I descended, cupping my hands around my eyes in an effort to improve my vision. Perhaps halfway down, my hands cupping my eyes, I saw, for a half a second, so clearly and so perfectly out of my right eye, that I drew water into my lungs. Just before the vision vanished, I saw the streak of something red, a kūmū, or more specifically a kūmū a'e, which is the adult of this fish. It passed under the end of my spear.

I surfaced coughing, gasping and frightened. I had seen under the water, but did not know how I had done that. I had seen the kūmū—it was Kū'ulakai, The Red One of the Sea, showing himself. He had allowed me to see, if only for an instant. Perhaps this was what the dreams had been telling me, that I would see for but half a second. But see I did, and the fright I felt was from the realization that Kūʻulakai would now eat me.

I left my spear where it was and swam toward the shore, imagining that a shark was following me, smelling the fear I left in the water. Then I stopped. My right eye itched, felt the fading irritation one feels upon emerging from the water. Air aggravates the sting of salt. I understood suddenly what I had done. While descending and emptying my lungs of air, I had trapped a bubble in the palm of my hand, which had been cupped around my eye.

After realizing what I had done, I tried repeating it, but unsuccessfully. The bubble would leak through my fingers, or out the side of my eye-socket. Then I thought that perhaps the deep chill in my flesh had made my hands unsteady. I went back to the coral formation where I had lost my spear, and tried again, this time emitting the air from my lungs up the right side of my face while I descended slowly, and I saw my spear, saw a yellow fish, a little crab scuttling over the pebbles, the small cave in the reef where the back half of my spear sat. As I lunged to grab it, the bubble left my hand.

I walked toward our kauhale. I had no fish, it was true, but I had received the gift of seeing under the water, and I wanted to tell my father about this. I did not want to tell my brother, because he was superior to me in so many ways that this one advantage I had somewhat mitigated against my inferiority. As I walked, I felt somewhat disappointed, because the gift of sight under the water was not Kūʻulakai's magic. Rather, it was his information about something that was quite simple. If you can see through water from the air above it, then manufacture air to be above water while you are in it. It was as if, after much mystery, with his suggestive whispering in my dreams, the god of the sea had laughed and said to me, "And by the way, fool, here is how you see under the water."

I found my father pulling kalo and saving the tops to plant again. He rose up from his work and saw me. I went to him, and said, "Kūʻulakai taught me how to see under the water." He did not change his expression. He looked at my spear and then at me, very thoughtfully, and said, "And Lono told me that insects are eating the sweet potato tops." Shamed, I went to my work, my fingers wrinkled from the water.

In the succeeding days I tried fishing whenever I could, but kept watch on the sun to determine the time, so that I could return home to something other than his thoughtful, disapproving stare. As for seeing under the water, because I had to keep my hand around my right eye so tightly, the vision was more a small window rather than the panorama you might expect, and after doing this for long periods of time, I felt a terrible ache high on my cheek, as if I were bruising myself with the repeated activity. Friends of mine began to shun me, because they felt that my fishing was an anti-social thing, and one even pointed at me one day as I was walking toward the beach, and said to another something to the effect that someone had given me a black eye.

One day, I floated over a formation that was about two bodies' length down, and saw something blue in a depression at the base of a formation, and letting more air into the palm of my hand, I saw that it was something as blue as a slightly hazy sky inside a shallow hole. I took a series of sixteen deep breaths, and I know that you might wonder why that number. An English boy might think ten or fifteen because of your numbering system divided by tens. Our system is in fours, so it would occur to a boy to take eight, or twelve, or sixteen. I took sixteen, because another thing I had discovered playing with my sisters was that you can, in a way, saturate your lungs with air, so that you can remain under the water nearly twice the time you might otherwise have before your air is exhausted.

Once I had taken my breaths, I began to descend slowly by letting the air out, and the blue patch, upon closer inspection, was the scaled side of a large fish, the scales on the right side of the patch leading to the large, slowly pulsing gill opening. I hesitated a moment, considering the kapu that could regulate this act, and when I began to feel the little halting, instinctive twitches of my lungs wanting air, I put both hands on the spear and thrust as hard as I could at the vague blue patch shimmering against the indistinct greenish side of the reef, my right knuckles scraping the coarse lip of the cave.

The billows of sand and debris told me that the spear had gone into the fish, and when I felt the spear being levered sideways, I drove it hard again, feeling the point strike the back of the cave. The panicked convulsions in my chest meant that I had to surface for air, so I ran my hands down the spear, and when my fingers touched the slick side of the fish, I slid my left hand up over the top, felt the dorsal ridge and a soft dorsal fin, then the spear barbs, and drew the fish out of the cave.

I surfaced heaving for air, drawing some water into my throat and then coughing, and lifted the fish. It was a blue uhu, with the solid tooth plates and yellowish bands on its nose, a yellow spot near its side fin.

With one hand on either side of the fish and gripping the spear, I swam into shore, the fish flapping powerfully. My legs shaking, I ran to our kauhale, my hands gripping the spear, the fish heavy and slimy, dancing on the shaft. Beak open, he seemed to stare at me, and every few steps he flapped his tail, sending fish-smelling water and excrement onto my chest and face.

My father's eyes widened when he saw the uhu. Breathless, I held it out to him, and he slid his fingers into one gill, his thumb into the other, and slid it off the spear. "Did you remove this from someone's net?" he asked.

"No," I said, trying to get my breath. "I speared it. Kūʻulakai taught me how to see under the water."

My father stared at the fish. He touched the spear-hole on the exit side, bits of pinkish meat hanging there, the light of the sun making it flicker with tiny blue, green and gold reflections. "See under the water," he said. "And how is this possible?"

I said, "I held my hand by my eye. I was halfway down and clearly saw a kūmū. Then—"

My father's fingers rose from the spear shaft. "No," he said. "I will ask this once. Are you lying?"

I said, "No, I am not."

He stared at the uhu, thinking. "When?" he asked.

I told him a few days previous. "Then I practiced what he taught," I said.

He held his hand up again. "Tell no one of this. Do not tell me. Should anyone ask, say only that you found the fish."

Why could I not announce that Kūʻulakai had taught me this? Was it not an achievement for a boy my age? "Yes," he said. "I see your face. But I do not want you to be selected as food for the gods. This fish I will cook, and feed to the gods the portion that belongs to them, and we will eat the rest. Remember, you must not distinguish yourself in any but a noa feat—boxing, or as a warrior, or at any Makahiki game. This carries much danger with it. You must do this no more."

"Ever?" I asked.

He thought, for some time, then said, "For the present time. If you do, you must have ready an explanation."

"But may I explain it to you?" I asked.

When I put my hand to my face and began to explain, he held his hand up and said, "Aʻole!"

I think that I understood, when I returned to the sweet potatoes. He wanted to protect me from the hazards of my achievement, and knowledge on his part, a secret he would be forced to keep, would make him somehow defiled, not properly in harmony with the gods and with the society he was a part of. He would have no pono. Makaʻāinana were forbidden such talents as mine, as they were forbidden the clear lines of their own pasts. My father had enough of a burden to bear in having inherited a disenfranchised past, a burden that he nevertheless cultivated like his kalo. As for my seeing under the water, for my sake and his, he would best know nothing of it.

4.

If you gentlemen are ready, I will continue, assuming that Mr. MacFarlane's hand will hold up today. Yes, I see by your expression that this is an insult, and I apologize for doubting your ability or your endurance, sir. You did ask me why we haven't seen, yet, any of the more notorious things known to you. The truth is that we lived a sedate, calm life. The stories about sacrifices and infanticide and cannibalism must be placed in their proper context: sacrifices took place every day, but these were sacrifices of parts of fish, bits of cloth, food, which was merely giving back to the gods what is theirs. We had a small shrine in our hale mua, or men's house, and there these sacrifices took place.

Sacrifice of humans was not something common people saw. It was the responsibility of the high ali'i, of kings. Infanticide may have been committed by women who bore children with flaws, and of cannibalism I know nothing, except for a myth in which a man's eyes were eaten. I can see that you experience a bit of disappointment at this claim. It is true that I did witness human sacrifice, but that is another part of this narrative.

So I will continue the story, which we left during my eleventh year. When I was twelve, I discovered a cave on the mountainside above our kauhale. The opening was small and hidden by brush, but inside it was perhaps half the size of this room. This cave gave me a broad view of the ocean and our kauhale, the kalo laid out so neatly, my sweet potatoes there just up the slope. The cave was noa, for there were no bones inside. Had there been bones, I would have avoided it.

The floor of the cave was a fine dark silt, the walls and ceiling basalt. There I worked on my ihe, and decorated the walls by scraping images of fish and war implements on the stone with pieces of coral. This was my hale mua. I gathered stones and built a shrine at the back of it, which was lit by filtered sunlight. I found a dead apapane, a red bird with beautiful feathers, and made a tiny kahili on a twig, and offered its slightly putrid head, the eye-sockets black and empty but for tiny, crawling ants, to the gods. I believe that this activity was like those of boys all around the world, the establishment of a place where they can dream of glory, look into their futures, and so on.

My exclusive dominion over this cave was short lived, however. One day when I was inside working on the image of a turtle, our 'aumakua, I heard giggling outside, and in came my sisters, crawling in on their knees so that their recently grown breasts swayed slightly under them. "You are forbidden to enter," I whispered. "This is a hale mua." They were not impressed by my warning. The now somewhat crowded cave became filled with the scent of their bodies, Ka'ahupāhau with maile leaves in her hair. The fragrance of the leaves gradually became mixed with the scent of their oil, something that excited me at the time, for reasons I did not yet understand.

Our conversation was what one might expect, and a brief translation can be reduced to the following: "This is a wonderful cave," and "I'll bring 'ōhi'a 'ai and we'll eat it here," countered vigorously by, "No, this is forbidden—women may not eat with men!" countered by, "That's why we'll do it. This would make a wonderful hale 'aina."

As you recall, hale 'aina is 'women's house.' I was of course livid with indignation at them for their having defiled my cave. Then, their eyes having adjusted to the darkness, they began seeing the shrine and the images on the walls and ceiling. "Our 'aumakua has big feet," and "Is that a war-axe or is it a warrior without a nose?" My leiomano was too thick, and resembled the profile of an ali'i, and it was true that he had no nose. This made me laugh, and with that laughter, my child's kapu was broken.

Laka and Ka'ahupāhau came to the cave a number of times, and there we would eat 'ōhia'ai and talk, first honoring tradition by offering small portions to the gods. It was during these times that I began to look at them more closely. Laka frightened me in ways because she so resembled my mother, both in appearance and in bearing, and at times, sitting there in the cave, it was as if she were an adult indulging children. Ka'ahupāhau, on the other hand, was more mysterious. She was reserved, always with a doubtful expression on her face, as if she had been born asking a question that had, as yet, not been answered.

Then, when Laka began anticipating her betrothal, she became much less interested in these games, leaving Ka'ahupāhau as my only company. When I was there I sometimes became excited anticipating the sound of her surreptitious movement through the brush, and became angry when she did not appear. Was she, too, anticipating her betrothal? I would stare out the entry at the water and laugh derisively at the idea. They were abandoning one of the great discoveries and one of the best secrets of our childhood, and at our kauhale when we ate together in the hale 'aina, I would be surly and short with both of them, much to my mother's mystified confusion.

I believe she described this blight on the family order to my father, because he seemed to understand that it was nearing the time for me to leave the company of women and enter the men's house. This would involve a ritual that needed proper preparation, and I believe I began to understand why, in the future, my sleeping in the hale 'aina would be forbidden. At the time that Ka'ahpāhau visited me at the cave, I began waking up in the middle of the night, lying there still, the scent of their bodies in the air, and because I slept next to Ka'ahupāhau, and had sought warmth from her all my life, that familiar body now had become an object of a powerful but confused desire. I would awaken to find my member engorged and painfully hard, and would stare into the blackness. Then I would reach over and have my hand meet some part of her body—her side, hot under the cloth, her shoulder, cold out in the air, the soft mound of her belly if she slept on her back, and her breasts. Sometimes she simply brushed my hand away and rolled over, others she remained asleep.

I would anticipate sleep because of this. One night when I was awake and in that state of almost maddening agitation, I ran my hand slowly up her stomach and rib cage, and then over her breast, the large nipple sliding under the palm of my hand, and I believe that because I felt a strong heartbeat under my hand, without realizing what it signified, and then did realize what it signified, I made a sound, a soft moan, and felt her tense up and then heard her whisper, "Tsst," very softly. That she had been awake while I touched her shocked me. She was and had been very much awake this night, and perhaps others. I lay there tense and shamed, grateful for the snoring sounds from my mother and Laka. I realized that I had to avoid Ka'ahupāhau from then on.

This conviction would have been sealed in my mind had she not moved toward me. I felt her hand pull at my shoulder, then felt the warm wind of her fish-scented breath on my face and chest, and then she moved her body over and against mine, the heat of it shocking to me, and I felt her face against the side of my neck, felt my groin pressed against her, and smelled a fresh but alien scent between us as she pushed her body harder against me, and then, unable to control myself, I ejaculated up between us so that our stomachs slid against each other wetly.

I had never felt a sensation like that before. The shame I felt as that fluid began to cool, and then dry on our skin, was so deep that I turned it into anger against her. Was this sorcery? For women kept the secrets of sorcery, not men. She remained against me, her breath hot on the side of my face, her heart beating against me, and when I put my hand on her hip to pull us apart, she tensed herself against me, found my hand and pulled it down between her legs, where I was surprised to discover that she too had produced some liquid, which, when I moved my hand, made squishing sounds in her hair. For a moment my finger was encircled by a soft, hot ring of flesh, and I pulled my hand away and found that the rich, dense aroma I had smelled before was from there.

I rubbed my hand dry on the cloth. She was awake and watching me. I moved away from her, our stomachs parting to cold air in a slow and gentle peeling away of the strange glue that seemed to hold us together. I uttered a soft giggling exclamation because of the coldness of the air on my skin, and felt two fingers press my lips. "Tsst." That was all she said. Within the time it took me to compose myself, I realized that the organ which had so recently deposited that fluid on us was erect again, but now it caused in me a sort of baffled anger, as if this sorcery were visited upon me by a sister whom I no longer knew.

Then my mother sat up, muttered something into the darkness, and lay back down again, flopping her arm out so that the back of her hand struck my shoulder.

The following morning, as we ate in the hale ʻaina, Kaʻahupāhau did not look at me. I went to tend the sweet potatoes, and my sisters and mother sat outside in the sun plaiting hala, making mats for Makahiki offerings. I remained in my crouched position, studying the leaves, aware of the dry stickiness on my skin, and once, when I sneaked a look at Kaʻahupāhau, I saw her look down at her stomach, then pick something off and flick it away, at which she then looked up at me. I did not look down, nor did she. It was as if we had now entered a shaming contest, that the first to look downward would lose. I looked back to my work.

Gentlemen, please forgive the frankness of this account, for I observed some discomfort on your part. I do not mean to shock you, or to cause you, Mr. MacFarlane, to produce blots in your ledger book. I believe that the truth of one's experience must be honored regardless of the nature of that experience, and to have you see, feel and smell that experience is important to me. Delicacy would violate that truth, and I see no reason for summarizing in order to avoid the specific details of such experiences.

I must depart now from the account of my strange relationship with my sister. The time of the yearly festival was approaching, and with it the preparation for my consecration to the hale mua. If there existed between Kaʻahupāhau and myself a tension, it was quite suddenly superceded by the preparation for Makahiki. Some description is necessary here, information about it so that you may understand the meaning of this festival to the common people such as ourselves.

First, each month we have a day that equals twelve hours, all in darkness, either the last day, Muku, which means 'cut short', or the first day Hilo, which means 'new moon'. For this reason, and because our calendar is lunar, our yearly festival begins at different times, either in the last month of the dry season, called 'Ikuwā, or perhaps in the next month, the first month of the wet season, called Welehu. These correspond somewhat to the months of October and November in your English calendar.

The king, with his priests, performs a series of rituals I need not describe in full here. There is one in which two green coconuts are broken, it is said, by the king, who then washes his hands in the water, and anoints the god figures. This is done with the first rise of Makali'i, what you would call the Pleiades, in the month of Ikuwā, or so it was when I was a child. With this rite, and others, the temples are closed. The return of the Pleiades is the return of Lono, who, during the festival, is called Lonomakua, or Lono the Provider, the god of fertility, agriculture and the like. Hence the festival begins in the season of life-giving rain.

The closing of the temples is in effect a temporary release from the dominion of the king and the ali'i, and for the maka'āinana it means the lifting of many kapu, but Makahiki has other kapu that are in force for its duration of around three months, such as prohibitions against fishing, against war, against, in one case, for one night, the lighting of fires or the making of noise. It is, therefore, an extended festival in which many of the rules of behavior are suspended. It always caused much exhilarated anticipation in the people, for the breaking of the bonds of propriety in a sense liberates them, and when the festival is over, they go back to their regulated lives, always knowing that this regulation, too, is temporary.

The aspect of Makahiki that will likely interest you most is the procession of the king's feather god, on a long pole, perhaps five meters, with a carved image of Lonomakua on the top. It is decorated with feather wreaths, skins of certain sea birds, and other objects, the result a colorful, mostly red and yellow display. This god is carried in a procession around the entire island, in effect around the kingdom, in a direction that keeps the interior of the island on its right side. This god is called akua loa, or 'long god.' A smaller god very much like this one, in its decoration, is called akua poko, or 'short god,' and belongs to the district, and is tended by the district nobles and priests. This god proceeds with the ocean on its right side.

As you can imagine, the journey of the akua loa lasts many days, more than twenty in fact. The journey of the short god lasts four days.

The reason for this circuit around the island is to collect offerings to the gods and their closest tenders, the ali'i, priests, warriors and various favorites of the ali'i. I see that you adopt an expression of jovial distaste—yes, it is a tax, in ways. The common people had to pay it, or suffer the consequences. Is it not true, though, that in England your debtor's prison is a consequence of just such a failure? Where, in fact, do your English ali'i get their wealth?

The preparation for the arrival of the long god is busy and joyful. My mother and sisters made kapa cloth and hala mats finer than those they made for our own use. My father consulted with other men on the recipes for special sweet foods that would not spoil, and one day he stopped me from my work and asked, "Do you still see under the water?" When I answered in the affirmative, he said, "Then go catch he'e," which is octopus. I asked him if he'e was noa, if it was an 'aumakua to our family, if he'e was kapu to thirteen-year-olds, to which he said, "No."

This order would ordinarily mean a sweet blast of vigorous anticipation in my flesh, but I feared that the catching of the uhu was so much a coincidence, perhaps a perfunctory whim on the part of Kū'ulakai, that I would fail. I went to the ocean with my spear and a float I made of wiliwili wood, which is very light, under which hung a short cord made of my sisters' hair attached to a sharp kauila stick, to stick through the he'e as I caught them, an idea that caused in me a feeling of rueful humor, for my father's assumption seemed now to be an attack of demented hope on his part.

I floated, my hand cupped over my right eye, and Kū'ulakai's perfect vision returned. After some time I went back to the beach, shivering with a deep chill. A man emerged from the water nearby, carrying a large, grayish lump, tentacles hanging down and dripping. It was perhaps four or five he'e. I ran over to him carrying my spear and float. He smiled when he saw me, for his kauhale was near ours. I said to him, "You have done well. How do you find them?" He answered by saying, "He'e keep their houses clean, and will sometimes decorate their entryways. This is how you find them."

I went back into the water, and assuming that he had caught his by looking down through water that was waist-high, I swam farther out, and again cupped my hand around my eye, looking for their clean houses with decorated entryways. His explanation had come in the form of a riddle, but we often answered such questions with riddles. It was not long before I understood what he had meant. At the base of a gray formation was a small opening, a hand's length wide and perhaps three inches high, and this opening had no silt at the base, and no webbing of silt at the edges. There were four stones just out from the base, arranged in a line. I surfaced and drew sixteen deep breaths, and then, my hand around my right eye, descended to the opening, where, transferring the spear to my right hand and thus blurring my vision, I jammed the spear into the opening several times, hitting sand, then rock, then something strong but resistant, which I thrust at as hard as I could, at which the spear began to twist in my hand. My air exhausted, I rose to the surface, leaving the spear. There, I cupped my hand around my eye again and saw my spear moving, then shortening as it was being pulled into the opening.

I dove down again and grabbed at the indistinct line I knew to be the spear, and thrust it several times, at which a cloud of silt, then what appeared as blackish purple smoke, bloomed out of the opening. I pulled at the spear and felt the strong resistance, so I pivoted it side to side, and even with the indistinct vision, saw the he'e burst from the opening. I surfaced with it lumped on the end of the spear, the tentacles sliding up the shaft and over my knuckles. Sputtering in the water, I realized that I did not know how to get it off the spear, so I pushed the spear out before me, grabbed at the cord of the float, and made my way into shore.

My father bit its eyes. He told me that if I did this whenever I caught a he'e, I would take the he'e's mana and would be able to see them better. Then he stuck his fingers into the slit under its head and in one motion, turned it inside out, so that dark organs showed through a light grayish-tan layer of skin that undulated with color changes. "This we will dry," he said. "The gods will smack their lips."

Recall that I told you that within the moku, or kingdom, there are districts called 'okana, with their ali'i and priests, then ahupua'a, or divisions within districts, each with their leaders, and finally the 'ili'aina, or sections within ahupua'a. Much of the excitement in our family had to do with my father's responsibility, to oversee our 'ili'aina's 'auhau, or tribute, to be collected and taken east to the border of our 'okana, where our ahupua'a's riches would be placed at the akua loa of the king. The akua loa would be wearing the king's niho palaoa, which is the symbol of his royalty and divinity. The niho palaoa is a necklace made with whale's teeth, and the king's giving it up for Makahiki means that he transfers his power to Lonomakua.

The procession of the akua loa begins on a specific day, in the Welehu month. The day before this procession begins, the gods are decorated and prepared, and the people, common and noble alike, gather, in our case at the district border, along the beach. The district akua poko is there, as are the ali'i, warriors, priests, and common people. From our 'ili'aina, this was a quarter of a day's walk, all of us carrying our 'auhau for Lonomakua. Many other people made this journey too, and I recall our walking that day, I carrying the dried he'e and rolls of kapa, my sisters walking before me carrying rolled mats, two carefully made malo, my father and mother and brother in front.

Ka'ahupāhau walked directly in front of me, her pa'u riding low on her hips. I recall being slowly captivated, and then mesmerized, by the sway of her hips, by the soft bouncing and swinging of her long, black hair, so that once again I became afflicted by that same agitation which I hid from others by carrying my offerings at waist-level before me. Ka'ahupāhau was aware, I believe, of what was happening behind her, because from time to time she jerked her head around to glance at me with a petulant frown.

To our left, the surf broke to a steady, soft roar, and ahead the bright sunlight baked the wide path. We could see gatherings of people, but the journey seemed to me endless, a steady march, always with my eyes falling to Ka'ahupāhau's hips, which, as the sun rose and the heat intensified, began to glow with a sheen of oil and perspiration.

Laka's hips and back were the same, but when I looked at her, I saw no more than practical, womanly strength. I did not marvel at this difference in perception. At my age I probably did not understand it—Laka was womanly strength, Ka'ahupāhau was a mystical, even frightening being of heat, softness, of fluids and breath, of strange, alien aromas, and unreasonable as it sounds, or perhaps strange, I knew that more than anything else I wanted to immerse myself in that softness, heat, and aroma.

Our destination was the akua poko at the district border, where, as happened each year, our waiwai or riches would be placed, and where, later, the Makahiki celebration would begin, with dancing, the singing of cursing songs, and a general revelry.

My mother was known for her composition of songs insulting the ali'i, which she offered this day every year. These were not direct insults, but rather carefully hidden suggestions that the song referred to a particular noble. In any case the spirit of joy made it such that there were no class differences during this time—the people, ali'i and maka'āinana alike, enjoyed each other's company in a more or less equal manner.

I could see the akua poko in the distance, surrounded by a gathering of perhaps a thousand people. My sisters' shoulders then straightened, showing their excitement. My affliction, which had forced me to carry my burden at waist-level lest someone should see, simply receded as this other stimulant took over.

There are three phases of this festival beginning. The first phase is the placing of the offerings at the akua poko, overseen by priests and ali'i, who assess the quality of the objects. In general, this is a jovial affair, tinged with some solemnity akin to the seriousness of the occasion. We would be offering our wares to the gods by offering them to those closest to the gods, their curators, so to speak. The konohiki, or leader of our district, stood before the god figure on the pole, the figure bedecked with feathers and, below the fierce mask, the skins of birds, more feathers, and shells.

Then, from the west, we saw the tall, feathered image approaching, on a pole high above the following crowd. It was the akua loa, the king's god-image, making its way along the shore, the priests bearing it flanked by warriors, and the ali'i dressed in their finest cloaks. The meeting of these two crowds took place a few minutes later while the priests of the akua loa found a place to put it up. The priests pounded posts called ālia marking a kapu area before the tall akua loa, which was decorated with bright feathers, mostly red and yellow, and, below the large, open-mawed wooden visage, the king's niho palaoa, a lei of bright whale's teeth slowly turning in the ocean breeze. We then waited for the arrival of all the gift bearers, so that our konohiki could then place the gifts at the altar, in this case the kapu space between the two wooden posts.

My father and brother approached our konohiki, an obese man who was perspiring in the heat. My father and he knew each other well, and touched their foreheads and noses together in greeting. The konohiki then inspected our gifts, and indicated where they should be piled in preparation for the offering to the akua loa, along with all the other gifts, which created a rather impressive mound a short distance from the ālia posts. The food was separated from the kapa and other inedible things. This food, I should say, would be eaten by the large crowd that followed the akua loa on its way to the next ahupua'a on the following day.

In the loud, gabbling din of all the voices, stunned by all the colors and movement, I found myself staring at one of the priests, who appeared to be young, with long red-brown hair and a sparse beard. I wondered if I should enter the priesthood and escape the defiling effects of my fascination with Ka'ahupāhau's body, if it would separate me forever from the sorcery residing in that hot, liquid flesh. The priest saw me looking at him, because he stared at me once, quickly, with a suspicious and irritated frown. I looked down then, recalling a warning from my father, that you remain safe by obeying all the kapu and by remaining unremarkable in the eyes of any ali'i or priest.

I saw Laka staring at the akua loa and I think particularly the whale's teeth, while Ka'ahupāhau seemed frightened in the presence of all the people. She looked around, her shoulders hunched, that doubtful expression of hers exaggerated into a gaping astonishment, but one having no delight in it. In my stunned, dreamlike state, I again stared at her, this time because of all the visual and auditory stimulants, drunk with desire for her.

We waited, escaping the heat of the sun in the shade of a small tree, under which many had already gathered. People we did not know moved in order to give us space. My sisters sat with my mother and I sat with my father a few paces away in another generously offered patch of shade, while my brother went off to look around, that forceful and arrogant stride the emblem of disobedience of my father's warning to me. All looked at him, the powerful, well-muscled body, the challenging eyes. I believe that had he stared at the young priest, the priest might have inwardly cowered. Eighteen years of age, he carried the glorious aura of royalty. This day, he wanted to arrange a boxing match for himself. He was not the champion of our area, for there was no agreed upon champion, and he wanted to consult with the konohiki's men and, in effect, volunteer.

As we waited, I furtively looked at Ka'ahupāhau. Whenever she shifted on the ground, moving her legs, my eyes darted down between them, and I believe she was aware of this, as she jerked her pa'u around and more or less stuffed it there, then looked in the other direction. In time we heard the chanting, which was the call for us to gather.

Then, amid some rituals I will forego describing, the offering was made. The food went to one side, mats, malo, some of the dried foods that would not spoil on the other. The young priest then spoke a prayer to Lono that signifies that the land is free of the kapu: 'your bodies who are in heaven—a long cloud, a short cloud,' and so on and then ends with an invitation: 'Arise, put on your malo, and play.' The people gathered around the god-image respond by saying in unison: 'Play!' or better translated, 'Enter into action.' The priest chants, 'Lono!' and the people respond with 'The wooden god.' The priest calls, 'is raging,' and the people call, 'raging, oh Lono.' Then the god-image is taken down, and another image, the akua pa'ani, is put up. This is the god of games, and with this prayer and response the people prepare to enjoy themselves.

The second phase of the festival opening is called the hi'uwai, which means 'purification bathing.' It is the culmination of an evening of revelry, in which the people are invited to swim in the ocean, and this play goes on until dawn, at which the ocean belongs to Lono and is kapu to all. One cannot go in the ocean, or the penalty is death, or at least a penalty like the sacrifice of a pig, depending upon the state of mind of the priests who oversee this process. The people continue the games and eating and general revelry. The third phase is the kapu Makahiki. No one can fish, pound kapa, or till the soil, because all is sacred to Lono. One's responsibility is to eat and enjoy oneself.

I will describe for you a period of perhaps twenty-four hours, from that late afternoon after we had arrived at the site of the akua loa until the same time the following day. We were, the six of us, quite exhausted from our long walk. After the offering of the gifts to Lonomakua, many fires were built along the beach, so many that the flames seemed to match the waning sun in their magnificence. My mother placed a large mat on the sand, and immediately went to visit other small groups, families whom she knew gathered around different fires, to offer dried heʻe and other prized morsels in trade for dog meat, by then already cooking, for herself and my sisters, and noa fish, whose aromas we could smell in the breeze from the ocean. To call this a 'trade' is perhaps misleading—people generally wanted to demonstrate their generosity by giving food to anyone who might appear hungry.

The combination of the din of the sounds of laughing and singing, along with the color, the movement of people, robbed me of a full grasp on reality. Everything took on the character of a dream, and as if to acknowledge that development, I flopped face down on the mat, drawing the fragrance of its fiber into my nose, and fell asleep.

I awakened perhaps two hours later to meat-scented breath, and opened my eyes. There, next to me, lay Kaʻahupāhau, her folded hands under her cheek, a line of saliva connecting the corner of her mouth to the mat. I stared at her closed eyes and eyebrows, her nose and lips, for some time. It was just past sundown, and the light made her face appear as grayish, a flat, almost colorless mask faintly illuminated by the firelight, but one I thought beautiful.

The disorganized medley of sound from before had been replaced now by the calls of hula dancers from one direction, the singing of a song from another, and the sand around our mat was not occupied by the multitude of bodies as before. We were missing one of the more enjoyable parts of the evening. Laka, much more energetic when it came to socializing, was most likely in one of those crowds.

I blew on Kaʻahupāhau's face, and she opened her eyes. "We are missing the songs and dance," I said.

"I ate too much," she said. In her sleepiness she stared at me without any hint of the shame I was sure she should feel at our nighttime adventure, now weeks back in our memories. Her stare made me nervous, because it seemed that she was thinking, perhaps slowly remembering the imagery of that night. She sat up, then touched her finger on a series of small squares, just visible, that the mat had imprinted on the fronts of her thighs.

"You have a tattoo," I said.

She laughed. "I want to hear her song." She was referring to my mother's insulting offering to our obese konohiki. We got up from the mat, and approached the closest gathering, a group of dancers lined up before a crackling fire, retelling a legend, and by the movement of their bodies and hand gestures, I could tell that it was about the demigod Maui.

We made our way through the cooling sand to another group, and there, on the far side, were my mother, father, and Laka. 'Iolana was not there. We had to wait through four songs before my mother, accompanied by Laka, who created a tempo with two hardwood sticks, sang her song, which she introduced as the story of the two-headed turtle. I do not remember specifically the lines of this song, only the story. It was about a turtle named Loli, which in our language means 'sea slug,' and 'changeable,' and if spoken twice, 'soggy or gummy.' This turtle grew so fat that his male member disappeared into the folds of his flesh, which then grew together leaving the poor turtle with no place to have his ule even peek out, much less satisfy any female turtle. Our Konohiki's name was Kalololo, which means 'the intelligent,' so her name for this turtle was suspiciously close to his in sound.

The turtle Loli would become excited by a female, but with no natural place for his ule to go, it peeked out from the side of his shell, or next to his wrinkled neck, making him appear as a two-headed turtle. Loli became bitter and miserable because when he became excited, he waited ruefully to see where his ule would appear. And it appeared peeking out of the folds of fat under one of his flippers, and another time he found himself garbling his speech, and found that his poor ule, so desperate to emerge in some useful if not fulfilling place, had now crowded his tongue to one side of his fat mouth. Sad was Loli, sad and tongue-tied, for his eager ule, seeing the light, burst forth toward it, pushing his tongue aside. So sad was Loli that he shut his beak, taking the head of his ule off, and in his misery he stopped eating. He became thin, and one day did the folds of his great 'ōpū recede, leaving his incomplete ule there, blind now without its head.

Gentlemen, you are obviously amused by this story. The crowd was too, our konohiki laughing with delight, women going over to stare between his great legs, and my mother, while she sang, stepping to him to open his mouth and look inside, at which the wily konohiki stuck his tongue out and grabbed her between the legs, causing her to shriek with surprise, much to the delight of the audience.

The song ended, however, with a kindness on my mother's part. Young female turtles, she sang, took pity upon Loli with the blind ule. Because of its shortness, the ule was recommended by grandmothers all across the turtle-kingdom to young virgin turtles yearning for this wonderful experience, and so Loli with the blind ule was never again alone, the young and comely turtles following him from sea-cave to sea-cave, yearning for the blind ule. Older women turtles also discovered that a blind ule tells no tales, and so sought him out whenever they wanted to steal across the stream for a while. Blind as Loli's ule was, it nevertheless functioned normally, and Loli fathered many, and was so the envy of other male turtles that they all became fat, waiting in vain for their ules to vanish into the folds of their flesh, and they were too slow to catch the nubile females, most of whom were in quest of the legendary blind ule anyway.

Although my mother's song was an insult to our konohiki, you can nevertheless see the kindness in it. Doubtless he enjoyed the favors of women that night.

The air had cooled considerably by this time, and Ka'ahupāhau made her way around the gathering to join my mother and Laka. As darkness made the fires brighter, the yells and laughter of people drunk on 'awa became more frequent. With Ka'ahupāhau having joined the others, I was alone, and wandered toward another gathering, this one a group of young women dancing a seductive hula, their bodies rich in color from the firelight. I made my way up the beach some distance from all the activity.

At times like these, alone but among other people, I always felt a peculiar social dislocation, as if I were an invisible observer of all around me. I was amazed by the number of fires on the beach, perhaps fifty, stretching for a quarter of a mile. I did not know where the ali'i were, but assumed that their fire was one of the ones in the center of the line of fires. I heard sounds coming from the brush behind me, some close, some from beyond the wide path that had seen the royal procession earlier. The sounds were those of young men and women engaged in a sort of joyful, squealing and grunting sexual activity. This made me think of Ka'ahupāhau, then shamefully shake my head.

A figure appeared in the darkness. Warily, I began to walk toward the beach by making a wide arc around the figure, but it moved to the side, as if to block my path. Then I heard an inebriated giggle. That this was a woman reassured me somewhat, so I walked on, toward the fires. She moved to interrupt my path.

She laughed again, and lightly slapped a gourd, producing the sound of liquid sloshing inside. "Oh lonely warrior," she sang, "are you pining for your love?"

"No," I said.

"Warrior, this will soften the ache and harden something else," she said, approaching. Then she raised the gourd to her mouth and drank, and made a satisfied smacking with her mouth. "Drink, oh warrior," she said. I could not see her face because of the glare of the firelight. She handed me the gourd, and even before I got it to my mouth I smelled the 'awa.

"But 'awa belongs to Kū," I said. "It is forbidden for you to drink, and for me." The gourd was warm from her hands.

"You are large for a boy," she said.

I looked at the black silhouette of the gourd, feeling the sensation of a mischievous rebellion tickling my chest.

"It is noa," she said. "We are noa."

I drank. It was both bitter and sweet, heavy and thick, the taste both sumptuous and repulsive. I moved to the side, so that the light from the fires might illuminate her. When I saw her face, half an orange-brown and then black on the dark side, I said, "I don't know you." She was Laka's age and size, but her hair was short.

"And I don't know you," she said. "Do you feel something yet?"

I was about to say that I did not, but discovered that my mouth had become somewhat numb. Then came a strange expansion, as if the fires were farther away and the silence enfolding us were somehow impenetrable. I said, "We are noa," and then did not know if I had said that, or thought it. There was a disembodiment, some odd displacement of my awareness centered in my po'o away from my body, which felt either numb or perhaps nonexistent. I thought that I should continue speaking, because it occurred to me that I had stood before this woman for perhaps half the night as she waited for me to speak. "Kū'ulakai taught me to see under the—" Then I lost my thought. What had he taught me?

She laughed. "Kū'ulakai is sleeping," she said.

"Water," I said.

"Very well, Kū'ulakai sleeps under the water. Now, I'd like you to come with me."

I stood there, not knowing how to move my legs. I drank more 'awa, waiting for my feet to function as they were designed to. The woman grabbed my hand and pulled, and thus did my feet wake up and produce a motion that fascinated me, one out ahead and placed, then the other past the first and placed, this process repeated perhaps fifty times before we arrived at a grassy hummock perched just above the sand. We were now far enough from the fires that, oddly, I could see her more clearly. She was older than Laka, perhaps eighteen or twenty, the pa'u she wore a fine one. It occurred to me that she was an ali'i woman, and when she sat down on the hummock I said, "It is a warm night."

I will admit here that at my age, and in my state of 'awa induced drunkenness, a most pleasant state indeed, that I did not have any idea of what she had brought me there for. I must also I interject that for anyone who is acquainted with any of your strong English spirits, 'awa would probably have no more effect than a numbing of the mouth. But for a boy, never having tasted anything that has these effects, 'awa is a strong drink.

She took the gourd from my hands and drank, put it down beside her in the grass and then entwined her fingers in my malo and pulled it down to my ankles.

"A sleeping turtle," she said.

I laughed. "That was a good story. It was recited by my mother."

"Story?" she said, looking up at me. Then she woke the sleeping turtle with her mouth, the act preceded by a strange sensation, of her hot breath on my skin down there. I must say that the effect of the 'awa, which I of course had never tasted before, delayed reactions on my part. At first I did not know what she was doing, and then, when I reasoned it out, I thought of Ka'ahupāhau, and that caused the sudden explosive pulsing of that same release I had experienced with her. The woman shrieked, and I had no tension whatever in my legs, and wilted to my knees. Laughing, she reached behind her and pulled out a handful of grass and wiped her face.

"Warrior," she said, "you have not paddled this canoe before."

"No," I said.

"We shall wait," she said. I was still on my knees before her, and found my upper body propped up by her knees. She held the gourd out to me, and my hands shaking, I took it and drank. "Well," she said, "I shall need to unwrap myself. If the next one goes twice as long, I believe I will feel only half of it."

I said, "My name—"

She said, "Let us not concern ourselves with names," and undid her pa'u. To our left, a man and a woman emerged from the bushes laughing and whispering to each other.

"Remain still," the woman said, the pa'u in her hands. "Don't attract their attention." When the couple's silhouettes became small against the firelight, she said, "How is the turtle?"

Even as she spoke, I was aware that it had awakened. So I said, "He is not blind, for he still has his head."

"My warrior speaks in the strangest riddles," she said, and pulled me by my wrists toward her. Then she opened her legs, and I felt the warmth of her thighs on my hips. She pulled more, and said, "The turtle seeks warmer water." I felt cool fingers on my ule, then its contact with something, at which she put her hands on my buttocks and pulled up, causing the complete immersion into a sensation of being constricted by a soft, liquefied heat that startled me. "There," she said, "it is the hot season for the turtle." After that moment, I was informed by the instincts of the race.

We repeated this three times more, and in order to avoid unnecessary repetition, I will leave it to your imaginations.

You have been, in the past, suspicious about my capacity to remember things, and now might be even more justifiably so, given that I was drunk on 'awa, and still drunk when the woman later directed me to other features of this act, for example, what, specifically, one who knows how to paddle this canoe does with his tongue and hands. 'Awa's inebriation causes a strange, lucid detachment, where the thinking processes separate themselves from a body that, at least for me, stumbled behind those processes in an attempt to keep up. I knew what I was doing, was a good student in learning what the woman was so studiously teaching me, and after, I recalled every detail with a clarity that makes the experience seem like one of yesterday or a week ago.

Finally she began to look frequently toward the fires. The time of the ocean bathing, called hi'uwai, was near, and she had apparently become sated both on the 'awa and on that act where she had wanted that organ pushed again and again up her body.

"I must go," she finally said, wrapping the pa'u back in place. "I will go first, and you must wait until I am but a speck by the fires before you return." She looked at me once, and then made her way around bushes toward the fires.

When she was indeed a speck, visible now only as a tiny undulating blotch against one of the fires, I made my way back.

The hi'uwai was already in progress—more than half of the people were in the water, their heads above the dark plane bobbing, appearing a dull orange color in the reflection of the many fires, all seeming oddly like tan coconuts floating there. I was hungry, and looked among the many mats, some occupied by sleeping people, for ours.

That, too, was occupied, by Ka'ahupāhau and my mother. My mother looked up at me, one hand on my sister's shoulder.

"She ate something that made her sick," my mother said. "She has been vomiting and running to the bushes. Sick at both ends." Ka'ahupāhau moaned, then writhed on the mat. "Stay with her," my mother said. "I am going to find a kahuna lapa'au." This term is the same as 'doctor.' My mother left, and I sat down next to Ka'ahupāhau, who was folded up, her arms around her knees, under a kihei, which is like a shawl.

So I sat there, Ka'ahupāhau groaning, her forehead shining with sweat. When she realized it was I who sat with her, she moved over and put her upper body against my chest, and trembling, continued groaning and then tensing up when the pain twisted in her stomach.

"I ate too much dog," she said. "I think the meat was stale."

"I don't like dog," I said.

"I smell 'awa," she said.

"I drank 'awa," I said.

Then her stomach began to tense again, and she held onto my forearm. My mind lapsed into that peculiar intellectual detachment, as if my body cradling Ka'ahupāhau's body was not my own, and my mind floated somewhere else. How was it that this had happened to me? The sensations I had experienced clearly told me why it was that the first coconut tree had two coconuts, why the fire-stick belongs to Kū, why the various pleasures associated with this act formed the very basis of our world. Was it not the most important of all things? Surely my misdirected desire for the sick girl I held was, I thought, only the early manifestation of a desire that, now, had met its more appropriate fulfillment. The well known illicit cohabitation of those of our race was more a habit of the high-born, in which the desire to preserve their divinity and separation from those of lower birth makes logical the marriage of, say, a brother and sister. There can be no pollution of the blood of the ali'i if they confine their procreation to themselves.

Thus the activities of my 'awa elevated mind went, while Ka'ahupāhau went through her periods of wrenching stomach pain. Once she jumped up and ran in small steps up the beach to the brush. When she came back, wan and wiping her eyes, she said, "Come with me to the water."

I did so, thinking that the stickiness about my loins would be washed away. For Ka'ahupāhau, it was cleaning herself up from her trip to the brush.

The hi'uwai is the cleansing that inaugurates the Makahiki proper. This we did, Ka'ahupāhau splashing water at me because she felt much better, as she said, and in a restoration of the games we played a few years ago, I dove under the water and swam, hands out, to get her legs.

When we left the water, Ka'ahupāhau complaining of a chill, we went back to our mat and she wrapped herself in a kihei, shivering. The 'awa was wearing off, to the east, the faint hint of dawn made the division of water and sky visible. Ka'ahupāhau slept. Shortly, my mother returned, without a kahuna lapa'au. "Is she well?" she whispered.

I told her that she was, and so my mother left again. I wilted over in fatigue, and slept, facing Ka'ahupāhau.

When I woke, the sky was a bright blue, and all around the groups of people sat eating. I thought about the previous evening, and found myself looking around for the nameless woman I had been with. No one was in the water, because the water was kapu, sacred to Lono, and this would last four days. No one would till the land, no one would make kapa, no one would fish.

My father and brother approached the mat, and their conversation woke Kaʻahupāhau. My father appeared angered by something, my brother perplexed and thoughtful. "This is why we must never forget the old times," my father said. "This is what has happened because we allowed them to exercise their will." I stood up. My brother was still nodding thoughtfully at what my father had said.

When my father sat down on the mat and looked at my sister to see if she was well, ʻIolana jerked his head to pull me aside. "The priests killed a man," he said. "He came to shore in a canoe, not long ago, after sunrise."

"Where is he?" I asked. I had as yet not seen a dead person except for a few people being borne in kapa to their places of burial, and then only from a distance.

We walked along the beach, toward the west. "Why is our father angry?" I asked.

"He is angry because it is against the spirit of Makahiki. The man should have been required only to give up a pig in his place."

I felt manly walking with ʻIolana. Young women followed him with their eyes. He walked in great muscular strides, swinging his arms. I had to step quickly to keep up. We were near the spot where I had been with the woman. I looked around to see if I recognized the area, but did not. We were on dunes interspersed with hummocks of grass, above the beach, but in daylight all looked different. Yes, there was a hummock, and over there too. On one of them she had placed her buttocks and then leaned back. Surely the grasses were flattened by what we did. But I saw no flattened grasses.

"I had a woman last night," I said.

"Did you?" he said, and then he laughed and slapped my shoulder. "Well, you are a man now, little brother. Was she young and ripe?"

"Yes," I said. "She had soft flesh and smooth skin, and short hair too. I think she is high-born. She taught me how to please her."

"And did you?"

"I think so," I said doubtfully. He laughed again.

We walked on, now far past the last of the mats, many occupied by sleeping people, flies buzzing around the partly eaten food. We went up a bluff near the wide path that encircled the kingdom, and he led me between clusters of naupaka bushes. Naupaka is a beach plant that has fleshy light green leaves, and a white flower with half a bloom. That is, it appears as if someone had plucked the petals of one half of the flower.

We came to the man, who lay on his back in the sand. He had flies on his eyes and mouth, the mouth drawn back in a leer. Flies also moved on a wound in his chest, on his left side where, I assumed, the priests had pushed their pahoa in to puncture his heart. One testicle had popped outside the man's malo-cord and appeared a pale gray blue against his thigh. I made a wide circle around the man. Any close contact with death defiles a person, and viewing him from a ten-pace perimeter would keep the flies off me. There was a man, who had been breathing only a short time ago and who was now dead, all the functioning parts of his body, beating heart, eyes that beheld things, a brain that had so many memories in it, all of that nothing but cold flesh left there to rot in the sun.

I recalled some of what my father had told me, that for many generations now, the new settlers had imposed upon us this lot, to go through our lives treading lightly lest we should end up food for the gods or simply stinking refuse as this man now was.

After I was finished satisfying my curiosity, we walked back. As we went over the bluff to see the colorful gathering of people, 'Iolana said, "I do not fear them."

"Nor do I," I said. "Did you see the priest who killed the man?"

"He came along the beach with two koa. The warriors were looking at each other, as if what they had just seen was wrong. The priest was young and hairy."

"I have seen him," I said. I shuddered at the thought of the young priest. I did not know why it was that he would be the one to take the kapu to its strictest limit. Should I ever see him again, I thought, I would avert my eyes.

Because the function of the Makahiki was the temporary overthrow of the gods and their power, the results of the boxing matches, which we called mokomoko, were most of the time preordained. This was my father's opinion. The ahupua'a champion was supposed to beat the king's boxer, but much in the way of preliminary verbal jousting was a part of it. Later in the morning, there formed large circles of onlookers, some to watch wrestling matches, some boxing. Inside the mokomoko circle, two or three matches would take place at once.

At the head of the circle stood the akua pa'ani, ali'i and their punahele, or close friends, gathered below it, some sitting, others standing. 'Iolana stood by our fat, merry old konohiki, waiting for the king's champions to be called out, and their names recited to the large crowd. These games would go on for a few hours, after which the akua loa and its large crowd of followers would proceed to the border of the next ahupua'a.

As for the match itself, 'Iolana and the champion, an older, more muscular man than 'Iolana, faced each other, but without much elaborateness in terms of physical stance. The men face each other with both arms straight out, fists almost meeting. The right hand is for striking, the left for parrying. Thus

'Iolana and the man readied themselves, but first the king's champion looked at 'Iolana while the crowd waited for the first insult. The man was perplexed, gazing dramatically and in wonderment toward 'Iolana, and then he said, "But I see nothing! Is there a man before me?"

The crowd laughed. 'Iolana's fierce expression took on a joviality. He feinted once at the man, but the man continued gazing before him. Then the man swept his hands through the air as if making his way through darkness. "Bring an opponent!" he said. "There is nothing here! I see nothing. But wait. I smell something."

"'Ōhi'a 'ai," Iolana said.

"Did someone speak?" the man asked. "Was it the voice of a spirit?" He gazed around, seeming almost angered by his own perplexity. "I am hearing noises," he said.

"And smelling 'ōhi'a 'ai," 'Iolana said.

"There it is again," the man said, his hand cupped around his ear. "What is that smell?"

"'Ōhi'a 'ai," 'Iolana said. "It rises up your chest, from all you have in your malo."

The crowd produced a lusty roar of laughter, and even the king's champion seemed to appreciate the insult. He pulled the front of his malo out and studied what he saw. "But the voice lies," he said.

"Your eyes lie," 'Iolana said. "They are 'ōhi'a 'ai."

The man gasped. "I now see someone. He stands tall and strong, with bright teeth. But alas, my eyes lie, I am told. He stands small and weak, with yellow teeth. Let us begin." He then blew at 'Iolana, stared at him carefully, and reeled back in exaggerated surprise. "You are still there!" he said in mock astonishment.

'Iolana laughed. Then it seemed that both 'Iolana and the king's champion were through with the customary verbal insults. They advanced, fists out. 'Iolana punched at the man, who deflected the punch and laughed. Then the man seemed distracted, and with his right hand, left fist still out, pulled his malo out again and looked down, allowing 'Iolana to punch again, but the man feinted to the side and threw his right fist out, striking 'Iolana on the forehead. 'Iolana returned a punch that slid off the man's shoulder, and continued, but the man parried each punch, and at random times, with amazing speed, sent his fist into 'Iolana's face.

Finally 'Iolana threw a punch that hit the champion on the jaw, at which he raised his hand and rested it there. "Enough!" he said. "I have been beaten."

'Iolana stared at him, surprised. Still holding his jaw, the man walked to the edge of the circle. "I have been beaten!" he wailed. "Auwe!"

The laughter that erupted was at 'Iolana's expense, and he did not take it well. My father, closer to the rim of the circle than I, went to 'Iolana and calmed him down, all the time laughing and shaking his head.

This was, then, not memorable as mokomoko. It was more in keeping with the spirit of the festival, and in addition, the akua loa was being prepared to continue its journey, along with its large crowd of followers, to the border of the next ahupua'a, leaving the rest of us to continue our play for three more days.

'Iolana's face was bruised and scraped from the champion's punches. He remained angry, standing there with his arms folded, watching the boxers make their way to the place where preparations for the raising of the akua loa were taking place.

Thus the akua loa left, borne by priests and flanked by ali'i, then followed by the bearers of the people's gifts and then by the large crowd, all of whom carried their mats, gourds, and food. The people of our ahupua'a watched, and walked for some distance flanking the god's movement. They would accompany the colorful parade for a while and then return to their play. I walked alongside, somewhat awed by the pageantry of the group in front. The day was warm and sunny, so those following carried their kihei, the women in their fine pa'u and bedecked with shell leis and other ornaments.

I decided that I had seen enough, and feeling somewhat weary from the previous night, turned to go back. As I passed the people, someone watched me, a woman walking beside a tall, magnificent looking man. The woman followed me with her eyes, then shifted her mat to the hand away from me and with her free hand next to her hip, came out with a gesture that appeared to be the imitation of a turtle flapping a fin.

I walked toward her, but she grimaced and shooed me away with her hands. So it was the woman I had been with. I watched her slowly vanish into the huge procession. Yes, she had the short hair of the high-born woman, and yes, she was lithe and sexually appealing. I wondered who the man was. Perhaps her father, or her husband?

I made my way back, a slowly growing astonishment consuming me, until I laughed. I had had congress with her. The image of her face now returned—it was clear to me that should I ever see her again, I would easily recognize the broad nose, full lips, the special individual set of features each of us is blessed with.

Following this day, our play was sedate. Much time was spent playing group games such as puhenehene, a guessing game involving a stone and up to twenty or more people, with two teams competing. The stone is concealed on a person from one team, and the other team must guess who has the stone. It seems very simple, compared to some of your elaborate games, but it is not—it requires considerable skill to fool ten people. We played other games, too, and over the three-day period, Ka'ahupāhau gradually recovered from her sickness, and seemed, like Laka, able to spend all day at puhenehene.

When it was time to return to our home, we gathered our things and, like other people, began the long walk. I remember feeling in a way saddened, because the woman I had been with was now somewhere else in the kingdom, and as we began our journey, I walking behind my sisters, we passed that area in which I had had the experience with her, and I looked toward the beach at each grassy area, studying those hummocks we passed for flattened grass. Ahead of us others were on their way home, and they talked, sang some of the songs they had heard and chatted amiably. Then each group passed a certain spot on the path and stopped talking, and put their heads down or walked faster. We passed that spot, and because the wind had shifted somewhat, we smelled air fouled by the heavy stench of the dead man, being consumed by rot now for nearly four days.

So ends the description of this Makahiki festival, the last impression, for me, the smell of death. I suppose that at my age, I was just then beginning to understand something about the way our world was ordered—joy and death, two extremes that mark beginnings and endings. As I walked behind Ka'ahupāhau, I believe that despite the fatigue that rendered my limbs loose and flaccid and reduced my mind into that state of languid stupefaction, inside my mind I was perceiving, perhaps for the first time, all that my father had carried as his personal burden.

$$\S$$

MacFarlane's pen hovered over the ledger, the wind spreading the fissures in the thatch and admitting small planes of light and riffling the corners of his page. Then he looked up at Pono, whilst I, my brain trying to find a difference in the battle-story I had now heard a second time, sat in befuddlement. How could it be, I wondered, staring at that dark visage now lost in some deep contemplation, that his narrative showed not the faintest variation from the one I had heard so many days ago?

"And may I ask what happened then?" MacFarlane asked.

Pono nodded slowly at some personally fascinating space before him. MacFarlane looked at me, his expression one of an awed curiosity, as if Pono's failure to continue would frustrate him, like a child arbitrarily denied the end of a bedtime story.

"If you will," Pono said at length, "place an X under that final sentence."

MacFarlane did so, blew on the X, and closed the ledger.

"Ah, Pono," I said. "It very much interests me that your account today seems indeed identical to the first story you told me the day I met you. How is this possible?"

He thought for several seconds. Men walked by outside, talking roughly and laughing. Then he said, "My memory of these events seems in my mind a fixed entity. My language, as I judge it at this moment, is as it was when I first met you."

"Yes, but would there not be some forgetful phase and a consequent variation?"

"Perhaps, although I do not remember any such phase."

MacFarlane laughed.

I looked at the young American. There had been growing in my mind a kind of uneasiness about him. In the execution of his duties as transcriber, he had, over the telling of this tale, begun to manifest a sort of affection for the storyteller, as if the story impressed him, indeed carried him into phases of staring with his imagination obviously enflamed by the imagery manufactured therein. This, I should say, to the point of his forgetting what it was he was sitting there to do. Oddly he seemed at the same time resolute in his writing even in the most prurient sections of Pono's narrative, writing such words as 'ejaculated' without the slightest hint of agitation.

Pono would pause, and then wait as the young man's wide-eyed gaze showed a kind of completion of the formation of this imagery, after which he would again dip and lower his quill, waiting for the next sentence.

"So," I said. "We have left you then at the age of fourteen, a wooden knife in your hand—indeed the tale may take us in our time here into the next year."

"I'd sure like it to," MacFarlane said.

The old storyteller smiled with a benevolent introspection. He sighed and placed his dark hands flat upon the table. "Such recollections do cause some discomfort," he said. "Particularly as Mr. MacFarlane asked, in terms of 'what happened next?'"

"Say," MacFarlane said, "you fellas like to come to my place? I'd like you to meet someone."

Instantly I surmised that it was a woman. The expression on the young man's face was one of a guarded if not somewhat embarrassed hope that we might comply.

Pono looked at him and said, "Certainly. Where is it that you live?"

"Well, our place is not 'elegant' but it is a home nevertheless."

"Your utopia," I said by way of jest.

MacFarlane then seemed to lapse into some brief but pleasant reverie, after which he came out of it and nodded thoughtfully. "If I may be frank," he said, "my digs are no more than a rude hovel among many such places, but I do in fact regard my circumstances as a kind of utopia." His face took on a somewhat troubled appearance. "We—I mean myself and my, shall we say, companion, are lacking in means." He looked at Pono. "Which is why this bit of employment is important to me."

"Very well," Pono said. "Let us go, then."

I paused as they rose from the table. Dust made its way through the fissures in the wall, and I smelled it, a dry, metallic smell, perpetually delivered here by the prevailing winds. For some time now my eyes had been affected by it.

"In which direction is your place?" I asked, as we began walking.

MacFarlane pointed to the east. He may have been referring to a slum I had heard about located in the direction of marshes on the west side of the crater called Leahi, or Lay-ah-hee. Sailors called it "Diamond Hill." This slum, I had heard, was a place wherein women ridded themselves of unwanted babies by casting them into the sea or burying them alive, where iniquity reigned, where natives picked lice from their skin and slept on the ground amid filth, raised pigs inside their dwellings, where mothers sold the bodies of their adolescent girls to lustful sailors for a pittance. And so an anthropological interest took me over there, wherein I weighed the threat of vermin against the lure of this interest in verifying for myself the truth of these allegations.

At length the hot dirt road we traversed narrowed to a footpath. Walking behind Pono, who was behind MacFarlane carrying the heavy ledger-book, I looked about and saw in amongst the dusted brush and trampled patches of grass the pitched roofs of small, grass-topped hovels more fit for animals than humans, and in the narrow spaces between them chickens of different colors ruffled themselves in dry dirt depressions, and muttered upon seeing us, their flat eyes regarding us warily. Somewhere to my left I heard the grunting of a pig. I looked down at my clothes and found myself envisioning lice, or perhaps itch-mites, and contemplated an apologetic taking of my leave from the two men. I was about to stop, to ask just how far MacFarlane's 'digs' were, when I beheld a white woman in a full dress coming our way. She carried in her right hand a woven basket, and in her left, a white parasol.

"What on earth?" I said. MacFarlane and Pono stopped and moved off the path to allow the woman to pass. Upon closer inspection, I saw her to be plain, perhaps too thin, and evidently weary, but of a pleasant demeanor.

"A missionary lady," MacFarlane whispered, at which Pono nodded.

"Gentlemen," she said, approaching. Then she paused, tipping the parasol to the sun. "And may I enquire as to what you seek here?"

MacFarlane seemed taken aback. "I'm going to my place," he said.

"And what ship are you with?"

"None," he said. "I live here now, up there a ways." He shifted his ledger-book under his arm and pointed behind her.

She studied us a moment. "You are Americans then, I assume?"

"No madam," I said. "I am British."

"Ah," she said, thinking. It struck me how self-possessed this woman was. "Please excuse my tendency to become inquisitive," she went on. "Our work here is difficult, and I suppose I am given to such behavior for reasons you are not aware of. I am not particularly jolly today, considering that I have met and counseled yet another native woman who has found herself with child."

She studied us once more, and then sighed rather quickly. "I bid you good day," she said, and passed by us, the parasol still tipped to the sun.

"Meddlers," MacFarlane said. "She assumed we're here for only one reason. Anyone not carrying the Good Book is assumed an eager visitor in a fleshpot."

Standing as we were, I felt the discomfort of a slight perspiration, which I did not want—it raised a disagreeable odor from my clothes. "Gentlemen," I said, "if we are to stand here like sentries, shall we look for some shade?"

"Oh," MacFarlane said, "come this way." MacFarlane then talked over his shoulder. "Some," he said, "have honest motives."

"Come," I called over Pono's shoulder to him, "admit that the origins of your interest in this place had visions of flesh occupying it."

MacFarlane stopped again, now in the shade of a single, bright cloud that had moved off the mountains to our left. "Visions of flesh occupy the mind of a rich man watching his maid change a bed, sir. There is nothing unnatural about that."

"Yes," said I. "But in England, or I suppose in your Boston, that rich man must negotiate layer upon layer of fabric in his quest, a complicated navigational problem, am I correct, in his quest for that grassy, tropical delta? Here, one needs only to dangle a bauble, or simply ask. Is that not what your meddler would call 'iniquitous'?"

"In London one can dangle a bauble or ask, too," MacFarlane said. I detected some annoyance in his voice, and was at the same time interested in Pono's noncommittal, amiable stare. Why it was that I could not stop myself from goading the young MacFarlane, I do not know. Perhaps it was engendered by my part in a collective shame having to do with the late war and our loss of that rich colony.

"Sailors tell me that they scarcely had the opportunity to ask," I said. "In fact, I saw an old filthy sailor enjoying the oral ministrations of a thirteen-year-old, behind a grog shop I might add, and in daylight for all to see. And a plump, well-endowed slut she was, apparently quite good at her work." Again, we were in the harsh sunlight.

"Very well," MacFarlane said, shading his eyes with his hand. "In London it's done behind closed doors. The difference is no more than a panel of wood and plaster."

"Ah," I said, "you claim that a bit of wood is the only difference? That young girls in London might do the same for a bauble? I am skeptical of this."

"Perhaps we should ask our storyteller then," MacFarlane said dryly.

Pono smiled. "That particular pleasure," he said, "is so esteemed by all men that they must manufacture various means of denying it to others, after which the unregulated act is defined as a crime. For it is in our nature to claim ownership of things—individuals and nations. We must then claim this access to that particular pleasure. Secretly, we desire it for ourselves, and at the same time are jealous of its fulfillment by others."

"There," MacFarlane said, pointing his finger at me.

"A curious sentiment," I said. "How can one 'own' a pleasure?"

Pono was about to speak when a boy came along the path with a brown chicken under his arm. Pono held up his hand and the boy stopped, and Pono looked at the chicken. He spoke in their native language a sentence I cannot reproduce here, but the boy's response was to think carefully and then say, "My chicken is grand," after which he went on down the path, leaving Pono to laugh with a contemplative merriment.

"Very well," Pono said. Then he thought a moment and said, "Perhaps by creating for oneself and for others, rules and regulations for its fulfillment."

What had he said? Then I recalled that I had indeed asked him a question before the boy came down the path, and he was answering it. I had to work my mind to grasp this. "Regulations are in place to prevent such things as disease," I said.

"And then would one regulate a man's desire for adventure to prevent his being harmed by it? And then if he is harmed, consider it a crime committed by the victim?"

"The analogy is suspect," I said. "But we must continue."

"Yes," MacFarlane said. "This way."

We passed many huts, simple structures that afforded little in the way of privacy, and I beheld more people, natives sitting in the shade, many children and enthusiastic dogs. There were flies everywhere, but I did not have the impression that this was a stinking slum, as a sailor had described it to me. I did not see evidence of any industry here, but did smell the pleasant scent of cooking, not meat so much as perhaps potato or some vegetable. Nor did I see the wanton nakedness that had been described to me. Perhaps the sailor had been talking about the legendary nakedness men had beheld in the past from the rails of their ships—brown wenches climbing over those rails, their parts animated lusciously by their vigorous motion, water dripping from their hair above and below. He had seemed to me older, and was perhaps in a reverie of recollection when he said, "Aye, an' she pushed me down into me bunk and pulled me pantaloons down an' sat on it, an' after months of it being me an' me, I tell you sir, it was a dream. I tell ye, clean they was, all of 'em beautiful clean an' naked as ever, takin' it like dogs an' takin' it underneath and up top of us."

These speculations rested in my mind as both delicious in their imagery and at the same time indecent to the point of perversity. The broad shoulders of Pono, who no doubt had enjoyed much of precisely what confused, disgusted and at the same time enflamed me in a vicarious sense, brought me back to the activity at hand. Before me were children watching us with their dark eyes, chickens pausing in their scratching to watch us pass, as if assessing us in some fascinated speculation, and as before, the hovels of the common people.

At last we arrived at a structure approximately the same size as the others, but erected more of wood than of thatch. MacFarlane's approach signified that it was indeed his dwelling, and at a low doorway we paused.

"I'll see if things are in order," MacFarlane whispered, and went inside, ducking down quite far to pass through the doorway. In a moment his face reappeared, tipped sideways as he looked up at us. "Please, come in," he said.

The hovel I assumed I was entering was not what I rose up to behold: centered on a raw wooden floor was a tan woven mat, upon it sitting a girl of perhaps eight or nine wearing a skirt but naked above the waist, above her a dark woman in a white dress, a not unpleasing countenance—full lips, a high forehead, and dark copper hair tied back. Her eyes were dark, her nose somewhat broad, almost negroid, and her upper lip had upon it a vertical scar off to the right side, which gave her mouth a saucy aspect that her apparent shyness could not hide. She stood next to, of all things, a desk, MacFarlane's I assumed, and indeed there was a rather fine picture on the wall, of a red bird sitting on a branch that ended in red globular flowers.

"This is Heneliaka," MacFarlane said, indicating the woman, and then he looked down at the child, who was I now realized reading a book. "And Loke."

"And what book is this?" I asked the child. She ignored me, her finger on a picture of a schooner.

"Ship," she said.

"Indeed," I said. "MacFarlane, this is a pleasant little house."

MacFarlane nodded, his face briefly crossed by a smug and proprietary expression. Pono took a couple of steps along the wall, not stepping on the mat. He spoke something in his language to the woman, who spoke back to him in a whisper. She looked at him then, thinking. Pono stooped down to hold the edge of the mat. "This is fine lauhala," he said. The woman continued to look. A strange expression, I thought. Did she see in him a partner for her pleasure that she might prefer to MacFarlane?

"If you only knew how far we had to go to haul the materials back," MacFarlane said, "you'd wonder about my sanity." He looked around. "But we have put a good deal of work into this. Much of the wood I bought or begged down at the port. The lauhala Heneliaka made. Her name in English is Henrietta, the respelling into their alphabet common here. Her mother was from here and her father unknown, but French, she believes."

"And the child?" I asked. I then felt a strange shame, making that assumption about the woman, for she had no parents, MacFarlane and the girl her only family, I supposed.

"Her sister," MacFarlane said. "Come this way. I'll show you the rest." The sister seemed to me sickly, thin and passive, as if underfed.

There was a small anteroom that served as a bedroom with, of all things, a bed, constructed of planking and topped with a thin mattress, which was covered by another mat. Sitting upon a small stand under a wall-mounted mirror there was a heavy, practical, white ironstone washbasin of the sort made by the English potter Miles Mason, a crack stained as though by rust running from its center to its rim, and inside was an ironstone pitcher lacking a handle.

MacFarlane took us behind the structure to show us a small garden, which made Pono laugh and then stoop down to study the dark green foliage of a low vine-like plant.

"'Uala," Pono said, holding the soft tip of one of the vines. "Hāpu'upu'u," he went on. "Sir, you are a more-than-competent farmer."

"What is this?" I asked.

"It is sweet potato, what I was given lordship over as a child," Pono said.

"Ah yes," I said. "I recall your narrative."

MacFarlane was at the moment studying some dusty brush beyond his garden. Then the three of us went back into MacFarlane's dwelling. The woman was now sitting with the wan child, both of them studying the book.

She was sitting with her legs crossed, her head bowed as they studied a picture of a horse. I caught one glimpse then, inside the slightly open white dress, the rich flesh of her breasts moving with a brief, jiggling animation therein as she flipped a page to a picture of a house. I saw the shape of sumptuous hips, and experienced a sudden vision: the unkempt youth MacFarlane and this savage in that jury-rigged bed. And what, thought I, what other iniquities did that vision portend? The child? MacFarlane was after all an American, like his kind given to secret perversities that indeed eclipsed anything that occurred behind wood and plaster in England. Even their Mr. Franklin was a renowned lecher. But I cast aside that speculation, again somewhat ashamed. Pono was observing the two of them. The woman, I believe, had engaged in this activity with the child out of shyness.

We took our leave. MacFarlane spent a few moments with us at his low door, explaining that the child was sickly with some digestive problem that caused her to go into fits of cramping with the production of bloody stool. Pono, listening, let his eyes drift to the dark square of that door, and nodded thoughtfully as MacFarlane spoke.

My mind again drifted to that question: what on earth besides pleasures of the flesh could have motivated the young man to set himself up this way, especially with a woman who was perhaps too dim of wit to provide much in the way of company for him? I concluded that the young man's 'utopia' was little more than a sexual dalliance that he had cloaked in the garb of propriety. It was true that she showed unbeknownst to her own sense of shame a sumptuous attractiveness of the body, perhaps more attractive in her charms than a woman past the inconvenience of shame, a harlot, say. Men like MacFarlane, I supposed, would be vulnerable to falling over themselves in the presence of the dim-witted child unaware of what she possessed in the flesh, for that inconvenience, shame, stood always in the way of men's fulfillment of their desires.

But in the evening I found myself once again alone on the ship, gazing at the numerous faint winking of lights, and hearing the mindless pandemonium of men made insane by drink. Are we civilized? I wondered. Or are we like the very savages we visit here but for the formality of our clothes?

5.

*G*entlemen, *we left this story* with the picture of a boy on a bluff overlooking the ocean which was blue and clear under magnificent clouds, and in his hand was a pahoa, or wooden knife. I use the word 'boy' because that is indeed what I was, thrust for one day into the violent world of men. Standing there, the knife heavy in my hand, I understood that 'Iolana was dead, my father too, and my mother and sisters were gone, I knew not where. I sat down and wept like the boy I was, my head bowed as if in invitation to any of those warriors to walk up to me and cleave my skull with a war-axe. I was looking through wet eyes at the ground under me, the vision lucid and watery, and beheld there a broken mo'o egg, apparently from my having stepped upon and overturned some piece of rotted wood.

The mo'o, or lizard you would call it, was curled inside the white egg the size of a pea, and I could see him through a delicate, translucent membrane left exposed when part of the egg broke off. The boy in me momentarily forgot the horror and enormity of the situation, because the mo'o had begun to move, to writhe inside that delicate membrane. The world around me became silent and remote as I stared, and in time the mo'o broke the membrane, and emerged, slick and tiny, no longer than one joint of my finger. Ants appeared, attracted by the tiny stain of fluid from the egg, and the mo'o, still wet, stood on its tiny feet, and then his tail rose up in an alert quarter-arc. I held my breath, watching, and magically the tiny creature walked away in its curving side-to-side walk.

Sounds returned to me, laughter, yells of warlike exultation, and down along the water, the deep thumping of wood on wood, canoe hulls sounding like random drumbeats from afar. I looked and saw people pulling fishing canoes down the sand, while to my left, the victorious warriors walked over their spoils, pointing at lo'i, at dwellings. Those trying to escape would soon be overtaken and killed, the men and perhaps even some of the women were they to try to stand by their men in defense. As my faculties returned, I began to sense the slow onset of a different fright, one which consumed my flesh with so horrible a dread that I began to moan, and again to weep, sitting there holding the knife. One canoe was now out in the water, inside the half-circle of reef that was now becoming exposed because of the waning tide.

Remaining low to the ground, I moved on the bluff toward the water, and as the sand came into my vision, I beheld three people dragging another canoe toward the water. I doubted my eyes, because the three were my father, mother and Laka. I was but two hundred paces from them. Behind me the victorious warriors moved over the bluffs, their line of vision apprehending first those dragging canoes farther down the beach to my left, and upon seeing this activity they began to run, their spears and war axes in hand.

I ran down the bluffs to the sand. Upon seeing me my mother screamed and ran toward me. She was shaking and breathless, and grabbed me, turned me around, studying my body. Then she moaned, "Auwe! It is a miracle!"

Laka and my father struggled with the canoe. I went to help, the knife still in my hand, and put it under my malo cord. There were three paddles in the hull. Pushing, tugging at the ama, I said, "Where is Ka'ahupāhau?"

"She was struck. She ran," my mother said. "Something struck her."

I turned and looked up the bluffs.

Then we pushed more, and the canoe slid into the water. We climbed in, and Laka, my father, and I began to paddle, Laka in the middle and I in the back. Not fifty paces into the water we heard hoarse laughter behind us. Four men, large and shining with sweat and oil, were carrying another canoe to the water. Their spears were in the hull, points just visible above the manu, which is the forward upward projection of the prow, and means *bird* because it resembles the straining neck and head of a bird in flight. My mother looked back and then put her face in her hands and wailed. We paddled straight away from the shore toward the exposed reef, and it was clear that we would be quickly overtaken. They came after us, the four men stroking smoothly and powerfully. There was no means by which we would escape. We 'men' would be killed, the women taken, Laka a prize for one of them.

It is perhaps one of the mysteries of the mind and body that strenuous activity seems somehow to stimulate one's cleverness, but paddling with as much force as I could wring from myself, I conceived a plan. The reef, appearing closer before us, would be a barrier we and our pursuers would have to cross by means of getting out of the canoes and sliding them over into the deep water.

I said to Laka, "Tell father I will stay by the reef as you paddle away."

"Why?" she asked.

I was breathless. I kept paddling, then heard deep laughter behind us. "Do as I say," I said. She leaned away from me to speak to my father.

I felt suddenly and somewhat irrationally ashamed, for having ordered her to do this. My father must have heard, because he turned to look at me, the expression of fright and awe and exhaustion showing also a hint of questioning, if not a faint hope.

When we reached the reef, the canoe bumped it and rose up, spilling my mother back onto Laka's knees. My father got out and, his motions rapid and agitated, pulled Laka and my mother onto the seaweed-covered reef. From behind, standing on a shoal under me, I pushed at the canoe, which slid over the reef and into the deeper water.

As they scrambled back in, I went along the side, and pulled the knife from my malo cord. "Paddle out a hundred paces," I said. "I will stay."

"Why?" my father asked.

And I said, "Do this. Do as I say."

They did so. Now in the water, clinging to the reef on the outside, I peeked over and saw the approaching canoe, the men stroking and talking at once, apparently gleeful, perhaps having seen Laka and discussing her. I believe that the feeling of water holding my flesh as it did gave me a resolve I would not have had out of water. It was after all the place I had chosen to die.

The four warriors had chosen another lower spot in the reef to slide their canoe over, so I dove down and swam underwater toward that spot. There, wedging myself between two protrusions and pulling out the knife, I waited, staring at the seaweed settled upon the rock. Inside that seaweed was a sea-urchin called wana, with many sharp spines on a half sphere, each spine with a painful venom. Hearing the thumps of wood on wood as the men dropped their paddles into the hull upon their approach to the reef, I put the point of the knife in the hole in which sat the wana and pried it out. Then, putting the knife back inside the malo cord, I waited, cupping the wana in my hand.

I looked once to the ocean, and saw my mother, father and Laka out more than a hundred paces, the canoe moving at an angle, as if they were waiting for me. Just as I turned back, the wood of the canoe moved past my face, so close that I wedged myself farther back. Fearing that I would be seen, I used the reef wall to pull myself under.

The sound under the water was of faraway voices, excited but remote, and the sound of that koa wood sliding, then a thump. I watched. A leg came down and then swept up. Then the wood's angle tipped toward the ocean. I felt my chest tighten for want of air, and paused there in horrible indecision. My plan, so firm in my mind as I had ordered my own father to do as I said, had faded in the water as a handful of dirt fades, and had been replaced by a fear so debilitating that I considered allowing myself to drown rather than rise with my feeble weapon, still cupped in my hand.

Indeed I might have, had a foot not come down and struck my shoulder, and that was followed by a sharp yell, at which my breath was gone and I rose out of the water.

I rose hands up, my luck that my right foot found purchase on part of the reef, thus making my emergence fast, and upon breaking the surface I smelled sea-foam and aimed the urchin at a shape I knew to be a man. Their yells of surprise were sharp and loud as the hand holding the urchin met a face, and the man fell back with a roar of anger, and I reached for the only thing within reach, one of their paddles. At the moment my hand felt the round shaft, a sharp, glancing blow to my head stunned me, and the force of it made me bite the side of my tongue at which the rich taste of blood visited my mouth. I either fell or dove, I am not sure, and with the paddle before me swam down into the deeper water, frustrated that the blade of the paddle hindered my progress until I allowed it to trail behind me. I swam as strongly as I could in what I assumed was my parents' direction. I had not even clearly seen my adversaries' faces, although I knew one of them at the very least was deeply insulted by my thrusting the wana in his face.

I swam under the water perhaps the depth of a man's height, and when my need for air again overcame me, I swam upward and again broke the surface. I was more than halfway to the canoe. When I turned, I saw the four once again making their way into theirs. I swam in my parents' direction, and I believe that my father, upon seeing the paddle above the water, understood what I had done. The canoe turned, and they paddled toward me, and I swam, exhausted now to the point of breathlessness. I reached our canoe when that of the warriors was not fifty paces from us.

It is a simple yet fascinating principle that four powerful warriors with three paddles chasing four people of obviously limited strength ought to overtake them easily, but this is not so. Four paddles meant perfect balance, and our combined weight was less than the weight of those large men. They pulled ferociously, at first so close that one seemed ready to launch himself into our canoe, in fact the one with his hand to his cheek and an expression of vengeful rage on his face.

But within a few seconds it became clear that no amount of strength would compensate for the loss of that paddle, and we were able then to slow ourselves and look back. The warrior whose face I had punctured with the wana now pulled the front of his malo down and urinated briefly into his cupped hand, and raised his hand to his face to rub the urine on the many tiny holes there. One of the properties of urine is ammonia, and is a remedy for wana and jellyfish stings.

My recollection of the hours after our escape is flawed, I believe.

Ah, I see that you manifest a good-humored shock at this admission. Mr. MacFarlane's hand pauses. But gentlemen, you yourselves know how one's memory operates. Sequence is sometimes reversed in the recollection.

I know that in my exhaustion I laid my head on my knees and slept, and I dreamed, and in my dream the man I killed talked to me. I know that under that bright sunlight my mother swung her upper body down and slammed her forehead onto the mo'o, or gunnel, of the canoe and, bloody and dazed, was comforted by Laka, who wept miserably and held her. I know that she asked me to assist her out of her misery by putting my pahoa into her heart. In my dream, in which the man I killed stood before me with an anguished expression on his face, holding his glistening entrails against the large wound in his stomach, I knew that Ka'ahupāhau was alive and waiting for us to come and get her. I heard the sound of her weeping, and I can connect parts of this day together by saying that when I knew Ka'a was alive, I came more to my senses and looked at my mother, who, her face wet and the welt leaking dark blood, held her hands out to me and said, "Will you help me?" and I said, somewhat thickly because my tongue had swollen because of that bite at the reef, "Don't you want to see Ka'a again?"

The silence on the part of the rest of my family was, to me, amazing, as if I had said something that had indeed caught their attention. Having killed a man and survived the battle, two unlikely events, had changed their opinions of me.

At length my father said, "What gives you the impression that she is alive?"

"I do not feel the absence of her yet," I said.

My father's face went into an expression of suspicious contemplation, that same look he had manifested when I had told him that Kū'ulakai, The Red One of the Sea had blessed me with vision under the water.

"What do you mean?" he asked.

"That I know where she is, and that she is alive," I said, and as I said that I also doubted it. The boy with his fantasy was at war with the man and his practicality. How could a dream be regarded as credible?

I could not simply go back. Our dilemma was complicated. We were homeless, reduced to outcasts, kauwā, the lowest we could become. Could it be that, somehow, we had returned again to the predicament my father often described of our line of many generations ago? I could see in the wretched and confused expression on my father's face that the question of whether or not Kaʻa was alive was irrelevant, for what kind of a life would our family have to offer her if we did find her?

We made our way along the shore, at a distance of one mile out. This was dangerous, because the warriors we had humiliated could easily have gone back for another paddle. But my father reasoned that they would desist in favor of going back to discuss the spoils of their victory.

Nightfall found us far to the west of our home, at an uninhabitable point of the island, the rocky shore beset by great waves and a steady driving wind. The landscape was arid, the small population dwelling somewhat inland of those rocks, and we discussed what we should do. I could think of nothing but the sound of weeping, not my mother's or Laka's, but Kaʻahupāhau's. She was alive as surely as I was alive—life was more important than the problem of a dwelling place.

We decided to beach the canoe at a place where, it was clear, it would be discovered in the morning. My father decided that we would make our way back out to sea before that discovery was to be made. We had to gather material to provide shade for us as we languished out there on the water.

"I am going back for Kaʻa," I said.

"You cannot," he said. "Once we are separated—" He did not continue.

"We are separated," I said. "I am going back to find her."

My father sighed. I saw a grudging acquiescence, as if my pronouncement pleased as much as irritated him. "And how will you find us?" he asked.

"You will come to land at night. We will see you by day and wait."

We made our way in darkness toward the shore. We did not know the nature of the breakwater, and feared injury to ourselves and damage to the canoe. My father instructed my mother and Laka to go over the side and swim in while he and I would get in the water and ride the canoe from behind, my father at the end and I on the ʻiako, which is the boom attached to the ama, or float. We would be dragged through the water, but would prevent the canoe from turning over, which would certainly damage it should the ʻiakos and manu hit the bottom.

Our arrival at the beach was smooth, effortless, as if we had done it many times. Because the tide had been low we had escaped the half-circle of reef in the morning, and we were again on a waning tide coming into the beach.

My mother and Laka stood together shivering in the darkness. In that pause, breathless from having been dragged through the water by the canoe, I perceived the bleak horror of our situation. What could we do now but die? My mother's hunched shoulders seemed to say this. Perhaps she was right. We were without connection, without claim to any patch of soil, forlorn and lost. I felt willing to accede to this dark sentiment but for one thing—Ka'ahupāhau, that girl who for me had taken on so mysterious and magical an aspect. Now she was my sister, whom I was bound by duty as a brother to rescue from the lustful desires of such men as we had escaped from hours ago.

I produced a fatigued laugh at the thought of my insult to that warrior, who at the very moment I stood there shivering, was rubbing urine on the painful stings on his face that would keep him from the comfort of a peaceful slumber, at least this night.

I felt that I had to leave immediately, but I was unsure as to how far we had come, and if I would recognize the place we lived, at night. I asked my father, who told me that I would sleep first, while he would move inland in search of some source of water, perhaps food. We had other matters to be concerned about: those warriors would, upon finding little to do the next day, come after us. The man whose face I had punctured with the wana would, my father said, spend many days looking for me so that he could kill me, and by means that he would enjoy, perhaps using a strangling cord. I had to be extremely careful not to be seen.

Then my father sighed, an ashen specter in the moonlight, and thumped his chest with his fist. "As for me," he said, "it matters not if I live or die."

We moved inland by moonlight. Here the terrain was dry and stony, and before us were the descending remains of the mountain range, a series of stark, rocky outcroppings devoid of vegetation but for dry grasses making their flat scraping sounds in the wind. We found protection from the wind in a sandy area behind some boulders, and there I slept, aware as I drifted off that my mother and Laka sat there beside me.

In that vast and flexible land of the imagination, aided by fatigue and darkness, the man I killed returned, and introduced himself to me, all the while holding his bloody entrails against his stomach, which surged and changed color under his fingers as he spoke. He told me that he had a family, that he had experienced much in his life, that he had never intended to nor wanted a battle over an insult or a handful of fish. It was at the behest of men of power that he and I had met at the river, and it meant little which of us was to die. In this case he was surprised by someone much smaller who, after having thrust his barbed spear, wanted it back and thus took entrails and organs from him, a long painful drawing that sucked the breath from him, and upon seeing that frightened boy's face, he, the dead man, knew finally how the vagaries of chance dominated all our lives. "Should you," he said, raising one hand from his horrible wound to point at me, "begin to elevate your opinion of yourself as men tend to do, you too will discover how without meaning or reason your life is and shall be."

I woke to the sound of my father's voice, spoken in the faint light of a flat, gray dawn: "There is a small cave just up this mountain, and I have found water, a trickle of water, but enough for us. There is soil up there in flat areas, enough perhaps to grow 'uala. In the forest above I found 'ōhi'a 'ai. I did not take any because the tree was across a ravine from where I stood, and I saw people there. In time I will travel farther around the end of the island and shall beg for the kindness of others."

"I want to die," my mother said.

"No," my father said. "I forbid you to cultivate such thoughts."

"Half of my children are dead," she said.

"And half are alive," he said.

I tried to orient myself to this new day. My tongue was thick and dry in my mouth. I sat up, and when my head went above the rock I had slept under, I understood why it was that no one lived in this area: the wind drove off the ocean with a steady force, a force I realized would be bothersome after but a few minutes. My father sat with my mother and Laka, and on a stone near his foot was a large wad of moss that leaked water onto the stone. When he saw me, my father said, "Come, there is little left."

I rose and made my way to him, stiff in my joints and weary, my feet sore, and he told me to lie down in the sand and open my mouth. When I did so, he picked up the moss, and very slowly squeezed it, producing a bright line of water that I watched as it ran over my tongue. "Enough," he said, laughing. "You'll become bloated."

This levity on his part was understandable. We were in the middle of a catastrophe that might mean our deaths. What else to do but approach it with good humor?

"I will go now," I said.

He nodded. My mother looked at me, then at Laka. That I would go no longer seemed impractical. My father told me to move lightly, and to avoid injuring my feet. He asked me to look for 'uala, and plants to snap off the tops from, a forearm's length so that we could eat some of the tops and plant the remainder. If we were to stay in this place, we should attempt to provide for ourselves. 'Uala grows rapidly, and the tops of plants are edible. He told me to eat what fruit I found and not to try to carry any back, because he had located some above us, hidden in ravines.

"Do not allow yourself to be seen," he said.

And so I went, moving into the rising sun, the pahoa secure under my malo cord. Because our valley and stream had been among the last of the populated areas before the windswept end of the island, I saw little for some time as I made my way down into dry ravines and over stark, rocky ridges. To my left, the ocean and the bright clouds beyond were just as they had been the previous day, when I had killed a man and had survived a battle. If I could find and bring Ka'ahupāhau to my mother and sister, then I would believe in my own resourcefulness and strength, rather than luck. It would be proof to my father, and more importantly to myself, that I was a man.

At length I saw the smoke of cooking fires in the distance, and studied the terrain from a ridge. Those darker collections of trees, those terraces on the mountainside, were the beginnings of our valley and stream. In fact, I thought I recognized, from afar, some arrangement of terraces that could have been those above our former home, and with this recognition, I turned my attention to the ridges above those arrangements of terraces.

As I moved closer, I became aware of an odor in the air, a rich smell of slightly turned meat. It was the valley of the uncertain winds, and this odor stayed in the wind a few seconds, and then vanished, then came back. I made my way up a grassy ridge, and lowered myself to my belly upon reaching the top. There, below me, was an area separate from the dwellings where the bodies of the dead had been dragged to rot in the sun. I could see them beginning to bloat and subtly shifting as if in movement of some kind until I understood that clouds of flies hovered over them, creating a strange grayish veil upon the arrangement of torsos and limbs. There, I imagined, 'Iolana lay, rotting by day, being gnawed upon in the night by rats. I concentrated on the bodies, trying to see if Ka'ahupāhau might also be among them, and then stopped myself, recalling that I had not yet felt her absence. I believed I knew where she was.

The first inhabitants of the area I saw were busy tending my garden, two women and a boy, and a foolish thought occurred to me: make sure to pick worms off the 'uala. Those people had simply crossed the stream and taken over our hale. I made my way up the ridge, out of their sight, and into wooded areas I was familiar with. Here I felt secure, but for the possibility of being seen by anyone collecting wood or hunting birds. The smell of the bodies was stronger up there, the wind having carried the odor up the length of one of the ravines. But I ignored that odor, because I was near my destination.

Within perhaps twenty yards of my secret cave I experienced a sudden morbid fright, for I now felt a strange dreadful pressure in the air, as if my closeness to the cave made understanding clearer. My heart labored in my chest, the foul, acidic vacuum of hunger in my stomach replaced now by the anticipation of her death. Those earlier experiences in which I had confused and misplaced my lust were no longer important. She was my blood, and her mana was my mana. I moved toward the cluster of bushes hiding the cave entrance. When I stooped down and crawled through the brush, I was shocked to behold her form in there, her feet toward the opening. She was lying on her side, apparently asleep. I made my way inside, into the cooler darkness, and crouching, made that same noise she had made to me in the night: *tsst.*

She did not move. When I touched her leg, she moaned softly, and I saw then where she had been struck, between her neck and her right shoulder, a deep cleft there left perhaps by a war-axe, the v-shaped hole showing pale bone. The wound was hidden below that cleft by her arm, which was pasted to her side by blood. As my eyes adjusted to the darkness, I began to see the insects, ants, even a slug, gathered around that wound, and the black, glistening lines that crossed her chest and ran over her right breast were lines of drying blood, their ends clotted and dangling with torpid thickness. I placed my hand on her side, and she moved weakly, her eyes remaining closed.

"Ka'a," I whispered. Her head moved slightly, and I could see that her eyes were glued shut, so I put spit on my finger and touched them, moving the lids so that she might open them, which she did. In that airy blankness in which I tried to make my mind conceive of something to do to help her, I began to shake, because I understood that she was beyond my help. The wound was too severe, the dark blotch under her a thick, pasty and jellyish mass, insects crawling at the edges. She was near death.

I sat beside her. Her eyes were open, and I saw the hint of a smile, or perhaps evidence of a feeling of some comfort on her part. When I put my hand to hers, she closed her fingers around two of mine, and held them. Then she whispered, "Wai."

"I will get water," I whispered.

I left the cave, and blinded by the sunlight, sat in the bushes waiting for my eyes to adjust. The stream was perhaps five hundred paces from where I sat, and I knew that there were coconut shells there, in which I could carry water. I made my way toward it, forgetting that I was to remain hidden. Near the stream I heard the voices of children, and then saw three boys, younger than I, playing in a pool formed by rocks. I ignored the boys and looked for coconuts. I found a large one that had no dried meat or dirt inside, and holding it under the water, began filling it up while they watched. The three holes on the end of the shell are small, and I shook it under the water so that it would fill all the way. I drank while I held the coconut shell under, drank until my belly felt bloated. The boys watched in silence. One of them made his way up the stream toward me.

"Who are you?" he asked.

"I am a ghost," I said. The word for ghost is *lapu*. At the sound of that word, the boy turned and went back to his friends, and then they vanished. Doubtless they would report me to their elders, so I made my way back toward the cave, the hard shell full of water.

I dripped a thin stream of water on her lips, and she drank. She seemed to awaken, and she then began to weep, and to moan, a soft, high-pitched, exhausted wailing. I tried to clean the ants and other insects off the wound, and apparently it caused her no pain. She was numb to it, numb to the water I dripped at the edges and numb to the touch of my fingers. I thought I should clean the wound more thoroughly, so I tried carefully lifting her arm, and when I did so, I saw that the wound continued under it, so large that it seemed as if whoever had struck her had nearly removed her arm. I could do nothing for her. So I sat, and held her hand.

"Pono," she whispered.

I leaned over on my elbow and put my face close to hers. "I am here."

"He has one ear," she whispered. "He is only a boy, a big boy. He said he would have me and told me to sit and spread my legs, and I spat in his face."

"I will find him," I whispered. "I will make fish-hooks of his bones."

"He hit me with the axe and then he laughed. He has one ear, and one stub. He laughed at me."

"I will kill him."

She sighed. I was about to say more when her grip on my hand relaxed, and then that sigh changed into jerking breath, as if she could not draw air in, and her face, as much of it as I could see in the darkness of the cave, changed into a clench-toothed tension, as if she were cold, and then she was still.

I did not know if what I did was right, but I poured the remainder of the water along her hair and divided it into three sections, twisting it carefully, and braided her hair all the way from the back of her head to the trailing end, and tied knotted the last points of hair. Then I found two stones, one flat and the other sharp-edged, and moved her head so that it was close to the flat rock, and with the other, ground the braid off at the back of her head. It took some time, and when I was finished I found grasses that I wound around the thick end of her braid.

Then I sat. I did not weep. I began to groan softly, rocking on my folded legs, holding the braid across my thighs. I felt responsible, for I had killed a man, and now Kaʻahupāhau was death's manipulation in favor of some grotesque symmetry. I felt small and soiled, and went on with my humming. I placed my hand on her hip and felt the coldness. The braid, now hot in my lap, had sucked the mana from her dead body and assimilated it into its thousands of tightly bound hairs. She had escaped into her braid.

I do not know how long I would have remained in our cave, now her burial place, but I heard the voices of men, and the tramping of feet through dry leaves. They were coming for me. I did not care. The only feature of this horrible turn of events that urged me into action was the responsibility I had, now, to deliver Kaʻahupāhau to my mother. So, touching her one last time, I made my way carefully out of the cave. The men were by the stream. I wound the braid around my hand, appreciating its weight—she was indeed in there, and made my way to the west.

Walking, I felt hollow and small, and then felt a powerful desire for vengeance against that one-eared boy who had killed her. I vowed that should I ever have the opportunity, I would kill him, perhaps strangle him with the braid I carried, after which I would dig out his eyes and urinate on them. At the same time I understood how small I was, how insignificant. I understood also that what was left of our family were Kauwā, the lowest of the low. In that vast expanse, the sumptuous white clouds sitting off to the north above the water, I felt the growing recognition that life itself, that mysterious gift we all must speculate on from time to time, meant little. We were as insects. How did this mix, I wondered, with what I understood to be a perception so complex, an ability on my and all other humans' parts to dream, to feel pain, to hope, to feel pleasure? Were we doomed to our own stupidity? Why, after all, had we fought? I went on, my poʻo tumid with such speculations.

So ends this part of the boy's life. I assure you, gentlemen, that the degree of detail I offer in this reconstruction shall diminish for a time, and that given how many pages Mr. MacFarlane has produced, you may be reassured that each year of the life I describe shall not be as rich in description, for were it, we might assume that this room would fill with ledger-books before we are done, and Matthew's resources exhausted.

True it is that the tale fascinated me, but at times I felt a peculiar agitation at the care with which Pono rendered his narrative. I needed a break from it. The rude chair I sat on, and the constant dry wind, bearing red dust that settled upon my clothes, had become unbearable. In addition, the sound of the sailors of the area yelling obscenities and fighting, and complaining about the missionaries, and trading stories about their dalliances with the brown girls, all of this made me feel as if I were exiled into some raucous penal colony. I did not know of MacFarlane's disposition in this matter, for he scratched away at his ledger-book with no indication of a like agitation. Besides, I thought, each night he went to his humble little digs and his woman.

I'll admit that I dreamed of her, and engaged in rueful cogitations about my own frustration where activity with women was concerned. In this place, one had not the slightest prohibition concerning this matter, and I wondered what it was about me that prevented such activity.

I do not know what caused these ruminations to visit me. Perhaps it was the atmosphere of the place, ugly at times because of the heat and the irritating humidity, which would cause me to perspire in my bunk at night. But at other times, the cool air of mornings and evenings would awaken in me a luscious swoon of excitement at my presence here, as if energized at my joy for being in a place wherein prohibition itself had been ignored or banished but for the presence of the much disliked missionaries.

As to Pono's tale, I had begun by this time to expect some more efficient movement toward the aspect of it that interested me most—Beckwith. But Pono was, in his tale, still but fourteen years of age. I believe that my frustration at this caused me to look outward, and so it was that I requested an invitation to visit the house of Don Francisco de Paula Marin. George Swift was a paying guest at the house, and suggested I visit and meet some of the men of the shipping business there. Indeed I should have seen the opportunity, because my family was part owner of *The Clarel*. A product of wealth, I had little interest in the exploitations of this place, but I understood the eagerness of others who saw possibilities here beyond the women.

They were British and American, these men, and were not the type to arrive at Marin's rather opulent house in pantaloons and bare feet. They were quite splendidly attired, rigged out I should say in a manner befitting an audience with George IV himself.

I stood by Swift, who engaged in a discussion with a shipping company man named Traynor, and we drank Marin's wine, made from vineyards on his own property. Traynor went on about the Queen and her alliance with the missionaries, and about Britain's interest in this place. At length he went into the problem of the denuding of the area of sandalwood and the drying up of the opportunities for profit there. Finally he looked at me and said, "So what brings you here then?"

"I am interested in botanical matters, but was lured by another project."

"And that is?"

"I met a most fascinating man, a kanaka who sailed with Roger Beckwith."

"Hide your purse," he said, and both he and Swift laughed.

"I am recording the tale of his experiences."

To which Traynor said, more to Swift than to me, "Say, did you see Marin's daughter? She bears the odd name of Lahilahi. A wonderful creature she is."

So, the revelation of my activity fell upon deaf ears. I had seen her too, a girl of perhaps fifteen who aroused in me, as she probably did in all men, that same sensation of the hint of wanton release. She was a 'creature' indeed, of this place and at the same time not, a mixture of the darker European and the brown flesh of this place and people. Indeed the image of those sumptuous breasts, here of course covered by fabric and lace, and the dark, innocent, seductive eyes, visited me later as I languished in my bunk.

But alas, the sporting of such creatures was not my aim or inclination. I felt more and more alienated from my associates because of this, and was left, again, with Pono and the young American whom, I will admit, I had begun to envy, considering his access to the luscious, dimwitted savage he had taken into his bed.

Another concern, merely academic, visited me: where did Pono live? I asked MacFarlane if he knew, and he said that he did not, although he knew the direction Pono approached from, the east. Farther out there, he said, between the marshes and the beach, there were other huts, some of them beachcombers' dives.

"I suppose what he does with his time is his business," I said.

"Well, he said he looks around for folks he knew," MacFarlane said. "Might be that he spends his time at that."

"Might be," I said, and then laughed inwardly at my picking up an American expression.

6.

As you recall, I had promised a more efficient advancement of this narrative, and so it shall be.

I presented my father 'uala tops, and my mother Ka'ahupāhau's braid, and in the days following, observed the process of her and Laka's grief, doubled now because they had already been rendered dull with misery because of 'Iolana's death. I told my father what she had told me, and he said, "I know that you desire vengeance as I do, but it will come to nothing. Everything we are will come to nothing."

He said this with thoughtful equanimity, and I looked around at the harsh surroundings. He had found a cave with no bones in it, he told me, farther toward the wild, uninhabitable point at the end of the island, and up into the side of a bare, windswept mountain. They had been waiting for me to return before going to the cave. My father had broken branches off brush and hidden the canoe, but he surmised that we would have no use for it. So, within an hour of my return, the four of us made our way up an old path toward that cave, and here this account shall accelerate forward.

We lived in that cave, and established a pattern of activity that restored some modicum of order to our lives. We planted 'uala in protected areas near the cave. I fashioned spears out of harder woods, using stones to shape and sharpen them, and on mornings when the tide was favorable, I used the talent Ku'ulakai, The Red One of the Sea had taught me, and made my way to the ocean, to find coves where the water was not so violent. I was able to provide fish and octopus for us, along with limu, which is a tasty and I believe nutritious seaweed eaten as a matter of course by the kanaka maoli. I also used my pahoa to dig opihi, which is a delicious limpet, from the rocks.

We lived thus, for the turn of a year. Yes, I see your facial expression manifest a sudden brightening, as if watching a wagon long stuck in the mud suddenly moving. My father made surreptitious forays back toward our former living place, thinking that perhaps conditions had changed. On one trip he talked to a fisherman who warned him that our valley was now under the leadership of a cruel monster who made a mockery of the privileges of leadership. My father was equally curious about what lay beyond the end of the island on the other side, but reasoned that death was as likely a result of too much curiosity as the discovery of a better life for us. He had been there years earlier, he told us, and said that the land was not as full of vegetation as our north side of the island.

All of this would have been better for me had it not been for the frequent nocturnal visitation of the man I had killed, always holding the gruesome wound in his stomach, and I also had like visitations from Kaʻa, who whispered to me that she wanted satisfaction for her death, and I would argue with her, offering the logic of the man I had killed as cause and her death as effect. She sometimes became seductive, and in these confused dreams I blended with her as she cleaved to me, she explaining that in her state it did not matter if a child resulted, for born in the nether world, it would be aliʻi, and when I awoke, I would find myself wet down there.

I would sometimes be shaken awake by Laka, a light sleeper herself. She accused me of talking in my sleep. I knew she was right, but wanted to hide from all of them the fact of these visitations.

As Makahiki drew near, we discussed whether or not we might participate, and decided against it. True, a colorful parade would pass on the path far below us, but we felt that any revealing of our circumstances might bring about results we would regret, for example, the recognition and then selection of Kauwā for the sacrificial stone.

So Makahiki passed. We did see the line of people and the banners, and the dots of red and yellow of the cloaks. They passed in an hour, making their way to that area wherein I had grown up and where Kaʻa lay in her burial cave.

As our residence in the cave passed one year, my father began to speculate more deeply on our state. Should we not explore more of our surroundings? Was our hesitation no more than cowardice? I agreed with him. Living as we did, in our profound isolation, had made us a little batty. My father was always lost in thought, my mother was indolent and thin, and Laka dreamt away the days, lapsed into some reverie in which a stout warrior would somehow come to claim her.

One day my father and I walked the path toward where the sun set each night. The path we took was not the one that ran along the beach, or wound in amongst the giant rocks the water crashed against, but one three hundred paces up the bluffs. This, he reasoned, would afford us a better view and some protection should someone see us. The sparse woodland was just above us.

I was anxious with excitement at this adventure, my mind tumid with visions of stable clans whose hale would dot the hillside ahead, people who would welcome us. But as we walked that path, we saw more windswept foothills, and huge waves crashing against rocks below us. Oddly, the path looked well used, and this my father noticed. He spoke to me in whispers. "Look here, an 'ōhi'a 'ai seed, and there, an overturned stone." True, the stone did not have dust on its exposed bottom, and the brown 'ōhi'a 'ai seed was wet, some of its white pulp still attached. We continued on the path, as we did so seeing the land begin to open before us. The pale sand of a beach increased in length as we passed the foothills, and I was aware that we were turning as we went.

I then felt a hollow, awful fright. My father must have been aware of something too, for he stopped and held his hand up to me. Then, from behind a boulder rose a man divided in half, brown skin from head to foot on one side, blue-black on the other. My father motioned me down. The man stepped toward us, and then other men appeared, seeming to materialize out of nothing. The man divided in half looked at me, then, and I stared in shock at him, for he was much larger than I, and muscular, and the amazing tattoo that covered half of his body cut his nose and forehead so precisely that I could not keep myself from looking at him.

He smiled, his teeth bright, and laid out his tongue. Half of it was also blue. "Am I not your most fearful dream?" he asked, and laughed.

My father groaned. "We are harmless fishermen," he said. "Do not hurt us."

"Fishermen?" the dreadful man said. "Until today."

The men would kill us. My father had told me of the pahupu, the cut-in-half warriors skilled in the quick death. For us there was no escape. More men had shown themselves, and it became clear that they were in the area for a reason. The cut-in-half man turned and looked away at the path. His back was divided, and his buttocks. Then he turned to look up along the bluffs, his blue-black side to me. The white of his eye was stark and bright against that skin.

"He is a koi," my father whispered. "A warrior, but I do not believe that he intends to kill us."

The path was then brightened by a feather cloak, and I did as my father did, put my face down on the hard dirt. With my tongue I tasted a round pebble, and watched the shifting shadows on the dirt before me.

"Rise," the cut-in-half man said. My father and I stood up. I was aware of my heart thumping so strongly that it was visible in my foreshortened vision of myself.

"Where are your women?"

"Behind us a quarter of a day," my father said.

The cut-in-half man looked at my father. "You are kauwā."

"No, we are not," my father said. "We fell upon bad times because of a dispute."

"You ended the loser in the dispute, then."

"Yes. I lost a son and a daughter."

"Boy," the cut-in-half man said, "what do you think of me?"

I looked at my father, who nodded with a doubtful, fatalistic air. Turning back to the cut-in-half man, I said, "I think you must be a great warrior."

"Why?"

"It is not your skin," I said. "It is your eyes and hands."

The cut-in-half man stared at me, and then laughed. "A clever answer. You are a clever boy. What should I do with a clever boy?"

I thought a moment. My father nudged me. "Use this cleverness like a digging stick," I said.

He narrowed his eyes, thinking. The ali'i in his feather cloak had walked up the bluff a few paces and watched us, his arms folded.

"My blue side thinks about this answer," the cut-in-half man said. "My brown side is waiting." He pointed at the path. "I have no use for digging sticks. I am koa."

"I used a digging stick," I said. "A farmer sees a digging stick as a weapon."

"What kind of a weapon is a digging stick?"

"A spear to pierce the heart of hunger."

I heard the ali'i say, "Ah."

The cut-in-half man stared at the dry path. "Makua," he said, to my father, "you have raised a good and clever boy. But is this the cleverness that hides weakness?"

"No. He killed a man in our dispute," my father said.

The cut-in-half man looked at me. "And are you proud?"

"No."

"Why are you not proud?"

"He visits me in the night. He holds his wound and tells me that he was a man."

"Yes," the cut-in-half man said. "Our dead follow us. You are not lying." He turned, as if distracted by something, his blue side facing us. Now I saw men moving in the brush on the slopes of the foothills. I saw a priest, then another. The priests were watching the men as they moved in the brush.

"Tell me," the cut-in-half man said, turning back to us, "what is it that you can do for me that no other man can do?"

I looked at the path between us. The cut-in-half warrior folded his arms across his chest, one blue forearm crossing the brown skin, one brown arm the blue.

My father nudged me. I had no answer.

"I am becoming impatient with this," the cut-in-half warrior said. "Tell me."

I tried to understand what this riddle meant, how it was that I should answer. Should I admit that he had bested me? And would this mean our deaths? This game we played had seemingly run its course. I stared at the path.

The cut-in-half warrior clapped his hands together, and I jumped, my heart banging in my chest.

"You are frightened by a mere sound," he said. "You cannot answer my question."

"I can."

"Then answer. Speak now."

"Kūʻulakai The Red One taught me how to see under the water." My father drew in a sharp breath.

The cut-in-half warrior stared at me. I was aware, too, that the aliʻi had turned back to us. I looked at my father, whose face was now grim, his eyes closed.

"If you lose a fish-hook in the water and it falls on pale sand, I can see it," I said.

"Hoʻopau," the aliʻi said. The word means 'cease'.

The cut-in-half warrior smiled at me. "I shall consider whether or not I believe you. But I have no fish-hooks to throw in the ocean." He looked at the bluffs. "And you claim that The Red One would speak to a Makaʻāinana boy like you. Why you?"

I thought a moment. "Perhaps he thought he was speaking to someone else."

"Beware that someone might require you to prove this," the cut-in-half warrior said, and walked to the aliʻi. My father let out his breath.

"Your words were as skilled mokomoko," he said. "You dodged each strike. But now you have distinguished yourself, and I do not know the consequences of this."

The cut-in-half warrior came back. "You will collect your women and return here by dawn tomorrow. If you do not, we will find you and pluck out your eyes." He looked at my father, and then raised his blue hand to my father's face. "I would take one now as proof of my resolve," he said, and ran his finger over my father's eye-socket. "But you will need them."

"May I ask," I said, and my father whispered, "Aʻole," harshly, at which the cut-in-half warrior held up his hand.

"Let the boy ask," he said.

"May I ask what you want us for?"

"Fish-hooks," he said, "of your bones." He paused, studying us, and then laughed. "No. I will tell you." He swept his blue arm to his right, indicating the bluffs. "We are building a great heiau," he said. The word refers to our worshipping place. "The heiau is being started a quarter of a day's walk from here. Each stone is selected by the kahuna, and consecrated. You will join us in this great enterprise."

"We shall be honored," my father said. "We shall do as you bid."

"Very well then," the cut-in-half warrior said, and looked at me. "One day I will drop the fish-hook, and we will see if you keep the eyes Kuʻulakai blessed."

"I am ready," I said. I looked up the bluff. There, standing with the aliʻi, was a kahuna. The aliʻi pointed in our direction, and the kahuna looked at us. I felt my heart begin to pound again, for I both recognized him and saw the expression of incredulity that had crossed his bearded face. His hair was long and more tangled, and he was larger, but he was the same kahuna I had feared more than a year earlier, the one who had killed a poor fisherman for being in his canoe during a kapu time.

I averted my eyes. I began to tremble, because I still felt his eyes on me. We turned and walked on the path, and the figure moved on the bluff above us, walking parallel to us and looking at me, his face still held in that expression of wonder.

"Do not look at him," my father whispered. "He does not like his divinity questioned, and your claim has angered him."

"I should not have made it then," I said.

He laughed ruefully. "Then we might have died."

Upon our return to the cave, my mother did not want to leave, and my sister did. My father had to order my mother to roll the mats and gather the gourds, the fire-stick and wooden trench, and other tools, and dried fish and ʻuala. The sun was setting over the water, soon to sink into it, but we were ordered to be back to the cut-in-half warrior by dawn, so we left. We walked under a nearly full moon, the landscape an ashy gray, the calls of the ocean night birds coming from above. Our vague shadows swept in dreamlike undulation over stones and small bushes. We arrived long before dawn. I recognized the area my father and I had been in the previous day, and so we found flat rocks to sit on, and watched the moon drop as the faint light of dawn began to define the outline of the bluffs behind us.

The first figures appeared far away on the path, and I saw the look of apprehension on my mother's and Laka's faces. And when the cut-in-half warrior approached, his blue side facing the rising sun, Laka began to moan, for so fearsome was the man that she probably thought she would die. When he was within twenty paces, my father and I rose to greet him, leaving my mother and Laka sitting on the flat stones.

"You shall keep your eyes!" he said. "Maika'i."

My father looked pleased with the cut-in-half warrior's joviality. The sun had now risen, and in the morning light the warrior looked rich in color, dense and magnificent. I stepped back to watch the others who had begun to make their way up the bluffs. Laka stared at the cut-in-half warrior, her eyes large and her mouth open.

Some time later, while we were being instructed as to what was expected of us, the cut-in-half warrior stopped, distracted. It was Laka, who had left the flat stone and had walked up the bluffs, apparently in search of some bush behind which she could relieve herself. As she walked, the swaying of her hair and her hips had caught the warrior's attention, and he watched until she had vanished behind higher brush.

"And so," he went on, "you are to move selected rocks that way," and he pointed at the path which he had come down. "In time you will arrive at a small collection of dwellings, and there you are to leave the rock. Others will move it on to its destination."

"And where are we to live?" my father asked.

The warrior pointed up the bluffs. "There are dwellings in the ravines above us. We will provide some food, and you and your family will provide for yourselves, fish, perhaps kalo, if you can establish dry patches up there." My father looked up the bluffs, nodding skeptically. "Yes," the cut-in-half warrior said, "this is a harsh land, dry and windy. You will be rewarded for your work. It may take some time for the building of the heiau, but those who work will not be overlooked by the chief."

"Is he the moi of O'ahu?"

"No, he is a relative. His kauhale is that of the first high chief, and he wishes to erect a heiau that will rival the greatest here."

My father nodded. It seemed best not to further question the cut-in-half warrior.

"I am called Konapiliahi," the cut-in-half warrior said. The word means, simply, 'powerful', and there was no more fitting a name for this man.

My father introduced himself by his short name, Kahu, and mine, Pono.

"Wait here," Konapiliahi said. He turned to leave, and then turned back. "Your daughter," he said, "what is her name?"

And so it was that we began residence in a new place, and Laka found a man. The house was a small, thatched dwelling up a ravine, one that had been recently occupied but was now empty. We speculated only briefly on the question of who had lived there and why those persons were gone, and I recall feeling a strange uneasiness. Where, after all, would a stone-carrier go if not the other world? There were other houses in the ravine, not visible from the path, occupied by a strange collection of people, none of whom were directly related by family. We were, I thought, castoffs like the rest of them, bound together by the great enterprise of the erection of a magnificent heiau. But the sense of a social order came with this, and at the outset my mother and father seemed pleased with the arrangement.

Laka, upon learning of the cut-in-half warrior's interest, lost her womanly confidence, as if so awed by this development that she could not compose herself. My mother spent much of her time advising Laka on her deportment any time the magnificent man was around, and working on Laka's hair, braiding and re-braiding it, and applying oils to make it shine.

I had assumed that I might be able to do something pleasant, perhaps fish, but we found, soon enough, that the work expected of us was hard. The young, wild-haired kahuna would arrive every third or fourth day, and study and select rocks for us to carry. The rocks were sometimes large, weighing as much as a man, and it was left to us to invent ways to get the rock to its appointed destination, which was, in miles, perhaps four. The path wound its way around dry, windy ravines, and under short, rocky cliffs.

The young kahuna did not seem to remember me or my arrogance about my association with Ku'ulakai, because he focused on his task. This made me feel more secure, for all who saw him became wary and afraid.

We learned what it was that made the rock-carriers afraid. The kahuna, named Kahimoku, was known to have special dreams and visions that instructed him to kill, and the selection of one to kill was both practical and mysterious. The man who had dwelt with his wife in our little house had been a rock-carrier. But he weakened under the strain, and one day Kahimoku the Strange, as they came to call him, noticed the man's weakness and later had a dream in which he perceived the man to be impure, and bitter about his lot. Kahimoku the Strange had him held down on the ground and he had workers place a large, flat rock upon his chest. Then he sat and watched as the man attempted to breathe. When the man wheezed his last, and the air was befouled by the smell of excrement, his limbs shuddering and his teeth bared, Kahimoku the Strange rose and nodded, as if satisfied that his test had been successful and his dream legitimate, and had the man dragged down the bluffs and cast into the ocean. The man's wife left the little house we lived in.

I soon learned that I would do no fishing. We carried our rocks, using an implement we devised and built of strong vines and lengths of hau, a very strong, but light wood. It was in effect a litter, that we could carry either holding the ends of the hau pieces in our hands or resting them on our shoulders. Our work was done largely in isolation, struggling under our litter on the path, passing the dry ravines and little cliffs. We would greet those carriers on their way back for more, and at times we would carry on conversations, the smaller the rock, the more loquacious the conversation.

Always interested in the complicated politics of the aliʻi, my father speculated thus: "Remember Kumahana," he said, adjusting the hau pole. I walked in front, and would turn my head to hear him. "The people deposed him, and Kahahana became moi of the island. Perhaps the mad engineer of this enterprise will meet the same fate."

"A man told me that the chief is indeed mad," I said. "He is a pretender to a greatness he envies in others."

"Yes. What use is the conscription into misery of those like us? I hear whispers every day. It is said that Muapo—that is his name—emerges from his hale only by night and buries his excrement in secret places, and so divine does he think himself that he does not let anyone within an arm's length of him. The whispers shall grow louder."

"Don't whisper yourself," I said. "It is wisest to stay out of this."

"Yes," he said. "You are a wise boy."

We would deposit our burden at an open area, the beginning of the beautiful land on the leeward side of the island where, as we rolled our rock off into the grass, we would see a fine, bright beach, and many people playing in the surf, and canoes on the water. Although it was not as green and plentiful of foliage as our original part of the island, we could see the careful arrangement of kalo patches and clusters of niu trees in the distance waving above fine houses. Large communities of people lived there, people whose lot was far more pleasant that ours. We heard from that grassy area the barking of dogs, the rapid squawking of chickens and the pleasing squeal of pigs.

But we were not allowed beyond that point. Far away down that beach lay the lands of the high chiefs, the rivers and bays of legend. My father had seen these places when he was younger. He told me that I would be astonished at the difference in wind and surf, were I to see these areas. Imagine the most beautiful, calmest day you've known, and then multiply this into most of the days of the year.

Days passed, and our feet and backs hurt, our shoulders became chafed and bruised, our hands sore. On one trip, bearing an exceptionally heavy rock so that our conversations were brief and delivered through clenched teeth, we passed under a cliff and an ʻōhiʻa ʻai hit me on the head. I looked up, and there, sitting on a rock some fifteen feet above us, was a girl with a head of magnificent hair, staring down at us. She was ten or eleven. She giggled and vanished.

I believe it was that same evening, upon our return, that Konapiliahi, the cut-in-half warrior, presented to my father the request that he take Laka as his wife, his second, he said. His first wife desired a meeting with Laka. You gentlemen have of course heard much about our polygamy and what you call incest. Incest, first, is the habit of the high-born, to preserve and not to sully their divinity with alien blood. It was frowned upon by Makaʻainana. Should a brother and sister marry, one would say, 'relatives that mate and hatch like chickens'. Should a stepfather take his wife's daughter, people would say, 'Auwe! From the privates of the mother to the privates of her daughter'.

Polygamy was common, more so among the high-born, and no one remarked it. The wives were usually friends, sometimes sisters. In the case of Laka, Konapiliahi's wife was older, and desired the company of someone like Laka. My father was excited about this. Konapiliahi was close to the chief. Laka was pure, and this made her more desirable. Weddings among the Makaʻainana were not elaborate affairs, but if they were connected in any way to the high-born, then they had other rules and practices. One which may be of interest is that should Laka accept, and the look on her face told my father that she would, then she would be taken to the chief who would take her virginity and then pass her on to Konapiliahi, who would be greatly honored. Should a child be the result of the chief's act, then Konapiliahi and my father would be honored, for my father's grandchild would be of high blood.

This made me see Laka in an altogether new way. She sat outside the thatched hut, my mother and an old crone of a neighbor talking, and I saw in those thighs, those brown, well-formed breasts, the sloping shoulders and dark shiny hair, a woman perfectly fit for her glorious good fortune. And I am sure she was perpetually amazed, frightened and excited at the thought of being made love to by so fearsome a man. She and my mother would whisper, producing in Laka a shy, frightened giggle, after which her mouth would drop open and her eyes would widen, her mind I suppose envisioning that great member she had seen curled in repose inside the muscular warrior's malo.

My father and I went out the following morning to our next burden: this rock medium-sized but of a pleasing shape and character, pale green lichens blooming on one side. My father's happiness was clear to see. We walked at a steady gait, the hau poles on our shoulders and the rock bouncing in its mesh cradle.

A piece of dried he'e bounced off my head. I looked up, and the impish girl sat there staring down at me. I lowered the hau sticks as did my father, and picked up the hard section of tentacle, the pink suckers large and perfectly round. I bit half away and gave the rest to my father, and looked up again, and again she had vanished.

So it was that Laka was taken to the chief, and then went to Konapiliahi's hale. His wife became her good friend, and in time we learned that Laka was with child. As to whether or not my parents could visit or if she would visit us, Konapiliahi told us that for the present, we should not cultivate such thoughts. My father understood this.

In the meantime, my father and I carried our stones, on through the blazing summer heat, and each day I would be struck on the head with fruit, dried he'e, dried fish, even chunks of cooked kalo. The girl would stare at us from her perch then vanish. My father speculated that she was dim-witted but sweet, for the food she so expertly bounced off my head was welcome.

My father and I labored thus for two years. Even Makahiki, kapu time where work was concerned, was compromised on the advice of Konapiliahi. The great project was halted at its site, but it would not be out of the question if the rock carriers took walks, and as an afterthought carried rocks and deposited them at the opening to that stretch of magnificent beach on the beginning of the leeward side.

We took the advice, but I was also able to fish, as per my mother's instructions for things that could be dried—he'e particularly. My father allowed me to do this a few times, and then ordered me not to. Some traditions, he said, had to be maintained. So Makahiki came, and in keeping with our desire to remain anonymous, we watched the procession pass toward the more populated area where we had once lived. I wondered, too, if the high-born woman with whom I had had that experience might be one of those walking behind Lono's banner. But our lives were different now.

And so the procession passed, and we went back to our house. As I said, during this time I did not fish, because it would have been an affront to Lono himself. I had to agree, finally, with my father. In time we were back at our work, overseen by the warriors and the wild-haired kahuna. In this time we did not attract the attention of Kahimoku the Strange, although others did, men who had begun to wear down and who not so mysteriously became the subject of his dreams. The boy kahuna was no longer a boy, as I was no longer a boy. We both grew taller, and although I was somewhat underfed, my body became well formed but somewhat thin. The kahuna was thin, too, with a very large and tangled head of hair, and every month or so his dreams led him to another failing man, whom he would order his personal warriors, two of them, to hold on the ground while he strangled or beat them to death with rocks, or, as he had done so long ago to the hapless fisherman, pierce the man's heart with a pahoa.

We did not see him do this, because his appearance always made the rock carriers wary, and they would move away from him, feigning some urgent responsibility connected with the work. How many stones, I would ask, does one need to build a great heiau? And my father would laugh and say, a lifetime of stones. He had once seen, he said, the great heiau at Kailua, a favorite place of the ali'i, a pile of stones as tall as a tree and all expertly fitted together. Would we ever see the fruits of our labor? No, he said, because we are common people. Those near the great chief do not want to be sullied by our presence, even if Laka is now the great warrior's wife, so they might wish to keep Laka's background secret. This, of course, is a cruel joke fate has played on us, for, and here he shifted the hau sticks on his shoulders, for our genealogical line is as great as theirs. This they do not know, he said, and then stubbed his toe on a rock. Auwe!

And as I grew, so grew the dim-witted girl. Some days I walked under that ledge, slightly tensing myself for the food that would bounce off my head, and none would come down. Upon looking up, I would see that she was not there, and say to my father, "So, she has tired of her game," and the next day, magically, a piece of dried fish would hit me, and she would be gone. She grew breasts, and tamed her hair, and rose from her perch to run off showing well-formed legs and a strong back, her pa'u of a fine weave. And one day she spoke. We walked under the rock ledge and I waited for the food to bounce off my head or shoulders, and she said, "Look up. I do not wish to knock you to your knees," after which she dropped a large, round kalo root, cooked, what we called 'ai pa'a. Holding it, I looked up to thank her, but as was her habit, she was gone.

My father also stared at that space she had occupied. "Well," he said, "our benefactor is after all not a dim-wit."

That she had spoken changed my attitude toward her. Now, at night, I envisioned those breasts and those dark, beautiful eyes, those shapely legs. Was she a child of the wild area? Or was she the child of an immigrant rock carrier? I became anxious to get to that ledge, pulling my father along. He became frustrated with me, and ordered me to slow my pace. And there she was on the ledge, holding a piece of dried he'e.

"Who are you?" I asked. The he'e came down at me, and she vanished.

"She is shy," my father said. "But the more I see her, the more I see what a fine girl she is. And indeed she has tamed that mountain of seaweed on her head."

The work continued. I must say that I became moon-struck over the mysterious girl. This made our work more pleasant, while my father, unfortunately, began slowly to weaken. My brooding fascination for her was now mixed with a fear that one day Kahimoku the Strange would notice him and his thinness and lack of vigor.

I looked at all the other carriers, assessing their strength, picking out ones that would be more attractive to Kahimoku the Strange. And indeed, from time to time, one would be selected to die in some new way.

One man I saw was grabbed by Kahimoku's warriors and simply relaxed and sighed with apparent relief that his misery was finally over, and all that was left for him to endure was the feeling of cord crushing his throat or of rocks caving in his head. He was walked toward the water, compliant and tired.

Life, my father told me in the evening as we sat outside our humble dwelling, is aught but fleeting good fortune, and those who wield power fool themselves into the conviction that theirs has meaning. We are creatures capable of dreaming, and that is our curse. We believe we matter.

And I said, "Tomorrow I will climb those rocks and find her."

He laughed. "You are young," he said. "Enjoy it."

He now no longer seemed bitter. His demeanor bespoke a horrible resignation which frightened me. My mother, too, had seemed to age, her hair with bright gray strands, her body flaccid and passive. She did, however, have women friends with whom she spent her days, likely reminiscing about a time when life was more orderly and full.

During the hottest and driest part of that year, we suffered. Bathed in our own dirty, acrid sweat, we carried our rocks, the sun searing us with merciless force. My father was less able to bear it, and at times we had to stop and rest in the shade of whatever bleak, parched brush we could find. On one of these rests, my father staring keenly in both directions for any warrior who might see us, I hatched a plan. We would rest near that ravine fronted by the girl's ledge, and I would steal up there.

We carried a particularly heavy, round rock, blooming with green lichens, to a place two hundred paces before the cliff she would be sitting on. We were on a curve in the path and not visible to her. My father sat down heavily between the hau poles, wiping his brow with his hand, and said, "Very well, go and find her."

So I made my way up through the grass toward what seemed like a dry ravine, but upon reaching it, I found a narrow, deep cleft in the land, rich with brush, and to my astonishment glittering at the base with a small trickle of water. I considered where that water went, if, as my father had once told me, water sometimes vanished into hollows and underground streams created by fissures in the once molten rock.

I went down into the ravine, got on my hands and knees and drank some of that water, and then climbed the other side. There, I looked around. A path crossed at my feet, the one she probably used to make her way to the cliff. I followed the path, and upon reaching the cliff, found it vacant. On a patch of stone overlooking the rock carriers' path I found 'ōhi'a 'ai seeds, a piece of chewed up sugar cane, and a single glossy black hair, which the wind stole as I raised it from the stone.

So this was one of her days of absence. I stood up, looking out over the windswept grasses to the ocean and the pounding surf. In the far distance to my right, I saw figures moving, perhaps a thousand paces. I had time enough to make my way back.

"You are tall."

I turned quickly, my heart pounding in my chest. For a second, standing there staring at her, I experienced a fit of bashfulness. "I cannot stay," I said.

"You will come back."

As I calmed myself, I was able to look at her, and when I did, I was overcome with so powerful and so nearly breathless a flood of desire that I must have shown it in my face, because her dark eyes relaxed, and her face composed itself in a direct stare, the aura of a hot, shamelessly luscious desire frightening me even more than when she had first spoken to me. This stare made me look at her more searchingly, my mind unable to control my eyes, which swept to her shoulders, her body, the hips and legs.

"They are like hands," she said.

"What are like hands?"

"Your eyes. I feel them like oiled hands."

She moved toward me, and for one insane moment I considered jumping down to the path. But I stood my ground, holding my breath. When she moved directly before me, so that the shadow of my head swept in a strange, warping darker ball over her belly, and then her breasts, I smelled the faint aromas of fish and coconut oil in the air, and then felt the radiance of heat from her body.

"Take this," she said.

I looked at a piece of dried he'e. She took my right hand and turned it over, and placed the dried he'e in it. "I am Pekau," she said.

"Ka'alokulokupono," I said over my shoulder. "I cannot stay."

"Pono," she said. "Return here in the night. A while after the sun drops."

The figures I had seen were likely to be very close, so I made my way past her, again catching the scent of fish and coconut oil. "I will be here," I said.

I do not wish to bother you gentlemen with narratives of gratuitous prurience, but I feel it just and pertinent that I attempt to give voice to this experience. Perhaps once in a person's life a match of such magnificent purity becomes nature's gift.

Walking once again, the hau sticks on my shoulders, I told my father about our conversation, and he said, "As long as you carry stones tomorrow."

So the sun dropped. The sky was clear, and above our hale I could see the glow of a rising moon. I ran on the path, my shadow bouncing in the grass to my right. The sky was ablaze with so many stars that, with the moon, I could have seen a single hair. When I got to the ravine and made my way up, I realized I was so early that I would have to wait in anxiety-flushed nervousness for some time. I sat down on a flat rock, and waited while my heart calmed itself. It was a cool evening. So bright were the moon and stars that I thought of it as another variety of day, so lucid as to make visible every leaf and every pebble, each with its tiny elongated shadow.

I caught the scent of coconut oil first, but heard nothing. Then, like a furtive ghost, she was at my side. I was about to speak but stopped, for she removed her pa'u and walked over my knees.

"I know nothing," she whispered.

I pulled the malo off, the erection straight up, and she walked over it, lowered herself, and with no help from me, pushed the head into the moist opening. There she paused, and tipped forward and came against the top of my chest, her hair draped over my shoulders, her hands on my back. She relaxed downward, and I moaned, fearing some injury because of the force of it, and then she slid down on my lap, shuddering as the head broke through and the shaft sank all the way into that almost scalding, liquefied constriction, and she moved against me, moaning and gripping me around the neck, after which the powerful pulsing of release robbed my muscles of tension. We sat thus for some time. I felt the wetness down there, but did not want to move. Her face was down in the hollow of my neck, on that bruised patch of flesh that bore, each day, the hau pole's end.

"I will speak to my father," I said.

"I will speak to mine," she said.

7.

As you might understand, Pekau and I were not loquacious, for our conversation was one of the flesh and the spirit. And this conversation resurrected itself twice more before I left. One odd image that remains is of her with a handful of grass, running it slowly up the inside of her thigh, upon which was a glistening black line—that line was her own blood, and as the tuft of grass rose, the line vanished into it, and she rose and looked at me, her face a mask of a curious wonder if not calm astonishment. Because of those myriad sources of light, and the moon, blazing white so as to hurt the eyes, we were in a world unto its own, the two of us and nothing else, no past, no prohibitions, no reason to halt in our bodies' reveling in this act.

Walking the path back under that dome of stars, with the phosphorescent surf blasting off the rocks, I understood both the beauty of what we had done and the predicament we faced, for what would happen when the heiau was finished? Would we be sacrificed on its sacred stone? The world we lived in was owned by, and lorded over by men who had little regard for our lives, and when they had no more use for us, we were at their mercy. I laughed bitterly. I had been a fool not to adopt my father's fatalistic cynicism, or my mother's wan and brooding resignation.

The image of Kahimoku the Strange visited me there, and I wondered how a man could enjoy killing in a world that could be this beautiful.

My father approved of the match, as did Pekau's father. It was custom at the time that when a man and woman married, the man moved into the house of his wife's family. It was fortunate that my mother had gathered around her a number of friends, and my leaving, to a small valley but two such valleys away, did not disturb her. After all, I would be working each day with my father.

In a somewhat fortunate correspondence of events, my father and I were beneficiaries of events elsewhere in the world. My blue and brown brother-in-law informed us one day that work on the heiau was interrupted by a council of chiefs, who were meeting in Waikīkī, far down the leeward side of the island. Rumblings of conflict were passing among the ali'i, and although we were advised to nevertheless carry rocks and leave them at the opening of the leeward side, we would have some freedom during this time. This allowed me to go up the ravine during the day to meet Pekau's father.

I met her first at the little cliff. In the daylight she was shy, and not at all talkative. She whispered, "Come," and I followed her up the narrow ravine. I was surprised at how far it was, but also lost my sense of time watching those legs, that back and swaying hair before me. At length the terrain leveled, and the narrow ravine widened, the dry brush gradually replaced by taller trees, 'ōhi'a and kukui, the latter the tree that yields what is called 'candle nut.'

All the way, that small trickle of water showed in the cleft of the ravine, and that upon reaching the location of their kauhale, I stopped to behold a small but lush patch of land, dappled sunlight moving on the leaf-strewn ground. Pekau pointed to one thatched dwelling and said, "My father's," and to smaller one, and said, "Ours," after which she looked down somewhat bashfully.

Pekau's father, Manomano, was far older than I imagined he would be. He was small and shriveled and very dark, perhaps sixty-five or seventy years old, and the first time I beheld him he was sitting outside his house blowing gently on a tuft of dried moss, and then placing twigs on the flame engendered there. He skipped formalities—simply pointed to a spot opposite him, at which Pekau and I sat down.

He looked at me without speaking. I was afraid for a few moments of his eyes. He looked into and through me, and the skin on my face felt a hint of some tangibility on it, as if the power of his eyes were physically actual. Then, while I sat still trying to manage my discomfort, he smiled, reached across the fire, and slapped me on the knee. "You are as your name," he said. "You are welcome here."

As I looked around, I saw the shapes of carefully constructed coconut fabric bags—the seed covering, I mean—protecting the drying he'e from the flies.

"You have he'e," I said. "Where do you fish?"

"Yes." He got up and went into his house, and came back out with two hook and lure contraptions that had cord attached.

"But we never see you," I said.

He smiled again. "I make myself invisible."

Pekau laughed. "He fishes early, before dawn."

"With your name," I said, "I believe it." Manomano, by the way, means 'many, numerous', and also 'to aim at and hit a mark'. "There is so much he'e that there must be many of you."

Manomano laughed. The more I watched him, the more fascinated I became. Sometimes we encounter men who have a spiritual glow about them, as if they wear their mana on their skin, and so it was with Manomano. I felt that I was in the presence of a great man, and wanted very much to have my father meet and talk with him. I knew also where Pekau got her eyes, which at times I felt to be somehow physically tangible when she stared at me.

When I returned to our hale, I described Manomano to my mother and father, and both of them, upon hearing his name, looked at each other in growing wonder.

"How old is he?" my father asked.

"Old," I said. "And small, with very strong eyes."

"He is Manomano, an advisor to Kumahana."

I recognized the name of the island's highest chief, or moi, from my childhood. He was deposed perhaps a year before we lost our kauhale, for being frivolous in his habits. He had alienated his people. Manomano, my father told me, was known as a seer, or prophet, reputed to possess great wisdom. I believed that this was indeed the man, and wondered how it was that he had ended up so far from the position he had held.

"Kumahana was not killed," my father told me. "He merely left, and those close to him left also. You are marrying the daughter of a once very important man."

And so I began life with Pekau. You needn't hear of our personal life beyond what I have told you, but suffice to say that each night, in our small dwelling, we repeated the same pure, beautiful act I have already described.

By the arrival of Makahiki, she was already with child, and I saw myself as a step in the grand design of life, that in our world, I was taking part according to the ancient principles of the continuation of my family. And Makahiki that year was as other recent ones in that we practiced its kapu without the oversight of anyone except my father and Manomano. Some day, my father believed, we might return to our proper place in this world. We did not have to accede to the lure of the slovenly behavior of the kauwā. We were not kauwā. We were simply displaced from our rightful status by men who put greed before morality.

After Makahiki, a strange story circulated among the rock-carriers. The claim was that the person of the god Lono had arrived at Waimea Bay, on the island of Kaua'i. Lono was the master of a great floating house, and he came ashore with a host of his kahunas and warriors. As a demonstration of their power, one slew a man with a wand, or a long stick that spat fire so hot that it pierced the man's chest. Lono and his warriors, it was said, were pink on the face but a strange, almost iridescent white otherwise. Their house floated, with great standards atop, white flags that surged round with voluptuous repetition in the breeze, making some think that the marvelous thing was a moving temple. Others were skeptical. Was it some madman's dream invading the reason of men? Had a kahuna made feeble-minded an entire population of a bay, a spell delivered like a billow of invisible smoke over everyone?

The story fascinated my father. He wondered, would Lono come and set straight the erring ways of our cruel and pertinacious ali'i? Would Lono restore order and perhaps status to those who had such status so injuriously removed? He wanted, first, to speak to Manomano, who by this time had become a good friend to him, a man he respected.

If I had made assumptions about the world and its order, or lack thereof, then the long conversation he had with Manomano turned these assumptions over. My mother accompanied us, and she and Pekau stayed off by themselves talking, my mother, I believe, instructing Pekau about the mysteries of the coming birth of our child.

We sat around the small fire, the orange light dancing on our faces. Manomano had a habit of remaining silent until a question was asked of him. My father had the question ready, but waited in deference to the old man, as if afraid that Manomano would manifest some inappropriate behavior, such was the somewhat merry, mischievous visage he always presented.

"May I ask," my father said, "if he is Lono?"

"He is not Lono," Manomano said. "He is a man of another place."

"And may I ask what place he is from?"

"He is from the land of mist and fog, of great heat and cold water."

My father thought about this. "Is this Kahiki?" he asked.

The word *Kahiki,* it should be interjected, referred to the place of our origin or to any other place or foreign land. Our concept of foreign land was of a land in the sky, a mythical land unreachable by us, or the sacred place of our origins.

"It is another Kahiki," Manomano said, "one strange to us, with people who are white of skin and unfamiliar of language." He shifted, resting his chin in the palm of his hand, his elbow on his knee. "Some generations ago a chief named Kuali'i went there and composed a long mele. In it he tells us of a place that is not like our world, where the weather is harsh and attacks you in unacceptable extremes, a land whose inhabitants speak not one word of our language or of the language of our Kahiki. Wait."

He rose and went behind his hale, and we saw him dig in the soil with a stick.

"He is mad, I think," my father whispered. "The world is the world. This is what we have always known."

Behind us, my mother and Pekau were laughing softly and whispering. Manomano returned to the fire carrying a rolled piece of coconut fabric with something inside. He placed this on the ground and opened it, and inside was a black stick the length of my forearm pointed at one end, and growing wider until it ended on the other with a round knob. Manomano looked at us. "You may pick this up," he said.

I looked at my father. He nodded, so I reached out and touched, and quickly withdrew my hand. "It is cold," I said. I picked it up, astonished at its weight. "What is it?" I asked. Carefully, I held it out to my father, who had the same reaction I had.

"It is a special weapon," my father said. "I have heard of twigs that do not break, found in floating wood."

"This was found in floating wood," Manomano said. He took the stick and held it over the fire, and then placed it on the ground. He stared at us, saying nothing. Then he picked it up by its thinner end and held it out to me. I took it.

"It is hot," I said.

"It will remain so for some time," Manomano said. He leaned away and found a fist-sized stone, and placed it on the ground. "Break this," he said.

"No," I said. "I will damage this."

"Break the stone," he said.

Holding the thin end, I raised the stick and brought it down on the stone, which shattered into five pieces. "It did not break," I said.

"It will not," Manomano said. He leaned back, lost in thought. "I have dreamed troubling dreams. The seed of these dreams is this stick, and legends I have heard. These legends portend a world of strange people, multitudinous in their land, a land forty-four hundred times as large as ours. Some fourteen generations ago, on another island, men found these haoles crawling in the sand, wan and tired and afflicted with great thirst. They took them in, including a pale woman, and thus did she cohabit with a kanaka and become a chiefess. Whether or not she is to be believed has remained a question all these years. She spoke of lands that would require entire years to traverse, people who spoke languages strange and without sense as her own. She described the very substance you see here, and alleged that it was made with fire. It was thought that she was giving voice to strange dreams and visions. The priests I knew preferred that these legends remain secret. But this madwoman was loved by the people, and her dubious proclamations were eventually ignored and forgotten by all but seers and men of tortured thought like myself."

We stared at him in silence.

"Our world is small," he said. "It is not the world centering a universe of water."

"And what of Lono?" my father asked.

"He is a man."

Behind us soft laughter continued. I did not know, at the time, if this information was connected to me, and as if Manomano knew what I was thinking, he said, "You are young. You will see them. You will live to know my visions. I have watched you and know the scent and shape of your future."

"May I ask—"

"No," he said. "It benefits a man not to know. You are the father of my blood, over there curled in the belly of my daughter. When I am gone from this old flesh, I will whisper to you."

"A man whispers to me," I said.

"A man you wish would not," he said. "I will make my way to the world of the gods and I will send him away."

He picked up the heavy stick, and touched the point.

"Will this man return?" my father asked.

"Yes. It was said that one of his warriors used a fire-spitting stick. That stick was as this stick. There are things about these strange men that we do not know. Kuali'i discovered the land of mists and fog. Now those of the land of mists and fog are to discover our world. I do not know what the result of this will be. But I am troubled nevertheless by it. My dreams are sometimes tortured by visions of death."

"But it was a single floating house," my father said.

"I understand that there were two," Manomano said. "These have been seen before, by fishermen who described them in different ways, as a moving temple, a small island, as far as twelve or more generations back. How is it that they have been here so long, and we in our world have been to the land of mists and fog but once?"

My father considered this. "And where is this land?"

"Kuali'i's mele says the land of mists and fog is to the east," Manomano said.

"And what shall happen now?" my father asked.

"Nothing," Manomano said. "Such events are quickly forgotten, or passed off as of no importance. So it shall be with the appearance of these men." He looked into the fire, thinking. "We will continue to act on our hatreds and our greed."

As if to verify Manomano's prediction, we were back to our rock-carrying and my father was back to the cultivation of a dismissive skepticism about men from far away places and strange lands unknown to us. Laka had borne the cut-in-half warrior a son, which buoyed my father's spirits and at the same time made more stinging the unfair displacement of him from his rightful status.

I, too, pushed the odd story to the back of my mind. The birth of our child was nigh, and my father and I lived each day with wary industry, our main objective that of remaining invisible to Kahimoku the Strange, who continued selecting the thin and enfeebled for his inventive deaths. And as the birth drew nearer, Pekau so huge in the stomach that I feared she might split open, Manomano reassured me that when Pekau's water broke, whether I was present or not, he would summon an old woman who lived further up the ravine, to assist in the birth. So each day I left, first spending time with Pekau, looking gape-mouthed at the size of her stomach. I walked with the hau poles on my shoulders hoping that the baby would wait until I got back. There was no point in requesting any time away from the work because of the birth. Indeed, that might have resulted in a cord wrapped around my neck.

My mother joined in the activities of the expectation. I would leave the ravine at dawn just as she entered it. Now the wan, dismissive and fatalistic bearing had been replaced by a busy, anxious glee, for she had never seen a grandchild, although Laka already had two. This one was hers, and I appreciated her presence while I was gone.

On one of these days, I left the ravine hearing my mother's footfalls behind me on the path, and went down as usual to what I assumed would be our next stone. My father was there, waiting with a contented smile on his face, for he saw the child as more high blood in the family, and credited me for being the agent of this development.

We had borne two rather heavy stones to the opening of the leeward shore, and arriving back, saw a warrior and Kahimoku the Strange looking down at a man who sat upon the ground laughing, apparently Kahimoku's next victim. We turned and made our way to our next rock. "Ho'opau," a voice called out. We turned. A warrior beckoned us, and we walked toward him. "You will join us and do as you are told."

We did so. I felt the heat of fear rising into my face. Kahimoku the Strange stood looking down at the man, who was large and soft around his middle, a man about my age. His face was streaked from weeping, and he stared at the ocean as if there were something fascinating there. "Excellent," he said. "Ah, excellent!" Then he laughed again, his face contorted and flushed, his mouth wet.

I dared not meet Kahimoku the Strange's gaze, so I looked down at the man. He had wet his malo. "Excellent," he said. "Ah, it is excellent." He laughed, and ended the laugh with, "Ahh." Then he said, "One day I went walking."

"The rock," Kahimoku the Strange said, pointing to his right. There, on the ground, was a large, flat rock, too large for one, or even two men, to carry.

"One day I went walking," the man said. He looked toward the point around which lay our former place of residence.

My father's expression was of a wary, guarded patience, as if he were ruefully eager to assist in any way required of him. The man would not rise, and the wild-haired priest, his dark eyes pulling into themselves in a strange, visionary lapse, was inventing a death. I could see, too, the grim recognition on my father's face. He knew what was happening, and was steeling himself to the idea of being a party to it.

"You," Kahimoku the Strange said, "bind him thus," and he put his hands behind his back. The warrior gave me a length of cord, and the victim put his hands behind his back. I tied his wrists together, careful not to do it too tightly, for his comfort, absurdly.

"Now you two shall hold his arms," Kahimoku the Strange said.

"One day I went walking," the man said. "Around the point." I went to his side and stooped down, awaiting my instructions. I then looked at the side of the man's head, and there beheld a ruined, reddish stump where his ear should have been, a bloom of flesh resembling the surface of a tiny, malformed sweet potato. If he had walked around the point, as he had said, then this was, I realized, Ka'ahupāhau's murderer.

You might conjecture that I was happy that her death was going to be avenged, but I was not. All I felt was a dread for my part in this, and sympathy for this poor common man who had walked too far from his home and ended here, carrying stones.

Two more warriors had been summoned, and stood waiting with the first warrior. "Part his legs and each of you sit on a leg," Kahimoku the Strange said to the two recently arrived warriors. The other warrior, apparently understanding, positioned himself behind the sitting victim, while Kahimoku the Strange went to his knees before him, so that his face was but a hand's length from the victim's. The victim, his face now reduced to a bleary half-comprehension, lowered his eyes.

"Proceed," Kahimoku the Strange said. The warrior above us looped a cord over the man's head and then drew his pahoa out and slid it into the loop and began turning the pahoa until the cord tightened in on the man's neck.

"One day," he said.

The cord drove into the flesh, and I felt his arm tighten, then surge up. Kahimoku the Strange looked deeply into the man's eyes, searching them as if looking in grass for something small he had dropped. The warrior twisted the knife, and I heard and felt a horrible popping sound from the victim's throat, at which fluid ran from his eyes and nose and powerful convulsions wrenched from inside his chest. His eyes closed, and then a knot surged in his malo, and Kahimoku the Strange reached up and with his fingers held the man's eyes open, and there, as the body began to jump, the arms vibrating with such force that the one I held nearly tore itself from my grip, Kahimoku the Strange stared deeply into the man's eyes, his own beginning to show a lapse into some mystical, detached and visionary distance, and when at last the man was still, the air now befouled by the smell of the excrement I saw rolling out from under him, Kahimoku the Strange sat up, and then turned and stared at the horizon, his face still held in that deep trance.

We were able to let go of the man's arms, and the warriors dragged the body, the head bouncing on the ground, to the water. Flies appeared on the excrement that had been troweled out into a brown swipe by the man's back as they dragged him over it. My father and I turned away.

"Wait," Kahimoku the Strange said languidly, turning. "Fish-hook in the sand, there is your stone."

I knew at that moment that we had two problems: one was the stone, too large for us to carry and not an approximation of roundness, as of a disk, to roll. Secondly, the fact that Kahimoku the Strange had referred to me as 'Fish-hook in the sand' meant that I had not, as I had hoped, become anonymous in his memory.

I turned to my father, but he had moved away behind a bush and was vomiting into the dry grass there. I waited while he coughed, and then pulled reeds of grass out, which he folded into his mouth. He looked at me then, his face wet and his body trembling.

I had not felt the revulsion my father had, because I had lapsed into a brooding consideration of our fate. Were we not human beings, with senses, memory, and the capacity to experience joy and pain? How was it that this man, this hairy, insane freak, could decide our fates on his own experimental whim? What was he looking for in the one-eared man's eyes as he died? And what was he thinking of as he gazed out at the ocean? Surely, he could commune with the nether world without having to kill to do it.

But these speculations lasted only a few seconds. My father, having recovered himself, made his way to me. Kahimoku the Strange, meanwhile, had gone on his way.

"It is foolish to assume we would be allowed help with this," my father said.

"We'll build a sliding bed," I said. "But if we try to do this now, I think we might become the next subjects of his study."

"His study?"

"Did you see how he stared into the man's eyes? He was experimenting."

"I closed mine," he said. He sighed. He looked, then, at the water, thinking. "How many of us would consider it a useful thing if he died?"

"We would die, too. His ali'i are capable of finding anyone. We must go on carrying our stones."

"Yes, but I am growing weary of it."

"When the temple is done, we can hide in the mountains to keep from rotting in it. We will keep carrying stones."

"If—" He stopped. "If they knew who we were." That old phantom had reared up again, the generations long bitterness that had tortured him in the nights.

"These are the same people who gouged your forebears' eyes."

"Yes, the same."

That day, we began moving the large rock by rolling it on its edge, so that it slammed down on the path, three edges directly, and one side with a lump on it, in such a manner that it would roll one fourth farther. We discovered quickly that if we let it do that, cover half its circumference and then fall down, we had to raise it up, and within a quarter of a day I began to lose skin on my fingertips, and my father began to look more and more like a candidate for Kahimoku the Strange's deadly loop of cord. But we could not stop, because of the bland and watchful eyes of the warriors interspersed along the path.

It became clear that a sliding bed would not be practical, but I realized that we were not necessarily expected to have the rock at the opening to the lee side within one day. Other carriers passed us from both directions, and they would whisper to us: "You are progressing well. Aloha to you," and "if your hands become sore, wrap them in ni'u sheath fiber and urinate in the fiber."

My father knew of this, and upon finishing our day, told me to do this as he said he would. I went up the ravine, my hands chafed, with one spot at the base of my right index finger nearly skinless and oozing tiny spheres of blood, and upon approaching the two thatched dwellings, heard the lusty cry of a baby.

So was born my son, whom we named 'Iolana. He was a fat baby with fine black hair, suckling at Pekau's breast, while Pekau, her face directly above the strained visage of the boy who worked at feeding himself with a mindless vigor, looked up at me with pride and an exhilarated smile of achievement. My mother sat staring wistfully at them, while old Manomano sat outside over a fire-pit in which he cooked sweet potato.

The baby was born, it seemed, at the same time I sat and assisted in the ushering of that poor one-eared man into the land of the dead. I did not know if there was any point in seeing some mystical symmetry in this, but realized that had the child been a girl, I would have wanted her named Ka'ahupāhau.

Pekau saw my hands and understood. "Eat," she said, "and sleep."

The results of the urine-soaked fiber were as predicted. The second day of this project, both our hands were hardened somewhat.

I came to know every lichen, every irregularity of that rock. One lichen, light green and silvery against the stone, resembled at a certain angle that part of Pekau's body I had eagerly visited in the night, and indeed I waited for it to rotate into my vision after the second flat thump preceding the half-circumference forward surge, which we shepherded carefully lest the rock fall over. And that the lichen appeared to me just before the forward surge seemed an appropriate pattern for the work.

As the days passed, I began to see the eager expression Pekau would greet me with, and before long we were again reveling in that activity that had produced 'Iolana.

We rolled our rock every day, the labor brutally hard. The suggestive lichen turned ahead while, bathed in sweat, we struggled. And when, finally, we saw the gap between the foothills and the ocean narrow, we had rolled that rock for nearly a month.

It occurred to me during those days that my son, showing a vigorous health, was both a responsibility I enjoyed but at the same time vulnerable to my fate. What would happen if Kahimoku the Strange decided to loop his cord around my neck and stare deeply into my eyes as I died? I had found myself awake at night, locked inside these rueful meditations. And as he began to show more and more of that beautiful human vigor, I sank into more horrific speculations about myself and my mortality, my very worthlessness in the eyes of the powerful. Were I to be observed so keenly in my death, soiling myself and fouling the air, what would happen to Pekau and 'Iolana?

One night I was awake, and Pekau whispered, "What is it?"

"I want you to remember something," I said. "One day I might go to my rocks and not return. I have been thinking about what would happen."

"We will stay here," she said.

"But 'Iolana will—" I paused, trying to find the words.

She moved closer, and I smelled, as always, the odor of fish and coconut. The sumptuous warmth of her presence against me confused these awful speculations.

"We will be here," she said. 'Iolana stirred, and she rolled away to resettle him. "You will be here too."

"But if Kahimoku the Strange picks me out, I will not be here."

"You will be here," she said.

I carried that conviction with me. Even if I were dead, I surmised she meant that I would still be with them. I told my father of this, and as we hoisted a small rock, gleeful at having delivered the large one the previous week, he told me that Pekau was a spiritually and physically superior woman, that she had the heart of a warrior and the blood of the ali'i in her veins. No matter her age, no matter that she is a mere girl. Were you to die today, he said, your son would grow up to be as formidable as his namesake.

"The spirit of my 'Iolana lives in that boy," he said. "And his mother is—" He slowed his pace. "She is like your mother when she was young—strong and intelligent. It does not matter that she speaks so little."

"She speaks with her eyes and her flesh," I said. "An endless conversation."

He laughed. I appreciated this, because he rarely laughed.

So did we haul our stones through the hot season of that year and on again into Makahiki, and like the Kauwā we were convinced we were not, we watched the proceedings from high on the bluffs while old Manomano, brave and forward, met the small procession as it made its way around the point, and bestowed upon them a rather impressive quantity of dried he'e, and a fine mat woven by my mother, who, I suppose wistful about former days, wished to participate even if from a distance.

And Manomano returned with the information that indeed our hairy kahuna was part of the entourage, no doubt going along with a sharp eye out for a transgressor he could kill in some new, debased fashion.

And as in past years, we went for walks during the kapu season and as an afterthought, carried rocks to the appointed place where, because others had heeded the advice, a pile of stones grew to impressive proportions. It was this year, I believe, perhaps one year after the appearance of the man, or god, from the land of mists and fog, that he returned, and so the story came to us that he was killed on the island of Hawai'i, the largest in our world. It was said that he they called Lono had ordered a man killed, had attempted to recover a small fat canoe for his floating shrine, one of two such huge shrines, and in a fray on the beach he was killed and his body stripped of its meat and his bones divided amongst the chiefs. His mana now belonged to them.

Manomano was party to another story. "This event I have heard about, upon good authority," he said, his face orange in the firelight. "This happened either on his first visit, or recently. The man I talked to was unsure. Upon his arrival, he was escorted to a heiau by a priest named Koa, and there amid great solemnity, led to a sacrificial stone upon which lay a putrid pig. Then did Koa raise the pig and chant honors to Lono, who stood and listened, wearing a glorious feather cloak given to him earlier."

Manomano paused, and my father put twigs on the fire.

"Then did Koa invite Lono and his warriors to sit. A freshly baked pig was brought, and Koa pulled pieces of the meat off the pig and held them to Lono's mouth, but he did not deign to eat of the pig. Koa saw his displeasure, and proceeded to chew the meat for him and then hold it out to his mouth, but each time, Lono declined the gift, and in this subtle way brought shame to Koa. What had irritated him? And why, wondered Koa, did he decline to partake of the sacred meat? It was then that Koa, and those in attendance watching, began to wonder—was Lono displeased with them, or was this indeed Lono?"

Manomano paused once again. "He was a man. He was from the land of mists and fog." He stared at us, and then into the fire. "These are not the only ones from that distant land. There are others, and they carry death."

He believed this, he said, because of another story that had meanwhile circulated, over the past year—it had to do with a sickness men and women caught, in which the malaise caused a fever, and caused pus to drip from men's ules, caused women to lose their unborn, caused the gums of the mouth to rot and teeth to fall out. This affliction, it was said, was visited upon those women who offered up their flesh to Lono's warriors, and to those men who slept with such women. What did this mean?

Again, as we worked on, the story faded in significance, skepticism creeping into our minds about all such stories. As my father had said, the world was the world and that was all we knew. We had our burden, and the enterprise continued, the strange story fading from the memories of all who had to face the next lichen-decorated rock.

My father's strength was failing. In the evenings he was more prone to sleep rather than sit with Manomano at the fire. I urged him to eat, but he frequently declined, complaining of disorders in his stomach, and he grew leaner as we worked.

'Iolana, however, flourished, and but one year after 'Iolana's birth, Pekau was again with child. So long had we now worked carrying stones that I had begun to see our life up that ravine as pleasant, and rich. Were it not for my father's declining state, it would have seemed to me nearly perfect. We had our sweet potato patches nestled in flat, well-soiled areas above us, we had a source of water, we had the ocean, we had, further up the ravine, established dry-land kalo patches fed when necessary by a careful rationing of water from the little stream. It is true that the wind lashed our hale, that during the dry, hot time it dried up our crops so that Pekau and my mother had to go out on long forays into the woods to find food. And when our stream was reduced to a mere trickle, they would divert, drop by drop, what water there was, into storage gourds.

All these problems had their solutions, and our life went on, and was as I said, nearly perfect, but for Kahimoku the Strange. Without him and the threat he represented, it might have been far better. And then we did not see him for weeks, and we hoped that perhaps he had taken ill, or had been sent elsewhere.

"Do not assume that his absence is a blessing," Manomano told us one evening as we sat at the fire. "I have heard much, recently, and I am troubled."

My father, once skeptical about the old man, had by now come to revere his intelligence. "And why are you troubled?" he asked.

"If what I have heard is true, then a great catastrophe is to visit us."

My father looked at me. Then he waited. Was Manomano to continue? We sat in silence a few moments. Then my father cleared his throat. "What have you heard?"

It should be noted here that with old Manomano, one was required to ask the right question. *And what catastrophe will visit us?* would have been the wrong one, for the answer would have been, *A great one, as I have said.*

"I have heard on good authority," the old man said, "that the great chief Kahekili has designs on our island. We have had years of peace, while those islands, Maui and Hawai'i, have been embroiled in wars. But as Kahekili's power grows, so grows his desire to claim as his own what he can."

"Our island has many great warriors," my father said. "Are we not more populous than Maui?"

"True," Manomano said, "our island is more hospitable, while his has the high mountain and much rock spat hot from its belly to cut the feet of all who would walk on it. Is it a surprise, then, that he would want the fertile soil and the calm waters of ours?"

"But he must come to us."

"Yes, but he is a fighter, the taste of blood and victory hot in his mouth."

"And Kahahana?"

"Our chief ascended without blood. From Peleioholani to his son the lazy Kumahana, who was so easily and bloodlessly deposed, the idea of conflict is to Kahahana alien and no more than a dream he respects. This boy," and he placed his hand on my knee, "knows more of conflict than Kahahana." Manomano stared into the fire. "Kahekili is cut-in-half. The very skin of the warrior encases his bones."

"And why has this happened now?" my father asked.

"Relationships of blood are as much a curse as a blessing," Manomano said. "Kahahana is Kahekili's cousin's son, and Kahekili regards Kahahana as a son. In addition, Kaopulupulu, Kahahana's high priest and advisor, is the older brother of Kahekili's high priest Kaleopu'upu'u, the latter jealous of his brother's wisdom and influence. I have learned that after a consecration of a heiau on Moloka'i by Kahahana, who met there with Kahekili, the long and fruitful friendship of Kahahana and his high priest has been severed."

He went silent again, and poked at the fire with a stick. My father, I am sure, was honored to be party to such information, that such talk, not for the ears of the common people, was freely offered by the older man. But again, the revelation of why this was important awaited another question.

"And what is the significance of this rift in our moi's friendship with his high priest?"

"Kahekili has used treachery to confuse and make ineffectual his next victim. Kahahana is doomed. There will be a war, and many will perish."

My father leaned back, his hands on his knees. How could the old man be so certain? The absence of Kahimoku the Strange now seemed to me to be logical, for the chiefs of our island must have found it necessary to meet, to discuss something, and here was that something to discuss.

"And when do you believe this will befall us?" my father asked, his eyes intent upon the fire.

"Soon. Kaopulupulu has returned to Waialua, and he and his people each have a tattoo on their knee." The act was, I should say, a sign that Kaopulupulu had accepted the loss of friendship with Kahahana, and wore his tattoo as an expression of his loss.

My father continued to study the fire. How, I wondered, did Manomano get the information, and from whom? Surely not some loquacious he'e. The wily old man tended to be absent even before my father and I made our way to the stones, and sitting there, I saw what it was. His feet were thick and hard on the bottoms, and despite his age, his legs were lean and muscular. While we carried our stones, I surmised, he traveled great distances to see people, perhaps even colleagues of his from the era of the now long deposed Kumahana.

"May I ask a question?" I said.

"I see your eyes," Manomano said. "It is a special question. Please, ask."

"When you walk, how far do you go? All the way to Waialua?" Waialua is the location of the ali'i closest to our former living place.

Manomano's eyes widened in apparent surprise. "Indeed," he said, "you are observant." He thought a moment, staring into he middle distance. "Waialua? Perhaps."

"And the information comes then from a trusted friend?"

He looked at me. "My daughter bears the child of an intelligent boy."

Gentlemen, I realize that accounts of stone-carrying are not fascinating for those who want a story. So we shall move ahead more than two years. Does that shocked expression carry with it some unexpected disappointment that the details of those years are not carefully presented month by month? Ah, apparently not.

What of Kahimoku the Strange? It is true he remained the calculating predator, garroting the old and the infirm, but we carried our rocks effectively enough despite my father's physical decline, using a technique I instituted and he protested against, that of rigging our carrying litter in a manner in which I would bear most of the burden.

And as for Manomano's prediction about a war, we gradually forgot it. Kaopulupulu, he told us, was living in different places, and the cut-in-half chief of Maui, Kahekili, was biding his time.

'Iolana became a stout, happy mountain boy, at three years old crawling over rocks and running in the ravine, watched by the large, dark eyes of his sister Ka'ahupāhau, born two years after 'Iolana. Pekau and my mother had become the greatest of friends, and old Manomano seemed not to age— indeed, it appeared to me sometimes that he grew in reverse, manifesting an agility and youth that questioned the dark, mottled skin and the white hair.

And one day we heard that Kahekili had landed at Waikīkī. The reason was that Kaopulupulu had died, and Manomano explained that with Kahahana's former advisor now gone, the way was cleared for him to take our island.

Again, the problems of the outer world of ali'i and great concentrations of people and magnificent houses seemed not to affect us. We assumed that we were to continue carrying our stones, whether or not our land would be taken over by this great chief. And if the island were taken over, would the new chiefs see what we were doing and order us to continue? Probably, for the business of making war was largely the ali'i's business, and projects such as the heiau would be taken over and continued by the victor.

It should be noted here that our island had its many chiefs, each with his retinue of warriors and priests, the rights they enjoyed divided among them according to the land divisions I have already described. If Kahekili were to make war against Kahahana for the right of becoming moi of our island, then the battles between their two armies would determine the victor, while the common people and the lesser chiefs would watch, in effect, from a distance. This would include Muapo, who would wait, and then pledge fealty to whomever emerged the victor.

And so it came to pass that Kahahana made up his army and met the army of Kahekili on the bluffs and flatlands of the eastern leeward side of the island, and the result was a rout, Kahahana's army bested quickly, the first warriors slain put on the sacrificial stone, the rest who did not flee to the mountains slaughtered, their bodies stripped of flesh and bones carried off as the fruits of Kahekili's victory.

What would this mean for us? My father and I discussed with Manomano the possible outcomes, but there were none. Kahimoku the Strange reappeared and we carried our rocks. Frustrating as this may be to you who expect the accounts of pageantry and conflict, of armies meeting and the lusty clash of weapons, I can only say that I was not a party to any of this, and that, magically, the ravine we lived in and the hard path we traversed remained as before. Could any event, any change in power, interrupt the awful obsessions of Kahimoku the Strange? It seemed not, and if there were any compromise in the chief's sovereignty over his own land, we were not aware of it.

Manomano told us that Kahahana had escaped to the mountains with one wife and a small group of warriors, and in the mountains he wandered, helped by the common people, while Kahekili's chiefs placed themselves in the more desirable areas, Kailua on the windward side, Kualoa, and on the leeward side, Waikīkī and Ewa.

Our labor went on unabated. Kahimoku the Strange selected and executed the weak and the infirm, and recruited new workers by conscripting growing boys to join in the work, and by abducting other common people who decided one day to go walking. Over time he became more strange, in that he began selecting rocks with greater discrimination, sometimes staring at one for long periods of time before ordering it carried away. This benefited my father in that we stood, or sat, for long periods of time, while the hairy priest meditated over these rocks. His warriors stood patiently as he did this, sometimes whispering to one another, and we surmised that they were whispering such speculations as to judge the priest as insane, or at the very least eccentric to the point of ridiculousness. And his thirst for men to study as they died abated somewhat, so that those of us who had time to discuss these developments wondered, was the heiau near completion? If it was, then we speculated on our liberation from this work, or perhaps our deaths on the very stones we carried. Which would it be?

Manomano drew us, one night, to the fire. We had developed the habit, by this time, of joining in our ravine as an extended family to eat and to enjoy the evenings. My mother could not get enough of the children, and Pekau enjoyed her company. Thus as they played with the children, Manomano poked a stick into the fire and told us the story of Kahahana's demise and death. As I have said earlier, relatives among the ali'i might ordinarily be thought of as close, and protective of each other, but in truth, when power intervenes, what one would assume would be a familial bond turns out to be a greater hatred than those engendered by a bitter enemy. Thus, Kahekili felt that Kahahana's being alive, despite their close family connection, was a blight on his regency.

To put this in historical time, it was thirty-nine years ago, in the year seventeen and eighty-five. Kahahana's wife's brother was named Kekuamanoha, Manomano told us, and he was urged by those close to Kahekili to find and lure Kahahana out of the mountains, and through his sister, managed to do this. Then was Kahahana killed by Kekuamanoha's warriors, and his body taken by canoe to Kahekili, who was living at the shore far to the east. The depravity of this act, Manomano said, is such that no man can endure it for long. "There will be a retaliation," he said, looking over the flames at us. "And it troubles me that it may somehow involve you." That he was looking directly at me came as a surprise, for I could not imagine how I would ever have anything to do with such a retaliation. The soft voices of my mother and Pekau came to me, and I thought about what he had said.

"And why might it involve me?"

"Warriors will be gathered in secret, and they will kill Kahekili and his chiefs. I have it on good authority that your brother Konapiliahi will be coming for you. He who is cut-in-half will lead a group of men to kill one of the cut-in-half Kahekili's chiefs."

My father looked at me, and then at Manomano. "May I ask where this information came from?" he asked.

"As I said, from good authority."

My father stared at him. Very well, he had received the answer one might expect from the wily old man.

I worked on the formation of a question. "Then may I ask why they would require my involvement? I am but a rock-carrier."

"Chief Muapo is careful," Manomano said. "He wishes his involvement to be secret. Konapiliahi was given the task of inviting, shall we say, anonymous warriors, to participate. Those involved should have no known connection with any family member of his, or those in his retinue. Konapiliahi is the one person he has allowed, who is close to him, to become involved. I heard this, I should say, from another advisor to Muapo."

"But I am still a rock-carrier."

"No," Manomano said. "You have been tested in battle." He turned to my father. "As have you, but you, I am afraid, have become too old for this business."

"I will go if ordered," my father said.

§

One day our storyteller failed to appear. I waited with MacFarlane in the shed, the little circles of sunlight penetrating the roof shimmering upon the table. Indeed I felt awkward sitting there with the American, considering all the strife our two nations had undergone, the word *nation* in my mind not applying to the insurgency in the Americas that had, as of that man Jackson's victory at New Orleans, left Britain without its colony.

"So, what brings you over here when so much is happening on the continent?" I asked him. "Mr. More's utopian pronouncements notwithstanding, that is."

"As I said, I came out here more to explore, but upon getting my feet on the ground, found that it pleased me enough to stay."

"Do you have plans of capitalizing on opportunity here?" I asked. It seemed an obvious motivation, considering the disorganized nature of the place, along with the opportunities anyone with a little ambition might conceive. "I think it's an excellent place for anyone interested in agricultural possibilities, or perhaps shipping. My family is a part-owner of *The Clarel*, and I've been considering staying here a bit myself." I paused, considering the idea. "It would take no more than a promissory note to erect a little house I suppose, and I'm quite amazed at the industry of this port here."

"You ought to talk to Mr. Jones."

"Indeed. I have heard of him. What is his full name?"

"John Coffin Jones," MacFarlane said. "He's a consul, and has all sorts of power here. The Calvinists hate him."

"I do not quite understand," I said. "I am aware of the missionary influence here, but why would they be at odds?"

"Jones likes the women here," MacFarlane said, at which I almost laughed, for MacFarlane was not immune to such preferences himself. "I know by that look," he went on, "that you see me in the same light. But Jones was already married, and took a young wife, Hannah Davis, much to the displeasure of Mr. Bingham and his cronies."

"I see, and you were not married before you came here?"

"No," MacFarlane said. "I consider Henrietta my one wife."

"I hope you haven't thought of me as badly judging here. I was merely curious."

"Well, Liholiho and his wife are visiting your king. These islands are right now considered to be under the protection of the British Crown. In fact, a lot of the chiefs went with Liholiho, and left a nine-year-old boy and old Ka'ahumanu to run the place."

"I've seen the queen," I said. "An extraordinary display, I should say. She had men pulling her coach."

MacFarlane nodded, thinking. "You might think her simple, but she is not," he said. "She knows whom to ally herself with. She's thick with the missionaries."

"So it's Americans and British squabbling again, eh?"

"Something like that," he said. "I think more interesting is the connection here. Ka'ahumanu is thought to be the child of a chief named Ke'eaumoku and a woman named Namahana, who was the wife of the very chief Pono tells us about, Kahekili."

"Indeed," I said. "We have our story brought forward in time to us in the form of the queen, then."

"I should return home, though," MacFarlane said. "I'll leave the story of the queen alone in case Pono includes her in his narrative." He closed his ledger-book and wrapped his pens in a rag. Then he stood up, sighed, and looked out through the thatch at the dirt path that ran along it. "Tomorrow, then. I don't want this story stopped here."

"Nor do I," I said.

The prospect of returning to the ship caused in me a sensation of wan boredom, so I made my way in the direction of the beach to the east, toward Diamond Hill, and decided to walk a bit on the sand. It was a pleasant day, and as I made my way, the sounds of the sailors in the grog shops receded behind me. I was moving near the dwellings of the missionaries, a cluster of buildings just a few hundred paces inland from the water. The climate had become more bearable, and with this came the speculations about how I might benefit in a business sense from remaining here. True it was that I was not like the sailors at that moment drinking themselves into stupefaction, and passing out coins for the pleasures of brown girls, but I had, at night, thought that should I remain here for some time, I might naturally strike up a liaison with one of them.

I was not interested in a 'professional', for the thought of those women, I must admit, somewhat unmanned me. Not only was there the tangible prospect of disease, they also struck me as brash and forward, and I had conceived in my mind the image of a passive woman, young, perhaps connected to a family for whom some compensation would be welcome. It seemed to me that these people were mired in a stultifying poverty, and found escape from it only in the various simple joys nature might provide them. Sea-bathing, for example. I had seen the people frolicking in the sea, the women either bare-chested and wearing only some sort of loincloth, or trussed up in dresses, those I assume connected somehow with the mission, and unfortunately made unavailable because of the imposition of an alien morality upon them.

Suppose, I thought, some young woman, connected to a family in much need of financial assistance, were to know that I could provide just that? The seeming availability of these women had caused me to lose sleep, thinking late at night amid the soft squeaks and groans of the ship, of the sight of water streaming down their bodies, of the saucy expressions as they played in the waves. As I walked along the sand, I indeed saw small groups of people sitting, and others bobbing in the water, their voices high, but upon seeing me, they became quiet and watched me as I passed. Of course I was an alien to them. And of course they could not have known that there were benefits I could offer them for that access I dreamed of.

When I found myself standing upon a bright beach that was at least a hundred and fifty yards of fine sand between the water and the first low shrubs, I stopped, and decided that indeed it was time for me to arrange for a longer stay in this place, for those delights that seemed so available should not be passed by. Pono's fantastic tale notwithstanding, and I will say that I doubted its truth and felt that in ways both MacFarlane and I were being handed a tale fabricated by a clever dreamer, I had other things to do here, and now that I understood the truth of the place, that it was a world-traveler's dream in which the most luscious desires could easily be fulfilled, that the access to the firm and healthy bodies of women whose childlike ignorance superseded any irritating social regulation, I decided that I would accept what was apparently so readily being offered me.

8.

Now, with my apologies for my absence accepted, and if you
gentlemen are settled, I shall continue this account by moving ahead
somewhat, and then as needed, filling in where necessary, so reordering what
you assumed was to be linear into something else. And yes, that expression
of faint hope that this might somehow advance the account more efficiently
shall, I promise, be realized.

I am walking at a rapid pace behind my cut-in-half brother, my pahoa
secured in the cord of my malo and carrying, to my diminishing astonishment
since he bestowed it upon me hours before, a beautiful leiomano, the weapon
of my brother ʻIolana and the object of my boyhood dreams. My mind is a
tumid, scrambled mixture of many emotions: fear and dread, awed curiosity,
a horrible fear about Pekau and the children should I die, and a troubling
conviction that what I am doing is wrong. Why should I, a commoner,
participate in this act of vengeance against Kahekili?

But I had no say in the matter. We traversed a narrow dirt path that
wound around mountain outcroppings and through wooded areas, always
above the ashy and dark panorama of the leeward side of the island, a place
I had never been. Movement by night, he told me, would go unnoticed, but
we had to move fast, for our appointed meeting with two other anonymous
warriors was to take place on the bluffs above the vast flatlands of Ewa, in the
center of which lay a cluster of great houses and a sleeping chief, whom we
would kill. The two warriors we were to meet knew a way to sneak into the
guarded compound of this chief, and my cut-in-half brother told me that we
would not know the names of these warriors, and they would not know ours.

My cut-in-half brother slowed his walk. In the distance ahead two
figures arose, both bearing objects I could not identify, but clearly they were
weapons. When we approached, the two men set themselves side by side,
and Konapiliahi raised his hand. One of the men raised his, and launched
into a strange speech in which he identified his moʻo, a word which means,
among many things, lizard, genealogical line, gunwale board, and so on. He
said that his line carried him back to before the arrival of the aliʻi, and what

we were doing was an act of vengeance centuries old. "I care not if I survive," he said. "I care only that I draw the blood of Kahekili's favored dog. May he cry out and slide in his own shit." He then held up his 'ihe, a beautifully barbed instrument, reflecting the moonlight along its smooth shaft. "There is another small group approaching from the sea," he went on. "I will know them and tell you. Together we shall wipe the land clean of this curse."

Konapiliahi raised his war-axe, and in imitation of his resolve I raised my leiomano. The second warrior held a leiomano also. "Follow us," the first warrior said, and the four of us, in a line, made our way down a ravine with a trickle of water in it, laboring over slippery rocks amid the soft sounds of the water beneath us. I recall that I had become badly frightened, and my feet did not seem to work properly, my body strangely out of balance and my heart pounding in my chest.

As we descended in that ravine, I saw from time to time over its grass-tufted lip the hale we would attack. Finally we reached a place where the lead warriors stopped, and crouched down. There, tall amongst smaller hale, was the chief's house, and we saw no movement around it. "Why are there no guards?" Konapiliahi whispered. The others considered this, and I could see the doubt on their moonlit, sweating faces.

"They are comfortable in their sleep," the lead warrior whispered. "We shall help them dream forever."

He moved out of the ravine toward the hale, and we followed, I trying my best to steel myself, my hand now tightly gripped on my leiomano. Ahead of me Konapiliahi gripped his war-axe, walking quietly in a low crouch. The two in the lead stole to the hale, and stood on either side of a low doorway. Konapiliahi moved toward the doorway, myself behind him, but just as we were about to enter, a standing figure appeared there, the upper part of his body parting thatch above the doorway, and there emerged his head, the sockets of his eyes empty, black, and oozing blood over his cheeks that ran black in the moonlight. Konapiliahi raised his axe, but the figure toppled forward and landed face down on the dirt, and when his body thumped there, producing a flat, dead cough, the point and then the shaft of a spear appeared coming from the stomach of the lead warrior standing against the thatch. With a sharp yell that warrior fell forward, the spear vanishing back into him, and men broke from the doorway bearing axes and spears.

Konapiliahi swung his axe, breaking one of the spears, and I moved forward to swing the leiomano, and its white teeth shattered off the shaft of another spear. The second warrior swung his leiomano at the head of one of the men, and it glanced off the crown. Konapiliahi roared, pulling away from a spear that had gone through his thigh. I crouched down and swung the leiomano at a man's leg, hitting it squarely, and when he fell, there was a moment of confusion at that doorway, at which I was grabbed roughly by the arm and pulled back toward the ravine. It was Konapiliahi. The remaining warrior had run away toward the water, and just as we reached the ravine we heard his screams. He had been caught, and then we heard the sound of wood on bone, the awful cracking sound of a head being crushed flat, blow by blow, sharp and clear first, and then softer and flatter in the sound of increasing liquefaction.

"Wait," Konapiliahi said. I could see black lines on his thigh, blood running down.

He groaned, putting his hand on the wound. Then he looked up again, and we could see many figures moving around the hale, spreading out over the moonlit landscape, their weapons ready. "We have been found out," Konapiliahi said. "Someone has alerted them to this." He looked up the ravine. "We must go higher."

We made our way up the ravine, but it was too shallow to afford us proper cover. As we moved over the slippery rocks, we heard voices above us. It seemed that the warriors had moved ahead of us up the ravine, on the firm earth above, and we were trapped. But Konapiliahi's leg was giving him trouble. We kept moving, more slowly as he struggled to stay up on his feet. At length we found ourselves in a deeper part of the ravine, the overhanging rocks and brush thick enough that we were able to find a hollow there, under the lip. We crawled into that hollow and rested. And as we rested, we still could hear the voices, farther away this time. There were many small hale dotting the landscape, and the warriors were looking for us by demanding entry. We waited.

Our wait lasted the night. Konapiliahi groaned over his wound, and when he did not do that he speculated on our fortunes. "My leg becomes worse," he whispered, "and I think that when you can, you must run and leave me." I held my hand up to him and whispered back, "I will wait for you. I will carry you." He laughed softly. "Boy," he said, "I am large." And I held my hand up once again. "You are my sister's husband, my brother. I have carried rocks for years. You shall become my next rock." To which he said, "Indeed, you look strong, but I do not know if you are that strong. Perhaps you look stronger than you are." And I said, "Perhaps I am stronger than I look." And he laughed.

Thus passed the night. When the sky lightened, I was tempted to peek over the edge of the ravine, but Konapiliahi cautioned me against doing that. We were hungry and thirsty, and I found a large leaf and folded it into a cup, and stole down to the little stream and drank, and took water to Konapiliahi.

He told me to stay out of sight. Because the plan had been detected in advance, and they had a couple of people to enjoy killing, the entire matter might end up a trifle in their eyes. We would wait out the day, and steal away in the next nightfall.

For a time we slept, sitting inside that little hollow. I picked up my leiomano and studied the section where four of the white teeth had broken off. I noticed, sitting there, that this was a place were children played, not unlike the cave I had so long ago played in with my sisters. The dirt floor had been smoothed by the feet and buttocks of the children, and little carefully manufactured toys lay around the edges: sticks bound together and knotted with strands of hair, odd pieces of coconut fiber folded in the likeness of houses and canoes. I drifted into sleep, and then awoke to the sound of Konapiliahi's moaning.

The wound, blue-edged and leaking, had surged into a pout, the thigh swollen. He would not be able to walk. I was tempted, again, to peek over the edge of the ravine, because the earlier silence had now been replaced by the sound of men's voices. Apparently their search for us had not dwindled in importance. In fact, now the inflections and tone were of an angry timbre. I moved to stand up, and felt Konapiliahi's hand on my forearm.

"We must stay here," he said. "This kīmopō involves chiefs all over the island. Kahekili is in Kailua. Although our attack has failed, others may not have failed. Someone may have informed on us and on others. Either all die, or none. If some chiefs died, then there will be much bloodshed." Kīmopō, by the way, simply means 'night killing', or 'secret rebellion'. "Kahekili is vengeful," he said. "If someone did die, then messengers would take the day to get to him. We must wait."

And wait we did, until the evening, at which Konapiliahi tried standing, and found that his leg was numb and would barely support him. We readied ourselves to go farther up the ravine, but upon raising my head above the lip, I saw figures not fifty paces from us. They stood in a small group, their bodies a rich orange color in the fading sunlight. Perhaps they were common men talking, or perhaps they were warriors on the watch, waiting for just such people as we so that they might split our heads with their war-axes.

Thus did we remain into our second night. Konapiliahi's wound caused him great pain, and he spent long periods of time writhing and moaning, and I considered our predicament. I could carry him out, but the stillness of the night, the lack of wind, and the sound, here and there, of voices too close to us, meant that we would be too easily seen. He then drifted into a fitful sleep, and I sat next to him, wary and alert, as long as I could, before I, too, fell asleep. I awoke hungry and thirsty, as Konapiliahi was. In the advancing dawn I crept down to the little stream to carry water back to him, and drank of the stream myself. I understood that we could not sit there forever in that little hollow. "Brother," I said, "it is time to go. Can you stand?"

Stand he did. I instructed him to drape the top part of his body over my shoulder, but he held up his hand. "I shall try walking," he said. I looked over the lip of the ravine. Around the small dwellings there was the movement of people, women it appeared, and children. Konapiliahi made his way to the stream, and cupped water with his hands and ran it down over his wound. I looked up along the edge of the ravine toward the mountains. We were far from any place where we would not be seen. Between us and the mountain lay a cluster of larger dwellings, perhaps the kauhale of some lesser chief. We speculated on this, and Konapiliahi believed that the best thing to do, at this time of the day, was to walk toward the mountains and behave as if we belonged where we were.

We made our way up out of the ravine. Walking on firm earth rather than the rocks below was preferable, and Konapiliahi was able to make his way, one hand on my shoulder, his war-axe in the other. The sun was up, our shadows long on the ground. We caught the attention of some common people, but just as we did, something drew their attention eastward. Under the bright sun, there were fires, apparently some of the small dwellings in the distance burning, and then, as we walked along, we began to hear the sounds of yelling, and screams, and the flat reports of weapons clashing. Konapiliahi shaded his eyes, as I did, and looked out over the plain to the east.

"It is as I feared," he said. "We must get to the mountains."

We made our way along the ravine. The larger cluster of dwellings above us now began to show activity, men with weapons standing facing east, women and children vanishing inside dwellings.

We stopped, and found some low brush in which to crouch down. From between the dry branches we had a good view to the east, and there, we beheld the armed figures moving over the plain, behind them a series of kahilis, or standards. I cupped my hands lower over my eyes. There was color, too, red and yellow. Ali'i. "Why?" I asked.

"I had hoped none would die," Konapiliahi said. "It is Kahekili's army. There can be no other reason for this than vengeance. If the plot to kill the chiefs failed, then it would be less important. But it may not have failed."

In the lead now came warriors who were running, and I looked around to see what army they were running at, but saw only the men at the cluster of dwellings above us pointing, hardly enough to pose a challenge.

Then a cloud blocked the sun, and my vision was suddenly sharp and lucid. Six or seven warriors converged on a small house and went inside, and a man, a woman and two children emerged through the thatch at the back, caught then by warriors who had quickly circled the house. Then weapons were raised, one an object with a flattened loop of white, a leiomano, and it came down on the woman's head while the man struggled with another warrior who pushed him down, stepped on his chest and brought a war-axe down on his face. A girl child had run away, now pursued by another warrior, who quickly reached her, picked her up by the ankles and swung her over his head and down, so that her head bounced on the ground. Then he pulled a pahoa from his malo and drove it into her chest, putting much weight on the handle. My mouth became dry and my stomach surged with sudden nausea. The other child, a boy, sat against the thatch, watching, perhaps too young to understand, and another warrior who had come around the house saw him and aimed a long spear at his back. He drove the spear partway in, and the boy screamed, and then the warrior pivoted the spear on the ground and raised the boy the height of two men off the ground, the boy struggling at the top. The warrior picked the spear up and then slammed the butt down into the soil, at which the boy, impaled through his back and out the hollow of his shoulder, slid down the spear, limp.

They were a hundred fifty paces from us now. The brave defenders of the cluster of houses above us had gathered, a few of them moving outward toward the advancing army. Konapiliahi grabbed my forearm and said, "We must get back into the ravine." It was true. There was no other place to hide. We made our way back through the brush to the lip of the ravine and made our way down, and then back toward the ocean to the hollow where we had hidden for the two nights. There, we waited, and shortly, we began hearing the clash of weapons and the screaming from above us, the shouts of the warriors, the shrieks of children, the awful sound of wood on bone, and then the smell of burning thatch came down the ravine. I closed my eyes, listening, until a hand touched my arm. Konapiliahi pointed downward. The little stream in the bottom of the ravine was running a faint reddish hue, which changed in density as we watched, until the water was a dark reddish-black that gradually became enriched with the bright hue of blood.

There was the sound of activity above us. We shrunk back into the hollow, and heard a man laughing, then grunting, after which the body of an infant child soared in a fast rotation, tiny arms and legs out so that the body formed a spinning X, and landed on the rocks in the streambed. I looked at the figure there, waiting to see if it would move. Its head bobbed in the red water, as if the tiny boy were slaking a powerful thirst.

Then there was silence above us, and the faint sounds of screaming and the clashing of weapons to our west. Konapiliahi listened carefully, and then said, "We may be able to get to the mountains now. Go up and look over the edge."

I did so, my legs shaking and my heart beating rapidly. I saw in the near distance the bloodied bodies of women, old men, little girls, and up to my left, the smoldering remains of the cluster of houses, their stick frames still standing. To the east one small group of men were crouched over a body. One man, a kahuna it appeared, held up the leg of a dead man while the other used a stick with shark's teeth in it to saw down along the thigh bone, separating a large slab of flesh from the bone. They were stripping the body of its meat, collecting the mana of the dead. I went back and reported what I had seen to Konapiliahi, and he nodded.

"We will move up the ravine," he said. He tried to stand, and used his war-axe as a short walking-stick, and we made our way over the rocks, past the dead infant boy, and along the stream, which had lost its bright red hue, toward the mountains. Near where we had hidden, we saw more bodies in the ravine, piled five or six deep, limbs splayed, faces stilled, the woman nearest me with her head resting on the shoulder of an old man, the top of her head misshapen from a heavy blow, her eyes open and staring at me with an expression of wondrous contemplation. The water coming out from under this brown-skinned dam of dead now ran clear, bubbling swiftly along the rocks and pebbles.

In order to traverse this obstacle, we walked partway up the side of the ravine and then lightly, gently stepped on the back of a boy whose wound pursed out and leaked fluid and blood when we put pressure on with our feet. At the greatest pressure his head rose slightly, as if he had awakened to address us when we stepped on him. On the other side of this dam of dead we beheld other bodies, throats slashed, heads caved in, and beyond them, a black piglet rooting in the mud by the stream. He saw us and squealed, and then clattered over the rocks up the ravine on his tiny hooves.

We rose from the ravine at the burned house. There, hidden somewhat by the remaining smoke, we were able to make our way past those remains to a place where the terrain rose toward the mountains. Konapiliahi struggled along on his war-axe, his blue half unharmed, his brown half appearing weaker on its damaged leg. We had seen so many dead by this time that the sight of old women and children with their heads ruined and their bodies bearing horrible wounds, already now drawing flies, did not cause us to pause or comment, for our minds were now numbed to the carnage. I recall being in a stunned, contemplative trance, walking slowly because my cut-in-half brother walked slowly, hopping over his damaged leg with each step. The slaughter had carried itself far to our west now, and when Konapiliahi had to stop to rest, now in the shelter of some short trees, we turned and looked out over the vast plain, seeing far below the hale of the chief we were supposed to kill, of course undamaged and as it was before.

It occurred to me there, for the first time, that Muapo would be killed, which would mean that Kahimoku the Strange would die with him. The warriors on their rampage might make their way around the corner of the island and continue their killing in the mountains, where Pekau, the children, and my parents were. With this thought, I was overcome with a sudden, debilitating fright. It made my hands weak, and I experienced a light-headedness that Konapiliahi must have recognized, for he said, "Do not worry. Your family will be safe. Those on their killing spree will weary of it."

"And what of Laka and the children? Are they not in danger?"

Konapiliahi gazed out over the plain, standing on his blue foot. He thought about this. "I shall tell you," he said. "I do not know if this is true, but I have wondered since we were attacked at the hale, about this. Muapo is crafty, and calculates his advantages carefully." Then he shook his head as if he were disagreeing with himself.

"But what does that have to do with Kahekili's intentions?" I asked.

Again he thought, and then winced, looking at the wound on his leg. "I may not be able to walk," he said. He held up his hand. "Listen to me," he said. "Someone informed on us. How better to ingratiate yourself to Kahekili than to become a part of this plot and then inform? This was carried out in the utmost secrecy. I am beginning to believe that I know why." He nodded. "I believe he is safe, and Laka and the children are safe. If this is so, then we may conclude that we have experienced the reason."

"We are near the path we took," I said. "It is time for us to go."

"You will go without me," he said. "This begins to fester. I will die."

"No, I will carry you."

He considered this. It was obvious that he thought I could not carry him. I told him to hold my leiomano in his hand with his war-axe. The best way, I thought, was for him to drape his body at the waist over my right shoulder, which we tried, and indeed, when he had released his weight on me, I was able to stand and struggle awkwardly along the path, the two weapons in his hand clacking together, his wound dripping on my knee and foot as I walked. The jostling hurt him, and he groaned, then seemed to be holding his breath against it. "You are indeed stronger than you look," he wheezed out.

Thus I carried my cut-in-half brother on that same path we had traversed by night, the great weight of his body hurting my tired feet as they met any irregularity in the ground.

He advised me to rest at one point, but I pressed on, panting under the burden, because I did not want my sister to be without a husband. The leakage of his wound had slicked the right side of my body, and I felt it slippery between my toes. The kauhale of Muapo would appear below the path, he told me, beyond which, from the same path, I would be able to see the project I had so long labored for.

At length, I beheld the kauhale of Muapo, and it was undamaged. Konapiliahi looked in the same direction, his head nearly inverted, and said, "Yes, I believe I was right." He instructed me to put him down. I did so, and he stood on one leg. "I will not forget you," he said. "In all of this you have shown yourself to be a warrior indeed."

"Will you be able to go the rest of the way?"

"Yes. As for you, I think it would be best if you stayed out of anyone's sight. This path moves into the mountains farther, and then ends near the end of the island. Take it, and rejoin your family."

I left him there, and, gripping my leiomano, walked the path, the sensation of lightness in my body not unfamiliar, because I had so many times felt this same way after having deposited my rock at the opening to this part of the island. And indeed did I see the project. The heiau appeared, from above, to be nearly complete, a vast square that was built across a shallow ravine, baking there in the sun, some of its black rocks the very same ones I had carried. Its ocean-facing wall must indeed have been high, perhaps the height of five or six men, for beyond that lip I saw the tops of niu trees waving in the breeze. But I hastened along that path because I now had become anxious to get back home, to verify for myself that no one in my family became a victim of this slaughter.

The path wound into the low woods, in which I looked for fruit but found none. Then it went downward toward the plain, and when I came to a place from which I could see over that plain, I saw more burning houses, the dreamlike glinting of polished weapons, and movement, although it was so far away that I could not discern anything specific, and thought, somewhat dimly, that yes, people were dying down there. I made my way along, my stomach cramping with hunger and my throat dry. The path turned downward toward the ocean, where the plain had thinned and now vanished, the mountains looming closely over the water. I walked as if in a dream, waking myself only to look for the place where we had for years deposited our stones.

In that dreamlike walk, I had assumed that I was past danger, that indeed these warriors had wearied of their slaughter and were now making their way back to their chiefs and their exultation over their victories, however unmanly they may have been, considering the nature of their enemies. But in a period of two or three heartbeats, I found I had been wrong, for I first smelled something odd, a rich smell of sweat and blood, and the hint of putrefaction. I was knocked off my feet onto the ground.

Above me stood two warriors, begrimed with dried blood and the filth of human slaughter, arms and legs glistening with the visceral grease and fluid of dead women and children, their teeth white as they leered down at me, one of them holding a blood-blackened club, the cord of his malo holding several long braids with glistening bits of scalp attached. I scrambled backwards like a crab, but met the knee of another warrior, this one bearing a short spear, his body also slicked with a mixture of his own sweat and the blood and bits of tissue of those he had murdered. I made a motion to raise the leiomano, and one said, "It is missing teeth."

Other warriors appeared. Their bearing was of a satisfied fatigue. I vomited a string of brownish bile into the grass, and slumped down, awaiting the blow.

"Stand," the warrior with the short spear said. I did so, weakly, my hands shaking and my vision blurred. "Defend yourself with your toothless weapon," he said, pointing the spear. It appeared that he intended to drive it into my belly, and was about to do so, because I was offering no resistance, my mind already settled on the idea that I would now join the numberless legions of the dead.

"Ho'opau," a deep voice said, and all the warriors turned. There, standing above us and holding a bloodstained war-axe, was a muscular warrior who was blue-black in his entirety, his body a nightmare of tattoos, swirls on his pectoral muscles, blue lines around his heavy thighs, his face blocked out in a rectilinear pattern of small squares, his arms each with a single line encircling and rotating downward to his wrists. The deference shown him by the filthy warriors meant that he held some exalted position, and I stood there, dizzy and amazed at the riot of shapes on his skin, so that he resembled a giant, hideous lizard.

He stepped down toward me, and as I stared, I thought again of raising the leiomano, but the spectacular warrior unmanned me. I dropped the leiomano.

As I stood there awaiting the blade of the axe, my eyes moved over the shapes, and then seeing beyond the amazing patterns to the body itself, to the eyes and the visage hidden behind the patterns, and then my eyes must have shown my astonishment, for he said, "Brother, we will meet some day, perhaps in some other place, but today you shall go home unharmed."

I wilted to my knees, nearly fainting with the astonishment. Above me stood the most terrifying warrior I had ever seen, my brother 'Iolana.

"His name," Manomano said upon our return home, "is Mo'omake." The word means 'deadly reptile', or perhaps 'serpent of death'. "He is legendary for his ruthlessness."

"How has this come about?" my father asked. "He was not given to this as a boy. How has this happened?" Away from the fire sat my mother, weeping with a commingling of joy and sorrow, joy at the information that her son was alive, sorrow for who he had become. Pekau comforted her, and the children lay sleeping in the house.

"Your story about the battle at the stream many years ago suggests to me that he was captured," Manomano said, "but his life was spared for one reason or another, perhaps the intervention of a high-born woman. But he is now one of Kahekili's warriors, and I have heard of his exploits. All who face him die." The old man thought, the little flames from the fire illuminating him from below so that his eyes appeared unnaturally bright. "The savagery of the slaughter is fitting for Kahekili. One of his favorites was killed, Kiku-Hueu, a chief much loved by his retinue. This vengeance may not be over." Manomano looked at me. "Have you filled yourself yet?"

"No," I said. I continued eating, chewing on a large piece of dried he'e, and then paused. "And what of rock carrying now?" I asked.

"I assume it continues," Manomano said, placing more sticks on the fire. "For two days now all has been quiet, but Muapo remains in his hale, safe and prepared to continue on his great enterprise. Konapiliahi's suspicions are correct."

"It is as it must be then," my father said. "But as for 'Iolana, I must not see him. I must never see him."

"I understand," Manomano said. "The story you told me of your family curse carries with it, now, that possibility. It is true that fate visits these things upon us. We must bear up under that burden." Then Manomano looked at me with that mischievous smirk of his. "Unless it is your son Pono who shall perpetuate it."

"No," I said. "My father shall not repeat the tragedy of his forebear Kamale'e on my account."

This seemed to surprise my father. "I told you that story when you were a boy. How is it you remember it after all that has happened to us?"

"I remember," I said. "It is interesting that without memory, we would be as sea-slugs." I finished my he'e. "'Iolana said that we will meet someday, but that this day I was to be allowed to go on. I think he means that when we meet, he will kill me."

"He will," Manomano said. "Once one is turned to outside allegiance, his former sympathies sometimes become hatreds. Remember Kahekili and Kahahana."

"But you are strong," my father said.

"I do not believe that I am a true warrior," I said.

"He who does not believe he is a true warrior may be the truest of warriors," Manomano said.

So my father and I made our way to our appointed place in the morning, as did other stone-carriers. The word of the slaughter had spread, and all who waited appeared fearful and anxious. Perhaps the worst irony of it all was that Muapo, and therefore Kahimoku the Strange, emerged somehow untouched by all the bloodshed. And indeed Kahimoku appeared with his small retinue of warriors, and he went out on the bluffs overlooking the ocean to study rocks. Apparently the project was nearing completion, for he wanted only flatter rocks, and seemed to mesmerize himself studying lichen patterns in the stone before pointing and ordering a rock moved.

One was assigned to us. It was another of the type that would need to be slowly rolled on its edge, and my father and I somewhat gladly took on this job, because all who were left idle standing there on the bluffs felt the worming of anxiety under their skin.

We met old rock-carriers on the path as we rolled ours. They were returning, fatigued and silent, looking down at where they placed their feet on the path. When they saw us and moved to the side, one addressed my father: "Leave that stone and come back. Do not rest, for the great butcher-chief is not yet satisfied."

"And whom are you talking about?" my father asked.

"Kahekili's warriors litter the mountainside, studying people. Anyone who appears capable of the slightest resistance to his regency has many eyes on him."

"My thanks for that advice," my father said. "We will turn quickly."

"They hunt in the mountains above the plain of Ewa and kill those they missed. In time they will come here."

"We will be careful," my father said, and we continued rolling our rock.

So went our work, always done with watchful eyes and studious concentration lest we attract the attention of Kahimoku the Strange. Manomano understood the odd tenor of the daily atmosphere, for he informed us over the fire that he had been assaulted at night by troubling dreams. He felt more and more strongly that we had to move our kauhale farther up the mountain, in more remote places where Pekau had played as a child. He had explored the ravine as it approached the clouds, and had found a large shelf with good soil and even a small pool at the base of a fall, and there, he believed, we could cultivate our crops and live without fearing the appearance of warriors convinced that we were part of some plot to topple Kahekili from his regency. The crops we raised at our present location could be tilled, and if circumstances changed, we could move back down.

He showed my father and myself this shelf one evening when the sun, a large orange ball sitting on the ocean's lip, shed its rich orange light on our skin. Pekau came with us, nimbly jumping up rocks and then waiting for me to struggle up, teasing me and laughing when I paused and looked down off the seeming cliff we had just climbed.

The shelf was large, perhaps thirty paces by thirty paces, and fringed with brush, with 'ōhi'a trees and other mountain plants that I did not recognize. Looking downward at the ocean and at the bluffs above it, I could see the path we traversed each day as we carried our rocks. Should defense of this place be necessary, it would be easy to prevent warriors from climbing the faint path. We would need only to roll rocks down on them, and if they lost their balance, they would roll halfway down the mountain. I mentioned this to my father, who agreed. Manomano said that defense was not the advantage. Invisibility was the advantage, for if warriors wanted to come up and kill us, they would do it. Therefore, the use of fires up here was to be considered carefully, and we would all learn the skill of making a smokeless fire.

"How does one make a fire without smoke?" I asked, still a bit breathless.

Manomano nodded, smiling at me. "Carefully," he said.

"And my mother," I said, "how shall we bring her up here?"

Manomano smiled again, but said nothing. I understood what the answer would have been should he have spoken: carefully.

And so we moved to that high shelf in the ravine. My mother, so spiritually debilitated by the loss of our home, the loss of her youngest daughter, and now the confusing problem of 'Iolana and what had become of him, walked around on that firm earth so far above the ocean and then wept. She looked down to the bluffs, and said, "I am exiled to this place and I shall die here." My father shook his head and tried to comfort her, as did Pekau and the children, who gathered around her and patted her and tried to lift her spirits. I stood off to the side, thinking that it was a pity that my mother, the great storyteller, the favorite of those old people who had lived in a world far more sedate and enjoyable, was correct in her complaint. We were all exiled here. But upon observing the children, I realized that, like Pekau, they had mastered the nearly vertical terrain like crabs crawling up rocks. They were children of the mountain, and therefore we who once lived near the water on level ground were now people of the mountain.

Work on the heiau underwent suspensions for as many as four or five days at a time. Had Muapo grown weary of his project so near its completion? We did not know. We waited at our appointed places, talking with one another about what this might mean. Was the project finished? If so, would warriors now come to select subjects for sacrifices? Certainly Kahimoku the Strange had in mind many who might qualify.

Far up the ravine in the evenings, Manomano built his smokeless fire, a simple technique of making a small one, but hot, and then building it in small degrees, so that only faint wisps of smoke rose from it. He also blocked one side of the fire so that it would not reflect on the sheer cliff above us. The water trickling over the face of the rock, he said, would reflect this light, so he would establish his fire-pit against a shrub that shadowed it. Manomano did continue fishing before dawn, and as before, he'e hung from the branches of little trees, salted and drying.

These delays in our work continued on through the spring season and into the hotter part of the year, and Kahimoku the Strange stopped selecting men for killing. His obsession with the perfect rocks had become so deep and so mysterious that all rock-carriers, who perhaps should have suspected some wondrous, humane change in his state of mind, fell into such an anxious depression that it was as if the delays were driving them mad. Where earlier the older rock-carriers had kept up their strength by carrying rocks, they now seemed to age rapidly, to become enfeebled to the point of appearing useless, left to stand in the grass and watch as the insane priest wandered over the bluffs deep in some mystical contemplation, unable himself to find rocks that satisfied his increasingly rigid aesthetic standards.

One day as we waited, I saw my father standing there in the grass, his shoulders hunched, and his body lean and debilitated. He stared at the priest, seemingly angry, and I did not understand his anger until he stooped down and picked up a rather heavy stone, and began walking toward the path. I quickly went to him, fearing his being seen by one of the warrior attendants of the priest. "What are you doing?" I whispered.

He stared blankly at me, then down at the rock he held. "I do not know," he said.

"Put the rock down," I whispered to him, looking around toward the warriors. He did so, and then began to tremble. I gently put my hand on his shoulder.

"Pono," he whispered. "I am dying."

"You are not dying," I whispered. "You are waiting."

He looked out over the ocean. "For death, yes." He looked at me with both wonder and affection. "But for you, I would be dry bones."

"Stay with me. We will endure this."

So it went, into the hot season. Two old rock-carriers died, four days apart. They were found in the grass at the end of the day. Other rock-carriers decided to walk away from the project, but that proved a mistake, because they were hunted down and killed by Kahimoku's warriors. In the evenings we discussed the strange tensions of our situation, and Manomano explained that the rocks now being selected by the priest were those to be used to finish the project, refinements as it were, and when Kahimoku selected the largest of all the stones yet, that one would be the sacrificial stone. He speculated that Muapo wanted all these stones from this area because of some youthful connection to the place, but regardless of how inefficient the entire enterprise was, some motive none of us would ever understand had been and would continue to be the reason for all of this. We had only to hope that once the project was done, we would all be released.

Then Manomano's eyes fell upon me. "I have watched you now for some time. You will live, and see many things. Remember that old Manomano's whisper will visit you from time to time."

"I will remember."

And inside our little hale in the middle of the night, Pekau became aware that I could not sleep, and put her head on my chest and said, "We will always be here."

"Manomano may not be right," I said. "Kahimoku may take me to his stone. I fear this not for myself, but for you and the children."

"We will have another," she said.

This kept me awake, even as she slept, and I lay there listening to her breath and smelling its sweet aroma, and listened too to the fitful sleeping of 'Iolana and Ka'a, both of whom would from time to time voice their dreams in nonsensical pronouncements. The horror of my situation was now to be aggravated by the gift of another child. This sentiment was a mixture of joy of the highest measure, along with fear and misery of the most exaggerated, for enduring our situation was a daily struggle that had its measurable parts, and this added information from her upset the delicate balance of what I most cherished and what I most feared.

Late in Makahiki, after we watched the small procession from our shelf high on the mountain while Manomano boldly offered dried he'e to the passing ali'i, we learned that the stone had been found. It was during a period of unpredictable weather, with heavy, driving rainstorms coming off the ocean to our west, unusual for our world, and my father saw it as a portent of doom. We had so long lived under the strain of Manomano's troubling dreams, that yet another portent seemed so ordinary that I ignored it, for one could not live reading doom into every change in the weather. There were signs everywhere anyway, and what did it matter that the weather had now offered one? So I watched the rain come in over the ocean, and then felt it as it lashed our living area, and caused the little trickle of water running down the rock face to become a heavy sheet that bubbled over the rocks near our little dwellings.

My father and I made our way down the cliff in the rain, and stood waiting for Kahimoku to arrive. When he did, he went directly to a place partway up the bluffs and then sent his warriors out toward those of us who waited. My father and I were ordered to go to Kahimoku, and when we arrived, unsure of what he wanted of us, he pointed down at a rectangular stone longer than a man's height and nearly as wide as a man's height, that the pounding rain had revealed, perhaps a hundred paces up the bluff from the ocean. "Dig here," he said, and a warrior handed me a digging stick. Kahimoku wanted to know if the rock, submerged in the soil, was flat on the bottom as it was on the top facing us. I got down on my knees and began undermining the rock, my knees squishing in the muddy water.

At one point I reached for the stone to steady myself, and was kicked on the shoulder so hard that I fell over. "Do not touch it," Kahimoku said.

He did not want the hands of a commoner to defile this stone. As I dug, I wondered how it was that we would ever carry it without touching it. I wondered how many men it would take, if we would drag it, or try to lift it to our shoulders. It did not seem possible. I worked thus for much of the day, tunneling under the rock and putting the stick in the tunnel to see if its shape changed there, but it did not. They had me dig a tunnel the length of the rock, and then crossways, and both times, the stick slid along the underside without pivoting in my hand, which proved that the rock was flat on both sides.

Kahimoku stared at the stone for some time, and then left, his warriors ahead of him and behind. We were left with the rest of the day free for ourselves, but my father, convinced that any change in the schedule was a bad idea, decided to remain on the bluffs until the sun went down. I climbed up the ravine to our kauhale.

There, watching while Pekau and the children worked arranging stones for an expansion of our system of kalo and potato patches, I looked out at the dark clouds on the horizon, the large red-orange ball of the sun moving down out of one of them and touching the ocean's lip. For a few moments, the colors around me were faint but rich, Pekau's and the children's skin a deep shade like polished wood, and I wondered if this would be the last sunset I would see.

There, as the bottom of the beautiful ball dipped below the lip of the ocean, odd shapes played on that straight line on the bottom, and I thought I beheld a shape there that interrupted the line, the undulating sail of some ghostly voyaging canoe perhaps, the one which would bear me to the land of the spirits. I shaded my eyes. There was something there, on the very edge of the horizon. And then I thought, another omen. What of it?

The following day my father and I stood waiting for Kahimoku to arrive. The weather had gone bad, with intermittent rain coming off the water, and then, a mist moving in toward the shore, soft but thick, and little was visible out over the ocean past two hundred paces. Our path vanished into it also, and my father and I waited along with other rock-carriers. In truth, carrying rocks was better in weather like this, but we knew that we would be carrying no small ones. Those days were over. The last rock was immense, and might be the one upon which some of us would have our heads beaten in.

We waited on into the early afternoon, while the thick mist continued to fall. Then one of the rock-carriers came running along the path. He stopped to talk to the first workers he got to, and they then turned and ran in our direction. My father stood up from a rock, and stepped forward to address the first man to get to us.

"They are coming," the man said. "Ali'i, and warriors." Others appeared on the path, looking back frequently as they walked. "Two in full cloaks," the man went on, "and attendants, priests, many warriors."

We waited. The first man to appear out of the mist was Konapiliahi, limping slightly but otherwise as impressive as the first time I had seen him, his blue half nearly black in the fainter light. I felt an immediate relief at this, for his presence might help guarantee our safety.

But as he approached, waving the rock-carriers back away from the path, I saw that he bore himself with a wary distraction, as if he, too, had something to be concerned about. When he was near, I nodded to him.

"How are Laka and the children?" I asked.

"Well," he said, and then he held his hand up. And then speaking so that others could not hear, he said, "It is Muapo and Koalaukane, one of Kahekili's great chiefs." He stepped away from us to shoo other workers back, then returned. "Auwē," he whispered, putting his hand on his leg. "It still becomes stiff when I walk." He looked at the path. "Muapo does not emerge by day, but today he wants to see his stone. This is the place where some of his forebears were killed in a slaughter some six generations ago."

I looked at my father. Manomano had been right. A motive we did not understand drove Muapo to take rocks from this place, and now we knew.

"They are led by some of Kahekili's warriors," Konapiliahi went on, "one of them Mo'omake, whom you will see presently."

My father backed away, and I put my hand on his shoulder and said, "We are but rock-carriers. He will not notice us." But already my heart was pounding in my chest.

"Here, you can see them now," Konapiliahi said. Emerging from the mist first were warriors bearing their weapons, spears and war-axes, after which we saw two kahilis, and two figures underneath wearing pale kapa cloaks covering their red and yellow ceremonial cloaks, and red and yellow helmets. One of the ali'i was tall and one short. "Muapo is the smaller of the two," Konapiliahi said. "He is experiencing a digestive fit, but insisted upon coming out today, an anniversary of sorts, for him." Konapiliahi watched as the group moved with a steady, regal dignity, some of the priests trailing the ali'i looking down with annoyance at their feet, which were dirty from the mud on the path.

The one Konapiliahi identified as Muapo stopped, and then turned and went into the brush, followed by an attendant carrying a gourd. Muapo spent some time there, and when he was finished, the attendant passed the gourd into the bushes that hid him. "That is to collect his excrement," Konapiliahi said. "He believes he is divine, and even his excrement is mana that can be stolen from him. It will be buried in secret later on. The gourd-carrier is the custodian of Muapo's excrement."

The taller ali'i laughed, watching the proceedings. "Koalaukane thinks this is amusing," Konapiliahi said. "He is allowed to mock Muapo because he is superior to him in the regency."

"Where is Kahimoku?" I asked.

Konapiliahi raised his hand once again. "Do not talk," he said. "I shall do the talking. Kahimoku is in there amongst Koalaukane's priests."

My father's face had gone pale. There, emerging from the group as if he did not want his forward motion impeded by a chief relieving himself, was 'Iolana, in the dimmer light nearly black with his fantastic patterning of tattoos, the only bright parts his teeth, eyes, and the serrated teeth of his leiomano. The force of his gait, the powerful proportions of his body, made the workers near us lower themselves instinctively, their faces crossed with shock and terror.

It struck me there that I should no longer think of him as 'Iolana. He was Mo'omake, the lizard of death, in that light mist glistening and peculiarly indistinct, like some figure from a nightmare. I felt both calm and wary, in that I realized that if he saw me he could simply split my head with his weapon.

But my father's reaction was different from mine. I saw his face suddenly crossed not with fear and submissiveness, but a look of amazed questioning on his face, as if he were ready to approach his son and ask if he recognized his father. I put my hand out and held his upper arm, but he pulled his arm free and took a couple hesitant steps toward forward.

When 'Iolana swept his eyes back over the lowered workers, he saw my father, who stood there with his hand raised, trying hesitantly to catch his attention. Then did 'Iolana stare, the irritation on his face now a righteous anger, and he pointed to the ground. My father said something I did not hear, at which the angry warrior said, "Kauā make loa 'oe!" and raised his leiomano. "Down!"

My father fell backwards into the mud, and then lowered his body forward into it.

The sentence my brother spoke means, in effect, "You are an outcast to be killed," or "I will kill you."

I did the same. On the wet grass, I was able to see 'Iolana turn and walk back to the group approaching. The other workers were on their faces in the grass, too, and my father, ahead of me, had his face in his hands, the bottoms of his feet toward me, fringed with muck. So it was that the curse he so feared had come to its lurid fruition. I hated 'Iolana at that moment, vowed to someday be allowed to face him, and if death was the result, I wished only for a wound I could put on him that he could remember me by.

The group went to the large rectangular stone, perhaps for a consecration. We workers stayed where we were, face down on the ground, the mist cooling our backs. It occurred to me that perhaps 'Iolana did not recognize his father. As the group passed us, though, I lay looking up at them, and saw 'Iolana at the lead look once down at the prone figure ahead of me with an expression of such haughty superiority, such arrogance, that I knew that he had recognized him. For why else had he singled him out for this glance?

Thus did we lie on our faces for some time, while at the rectangular stone, we could hear chanting. For a time I was near sleeping, but for the chill from the mist. When the group finally gathered and left, the workers rose up and looked around. It was late enough in the day that we decided to return home, because it appeared too wet for us to try to get that large stone out of the mud for its trip to the heiau.

I followed my father up the path. He said nothing. From time to time he stopped, turned, and looked down at our work area and at the fine rain making the ocean vanish in a gray wall. When we reached our abandoned living area, he stopped and looked around at the brush. "What are you doing?" I asked.

"I am going to make a spear," he said. On his face was the appearance of a more youthful vigor than I had seen in some time. Slicked with rainwater, his hair matted and wet and still holding bits of mud that he had put his face in, he had a bearing that bespoke some new-found will. "I will not work tomorrow," he said. "I am sorry. I know this may put you in some danger, but I cannot go down there again. If they come for me, I will do my best to bury a weapon in their lofty guts. I do not care."

"I will not try to discourage you," I said.

At that his face took on the look of affection I had seen so many times all my life.

"Pono," he said. He shook his head. "I feel that I am leaving you, leaving this family now. Lying there, I felt pain in my chest that made my hands and feet numb for some time. I have had the pain before, and my breath becomes weak. I am sick, and I am dying. I will make my own peace with it, but I am sorry to be leaving you."

"You will be with us," I said.

"You, too, may go to work and not return. Any day you could end up on the stone, or thrown into the sea with your neck broken. I can no longer live with this."

"Pekau and the children are prepared," I said. "Pekau is a woman of the mountains. I am prepared, too. I have made my own peace with it."

He nodded. He did not look distressed or melancholy. He had indeed made his peace.

"Come," I said. "If you can make it home with me, I will make you a fine spear."

§

At times my attention lapsed during the voicing of Pono's tale, but not because of any failure in its capacity to entertain. It was the press of other interests upon my mind. Indeed I had begun to appreciate this remote place more, to speculate on its alluring features, at least once I was able to look past the filth and the depravity of the large area of the port, a place that made me more and more aware of the essential heart of the commerce of this place: men coming on ships intent upon consorting with women intent on offering themselves to these men.

I vacillated, I shall admit, between being repulsed by these thoughts, and being involuntarily stimulated by them. The wretchedness of the port was an odd contrast to the beauty of the water and the deep colors of the mountains to the north. I am not a prude, but some aspects of this contrast concerned me in a moral way—*was this right?* I wondered. Americans, I suppose, might do anything short of cannibalism in places such as this, but acts of indecency on the part of British men caused in me a deep shame. I did not like seeing them drunk, much less paying for the oral ministrations of a child behind a grog shop.

I had by this time familiarized myself with the white community in the port town, particularly two British gentlemen who had come here with an eye for business opportunity. Like my father, I was never a man stimulated by such notions, for the more passive activity had been more my preference, but here, it seemed, the notion stood front and center, what with the rawness and beauty of the place.

Another matter which piqued my interest was a woman. While other men found the willing natives attractive, and appreciated the immediacy with which they yielded to these men's desires, I found them rather unattractive in their licentiousness, the lot of them almost Negroid in feature and hue. This is I might say, not a comment by way of any unreasonable distaste in terms of race, for the world, I knew, was composed of many races, but rather simply an instinct on my part for association with those of my own.

She was a young American widow, which, with women, did not cause me the same consternation that MacFarlane's being an American did. Her name was Rebecca Searle. I first saw her early one morning a little before our appointed time in the thatched room, as I was making my way along the line of grog shops. I had stopped to look down at a sailor asleep in the dirt beside a broken barrel and a mound of refuse thrown out the back entryway of one of these places. He had a wound on his face, scabbed over and drawing flies, which rose away from the wound each time he breathed out.

"A friend of yours perhaps?" a voice to my left asked.

"No, madam," I said, turning. "I am merely fascinated by all this." I beheld a woman standing under a stained white parasol she held in her right hand.

"Yes," said she. "Fascinating at first, I suppose."

The man groaned and put his hand to his face. He looked up and saw the woman. "Get the bloody 'ell away from me," he said hoarsely. He rolled a bit, as if to reposition himself for a more comfortable sleep. Then he broke wind somewhat loudly.

"Ah," she said, and turned.

"He is British," I said. "So I apologize for him."

"Thank you," she said, and went on her way. As I had some time, I walked after her as she went along the rude dirt path.

"What, may I ask, is your business here?" I asked her, moving up to her right side.

"I work with the mission," she said.

"And how long have you been here?" As she looked briefly off to her left, I studied her profile. It was well formed, not lined, and she had blue eyes. There was the hint of a certain sauciness there, hidden within the appearance of a rather proper bearing.

"Two years," she said. "My husband, rest his soul, died of a digestive ailment a year ago, but this is now my home, and the people my family."

"Ah," I said. "I am sorry. But you seem much in possession of yourself." I went on to introduce myself, and to briefly describe my business here, including the recording of Pono's tale. This she seemed quite interested in, for she listened intently as I spoke.

"And what will you do with this tale once it's done?" she asked.

"I am not certain," I said. "The story itself is my main concern at this time. But perhaps I shall put it into print someday, for its historical points are quite interesting."

She then got a mischievous look. "It has, I suppose, its salacious elements?"

"Well," said I, "yes, but it is all woven into the narrative in a manner that represents a reasonable picture of the man's life."

"Were I to read this tale, would I blush?"

She was toying with me and I enjoyed it. "Perhaps," I said, "and perhaps not. You were married, so I suppose little would surprise you."

"But it is a tale told by a man," she said. "Suppose it were told by a woman?"

"Then the settings would be so altered that it would be another tale." I paused, aware that it had become somewhat warm. "I am sorry, but I have an appointment, indeed to listen to the next part of the tale."

"So, Mr. Davis, it has been most interesting to have talked with you. Each morning I walk in these parts and near the beach looking for young girls who might join my group. You see, I teach the language, and also the customs and habits of our world to these girls, and do my best to keep them from quickly expanding around the middle or dying of some invisible gift brought by men such as the one we just saw sleeping off his inebriation back there. Should we meet again, I might enjoy more conversation." She then briefly introduced herself and bade me good day.

I will admit that the distraction of meeting this fine woman extended itself even into the continuation of Pono's tale, for I had much difficulty driving the image of that proper but at the same time coyly playful visage from my mind. If I were to stay here, I thought, I might cultivate making a companion of a woman such as she. There was a certain, perhaps innocently salacious manner in which she pronounced the word 'salacious,' as if behind that wall of apparent propriety was a person for whom the salacious might be attractive, given the right circumstances. This was a coyness appropriate for my world, and unappreciated by men here. It was as if I had had this conversation somewhere in London, on an elegant street. But as she herself said, this very narrative is one rendered by a man, one given perhaps to the over-interpretation of facial expressions. What likelihood was there, after all, that a woman of her physical grace and refined manner would be interested in me?

In any case, I watched her walk away on the path, fascinated that below her dress, which she held up a bit to prevent dirt from fouling the hem, I saw that she wore sandals on her bare feet, each heel rising and the pad of the sandal following to slap it softly, producing a puff of dust with each step. I stood there for some time before recalling that Pono and MacFarlane were probably waiting for me.

9.

*G*entlemen, we arrive now at that part of this narrative that connects to the world we know now. The year, in your numbering of years, was 1786, which as you know is the year in which the great floating shrines of the people of the mists and fog appeared once again, first at the largest island in our world, and then later on this fair island where we now sit.

That morning following the fulfillment of my family's curse, when my brother 'Iolana did deliberately and foully reject my father, I went by myself to our work place. I did not know what his motives might have been. Perhaps it was, as Manomano said, that a woman of high rank had saved 'Iolana from the war-axe, and in his gratitude or perhaps his infatuation, he abandoned all of his origins in favor of a new life that required he reject those origins.

The absence of my father made me feel somewhat light in the head and short of breath, as if I knew I were going to my execution. Pekau knew it too, for before I left, I stood with her for some time, as if we were wordlessly saying our farewells. We did not speak of it, but in those deep, expressive eyes I could perceive what she felt.

This day was like the previous: dark, with a fine rain falling, and when the other rock-carriers saw me without my father, they showed their concern and asked after him.

I told them he was ill. Kahimoku's warriors could, if they wished, go and look for him, but I reasoned that because we were at perhaps our final rock, what Kahimoku needed was a number of younger, stronger men, and would not notice my father's absence.

And indeed it seemed he did not. I saw the group of men approaching, Kahimoku at their lead. These men were large and appeared strong, and it became clear that they would be the ones to carry the stone, although there were too few of them to do it. They carried numerous large lengths of cord, and large sticks. The mad priest looked around, and began selecting from among the rock-carriers, younger men, and shooed the older away. They gathered nearby and awaited whatever new orders he might come up with. Kahimoku waited too, as if expecting even more men to appear on the path.

It was then that he seemed to notice me as I waited down the bluff closer to the water.

He looked around, and then walked on the path, stopped, and then walked the other way. Then he turned and went back to the group of men near the flat stone. He conferred with them, pointing in my direction, and they looked. I felt myself weaken, and found a rock to sit on. They had selected me, I assumed. I thought of running, or of jumping into the ocean, but clung to the faint hope that they may have wanted me for some task, perhaps to dig under the rock again, as I had previously done.

Kahimoku and three warriors approached, one carrying a war-axe, one carrying a length of cord, and one without a weapon. I was but twenty paces from the water, and understood that my opportunity was fading, but some malaise, some strange lapse of will, kept me sitting on the rock. I looked at my hands on my knees, the skin of my legs so dark from so many years in the sun carrying rocks, and then looked up at them as they positioned themselves around me. From the direction of the water I felt the presence of something, and even thought that I had from my peripheral vision perceived a shape, a manō perhaps, or shark as you would call it. Something was there. Oddly, the idea that something was there fascinated and distracted me, as if this little mental escape from what appeared to be my execution had taken over my logic and will to survive.

"Where is your other half?" Kahimoku asked.

"I do not know," I said. "Are we to carry—"

"Do not speak to me," he said. "Muapo's house is not clean. The wife of Konapiliahi is your sister, and Muapo wants the filth swept from his house. Konapiliahi's issue is much loved by Muapo, but you, the filth, must be removed from their skin."

"I am not filth," I said.

"You are. It is a trifle for him, but he wants the filth swept from his house. How else to do it but remove that which makes his house unclean?"

I looked up at him. I was to be eliminated because the very existence of me tainted Muapo's house. I thought of telling him that Mo'omake was my brother, but as I framed this information before speaking it, he reached inside his cloak and drew something out. It was a white, finely wrought fish-hook.

"I know you," Kahimoku said. "I know you from long ago. That you sometimes occupy my thoughts, and corrupt those thoughts. That you credit your eyes with a gift from The Red One insults The Red One. Your eyes shall be offered on the stone, but because I feel a warmth for you whom I have known so long, we will relieve you of your life first. It remains only to discover the lie or the truth." He pointed toward the ocean, and the warriors walked behind me out onto a flat section of rock with water sloshing against its leading edge. Standing there, the spray hitting my legs, I looked down, and saw the faint pale color of sand, perhaps three lengths of a man's body down. To my right, rock outcroppings hid caves and other inlets, and I thought that I would dive under and then swim toward those caves and escape.

"You shall retrieve the hook," Kahimoku said. "If you do, then we shall know. If you don't, we shall know. If you do not come back, I will find your woman of the mountains and your children of the mountains and take their eyes to the stone. I will take the eyes of all you know to the stone. It shall be your eyes, or the eyes of many."

He dropped the hook in the water. So it was that I understood, and I resolved to find the hook and bring it back, if for no other reason than to prove that The Red One had indeed told me how to see under the water. Then my death might have meaning.

I began to breathe deeply and rapidly, to suffuse my lungs with the air. When I felt nearly dizzy, I jumped into the water and surfaced, and continued breathing. Then I cupped my hand against my eye-socket, and made myself very still, and because the water was calm, I was able to produce the bubble of air that caught in the palm of my hand, and holding it thus, I looked at the sand below.

The hook appeared tiny, sitting on the sand, next to a rock that would be easy to identify without the bubble. I let the air out of my lungs slowly, until they were nearly empty, at which my body began to float down. During this descent, my lungs twisted inward for want of air, but as the hook grew larger through the little lens of that bubble, which then closed up, I kept my eye on the patch of sand upon which the hook lay. I slowly let my free hand out to clutch it. As I did, preparing to put my feet on the sand and spring for the surface, I heard a strange tapping through the water, as if some large crustacean were breaking shells, or perhaps one of Kahimoku's warriors, eager to split my head, had hit his axe several times on the rock. Rising, the hook in my hand, I was nearly robbed of consciousness, and burst out into the air, holding the hook aloft.

I climbed out holding the hook. "Throw it in the water," Kahimoku said. "I will not touch what you have touched."

I threw the hook in the water. Kahimoku pointed down at the rock. I felt airy and distant from these proceedings, still breathing heavily from having held my breath so long, and now they would hold my breath for me, unless the axe were to be the weapon. I assumed that it was, because the warrior carrying it went behind me, so I lowered myself to my knees, focusing on the wet stone under me, and closed my eyes and relaxed.

The blow came as a deafening shock of sound that sent me forward, the heels of my hands meeting the rock, and the second blow was as loud, and the air filled with an acrid smell, and I reached up to feel my head. But my arms were held, and when I opened my eyes I saw Kahimoku sitting near me with his mouth open in shock, blood coming from his neck, while one of his warriors ran away through the grass. The war-axe was on the rock beside me. My arms were trussed behind me and something covered my head. The same acrid smell assaulted my nose, a salty, rich odor, and then I was lifted by many hands, and felt suddenly weightless, after which I hit the water. Then hands pulled me out of the water, and over the edge of wood, which struck my shin so hard that I cried out, but my voice was muffled inside the foul-smelling fabric encircling my head.

The hands held me by my shoulders and I found myself sitting on a flat surface, and then I felt movement, the softly surging movement of a canoe in the water, and my feet were in shallow water on a slightly curved, slippery surface, and I heard the thumping and wheezing sound of paddles being pulled along wood, and I tried to understand this peculiar squeaking sound when voices came through the fabric of my head's cloak—odd sounds, the weird, rapid rolling of deep voices trying to imitate the sounds of a storm, or of the chortling calls of seabirds.

I tried to gather my senses. I was alive, and had that war-axe split open my head, Pekau and the children would do as Pekau said they would do. So be it. They would be safe, even if what was happening to me now meant my death.

The soft surging of the canoe caused me to rock, and then did these men begin to chant, and their voices rose and fell in unison, strange rolling sounds that matched the surging of the canoe, plosive utterances beginning with *gah* and *roe* and *bah*, that sounded like yells from a strange dream, and I heard the sound of rain racing across the water, and then felt it softly stinging my knees and feet. The men produced whooping sounds and then deep laughter, which was followed by a rich odor coming under my head-cloak, of sweat and the hint of cooked fish, and the entire of my skin shuddered so that I felt hair moving on my head and legs, because at that moment I understood that these men were from the land of mists and fog. Manomano had been right.

How can I recall the amount of time I sat there, my legs flexing, my body rocking as those men chanted? Perhaps one hour of your measurement of time. But at length the canoe stopped, and other strange voices called from above me, many voices. I was grabbed and then felt myself being wrapped, so that my thighs and lower legs were tucked against my chest. Then I felt myself rising in a series of jerks, hauled as it were, and these jerks were punctuated by the sounds of men calling, "Ho, ho, ho!"

I felt myself sliding over the edge of something, and then carried and set down, and the thing that had held me wrapped was pulled away from me and my hands were untied from behind my back. I put one hand out, and it met a round pole, cold, colder than wood, and I knew it to be the material Manomano had showed us. The hood was pulled from my head.

Then through the cold poles surrounding me in vertical lines did I behold, with fright and a horrible dread, men with faces either a pale, death-white, arms the same, or faces an unnatural reddish-pink, black stubble on their jaws, teeth stained yellow, and they wore all manner of colorful kapa encircling their upper arms, their torsos and legs. Then I saw their surroundings, a long, curved rail of polished wood atop a low wall, the great canoe's gunwale, and wood lengths close together coming out from under the floor of the cage I sat in. The seams between the pieces of wood and that rail all swept upward to a point where I could see that the same wall went along the other side of the canoe, and next to my cage rose a house in the middle. Then I looked again at the men. I shrunk back from those faces, leers of a bestial merriment, some laughing so that visible were their red, open mouths with spaces where there should have been teeth.

It came to me that they were going to eat me. Their appearance was so disgusting and frightening that I could think of no other reason why they wanted me.

Then I recalled that Kuali'i had gone on a voyage with the men of the mists and fog. These men, I thought, could not have been those Kuali'i had referred to. To my recollection, nothing was said of the loathsome hue of the skin, or of the bony, leering emaciation of faces, or of the bizarre and fantastic array of colors of their dirty garb.

At length they moved away from me, one by one, and sat on the wood or leaned on the rail. I sat in the cage with one hand on each side of me clasping those cold poles. Some time passed as they sat. I heard water sloshing softly against the side of the great canoe. One small man sat at a strange slowly spinning wooden circle. He held pieces of thin cord that he fed into the center of it, and at the same time pumped his foot on a piece of wood on the floor. I watched him, wondering what he was doing. And then all the men who had been sitting and standing stood or turned, looks of deference on their faces. I leaned forward to look, too, for I understood that their ali'i was approaching.

I heard his footfalls on that wood. And then two legs encased in blue kapa were before me. They bent, and down came the man's upper body, encased in a strange blue cloak that had a line of equally sized lumps of some yellow material going up his chest to the base of his neck, where the cloak split slightly, revealing a tuft of hair emerging from therein. I beheld a not unpleasing countenance, because, despite the large nose and the lean face, I saw eyes that showed both sympathy and interest, deep and expressive eyes not unlike those of Manomano. The man stared at me for some time, and then sat down and crossed his legs.

He cleared his throat. Then he reached through the poles, making me shrink back. He held both hands up, and reached in again, and touched my foot. "Phu-ut," he said.

I stared at him. Then he touched his head with his finger. I did not at first understand, and then did.

"Po'o," I said.

"Head," he said.

"Head," I said.

He patted his chest. "Roger," he said. As you may have already surmised, this of course was the infamous Roger Beckwith, the man with whom you are so fascinated.

I patted my chest. "Pono," I said, and he clapped several times, and laughed.

He reached inside the poles once again. "Ponoze-phut."

I understood. I reached through the poles and touched his foot, which was encircled by thick strips of what I assumed to be the hide of a pig. "Rogerz-phut," I said. This brought out a burst of laughter from all the men, the ali'i laughing with them. He seemed delighted with the game. He reached through the poles once again, and pointed.

"Yoo," he said, and held up his hand. He again patted his chest. "Me" he said.

This confused me, until I thought about it. Then I reached out, and pointed at him. "Yoo," I said, and patted my chest, adding, "me." Then I understood. I shifted my position inside that cage, and cleared my throat. "Yu, Roger. Pono, me."

"Ah!" he said. Apparently this was not expected by the other men observing our game, for they gathered closer, talking amongst themselves in their strange tongue. I saw then that these men were introducing me to their tongue, and realized that had they wanted to eat me, they had no need of this exercise. I shifted once again, and patted my head and said, "Head," and then my foot and said, "Phut."

Sitting there outside the poles, that person who was called Roger stared at me. Then he looked behind him, and then off to his right, thinking. He rose, walked out of my sight, and then returned carrying a shiny brown gourd cut off at the top as of a bowl, which he placed upon the rail of the great canoe. Then he spoke to some of his warriors. One went down on his knees while another stood behind him holding an imaginary weapon over his head. At once I understood that these men were enacting my execution, and the one called Roger looked back at me nodding, pointing to the man on his knees.

"Me!" I called out. This brought more laughter, and expressions of apparent surprise from the men watching. Roger then disappeared from my sight and returned bearing a long, slightly bent stick, which, when I studied it more closely, was a complicated arrangement of finely polished black wood in curious shapes—a long black stick vanishing into a lighter colored wooden plank, or I should say, a carefully wrought wooden object not unlike the handle and body of a leiomano, which toward one end was mounted with a circle of black wood under another piece shaped like a bent lizard. The man standing behind the sitting man again raised his imaginary weapon, and Roger then raised this object to his cheek and pointed it toward the man holding the imaginary weapon aloft. Then did Roger turn to me and point to the shiny gourd sitting on the rail. He backed away three paces, and placed the object once again against his cheek, and with his thumb pulled the lizard-shaped part of the device back, producing a strange clicking sound that suggested to me that this was not wood but the very material my hands were now grasping as I watched.

There was a pause amongst all the men, some watching Roger and some with their eyes on the gourd, and then from behind me I heard a sound— "Aarrr!" at which two legs passed the poles I held, and a wizened old man went to the gourd, picked it up and held it against his chest. He yelled out a single sound, "No!" Then did he address Roger with a string of sounds, yells in fact, while Roger and the men listened to him. The old man was angry, and addressed his anger to his somewhat penitent looking aliʻi, which surprised me. After he finished yelling, he brushed past Roger carrying the gourd against his chest, and vanished, leaving the men staring after him.

Roger groaned and shook his head. He looked at me, and then pointed at the sitting man, held the device up pointed at the man above the sitting man holding the imaginary weapon, and said, "Boom!"

This I did not understand.

10.

Gentlemen, I will forego an extended narrative of the various word-games we played that first day. Suffice to say that my capacity to absorb these utterances and their various meanings was aided by the fact that I was locked inside the cage watching those strange men going about their business, which, during this time, did not amount to anything urgent. They sat on the floor of the great canoe in languid repose, from time to time getting one or another idea and approaching my cage to offer another carefully constructed naming of an object: one man who was tall and bore himself with a quiet, oddly detached manner in respect to the other men, came and sat down outside my cage and stared at me for some time. I stared back. Then did he remove from his foot a brown, supple encasement of pigskin and held it before me, saying, "Boot." I repeated the word, staring into the black hole of this object and leaning back somewhat from the odd stench that wafted up at me from therein.

As the first day waned, I began thinking of home, Pekau, the children, and my separation from them. Would these men let me go once their interest in instructing me as to their language faded? I thought it unlikely, and repeated again to myself that Pekau and the children would remain in the mountains and would be safe. Did the others at our workplace see the men from the land of mists and fog? That blood issuing from Kahimoku's neck meant that he was very likely dead, but what help would that be? Others would take his place, the project of the great heiau would be completed, and if I did go back, I would very likely become one of those sacrificed upon the stone, because whether or not Kahimoku was dead would not change Muapo's desire to rid his house of its filth. But as the flat, gray light faded that first day, the sky that I could see was heavy and shrouded in a light, misty rain.

With the dimming of the light came a chill that made me tremble, sitting there with my arms around my folded legs. I could feel movement under me, the subtle rising and sinking of the great canoe, and with these movements it groaned and made soft popping sounds. The old man who had been so angry at his ali'i appeared bearing a kihei which he thrust through the poles, and I wrapped myself in it warily, for it reeked of odd odors, as if it were formerly used as the wrapping cloth for a dead person. As darkness descended upon the great canoe, the men slowly disappeared elsewhere in its bowels, for I heard thumping sounds and the muted sounds of human voices.

I sat there leaning against the poles periodically drifting into fitful sleep, a strange gabble of voices in my head, and the recognition of a strange grief awakening me, for it was likely that I would not see Pekau and the children, perhaps ever again. This day of my separation from everything that was important to me had arrived, and the only means by which I could identify that feeling was to think of it as dying, as a kind of death in which I would remain sentient but without spirit, without any mana.

As did the previous day dim in shades of gray, so did it brighten in shades of gray. Before I saw any of these men I shook the stinking kihei off and addressed the poles surrounding me. Two of them turned in their sockets, and I saw that they were encased in wood top and bottom, and thus did I lower my face to the base of one of the poles and chew on the wood. Bits of it ended up in my mouth and I spat them out, reasoning that if I could eat away enough of this wood, I could tear the pole from its socket. I would jump over the side of the canoe and swim back to shore. The light grew on one side, and I assumed that I should swim toward the growing light. Once on land, I would escape to the mountains and remain there the rest of my days with Pekau and the children.

Had I been able to chew on the wood for another two or three hours, I might have made good this plan, but I was seen working at this task by a man bearing a small cut-off gourd from which steam emanated. He was the same old man who had given me the kihei, and who had yelled at his ali'i. He passed the gourd between the poles, and I smelled an odor that reminded me of soil, and grass sap. In the gourd, which felt hot to my touch and seemed made out of a pale stone, I saw what appeared to be rotted poi, lumpy and shimmering with a viscous appearance. I dipped my fingers into the hot material and tasted it. The material was not unpleasant, some mash mixed with what seemed to me to be sugar. Hungry as I was, I ate all the gourd's contents, at which the old man, who had watched me, smiled and nodded, then patted his own stomach.

Then a change overcame the men who had appeared one by one rubbing their eyes, coughing, urinating over the ship's great rail, and talking softly amongst themselves. The sky was clearing, for above the gray, materializing out of it, a deep blue sky tinged with pink showed itself, and at length the men became more animated, and seemed for some reason alert to the clearer dawning day. One man appeared at the rail bearing a shiny tube, which upon his interest in some object he had espied off the rail, he held and then magically extended to twice its original length, after which he held this tube to his eye and exclaimed something to other men, all of whom came to the rail to look outward. Then Roger appeared, and took from the first man the strange tube, which he then placed against his eye. From his mouth came a series of sounds in his language, hoarsely exclaimed, so that the men did suddenly run about, shouting at one another and looking up.

I rose from my sitting position into a crouch, frightened. Over the rail I beheld the top of a mountain, the very mountain, I thought, on which our hale stood. I imagined that I might see the movement of people, Manomano going up the path bearing fish, or Pekau and the children. Then sounds came to me, the groaning of the great ship's wood, the sounds of cord snapping and then the lusty pop of sail fabric catching wind. At a sharp angle just inside the ceiling of my cage, I saw a great billowing square of whitish fabric held at one corner by a vibrating cord, at which the ship tipped, leaned down on the side of the rail I was close to, and after that there was more popping of fabric, then the rapid clicking of something as of a stick being drawn quickly across a series of poles. We were moving, and as the great canoe tipped, the floor under me issuing groaning and popping sounds, I saw the mountaintop outside the cage sweep along the rail and then vanish under it, and as the great ship turned, groaning, more land swept past the rail, and then I saw the dark line of the ocean under brilliant clouds that, gathered as they were, appeared smaller and smaller as they vanished into the farthest distance above the water.

My heart thumped, and the hair on my head had stood up. I nearly vomited the food given to me, but held it in, and my hands were gripped tightly on the cold poles of my cage, the entire of my body trembling. As the ship continued its turn, I beheld in the distance a brilliant day, and understood what was happening: we were sailing away from my world toward what my great voyaging forebears had called 'the hanging sky.'

Gentlemen, this narrative must now advance as a summary, for it concerns a string of days in which the distinction between one day and the next has been lost to my memory. I remember it as an accumulation of days. We were at sea perhaps forty-five days, the ali'i Roger wishing apparently to cross great distances in a two-day span, the men busy all day, then changing his mind and resting for three days, the great sails rolled around their poles and some of the cords slack in the wind, others taut against smaller, half-folded sails.

I believe that because of the general lack of activity for the men during the majority of these days, I quickly learned how to speak their strange language, twisting my mouth and tongue into awkward and unfamiliar positions in order to imitate their phrasing.

Amidst the pastime of the naming of things was my frequent inquiry: 'Aha?' or 'I ke aha?' in its various forms in my language. But the abstraction 'Why?' was lost on those who were so busy shepherding me into the intricacies of their language. That first day, after perhaps two hours of movement under sail, I endeavored to make clear to those men who one by one came to my cage with new and more clever means of the naming of things, that I had to relieve myself. This was communicated to them through a series of gestures and mimicking until one of them, the tall man who bore himself with a moody, distant demeanor compared to the animation of the others, seemed to understand, at which he communicated to Roger. The ali'i then came to my cage and mused over some decision he was apparently in the process of making.

Then did he draw from his blue cloak a strange twig that I understood was of the same material as the poles of my cage. He raised it just out of my sight and I heard a clicking sound followed by a soft squeak, at which the entire line of poles before me drew open.

Roger backed away and stood watching, as did the other men. I moved out of the enclosure and stood up straight, my back somewhat stiff and my legs unsteady, and there got a better view of the canoe. I must say that it startled me at first: the wood under my feet was smooth and swept off along the shiny gunwale back perhaps fifteen paces, while in the other direction it swept for perhaps ten. Over the rail, the water was the distance of three men's bodies down, and instead of a manu at the front, there appeared to be a great pole jutting up and outward, like a giant pololū. I turned and again beheld the rear portion of the canoe. There, sitting above the curved rail on the fattest part of the canoe, to the rear, was the house. And then above me rose a riot of cording, poles and cross-poles, and many more of the same sail I had seen part of from my cage.

Uncertain as to what to do next, I took a step toward two of the men, who warily drew back, as if afraid of me. I looked down, and mused upon the observation that, unlike the rest of these men, I was naked but for my malo. They stared at me, Roger still contemplating something. Then he uttered a string of sounds to someone I could not see, and shortly the same old man who had fed me emerged from a hole in the deck of the ship bearing kapa of various colors, which he held out, approaching me. Still uncertain, I held out my hands and he placed these things in them. The material was soft, and

I raised it to my face and sniffed, and there arose from this material an odor not of cooked meat or human filth but a dry, nearly sweet smell. I was to don these things, I understood, so that I might resemble these men.

The process of my reasoning out how to put these things on brought from these men a merriment that shamed me somewhat, until I had successfully slid these fabric tubes up my legs and over my arms, at which Roger approached and put his hands to my chest and then slid round shell ornaments, already attached, through tiny slits in the fabric, thus enclosing me in this material. He then pointed down, at which I understood that I was to do the same with that open part of the fabric covering my malo.

It took me some time to accomplish the process of sliding the round shell ornaments in their places. Then Roger had me step into sandals that resembled those of my world, but made of thick blackish animal skin, quite hard and heavy, their most interesting feature being straps held closed by clamps of the same material as the bars of my cage. Finally, upon my looking down at myself once again, the men produced a collective barrage of laughter and clapping of their hands.

Roger held his hands up and quieted the men. In the silence that followed, he walked to the rail, put his hands together, and then mimicked jumping over, as if to dive into the water. Then he waved his finger before my face and said, "No." I understood this, and said, in my language, "No, I will not try to swim back to my home."

Satisfied, he nodded slowly, and ushered me to a wall, a man-sized portion of which he pulled open, to reveal a tiny room with a plank across the back, that plank centered by a round hole. I was to use this to relieve myself. He pointed to a fat bag of some sort hanging to the right of the hole. He turned a tiny device on the bottom of it, at which water streamed forth. Then he mimicked cleaning himself with his hand rubbing in his crotch. I understood this, and went inside the tiny room, and he closed the door.

As for the succeeding days, I should say that my facility with their language advanced with a pace that seemed continually to interest, and sometimes apparently amaze, the men who were teaching me. They put me to work with what they referred to as a holystone, a flat, rectangular rock, finely grained, with which I scrubbed the deck. I enjoyed this work, and understood that it was appreciated by those who would otherwise have to do it. *I ke aha,* was the question I held there in my mind, but as I said, such abstractions would have to wait.

I slept in what was identified as a hammock, which in my language might be a 'kōkō,' or a cord net usually used to carry the very old. Roger and two of the men took me, that first day, down under the deck, where I beheld a most complicated and fascinating arrangement of tiny rooms, large rooms, a kitchen with a large fireplace and crowded with many gourds, or I should say now, pots and pans, and crockery. I was being asked where I felt I might feel comfortable sleeping, but the atmosphere of the dark bowels of this ship made me frightened, as if I might become lost there. Amidst various gesturing and questioning expressions, we settled upon a place outside on the deck, very near the cage I had occupied the day before, and the men worked at rigging my hammock in place, so that I might sleep under the stars, and if rain should come, an overhanging plank would keep me dry.

And so I did sleep, for short periods, because when the ship was under sail there were always noises, orders yelled, sails popping, and in those waking hours before sleep and before rising, I waited for Manomano to speak to me, but he did not. I waited for Pekau's whisper to make its way over the water to me, that he'e enriched breath, but it did not. I was lost, and without mana. This death, however, was one in which I remained sentient, and I labored over certain ideas: if these men had sailed to my world and now had sailed away, would they again sail to my world? I envisioned Pekau and the children, and my parents, living in the mountains, and cultivated the thought that if I were blamed for Kahimoku's death, then Muapo's warriors would go up the mountain to find me, and if not me, then Pekau and the children. If Pekau knew of this danger, then they would go farther up the mountain, up into the clouds if necessary.

So went the days, and I continued carrying with me the quesion 'I ke aha?' It may be that the rapid advance in my facility with the language was driven by a desire to have this question answered, and after that, other questions: would we return? If we would, when?

By perhaps the twenty fifth day of our sailing, I had begun to memorize the parts of the ship, had seen the operation of such fascinating objects as the 'spun yarn winch,' operated exclusively by a little man they called Jack, whose job it was to fashion rope from scraps of other rope or old clothes. I had begun to practice climbing up the mast pole, had learned the names of some of the men on the ship, the ones whom I associated with most closely a man called 'The American', whose name was Dick Burrrows, Owen Bew, the old man who had first fed me and who was the cook and physician of the ship, and Don Bentley, an Englishman who was described by Bew as a 'malefactor and cutpurse,' and Ben Fowles, the 'carpenter.' There was also a group of five men referred to by the other sailors as the 'gentlemen of leisure,' which would take me some time to understand. They were gamblers. They spent their free days grouped around a small table upon which they placed, while holding others, small square pieces of bark adorned with pictures, and they would spend entire days doing this if the ship were idle, or if not this, then they would group themselves around a wooden board with squares on it, upon which they placed tiny statues that they would study for hours on end. By this time, the concept of 'why?' had formed itself, for I had observed the men using this word when one did not understand the motivations of the other, and the word interjected would cause the man to halt and explain 'why' such and such was being done. So 'I ke aha?' was 'why?' What, sir, motivates you to do this? Why?

The day I believe to be perhaps the fortieth of our voyage, I was on the deck eating with the other men, and Roger ate with us, enjoying a fair day with the beginnings of a golden sunset. A small group were dividing up a dark moss, or a dried and chopped leaf of some sort, which they then pressed into tiny wooden gourds with long handles jutting from their bottoms, the ends of which they put in their mouths. Then did they draw on these handles and puff out smoke, which had a peculiar, rich smell. "Backy," Dick Burrows said to me. "We're out of it, and need more." I did not know what he meant, and turned again to Roger Beckwith. I put down my 'bowl,' as I now knew it to be, and stepped before him, and said, "I am on your ship. You have put me here. Why?"

Then did Roger put his bowl upon the rail and think, staring at me. "Pono," he said. "If you would labor to understand me, I shall tell you." The men turned, one saying "Aye," and others moved toward us. One of the gentlemen of leisure leaned up from the little table and looked in our direction, and then went back to the staring at the table.

"Labor?" I said.

"Try," he said.

"Sir, I shall try," I said. "I shall labor to understand you."

He then spoke to another of the man named Will Kelsey, who called down the stairway, at which cups and a dark liquid were brought up for the men, grog, it was called. This ritual was carried out on certain days, and more-so during times when we lay idle upon the water. Roger Beckwith apparently wanted cups of this material distributed to the men, even offered some to me, which I declined in favor of water.

So he told me a story. There was much in the way of interpretation, translation, and mimicking in this process, provided by the men who, upon hearing that Roger would explain the 'I ke aha?' to me, gathered around and prepared to listen with great interest.

In favor of making clear what motivated Roger Beckwith to become what he was, and what motivated him to take me to his ship, I translate this tale into a smoother narrative than the much mimicked and obliquely explained tale he told me that first time, for I was to hear this story again more than once, after having mastered the intricacies of your language.

Roger Beckwith sat and thought, and placed his hands upon his knees. The men watched, remaining silent. "My father and I were held at Newgate Prison and condemned to death as petty criminals," he said. "It was all because of a cane. I'll allow that my father may have committed other minor crimes that justified our condemnation, but the matter of our landlord's cane tipped the balance against us. Our trial, if the farce that it was could be called that, lasted but a few minutes: Mr. Bowley testifies that his cane was quite valuable, the handle made of pure gold. No, my father said, it was not gold. Show the court the cane in question and the matter shall be settled. But Mr. Bowley says he no longer has the cane. You were in his house, sir, and ye be accused of being a footpad. He needs only to produce the cane, said my father. He no longer has the cane, testifies that it was again stolen, perhaps by you, the thief of same the first time. Ye be footpads. At length I, at a mere fifteen years of age, did raise my hand and claim that I took the cane, at which the judge, bored at the proceedings and perhaps hungry for his noontime meal, said, then ye be footpads the both of you. The jurors nodded, and I surmised that at my young age, they might take kindly to me. But they did not. Then be ye the spawn of Beelzebub, said the judge, to the affirmative grunts of the jury. We were sent to Newgate and placed in what was called The Lower Ward, amidst filth, darkness, creepin' insects, a place peopled by the worst ruffians and scoundrels, drunks, malefactors of all kind. So dark was this dungeon that the lighting of a candle did hurt my eyes. The smells of tobacco, liquor, human waste, piss and sickness assaulted our noses, and because we had no money, we had to beg from the ruffians any scrap of food they found unpalatable to their own detestable taste. I chewed on cold gristle that smelled of rot. I ate bread that had fallen into human waste. We drank water that came from a putrid stream that ran under the prison, and we both became ill in our insides, pukin' and shittin' thin gruel, our stomachs twistin' with an awful pain.

"This, my brothers, is the England of our time, the England of great poetry, of elegant refinements of life, of enlightened philosophy and advanced science. This is our England, a great sea-power, a place of Lords and Ladies, of great musers on the perplexing questions of life. But it is a place in which a poor man and his son can be condemned to death over a dispute involving a worthless cane, a lie concocted by a landlord annoyed with the presence of that father and son. It is a place in which life itself, at least among the poor, is of no value to anyone but for the spectacle their deaths might provide.

"I'll allow that I fumbled and was unable in ways to perceive the reality we were faced with, because as a boy I was a dreamer, but after a week in this detestable place my father and myself, and seven other men, were ordered to stand together near the heavy door of the Ward, at which it opened and a man appeared, and raised a parchment before his face, tipping it into the faint light of the dungeon so that he could read: 'You prisoners that are within, who for wickedness and sin, after many mercies shown you, are now appointed to die tomorrow. Give ear and understanding that tomorrow morning the great bell of St. Sepulchre's shall toll for you, in form and manner of a passing bell, as used to be tolled for those that are at the point of death, to the end that all godly people hearing that bell, and knowing that it is for you going to your deaths, may be stirred up heartily to pray to God to bestow His grace and mercy upon you while you live.'

"One might have imagined that some mercy would have been shown us during that day and night, our being notified of our deaths known to the ruffians in the Ward, but indeed they jeered and laughed at us, some singing, 'ye be turnin' off the cart tomorrow, me gentlemen, off the cart ye go under the Tyburn Tree, ye be messin' yer breeches 'fore the crowd, me gentlemen, yer limbs twitchin' and jerkin', me gentlemen, off the cart ye go!' My father became numb to it, sick as he was, and I, dreamer that I was, did not perceive my death as any more than the next thing I would do in my life. Would I go to God? Would I see my long dead mother there? Would I be issued, in this wonderful place, clothes that did not shame me?

"And so dawned the day, unseen by us the condemned because of the darkness of the Ward. I was relieved of my filthy clothes and given a foul-smelling woolen smock, as law had it that those turned off the cart must wear wool to their deaths. And behind us as my father did also don his smock a ruffian called out, 'ye gentlemen goin' to the Tyburn Tree, ye be a surgeon's toy now,' for he was referring to the probability that our bodies had already been purchased by a surgeon and anatomist for use in teachin' the young learning the physician's trade, us toys to be sliced up for their practice. I believe this was all lost on my young dreamin' mind until those great doors did open, and oh my brothers, we walked out of that darkness into a day so blindin' in its beauty that I couldn't open my eyes for it. A length of rope passed under those blazin' slits of vision, and then did I feel the prickle of the noose around my neck, and I believe there understood, finally, that I was to die, and when I did open my eyes, oh my brothers did I behold one of those days in England that makes all look up, so beautiful and blue was the sky, with immense, gorgeous clouds a lined up on the horizon. Blinded as I was for a while, I allowed myself to adjust, and then did see this day, and it was unlike any day in England I had ever seen. So beautiful was it that my father prayed, his hands clasped under his chin, the rope a hangin' down his back and lyin' on the cobbles, and thus did we drag our ropes to the carts.

"We were pushed up into the cart, the third man in ours, my father's age, with a gleeful grin upon his dirty, pockmarked face, and he says to me, 'Boy, there isn't a soul here to pray for us,' and I said, 'We are poor. No one prays for us,' to which this man smiled at me, showing gaps where teeth should have been, and said, 'Then boy, I hope what you did was worth this.' I wanted to say I did nothing but felt the cart jerk and then move, for we were on our journey to the Tyburn Tree. And oh what a gatherin' of the curious and the devout we drew, the old and the young, the children laughing and pointing and singing and runnin' alongside the three carts enjoying that beautiful day, a followin' us along toward the Tree, for they were going to watch us die and celebrate.

"Boys mimicked the twisted faces of the dyin' and holding a fist to the side of the neck emitted awful chokin' sounds and pointed and laughed. And there, I think because of how pleasant the day was, I understood, and then did I begin to tremble and weep. And the way I was standin' there with that rope prickling my neck, the cart did bang my hip again and again, and I laughed, because I knew now that pain was an affliction of the living, and I was to die. And as if to let me know there was not the least chance that this could turn out in my favor, ahead of us the great bell of St. Sepulchre's church tolled, and then the carts stopped at the church, and the bellman leaned over the churchyard wall fronting the road and called out, 'All good people, pray heartily unto God, for these poor sinners, who are now going to their death, for whom the great bell doth toll. You that are condemned to die, repent with lamentable tears. Ask mercy of the Lord for the salvation of your own souls.'

"And so did the carts proceed toward the Tyburn Tree. In that last stretch of bumpy road, the cart banging my hip and me now silent, I stared ahead stunned into a fright, for a great gathering was afoot, hundreds of people all waitin' around the Tree, just beyond which was a gallery of seats already fillin' up with gentlemen of wealth who paid for the privilege of watchin' us die. I tried to understand it, to find one kind soul in that rabble, but a kind soul there was none. For me, a boy who could weep at the death of a small bird, this was a revelation. I had lived, without knowin' it, in a world without human kindness, and now was to leave it. A blankness and a tremblin' serenity overcame me, and I beheld ahead of us in the next cart a man bein' read to from a bible by a holy man in a gray frock, and the man stared down, and dressed in a fine wool suit he was, goin' to his death. And then did I look to the side over the heads of the runnin' children and the hobblin' of old women hastenin' to the Tree, and saw there a strange, hooded man on a horse, a canterin' along and watchin' us carefully, and the man did frighten me, for I thought he must be the hangman, but he was not, for the hangman was in the first cart, which had stopped now just past St. Giles's Church and was offerin' to the condemned a last drink, the benefits of which was denied us in the last cart, much to the leering displeasure of the third man, who adjusted his noose as if it were a cravat. 'Aye, so they ignore us,' said he, 'the blighters. Are we not to imbibe a last time, or are we just not worth the trouble?' Apparently we were not, for the carts rumbled ahead to the Oxford Road, and again I watched that strange man, dressed dark and hooded he was, and wearing what appeared to me an awful, black military uniform of some sort, and he had stopped studyin' the others and had apparently locked his eyes in on me. Perhaps, thought I, he is the anatomist looking after his surgeon's toy, and the fright I felt was at the picture in my imagination of that hooded man cutting my innards out for study.

"And oh did the rabble become loud and joyful upon our approach to the Tree. It put me in a fog, it did, the women sellin' fruit and the men slakin' their thirst with liquor and the screamin' and yellin' and the children laughin' and pointin' at us who was to die, the whores plyin' their trade at the fringe, and ahead the hangman lightin' his pipe by the Tree, the magistrate's officials a readin' papers and announcin' the names of the soon to be deceased, and then did the first cart move under the tree, for it was wide enough with its three legs and its triangle of beams atop.

I closed my eyes and waited, the screamin' increasing until there was a brief hush, and I heard the quick clatter of wheels that was drowned out then by a collective gasp, for the spectacle apparently did captivate the audience with awe, so that the gasp did then recede into a sigh of pleasure that sounded to me like the practice of an untrained church chorus. I opened my eyes to see the man swingin' closest to us with his bulgin' eyes and tongue stickin' out and his mouth stretched in a shocked leer, whereupon a woman, his wife probably, did run to him and hang on his legs so that I could see the rope crush in on the man's neck and vanish under his jaw and he was kickin' and jerkin' as she tugged down to hasten his death, and the air was fouled by the smell of excrement which had burst from his body and run down the inside of his pantleg onto his wife's dress. Then did our cart move again, toward the Tree, and off to my right, just below me, a woman was yelling at a man for having stolen a biscuit, whilst other men yelled at her to hold her tongue. And a man was laughin' and gropin' his hand under a whore's skirt whilst she stood, eyes open and mouth agape with pleasure.

"I was then shocked to see how close we had come, now, to the Tree. A space had been cleared for the official announcements, that space ringed by those who had rights to the bodies, and near us stood a woman finely attired, and what appeared to be her son, who stared up at me flat-faced and contemplative, and I did not understand why he was staring at me until I saw his right leg, an awful growth of some sort on the outside of the knee, and I knew their reason for being there. The woman did then whisper to a rather imperious gentleman flanked by younger men, all of whom stared at me as if assessing a purchase, and I understood that I was looking at the anatomist, whose claim to my body was evident on his face, the woman and her son beside him mere irritations. The woman was displeased with him, and just below the gabble and the jostling and the sounds of people yelling out at the edge of the crowd and the activity of other men dragging off the bodies of the first 'anged, she leaned toward the imperious gentleman and said, 'You'll get him when we're done. I paid good coin.' I understood then, for I had heard of this: before he could claim me for his experiments and teaching, she would be allowed to hold my twitchin' leg on the boy's wound for a cure, that is, after I was cut down and the life choked out of me, for it was believed, and may be still believed, that the twitchin' limb of a dying felon held against an affliction of a like limb on a living person might effect a cure.

"Again did the cart lurch forward, for it was now our turn. My father was praying, as was the leering gentleman with us. They had escaped inside themselves, and I longed also to do that. I was trembling and breathless, my heart high in my chest, the prickle of the rope now burning my neck. And piss did run down my legs. Above me I saw, sitting in the gallery, an array of fine gentlemen, wonderfully attired and enjoying the beautiful day, packin' their pipes, and laughin' amongst themselves.

"The woman and her son followed the cart these last few paces, as did the anatomist and his students. On their faces was the expression of a proprietary smugness, as if the good coin they had paid rated deference toward them. Under the Tree the cart moved, the hangman up on one of the beams a waitin' to tie us off. Then came a hubbub of some kind down on the ground, for the strange man on the horse had advanced through the crowd, and upon seeing him I began to shake with such a fright that I lost my breath. 'What business have ye here?' yelled the hangman, whilst others in the crowd did protest and jeer at the horseman, as if he had wandered out upon a stage while a play was on, and the horseman drew from his cloak a folded up piece of parchment, which he then cast to the ground, saying, 'This!'

"In the confusion of people moving to pick up the paper, the Sheriff's men did then advance, shouldering their way through the rabble, but before they could make their way to us, the horseman knocked the anatomist aside and swept by the back of our cart, and I felt a powerful jerk of the rope on my neck, and fell off. I would have fallen to the cobbles but a powerful arm did catch me and slide me upon the great sweating haunches of the horse, and with the rope in one of his hands, he both kicked the horse and jerked the rope so that my head slammed against his back, at which the horse rose in a powerful surge, and amidst the yells and hoots of the onlookers, it galloped out of the crowd, my face banging against the man's back.

"We rode at a brisk pace for some time, myself aware of the strange, hooded man looking backwards, for we were being pursued by the Sheriff's men. But the horse, its powerful flanks surging under us, carried us away. At length the man slowed the horse down. I was aware that in my fright and sickness I had a fit in my bowel, dirtying the horse as we rode. 'Sir,' said I, 'I have befouled your horse.' And he said to me, 'Boy, my horse befouled by a corpse would irritate me, but you are alive to befoul my horse, are you not?'

"We arrived in a woods, and the horseman dismounted and pulled me off. I picked up leaves and wiped the soiled part of his horse with them. The horseman stood for some time, my rope in one hand, and studied the surrounding countryside. Satisfied that no one followed us, he looked at me and removed his hood. I beheld there a countenance that bespoke a peculiar contemplation, as if he were wonderin' why he'd done what he'd just done. 'Let me remove this,' said he, 'on one condition, that you do not run.' I said I would not, and thus did he remove the prickly rope and cast it to the dead leaves of the woods' floor. 'Why have you done this?' I asked. And he said, 'Because it was my desire to do so,' and then did he laugh. 'And what will you do with me?' I asked. 'You are going away on a ship, to see the world,' said he. 'Aye,' he went on, 'you shall live to see the world, as I have, for once a long time ago a man did the same for me, did cheat the rope on my behalf.' I thought him daft, but was aware enough to be grateful. 'Yes,' he said, 'the captain of my ship Edward Morley collects the condemned, and then do those condemned become students of the world.'

"Daft though I thought he was, he packed me once again upon his great horse and we rode for some time, so long that I felt myself bruised from bouncin' on the horse's hot, rippling haunches, but at length it slowed down to a rhythmic walk, and then its hooves did clop on cobbles, and indeed ahead of me I beheld, my hands locked around the horseman's trunk, the top rigging of a ship. The horseman turned to me as I gazed at it, my heart pounding and my mouth unable to form a word, for the blazing sunlight and the huge, voluptuous clouds behind that shimmering riot of ropes made the ship appear to me as a bright, rippling dream. I did then understand what had happened, and drawing my eyes down to the dark fabric of the horseman's tunic, I could no longer control myself, and wept."

So affected were the men by Roger Beckwith's story that they mused in silence, or went to the rail to gaze at the sunset over the water. Some talked softly amongst themselves, nodding and seemingly affirming that story's content to one another. I believe that my memory is perhaps fogged as to how much I understood of this story, but I did understand the connection between myself and Beckwith, who, upon finishing his tale, went also into a contemplative musing, shielding his eyes from the sunset.

"These men," said I. "Have these men all cheated the rope?"

"Aye," said he. "It is my life's work. We are here to study the world's design."

"Design?"

Roger Beckwith stared at me. The meaning of that word, upon his first rendering of his story and his life's work, was perhaps too complex for me.

"And how did you find me?"

"Long out at sea we saw the white line of a waterfall, just a tiny thread it was. I sent men in a small boat, to find where that water entered the ocean so that we could collect it, for we didn't have enough on our ship. As it happened, we were able to collect water on the ship, what with the rain. But the men hid in the rocks at the water's edge and watched for a day, and saw three men place a rock on an old man and kill him. You should know that they did this where I lived as a boy, in England. If a prisoner denied his crime, he would have a rock placed on his chest until he died. And the men saw and reported this to me, and I was amazed."

"And the animal you called ''orse.' It did carry two men?"

"Horse. Huh-orse," said he. Beckwith then stared at the wooden door to the interior of the ship. "Ye shall see one," he said.

I believe that equal to his story's perplexing details was the mention of, and acting out of this ''orse,' as he called it during the telling of the tale. One of the men had gone down on his hands and knees whilst the other did straddle him, at which the first crawled around on the ship's deck. That, they said, is an ''orse.' But the claim of a four-legged creature that could run with two men atop, was one I could not believe, for it suggested to me a pig of immense proportions, a creature from a fantasy.

I thought no more of it then, for the sun was setting and I had a sudden sense that I was lost in a universe whose very vastness brought out such fright that I began to tremble a bit. What world was he describing to me? Men suspending boys by ropes and crushing their throats over this stick they called a cane? Was it the land of mists and fog? And how was it that this vessel should now be peopled by these men, each of whom had 'cheated the rope,' with the help of Beckwith. And then did a strange recognition settle on me: Beckwith told of a man who helped him cheat the rope, a man who had been likewise helped when he was young, and now Beckwith had done likewise for me. How many generations back in time did this story go? As many generations as my father's curse? It was as if I had begun to perceive, for the first time in my life, the design of the world, but as I said, these ideas were in ways fleeting and unformed. I had much to learn about this world.

Another 'I ke aha' began to trouble me in the days following his tale. We did not move at a fast pace, did not open all the sails and catch the wind. Each day the sun rose into sumptuous white clouds, and each day I saw those clouds I recalled the morning of the fight at the stream, so long ago, when Ka'ahupāhau had been lost and I had cheated a war axe. Why were we sitting still upon the water? One day I made my way along the rail to stand beside 'the American,' Dick Burrows. A tall man, and silent, apparently musing over various mysteries as he stood at the rail. He looked once at me, nodded, and then stared out over the water at the clouds and shafts of white sunlight dropping out of their bottoms upon the water, creating a blinding glare on the horizon. "We are not moving," I said. "Why?"

He nodded again. "We move by night, and in bad weather," he said. "Why?"

Burrows stared at me. "You have heard the story of the rope."

"Yes. I am not satisfied yet."

He said, "You mean, 'I do not understand yet.'"

"Yes, I do not understand."

"Roger Beckwith moves over the world, but must not be seen by another ship."

"Where is the another ship?"

"There are many." He held both hands up, fingers splayed. "This," he said, and moved his hands. "And this, and this, and this, many many times over."

He had indicated perhaps fifty or sixty or seventy, but I did not understand. "Understand me 'many times over,'" I said.

"Explain 'many times over', you say. How many days are there in your life?"

"Many many," I said.

"Ten that many."

I understood. The life-days of ten men. I placed my hand on the rail and thought about this. Great ships such as this, many thousands of them, so many, I perceived, that they must crowd the very world we were learning, but all around us was the blank vastness of ocean, and not one in sight. "And when will we see another?" I asked.

He laughed. "'fore they see us, mate," he said, and laughed again. "'fore they see us, godwillin'." Then he went back to his musing.

"And you," I said. "'ave you a story?"

"Aye," he said. "We all do."

§

When Pono's tale had advanced to the exploits of Roger Beckwith, I listened with great skepticism, for Beckwith was being presented to me as a man normal in his vision and perhaps inclined to a saintliness that so contrasted with the stories I'd heard, that I could barely believe what I was hearing. And indeed the American with pen in hand did look up at me from time to time as if I were somehow responsible for the unfairness that Beckwith had experienced as a boy, and I informed him that the jail in question was destroyed forty-four years ago in 1780, and that much had been done to reform England's judicial system. Drawing and quartering were punishments that had long-since been abandoned, and now the apparent abuses of judicial power were better under the control of thinking men. Was it not true, I asked, that America did also have its faults where the same was concerned? Note the abuses in Salem all those years ago.

But the argument was a trifle, for I had been enlivened by my chance meeting with Rebecca Searle, and had talked to her again earlier the morning of Pono's account of Beckwith's experiences as a boy. I had walked, first, toward that long stretch of beach to the east of the port. The day was pleasant, the wind coming from the east-northeast as it usually did, and I saw natives bathing in the small waves offshore. The sand was heavy and made my walking difficult. Men stood knee-deep in the water with nets draped over their right shoulders, at times casting them in almost perfect circles out over the water, after which they slowly pulled them up, apparently feeling the cords for the movement of fish.

Dirty sailors sat in the shade of palm trees, smoking and laughing and passing large stone bottles amongst themselves. They looked at me with languid and impudent gazes as I passed. I walked perhaps six hundred yards, but did not see Mrs. Searle, so I turned to go back.

A fine ship beat towards the harbor, its sails full. There, in that increasing morning heat, feeling perspiration begin to dampen my clothes, I felt the strongest presence of that idea concerning my remaining here awhile, for the beauty of the place did clearly outweigh its crudeness, and

I thought, what could a man with a bit of money do here? The options seemed numerous.

On my return to the port, I saw her walking at the edge of the largest cluster of buildings. She wore the same dress and I assumed was being gently slapped upon her heels with each step she took. She was having some difficulty controlling the parasol in the breeze. I approached her, and she saw me and raised her hand, then grabbed the parasol once again. As she grabbed it, her dress fell against her, revealing physical proportions that most assuredly convinced me that I had, as they say, bumped into a woman whose physiology would cause me breathless excitement.

"Good day," I called.

As the old kanaka storyteller was wont to say, so shall I move forward. We talked, standing there on the dirt path. And again did that wondrously expressive face move from nodding contemplation to levity to coyness, and I must admit that our second conversation was so much a corroboration of my earlier speculations about her that I found myself made somewhat shy. I learned that she was unattached, was not that well accepted by the 'stiffer elements' of the mission because she was, as she said, "Perhaps a bit too liberal in my thinking and behavior."

"Ah, Mr. Bingham and his crowd," I said.

Clouds blocked the sun, and she lowered and closed the parasol. "So," she said, "now I will go and do my teaching."

"And these 'stiffer elements' of the mission. What have they against you?"

The question drew her eyes, and fetching eyes they were, to the ocean, where it seemed some answer lay. She sighed and shook her head. "They choose to combat licentiousness with an extremity of prudishness, I think. Now, I do not think these women should bandy about with their breasts bouncing, and I do not think that they should offer themselves to any dirty sailor who jumps off a ship, but one must be just a bit more moderate in thought where conversion is concerned, don't you think?"

"More practical, do you mean?"

"Yes. Practical. Their language and many of their social habits are wonderful. Their dance is wonderful. I'm not inclined to think these should all be stamped out."

At that moment I thought, ah, so she is a sort of libertine. This, I will admit, excited me for the wrong reasons. I did then allow my eyes to drop to her chest, accidentally, and this I believe she saw. The various subtle displays of the body, eyes particularly, become their own language, and this made her blush a bit. I must say that the breeze, the smells of ocean and flora, the sultriness of the place, put the very licentiousness she referred to, between us like a humid, ticklish vapor. The subject she was discussing, in reference to the brown women in question, did then become a subject between ourselves. Pono himself once held forth on the subject of walls and licentiousness, and whether or not there was any significant difference between one social context and the other. I felt at the moment that this woman and I faced each other outside of our clothes and our cultural inhibitions. I became a bit flustered.

She laughed. "Mr. Davis, or Matthew," she said. "Something is on your mind."

"I am afraid that what is on my mind shames me."

"Ah," she said, her face brightening. "I know what it is. Doesn't it make you feel free? Doesn't it push you to feeling as if what we have left back there is somehow an arbitrary constriction, one that was given to us as a burden at birth?"

"In ways," I said.

"We have come here and spoiled it," she said.

"Spoiled it?"

"Eden before The Fall."

I believe it was I who blushed now. Was this woman mad?

She sighed again. "My apologies, I go too far. It is just that when I look at the people go about their business unaware of our presence, I see a wonderful balance of things. And we're spoiling it."

"Well," I said, "I failed to anticipate that degree of free thinking on your part."

"This is my problem with the other whites here. I recommend that we be at least somewhat understanding of this world and its people. But all of them think me insane."

The sun had slipped out from behind the racing clouds, making her squint as she talked. She fiddled with the parasol, and then looked toward trees some distance away. "If we had more time, I would enjoy more conversation, but I must go," she said. "Would you like to meet again and continue?"

"Indeed yes," I said.

"You say you are interested in botanical matters. One activity I like is walking, mostly up the valley there," and she pointed in the direction of the pass Pono had identified for me some time earlier, the one that leads to the other side of the island. "It takes much time to get all the way, but if you'd like, there are days that do not require my presence at the mission. Would you be interested in that?"

"Yes," I said.

"Then we might meet tomorrow," she said, and then frowned. "No, I have an appointment. Two days from now, at this spot? I prefer dawn myself."

"Dawn it is," I said.

Oh, did I dream of this woman and the idea of Eden before The Fall. I was left that day with a final image of her face, which preceded the sound of her heels being gently slapped, of a face composed and demure, yet bespeaking of the innocently salacious, as if somehow her having mentioned Eden before The Fall opened wide my imagination to a delicious freedom that did cause my heart to pound with an imprudent force, as of a primitive drum.

11.

As we waited out there on the ocean, each day dawning with beautiful clouds, I continued learning the language, and the duties of a sailor. My work with the flat stone was now accompanied by another activity, called 'picking oakum,' a process where one mixes separated threads of old rope or half-rotted sailcloth or clothes, 'junk' this material was called, into sticky wads of tree sap which becomes more and more pliable the more you work it with your fingers. The difficult part was separating the threads by pulling them apart, softening old rope by rolling it on your thigh, and so on. The sharp, sweet smell pleased me, and I understood that, like the holystone work, this was something the men were grateful to me for doing. But I slept with the smell of it on my sore fingers, and splotches of it stuck to my clothes and skin and blackened there. The product, oakum, was used to seal seams and cracks in the ship's wood.

It is likely to make one skeptical, but I should say that this total engagement in communicating with these men advanced my skill in their language at a speed that surprised me as it did them. And in those days I saw various marvels of their world. The 'looking glass' was one of particular amazement, for this sheet of hardened water, as of a pool in which one can see the clouds or one's face reflected, could be picked up and held vertically so that I could study, with a clarity I had never beheld before, my own face, noting that its sparse beard and dark skin and broad nose was quite different from those of my hosts. The men seemed to enjoy showing me these marvels. Another was the musket, which propelled a heavy ball at great speed using a controlled explosion inside the device, something I thought I could understand, recalling stones that would explode in a fire-pit. Another was the clock, a complicated device of yellow metalled gears and posts inside a glassed case, that ticked, moving a tiny spear in minuscule jerks around a white circle decorated with black markings.

One day I asked Roger Beckwith about the shining tube he had placed against his eye on that day after they rescued me from the war-axe. By this time, he and the other men had grown to trust me not to do anything that might damage any part of the great ship, or anything involving what appeared to be the men's personal belongings.

"Go to my cabin," he said. "You'll see it on my desk."

"Desk," I said.

Beckwith laughed distractedly, for he and two of the men were staring with considerable curiosity at dark clouds on the horizon, the bellies connected to the ocean by pale shafts of rain. "Aye," he said, turning to me. "See if you can find it, Pono."

So I went down the steep, narrow steps into the bowels of the ship. The cabin had been pointed out to me, so I made my way along a very narrow hallway bedecked with implements I did not yet understand, the most fascinating of which was a device that amazed me in its cleverness: a plate which hung upon the wall that held a candlestick, the stick suspended and rotating according to gravity on a shaft that allowed it to remain vertical when the ship tipped with wind in its sails. It now hung parallel to the face of the plate because of the calmness of the sea the ship sat upon.

Upon opening the door, I saw first the 'desk', which was a flat square of wood suspended by four carved wooden legs resembling stacks of a fruit, perhaps what you call breadfruit, skewered through, and atop this desk was the tube, in its shortened form. I was about to pick it up when I beheld another platform, smaller but higher than the desk, with a tipped flat top suspended by another stack of carved wooden legs. Upon this, as I related to you the other day, Matthew, lay a white object which looked like a bird's wings, soft curving shapes sweeping upward and out from a single point. I stepped to this object and saw that these sweeping shapes formed identically curved rectangles finely squared at the outside corners, each one centered by smaller rectangles of gray-black blotches, curving up from where they joined and then sweeping outward and down to the edges. I moved closer. These rectangular stains were a series of tiny shapes, lines twisted around resembling sections of 'uala vine or tree roots snaking through soil. Someone had placed these tiny stains in lines, so many that it seemed impossible to have done such exacting work of blotting these markings into the surface of these strangely shaped blocks. Whoever had done it had left spaces, as if wearied by the magnitude of his task.

Some marks after spaces were larger but of like shape, and I whispered out interpretations of these—a house, an eye half-closed, a woman with child, a mo'o. I touched this object, and moved a thin rectangle of material up and over, and then down upon the other side, a thin sheet tightly woven as of the finest kapa, revealing another two rectangles of markings. I was looking at a carefully constructed pile of these squares, all joined in the middle of the entire of the object. There were what appeared to be hundreds of these rectangles of attached kapa on each side. I laughed, and looked at the tube on the desk. My attention had been drawn by what was before me now, for there were more markings, I thought, than grains of sand in a large dune.

Just then Will Kelsey, the first mate, looked in. "Aye, Pono," said he, "what keeps you?"

I pointed at the object.

"Why, that's a book," he said.

"Book."

Kelsey walked back down the narrow hall.

I left the cabin without the tube. Back on the deck of the ship, I envisioned this marvelous object I had seen, but the men were studying the dark clouds on the horizon. At length I approached the man named Don Bentley, and said, "What is a book?"

"Bunch of bloody words on the bloody page it is—nothing for you to be concerned with, Pono. Nothing for me to be concerned with either, I tell ye."

Later, as the sun began to descend, I approached Beckwith. "Sir, I would like to see the book," I said.

"Indeed?" said he. He thought a moment, the appearance of a speculative merriment on his face. "Aye, did you see the one open on the podium?"

This must have been the object upon which the marvelous book sat. "Will Kelsey told me what it was."

Roger Beckwith led me to his cabin. Again, I stared down at the book, but he turned to study a series of brown upright shafts of wood lined up in his wall. From these he pulled one out, and I saw that it was a square object white around three of its edges. This object fell open in his hand to resemble the larger one on the podium, revealing one rectangular block of like markings on one side, and on the other a very fine ki'i, what you would call a glyph, or petroglyph as I have heard it referred to. "Elephant," he said. It depicted a pig with a nose that hung to the ground and legs overly thick as of tree trunks, and I laughed, studying it. "Big," he said, "big as this room."

"How is this done?" I asked, pointing at the tiny markings. Again I looked at the elephant, trying to imagine this animal. Surely his claim that it was 'as big as this room' was an exaggeration.

Beckwith drew me to his desk. There he pulled a feather out of a small gourd of black liquid, and drew a circle upon his thumb with this feather that leaked what appeared to be very dark berry juice out of its sharpened tip, and he then reached behind him to pull out another book, which he laid open upon his desk, and pressed his thumb on a blank rectangle of one of the leaves, leaving there a circle. "Kapa," I said.

"What is kapa?" he asked.

"Cloth we make, stained as you have."

"Ah," he said. He then wiped his thumb on his trouser leg and turned one of the sheets over to reveal large figures. He pointed to the ones at the top, I noticed each string of figures ending with what I thought of as the helmeted head of a warrior looking left. "Enclyclopædia Britannica," he said. "Or, 'a dictionary of arts and sciences, compiled upon a new plan in which the different sciences are digested into distinct treatises or systems.'"

"I do not understand," I said.

And thus he explained to me the function of these markings. The world is full of a host of great marvels, its very vastness one which occupied my mind for years, but upon my understanding of what he was showing me, I felt the presence of the one marvel that eclipsed all others. He used the word 'read' in reference to this, and pointed at a short string of figures: "And," he said. "Ah, then 'n' followed by the 'd' sound."

"You said earlier a word that ended with 'ah,' and then another ending in 'ah.'" I pointed. "These here."

"Indeed," he said, and stared at me. "You absorb this quickly, Pono."

"Absorb?"

"Learn."

"Yes, I learn."

"Pedi-ah," he said, placing his finger at the end of the first string of figures at the top, and then he moved to the other string and said, "Britannic-ah."

"So this ki'i is 'ah.'"

"Key-ee?"

And so this conversation went. The connection between a sound and a figure on this leaf was instantly fascinating for me. He put his finger upon another string of figures, and said, "Gentlemen." I looked at it. The word was long, and hence the number of figures representing it numbered nine.

"Men is here," I said, putting my finger under the end of the word.

"Exactly," Beckwith said. "I am amazed at this. You learn this so quickly."

"I absorb," I said.

"Ah!" he said. "You do indeed."

The magic of this 'book' was such that I fell into a musing about it. How could I get one of these? Beckwith seemed to anticipate this, for he said, "Would you like to take this with you up on the deck? Some of the men can read, and they will help you."

"Yes," I said.

And so I went to the deck with the book. There, sitting in my hammock with my legs crossed and the book in my lap, I turned the leaves and studied the figures, and studied the illustrations with a deep fascination, for in this volume was a long section entitled 'Anatomy,' a word that Will Kelsey helped me understand. "Aye, it's your body, Pono, all the bloody tripe inside, the bones and organs and such, the entire devil's brew of juices. Beckwith's story mentioned that blighter called 'the anatomist.' This is what the bloody rotter does, cuts up the 'anged and draws pictures."

Although the pictures were fascinating, it was the words and their meanings that I was drawn to. So as the sky darkened and the men continued to speculate on the weather gathering on the horizon, I asked one or another of the men to pronounce for me words that were listed in the very beginning of this book, just after the pages starting with the larger figures Beckwith and I had looked at. Many of these words, the various tutors would tell me, were old, and not of any use to me: 'abaco,' a term for mathematics, 'abactus,' used by physicians for a type of miscarriage, and so on. Then 'abaft,' for a thing, 'toward the stern of a ship.' Abaft, then, went into my memory. I still saw it in my mind as 'helmeted warrior looking left, pregnant woman, helmeted warrior looking left, tree in the wind, leomano pointing down.' The men helped me identify these as letters, and then gave me the sounds for each one.

I would have been content to spend every waking hour with this book, but the men began to show a gleeful agitation, for we were going to visit 'King Philip's land,' which was described to me as a place of many thousands of islands, twenty times larger than my world. "Aye," Will Kelsey said. "Beckwith wants chickens, and there are many there. And the people of the place are victims of the cruelty of the Spaniards." When I asked him to explain who these people were, and what Spaniards were, he thought, and said, "It'd take me days to tell ye, Pono. But we'll let you see it for yourself."

I was told that King Philip was an ali'i from a place called Spain, which was a part of a body of land a thousand times the size of my world. This King Philip had sent his warriors to this land, and visited upon the peaceful people a scourge of death, all in the interests of imposing upon them a new god. The story sounded to me strangely similar to the stories my father told me of the newer arrival of ali'i to our world, and when I asked when this had happened, it was old Owen Bew who told me that it was some two hundred years before, again corresponding to the time of arrival of the ali'i to my world. Were my ali'i, then, from this place called Spain? No, Bew told me. "I know nothing of your alee-ee as you call them. This is men who believe in a god that gives them the will to capture peacelovin' people and cut off their hands and noses and build their bloody churches and tell those peacelovin' people they don't murder to bow down to their god. Curious, it is, that this is 'ow these men see the world."

Just as the Dick Burrows had told me, we began moving again through a fog. I had understood by this time that Beckwith existed out of sight of anyone who could report his presence, for he was much sought after by various people, each of whom wanted to put a rope around his neck. Large as this new world was, so vast that I could not fix in my mind the sense of it, he was well-known all throughout this world.

Our movement through calm water, under a light wind with many of our sails partly folded or 'reefed,' as the men put it, was smooth and nearly silent, the great ship groaning and popping softly as the men operated the marvelous devices that gave it its direction. But the men, always peering intently off one side of the ship, or perched high up upon the yard arms, were more agitated, and I wondered why the procurement of a few chickens required such care and stealth. The men squinted into the fog, and I went to stand by Dick Burrows, the silent one, and said, "This getting of the chickens is 'ard then, is it?"

Burrows laughed. "You sound so like a Brit," he said. Then he looked at the fog. "No. It's Beckwith. He's a way of findin' strife, he does. Always wants to do somethin' on the simplest of pretenses, and uses them same pretenses to confront the horrors of the world. That business of his almost bein' hung warped his mind in the most peculiar direction, toward travellin' the world lookin' for evidence of human fault, and sure enough does he hate them Spaniards for what they have a desire to do."

We remained in the fog, although I was given to understand that land was near, in the direction those pensive men standing at the rail squinted. And so we moved, the ship softly mumbling down in its innards, Beckwith mostly in his cabin, but for times when one or another of the men would go down to report something seen off the rail. Then in a change in the wind, I smelled land, and it brought to me a powerful flush of memory of my world, the odor of soil and flowers and fish and the smoke of cooking fires, and then even the smell of hair and breath tinged with the hint of he'e. My heart made a strange movement in my chest, as if rolling over at the sadness of it.

So came the morning that Beckwith drew the men, nineteen of them, to the deck. We were going to take the smaller, fat canoe called a 'cutter,' to the shore, and there we would negotiate with the people of this land for six chickens. The cutter would be lowered by rope winches tied to a 'capstan,' or a wheel men walked in circles to turn.

"We'll take eight men in," Beckwith said. "If all looks well, we'll send four back to take six in, and all will have their feet on land. Aye, and Pono can come." He looked at me, thinking. "We'll arm this man with a sword." Beckwith's expression changed. "Gentlemen, we are in the south of the length of this place. We've first to find who populates it. If it's a center of commerce it's the Catholic faith. They've been warring with the southern people of this country for two hundred years. I smell no commerce here but wood fires and cattle. If it's the remote parts of the country, the people here might be the followers of Alla, of the Mahometan faith, so if they are, there'll be no cavorting with their women."

One man holding a sword, the one named Ben Fowles, dropped it on the deck. And amidst its clatter others sighed.

"Aye," Beckwith went on. "We'll find a place later where you can cavort with women, but these people are strict ." The men whispered to one another. "Aye lads," Beckwith said, "you're alive to experience that misery. But considering that long ago you made the acquaintance of yer 'and, I surmise that ye'll make do under the circumstances." This was followed by hoarse laughter and more snorting and sighing.

"S'pose I said I was a devotee of this Alla," Don Bentley said. "Would that 'elp?"

"You'd think it would, wouldn't ye?" Beckwith said. "If they see us, we might have to defend ourselves, for they're suspicious of anyone connected with the Spaniards. But it's chickens we want lads, an' I'll not have you cavortin' with them either."

And so we climbed down a heavy rope webbing into the cutter. The men, Will Kelsey and Dick Burrows and a man named Olney, who was one of the gentlemen of leisure, carried muskets, others carrying small hand muskets called flintlocks that they slid into their belts. I had strapped to a belt around my middle a short sword, longer than a leiomano but shorter than the one Beckwith wore. The sword was heavy, with a gleaming blade that fascinated me as the men rowed, and I tipped it in the faint light and caught reflections of my own face, and the colorful clothes of the men who rocked with the pulling of the oars. We had with us objects of barter carried in a sack by Don Bentley, including a hand musket, two kegs of gunpowder, and some glass baubles that Beckwith had brought from his cabin. We moved through a light mist, and into the smell of land, Beckwith at the front of this boat, peering ahead.

Then the darker shape of the tops of trees emerged from that mist, and the water sweeping by the boat turned a brownish color. The boat slid into brown sand that fringed what appeared to be a dense forest of low vegetation. I was surprised to see, above this vegetation, the faint gray shapes of niu, what you call coconut trees. So this land was similar, I thought, to my world, although the air felt sodden and heavy, humid beyond what I had experienced. We made our way out of the boat onto shore, our sandals in our hands, and the familiar sensation of sand under my feet caused in me a brief sadness, but the men were already making their way into the forest. I wiped the sand off my feet and put my sandals on.

Once inside the wooded land, we walked to the sound of singing birds, whose song paused as we passed. We walked for perhaps two hours, all the while Dick Burrows out in the lead, peering around with a wary and furtive caution, pushing branches away with the nose of his musket. At length I began to wonder about Roger Beckwith's sanity, for I had never seen so forbidding a place as this. At my feet I saw a giant, legless mo'o that raced past and disappeared into dead leaves. Will Kelsey called it a 'snake,' and it so frightened me that I found myself looking down with every step.

Upon reaching a clearing of high grasses, Beckwith allowed us to rest. "Aye," he said, "we've come to a remote part, we have. We'll go a bit more, and if we find aught but trees, we'll go back and move the ship."

Farther into the interior, though, we saw that the sun had broken through the clouds, sending fat shafts of light upon a plateau, the foothills of which we climbed, and upon reaching the top, I saw Beckwith and Dick Burrows gazing out toward that light. There before us lay a great field of the same plant, all of these plants arranged in rows. On the far side stood a low structure, but large, perhaps twice the length of the ship.

"A plantation," Beckwith said. "This is tobacco, which we'll harvest, eh lads?"

"You're blinkin' right we will," Don Bentley said, shifting the sack of barter he carried on his shoulder.

"But we can't be seen. I don't believe the occupants of that fort will harm us, first because they may not see us, and second because this area is, I believe, part of the land system, and that is the cabeza or headquarters. So that means there's a pueblo in the area, which is like a town. The capitan, or leader who lives in that place, is the plantation owner and wants nothing but his money."

Beckwith looked around, then back. "We've been seen," he said.

The men reacted quickly to this. Dick Burrows addressed his musket, and carefully checked its complicated works. "What'd you see?" he whispered.

"Way out there at the edge of the field," Beckwith said. "Two men, and when they saw us they vanished into the woods borderin' this place."

"We sh'll go back to the ship then?" Don Bentley asked.

"First we'll go there," Beckwith said, pointing to where he had seen the people.

Bentley appeared somewhat frightened by the prospect. Dick Burrows nodded, then spat. "Let's go on then," he said.

Burrows led the way, now with his musket's nose ahead of him. We walked in a line, Beckwith behind Burrows and talking softly to him as they walked. We entered a woods, and inside we found a wide path, which we followed. "Burrows has got senses unlike any man's," Will Kelsey whispered to me. "He knows what's out there."

As we walked, we became aware of a smell in the air. It was that of a salty putrefaction, perhaps of cooked pig left too long. Will Kelsey began shaking his head as we walked, whispering, "No lads, I don't like this at all. Beckwith's daft, I tell ye. 'e's determined to get us all killed over a bloody experiment."

"I do not understand," I said.

We continued on, Dick Burrows out ahead. The light breeze coming across that wide path carried hints of that smell, then stole it away. Dick Burrows then held up his hand for us to pause. He turned and addressed Beckwith, after which Beckwith gestured to us to gather near him.

When we were there, he said, "Lads, we're at the source of that odor. It's two men crucified up ahead and cooked by the capitan's police. We'll go look, but I want none of you running, for the people connected with those dead men are all around us."

"Dear God," Will Kelsey said. "They'll take us for the perpetrators."

Beckwith looked at me. "'Perpetrators,' would be those who killed those men," he said. And then to Will Kelsey, he said, "We have come alone. We remain together, and they'll understand that we're bringing no harm."

We made our way into a clearing, and there, erected in the center, were two wooden things resembling the letter 't' with the remains of men in blackened heaps at their bases. Dick Burrows went and studied the men from a few feet away, and looked at the trees bordering the clearing. Clouds of flies hovered over the two bodies. Behind these bodies was another stick driven into the ground, at the top of which was a brown leaf resembling those of the plants in the large field we had seen.

"We shall wait," Roger Beckwith said. "They'll come out of the wood soon. These men stole the *capitan's* tobacco, and were executed for it. Aye, a tiny crime is it not, for such a punishment?" Beckwith sighed, and I beheld him trembling somewhat, for the sight of those men seemed to have aggrieved him greatly. "Don," said he, "lay out the booty, will ye? Just lay it out there on the dirt."

Don Bentley complied, lining up the two casks of powder, the hand-musket, and some of the shiny objects whose function I had not yet been taught. We waited. Beckwith talked, as if to himself: "Aye, these poor lads went for a leaf or two of tobacco, and here's what's left of them. I'll say those two leaves of tobacco weren't worth even as much as a cane, were they?"

I moved toward the two sets of remains under the blackened poles. Below the flies, the flesh was black and glistened with maggots, and dry, pale bone showed through it, the skulls, and against the side of one pile of remains, a jawbone. I backed up a step because of the smell, and then Dick Burrows turned to Beckwith, saying, "Here they be."

From the trees fringing the clearing there emerged a group of men clad in loincloths and naked above the waist, all of them smaller than we, and with their heads wrapped in white fabric, the white tails of which went down their backs. The leader, who stood before them, held a musket, and looked fierce and angry. He was dark, and had very white teeth, and resembled the kanaka maoli of my world.

Beckwith rose and took a few steps toward the men, and pointed at the remains under the poles. Then he patted his chest. This the leader appeared to understand, for he handed his musket to one of the others and took a few halting steps in Beckwith's direction, all the while looking down at the two casks of powder and the hand-musket. Beckwith gestured to him to approach, and then lifted the hand-musket and held it out to the man. He then held it away from himself as if to fire at a tree, and the leader held both hands up and said, "Ah! Ah ah ah!"

Beckwith lowered the hand-musket. Then he put it down on the ground and pointed to the casks. "Bah!" he said. "Boom!"

"Ah," the leader said.

Beckwith turned to Don Bentley. "Please sign to him what we want."

Don Bentley squatted down and began walking around with his arms folded against his sides, his elbows pumping out imitating the flapping of wings. Then he found a rock, held it under his rear end, and dropped it, saying, "Awk! Cluck cluck!"

The leader laughed, as did some of his fellows by the trees. Beckwith held his hands up and indicated seven with his fingers. Then he nodded to Don Bentley, who drew the little wooden gourd from his tunic and held it up. He formed a circle with his arms, indicating the amount of this material he wanted. "We can steal and dry some," Beckwith said, "but they'll have it dry for us." The leader confered with his fellows. Then he held his hand up and nodded, at which two of his men vanished into the woods.

The leader returned. He sat down before the booty. Beckwith put his musket down and sat on the other side. Beckwith then pointed in the direction of the field, and imitated with his fingers in the dirt a sequential thumping, as of a pig running. The leader nodded, held his fist by his head and pulled up, imitating being pulled by the neck. Then he ran his hand across his throat and said, "Zeek."

"Aye," Beckwith said.

The leader pointed to the remains under the blackened sticks, and then stood up, and held his hands palms down next to his own shoulder. "Boys," Beckwith said. "These dead were boys." He turned and looked at the remains, then picked up one of the hand-muskets. He turned it over in his hands, and then reached across the remaining booty and handed it to the leader. Then he worked at opening one of the wooden kegs, and lifted the top off. Inside was what appeared to be black sand. "Good," Beckwith said.

"Ah," the leader said. "Good. Good."

Beckwith then looked back toward the field. "Hay-soos," he said, pointing, and then pointing at the wood, he said, "Alla."

The leader raised his hands and brought them down on his knees. "Alla," he said.

"So they been fighting for 'undreds of years," Beckwith said to us. "Killing each other over their gods. There ye have it, lads."

Beckwith had just turned back to the leader when a boy raced into the clearing and spoke a rapid string of their language to the leader, who stood up, and listened carefully. Then he waved us toward the woods. Beckwith looked back toward the field also, and then said, "Lads, we've got to hide ourselves in them trees a bit." We all followed Beckwith and the leader into the woods. Don Bentley quickly closed the powder keg and placed the booty in his bag and followed us in. The leader gestured anxiously to Beckwith to move farther into the dense woodland, and so we did, all the while looking back. From inside the wood, we had no view of the clearing. Beckwith turned to me. "Pono, ye like to see an 'orse? Slip back a little and stay on your belly, and if they see you, come back quick as you can. I don't believe they'll come in 'ere after us."

I made my way back to the clearing, remaining two body-lengths inside behind a small bush, and in the ground I could feel the sound of their approach. I could think of nothing but pigs, but when they broke into the clearing, they appeared at first to be men whose lower extremities were huge, moving at a pace no man could ever achieve running, and when they stopped, dust rising around the strange feet at the ends of very thin, delicate-appearing legs, four for each man, I saw that indeed the men were sitting upon these animals, whose brown hide with white markings shone in the light and whose strange faces, long and ending in huge snouts, moved their mouths seeming to chew upon shining metal devices attached around them. The men upon the 'orses, their muskets strapped over their shoulders, looked around, pulling on strings attached to the mouth-devices of these animals. Their skin, like that of the leader we were with, was dark, their hair black. Speaking briefly to one another, they turned and ran away, the huge buttocks of the animals rippling and their strange, thin legs carrying the men in great strides.

We waited until it seemed safe to return to the edge of the clearing. I noticed all the while that Dick Burrows and Will Kelsey stayed off to the side, their muskets at the ready, in case the very men we were negotiating with might attack us. At length we heard swishing sounds from the brush, and there emerged the two men who had run off, one carrying a large sack, the other a cluster of light brown chickens in each hand, their legs bound together, each chicken with its head turned up and peering around. The man bearing the large sack was breathless and glistening with perspiration. He dropped the bag before Beckwith, who lifted it briefly. "Three stone at least," he said. "That'll keep our pipes afire for some time, lads. And look, what fine 'ens we've got."

We left shortly after that, the booty in the hands of the leader and his men, tobacco and chickens with us. I carried the tobacco bag, which reminded me of carrying stones, and the memory of that brought back images of dried he'e bouncing off my head, of my father and then of Pekau with child. Perhaps I was wearied from all the walking, but I fell into a musing about this as we went, Dick Burrows again at the lead.

But Dick Burrows stopped. We had made our way to the wooded area near the ocean, and he turned to signal to us that something was amiss. He whispered back to Beckwith, who whispered back to Will Kelsey, who said to me, "He smells 'orses."

I smelled nothing but soil and vegetation. We gathered in a group, and Dick Burrows looked around, and then turned to Beckwith. "I'll go off to the side a hundred yard or so and pull them off. You keep movin' toward the beach."

"Pono," Beckwith said. "Give Will the bag and go with Dick."

I gave the bag to Will Kelsey, and Dick Burrows and I went into the woods, walking parallel to the beach. Burrows moved very silently through the trees, and I tried to imitate the stealth with which he moved. He stopped to listen, to sniff the air, and to peer ahead into the trees. We crossed clearings and went into more woodland, and to my left, I saw the ocean, not three hundred paces from us. Burrows stopped again, and held his musket with both hands. Less than a hundred paces away were two men atop their animals, both with muskets. "Stop," Dick Burrows said. He reached into a purse he had attached to his belt. "Pono, hold these," he said, and handed me a small, heavy ball and a piece of white fabric. "Hold it out where I can see it, and don't move your hand."

I assumed that the men would attack, and holding the ball and the piece of fabric, drew out my short sword with my other hand. The men on their 'orses laughed, one raising and addressing his long musket, then the other. "They're comin'," Dick Burrows said. "Hold that ball and wad where I can see it, and don't drop it."

"Yes," I said.

"They're waitin' for me to fire, and when I do, they'll come. They've got two muskets and I think I see a pistol in one of their belts. So they got three shots to our one. Just hold that ball out where you got it now and don't move. Their muskets've got bayonets, too, so if they get close, keep your senses."

The men moved their animals around, their feet thumping in the dirt. They talked to each other, then laughed again, one raising his musket and aiming.

"He won't shoot," Dick Burrows said. "He wants us to shoot what we've got." They moved their 'orses closer, perhaps five paces. "This ain't workin'," Dick Burrows said. "We can't let them get any closer." He raised his musket and aimed, and the men moved around on their animals and laughed again.

Dick Burrows continued aiming. "Don't drop that ball and wad," he said.

I heard the loud click followed by the report, and then through the quickly clearing smoke I saw one man grab his shoulder, his 'orse jumping backward, while the other galloped toward us, his musket up and aimed. Burrows pulled out his horn and pulled the plug with his teeth and shook powder into the musket's works at the close end, flipped something down, poured powder into the long tube's end while the 'orse had brought the man more than halfway to us, but Dick Burrows did not look up at him. Rather he quickly grabbed the ball and wad from my hand, stuffed it into the end of his musket, and pulled a thin rod from underneath, and as the man enlarged in my vision, not twenty paces from us and moving at a frightening speed, Burrows tamped with the rod, pulled it out and dropped it before us on the dirt and raised the musket and fired, the 'orse sweeping past us at a full run without the man atop, the man having toppled off his 'orse and falling with a thump on the ground that produced a loud cough from his mouth. The other man had fled.

Burrows regarded the man on the ground, and the man, looking up at us with a strange leer, wheezed and began to tremble, his teeth bared and clacking, after which blood pooled into his mouth and ran down his cheek into the dust.

"Pick up his musket," Dick Burrows said. "Get the pistol and his bag, willya Pono?" I did so, my hands shaking. "I believe we'd better get to the boat, for more'll be a comin' soon," he said. "That's your musket now."

By the time we had rowed halfway to the ship, the sun had burned off much of the fog we had seen earlier. Beckwith and the others looked somewhat anxiously around at the horizon, Beckwith dividing his attention between that horizon and the chickens lying at his feet.

When we reached the ship and climbed the ropes onto the deck, leaving Dick Burrows to attach the winch ropes to pull the cutter up, we were met by the other eleven men, all of whom appeared somewhat surly and petulant. Old Owen Bew was quite red-faced. "Aye," he said, "ye left us and went a cavortin' 'ave ye?"

"Owen," Beckwith said, climbing over the rail holding the sack of leaves, "y've been in the grog."

"We all 'ave," he said. "And it's our right too, damn our circumstances."

"What is grog?" I asked Will Kelsey.

"So we're to go find more grog are we?" Beckwith asked, a pained expression on his face. "So how much did you consume lads?"

"Tell ye later," Will Kelsey said to me.

"Hardly any," a man named Tom Crabbe said, "except for Owen. Tried to consume the lot of it, I'd say."

"I'd be lying on my face if I did," Bew said, looking down at the tied-up chickens. "So you went an' 'ad yer fun you did. And we here waiting for some relief, and what do we get? Chickens."

"Tobacco," Beckwith said, and dropped the sack on the deck.

"Indeed," Owen Bew said, his expression brightening up a bit.

Dick Burrows came over the rail, and then did the men pull smoking gourds from their clothes and stoop down to jam bits of the material into them. Owen Bew climbed unsteadily into the belly of the ship and emerged with a stick with a red ember on the end.

"Grog is mostly rum," Will Kelsey said, watching the men pass the fire-stick around, each touching it to the material. "The English started rationing it to sailors more'n a hundred year ago. Admiral Vernon I believe it was who started it up."

"What is rum?"

"An—" Will Kelsey stared at me. "Aye Pono, it's one of those things you'll just need to experience for yourself."

Roger Beckwith went on to explain to the men what had happened, and they seemed satisfied that indeed it had been better for them to remain on the ship. For my part, I wanted to retrieve my book and continue reading. Dick Burrows approached me just as I was about to settle myself in my hammock. "Let me show you this, Pono," he said, holding the musket to me. He explained how the device worked, and the most fascinating part of it was how a thing called the 'frizzen' was struck by a flint in a 'cock' which flipped this frizzen open to reveal the flash pan while simultaneously causing a flint to spark into the flash pan, thus igniting the powder, which burned quickly through a tiny vent and ignited the larger body of powder shaken into the barrel and tamped in behind the wad and ball. The cock, as he called it, was called that because it resembled a pecking chicken, and indeed it did. "I'll teach ya how to do this when we get the time."

"Thank you," I said.

No matter what I was doing, I thought of it as time not spent with the book, and each time I was done with what I was doing, I went back to it, even at night under a full moon, the light just strong enough. But then I was without the help of those who could read, because they claimed that they could not see what I was seeing on the leaf. When the sun rose in the morning, Beckwith ordered the ship moved out to sea, Will Kelsey telling me that because of our little depredations there on shore, he 'wanted to get us under the 'ill.' I did not understand this, and he explained that if we went thirty or so mile out to sea, we'd hide under the curvature of the earth. When I did not register an understanding of this, he said, "Pono, the world is round." It was, he said, a floating ball in the heavens, like the moon, but much larger. We were moving through water upon this floating ball, and this is what explained hiding under the hill.

I thought that surely Will Kelsey was mad, and dismissed the notion as a fabrication of a man who'd had too much of that grog that had made Owen Bew so stumblingly amiable once he lit his gourd with the crushed leaves stuffed therein.

So went these days. The men did partake of their grog in the evenings, a little of which I tried drinking, much to my rueful surprise, for it burned my throat and then sent me into a hollow, dizzying dream in which my own voice sounded to me faint and distant, and this reminded me of the 'awa to which I had had a similar reaction. I did not like the sensation, and once I was cured of the effects of this and emerged from that confused dream, I went back to my book. Still dizzy with it, I turned the leaves while the men watched, some of them laughing at me and whispering to one another.

Within a few days of our making our way under the hill, so that the outline of that place we had gone to was a faint shape stretched across the horizon, I had begun to try using these words. "You, then, are an adventurer," to which Beckwith said, "Indeed I am."

I would find appropriate occasions for their uses. Once, having in mind two words, I was sitting with the men, Beckwith this time among us, and was aware of a strange, languid atmosphere on the ship, as if all were growing weary of waiting for Beckwith to decide where we would go next. So I said, "I am doing only two things in the way of work on this ship, so I need an assignment of an agenda for additional work."

There was a brief silence while the men looked at one another, and then they all began laughing: "Arr ar ar ar! Agenda! Assignment! Arr ar ar."

"Or I can work in alternation with one of the other men."

"Arr ar ar ar ar!"

"The men are having a bit of fun at your expense, Pono."

"Aye, it is apparent."

And so I continued, storing each of these words in my memory, also words which I was told no one would ever use: asseveration, ataxy, attainted. I continued as Beckwith made up his mind and we set sail once again, this time north for the South China Sea. The season of bad weather would soon be upon us, and his logic was to find calmer seas to pass the winter. My immersion in the task of this language exhausted the first letter, 'a,' and went on to 'b,' which brought on more 'arr ar ar' from the men, who waited for my pronouncement of these words. We were moving, and had I many tasks to perform in helping the men navigate the great ship. I learned much in the way of knotting ropes, of the repair of such things as snapped clew-lines, of the preparation and treatment of ropes using liquefied tar, how to help raise sails and lower sails. As for the cannons, I was given to understand that I'd best leave those alone. I knew also that each day of that ship's leaning against the wind and sweeping through the water took me farther and farther away from my world, and each night I waited for Manomano's voice to come to me, but it did not. I was too far away, and I did ask Beckwith about this. "As we are bearing north—"

"Arr! Bearing!"

"Ignore them Pono," Beckwith said. "They've nothing else to do."

"When shall we return to my world?"

Beckwith mused upon this, sighed, and looked around at the blank sea. "Aye," he said. "You want to return to your world, and we'll do that. But it'll take some time."

One day I chanced upon something that I was given to understand later that I should not have seen. It was such that the task of learning their language caused in me a feverish need to make connections, so I would identify an object in the book and then go somewhere on the ship to look at it, to fix in my mind the object and the word. I have already mentioned Mr. Tom Crabbe, and now mention Jack Audrey, a small, passive British man whom Beckwith saved from the rope in a place called Mexico. Crabbe, a blustery man who carried on his face a perpetual leer of displeasure, spoke their language with his teeth bared, and appeared always to be thinking about something that bothered him. Audrey and Crabbe were friends, I knew, but that day I found a word relating to an object that I knew to be in the hold of the ship, beneath the men's sleeping quarters, and went down into the hot and uncomfortable atmosphere of the ship's innards. There, by the opening to the sleeping quarters, I heard grunting sounds as if someone were working down there, and stepped inside and saw them on a bunk, Crabbe atop the smaller one, both of them on their knees. They saw me and paused, and I moved out of their quarters. Returning to the deck, I thought words from my language: moi aikāne, or *friend mating*, and māhū, or in your language, *homosexual.*

Back on deck, I beheld Beckwith looking at me, and then he sighed. "Aye, you've been down there 'ave you? And you saw Crabbe and Audrey?"

"Yes."

"What do those in your world feel about men like that? What is their opinion?"

"Opinion? I do not know the word. It is in the O part of the books."

"Ar!" Will Kelsey said.

Beckwith waved his hands at him. "Opinion is how you look upon those who do this. Do your people dislike it?"

"No," I said. "People of my world know that this is how some are born. It is a part of the world of a few, not part of the world of most."

"In England if a sodomite is arrested, it is likely that he'll be turned off the cart for being a sodomite as much as anything else."

I understood the word because he had used it in reference to the two men. "In my world," I said, "they are who they are. Little else is thought."

"So," Beckwith said. "We all know these men, and we look the other way."

I thought about that expression. "Very well," I said. "I shall look the other way."

Roger Beckwith's interest in chickens, I discovered, was not as much for their eggs but for their acuity in catching insects. I had not, as of our trip to King Phillip's Land, seen the 'old, or hold of the ship. A portion of the ship's belly was a large room with walls sweeping up in graceful arcs from a low floor above the ship's keel, and that floor perpetually sloshed with stinking water, which at times we carried out in buckets to dump over the side. Beckwith's cargo was made up of three things: muskets, powder in small kegs, and a pile of what they called 'pelts,' various animal skins from what they called North America. But upon the chickens getting acclimated to life on the ship, Beckwith decided one day to put two of them to work in the hold. I was given the task of holding one of them under my arm as we climbed down. Other men went down with candles, so that the entire room was bathed in a rich light, not unlike dawn light, and the two chickens we carried were rigid with fright and confused by the proceedings. The men did this without removing the main hatch to let light in, because their 'prey' as they called it, would flee toward the darkness. The chicken I held looked at me with wary doubt as I placed my feet upon the planks suspended above the water in the bottom of the hold. One man then approached the large pile of pelts and drew one back, upon which insects appeared, and then my chicken became animated, struggling to free itself from my hands. I let it go upon the pale skin of the reverse side of this pelt, and the chicken raced around upon it pecking insects, its throat producing a high-pitched grumble of anticipation and pleasure. It would stop, staring at the hair at the edge of the pelt, and then strike, and then did it begin to scratch the pelt, much to the delight of the men, who then threw another pelt back amid the squawking and the flapping of wings, and the chickens continued their studious pursuit of the insects.

When these two were sated, Beckwith had us put them back in the pen and grab two more, and we spent most of the day doing this, the chickens unrelentingly industrious in their pursuit of the insects. After that day, the chickens who had been suspicious and shy upon anyone's approach, jumped against the wire of their cage each time a man passed. Beckwith did then bestow names upon each of them: Elizabeth, Mary, Catherine, Moll Jones, Amey Price, Mary Barton, and Madam Churchill. They were, I was given to understand, the names of queens of the country of their origin, England, those being the first two, and the names of murderesses, whores, and pickpockets, the remaining five, those 'anged for their misdeeds. For why, Beckwith mused, shouldn't these malefactors keep the company of royalty? This bit of levity brought rueful laughter from the men.

Upon our travel into what they called the South China Sea, Beckwith did again have the ship pause for days on end, then move by night, and again pause for days on end. This appeared to aggravate the men. One day Will Kelsey stood at the rail staring out at the blank ocean, and said to me, "This be a pointless enterprise, Pono. That man ain't going to become the Governor of nothing."

"I do not understand."

"Aye, I'll tell ye. The great 'enry Morgan was a pirate, and became the governor of Jamaica. Now you don't know what that is, but I'll tell ye it's a place bigger than yours." He looked out over the water and snorted. "And Beckwith? 'e'll end up like William Kid. Another pirate who went back to buy his way out of his crimes, and they 'anged him. Aye, they did that. We can never go home."

"And where shall we go now?" I asked.

"We'll move up the coast of bloody China until he finds a place where there's death, where there's the smell of the most awful of 'orrors I tell ye. Aye, but 'e's—" Kelsey stopped there. "Aye. We're alive," he said, nodding. "We're here."

12.

I suppose that the anxiety of the men was matched by a strange pause in me, for during some days I felt an odd sensation of a wispy beckoning of something I could not identify. During the nights I lay in my hammock waiting for sleep, and one of these nights I had either a dream or a vision, I cannot say, because I was between sleep and wakefulness, when a faint voice came to me across the water. This made me sit up, my eyes wide and searching the blackness, for I did not know what the voice meant, and then I realized that it was the voice of Manomano telling me that Pekau waited for me in the clouds.

I got up out of the hammock and stood at the rail. Did this mean that she was dead? Then I either remembered more of what this voice had told me or manufactured this, I do not know. Pekau waited for me in the clouds because she had been sought by the warriors of Muapo, seeking vengeance upon my family for the death of Kahimoku. And with that came the vision of a tattoo-bedecked warrior who would find her: Mo'omake, my brother. And what of my parents? I could recall nothing in the voice that told me what had become of them. But if Pekau waited for me in the clouds, what of my children? Did they wait with Pekau in the clouds? During the succeeding days I could not get this whispered message out of my mind, and noted that in the night, the voice did not return.

How many days would it take Manomano's voice to reach me? If the voice traveled at the speed of sound, where as I child I had been fascinated by watching from some distance a man break a coconut and noted the pause before the sound reached me, then Manomano's voice might have traveled mere days to get to me. But if his voice traveled at the speed of a man walking, then it might have taken months. I was tempted to grieve, but I did not know with any certainty that the voice told me the truth. And so we made our way toward bloody China. I assumed it was another place like Phillip's Land, shrouded in mist and covered by forest.

One day, far to the east, there appeared on the horizon a hazy shape that went from the left of the pale sunrise to the right, high and cloud-topped, and Beckwith had the ship move along this shape for days. I was told it was China, and I conceived of it as a large island, but as we sailed along this hazy shape, perhaps fifty miles out from it, I began to wonder about the size of the place. And then Will Kelsey told me it was an island called Formosa, which was off the coast of China.

Beckwith then had the men raise a square of fabric with a picture of a leaf on it, up the mast-pole near to the top, so that it fluttered in the wind, and Will Kelsey told me that it was a 'flag' that announced us as an obscure trading company, "in competition with British East India," he said. I asked him what that was, and he told me it was the great sea trading company of England.

And then we were inside what was called the Formosa Strait, the ocean between that island and a landmass I was given to understand was hundreds of times larger than the island we had spent so many days passing. Beckwith was looking for an inlet wherein he could hide the ship and 'winter over,' as the men called it. By this time I had seen maps in the encyclopedia showing all that was important in the world, and oddly these maps did not include the middle of the great ocean where my world lay. Because my world was not represented, I could not at first fix in my mind how large these other masses of land might be, until Beckwith one day showed me an approximation of my world, using his quill pen. He placed a series of dots at the edge of a page showing the great ocean we had traversed in order to arrive at King Phillip's land, and these dots, he told me, were the size of the great islands of my world. "They are small," I said.

"Aye," he said. "They are very small."

I understood the principle of the world as a floating ball, gravity the factor that made it such that things remained on that ball. Fascinating as this study was for me, I was aware also of the quiet, musing anxiety of the men. They greatly respected Beckwith, but the problem of his traveling the world in search of human fault put the men into a state of anticipatory fright, as if any day he might find that place on the coast of bloody China to drop the anchor near that horror and death they knew he was looking for.

Indeed he had to find some protection for the ship, for bad weather began to lash against its side, making me sway at night in the sound of my ropes grating the wood in the hammock, sometimes with rushes of rain hurled horizontally that would wet me as I tried to sleep. I knew this weather, for it was the approach of Makahiki time in my world, when the ocean became rough and fishermen stayed out of it, both because of the kapu and because the prospects of fishing were thwarted by that weather. Other ships, I was told, went to a place called Canton, a great port city wherein sailors could find excellent accommodations and women 'aplenty,' according to Will Kelsey.

But I knew by this time that we could be seen by no other ship. Thus did we move along the coast of China, with Canton to our south and a place called Shanghai to our north. Beckwith studied his maps, and settled upon the region of a place called Ning-po, a small port on the China coast inside a series of islands peopled by fishermen. We could not go to Ning-po, but we could find shelter perhaps in smaller villages that lay along that coast.

This plan settled the men somewhat, but one day early in the morning, Jack Audrey was up the mast, and saw sails on the horizon to the east. This animated Beckwith, who climbed partway up with his golden telescope, and for some time he hung there on the mast, his feet on the ropes, studying the sails. "Aye," he called, "she's British, lads. And you know they've seen us."

Beckwith jammed the end of the telescope in his eye and continued looking. "Will!" he called. "Where do you see the weather coming from?"

"West northwest, sir!" he called back.

"Aye, then we wait. She's a seventy-four."

This announcement made the men suddenly anxious, whispering to one another and staring out at the horizon. We could all see it now, not the body of the ship but its sails. Will Kelsey sighed, and looked back over his shoulder at the weather over the shape of the coast. "Aye," he said, "I can tell by the cut of her jib. It's a seventy-four all right, and we're in some trouble I tell ye."

"What is a seventy-four?" I asked.

"Man-o-war. Seventy-four cannons, and we've got twelve. We're a Corvette, which is near being a Brig, and that ship's got three 'undred men on it. Now they'll decide whether or not to come and board us. All we've got is a little more speed, perhaps."

Where first the sails of that ship moved slightly upon the sharp line of the horizon, they remained in one place, and slowly turned so that we saw their great width. I could not at first gauge the size of it until those sails enlarged on the horizon, very tall they were, and then I did sense the difference. That ship was more than twice *The Tiburon*, and although I knew nothing of these names Corvette and Seventy-Four, the cannon numbers for each was enough to frighten me: twelve to seventy-four.

Will Kelsey conferred with Beckwith. The weather, he thought, might bring a squall or two later in the day. The sails of the seventy-four sat there on the horizon, but within an hour it was clear that they had enlarged, and so Beckwith continued studying the sky above the shape of the coast on the opposite side and readied the men for action. The sky was darkening, and we felt wind from that side, colder than earlier in the day. "Aye," Beckwith said, "isn't it a wonder how the old girl helps us when we need it."

"Who is the old girl?" I asked Will Kelsey.

"Nature," he said.

"She's coming!" Jack Audrey called.

We could now see the hull of the great ship. I studied it as it enlarged on the horizon. The sails were immense compared to ours, billowed in that wind and tipping slightly away from its direction. The men looked at Beckwith, who stared in the direction opposite of the seventy-four. The squall had now blocked our view of the land to the north, and appeared to be moving down the coast and swelling out over the ocean toward us. "Will we set out to use our cannons?" I asked Will Kelsey.

"No," he said. "We will not."

"Twelve, fourteen mile!" Jack Audrey shouted.

"We will talk to them, then," I said, beginning to feel quite anxious about this.

"Lads!" Beckwith called, "bring her about and head for that coast!" Will Kelsey left, and the men began running about and climbing the booms, unfurling sails that popped open and rounded away from the wind, tipping the ship so that I had to place my hand on the rail. The men worked quickly, and the ship began moving toward the coast, the remaining part visible to the south, the part we were headed for shrouded in rain. The seventy-four had now enlarged on the horizon, itself leaning in the wind, and I could see white at the level of the ocean through which it carved its way. *The Tiburon* now moved at a lusty pace toward the coast, although Will Kelsey, now at the wheel, had to fight it into a slight tack. And it seemed that the seventy-four gained on us as we made our way.

Beckwith stood atop the aft portion, his hands gripped on a pole to which the mizzen was attached, and watched the seventy-four, then turned and studied the rain.

"Can I assist in any way?" I called to him.

"Aye, assist by hangin' onto the rail, Pono."

Dick Burrows, who had climbed down from the mast, had made his way along toward me, walking with one hand braced on the rail. He had a somewhat amused expression on his face, and said, "Watch the old magician at work."

"You boys at the ready?" Beckwith yelled.

Beckwith watched the seventy-four. It had become quite large, and it seemed that in ten or twenty minutes it would overtake us, for it was close enough now that I could faintly perceive the shapes of men at the rails, tiny in comparison with the great bulk of the ship. Beckwith continued looking off the stern at the seventy-four, and then toward the coast, that had now vanished in the rain. And then I felt the large raindrops on my face and arms, and it increased in its strength, windblown and heavy. Beckwith then turned. "Will! Port!"

"Aye!" Will Kelsey yelled, and then did the ship lean, so much that I thought it might roll over, and we were in the heavy rain, the seventy-four out there beginning to turn also, as if to overtake us at an angle, but the rain fell so heavily that it vanished into it, and I thought that the ship would right itself into a downwind race, but it did not.

"Hold to port!" Beckwith yelled, and the ship, leaning dangerously, righted itself quickly and fell to leaning the other way so that Burrows and I had to pull ourselves against the rail rather than push. Deep in the bowels of the ship I heard something clatter upon a floor, followed by a sound from old Owen Bew: "Arr!" Burrows laughed.

We were making a tight circle, and once that circle was completed, we beat to windward, Kelsey spinning the wheel one way and then the other, so that we tacked to the north in a tight pattern in which the ship tipped to one side and then the other. "There," Burrows said. "That Brit seventy-four is chasing us south."

Beckwith had waited until the seventy-four was close, cut to port just as the rain came and shrouded us from their view, and then had continued port in a circle. If the deception worked, then the seventy-four was moving in the opposite direction from ours.

We beat into this rain for the remainder of the day and on into the night, Beckwith on the starboard rail peering into the darkness for any sign of land, the men fearing running upon a shoal. The rain decreased, and I beheld faint lights off the port rail. It was the coast of China, and those lights were in the homes of its people.

And as the sun rose, we moved along that coast, which showed itself as a high, rugged cliff, the lower portions spotted with tiny villages that had clusters of dwellings perched upon rock outcroppings. We were perhaps two miles away from this coast, and I could see, standing at the rail, small boats moving parallel to us, as if inviting us to come in. Will Kelsey told me that these were fishermen and merchants eager for trade, for our ship was small enough, and square-rigged to appear to be what he called an old brigantine, no great threat to the villagers. But Beckwith was not satisfied with what he saw. We moved slowly, Beckwith at the rail with the telescope jammed in his eye, from time to time muttering, "What's this? Aye. It's not secure enough for us," and "Ah! The land's too low there, lads," and "Aye, charmin' enough I'll say, but a trap is what it is."

And so we moved along that coast for two days. Beckwith had a man high up the mast most of the time, scanning the ocean horizon for sails. But it was the nature of the land we passed that began to bring more anxiety to the men, for they seemed to know something was about to occur that they feared. And then one day we saw a cloud of smoke and dust that hovered over the high coast's profile, and no longer did boats move parallel to us. This interested Beckwith, for he wondered what it could have been that would make that coastline appear so desolate, despite the presence of little villages perched upon the rugged, stony outcroppings. Had there been a forest fire? What iniquity might have visited this place? he wondered.

We smelled the remnants of smoke, an acrid tinge in the air, and Beckwith, his interest stimulated by this, had the ship angle slightly along that shore, to bring it closer so that we might see what was amiss there. The men looked at one another with skeptical, sometimes fearful sidelong glances. Was it merely a fire, or something else? Inside that dead embers smell in the air, we began to catch the hint of carrion. Beckwith was now convinced that one of those villages was worth a look, and Will Kelsey, standing with me at the rail, turned to me and said, "Any other man would get the bloody 'ell away from this place, but him, ah, now there's a difference."

I clearly saw the dwellings of the people, the sparse strip of shoreline fronting the paths that went up to one outcropping or another, each with its cluster of buildings. Owen Bew was at the rail now, having come up from his stove, and he scanned the shoreline, then sniffed the air. "Aye," he said. "I'll wager we're staying here a while." He pointed toward the northern part of the coast we observed. "See that inlet there?"

It was a series of shoals and outcroppings offshore that appeared to provide a protected inner harbor of sorts, in which small boats were anchored, odd-appearing square-rigged canoes that resembled those canoes of my seafaring forebears, although I was not sure. The outcroppings appeared high enough to hide the entire ship, including the rigging. Beckwith decided that there was where we would anchor for a rest. I asked Owen Bew what 'a rest' was, and he said, "Months." Beckwith conferred with Will Kelsey and Jack Audrey on the possible hazards in that water, shoals and the like, and determined that we would lower the small boat and tow *The Tiburon* into the cove, for here, in the lee of the great rocky coast, there was no wind, and the water appeared calm.

Upon our approach, many of the sails tied off on their booms, we were assaulted by that odor, now stronger. Ahead, just below the jib boom, we saw a white body floating face down, its arms out and bloated, its legs splayed and its buttocks clearing the water, rounded and plump as if to burst. The person appeared to be studying with great interest something on the ocean floor. "'e's got no 'ead sir," Will Kelsey called.

"Aye," Beckwith said. "We shall keep at it then."

Tom Crabbe's face went into a doubtful sneer. "So, 'e's found it then," he said. Jack Audrey, appearing somewhat nauseated by the body, moved back behind Crabbe.

"Another!" Will Kelsey called. This one was smaller, perhaps a boy. I could not determine from up on the deck. It was not as bloated as the first we saw, but indeed, it had no head. Strings of a pale, mucous-like material drifted from its severed neck.

"Mr. Audrey," Beckwith said, "'ow's your Chinese?"

"I don't know what dialect they speak here sir."

"Our 'osts're out there!" Will Kelsey called.

Beckwith turned to us, smiling amiably. "Pono, you, Dick and the Seager brothers get out your muskets. Please bring out six more. We'll not need cannon I believe, but Dick, let Owen know that we'll 'ave to have the port cannons ready."

"Aye."

"And Tom," he said to Crabbe, "go on down into the 'old and pick out three nice pelts and one small keg of powder."

Our hosts, as Will Kelsey had called them, moved toward us in a small fishing boat, and appeared to be two old men, and a boy pulling on oars. The men were thin and bearded and dressed in pale tan smocks, the boy dark and naked to the waist, wearing a loincloth. I was fascinated by their facial features, eyes that were long and narrow, their noses and lips not unlike those of my world.

They maneuvered their little boat right past one of the floating corpses, the boy raising one of his oars so that it swept over the corpse, the drips off the blade dropping onto the exposed buttocks. Jack Audrey went to the rail, and with the help of Will Kelsey, rolled the net over the side so that the men could climb onboard. Two came up, the boy and one of the men, and just as they did so, we saw two more boats, slightly larger, leave the shore and begin making their way to us.

"Mind, lads," Beckwith said, watching them. "Be ready with the muskets should they be hostile." The two other boats, however, rested alongside the first, while Jack Audrey sat facing the man and the boy, and talked with them.

The language they spoke was melodic, with many drawn out 'o' sounds, and 'haa' sounds, and Dick Burrows stood next to me watching, his musket cradled in his elbow, but the way in which he watched had a special pattern: he looked up the high, rugged bluffs, then behind at the ocean, then to the village, then up the bluffs once again. I should say that he was a man with extremely keen senses and a brooding, contemplative bearing that never changed, as if even sleeping, he would somehow be alert. After some time he looked at me and said, "I don't get a thing they say, but we'll find out."

And in time we did. We learned, first, that we were free to come and visit this village, but the state it was in at the moment was not one particularly pleasing for visitors. I was to learn this later in the day, in effect a short history-lesson by Roger Beckwith delivered to those of us who were interested. The problem was as follows: the cloud of dust and smoke we had seen was from up over those bluffs, where earlier in the day and in the two days preceding those, some two thousand five hundred people, boys and men, had been beheaded because of their hair.

The country we visited was run by an emperor named Qian-long, who was identified by Beckwith as 'a Manchu,' the name given to the people of the ruling dynasty of this place. The people of this village identified themselves as 'Hanren,' or Han Chinese, the people who had lived here for many centuries. The Manchus had invaded the country from the north some hundred fifty years earlier, and imposed upon the people their way of life, their garb and their manner of sporting hair. At this information Beckwith sighed, and thought for a few moments. "There you 'ave it lads," he said. "All of this is over some hair."

It is an oversimplification to suggest that hair could have so much to do with the life or death of people. It is merely a symbol of a deeper imposition of will, Beckwith explained. This story fascinated me because of the similarity it bore to the history of my people, that certain conditions of our existence had been imposed upon us by people who had found their way to our world some two hundred years earlier, the awful fruits of our being found creating such stories as the one my father told me about his forebear who, upon presenting himself to the ali'i in hopes of regaining some contact with his lost wife, had his eyes gouged out.

The boy was the son of a man embittered by these impositions, a thinker and scholar living in a world in which thinking and scholarship were forbidden, as were other things: muskets, gunpowder, writing of any kind, in an edict identified as 'Wen zi yu,' and the aforementioned manner of sporting hair. So the man had taught, had written, and had cut off a braid at the back crown of his head, and his followers imitated him in a small, personal rebellion against the domination of these Manchus. The punishment was to have that offending head removed. The boy, laboriously trying to make clear to Jack Audrey the details of this story, ended it by saying that his father, mother, and sisters were somewhere up there over that bluff, and he hoped that they might still be alive. The villagers here were all hiding, for the emperor's soldiers might return to continue exacting the penalty until every head in the region was removed.

This information made the men wary, so that they looked up the rugged sea-cliffs, Will Kelsey taking Beckwith's telescope and aiming it at the top of the line of bluffs. "Beckwith's taken the bait I tell ye," Jack Crabbe said to me, his leer showing fright. "Aye, he has, and we're going up there to find that boy's family."

And indeed it was true. By the time the conference was complete, the sun had dropped to the horizon, so that the faces of the men glowed a warm orange. We would venture up those bluffs in the morning. In the meantime, we would secure the ship in the cove and request a source of water to fill our casks. Our visitors offered food, but were apologetic, for the smell in the air would do little to stimulate our palates. Beckwith declined the offer, instructing Jack Audrey to inform them that we would be ready to go up the bluffs just after dawn, if the boy and the two old men would be there to lead the way.

I should say here that as I observed these men, the men in the boats below us, and the boy, I was struck by the dignity of their bearing, the boy particularly, for in his explanation of the events, laboring over words to communicate with Jack Audrey, he bore himself with the thoughtful, intelligent presence of a man. His name was Tong Guan, named after, he said, a famous eunuch of literature, although he had no plans of a full imitation of the life and condition of his namesake. Will Kelsey explained this to me. So with the dropping of the sun, the men relieved one another so that some could sleep while others stood watch. I sat in my hammock, watching the black silhouette of Dick Burrows against the faint whiteness of the village houses, and that silhouette did not move for much of the night. Sometime before dawn, I believe, he found some time to sleep.

The sun rose behind the high bluffs, and we could see a gray sky behind the trees on the bluff's top, but little else except the faint colors of the dwellings in the village, and with the gradual lightening of the sky came an intensified version of the death-smell from the previous day. Beckwith selected five men: myself, Dick Burrows, Will Kelsey, Jack Audrey and Tom Crabbe, and instructed the remaining men to stay by the ship, keep the cannons ready to roll out, and keep watch on the surroundings. Should they wish to explore the little village, he said, they should do so in fives. There was no mention of cavorting with women. The men seemed to prefer to remain on the ship.

Because the older men had not the energy, the boy named Tong Guan led us up the bluff on a steep, winding path with narrow sections supported by carefully stacked rocks. To our right, as we climbed, I saw a strange device, a track with ropes suspended above it, every fifteen feet or so separated by a wheel affixed to the mountainside. It was a pulley, Will Kelsey told me between gasps for breath. At the bottom, or the top, he said, there was a platform or a basket that could be raised or lowered, fish from below, various goods from above. We had little else to say. The climb was difficult, the musket hanging on my shoulder rolling on by back as I looked for good footing. The farther up we went, the stronger was that smell of death, and I could see, from time to time above me, Tom Crabbe looking back down at the ocean with that doubtful leer on his face, his yellow teeth showing. Beckwith was just behind Tong Guan, who was in the lead. From time to time Tong Guan stopped to allow us to rest, and conferred past Beckwith to Jack Audrey, who in turn whispered interpretations to Beckwith.

Upon reaching the top of the bluff, we were all breathless, but remained wary and careful, for according to Tong Guan, the emperor's soldiers might be there in the town. But upon our waiting and looking down over a series of rooftops of baked clay tiles, we determined that the town was probably empty. Some of the structures emitted smoke, and had been burned inside. Dick Burrows looked at an opening between two lines of dwellings to a narrow path between them, and held up his hand. "Wait here," he said. He tiptoed to the first structure, and then looked around at the path, and then waited, listening. All I heard was the buzzing of flies.

Dick Burrows waved us forward, and so we moved to that opening. From there, we could see the first bodies, lying some fifty paces away, the heads lined up against the bases of some of the structures. "Aye," Tom Crabbe whispered, "this isn't a place for living people. I say we leave this place."

"We will," Roger Beckwith said, "in time."

Then, between us and those bodies in the distance, an old woman emerged from a building, threw a pan of yellow liquid into the street, and turned and went back into the building. "Well, how d'ye like that?" Crabbe said.

Tong Guan spoke to Jack Audrey. Audrey turned to Beckwith and said, "For the old, life continues as before, he says."

"He is a clever boy," Beckwith said. "Let us move on, lads."

We walked up to and past those headless bodies, the heads lined up against the base of the building in various expressions of deep thought, surprise, weariness, sleep, and one with his mouth open as if he were about to make a pronouncement of some sort, the splotches of blackened blood under them covered with flies. The stench was quite strong, and the severed necks of the corpses glistened with the movement of maggots. Some of the corpses were without clothes, the genitals swollen and dark as were the hands. We stepped lightly around them, myself glad that some time ago I had been given sandals.

At length we emerged in a widening of the lane between the buildings, and there we saw so many bodies that they would be impossible to count, piled as they were next to a smaller mound of heads. Old women sat around the perimeter of this opening, staring at the bodies and waving flies away from their own eyes.

Tong Guan stared at the mound of heads. He spoke to Jack Audrey for some time, gesturing, searching for words, and finally Audrey said, "He says it is useless. He knows his father is in there. His mother and sisters have fled, unless his sisters have been abducted by the soldiers. He does not know what he shall do now, for the condition of his own head is such that if he is seen, he will lie some distance from his head too, like these men." Then the boy crossed the opening to address another old woman.

As he did so, I walked to the corner of one of the structures and then along its side, to see what was behind it. The odor was not as bad there, and behind the dwelling I saw chickens scratching in dirt, and smaller structures, one of which had a line of dark disks leading to its door. Will Kelsey had seen me going back there and made his way along the side of the structure.

"What brings ye out here?" he asked.

"I was curious," I said. "I see bloodstains by that tiny house there."

"Hmm," said he. "Someone in there, I suspect."

I checked the works of my musket, ran my thumb on the rough patch of the frizzen, and then made my way to that small house. I pulled on a rope attached to the door, at which it opened, and inside sat a boy with a stick buried in his shoulder, broken off about half a foot from its entry point, which drew the fabric of a smock into the hole. His leggings were of the same material, and he had them drawn up against his chest. The smock was matted with blood, and the boy looked up at me with eyes like Tong Guan's, but strangely placid, as if he were assessing me with a thoughtful objectivity. I held up my hand and then knelt down to see more closely, at which the boy made a moaning sound of protest. I reached over his shoulder, and felt the point of the stick on the other side. It was not unlike the point of a pololū.

"There isn't anything you can do for her," Will Kelsey said from behind me.

"Is this not a boy?"

"Pono, it's a woman."

I looked again. The eyes stayed on me. I saw now that her hair was tied behind her head, and with it tight against her head in that manner, she had appeared to be a boy.

"Well, thirteen, fourteen year old maybe," Will Kelsey said.

"We must try to help her," I said.

"She's beyond 'elp, Pono. Come, we're going."

When I backed away, she continued looking at me, her mouth open slightly. The expression shook me, for I thought of Ka'ahupāhau, and that expression she had always worn, as if waiting for the answer to some question she had asked.

I closed the door and followed Will Kelsey out to the others.

Tong Guan was done conferring with the old woman. Beckwith listened to Jack Audrey's translation of what she had said, that all the men were dead and the women were either with the soldiers or in the forests. Thinking of the girl in the little house, I asked Jack Audrey to ask Tong Guan if his sisters were young, and the translation that came back was that they were not.

"We shall move on beyond this place," Beckwith said, "see if anyone's alive out there." Tong Guan, by this time, had gone to speak with another of the old women. After doing this he returned and spoke with Jack Audrey.

"This woman says the soldiers are out there rounding up more," he said. "Sir," and the expression on his face had changed to one of a pleading logic, "I believe we've done what we've come up here for. We should go back down."

"Aye," Beckwith said. "We shall. You and Tom go on back to the top of the bluff then. Take the boy with you. Will, Pono, Dick and I shall look around a bit."

Will Kelsey looked at me, and then studied the works of his musket. Then he snorted softly. "Aye," he whispered. "This is 'ow it is."

Tom Crabbe and Jack Audrey turned to make their way back, but Tong Guan was unwilling to go with them. This brought about the problem of translation, and Jack Audrey thought, shook his head ruefully, and agreed to accompany us. Tom Crabbe was unwilling to go back without Jack, and so we decided, all of us, to continue on.

Dick Burrows walked far ahead of us, over a brushy landscape spotted with vegetable patches. Once away from the village, I saw what beautiful country this was, with large mountains in the distance in a bluish haze, dark forests on their flanks. The village itself was set in a depression in the great bluffs over the ocean.

We walked for perhaps an hour, seeing little, and assuming that people were hiding, we turned to go back. The day had become warmer, and I think Beckwith and the others wearied of this exploration because we had become hungry and thirsty. At just the time that I had fallen into a speculative, almost dreamy phase, my feet becoming sore, Dick Burrows, out ahead of us, stopped and held up his hand. We waited while he stood there listening, sniffing the air, and thinking. I heard nothing but the distant squawking of a chicken, and birdcalls. Then he found a boulder and placed the side of his head against it, and remaining there for some time, his ear pressed against the stone, he gestured with his hand toward the ocean. "He's got something," Beckwith said.

Burrows came back. "It's wagons," he said. "And maybe a horse or two, I can't tell. They're over there toward the bluffs."

"Can they see the ship from the bluffs?" Beckwith asked.

"No, they can't, because there's those two high peaks there." He pointed. "They can't see it unless they climb up on them, and I don't think they will. But it's wagons."

We looked, but saw nothing. I could not determine how it was that he had come to this conclusion, and asked Will Kelsey, who laughed and said, "I don't know either. The man's got senses no man has."

"They're moving toward the village," Burrows said. "I'd say we get there first, because I don't want to fight my way to that path down the bluff."

"Aye," Beckwith said. "You've a point."

We walked toward the village, while Dick Burrows, his musket in one hand, ran toward the bluffs and then along some trees, paralleling our movement. At length he ran at an angle toward us, and with the village now visible in the distance, he came up to Beckwith. Somewhat breathless, he said, "It's a group of maybe thirty soldiers all decked out in their helmets and uniforms, mostly with spears and bows 'n arrows. Can't tell if there's muskets. There's a group of maybe forty village folk walkin' along with 'em, and maybe five men in a wagon all tied up. Led by one man on horseback."

"And what is the object, d'ye think?"

"I'd say there going to execute the men in the wagon down there to the village." Tong Guan spoke softly with Jack Audrey, who reported to the boy what Burrows had seen. The boy nodded, spoke more with Audrey. Then Audrey turned to Beckwith.

"Dick's right," he said. "Stragglers, they be. Hunted down and now to 'ave their 'eads cut off." And he thought a moment. "For their hair it is, then."

"Aye," Beckwith said. "'ow much time 'ave we?" he asked Dick Burrows.

"We'll get there ten or fifteen minutes before they will."

Beckwith looked at us. "Gents," he said, "I think we should not fire on these men, given there are thirty of them so he says. Jack, tell the boy we've got to leave, and that if he's got the will for it, he can come with us."

"You sure you want a chinee on the ship?" Burrows asked.

"If I've got an American on the ship, I'd say a chinee's about the same."

Burrows laughed. "You got me there, Roger."

Upon our return to the village, Dick Burrows turned back, and made a line closer to the bluffs to keep watch until he saw the soldiers. The stench of the bodies and heads was now quite strong, because it was midday. The old women had left. Jack Audrey and Tom Crabbe made their way back toward the steep path, leaving me with Will Kelsey, Beckwith and Tong Guan. The boy appeared anxious, I believe because he suspected that one of the men in the wagon could be his father. In those few minutes before the soldiers were to arrive, I went back to the last building in the line before the open area and retraced my steps to the little house wherein I had seen the young woman. I opened the door, and there she sat, as before, the broken end of the spear driven through the top of her chest on the right side. She looked up at me, staring with that same placid, waiting expression. "I cannot help you," I said.

She whispered something in her language, then blinked, and sighed. Then she continued staring, and began to make soft moaning sounds, as if quietly rendering to the air before her some drawn out, dreamlike chant. I heard a sound behind me. It was Will Kelsey gesturing to me to come back. The soldiers were coming.

We positioned ourselves in the lane where the heads had been lined up, hidden by the doorways of the little dwellings, with a good view of the open area where the larger mound of bodies lay. Beckwith reasoned that, even if we were seen, we could simply go to the path down toward the ocean, and the soldiers would not be able to follow us in any great numbers. But there was a change in the situation when the dust above the landscape drew near: Tong Guan had vanished. "Ye don't suppose he's going to fall in with that crowd of villagers, do you?" he asked Will Kelsey.

"I don't know," Kelsey said. "I understand that he wants to see if one of the people either in the crowd or in the wagon might be his father."

Inside a thatch dwelling with a good escape route on the other side, I could see the open area well, and the soldiers came into view shortly, on the curve of a wide dirt lane between trees. They appeared tall, and were dressed in red suits studded with metal, red leggings, and wore helmets shaped like the narrow ends of chicken eggs. They carried spears, and bows and arrows, which I was familiar with, because in my world boys made these devices and hunted birds and rats with them. All but one walked, while one, apparently the leader, sat atop a horse. The soldiers, weary and thirsty as they entered the open area, sought shade under the surrounding trees while the group of villagers entered the area. They appeared to be ordered by the leader to stand out in the sun, nearer to the mound of bodies over which hovered a cloud of black flies.

Then the wagon came in, pulled by another horse. There were six men in the wagon, bound so that their arms were trussed behind their backs, and all had weary, fatalistic expressions. Then I saw Tong Guan with the villagers, wearing a large conical hat made of reeds. He did not have that braid hanging down his back, and it was evident that he wanted to conceal this from the soldiers. I tiptoed to the lane doorway, and caught Will Kelsey's attention. "Where's Beckwith?" I whispered.

He nodded in the direction of the interior of the little house. Beckwith did then appear at the door. "Tong Guan," I whispered. "He is standing in with the villagers."

"Where is Dick?" he asked.

"In the back of your place," I said.

Beckwith vanished. Will Kelsey sighed, and looked mournfully at me across the stinking lane. "Aye," he whispered, "he's decided that the boy is coming with us to see the world. We're in for a fight."

The leader swung his leg over his horse's back and stepped to the ground, and then pulled a heavy-bladed sword from within the horse's colorful adornments. He stretched himself, looked around, and then studied the blade of the sword. He coughed, and adjusted his helmet. He stuck the point of the sword into the ground and looked at the men on the wagon, and then walked over to the shade to sit with the other soldiers. The heat was such that all in the sun appeared stultified by it, weary and without motivation. I saw Tong Guan move in the crowd of villagers, looking up at the wagon, and then he whispered to another villager and pointed. This did not draw the soldiers' attention, but I thought that if he was trying to conceal the lack of his braid, he should remain still. Then he turned and gazed in our direction, for he appeared to know that we were hiding in amongst the small dwellings.

The leader rose from the shade and with his hands dusted off his suit, carefully flicking debris off the fabric. He walked out into the sun, and then turned and spoke to the other soldiers. They all rose, some of them moving to the villagers and positioning themselves every five or so feet. Six of the soldiers moved to the wagon and two, putting their spears on the ground, reached up and pulled a man off the wagon. He landed in the dirt, and remained lying there with his knees drawn up. One soldier began prodding him with his spear, and he rose so that he was sitting on his knees.

I believe that because of the heat, the haze in the air, and the strange, dreamlike silence of these proceedings, the villagers watched with blank faces, and no movement save for Tong Guan, who looked around as if believing something might occur to prevent this.

My heart began beating rapidly, and it was made worse by the passivity of the villagers and the slow, languid movements of the soldiers, who seemed engaged in this with a weariness that contradicted the fact that they were about to kill someone. Only the leader seemed animated, but this was more a sort of blustery, self-aggrandized flourish of that sword, and then a studious pause to run his finger along the blade to test its sharpness. Then did he approach the kneeling man, raise the sword over his head, and in one quick motion bring it down through the man's neck, so that the head dropped in the dust while an arc of dark blood shot out from the back of his neck, at which the headless body flopped forward to its rest.

A soldier nudged the head away with his boot, so that the gaping, open-eyed face and the neck picked up dirt as it rolled. The leader stared at the body with a contemplative expression, and then two soldiers pulled another off the wagon. Tong Guan's animation now was such that he had moved to the front of the gathering of villagers, and when he turned to say something to one of them, soldiers saw him. Two went to him and pulled the large hat off, and then threw him toward the wagon so that he fell down. One of the men on the wagon began yelling, until a soldier prodded him with a spear, and Tong Guan then settled upon his knees, apparently accepting his fate.

The man who had yelled was pulled from the wagon. Tong Guan began weeping, and I understood that this was his father. The leader ordered the man to his knees, and he obeyed, and then did the leader repeat the swing, sending his head into the dirt after which his body flopped down upon it. Tong Guan did not move, and the leader turned to him, and then walked around to his side, preparing to behead him while the villagers looked on, blank faced and mute.

I wanted now to turn away from this, move away from this place. As the leader prepared to raise the sword, there came from behind him a loud, prolonged whistle, at which everyone turned. There, standing in the lane the group of soldiers had come down, stood a tall man in a grayish smock and a large, conical hat, and I saw the puff of smoke from a musket before I heard the sound, saw the leader's head jolt with the shock of the ball hitting his face, at which he sat down with a thump, the sword falling from his hand, and then all but a few of the soldiers yelled out and ran toward the man, who stood there, the musket across his chest. When the soldiers were within fifty paces of him, he turned and vanished into the lane. I looked back at the open area, and saw that Tong Guan was no longer there, and the remaining seven or eight soldiers were grouped around their dead leader. I understood. Dick Burrows.

When I got to the narrow path that would take me down to the ship, I saw Beckwith, Tong Guan, and the others already making their way. That Dick Burrows was not with them confirmed my suspicion, that he had donned the clothing of these people, shot the leader, and led those soldiers on a confusing chase into the forest.

He came down the path in darkness hours later. By this time the ship had been prepared to be towed back out to where we could have some wind catch the sails. Dick Burrows told us that the soldiers had picked up their leader and placed him in the wagon, and had struck out in search of the people responsible for his death. He had led them some distance down the lane, and "left sign," as he put it, that would make them chase this man for some time. In fact, the remaining people of the town had emerged from their hiding places to begin dealing with the many bodies strewn about.

I had thought we would leave then, but Beckwith held back on that decision, and because of this I found myself at the rail, staring into the darkness and wondering about the girl in the little house. I could not forget the horrible symmetry of Ka‘a in the cave and that girl, my sister's age, patiently waiting to die. And I wondered, why was it that no one went to help her? And why did she not seek the help of the people of the village? As the evening wore on, I was unable to think of anything else, and approached, first, Jack Audrey, and asked him if he might ask Tong Guan about this girl.

The two of them conversed for some time, the boy looking up the dark bluff, then back at Audrey. At length the latter turned to me. "He believes she is the daughter of the man who is responsible for the soldiers' appearance, a man not liked in the village, who cultivated pretensions of wealth and connection with the dynasty. He believes that either no one knows she is there, and perhaps if they do know, no one will help her."

"Is it her fault that her father is disliked by the villagers?" I asked.

"Of course it is not," he said. "But that does not alter the situation. Someone did this to her as an act of vengeance, he believes."

I fell again to musing, leaning upon the rail. Was I responsible for the depredations of my brother ‘Iolana? Clearly not. This girl was a victim as my sister had been a victim. I looked for Roger Beckwith. Will Kelsey told me that he was in his cabin, writing in a journal. I made my way into the hold past the sound of Owen Bew and his pots, and the sounds of snoring from the other direction, and found Beckwith's door open, Beckwith himself seated at his desk. He looked up at me. "Pono," he said. "What is that expression on your face? You are troubled."

Although so recently acquainted with this new language, I spoke, perhaps in the longest string of these strange words I had ever mustered. Upon finishing my account, I said, "I wish to go find her and bring her to the ship."

"She is not your sister, Pono."

"This is true," I said. "But I think of her as resembling a sister."

It was not difficult to negotiate the path by night, for the moon was out, creating a wide, undulating line of silver on the water. I carried my musket, and a small gourd of water, the gourd in this case a bluish glass bottle webbed with twine that hung from my side. Upon my reaching the top, I was assaulted by the stench of the bodies, and I noted as I stepped carefully into the lane that some of the little dwellings emitted light from windows. I made my way quietly past these dwellings. Some of the headless bodies had been removed. At the far end of the lane, I could see, still piled up in the center of the opening out to the fields, the same mound of bodies, Tong Guan's father one of them.

The little house was there, the door closed. I approached, and when I pulled the door open, I heard the sound of a quick, indrawn breath. She was still there, curled up, the broken spear-end still buried in the top of her chest. "I shall take you to the ship," I whispered. I reached down to touch her, and she drew back. I opened the water gourd and shook it a little, and her left hand fumbled at it. I opened it and held the gourd to her lips, and she drank. I believe she understood then that I was not there to hurt her, and after drinking some of the water, she sat there looking at me. I made my way inside and slid my hands under the backs of her knees and around her waist, and lifted her. She was light, and I could not believe that she was an adult. The movement of her body caused great pain, I believe, for she emitted soft, crooning sounds: "Ae, aeae, ae," and thus curled in my arms like a child, she submitted to the journey back.

As I carried her, she held her eyes on my face, her mouth open as if she were engaged in some careful speculation, a calm wonder that reminded me once again of Ka'ahupāhau's expression, that strange waiting as if for the answer to some cryptic question. Again I negotiated the path, without difficulty because she was so small.

Upon my arrival in the cutter, the woman cradled in my lap, Beckwith told the men to "belay your supersititons, for Pono is on a mission of mercy." Tong Guan did recognize the woman as the daughter of the much-disliked man in the village, but he did not seem displeased about what I was doing. Owen Bew emerged from the bowels of the ship while I climbed the rope mesh, the woman in one arm. Bew understood—we were to treat her, and he led me down into the kitchen, where, as I got there carrying the woman, he was busy lighting lamps. "Very well then," he said, "let's 'ave a look."

In the increased light I was able to see her clearly. She had very fine eyebrows, a broad face and large eyes, and pale skin, and wore some material that was shiny and strange to the touch. "That's silk," Owen Bew said, and pointed to the table. "Set her down here."

I placed her on the table, and indicated that she should lie down. She tried to, but it caused her much pain. Owen Bew pulled pillows off a shelf, and arranged them so that she could lie partway on them, her upper body supported. Then he picked up a pair of scissors and began cutting the silk top off her body, cutting a ring around the broken spear shaft, and pulling the material away, leaving a circle of silk pulled into the wound, the shaft entering her body above the breast. Bew gently touched the splintered end of the wood, and the woman tensed. "Aye, it's lodged between bones," he said. "It might kill 'er. We shall give her a sip of extract of mandragora."

"What is that?"

"A soporific. It is *Mandragora officinarum*, which is extract from a root mixed in alcohol. She'll sleep through this."

He went to a cabinet on the wall and drew out a brown bottle, shook it, then held it up to the lamplight. "Aye," he said. "This'll do it."

He poured a small amount into a glass cup, and held it to her lips. She stared at it, then up at me. I nodded, and she drank it in a single swallow.

The effect of this drink did not take long. Her eyes began to glaze over, and she relaxed. I tried helping her down to a more comfortable position, and noticed her feet. They were tiny, encased in the same material as her garb, that I thought she must have been the victim of some strange accident. "They are bound," Owen Bew said.

"Why?"

"Here they believe that a woman's attractiveness is increased by small feet, so they turn the toes under when the girls are little children. It makes for much difficulty in walking, but this is the practice here."

It seemed hard to believe, but her feet were no more in length than the width of the palm of my hand. Owen Bew stared down at the splintered shaft of the spear. "I shall hold her body down while you pull on that. We'll assume it is not barbed."

He placed his hands on her shoulder and mid-chest, and nodded to me, at which I held the pole with both hands and pulled. It was so stiffly lodged that I found myself pulling her body up, and Owen Bew pushed down harder, and I pulled harder, and out the pole came in a horrible sucking sound, and then we smelled a foul odor rising from the wound. "She is badly infected," Owen said. "I believe she shall die." The wound did not bleed, but it remained partly open, the skin around its edges bluish and swollen.

"I shall put an ointment on that, and we'll see," he said. He worked on the wound by passing into it a thin metal device dipped in a brown material resembling poi, which he had shaken from a bottle from a small cabinet behind him. When he was done, he looked at me doubtfully as if in anticipatory apology, and said, "It is the best we can do."

Bew left me with her, and I pulled a small stool to the table, and sat with her. Whenever my fatigue invited me to go up to my hammock, I reminded myself that my fatigue was a minor irritation while her state was grave, and required my presence. I watched the flame of Bew's lamp, and looked around at the objects of his place of work.

The lamplight in that room was muted but rich as of the light upon people's faces at sunset, so that in staring at the girl's face as she slept, I lapsed into a strange, trancelike hush, into some broader consideration of things. If Beckwith's plan was to have his charges cheat the rope and move on to study the design of the world, then I suppose his plan was nearing fruition here, because there must have been some reason for my chancing upon this girl, that being a perplexing symmetry of experience connecting her to Kaʻapupāhau. I began to see a vast, horrible order to this world I was learning. It was populated in its largest part by victims, and the small minority of what Will Kelsey called "perpetrators," were the masters of this world. The masters of my world were aliʻi, and that minority had been responsible for the life I had so far lived. And so it seemed true here, among the Hanren, that this minority in the form of thirty or so soldiers, came and beheaded some two thousand five hundred people all because of some hair.

I shook myself from this strange reverie and moved the stool closer to the table, and put my hand up to place it on the girl's arm. It felt hot to the touch, and again, I lapsed into that same reverie, but this phase of odd consciousness blended into something akin to a dream, or perhaps a vision, wherein many voices came to me in urgent and conspiratorial whispers: Kaʻa's, Manomano's, my father's, Pekau's, and forebears going back into the origins of time. These voices superimposed upon one another in a gabble of sound that both confused and enlightened me: the short form of my name, Pono, had in my language its meaning, but now I saw it as nearly dizzying in its complexity. Perhaps it was the benefit of this new language that made it so: goodness, duty, fairness. It meant order, hope, use, function. In the face of all I had witnessed, what was my use? What was my duty? Why indeed was I placed upon this strange world?

Near dawn, when the sunlight first appeared over those high cliffs, I woke from a fitful slumber and lifted my face from the table, my hand still on the girl's arm, but now her arm was cold. When I stood up to look at her, I saw that she was dead. Her face had swollen, so that the bloated features made her look all the more childlike.

Thus did a melancholy awareness settle upon me. This girl, like Ka'a, had been alive and perhaps felt the same things she had felt, and if her mind was at all like my own, it was, like Ka'a's, Pekau's, my father's, and all else who populated this strange world, a realm of the most amazing complexity, beauty, imagination, fear, love, fright, boredom, desire, and to have it go to waste as it had with this girl and all who died before their natural time, was perhaps the awful core of this design Beckwith wanted to show us.

§

As our storyteller had advanced his habit of making his narrative more efficient through the use of summary, so shall I, in connection with my association with Mrs. Searle. She invited me to 'take a walk,' which seemed to me harmless enough until she pointed in the direction we were to do so: those two mountains up the valley inland from the port, perhaps some six or seven miles from the dusty spot upon which we stood that day at dawn. "Are your legs quite stout this morning?" she asked, that saucy look on her face. I informed her that indeed my legs were stout, for I had tramped many places in search of botanical specimens, which, she said, I should do on this particular trip. I did not have my own small notebook, nor did I have a bag in which to carry such items, and I was not about to wait around for a cutter to return me to *The Clarel* to find these things. "If there is anything worth collecting," I said, "I shall use my pockets."

"Very well," said she. "Off we go."

I paused. She wore the same dress she had the previous times I had met her, and I inquired as to how she thought she might climb over boulders wearing that. Again, with a coy, secretive wink of her wonderful eye, she indicated with that expression alone that she knew what she was doing, so off we went, side-by-side on the barren pathway, the bottoms of her feet being gently slapped by her slippers.

Our journey took us up a beautiful valley, along a stream in which many native children played, all of whom called, "Aroha," or "Aloha," to us. Mrs. Searle did indeed have stout legs, and upon our reaching an area heavily wooded, above an area quite dense with 'kalo patches' as she called them, shallow ponds sporting lines of large-leaved plants, the source of their poi as it is called, that nearly tasteless grayish purple paste they eat and for which I did not have any desire, we stopped and looked back toward the harbor, *The Clarel* there in view. She seemed much impressed by the apparent industry of the farmers who peopled the valley, and paused often to speak to the dark, happy children, most of whom played naked in the shallow waters of the stream. Then she drew her skirt up her legs, and tied it around her hips, passing part of it under her so that the skirt very closely resembled the garb of the native women.

"Clever," I said.

"Practical, rather," she said.

She often stopped to show me plants, her favorite one she called an oh-hia tree, a rather gnarled plant with small, thickish green leaves lined up upon thin branches, some of these leaf clusters bearing bright red flowers with many tiny stalks, the entire of the ball of red resembling some strange brush. "You pick one of these and it remains bright for two days," she said.

Farther up this valley, the dwellings of the people resembled what I imagined dwelling places might have been prior to the discovery of these islands. Men wore those loincloths that Pono identified as 'malo,' and women were bare-breasted and unashamed at being so. They all called 'aloha' out to us as we passed, some of them calf-deep in the water of their kalo patches.

The higher lands we traversed were raw but pleasing, those trees she liked here and there, and the stream meandering along, small thatched dwellings on either side. That skirt that she had tied around her waist moved around her hips in the hot sun, her legs under it flexing with each step as she made her way over rocks and past brush in increasingly difficult terrain. We were quite high up now, moving toward a pass that went right over the mountain range to the northern side of the island. "There," she said, pointing. "Do you see those two squared-off notches on the right?"

"Yes I do," I said.

"It is alleged that their warrior king, Kamehameha, had those notches fashioned as you see them so that he could mount cannons in them."

"Ah," I said, somewhat breathless.

"Now," said she, "we move to the left, and go to a small widening in a stream."

She found no difficulty in finding this place, a pool hidden down among some large boulders. I caught up with her as she sat down upon a rock, took off her sandals, and put her feet in. "It is deep," she said, "but I warn you, it is quite cold."

"Oh, I shall not go in there," I said. "But it is quite pleasant a place."

"Sometimes people are here bathing," she said, "but I am happy to see that it is vacant today. Sit down there."

I did so. She stared at the water, and then up at the gap between the two mountains. "May I say something to you about my opinions?" she asked.

"Of course."

"When I first came here, I was given to going off exploring by myself, meeting the people and so on, and my husband was not pleased that I did this." She moved her feet in the water. "At the mission I was advised to tend to my duties and not go off in that fashion, for a woman should not be wandering about in the hills alone. But I continued doing this when I had the time. One day I chanced upon a gathering of people, just down from here perhaps a mile or so. I do not know what the occasion was, but I stood off to the side, not wanting to disturb the proceedings. A woman saw me and came to me, took my hand, and pulled me down closer to the gathering, and then had her children bring fruit and water to me. She seemed quite intent on my remaining there. Then I beheld something that I shall never forget."

She was silent a moment, moving her feet in the water. I saw that I was sitting in the sun, just two feet from a shadow made by a small tree, so I moved into that shadow.

"It was a dance involving young men and women. Hula. The women went up first, or rather, girls, for I believe they were in their teens. They stood in a line, called out something in their language, and beautiful voices they had. Oh, you cannot imagine! Then they began to dance, their motions in unison, stamping their feet and turning, their arms up, out, then before them as if offering something. I had heard of this, a dance of ignorant savages, lascivious and suggestive and evil. I sat there thinking of those horrid, wooden dances we learned as children, and I have seen even a ballet in Boston. But this was beautiful, perhaps the most beautiful movement of human bodies I have ever seen, and it was not evil or savage. It was so elegant and innocent and pure that I was breathless watching it, the rhythm and the perfection of movement, and when I thought of those dances we learned as children, I was absolutely thunderstruck that the meaning of the word 'dance' was being shown to me right there. The woman who invited me watched without showing any great appreciation or amazement, and I suppose it was because it was simply a part of her life and the lives of these people. And then the young men lined up to dance, with bits of vine, flowers, and so on around their ankles and wrists, and then moved in warlike poses, stamping their feet, and again I saw an elegance and a perfection of movement, although their motions suggested a warlike mime, where the young girls' movements suggested something both devotional and at the same time somewhat teasing.

This is what my mission wants to get rid of, this beauty and this elegance."

"I have heard of this dance," I said.

"I have seen it, and I fear that if our mission is successful, we shall see it no more. You know, when the people of this place convert themselves to our religion, they sometimes do it with such vengeance and enthusiasm that it strikes me as sad. I have been to the other islands, on one mission or another. There are all manner of new proselytizers tramping around the country ordering them to fall to their knees before our god. And these converts strike me as fools, pretenders, denying their own beauty for this. They are the people of this place, and they become quite arrogant and superior in their new role." She moved her feet in the water. "I despise this," she said. "I do."

"I believe I understand."

"Who are we? Are we so convinced of our superiority that we are blind?"

"Well, we did find this place. We are more developed than they."

She stared at me. Then she did something that convinced me that she was either daft or belligerently licentious. She gathered her skirts and pulled them off her body, the entire dress I should say, so that, sitting there wearing aught but white pantaloons and otherwise naked to the waist, she said, "I am going to bathe. Would you like to?"

"As I said," said I, probably quite gape-mouthed staring at the indeed healthily endowed woman, "I shall defer this time." I could not take my eyes off her and noted somewhat numbly that she was also quite well-colored on the skin, as if she had made a habit of doing this. Indeed she was physically endowed as of an artist's model, and I suppose she saw me unable to move my eyes away from those breasts.

"Oh come now Matthew," she said. "The water shall do you good."

"As I said—"

She slid down into the water, and there, shivering with pleasure, she looked somewhat doubtfully up at me. "I have shocked you and I am sorry."

"No madam, you have not shocked me. You have merely made a point."

This made her laugh, a trilling, explosive laugh caused I think by the coldness of the water. "Oh, I am sorry," she said. "Please forgive me. I have a request."

"Of course," I said. "What is it?"

"Would your Mr. MacFarlane make available to me the text of the story?"

I watched her as she waved her arms about in the water, her body underneath producing dreamlike, pale motions. "I wonder if it is a story a woman should read."

"Please," she said. "I am not easily shocked."

"Very well. I shall ask the storyteller and Mr. MacFarlane."

After she came out of the water and dressed, she led me to the top of the valley, upon a well-worn path, to a place where the wind blew so strongly that I could lean at quite an angle into it, and below us, spread out for many miles, was a fertile plain, the smoke of hundreds of cooking fires visible, and the multi-hued water beyond, and in the middle distance below, a marsh of some sort, much of it set out in those kalo patches.

I shall say that I remained confused about the woman, that, having made the point she had made, she left me wondering about my attraction for her. It was as if, having found her to be a woman of conviction, I had found myself now less attracted to her. The attraction was now colored somewhat by a new mystery: she had opinions, and those opinions were very strong. And her conviction that our presence here was destructive rather than helpful left me wondering if she were some eccentric, or perhaps one of those free thinkers who tends to enjoy embarrassing people such as myself.

But our conversation, upon our journey back down through the valley, was pleasant. She showed me plants I had not heard of before, and described to me their uses, many of them medicinal, and I fixed in my mind the personal vow to return to that enterprise that brought me here in the first place. I will add also something I hesitate to add, simply an image of her rising out of that water to put her dress back on. She did so with a demure awareness of my presence, but at the same time a kind of innocent pretending that no one happened to be watching. She stood up, the water streaming down that wonderful body, turned, and reached for her dress, and those white pantaloons pasted themselves to her buttocks and legs, and in the process nearly disappeared. To avoid presenting this with a salacious choice of words referring to those hips and buttocks, I shall say only that what I beheld was beautiful, those sweeping animated curves, an ideally wrought figurine on a Grecian vase.

13.

We stayed in that cove for months. At first I was convinced that the aliʻi of this land would send ships around the coast to find us, but Roger Beckwith told me that it was not likely, for this place, China, was once a great sea power, but no more. They barely had a navy, because the government was more interested in armies to defend the country from attack by land. As for cavorting with women, this did happen, but through a slow process during which the villagers became familiar with the men. Tong Guan believed that eventual vengeance would be visited upon the village, but because the weather had gone foul, so that I shivered in the night, wrapped up in a pelt in my hammock, the soldiers were most likely waiting until a trip out here might be more comfortable. But the force of the weather seemed to make that unlikely. The ocean blasted against those outcroppings, and the ship would rise, then sink, then rise again, so that, in my hammock, I would see the rock face of the land sweeping up and down.

Roger Beckwith detailed the rules of the men's life outside the ship. They were to report once a day, and they were not to bring their women onto the ship. He would operate by these rules too, he said. Work on the ship, sealing seams, keeping the deck clean, maintaining the ropes, would be divided out amongst the men. The men were inclined to do no more than nod eagerly at each rule detailed. The village was in such a dearth of men, they said, that some of the more lusty women engaged in this cavorting without any hesitation, and the men would come down the path in groups, laughing and imitating dizziness at how much cavorting they had done. Some days during fairer weather the ship was nearly empty but for old Owen Bew and the two who found cavorting with each other in the hold preferable to cavorting with the village women.

As for myself, I did not cavort. I suppose it was the memory of Pekau and the children that made it so. Pekau waited for me in the clouds, and I did not know what this message meant, so I held myself and waited. When I was not picking oakum or tending to the deck, I wrapped myself in a pelt to keep warm, and opened the Britannica volumes. But this time it was not the vast body of information that I wanted to absorb, but rather that information that pertained to medicine, anatomy and surgery. I could spend hours in pursuit of the definition of a single word, for some of the information about medical practices used words that, when I tried to find their definitions in the very volumes that used those words, they would not be there, and I would then have to ask Roger Beckwith if I might borrow his dictionary.

So went the winter. The men brought back pots containing strange, hot foods, mixtures in which pieces of chicken and pork were cooked in with what they called Chinese noodles, which made for some excellent eating. The weather became so cold that I was reminded of a story my father told me of the great Mauna Loa on the largest island in our world, where, he said, water froze white, and could be carried as a solid. We children of the ocean had all heard these stories, and now, wrapped in the large pelt with the book open against my knees, I paused from time to time to feel the chill air, and later, to watch as the white flakes descended and painted parts of that rock face white.

Roger Beckwith remained on the ship the majority of the time, but he would sequester himself in his little, cramped room, sitting at his desk, and he would do as I was doing: read books. He also spent a considerable amount of time writing in his log, but Will Kelsey told me that this log was more a record of his experiences. Beckwith was, he said, a thinker, and it was because of this that we tended to end up where we ended up. That the situation now was sedate, and the men were happy as larks satisfying their various urges, was an illusion, because as Tong Guan said, the soldiers would reappear sometime in the coming months. For these reasons, Will Kelsey told me that it would be wise if I pulled my eyes away from those infernal books from time to time to look out over the ocean or up those bluffs, to see if either a British or Spanish ship appeared coming through the water or those colorfully attired soldiers appeared standing on those bluffs. It would happen, he said, before we left, because Roger Beckwith did not want to leave until he found more human fault to study and record in his bloody log.

Tong Guan became one of the gentlemen of leisure. It became quickly apparent that he was very skilled at games, and Olney and his friends drew him into their circle every day, the men shivering over their table while Tong Guan, having learned the intricacies of chess, became very difficult to beat.

This then is how those months passed. I drifted into sleep each night picturing Pekau and my world, and awoke each morning in the frigid air, my breath expanding clouds blown from my mouth. And I positioned myself to do my reading in such a manner as to scan the ocean, or the bluffs, as I read. I might read, "The *fistula lachrymalis* is generally understood to be such a disorder of the canals leading from the eye to the nose, as obstructs the natural progress of the tears, and makes them trickle down the cheek: but this is only the first and mildest stage of the disease." This benign description followed by: "In the next, there is a mucus resembling matter itself discharged with the tears from the *puncta lachrymalix,* and sometimes from an orifice broken through the skin between the nose and angle of the eye. The last and worst degree of it is, when the matter of the abscess, by its long continuance, has not only corroded the neighbouring soft parts, but also affected the subjacent bone."

I remember this passage particularly because I had never imagined that the simple act of weeping could engender such a bodily disaster. The large section on surgery was rich in the many grotesque afflictions that visit the human body, and I resolved at the time to commit every sentence of this section of the book to my memory. Had I known all of this earlier, I speculated, I might have been able to rescue Ka'a from death.

While it is true that time itself may seem to pass rapidly, or altogether too slowly, according to one's mood or situation, I was aware that many days, and then weeks, were passing while the men enjoyed their lives as guests of the little village and I read and memorized the sections on surgery, anatomy, and medicine. It seemed to me that I had been in this hammock strung up on the lee side of the ship, out of the prevailing wind, for years, so demanding was the task of deciphering word after word in the books. From time to time, perhaps once every two days, I left this task to row my way to shore and climb the steep path, and to make my way to the tops of the bluffs overlooking the water. From there, I could get an excellent view of the ocean and the rooftops of the village buildings. And to make myself useful, I fell to carrying one after another of the chickens into the hold, to sit there in the dim lamplight and watch as they pecked away at the pelts, and when the chicken seemed sated, I would collect another to take down into the hold. I would talk to them as they worked: "Aye madam, there's a bloody beetle be'ind you there is. Ah! That's quick of you. Does the blighter taste good, madam?"

In the evenings, usually, some half of the men would be on the ship, and these months were spent talking, each of them telling his story, one example of which follows: Dick Burrows, after eating a large bowl of some concoction made in the village, of pieces of chicken in a soupy sauce and made of what Owen Bew called "strings of dumpling paste," leaned back, took a small sip of grog, and held forth for us. His English was different from that of the others in that it was softer, and in ways drawn out, melodic and, for me, in ways more understandable. I recalled asking him, "'ave you a story?" and so he put his elbows on the table we were sitting around, Roger Beckwith at the head enjoying the same dish, and spoke: "The war was one I wanted nothin' to do with, and me and my Tuscarora squaw was goin' east to see my family, and there near the ocean we was taken by Brits." At that Burrows stared around the table at all the Brits listening. "They wasn't interested in my story, that I was no more'n a simple trapper from a hundred miles inland and my wife here was travelin' with me because I didn't want to leave her back. There had been enough depredations by revolutionaries that they weren't about to err on the side of kindness so they figured it would be best to string me up. Shot my wife first, and there she was layin' bleedin' to death from the mouth, the ball havin' split a lung, and I was there under a tree with a rope around my neck, numb and lookin' at her lyin' there and not carin' when they'd pull me up. Looked off to my side at a Brit soldier studyin' my rifle, a beauty it was, could blow a turkey at two hundred paces it could, and then I waited, thinkin', the only two things worth livin' for were gone, the wife and the rifle, and so I made my peace. Not with God or anything like that. Made it with myself, because if there was a God, I'd'a rather shot the son of a bitch then and there if that Brit soldier'd give my my rifle back. Which he didn't. So I'm there with my hands tied behind my back an' two of them come up to just hoist me up a little so that they could pull the rope slack up and watch me dance. Five of them soldiers there was, and I tell you the expressions on their faces were a thing to watch, they were, because they looked grim and pompous like, as if they was blessed with the right to make the decisions they had, blessed with the right to shoot a woman who'd never done a wrong thing in her life. And me, who'd done some wrong, never done wrong like that. Mighta got drunk and fought, mighta even gouged an eye or two, but I never woulda shot a woman. So who gains that right? I guess it's like all's you need to do is put on a uniform, and like magic you get that right, to shoot a pretty little eighteen-year-old Tuscarora girl as if she's no more'n a deer or a turkey. But she was much more'n 'at, I tell you, just then beginnin' with child she was, so those who felt they had the rights to do it took two lives that day, and was just about to work on takin' the third when there was such a racket of musket shots and that smell a spent powder workin' across my face, and them soldiers was all dead. Just like that, with me standin' there tryin' to figure it out. Then I see an old man run up to my wife and look to see if he can help, Owen Bew it was, and I turn and see Roger Beckwith right there a starin' at me like I was both dangerous and somehow interestin' to his twisted sense of thinkin'." At that the men laughed, and looked at Roger Beckwith, who continued eating his food, nodding contemplatively at the story. "Spot here on my chest, you know, where, short as she was, she used to put her head. I remember that, always will, that spot, because I guess it makes me remember everything else, how what a girl she was, and how I woulda died to see her happy. My life ain't meant nothin' since then, 'cept for lookin' at the world. That's about it. So I got to keep my rifle," Dick Burrows said. "And my life, whatever use it is now. And so the rifle I carry is that rifle, an' Pono, you seen what it can do."

"Yes," I said. "And I appreciate your having expounded your tale."

"Expound?" Will Kelsey said. "Pono, are you takin' leave of your surgery to continue with your words?"

"Yes," I said.

"Exemplary," he said. "You've reached the letter *E*."

With the first hints of change in the weather, I began dreaming of Pekau, as if that cold weather during which I committed to memory the parts of the books on Medicine, Surgery, and Anatomy, had been some odd lapse, some strange, waking sleep in which words had dominated my mind. The men, too, began manifesting a peculiar anxiety, for they knew that Beckwith would one day announce our departure, to where, no one knew.

My dreams of Pekau were painful, as if the message that she waited for me in the clouds somehow implied her death, and with those dreams came speculations again about my children and my parents, about Laka and Kōnapiliahi and my life in that lost world. Manomano's voice was too weak to reach me, and I found that I had begun to dread returning to that world, for the likelihood was that naught but misery awaited me. But the desire to return did finally compel me to address Roger Beckwith on the matter.

His response was to tell me that I should hold forth on the subject, and with my improved facility with the language, I was able to do so, in a story which may be thought of as a shorter, summarized version of the story I have told you, up to the point of Beckwith's rescue of me from the war axe. The men who chose to be on the ship at the time of the telling of my account were Beckwith himself, Dick Burrows, Will Kelsey, Owen Bew, Crabbe and Audrey, and Tong Guan, who had spent the winter either with us on the ship or up in the village as the remaining populace put it back together and tried to reinstate their life's work, which was fishing. The other men, more inclined to mix with the village folk than languish on the ship, were absent.

When I was finished, having piqued the interest of those in attendance, Will Kelsey said, "Are we able to billet there, then?"

I misunderstood. "Is not 'billet' a word for heraldry or fox dung?"

The men laughed. "You're right, Pono," Beckwith said, "but a third meaning is 'soldier's quarters'. He is asking if we might establish a camp there."

"Yes," I said. "I believe that will be possible."

Roger Beckwith considered this, then frowned. "Pono, I did tell ye that the day we picked you up off that rock, we were looking for water, and the next day I guess it was, we left. We left because we saw another ship."

"From the land of mists and fog," I said. "Twice before ships came, and one with an ali'i my people killed."

"That was James Cook," Beckwith said. "But the presence of a ship means the presence of muskets, of the men of my world."

"They do not stay," I said.

"And you're looking for your wife Pay—I forget the rest," Kelsey said.

"Yes, and my children, my parents, Pekau's father Manomano. I fear I will be disappointed, however, for a voice in a dream told me she waited for me in the clouds."

Beckwith thought this over. "Aye, but dreams are not always omens."

"Omens?"

I had not made my way anywhere near the letter O, so I needed that explained to me. I believe that the men of the ship felt that my world was in ways more benign than the various worlds they had visited, for the presence of one ship was not enough to taint the pleasing image of the place. The idea of returning to my world, with its fair weather and its 'handsome' people, as they called my people, was not as threatening as, for example, visiting King Philip's Land. I did warn them of the ferocity of our warriors, but also described for them the relative remoteness of the area they had visited when they found me. This they thought over, and Beckwith, considering the various options, finally said, "Pono, this may take some time, perhaps the turn of a year or more, because the skins we've unloaded so far take only a third of the cargo. The chickens are still busy."

"Yes," I said. "I am most fond of Madam Churchill."

Sometimes on fairer days I climbed the bluffs, working my way past the little houses perched upon the rocks, to visit the village. There, I would marvel at the industry of the ship's men, repairing this and that, doing all sorts of useful jobs much to the nodding delight of the women. The village still had men, but very few of them. The three of our men most industrious in these enterprises were the Seager brothers and Ben Fowles, our carpenter, who were living up in the village during that winter. One image I enjoy is the following: Ben Fowles carrying a muddy spotted pig across the village center, flanked by two women chattering at him as he struggled along, the pig squirming and squealing, mud dripping on his clothes and then a string of thick pig saliva draping across the bridge of his nose, and Fowles sweating and flustered while the women talked in their strange language, Fowles nodding and saying,

"Aye, if I understand what you're saying madam, but could you please get out of the way before I step on your feet, madam? Please?" The Seager brothers spent three days down in a well, hauling wet silt from the bottom, the project overseen by women who ringed the well and peered down until the bucket was full, at which they hauled it up and dumped it and sent it back down.

And then I saw flowers growing on the rocky face of the cliff above the cove, and the men began spending more time near and on the ship than they had during the winter. The table belonging to the gentlemen of leisure came up on deck, and I continued with my reading. The enclycopedia seemed an inexhaustible world, and I reread passages I had seen earlier when my facility with the language was in its early development. Around me men were loading the ship with supplies, foods that did not turn, for they were dried, and much water. Beckwith also came into the possession of various 'trinkets,' finely wrought pieces of a green stone he called jade, and some coins of the realm made of gold, which was described to me by the men as the most precious metal in the world. I thought it attractive, but because of the values of things in my world, did not understand how it was that men would kill over this very dense, heavy metal.

If Beckwith were making good on his promise to visit my world, it seemed odd if not frustrating that he chose to sail the other way, south along the same coast we had spent the winter on. He was doing so to try one more port wherein ships like *The Tiburon* could dock without fear of the rope, a trading colony called Macau. Beckwith said that at this time of the year, the merchants were testing the waters, and it would be some time before the port would be crowded with Brits and Spanish and others who might take issue with our being there with them. We had to be careful because Macau was but a two-day sail from the great port of Canton, and our approach to Macau had to be from the south, so as to avoid any ships that might be sliding along the coast into the bay that led to Canton. Tong Guan had decided to go with us, for none of his family were left in the village, and he convinced Beckwith through the interpretations of Jack Audrey that his facility with the Chinese language would be of use to him.

Another development in connection with this southward journey was that one of the gentlemen of leisure, an older man whose name was Robert Baynes, informed Beckwith that his sailing days were over and he would now collect his share and live in Macau. I had not yet heard of what a 'share' was, and learned that Beckwith kept careful records of the booty in the ship, and whenever any of the men were ready to rejoin the world, the share belonging to that man would be given him so that he could go and establish himself somewhere safe from the rope. For Robert Baynes this was Macau.

I asked Dick Burrows about this. "Beckwith keeps everything in his cabin and he's honest, so nobody gets shorted. Seen it before—fella gets a good stake for his retirement." Words like 'stake' and 'retirement' needed explanation, but I understood. Beckwith shared the wealth of his trading with the men, and apparently wanted no more than anyone else got, for his share. As to what a 'stake' was made of, Burrows explained the concept of money to me, that certain objects of barter had an agreed upon value, gold mostly, and silver and other valuable stones and metals, and a man could establish himself with a house, even, using a pocketful of these items. I had come across much in connection with this concept in the encyclopedia, yet had not heard of it used in a practical way until this time. Men of great power got that power from the accumulation of these things, and they needed no more, not physical strength, not the ability to convince others to devote themselves to him, not the bravery to face another in battle.

And so we towed *The Tiburon* out of its cove under the rugged cliffs and set sail south along the coast of China for Macau. And as Beckwith preferred, we sailed into gray skies that produced rain each day, and inside the bowels of the ship the air was sodden and heavy. The men were anxious about this, for the possibility of being recognized by some warship tortured their dreams, and made them very tense and alert as the high coast slid past the starboard rail, that is, during those times that the rain abated enough for us to see beyond three hundred paces. Then Beckwith turned the ship from the coast, and we found ourselves in the middle of an ocean with no horizon, no stars, no means of determining where we were but for Beckwith's navigational skills, which I was told were considerable. We traveled thus for many days, and each day was like the one before, sodden and hot, so that the thicker skin on my feet turned a mushy pale color and weakened to the point that I could shave great wads of it off with a thumbnail.

I had assumed that Macau might resemble the little village we had spent the winter in, but was held in a strange astonishment at the sight of this place emerging out of the heavy mist, a small island, but with many great structures, 'churches' they were called, likened to our heiau. Beckwith wanted to do his trading forthwith and then sail away, for the limited visibility might just limit the visibility of an approaching Brit seventy-four. The men could explore the little port town, but only in brief stretches of perhaps a few hours, after which they were to return to the ship and be ready to sail.

Where my memory of natural settings, the vast Ewa plain or the long stretches of beach and surrounding foothills of my world, or even King Philip's Land, remains lucid and without flaw, my recollection of Macau sits as a confusing collection of odd images, all of them in a gray rain. I cannot place the port buildings in connection with Saint Paul's Cathedral, as it was called, although I know it was but a few minutes' walk from the port buildings. It was a vast building of stone, darknened by the rain, with looming spires and windows and much in the way of decorative design. Wet as I was, I decided not to go in. There was what the men called *Senate Square,* an area of stone walkways and a vast stone building of many archways, three tiers high, under which Chinese people hurried about, and here and there, men from a country called Portugal went about their business, which had to do with trading and shipping.

On one of those cobbled streets that ran throughout the port town, two men sat languidly against a stone wall, regarding us as we passed. One of them was covered with horrible sores, and had no teeth. His yellow eyes regarded us with a kind of wan merriment, and then he coughed horribly, causing the other man to move away from him. "Consumption," Will Kelsey whispered. "Our good luck that nobody on our ship's got it, or the clap, or any of those other 'orrible afflictions." I had to have the words 'consumption' and 'clap' explained to me.

Our adventure into the port town ended, we returned to the ship, where Robert Baynes readied himself to be left there. He knew Macau as he knew the areas of land north of it. He knew the Portugese well enough to establish himself in his original profession, that of tailor, and Portugese gentlemen of wealth out here in this trading post would appreciate the skills of a man just such as he. As for being recognized and led to the rope, he ventured to guess that the chances of that were about as good as his winning at chess against Tong Guan ten times in a row. This produced a few 'ar ars' from the men, and a nod of smiling recognition from the Chinese boy.

"Boys," Robert Baynes said, "ye've been referrin' to me for years as a gentleman of leisure, and I'm now making that a reality. And I thank ye for all, you most Roger, for having kept the cravat off me neck."

"It was just practical," Beckwith said. "What use would you've been dead, after all? I was just denying that surgeon his toy."

Thus did we sail off into the mist-shrouded South China Sea, Beckwith carefully navigating the ship south, and then east, to work between the northernmost island of King Philip's Land and the large island off the coast of China called Formosa. I had assumed that now, finally, we were going to return to my world, a journey I thought might take us a number of months, if what was explained to me in connection with Beckwith's maps was correct. But once out on that calm water, in the maddening humidity, we did not move, or if we moved, it was in a breeze that barely pushed the shapes of the sails into the roundness that meant movement. The men could not bear the hold of the ship and slept on the deck, arranged in uncomfortable positions upon the planking, muttering and snoring in the night. The visibility off the rails was no more than a few hundred paces, and there we sat, waiting for wind to carry us away.

During the days the gentlemen of leisure had their table set up, and glistening with perspiration, played their games. With one of their own gone, they began to educate Tong Guan as to the intricacies of operating the cannons. I observed as they told him the proper words connected with their operation: gun-worm, canister, ball, chain-shot, bar-shot, and so on. I sat in my hammock and turned the pages of the encyclopedia, and those pages were limp and moist, as of the limpness of some half dry fabric. All the men save Beckwith and Dick Burrows seemed to lapse into a miserable lethargy, and even the chickens remained sedate, standing in their wire enclosure muttering doubtfully in their throats. Because the visibility was so limited, I had the sensation that we were in the midst of some spirit world, and the sense that there was land out there somewhere faded as if this was the rest of our existence, that our food and water would run out and we would die here, slicked with our own dirty sweat and wearing clothes that seemed to melt to our skin, which, turning into paste upon our bodies, seemed to putrefy there. I could scratch my scalp through my hair and fill my fingernails with this melted skin. One day I ran my finger between two of my toes and came up with this paste that smelled of rot. Many times I thought of going over the side into the water, but was advised against it, for salt, they said, would suffuse my clothes and make me more miserable.

When we did begin to move, very slowly at first, the sails filling and then becoming flaccid, then filling again, I could feel the roll of movement in the planks, and this brought to the men the look of hope that there might be some relief from it.

I had learned not to question the direction Beckwith took, and assumed that the men trusted him, but they began to complain that they might be lost, or headed into some area where Brit Seventy-Fours might materialize out of that gray mist and chop *The Tiburon* in half. The lack of visibility made us vulnerable, and caused the men to grow short with one another and to sit muttering to themselves.

One night while we were moving slowly through the gray, misty nothingness, Dick Burrows stood near me at the rail, a strange expression on his face, and then turned and said, "Pono, will you go find Roger for me? I'm stayin' here." I wondered why Dick Burrows would send me instead of going himself. Beckwith was at the stern, sitting upon a small stool, because the hold was too hot. I told him what Burrows wanted, and we went back to where he stood looking out at the flat, gray, horizonless night.

"I smell spent powder and sweat," Burrows said to Beckwith.

"Land."

"No, it's a vessel. Not a trader either I think. And I get the smell of spices, like cumin, coriander, maybe pepper."

"What would that be used in?" Beckwith asked. "Is it a trader?"

"This is being cooked," Dick Burrows said. "It's that stuff they eat here, the way they cook meats. This ain't no trader."

"Curry? Is that what you mean? How do you know it's not land?"

"That's what it is. Curry. And I don't smell earth or greens. I think they're followin' us. I think they'll wait until they get just enough wind and come board us at night. You know what that means."

"What does that mean?" I asked.

Dick Burrows ran his index finger across his neck. "There ain't no quarter out here. If these is Malays or any of them others, it can't be good for us."

Beckwith stared at the wall of mist, musing. "Are you quite certain?"

"I am," Burrows said. "They'll wait weeks. Doesn't mean nothin' to them."

The uneasiness of the men now advanced into a maddening tension, as if the threat of that shadowy presence of another vessel caused sweat to erupt from the skin, and one's grasp on his sanity to become shaky and weak. We spoke in guarded whispers, close to one another, smelling each other's clothes, which reeked of fear and the unclean odors of rotting skin, not unlike the odor of the rotten water sloshing deep in the hold.

When the gray dawn crept over the water, the sky lightened a uniform gray all around us, and we stood at the rails peering into that flat, humid plane, looking for the shadow of any movement, but movement there was none.

Then a faint breeze came, and the men, Will Kelsey at the wheel, labored to turn the ship in order to catch some of it. This wind allowed us to inch southward, so that for periods of time the breeze crossed our faces, bringing some relief.

Dick Burrows informed Beckwith that smells were carried in that wind, of wood, of grease and the bodies of men. This time, I believe, I could smell it too, but so faintly that I might have thought that the odor had wafted off my own shirt.

"There's more'n one vessel," Dick Burrows said.

"Aye," Beckwith said. "There could be any number, is that what you think?"

"I make it that way," Dick Burrows said.

"Shall I have the gentlemen of leisure load the cannons?"

"No. Load 'em now and the powder'll foul. We've got to wait."

"How does powder foul?" I asked. "And why the gentlemen of leisure?"

"The wet air," Dick Burrows said. He ran his sleeved forearm across his brow. "I wouldn't even open a cask until I was aimin'." He looked at me, then at the men sitting at the table aft. "The gentlemen of leisure are not gentlemen when it comes to cannons."

And so we moved, slowly, through that water, and unnatural water it was, for it had no texture. It was flat as a pond.

As the gray dawn had opened all around us, so dusk and darkness came, with no proof of where the sun had set. Beckwith ordered that four lanterns be set up in the cannon ports, pieces of sailcloth hung behind them to throw that weak light over the water, and so we began that night staring at the dark, horizonless plane. I slept for a short time, then rose and stared off the rail. Other men tried to sleep, but the humidity made it impossible. When the fog began to lighten, again with no proof of where the sun was rising, it occurred to me that we needed to know more. Beckwith stood at the rail with Dick Burrows, Crabbe and Audrey, and Owen Bew. I approached them and said, "Dick says there are vessels out there, and that they are in the mist out of our sight. I shall go over the side and swim in the direction of the smell, and look."

"Ye'll be lost," Crabbe said, his leer tinged now with fear and a wretched pessismism. "The sharks'll get ye, or ye'll drown."

"I will not drown. I can swim."

"I can't," Audrey said, "nor can Jack or half of the rest."

This I found surprising. For how could it be that men of the sea could not swim?

"We'll rig a tether for you," Beckwith said.

"What is a tether?"

"A rope. Even if you go out of sight of us, you can pull yourself back."

Now it became the second time that the men saw me in my malo, but they all appeared unsure of the point of this. Will Kelsey brought out a roll of light rope, two hundred yards he said, and when I asked him how far that was, he said that it was about two hundred paces. He worked one end into a knotted loop the right size for my wrist, and told me I was to hold on to it and under no circumstances let it go. "I'll 'old the rope for ye, but I'm hoping it isn't a baited fishing line."

"Arr ar," I said.

"Now we'll roll the ropes off for you," Dick Burrows said. "If we're listenin' to them, they'll be doin' likewise with us."

I worked my way down the ropes, and slid into the water. I hadn't felt this familiar buoyancy in some time. The water was warm, however, not instantly invigorating as seawater can be. I began working my way off the rail while the men watched, Dick Burrows pointing, in the direction of the smells. I looked behind me as I swam, and *The Tiburon* grew smaller, and then began to become vague, and when I turned in the water, looking all around me, I saw nothing. I worked a bit farther, making sure the rope was secure in my grip, and continued turning my head.

Then, when I shifted my eyes across the water, I knew that I saw something. It was a series of shapes that materialized out of the gray wall, triangular but rounded somewhat along the shorter line of the triangles, sails. I moved forward slowly, and then it seemed as if these vessels were all around me. There were four of them, each much smaller than ours, their sails ribbed oddly, parallel to the water, and the faint shapes of men moved under those sails. I had seen these smaller vessels in Macau. Lower on the water were small cutters, some with sails and some without. I moved closer, and saw dark men naked but for white loincloths, moving about the vessels, and to my surprise, men like those I sailed with, white men dressed like the men of *The Tiburon*.

I made my way back, gathering the rope as I went. After I climbed over the rail, pulling the rope up behind me, I described to the men what I had seen.

"How many sails on one ship?" Beckwith asked.

"One," I said. I went to my hammock and donned my clothes, disregarding the drying salt water on my skin. "They had lines in the sails, ribs of wood perhaps."

"Small junks," Beckwith said. "The white men are privateers. We're in for a fight."

"Would a one-sail junk 'ave cannons aboard?" Will Kelsey asked.

"They would," Beckwith said. "And if they manage to board us, we're all bait."

"Problem here is that a small junk can turn faster than this ship," Dick Burrows said. "There're nineteen of us, and if there are four off the starboard rail, then there are that many off port, and more fore and aft. There could be fifty or a hundred men out there. And the small boats are the sampans, and they can row them if they want."

"We've got an ocean warlord of some sort then?" Crabbe asked. "Can we negotiate with them?"

"We can't," Beckwith said. "All you negotiate there is a slit throat."

"Touch of wind today," Dick Burrows said. "We've been moving, they followed. The wind increases, and they're comin', no negotiating that. Fact, they'll come by nightfall I'd guess. They're afraid to come now because of our cannons, but when we get wind, they'll come because we'll be pullin' sailrope and turnin'. They'll wait for the confusion of that."

"So what do we do?" Beckwith asked.

Burrows spat over the rail. "Say the wind picks up just a little. We keep the sails open. We lower the cutter and row into the wind away from the ship so they can't smell us. We move slow, and wait. We stay right at the door of clear seein' and when the time comes, we act. If we got four rowin' and three with muskets, we pick a couple of the white men off and turn the cutter and run back to the ship. We move the ship into the opposite side of their circle, cause our powder smell to go past us and they'll smell it on the other side and figure the firin's comin' their way. They won't know how far the firin' is because this here fog flattens the sound out. They'll have to decide what to do then, because them chasing us will be chasing, and these ones smellin' the powder'll have to decide." The men looked at one another, imagining this. "Look here," Dick Burrrows said, "if we wait till they decide to board us, we don't have the advantage."

"And when do you see us doing this?" Beckwith asked.

"Before dusk," Dick Burrows said. "After dusk we can't see them in the water."

"They'll hear us when we lower the cutter," Will Kelsey said.

"Get Owen to bang pots," Dick Burrows said.

"Are ye daft?" Beckwith said. "Why that?"

"If they was bangin' pots out there in that fog, would you attack them?"

Beckwith stared at him. "You got me there, Dick. And how do we see them without them seeing us? Your doorway of seeing. What is that?"

"You gotta blink, shift your eyes. We'll stay right at that doorway. Them's more to see than us, so we'll see them 'fore they see us."

So did we ready ourselves, and I will admit that I was doubtful and afraid. I told myself again and again that they were hostile, had to be if they were surrounding us and staying out in that fog. I stared down at my musket, taken from that dead horseman in King Philip's Land, and I raised and lowered the frizzen, and ran my thumb over the cock, shook the powder inside the horn given to me by Owen Bew to make sure it was still dry. Dick Burrows had taught me the intricacies of loading and firing a musket, and I would now use it against another man, and I did not like the sensation. On what is called the half-deck, and then inside the ship under the quarter-deck, the Gentlemen of Leisure opened the doors for the cannons and wheeled them slightly out, so that their muzzles aimed away, the ones in front angled out fore, the ones in back angled out aft.

When it came time to lower the cutter, Owen Bew came up on deck with some metal pots and a wooden spoon, and thus did he begin to beat upon those pots animating the chickens into an hysterical squawking while the men turned the cutter up and hoisted the ropes to put it over the side. Once it was in the water, Owen stopped. Beckwith selected the Seager brothers, Crabbe and Audrey, Dick Burrows, Don Bentley and himself to go out, the latter three each with two muskets. "Pono," he said, "you stay with Will and the rest, and watch Tong Guan. Some of them might be his people."

Tong Guan, meanwhile, understood what was happening, and joined the Gentlemen of Leisure at one of the cannons. There were but twelve of us on the ship, once the seven got down into the cutter, and I will say that without Dick Burrows, particularly, I felt more afraid and more vulnerable. Bob Olney, one of the gentlemen of leisure, stood up on the deck with his musket, and called across the planks to me, "You keep your eye on port, Pono. Once the shooting starts, anything you see you shoot."

"Yes," I said.

"Ben'll be at the fore with two others. Those manning the cannons can't see fore and aft, so swing your eyes around." Then he shook his head and said, "A ship like this could carry a crew twice our number, Pono, and now look where we are."

Thus did we wait. I thought that perhaps I would hear the reports of muskets within a few minutes, but much time passed without any sound, and I became more and more rigid and tense searching that blank wall of fog. I became so tired standing there that I believe I nearly slept, for at one point I jerked awake and looked down at my hands on the rail, and saw a warmth of color in my skin that seemed odd until I looked up, and there, straight overhead, the pale orange disk of the sun showed itself. Bob Olney had seen it too, for he stepped across the planks toward me and said, "Soon now."

After another minute of waiting I again looked up, and the sun shone more directly. The fog was about to clear, and I could now make out the cutter's faint shape. Just as I made out that shape, the reports of musket-fire came across the water, three reports, a pause, and then one. Then the oars of the cutter slapped the water, and in but a few seconds it had clarified, the men rowing quickly, and three other figures facing back, one in the stern of the cutter standing hunched over his musket, Dick Burrows.

The water between the ship and the cutter now became animated by small wavelets, the wind stirring it, and I smelled the odor of black powder. Something hit the water just thirty paces off the rail, and then I heard the sound of something hitting the planks on the ship's hull, these two followed by the more distant reports from beyond the cutter. I looked up and saw the shapes of vessels emerging from the fog, many of them, and it seemed that the cutter would not have the speed to get back to *The Tiburon* before being overtaken. The shapes of larger sails then appeared, and I understood that the fog was being blown away from the direction of the musketfire.

"Wait until they're closer," Bob Olney called.

I was nearly numb with fear, I will admit. The cutter approached, the oars slapping the water, and not fifty paces beyond it were small boats, six of them, then off the stern three others, and I saw dark men, naked but for those white loincloths, leaning over the rails as if preparing to dive into the water. The cutter bumped the ship, and the seven worked their way up the ropes, and just as the last, Don Bentley, came over the rail, there was a loud explosion and a section of the rail just beyond the men vanished, and a hole appeared in the wall under the quarter-deck, and with the squawking and flapping of the chickens in their cage, small feathers floated out upon the faint breeze.

"Fire as you see fit, lads," Beckwith called, and then leaned over, his hands upon his knees, and gasped for breath. "'Ave you got a bead on them?" Beckwith called.

From under the deck someone yelled back, "Narrowing, sir!"

Dick Burrows addressed his musket, checked the works near the trigger, and looked up and around. "Some of them is under," he said.

The smaller boats had pulled up about sixty paces from the ship, but now did not have their crews. A great belch of smoke appeared from one of the larger vessels, and the men drew back as a faint, rapid cloud of material raced over our heads and shredded the fabric of the aft sail.

"Port bow!" Bob Olney called. These smaller boats were close enough for Dick Burrows to make his way there, aim, and fire, at which one of the white-loinclothed men fell back into the water. I saw heads in the water, close, and then they vanished under.

"They're swimming under water to us," I said. I leaned over the rail and aimed the musket, waiting for a head to appear, but none did.

Beckwith turned to me, still gasping. "They're going to try to board," he said. "Aft in my cabin, the taffrail windows. Go there Pono, and—"

A powerful report followed by a gout of rolling smoke came from under us, and out over the water, one of the larger boats' mainsail folded into itself and vanished out into the fog, shafts of wood sailing behind it, and men went over the side into the water. "Aye, eat that!" I heard one of the Gentlemen of Leisure yell. Then one of our cannons went off on the other side.

"Down by my windows, Pono," Beckwith said. "They'll be trying to come in there. Owen'll be there."

I made my way to the stairway to the hold, and now musketfire came from all directions, and more cannon reports sent powerful shocks into the hold, rattling things in Owen Bew's kitchen and raising dust from the floor. Inside Beckwith's cabin Owen Bew stood by the small windows, now broken, a meat cleaver in his hand, and just as I raised my musket to fire at any head that appeared there, a hand wrapped over the sill, at which Owen brought the cleaver down so that half of the hand dropped on the floor. He picked it up by one finger, and held it out the small opening, blood dripping from the cut. He dropped it and turned to me. "Aye, Pono, come 'ere with yer musket."

I went to the window-hole, and saw more of the heads in the water. Then under the sounds of firing from above I heard thumping sounds through the wall by my feet. "They're setting axes in the wood and climbing," Owen said, holding his meat cleaver aloft. "You shoot some 'eads for me whilst I chop."

I raised the musket and aimed at one of the heads in the water, but a small boat swept past with three of the men in it, and I shot one of them off into the water, and others pulled closer to the ship, under my access to them. As taught, I pulled the cock back, flipped the frizzen, put a small amount of powder into the pan and closed the frizzen, and then addressed the muzzle of the musket with my powder, ball and wad. When I was done I shot one of the heads in the water.

"Go up to help, Pono," Bew said. "I'll watch here." I loaded the musket once more, and then left the cabin. Between me and the steep stairway stood a boy dripping seawater, crouched and wary in his loincloth, myself I suppose confused for the moment at what a boy would be doing in this enterprise. He stood up, his face crossed with an expression of beseeching anxiousness, and then he dropped his shoulders in a meek surrender. I looked once down at the musket and heard another cannon report that shook dust off the planks, and he moved quickly, his hand back, and before I could aim he threw something which clattered off the musket barrel and hit the floor behind me. He turned to climb the steps, and behind me on the planking I saw a bright knife.

That he had thrown it, and deceived me out of shooting him, made me more confused, until I understood that if he got onto the ship, others must have too. So I climbed the stairs and went out into the flat light into a riot of clattering metallic noises, chickens squawking, to see Beckwith, first, ramming a stock into the face of a man coming over the rail, and beyond him, others shooting their muskets or swinging them like clubs. Wood exploded next to my head, bits of it stinging my neck, and I saw one of the larger ships close enough to see clearly, one of the white men at its rail next to men hunched over a cannon. I raised the musket and very carefully aimed, as

Dick Burrows had instructed, and held the musket as firmly as I could, and pulled the trigger, the cap spluttering and then the musket bucking in my hands, at which the white man fell back, and those hunched over the cannon turned to see to him. Then another of our cannons went off, and the side of that larger ship exploded.

I loaded the musket once again, seeing to each step carefully, and then looked up to aim. Dick Burrows hurled a man over the rail, and then picked up his musket and shot down at the water. Beckwith stood looking around. I stepped away from the stairwell and toward Beckwith. The heads in the water were now retreating, and that one ship closest to us was sinking, parts of it on fire and hissing on the water as it went down.

"Pono me boy," Beckwith said. "Ye shot the white scoundrel did ye?"

"Yes."

"Then you're as competent a marksman as our man Burrows over there."

No one shot at the heads as the men returned to their small boats, some of which were now moving around the floating hull of the one that had begun to sink.

"Is Owen safe?" he asked.

"Yes. He was at the window with his cleaver."

The various sized boats and larger junks moved away, apparently through with the enterprise. We looked around at one another, as if each assessing the count—who among us has been hurt or killed? No one. And I wondered, what of that boy? I could not identify him among the heads moving away.

Dick Burrows came along the rail. He appeared quite calm. He spat over the rail and looked at the boats and ships moving out of sight in the thinning fog. "They ain't done," he said. "We knocked down one junk. It ain't enough."

"Pono put a ball in the chest of one of the whites," Beckwith said.

Dick Burrows stared at me a moment. "Ain't surprised," he said. "He's got steady hands. Hell, we was thinkin' that white fella was immortal."

"Which means?" I said.

"We threw six, seven balls at the son of a bitch," Dick Burrows said. "And you knocked him down. When we get to the Americas, we'll go huntin'."

"And why would they try again?" Beckwith asked.

"They almost got us," Dick Burrows said. "They got some on board, and they damaged the ship." He looked at the rail, missing one of its sections, and then up at the damaged rigging, one mast pole broken in half and hanging from its ropes. "They'll follow us and try at night. Can we sail?"

"Will!" Beckwith called. Will Kelsey came along the planks. "Can we sail?"

"A bit," he said.

"Then let's sail a bit," Beckwith said. "And tell Owen to break out some fine whiskey for these men, but not too much."

"Aye," Will Kelsey said.

"Well now," Beckwith said, "we've fought them off, and Dick here thinks we'll have to fight them off again." He looked out at the slowly receding armada of vessels. "Not a betting man am I," he said, "but this time I'll bet you a chicken they don't."

It will suffice to point out that Roger Beckwith won his bet. With the clearing of the fog, we made our way south, and it was clear that somewhere we would have to pull into shore to repair *The Tiburon*. King Philip's Land lay to the east of us somewhere out there off the port rail. Whatever became of the strange gathering of vessels that attacked us, I do not know, for once we passed out of their sight, we did not see them again. The only casualty of our battle with the privateers was Tong Guan, who made the mistake of trying to shift his position just as one of the cannons, called a carronade, was ignited, at which the recoil of the great, heavy device broke his right leg at the knee, so as we sailed, Owen Bew worked on Tong Guan's leg, Tong Guan himself inebriated on whiskey to the point of a giggling stupor. Then did he make his way around on the ship's deck in a splint, surly and of ill temper the morning after his leg was set.

The delay caused by the damage to the ship kept us from returning to my world for more than a year. First, we languished at sea under our partial sail for weeks. Beckwith wanted a well-wooded island of some sort where we could find the necessary quantity of wood to do our repairs. The broken mast, in this case a foremast, could be repaired without being replaced, but it would take considerable work on the part of our experts in carpentry.

We located a small island off King Philip's Land that had a cluster of tall trees in the center. Beckwith studied it, his eye jammed into the narrow end of his telescope, before turning to Will Kelsey and saying, "We may be able to use some of that wood."

"Not until it's cured," Ben Fowles said. "Best chance is a tree recently fallen."

I went in the cutter with six others. We had our muskets, and quite quickly men in loincloths gathered on the shore of that island. Just inland from where they gathered appeared to be a fishing village. Poles lined the shore strung with nets, and behind them were small thatch houses, and beyond those houses, a dense woodland. The men on shore did not appear hostile, for they waded into the water to greet us, and Beckwith, having anticipated this greeting, offered an old musket along with balls, wads and powder, to the man who seemed least afraid of our approach. He studied the musket, slapped the stock and spoke behind him to other men, who spoke amongst themselves.

"Where are the women?" Will Kelsey asked.

"In the woods lad," Beckwith said. "You'll not find them. And if you ask, these men will say there are no women here. It is an island of men."

"A lie if ever there was one," Will Kelsey said.

Thus did we engage in the repair of the ship. Along with the damage, there were other necessary tasks in the maintenance of the ship: pounding oakum in seams from the outside while the ship was pulled to an angle so that the seam would be above water, the Devil seam, they called it, a spot on the hull that took the greatest pressure during sail, and other such tasks involving stabilizing the hull. The food offered us during those weeks, then months, was good, based in large part on fish adorned with what little they could grow there, kalo among the island's products. Women did appear, but so as not to offend our hosts, the men stayed away from them. The men languished, for the humidity was oppressive, but because there was a reasonable source of water for the washing of clothes and refilling of our casks, the men often took off most of those clothes and waded in the shallows along that muddy beach.

Despite the discomfort, the men did remain alert to the horizon off that island, constantly scanning it for the shapes of sails, but there were none. We learned that one of the reasons was a series of shoals that had caused shipwrecks, and merchants knew the area well enough to avoid it, hence our isolation.

As the time passed, the repairs done under the direction of Ben Fowles, I was aware more and more of how much time was passing, indeed how much had passed since I was rescued from the war axe. I gauged it at more than a year and a half. In your calculation of years, I am referring to the summer, and then the fall, of the year 1787, and with the repairs taking so long, and a bad typhoon season in the seas we had planned to sail, the spring of 1788 brought my absence to two years. That we could not sail because of the weather struck me as an excuse, but I did not argue the matter, because proof came in the form of a series of storms that lashed at us for days, and undid some of the repairs that were in progress. Will Kelsey said he had seen it before, "like a pattern, one after the other, so you wouldn't remember which one took which tree or killed your 'orse." At night during the calm times, trying to make myself comfortable in the windless humidity, I calculated how much my children had probably grown, and how long Pekau had endured being alone up there in the mountains. These speculations tortured me, in part because I had never been able to settle in my mind what was meant by the statement that she waited for me in the clouds.

But the repairs went on, the gentlemen of leisure played their games, and I continued reading the encyclopedia when I was not carrying out some order or other, usually involving pounding oakum into seams or coating wood with varnish and tar. The island men were patient, and were amiable and friendly with us, thus rewarded by Beckwith in the form of small gifts that he brought out from his cabin. And one day the ship was declared seaworthy, and we prepared to sail, and when I asked Beckwith where we were going now, he told me that they were taking me home.

§

So progressed Pono's story, and while before this I had speculated on establishing a house for myself, I now found myself idling away the days lost in a dream of Mrs. Searle, the image of whom visited me in the nights whilst I lay in my somewhat dirty bunk being lulled by the soft movements of the ship. I did borrow the first of the ledgers from the somewhat reluctant Mr. MacFarlane, and bestowed it upon Mrs. Searle, who read the entire volume in two days. Pono's tale was taken to the death of his sister in that volume. I usually saw Mrs. Searle in the afternoons, after Pono had finished with his offering of the day, for Mrs. Searle kept herself quite busy in the earlier hours of the day helping the people who lived to the east, in the somewhat ugly collection of shacks there, all the way to the beginning of a putrid marsh.

When she returned the volume to me, I believe anticipating my daily movements down to a ten-minute span of time in the afternoon, she appeared to me somewhat tired, laboring along with what appeared to be a rather heavy bag. She saw me and waved, and walked along the dirt path between the low buildings toward me. "Tell your Mr. MacFarlane that he has fine penmanship," she said, approaching, and handed me the ledger from her bag. "And please tell Pono that I am more than impressed with his tale. He is a wonderful storyteller, and I find his story beautiful and in so many ways sad, but it is quite a window into the past, don't you think?"

"Yes."

"I should like the next volume, if that would be all right, but for the moment I cannot read it. There's an outbreak of something over there. I'm worried."

"An outbreak?"

"Influenza perhaps. It is the wrong time of the year for it, but I surmise that some sailor brought it up from Australia, which is in its own winter." She looked at me with a seeming perplexity, or curiosity, I am not sure. "I wonder if you'd come with me for an hour or so. I want to show you something."

"I don't believe it would be wise for me to go where there are sick people. You are talking about the grippe, are you not?"

"The people here call it Palū. Oh come, Matthew. We whites have an immunity to the worst of this. Please."

It is an odd picture, I think, of myself following this woman, the ledger of the first part of Pono's story under my arm. We made our way into an area far enough from the port that the moist heat became almost instantly uncomfortable, and the smells of cooking mingled with human and animal waste, that of pigs, dogs and chickens, hung in the air. The hovels were low, with low doorways, and the flies hovered over this waste, and the mires in which some of the pigs were lying. Naked children idled away their time in the meager shade of the grass roofs of the hovels, and in a few more open areas toward the mountains, nearly naked men tilled the earth with sticks. Here, the populace looked sullen, oppressed by the heat and the lack of any breeze. A few called "Aloha" from their doorways, at which Mrs. Searle responded in kind.

At length we arrived at a small cluster of hovels that appeared victims of greater desperation than the ones we had passed. At the door of one stood a white man and a white woman, speaking into the darkness inside. "They are from the mission," Mrs. Searle said. "There is a girl in that house the woman is fond of."

"Will the mission send doctors?"

"The mission has one, Dr. Blatchely. He serves the mission families and the high chiefs and their people."

"Are not these the high chiefs' people?"

"Sadly, no. They have only the kahuna lapa'au to help them, the native doctors. Their remedies for one thing and another worked for centuries, but we have brought the people new diseases." She looked at me, almost accusingly I thought. "I'm sorry," she said. "What we are seeing is repulsive beyond imagination, because they've no resistance. They are obviously a very strong people, but from our diseases, there is no resistance. We have given them Christianity and disease. Isn't that interesting?"

She turned and went to the two white people, and talked with them, while I stood there with the ledger under my arm. A distinct, foul odor came up from my clothes, of perspiration and turned food odors. I felt myself swooning with the merciless heat. It occurred to me that this matter of the introduction of diseases was inevitable anyway, for how could this string of islands remain remote forever?

Mrs. Searle did then return to me. "Please come this way," she said. "There are two houses down the way a bit here that are affected."

So I followed her, still perspiring and not at all enjoying this walk, my moist hand now darkening the leather of the ledger. At length we arrived at the two houses she had referred to, both of them perched at the edge of a marshy area above which flies hovered, but because we had come out of the dense cluster of hovels, I now felt a slight breeze. But just as that breeze refreshed me, I heard the sounds of weeping and moaning from one of the hovels. She turned to me outside the doorway of the hovel from which came the weeping, and said, "We must be silent, because a kahuna 'aumakua is praying."

I stooped low to enter, and my eyes adjusted first to the whiteness of Mrs. Searle's dress, and then to the forms of five people, one child lying on a mat with a native man above it, sweeping his hand over the child's bare chest, an old man and woman sitting against the thatch wall, and another child across the small room wrapped in a mat. The child being attended to by the man coughed, and that cough was deep and liquid, some catarrhal ague I supposed, but I had seen it before. What remedy might work? Rhubarb and calomel, or so doctors at home might prescribe. The kahuna chanted over the child, and Mrs. Searle watched, and then moved quietly to the old couple, who sat stone-faced against the thatch wall, the woman now wearied of her weeping, I supposed.

I wondered what was being done for the other child, and looked down at it. Something moved on the child's forehead, and I moved closer. It was one of those small, grayish-pink lizards, which jumped off the child's forehead and scuttled off. As Mrs. Searle whispered to the two old people, I leaned and touched the child's forehead, then recoiled in horror—the child was dead, and this mat was its winding sheet. I shuddered and looked at my hand. Warm as the air in this hovel was, the child's forehead was cold.

The living child coughed again, that deep, liquid hacking, and Mrs. Searle drew a rag from the bag she carried and wiped the thick mucous off the child's face. She turned and looked at me, and shook her head. The kahuna chanted, and Mrs. Searle moved to me, and whispered, "She is dying."

I had not known it was a girl. "What remedies is the man using?"

"He uses a fruit called noni, tree bark of some kind, sugar cane, and shoots of the hala tree that they make mats with. He uses other things too, but I'm not sure what. He boils them and administers this mixture five times a day. Everything is done in fives."

"And the prayer?" I whispered.

"He is appealing to some diety. Sickness comes from spirits, and cures come with appealing to them, along with the remedies they feed them."

"The other child is dead."

"Yes. And this one, too, will die," she said. "There is nothing we can do."

I looked at the child. The kahuna had finished his prayer, and now felt the child's chest, then said something to the old couple.

"Where are the children's parents?" I asked.

Mrs. Searle indicated that we should go outside, which we did. The sunlight was strong and hurt my eyes, which adjusted slowly to the line of hovels adjacent to the dirt path we had traversed. Mrs. Searle shaded her eyes and looked at me. "The fathers are at sea, most likely, and some of the mothers, well, they might be at the port."

"I see," I said. "Engaged I presume in a not-so-honorable profession?"

The look she gave me indicated that my statement was an insult.

She shook her head. "No," she said. "It is true, and that is the problem." She looked at the line of hovels. "And the other problem is this fever. I don't know what it is, but I do know what it is not. It is not the measles, or the spotted fever. But if it is an epidemic fever, then it will make its way throughout all of these houses and kill off a third of the people. I have asked at the mission if there were any help for this, and was told that the physician is too busy to come out here."

"MacFarlane's house is at the other end," I said.

"Then Mr. MacFarlane should be aware of this," she said. "He should take his family up Nu'uanu Valley and find a place to stay until this passes."

"And when it has passed, you say a third of the people will have died?"

"More perhaps. The race is dying."

14.

The world I was learning was indeed vast. I had familiarized myself with the five maps in the encyclopedia enough to know that my world was so remote as to be somewhere off two of those pages. Somewhere in that ocean was my world, and I was given to understand that our being able to find it was not a foregone conclusion.

The Tiburon cut its way through pleasant seas for days, and then through violent seas that hurled salt spray across the decks, tipped it so that the bow was awash, water blasting in and out the scuppers, so that the men remained awake through the night, holding onto one thing or another just to stay upright, after which, in calm weather, we would hobble around on the deck on legs so sore from being tensed for so many days that we all looked infirm and greatly aged. Even my hands and forearms, and my back, felt bruised, my neck and jaw tender from being tensed over long periods of time, and this soreness made its way even to my teeth. These storms blew us off our course, and extended the voyage to the point that I stopped counting the days and weeks.

On one of those days of calmer weather, we all noticed a more temperate atmosphere. We had left that humidity and made our way into days and nights that did not wear at us. The waters we traversed now took on a predictable pattern of swells, and the men went into speculations about where we might be. Beckwith used a device he called an octant, which I had seen him use before, but now he spent much time going over graphs with numbers on them, and over his charts, one of which had the handwritten heading 'Great Ocean.' I was fascinated by this process, for it was the science of his world. One might assume that we would simply go from King Phillip's Land to my world in a matter of a few weeks, but in truth we made a large, meandering pattern on that water, Beckwith and Will Kelsey hovering over their charts until they became short with each other: "Aye, it's north northeast for sure Will." "Are ye daft? You want to go taking on seventy-fours off the bloody

China coast?" "No, Will, I want to go to De Gama's Land and freeze my arse off is what I want to do." "It's dead east, man. Where the bloody 'ell'd you learn to navigate?" "From my benefactor, sir, and he was everything. Everything but a navigator that is." "Precisely my point. Leave this to me and go dream on the quarterdeck." "If I left this to you, my friend, we'd be lookin' for pretty maids in those islands at the bottom of the world." "Ar, and if we left it to you, we'd be tryin' to copulate with she-bears in the bloody Arctic Circle." "Will, you are a trifle overwrought. Go get yourself a drink." "Think I can't use an octant?" "I know you can't use an octant. You can use many things, but an octant is not one of them." "Very well then sir, I sh'll go get myself a drink. Very well."

Then we sighted land. In fact, at the time Bob Olney called down from the mast that he saw land, I began to catch the hint of limu in the air. The faint, but unmistakable scent of seaweed moved across the water. It was the smell of my world.

What Bob Olney had seen was a low rise of land, small, he said, but clearly the top of an island of some sort. As we moved *The Tiburon* closer, I could see, even from the distance of perhaps five miles, the white lines of surf breaking over reefs. But it was a small island, perhaps a mile long as we saw it from the ship, and rising out of the water no more than about fifty feet. And at first, sitting atop that island, there seemed to be a haze of dark smoke, which turned out to be birds, so many of them that their multitudes formed what appeared to be that dark cloud. We lowered the cutter. Beckwith took six of us with him, including Bob Olney, Dick Burrows, myself, Will Kelsey, Crabbe and Audrey. We spent perhaps two hours making our way along the island, listening to those birds, a rushing hiss resembling a powerful wind lashing through trees. We found an opening in the reef, and made our way through to a fine sand beach.

I looked around as the others walked up a high dune. The reefs looked like the reefs of my world, the water its proper color, but I had not heard of an island in my world this small and this remote. I walked along the beach, now paralleled by Tom Crabbe and Roger Beckwith. "Those are albatrosses," Tom Crabbe said.

"These are my birds," I said. "These are the birds of my world, but I don't know where we are." I looked out at the reef, and there, hopping amongst the exposed rocks, was another bird. "That is an ulili," I said. "They are said to inform on cheating wives."

"We'll go back to the ship, give the others a chance to walk around here," Beckwith said. "Can we eat the birds?"

"I don't know," I said. "I believe we can."

"Then we shall not," Beckwith said. "We must be careful." Tom Crabbe looked at him, I thought somewhat skeptically, as if he wanted to argue but thought the better of it.

"On the other side of that dune is some kind of a lake, or lagoon," he said. "Do we 'ave water enough?"

"We've enough," Beckwith said. "But I doubt that there's potable water here."

"Would you like fish?" I asked. "Or he'e?" They looked at me doubtfully. "I am sorry. I mean octopus. It is very good when dried and salted."

"I've 'ad octopus before," Beckwith said. "I'd appreciate that, Pono."

"I'll fashion a spear and take a look, then."

"Aye," Tom Crabbe said. "Now there's something we can eat then."

On the ship, I was invited to Beckwith's cabin along with Will Kelsey, Tom Crabbe and Dick Burrows. Beckwith laid a chart out on his table, blocked the curling edges down with two books, an inkwell and a pistol. "This is the great ocean, and here," he said, pointing with a quill pen, "is your island." It was a square he had drawn in the middle of an otherwise blank chart. Below the square to what would be the southeast on the chart were three other squares. "Tell me, Pono, what you know of the other islands."

I told him what I knew: that the largest island was the last, the easternmost island but also south, and that Maui and Moloka'i were between that island and mine.

"The largest being the last means smaller as we move northwest," Beckwith said.

"This means," Tom Crabbe said, "that we are at the other end of this line of islands. If Pono is right and the birds are the same, then we travel southeast."

"Very well," Beckwith said. "We shall remain here a while and rest."

Our sojourn on this island lasted two weeks. But for the perpetual din of all those birds, I recall this as a most pleasant time, for the weather was fair enough for the gentlemen of leisure to set their table up on the beach and to cover it with an umbrella of sailcloth, and for me to don my malo and go wading in the shallows with an old musket rod that Owen Bew filed to a point, and behind that point filed a barb. I probed into likely looking holes under rocks, and in one day saw, again and again, that billowing of purplish black ink block my own feet from my view, after which the he'e came out of the hole on the spear. I would then do what fishermen from my world did, bite the eyes to kill them, and then wade back and give the he'e to Owen Bew, who would salt it and prepare it for cooking. There was enough driftwood, and dead wood from the shrubbery, for us to have a fire.

The heʻe were plentiful, as were other fish, uhu that I could see hiding under rocks in those shallows, various small fishes that I recalled were edible, and in the reefs there was an abundance of limu, which the initially skeptical men quickly found delicious. Owen Bew wanted as much as I could find so that he might experiment with storing it in jars, or drying it. Dick Burrows found good water by tramping around the island, stepping around birds that did not deign to make room for him, and finding likely places to dig holes, in the bottoms of which pools of water formed. Owen Bew needed only to boil that water to cleanse it of anything that might make anyone sick.

I was not sure, however, of the logic of Crabbe's speculations about the nature of my world. I would find myself lying on the beach at night wrapped in a section of cloth, staring at the dome of stars and the moon, wondering if indeed we were anywhere near my home. I did not hear any voices in my dreams, not a whisper from Manomano, and this troubled me. It was either that Manomano was too far away, or dead, or I was somehow made deaf to his voice, and the voices of all close to me from that lost world.

One other observation about this stop at that low island: the men did not disturb the birds. In fact they became more interested in recording them in the form of drawings in small ledgers. Hostile or dangerous as they might be, they were still given to fits of scientific curiosity. I believe it could be that Beckwith's attitude about this place influenced them, for he approached whatever was natural and settled into its own order with a peculiar deference to that order. When we walked on the beach and came upon a huge seal, one I told him I had seen on my island, he approached it slowly, speaking to me with decreasing volume until he whispered to me, "What a fine creature this is, Pono. Look at its eyes. Are they not the eyes of a human, perhaps a beautiful, dark woman?"

"Yes," I whispered.

In the evening, I became interested in the question of food, and why it was that Roger Beckwith seemed so cautious about it. I sat down in the sand next to Owen Bew. "Sir," I said, "may I ask you a question? You are careful about food. Why?"

"Ar," he said, staring at me with a merry expression. "Pono, if you were sitting at court with the blinkin' queen, she'd think you a duke, she would. What an Englishman you've become." He leaned back and laced his fingers together over his knees. "Pono," he said, "I'll tell you a story, which shall explain in part how we think of food. Nearly fifty years ago when I was a boy, I sailed with Commodore George Anson down around the 'orn into this ocean, to take on the Spaniards. The men were hale and strong at the outset, but as the weeks and months passed, they began to show a change. I knew one well, James Smith, who was five years older than I and helpful, almost like a father. What happened to him happened to many.

"Each day this young man would stand at the rail grinnin' and eager for the adventure, but as the time went on that grin did change to a look of thoughtful melancholy, and I did what I could to keep 'is spirits up: 'Hey Jim, we'll get ourselves to the Spanish Main and get in a fight, we will.' And he'd say, 'Aye, we'll do that Owen, we will.' Day by day I watched that change in him, until one day I saw blood on his mouth and asked him what the trouble was, and he told me that his mouth hurt, his gums, and his teeth were comin' loose, and he showed me, his mouth agape, and inside there I saw the dark red swollen gums, recedin' up around his teeth to make them look long like those of some odd animal, and a little waft of that breath did cross my nose, and it was putrid and terrible. But he'd stand at the rail day by day, and soon his skin started a turnin' color, darker and darker, whilst some of his teeth did fall out, and worse, when they fell out, his gums grew, thickened and swelled, and kept growing until he would look out over the rail with his eyes locked on the horizon, moving his mouth over that awful growing inside there, that growing which rotted in his mouth, his face held in this appearance of a kind of permanent fright, or awe, or a muddled, hopeless desperation at what he felt, for he knew nothing of what was happening to him.

"Aye, and others began showing the same signs, the bleeding mouths and the rank and 'orrible breath, so bad that you'd have to hold yours in order not to be sickened by it. My friend James then underwent another change: a strong, hale and dutiful young man he was, but now, when an officer would chide him for being a slacker, he'd begin to cry, and would not be able to stop, like a baby he was, gone emotional over any little slight to the point that he would sit down on the deck and blubber through his rotten mouth. I could not console him. All he said was that he wanted to go home, had been dreaming of home and it made him weep, even the slightest thought of it. At length we sighted land, and from that land came the smell of flowers, and the smell of those flowers made all the sick men weep, the smell of earth drove them into an inconsolable melancholy, all these men hangin' on the rail sniffing the wind and crying, all of them with their bloody mouths and their skin gone nearly black, James's skin like that too, and now they were stiff and had trouble breathing to go along with everything else.

"One of the officers who wasn't sick loaded a musket to try to hit a bird swooping around the ship, and he stood five paces away from James and myself, aiming the musket whilst we watched, and there stood James, stinking and dark and his mouth swollen and his awful, haunted eyes running tears, staring at that land as if he'd fallen in love with it, and then did the officer pull the trigger, and the report of the musket, not any louder than usual, caused James to stiffen where he stood, his face locked in a terrible surprise, totter and then and fall on the deck, dead. So sensitive to sound was he that the report of the musket did kill him. He might as well have been shot. The officer missed the bird, but the report unmanned the rest of the sick so that they staggered and fell, cried out in agony, beseechin' that officer to refrain, for the sound hurt so badly. When those men got to shore, some tried to eat dirt. They pulled foliage off trees and brush and stuffed it into their bloody mouths. The experience of walkin' on land killed some, for they opened their arms and fell face down, dead. Others went insane with a mixture of joy and melancholy, their mouths full of leaves or dirt, their eyes popping.

"We know now that they were denied nutrients all men need. It isn't enough to eat dried meat and gruel. Over the years I experimented with this. Others did, too, tried to understand the nature of this affliction. A man named James Lind wrote a treatise on it, and called it scurvy. Others speculated that it had to do with eating the wrong animal whilst on your voyage, which explains Roger's superstitions about food. He's right, I believe. I tasted your seaweed, and it gave me a pleasure that convinces me that some of what we need is in that plant. Other places I have experimented with things: the soft tips of the branches of some pine trees, some roots, some fruits we find here and there. I trust the vegetable more than I trust any kind of meat. I believe I trust the creatures of the sea also, providing we eat only the flesh and not the organs. You've been a good sailor, Pono, in that you ate whatever I gave you, without complaining. Some of what I gave you was a mush mixed with dried pine tips, y' know, that burgoo the men groan about whenever I make it, various relishes made of such things as the cucumber, and so on. Lind would call these antiscourbutics. That the men are healthy suggests to me that we are eating the right foods."

"The men are healthy," I said. "Thank you for describing this for me. I hope my limu is an antiscourbutic."

"Aye, I hope so too," he said. "And Pono, remember, once you lose a tooth, you don't get it back." He then drew his lips back and showed me his, somewhat yellow and large. "I got most of mine," he said, "and I shall do what I can to keep them."

We chose a day with overcast skies to sail, and we sailed to the southeast in a snaking pattern, moving northeast and then southwest, and repeated in this pattern, so as to give the man up the mast pole a broader view of the ocean. The second day we sighted a peak off the port bow, and moved toward it. I recall a strong swell of emotion in my chest, for I expected that as we approached this peak, the larger island under it would materialize in my view. But it did not. What we found were three rock peaks emerging from the water, which blasted against the flanks of these peaks sending a white mist away from them, and after speculating on what it might be, Beckwith assuming that it was part of an archipelago, or line of islands, and so we continued on our meandering way.

After another two days, we encountered a very large area of paler blue water, interspersed with tiny islets, not unlike the interior of the reef at the first island where we had spent that pleasant time. I began to envision islands in the process of sinking, for this arrangement of islets barely broke the surface of the water. We sailed around the arrangement for a day, and all we saw were birds and low brush on the tiny specks of land emerging from that water.

Then did we sail in our snaking pattern for a week. I began to feel a constant anxiety about what we had seen, and could sense in the men, also, a strange tension, as if they had expected for weeks to find my island and were now baffled at its failure to appear on the horizon.

At last we sighted another island, one with two peaks, much higher than the first at which we had spent that pleasant time, but in land area, perhaps the same size. Beckwith's curiosity about the island frustrated the men somewhat, because the island looked too small to be populated. We lowered the cutter on the lee side of the island, Beckwith having identified a cove of some sort through the lens of his telescope.

The cove was a half-round inlet with a rocky shore, and there was little in the way of reef around the flanks of the island. I climbed out of the cutter along with Beckwith, Will Kelsey and Dick Burrows, and we made our way up through brush toward the depression between the island's two peaks. The others stopped to study some plant, and to look at the birds in their burrows in the patches of sand, and I went up the foot of one of the peaks. There, standing alone and looking around at the horizon, I felt the presence of something, as if I were unable to see something obvious. Then I understood that I had seen it: terraces that could not have been natural, for their geometric shapes matched those of the shapes of the kalo terraces of my island. I made my way through the brush toward one of these terraces, and came upon a stone foundation laid in against the slope of the mountain, and there, in its weedy center, were the remains of house-poles, and some distance away from the foundation, the blackened depression of a fire-pit.

I sat on the foundation. The air sounded to me in myriad whispers, perhaps of those who occupied this place, and then a deep, debilitating fear overcame me, for I wondered if these were my islands and they had worn themselves down to death while I was gone, and all the people I had known including Pekau and my children were around me whispering, *do you see what has happened?* Do you know how long you have been gone? So long that the soil and stone of your world has corroded in wind and rain and sun down into this tiny remnant, and this foundation you sit on, peopled for centuries by those who now make the whisper that invades your spirit, is all that is left.

I got away from there. As if to corroborate my suspicion, Beckwith had found carvings in the stone near where the cutter bobbed in the water. "It is a primitive picture," he said. He indicated a flat rock on an incline at the base of one of the peaks.

From a rough square four appendages extended, one holding a paddle, the head on the top of the square a small round thing. "It is a man with a paddle," I said. "Yes, this is my world. Or what is left of it."

"We went east southeast," Will Kelsey said. "We shall continue to do that and find more islands."

"It is my hope," I said.

We had languished long enough on the ocean that our water stores became low. This aggravated the men, as did the mystery of what had become of that island they had visited but three years earlier. Where the men had been ebullient and talkative in our journey from the South China Sea, I suppose imagining the women of my island, this exaggerated in their minds by some tales I had told them of their agreeable nature, they now sulked and became short with each other.

When the sea was calm enough for the gentlemen of leisure to set up their table, they played a game of chess for but an hour when Bob Olney, in a fit of anger at Tong Guan, swept the pieces off the board and stalked off aft, leaving the men staring skeptically after him and Tong Guan making unintelligible declarations in Chinese to the table.

Then we ran into a storm.

For two days the ship leaned, groaning and popping in its bowels, the wind lashing the lines above, the men finding handholds to stand there, legs splayed, riding it out. Beckwith's octant was useless, and I assumed that because of the wind, the ship moved, where, no one knew. If my world still existed, this storm would move us away from it until we were lost and without water, and we would all die.

One night during a strong phase of this storm, Will Kelsey claimed to have seen land, how, no one knew. "I saw a rocky coast!" he shouted at Beckwith. The men on deck, each holding onto something, looked at one another, faces dripping with rainwater.

"We were all looking!" Beckwith shouted. "There's nothing there."

"There was!" Will Kelsey yelled.

No one believed him. If we had been close enough for him to see a rocky coast, then we had been close enough to blast *The Tiburon* to sticks on those rocks.

We endured the storm that night, and in the morning, found the clouds somewhat higher and the wind abated, and unrolled sails. Beckwith could not use the octant, but he did use a small device he pulled from his pocket to determine magnetic north, and to turn the ship to the east southeast. Thus did we continue our journey.

How coincidence occurs, how events manufacture themselves in a way that convinces men that there is such a thing as fate, no one knows. But late that same day, when the sun had managed to penetrate the clouds, I was in my hammock stealing an hour's sleep, not having had any for two days, and heard men shouting. I rolled out of the hammock and stood on sore, unsteady legs, and then moved to the port rail where they all stood. At first I did not know what it was they looked at, until I focused my eyes into the distance and there beheld the immense, broad shape of my island, in fact that part of my island that was once my home, for in the center, barely visible against the faint black shape, I saw a thread of white connecting the high cliffs to the ocean, the very stream that fed the kalo that sustained my children. I wondered if my eyes deceived me, and concentrated on the sight for some time, thinking, yes, that appears to be the broad, grassy flank from which I and my father had carried so many rocks, and yes, that area at the right-hand end appeared indeed to be where we had been instructed to leave them.

"I was right," Will Kelsey said.

"What makes you think that?" Beckwith asked.

"There was another high island to the east northeast of this one."

"There was not."

"There is," I said, not taking my eyes off that faint, white thread, as if doing that would make it vanish. "It is called Kaua'i. This is O'ahu. This is where you found me."

Roger Beckwith's caution, mixed now with a strong curiosity, for my stories about this place had stimulated his imagination, brought about a plan for our stay here: we were merchants, and our ship was to be called *The Tyburn*, should any other ships be in the area. He respected the ship's original name, but at times practicality held sway. He had a way of altering the letters of the ship's original name on the taffrail to represent the new name, which bore enough resemblance to its original that even in its pronunciation, one could easily mistake one for the other. He had what he called 'forged papers' for this ship, so that should he be forced to show them to someone, the person would not have the wherewithal to verify these papers. The very remoteness of this place, he speculated, made it such that the likelihood of the presence of ships with many cannons was also remote. We would lay a few miles offshore while this bad weather passed, and work at taking water from the bilge, which now was twice what it was before and twice as putrid.

While all this planning was taking place, I was at the rail, staring at the white line of that waterfall, studying the places where it was broken, seeing in my imagination those flatter shelves against the mountain where Pekau and the children waited, at this very moment I imagined being inside the hale out of the rain, perhaps huddled in there with Manomano, and my mother and father.

At midday Beckwith called us all to the quarterdeck. "Now lads," he said, looking down at his crew, "we are to billet here for the time being. We must keep the ship out here, however, and if any of the natives wish to visit us, as Pono says they will, they'll have a long ride to accomplish that. In this way if there's any plan to attack, they'll be too tired to do so. I'll allow that it will become an irritation to you on the ship, for it's too deep to anchor here, and men must be on watch at all times. The water, however," and Beckwith looked off at it, "is so calm that the ship barely drifts. Should it become a problem, we'll pull her in and anchor."

In sum, we were to row the cutter in, nine of us aboard, and see what possibilities there were for setting up some kind of a camp. I had told them of the fair weather of my world, told them also of the generally unpopulated, or at least sparsely populated, condition of this end of the island. Should billets prove pleasant and workable in this place, then we might explore areas where there were more people. Beckwith had some difficulty believing that my people would be as welcoming and as amiable as I had promised, but I did caution him and the rest about the ferocity of our warriors, particularly those connected in any way with the ali'i, like my brother 'Iolana, or Mo'omake, the death-lizard.

I recall being nearly overwhelmed by a nervous excitement as we lowered the cutter, my hands shaking and my heart pounding, for the horrible speculations I had had concerning Pekau and my children were now to be tested. More than three years. How large would my children be? Planted on the plank, both hands on the end of the long oar and trying my best to match the strokes of my brothers in the cutter, I fell to holding my breath, as if when I let it out, my feet would be planted on firm ground rather than on the planks of the cutter, water sloshing forward and then back as we stroked.

The sensation of stepping off the bobbing rail of the cutter onto rock increased this anxiety. Dick Burrows came up after me, then Will Kelsey,

Roger Beckwith, Crabbe and Audrey, the Seager brothers, and Don Bentley. We made our way up rocks toward the path along the shore.

There was no one. The path was narrower than I remembered it, grass growing undisturbed toward the dirt center. I scanned the hillside and then looked up the mountain. We had pulled the cutter in to the north of the path that ran up the mountain along the stream, and tied it off on some rocks in a calm little cove.

"Well it's a fair enough place," Dick Burrows said. He wiped spots of water off the works of his musket, spat, and looked around. The sunlight had begun to dry the ground, and the land had begun to steam in the heat, that faint steam blowing to the south.

"Aye," Roger Beckwith said. "Looks like a deserted island from what I see here."

"As I said, this is a part of the island not well populated. I believe people still live in the hills above us, perhaps have seen us already."

"Your wife's up there," Dick Burrows said.

"I don't know," I said. "I will look now."

"Pono, take Dick with you," Beckwith said. "We'll walk about a bit, but we'll be no more than a mile from this spot. Get yourself back here before sundown."

"I shall be back before sundown," I said.

Dick and I went down the path toward the stream. Before we got to the stream, I stopped, and sat down on a rock and placed the musket across my knees. Burrows walked past me, stopped, and turned. "What is it?" he asked.

"No one speaks to me," I said. "No whisper, no scent. They are dead."

"I tell you what," Dick Burrows said. "If you believe in them voices, and you hear none, then we'll go back. Ain't no sense in goin' up here if nobody's there."

"Very well."

"All right then, let's go back."

I stood up, looked at him, and continued on the path toward the stream. A smart man, Dick Burrows. He showed himself there. A hopeful man, an optimist.

We came upon the rock carriers' path, and that, too, had all but disappeared under the grasses. We were near the area of the great sacrificial stone, and I told Dick Burrows of this, so we made our way into the tall grasses, kicking our way through it until we arrived at the spot it had occupied. "So, Muapo's worshipping place is complete," I said.

"You said this Moo-apo was one of them alee men, right? Which way's he at?"

I pointed my musket south. "Around the corner of the island, there."

"Well then, I'm keepin' my eye in that direction just to be safe."

Thus did we make our way up that path, overgrown, too, as were the others. Perhaps, I thought, some evidence might rest up there to tell me what had happened. Dick Burrows laughed at one point, and said, "So you lived then with billy goats?"

At the first shelf I found the remains of cooking fires, I found overgrown kalo patches, their water-sources no longer connected to them. This, I told him, was one of my homes, and there, where those sticks are lying in the dirt, was my house, before we moved up the mountain further. But no one had been here for some time, so we went on, negotiating the remains of a steep path farther up the mountain into terrain that to Dick Burrows seemed unlikely for human habitation, but on one of the highest shelves we again found the remains of a cooking fire and the pole-shell of a hale. Inside, standing on rotted grass that had once been its roof, I dug around in the dirt with the stock of the musket, but found nothing.

We stood on that shelf, both a bit breathless from the climb, and looked down at the ocean. Out perhaps a mile or more sat *The Tiburon*, and below us were the specks of the other men walking on the path along the rocks. "Hold up," Dick Burrows said. "I saw something. One ridge over, down there a bit. I saw movement."

"People?"

"Could be," he said. He stared at that ridge, as I did. It resembled the ridge next to the gully we had climbed.

"Saw somethin' drop down off the other side, like somebody goin' down the hill. Now he'd be what? Other side of that ridge there."

We made our way back down. The descent was as difficult as the climb, for, burdened as we were with our muskets, we each had but one hand free to steady ourselves. Once down in the high grasses, we saw the other men walking slowly along the ocean path, Beckwith looking up at us with one hand out, at which Dick Burrows shook his head. He made his way a few steps more, and then stopped and whispered to me: "They're behind us up that path. Looks like three men, older men."

I turned and looked, and saw nothing. Then I saw a tassel of grass move. "They are hiding over there," I said. "Dick, I'm going to move toward them and invite them out. Tell the others that they mean no harm."

"You sure about that?"

"I am certain."

Dick Burrows made his way toward the other men while I stood on the path, looking at that tuft of grass that had moved. I resolved two things before speaking to them in my language: one was that I would not reveal my identity and the other was that I would not specifically call any attention to members of my family.

"Aloha," I called out to the grass. "Show yourself. I mean no harm."

One man stood. I did not recognize him despite his age, perhaps fifty or so. He was thin and dark, a rock-carrier I thought. Then did two others rise from the grass, a boy about fifteen and another man older than the first, also quite thin and dark. His hair was white. "Aloha," the man said. "How have you come here?"

"On that ship, *The Tyburn*. It is a merchant ship come back from China."

"Ah, China," the old man said. "We have heard."

"I have heard that a great heiau was built near here. Is that so?"

"It is so. Muapo has built a great heiau, and it is finished. We helped in the building of this heiau. Now they leave us alone."

I moved toward the men, at which they began to back away. "I mean no harm," I said. "I merely wish to ask a few questions."

"You are haole yet you speak my language," the old man said.

"I am kanaka maoli."

"Ah, and of O'ahu?"

"Yes. I wish to know the story of the great heiau."

The men spoke with one another. In their subdued voices I heard something to the effect that they were concerned that I might be 'Muapo's haole.' At length the older man turned to me and said, "Why do you wish to hear the story of the great heiau?"

"I have heard of it," I said. "I have heard strange things about it."

This he considered. Then the eyes of the three left me and looked behind me, and I turned. The entire group from the ship was coming our way. The oldest of the three men looked once again at me. "They will not hurt you," I said. "You have my word."

Then did the three emerge from the weeds and stand on the path. Beckwith and the others stopped a few feet behind me, and I turned to them. "I will speak with these men for a while. Will that be all right?"

"Aye," Beckwith said. "Speak away, Pono."

I approached the men. Apparently they were interested as much in the musket as in me, for their eyes drew down to it, and then followed it as I shifted it from one hand to the other. We found a place to sit, myself upon a flat rock, the three of them on the grassy edge of the path. The boy seemed either excited, or perhaps afraid, I was not sure, while the others remained wary and somewhat suspicious in their bearing.

"Tell me of the heiau," I said.

Thus began a story of the terrible subjugation of the people of this area, of an arrogant ali'i wasting the lives of many in the quest of his self-aggrandizement. The old white-haired man told the story as if in verse: "oh did the people suffer, for the old and the infirm were throttled with cords, crushed with rocks and cast into the sea. Muapo's kahuna Kahimoku did have visions from the caves of death that made him kill those people. And oh did the heat of the day sear the skin, the rough surface of those rocks scrape and bruise, for no rest were the poor laborers in his awful quest allowed, and the rocks that dotted the landscape did vanish day by day as did the old and the weak.

So went his tale, until he arrived at the point that interested me: "And so did Muapo come in rain to the place where his ancestors had been slaughtered, to see his sacrificial stone. And the stone pleased him. And all but one dropped in fear, their stones shriveling in their sacs. All but one watched as Muapo did turn and leave, his warriors and the punahele of the great Kahekili with him, leaving Kahimoku and his warriors to complete the great task. And all continued in that task, until Kahimoku did select the one whose stones did not shrink, and endeavored to kill him first by casting him into the ocean and then taking him out and driving him to his knees upon a surf-splashed rock."

Here the old man paused, his hands up, while the other two looked at him as if in awe of what they were hearing. "He who would not drop his head rolled once again into the water and then after a confused pause by those who stood waiting to kill him, he emerged in a thunderclap and shot as a spear from the blue-black water, turned into a giant, vengeful needle-fish, so bright a silver as to close the eyes of all who saw him, to puncture Kahimoku in the throat and kill him, and then run his sharp, silver nose through the head of a warrior before vanishing again into the sea. Muapo was frightened, and enraged at this account by one of his warriors, and vowed to find the killer, 'Aha Ka'alokupono of the Sea."

The men stared at me. I was astonished at this tale, for I had become one of those minor gods of which there are, in my world, many, in fact thousands. If it were a story told to Muapo by the surviving warrior, the one I had seen run away, then that warrior had been somewhat liberal with his own imagination.

"It is an interesting story," I said.

"It is unfinished," the old man said. "Muapo desired vengeance, and so did select a warrior to find and kill the wife and the issue of the man turned fish, and then did Mo'omake and his warriors come to this place, for the Lizard of Death was for Muapo the one with the will and the power to do it.

Upon Moʻomake's approach did all vanish into the forest, for Muapo's desire for vengeance could mean the death of all who were near the place where the man turned fish had killed Kahimoku, and Moʻomake did learn of the mountain house of the man turned fish and strove to climb to it and kill his woman and his issue, and to take back to Muapo their bloodied remains to rot upon the stone so that the stench would please Muapo."

I did what I could to control myself during this tale, and believe that those three men did not see my shaking hands, nor the constricted throat, for the tale-teller spoke to the air before him, and the other listeners watched the tale-teller, faces held in that same look of awe and wonder they had shown throughout.

"Moʻomake and his warriors went up the mountain, and that woman of the mountain went up toward the clouds at its top, and then did Moʻomake see her and her children going up the rocks as young pigs, as if they floated laughing upon those rocks, and the warriors charged after them and looked up at a sky suddenly blackened by a terrible sight, of rocks rolling at them and striking them and crushing their skulls. And Moʻomake survived, and with the other surviving warriors did descend the mountain in humiliation. It is said that he became ill after this, his humiliation so deep that he was not seen for a long time. And the woman, Pekau of the Clouds, did vanish, not to be seen again. Some say she stays there, some say she and her issue turned into stout pigs and continue to roam the mountains. No one knows. And so the tale is finished."

I stared at the man. I was trying to control my elation, but the question of how she disappeared troubled me. Where had she gone? And what of my parents, and Manomano? "This is an interesting story," I said, "for I have heard of Kahimoku, and of Moʻomake. Do you know of the kupuna of this family of people turned beasts?"

"Yes," the old man said. "They vanished also, and all wondered if they, too, had changed themselves into other forms." His eyes fell once again to the musket. "And have you many of these?"

"Many, yes. And why do no people live in the location of this woman's house?"

"Anyone who lives in that space shall die," the man said. "Any who go up there to see the remains of the house shall be killed by Muapo's warriors."

"May I hold the musket?" the boy said. The elder shook his head.

"No," I said, "please, each of you may hold it."

I held the musket out, and the boy lifted it from my hands. "It is heavy," he whispered. He handed it to the elder, who held it, and ran his fingers along the barrel.

"There are many of these in our world, now," he said.

This surprised me. "Many? How many?"

"Traders come in ships, and men stay, haole men," the elder said. "They all have these muskets, and they are all favored by the ali'i. They are welcomed."

"How long has this been happening?"

"The turn of a year, or more," he said. "The possession of these," and he held it up, bouncing it a bit in his hands as if to appreciate its weight, "brings mana and then arrogance. Muapo has them. Kahekili has them."

"Are many ships here then? Ships with the larger muskets?"

"Ships like that one on the horizon," he said. "But on the other side of the island."

"What do they trade?"

"They come for water, food, and for the women," the old man said, and there I detected a look of distaste on his face. "They trade muskets for these things, remain here and rest, and stay with the ali'i, and then they go. Because it is near summer, they will be here for some time, and leave when the winter comes and the water becomes rough."

"Do the ships fight with each other? Are these men enemies?"

"No, they are not enemies."

"Are the ships larger than the one on the horizon?"

"No, the same. Are you that ship's leader?"

"No, the leader is there, behind me with the others."

"Your leader will want to stay with the ali'i."

"My leader will not desire to stay with the ali'i. My leader was looking for a place to rest for a time, here."

The man seemed surprised at what I had said, and looked, somewhat confused, at the other older man. Then he turned back to me. "Then you will stay here as our guests," he said. "My name is Ka'awela, named for a distant star."

"I am Aukai'ula," I said. The name means 'sea-traveller who is red,' or more simply, 'red sailor.' I laughed softly to myself, wondering how I had so quickly conceived of it.

I asked the three to remain while I talked with Roger Beckwith, and then related to Beckwith what the man had told me. Smaller ships, he surmised, meant that whatever traffic was here was not of the type he had spent so many years avoiding. The likelihood of a Brit seventy-four seemed remote, and although this place seemed to him somewhat rough, it did look pleasant enough to remain a while. I had told him enough, before this, about the ali'i and their habits. Now I added that while the weather appeared pleasant, it would not remain that way, and the rain would visit this place, or it would become parched and hot. But he seemed satisfied that, for now, this was the place we might remain a while.

The story the old man had told me, I thought, would wait until later. My goal was to find Pekau, and that might mean my staying here while my compatriots left, and should that be the case, then I would reveal that to Roger Beckwith later.

Beckwith put into work a pattern of coming and going from the ship. Ten men would remain on the ship while nine came in for four or five days at a time, and the ship would remain that safe distance from the shore. If that dark fellow over there had invited us to be his guests, then we would accept his offer, and in return that fellow would be the beneficiary of a few muskets and instructions as to how to use them. "Pono has told us of this alee-aye man who has brought so much pain to the people of this area," Beckwith said, nodding in the waiting group's direction, "so it would seem only fair that he should have the means to defend himself. And you say they live here, up those ravines?"

"Yes," I said. "As you look up the ravines, you can't see that there are shelves, flat areas that are quite habitable."

"It's purdy up there," Dick Burrows said. "Quite a view, I'd say, and if I were to want to make a camp, I saw two or three places where I could do it."

"And this alee-aye," Beckwith said. "He will be aware of our presence."

"He will," I said. "But he is careful."

I turned to the white-haired man and told him that we would indeed enjoy being his guests. The man turned to the boy and said something I did not hear, and the boy sprinted away on the path, running with astonishing speed, and after running perhaps two hundred yards he turned to the right without altering his speed and flew up the mountain, his legs under him a blur.

"Remarkable," Beckwith said.

Among the group of us, four volunteered to take the cutter back to the ship. Tom Seager did not like the openness of our position here, and his brother agreed. Crabbe and Audrey, upon discovering that the ship would have but a small crew while we stayed here, preferred to be on the ship. The somewhat crowded conditions on *The Tiburon* did not normally afford them the chance to be alone as they wished.

So it happened that ten of us were there to be welcomed by Ka'awela and his extended family. I should describe for you the customs that go with this: we were led up a mountain path to a wide, rather richly foliated shelf upon which sat five small houses and a large common area, a black fire-pit in the center. We were seated amidst some confused jostling and placing of muskets on the ground, the ten of us in a quarter-circle around this pit, which snapped with embers, ready to have wood added to it once the sun waned. It hovered upon the horizon, a rich orange disk with thin, pink clouds crossing it, and as we sat there, Ka'awela and his old wife, and his brother and son, the boy and the man we had seen before, waited with us, as if the dropping of the sun were some point we needed the patience to wait for. I explained to Beckwith and the others that there would be some formal process in this, but I became less convinced of this as we sat.

Then the people came up the mountain, from where I was not sure, but one by one, and then in small groups, young women and older men in malo and kihei, or shawls to ward off the cold, and older women, dressed in their finest pa'u, or skirts, but otherwise naked above the waist, gathered on the other side of the fire-pit, shyly regarding the strange haoles. When all had appeared, numbering thirty or thirty-five, they positioned themselves as if an audience to our presence.

Then, with an air of some solemnity, Ka'awela added wood to the fire. I leaned to my side and explained to Beckwith and the others that all of the men should be patient and respectful of this custom, for it was important to Ka'awela that he be a good host. The fire began to crackle, and in the increasing darkness the dark bodies of those on the other side of the fire began to enrich in color, so that the remarkable health of the women, particularly, became evident to the guests, and this was in contrast to the seeming ill health of the men.

Beckwith leaned to me and asked, "Where are the young men?" and I answered that many had died in the construction of the heiau, and others might have fled Muapo's warriors and might have thought of this event as a trap to get them back, for whatever their ages, all men feared Muapo's sacrificial stone.

Ka'awela did then stand above the fire and chant what we call a 'heahea', the exact words: "i kū ā hele mai i ka 'āina, he hale, he 'ai, he i'a nou, nou ka 'āina." Effectively it means: "If you wish to come to the land, there is a house, poi, fish for you, the land is for you." Then he went into an extension of this, fashioned for his guests: "welcome you from afar, you of the pale skin, you of the scent of far off lands, welcome, the house is yours, you of the hairy bodies, you of the scent of strange trees." When he concluded, I looked over at the confused expressions on my shipmates' faces, but then their attention was drawn back, for six younger women stepped forward and arranged themselves in a line facing the fire. Behind them, in the darkness by one hale, an older woman began slapping a gourd in a slow rhythm, and the young women began to dance.

Their motions were soft and elegant, gestures of invitation, gestures toward the sky, the slow stepping from one foot to the other, and in the soft, steady beat of the hand on the gourd, I could see the men staring, for I suppose they had never seen a display like this before. The paʻu the women wore bunched somewhat about their hips, so the movement of hips was exaggerated by that fabric.

Then a slow change came over this dance. The pat of the hand upon the gourd increased in pace, at which the dancers stamped their feet and moved their hips rapidly, and moved forward to the fire so that their bodies glowed a rich orange in the reflection, and they undulated their hips, hands out and breasts jouncing voluptuously, and the perspiration on their skin caused silver rivulets to appear on their stomachs, and the movement of hips all in unison caused those paʻu to become one mesmerizing shape of circular undulation below twelve outstretched hands, and they turned so that their sweat-slicked backs shone in the firelight, their black hair swaying back and forth so that their backs glowed and were hidden and glowed again in unison with the beat of the gourd.

At length they began to slow, to recede, and held out their hands once more under bowed heads, and I looked at the astonished men and saw there the expressions of amazed lust. "We shall eat now, I believe," I called to them, and they looked at me in confusion, as if the business of eating were something they had not heard of before.

The older women came forth bearing mats, bowls, ti leaves with fish on them, and gourds of ʻawa. I instructed the men as to how to eat poi, and how to pick at the fish with their fingers, but they were quite clumsy at doing this because they could not take their eyes away from the darker area over by one of the houses where all those young women sat in a circle, also eating. Then, behind me a few feet, there came the loud crowing of a rooster, at which two of the men jerked around, their fingers dripping poi. The rooster walked into the light of the fire. He studied the fire, and then shook himself, creating a small cloud of dander from his feathers, and strutted off into the darkness.

"Now there's a proud fellow," Beckwith said.

Kaʻawela, his brother and son, and two older men came and sat with us, but facing the fire, and ate. They ate with grave reservation, staring intently at the men, and the men appeared to me shy and cautious, and continued stealing looks at the women. Kaʻawela patted his chest and looked at Dick Burrows, on the other end of the line of sitting men from me. Then he said, "Kaʻawela." Dick Burrows pulled a fishbone from his mouth and placed it in the dirt, and patted his own chest. "Dick," he said.

"Ae, Dick, Dick," Ka'awela said.

Roger Beckwith reached behind him and drew up a musket. He moved away from where he sat toward Ka'awela, and handed him the musket. Ka'awela accepted it and placed it carefully across his lap, his mouth open in apparent shock. "Pono," Beckwith said, "tell him that he shall not try to use it until we instruct him as to how."

I did so, and Ka'awela nodded. "Mahalo nui loa, mahalo nui loa," he said.

"Well, yer welcome there, sir," Beckwith said, and returned to his place.

With the meal complete, the men looked at one another. The younger women rose from their positions, and walked gracefully toward, and then around the fire, and sat before the men, who backed away a bit, as if afflicted with bouts of sudden shyness. One young woman saw Don Bentley's belt-buckle and moved forward, and then reached out and touched it, at which Don Bentley removed his belt from and put it around the small waist of the young woman. He carefully buckled the belt, and all the other young women clapped and leaned over to look at what encircled her waist.

That act melted away any awkwardness, and within a few minutes the men had all paired off with these women, leaving me sitting there with Ka'awela, who looked at me and said, "May I speak to you privately?"

"Yes," I said.

We made our way out of the firelight toward the opening to the path, and there, after looking out over the black ocean, he turned to me. "I am honored that you have come," he said. "I fear saying this because I do not know your disposition where simple men like me are concerned." He considered what he had said, and then turned to me once again, the reflection of the distant fire in his eyes. "I know who you are."

"Yes," I said.

"Even in the worst of times I have maintained a grip on my belief in the gods. I wish to be forgiven for what I am about to say."

"You need fear nothing from me."

"The story of the needle-fish is one many believe, but I do not believe what I am told all of the time. There were many different accounts of how you killed Kahimoku, and the one most believe is told by one of Muapo's warriors, but I believe that the warrior was a victim of his own imagination, of the heat of his own fear."

"That is correct," I said.

"Pekau of the Clouds is alive, as are her children and we think also her father."

"I am pleased to hear this. Can you say more?"

"I fear the result of being the bearer of such information. I watched you during the hula, and saw that you looked through the women. You looked somewhere else, as you looked somewhere else when they came to your men."

"You are correct."

"The eyes given the gift by Kū'ulakai The Red One are eyes different from the eyes of other men."

"They are the eyes of a simple man, a rock-carrier."

I dreaded the information that he feared relating to me. Were they prisoners of Muapo, who waited for the right time to send them into death? I felt suddenly weary, and lowered myself and sat down. Ka'awela did so too, as if fearing remaining above me. I sighed, and looked down at the black water, and the faint change in the intensity of the light at the horizon. "You must tell me," I said. "Tell me where they are."

"Manomano is a wise man," he said. "Early one morning, some time after the rocks came down the mountain, he took the entire family away, in a canoe. No one knows where, but I knew Manomano, and he told me that they were going first to Moloka'i and then to Maui, to the region of his birth, which is Kahului. He asked that I not reveal this to anyone but you, should you ever return."

"You have my thanks for that."

"I know that the seas were calm the day they left. It is a dangerous journey, as you know, but Manomano is wise." He turned and appeared to listen. "There," he said. "Everyone is enjoying themselves. Will you not come back to the fire?"

"I shall come back to the fire," I said.

15.

Up there on the mountain I spent a night of troubled sleep, in a small hale provided for me by Ka'awela, who insisted that I use this house rather than sleep under the stars. The men of my ship went off with the young women, and I was happy at least for that, the hospitality of the people here that I had told them about months earlier.

On that shelf, morning was visible first as a brightening of the ocean far out, that brightness moving toward the shore and then illuminating the waving grasses of the flanks of the mountain. I rose early and sat at the head of the path, my eyes to the south, where Muapo's warriors might appear if they wanted to learn the reason for the presence of that ship on the horizon. I understood my predicament: I could not simply ask Roger Beckwith to take me to Maui, nor could I, once there, be assured of a willing person to tell me where Pekau, Manomano and the family had gone.

I heard movement behind me. Dick Burrows came my way, carrying his musket in one hand and eating 'ōhi'a ai. He came to the head of the path, and sat down.

"Eaten these before?" he asked, holding it out. "It's like an apple."

"Yes, all my life. What is an apple?"

Burrows stared at the brown pit in the center. "A fruit like this," he said.

"My wife and family are alive," I said. "They are on another island."

Burrows thought about this. Then he finished eating the 'ōhi'a ai and threw the pit down the hill. "Well," he said. "Maybe we'll talk to Beckwith about that. He's for helpin' us out that way." He pulled a reed of grass from a tuft next to him, broke it and began picking his teeth. "Can tell you that the men ain't wantin' to leave right away."

"It is as I have said then," I said.

"Par'ner, it's more."

I appreciated the word 'partner' from Dick Burrows. I suppose of all the men on my ship, Beckwith included, Burrows was the friendliest. As he picked his teeth, he scanned the water, as I had been scanning the water.

"Nope," he said. "Never seen people as generous as yours, 'cept maybe the Tuscarora, in their way. My Tuscarora is Injins, and in ways look a lot like you folks. You could pass for one."

"These people we are visting are common people. I cannot speak the same for the ali'i, although I do not know them well."

"I think we got company. Off down there to our left, mile, mile and a half or so."

I looked down in that direction, and then reeled in dread, I believe, for Dick Burrows stared at me in wonder. It was a procession of warriors and apparently ali'i, for there was no mistaking the kahili, that yellow and red feather standard borne by them duing Makahiki. This, however, was not a Makahiki procession, for there were no women or children with the group, of perhaps thirty people. They were warriors. Then Burrows leaned a bit forward, squinting.

"They got a couple whites," he said, and got up. "I'll get Beckwith. Looks like the ships's been seen and we been seen. We may have a fight."

My mind focused, first, on spears and war-axes and leiomano, on strangling cords and close, sweating combat, but I recalled that my men fought in a different manner, with muskets and swords. There were ten of us. Our cutter was hidden in the same little rocky cove it had occupied on the day of Kahimoku's death, and I hoped the sound of its hitting the rock face of that shoreline would not give it away.

Ka'awela hastened to the path opening, and looked down at the procession. "It is Muapo," he said. "He has seen your ship."

"We are ready."

"He will not harm you," Ka'awela said. Then, with the sound of some disappointment in his voice, he said, "He will invite you to his great hale."

Beckwith was not sure of the wisdom of going to speak with them. The whites, two of them, he did not mind. It was the look of the warriors that caused him some alarm. I translated what Ka'awela told me, and he said, "From what you've told me, your people are smart where gaining favor with each other is concerned. How do we know that this Ka-ah Vela isn't taking advantage of an opportunity here?"

"He would not lie to me, I believe," I said.

"So what are we to do? March down there with our muskets up?"

I turned to Ka'awela, and in our language, said, "I should not go down there. I shall be recognized by them."

"'Aha Pono," he said. "In your dress you will not be recognized. They will wish to talk to you, as all ali'i wish to talk to all haole. They will wish to get the muskets."

I turned to Beckwith. "They treat all haole well," I said. "You shall be treated like royalty."

"And get our throats slit at night, is that it?" Beckwith asked.

"No," I said. "The ship lies on the horizon. They know that great treasures are within it. They wish to get some of those treasures. Muskets, for one."

"And why wouldn't they attack us now?" he asked, holding his musket up.

"Three, four of them below have muskets," Dick Burrows said.

"They fear other men on the ship. If they harm us, they will have to contend with them. They do not know how many there are, or if you have cannons."

"Very well," Beckwith said. "Mates, go find those other rascals and bring them here. We'll go down and talk with them."

Ka'awela moved to my side. "That is Muapo," he said. "Do not prostrate yourself before him. If you do, he will begin to ask why, and you will be recognized."

The odd image of myself standing facing Muapo seemed to me unwise, yet I believed that Ka'awela was right. My deportment should be not unlike Dick Burrows', or perhaps Will Kelsey's, who faced everything and everyone with the same directness.

Will Kelsey walked to me. "Wear this," he said. It was his hat, in fact no more than a greasy leather bag with a rim that fit the head, and I held it, felt my thumbnail move the foul, black paste on the inside of the rim. It smelled, too, but I wore it.

The ten of us descended the path toward the procession. Ka'awela told me as we left that he was there should we desire to be his guests once again, and I assured him that we would do our best to return, and I thanked him for his hospitality. I think the man was made bitter by our departure, and he felt that Muapo's hale would make us forget his kindness.

As we reached the path along the shore, I moved in behind Will Kelsey, and saw a taller warrior walking with a limp. It was Konapiliahi, and indeed as they enlarged in my vision, I saw the dark side of him, bluish in the morning light, his brown skin on the ocean side. I moved up next to Will Kelsey. "I know the cut-in-half warrior."

"Cut in half?" he whispered. "Aye, I see him, the decorated one." All of the warriors had tattoos, but Konapiliahi stood out. The two haoles carried muskets, as did two of the warriors. Dick Burrows and Roger Beckwith were out in front of our group, approaching the procession cautiously, and then Konapiliahi and the two haoles moved out in front of the procession, which stopped on the path.

"Ahoy lads!" one of the whites called.

"Good day to you sir," Beckwith said.

"A right fine looking vessel you've got out there."

"It's *The Tyburn*," Beckwith said. "Fresh from China. Encountered much in the way of bad weather on the way."

I remained behind Will Kelsey, adjusted my filthy hat and studied Konapiliahi. He had not changed, still bore the regal, impressive bulk of a warrior, despite his leg, whose scar left a deep dent in his thigh. He spoke to the impressive group of warriors, who, holding their spears and war-axes, moved off the path into the grass. The haole who had greeted them smiled.

Don Bentley and Dick Burrows moved out into the grass, their muskets at the ready, and Ben Fowles positioned himself on the opposite side of them, holding the musket across his chest. All were cocked.

Muapo moved to the front of the procession, appearing flustered with the proceedings. In his red and yellow feather cloak and royal helmet he looked impressive, but small. He said something to Konapiliahi, who then spoke to the haoles, who conferred, apparently trying to understand what Konapiliahi had said.

"And are you Brits, boys?" Beckwith asked.

"I'm a Brit," the man who had greeted us said. "'e's American."

"Where ya from?" Dick Burrows asked the American.

"Virginia," he said.

"Right pretty country," Dick Burrows said. "You fellas aim to use them muskets, or am I right in figuring you ain't loaded? You don't hold 'em like they're loaded."

The man flipped the frizzen of his musket up. "No powder," he said. "Here they fight with spears mostly, like the twenty or so behind me."

"What you want to dicker for? Powder?"

"Yep. Got any?"

"Got 'nough on the ship to blow this island off the water," Dick Burrows said. "If that's what you're wonderin'. You might tell your folks that we got ours loaded. Tell your folks the first to get one in the face is that chief there."

"Cannons too?"

"Lays low in the water, all the cannons we got."

"Why are you telling him this?" Beckwith asked, somewhat softly.

"They won't hurt us if they know we'll dicker," Dick Burrows said to him. "Those fellas with the spears 'n clubs don't look scared 'a nothin', and that's bad. We gotta get our message out before they get ornery."

"How many cannons does a trader need?" the American asked. "Or are you privateers?"

"More'n the next trader," Dick Burrows said. "I wouldn't go out there and try an find out, though, if I was you."

The British man cleared his throat, and stepped forward. "My chief would like to barter for powder. Powder is scarce here, and what powder there is goes to the high chief some ways down the way there behind us."

Konapiliahi moved forward to stand next to the Englishman, and his eyes fell once again on me. I could see Beckwith and Will Kelsey studying his skin, somewhat awed, I think, by the ferocious appearance of the man.

"I don't like this," Beckwith said.

"He won't hurt us," I said to Beckwith. "I know him. He is my sister's husband."

"Indeed," Beckwith said, turning to me. I moved back behind Will Kelsey, because this movement of Beckwith's had pulled Konapiliahi's attention away from Dick Burrows to me, and I thought that, for a brief moment, he had begun to wonder.

"Who's the darkie?" the American asked.

"Injin," Dick Burrows said. "But he speaks a bit of these folks' language."

I did not think he needed to say that. The two whites conferred, and then spoke back to Muapo, who then spoke to Konapiliahi.

"If he speaks some of their language, then maybe he should do it now," the American said.

"We can do the speakin' for now," Dick Burrows said.

"How long you intend to stay?"

"Not sure. Gonna take in water, rest up a bit."

I moved a bit forward toward Beckwith. "They won't hurt us," I said softly. "The chief is interested in powder, and will treat you very well if you promise him some. Invite the cut-in-half warrior over to us, and I will speak to him." It occurred to me that Konapiliahi, who had always been a friend to me, would keep my identity a secret, as it occurred to me that he had already recognized me. I could now see the ferocity on his face crossed by that hint of wonder, and he looked, now, mostly at me.

"Does that make sense to you, Dick?" Beckwith asked.

"Long's he knows his chief gets his head blowed off, it makes good sense to me."

"I'll advise you to keep that finger limp, Mr. Burrows," Beckwith said. "We don't want to instigate anything here, is that clear?"

"I ain't instigatin' anything," Dick Burrows said. "If somethin' get instigated, their chief gets minus his brains is all I'm sayin'."

"Very well," Beckwith said. "Remind me to record some of the wonderful expressions I hear from you. 'Gets minus his brains' is a delightful conceit.

And tell me: why is it you Americans get at each others throats the way you do?"

"We're just sizin' each other up is all," Dick Burrows said. "Back home we'd be all right. Here I take care, that's all."

"My compliments on your prudence," Beckwith said. Then he turned to the two whites. "Send that big fellow over here, the one who's half blue. Our, ah, injin would like to confer with him."

"Somthin' he conferrin' on that we shouldn't hear?" the American asked.

"I can't hear it neither," Dick Burrows said. "You an' me, we'll just wait. Less you got a other idea."

The American snorted and looked away at the ocean.

I looked at Muapo. During these negotiations he simply stood there and listened, as if fascinated by the alien sound of their language. His warriors stood stone-faced, awaiting his order to attack, I suppose, but Dick Burrows was right. Muapo wanted powder, and it was on the ship.

As Konapiliahi moved toward us from the group, Beckwith and Kelsey backed away, and those on the fringes of the path spaced themselves out a little further, because Konapiliahi was larger than any of us, and his appearance kept everyone watchful. He saw me again, and nodded his head in the direction of the water, and then turned and spoke to Muapo, who flicked his hand at him as if waving away flies—yes, yes, confer with the man.

I walked off a few paces and sat down upon a large rock that faced another, upon which he could sit. I removed the hat and placed it on my knee, arranged it so that the filthy interior would not show. Konapiliahi approached, limping, and sat down, looked over his shoulder and then back to me. "Brother, I will not put my face against yours, although I wish to," he said softly. "My heart is high seeing you alive."

"Thank you. What of Laka? Is she well?"

"She is well. We have four now."

"That is good."

"There is much we could talk about, but little time now," he said. He looked back toward the men, the brown side of his face to me. I saw bits of gray in his hair, and the skin around his neck had become creased with age. His body, however, remained strong, the blue and brown knees pointing toward me large and muscular. "Muapo invites you and your men to his hale. But I do not know if anyone might recognize you, and if Laka sees you she will give you away, for she will be unable to conceal her joy."

"I will say that I must remain with the ship."

"Do you have the powder?"

"Yes, in many wooden gourds of the type haoles make, called a 'keg.'"

"Keg," Konapiliahi said. "And this 'keg' contains the powder. How large is it?"

I held my hands out, indicating two-thirds of a foot by a foot.

"Ah, this is much powder." He looked around once again. "Kahekili wants muskets and powder," he said, "wants the great muskets on wheels—"

"Cannons," I said.

"There are many haoles in our world now. Many. And they bring muskets and—and cannons as you call them. It would be a small matter but for one thing, and that is a warrior in the south who has many more muskets than we, a warrior who has been trading with the haoles more than we, and he now is moi of Hawai'i."

"But that is far away."

"This warrior is related to Kahekili. One of his wives is the daughter of Namahana, the half-sister of Kahekili. This warrior, who is named Kamehameha, will carry his desire for conquest to us. Kahekili knows this, and waits."

I studied his face, divided as it was, with both sides locked in a brooding perplexity. He seemed to care not for the presence of Muapo. Whatever visions he was cultivating at the moment seemed far more important than upsetting his chief.

"Many more ships travel to the south than to us," he said. "Those who come to us have little left to trade because they have already traded away muskets and powder in the south."

"I will talk to my chief about this."

"Your ship. It is far out on the water. Why is this?"

"My chief is careful. He left many men on the ship, to use the cannons if anyone should cause difficulty."

"I will tell this to Muapo. If he welcomes your men, he will get powder."

"Tell him that," I said. "And tell him that I will not join you at his hale."

Konapiliahi nodded and rose from the stone, somewhat slowly, his leg stiff. "How long will your chief wish to stay here?"

"Many days," I said. "Many."

Beckwith designated me as the man to stay near the cutter while he and the rest would go with Muapo to his house. Dick Burrows declined the offer to go, because he felt very much at home there up on the mountain with Ka'awela and his family and people, and a miss called Lana, he thought her name was, who wouldn't want to see him wandering off, just as he wasn't interested in wandering away from her.

And so we stayed, the water offshore calm enough that holding *The Tiburon* in place without its anchor down was not difficult. Within two weeks of our arrival, we moved the ship closer to shore, enough that the bottom of the ocean was visible off the rail through clear, dark blue water.

During those early days of our long stay, while I was on land, I rose early in the morning, stripped myself down to my malo, and walked up the mountain, I suppose thinking I would find Pekau higher up than our little houses. These trips took me high enough that, one day, I made my way through a strong wind up through ōhiʻa trees in bloom with their red flowers to where I could see far to the east and south of my island. Below me I saw the vast plain of Ewa, where so long ago, Konapiliahi and I became involved in the failed kīmopō against the chiefs of Kahekili. As I stood there in the wind, all seemed serene down there, hundreds of cooking fires visible across the plain, and in the far distance I saw the sacred Leahi, a distinct flat-topped mountain with a lump on the ocean side, a place I had never been. This was near Waikīkī, Kahekili's playground, and I could see, just offshore, tiny dots in the water, although from this distance I knew my eyes were deceiving me. When I turned, I saw below me, out on the calm water, *The Tiburon*, tiny figures moving along the rails. Far beyond Leahi lay Molokaʻi and Maui, and I felt that this strenuous activity of climbing was but a nervous release I took on as I waited to go beyond that distant mountain.

In the evenings I spoke with Kaʻawela, at first pressing him about how I might get to Maui and then return. He was a wise man, not unlike Manomano in his careful speculations. I told him that Manomano said that he would speak to me in the night, and Kaʻawela said that it was less a matter of Manomano's speaking than it was my hearing, that clad in the clothes of the haole, and living these years in their ways, I had perhaps lost my skill at listening to those voices. In any case, he told me, the future appeared too rife with friction—Kahekili rests in Waikīkī while the warrior Kamehameha becomes stronger. Kamehameha was a giant, perhaps the greatest warrior ever, and he not only commanded a devoted army of men eager to show him their daring, he had the haoles' muskets and even the cannon. Kahekili was older now, and perhaps too given to relaxation, as if what happened on the great Island of Hawaiʻi were of no concern to him.

One of the walks I took was from the location of our house, that first shelf where Pekau and I had begun our life. Little evidence of our having lived there was left—the blackened soil of our fire-pit, the remains of our kalo patches tucked here and there on level areas, and a few broken sticks which once had been frame-poles for our little hale. As Kaʻawela had said, no one inhabited this place after Kahimoku's death.

The path that rose above this area, leading to our more recent home, was overgrown and barely visible, but I made my way up, over that same treacherous terrain that my children and Pekau had little difficulty with. The higher shelf was empty of obvious evidence of habitation, although the fire-pit was more visible as were the arrangement of some stones delineating kalo or ʻuala patches. The remains of our house frame, now rotted and lying on the sparse grass, lay arranged as if someone had pushed it over. Above this area, the mountain face seemed vertical, although I knew of one path that rose diagonally to another smaller shelf high above.

I went to the base of this path, and, staring at the moss and lichen-spotted rocks, I experienced a strange haunted pause, but I shook that feeling off and made my way up. The reason for that uncertainty was perhaps fifty feet up the mountain face, where I pulled myself up onto another of those shelves created by thousands of years of flowing water—it was a bone, not that of a pig, I thought, for it was long. There were no other bones near that one, and I guessed that it had fallen from somewhere above. I looked up, and there was another interruption in the terrain.

The climb to the next level area was not difficult, because although the cliffs appeared nearly vertical, it was closer to a forty-five degree angle. I pulled myself up onto a flat area deeper than I had expected, one which might be large enough for habitation, and indeed there were the remains of a cooking fire grown over now with tough mountain grasses. I moved my foot around in that grass while looking off to the side where there was a rocky depression with the glint of water in the bottom, that same small source that journeyed all the way to the ocean some of the months of each year.

Then the sun was blocked by a cloud, which slid along the mountain face, chilling me. Near my foot, then, I saw something pale gray, and moved the grass aside to reveal a dry skull with cracks in the crown. I rolled the skull over to reveal its detached jawbone, and studied the top row of teeth. They looked like my father's teeth, or Manomano's. I shuddered, wondering now if elsewhere around this area lay Pekau's and my children's bones. Was that story told me by Kaʻawela a kindness on his part, telling me of Manomano taking her and the children to Maui? I did not want to know.

It became clear to me within weeks of our arrival that Beckwith and the other men would not be inclined to sail anywhere for the foreseeable future. They had altered the letters mounted on the taffrail of *The Tiburon* so that it now read *Tyburn*, and were parading as merchants of a fledgling company from England. Beckwith himself, who was not ordinarily given to cavorting with women, apparently was lured out of his monkish habits by one of the healthy young women who lived at Muapoʻ great kauhale. I could not fault him, as I could not fault myself for my monkish habits. So frustrating was waiting on land for the opportunity to sail, that I eventually preferred sitting on the deck of *The Tiburon* with a volume of the encyclopedia on my lap, for the broad view of my island seemed somehow more comforting. Indeed I was separated from Pekau by water, and so this place separated from our former home seemed appropriate.

It was perhaps two months into our stay that my situation changed. I had finished ten days on the ship, which was now anchored just offshore and beneficiary of frequent visits by my people on canoes. I helped row the cutter in, along with Owen Bew and the Seager brothers, Bew himself not particularly excited about being separated from his kitchen. Upon our reaching the shore, I made my way up from our little cove over rocks very close to that shelf where I was saved from the war-axe by Beckwith and his men. I rose up to look out over the grassy foothills that had held the rocks I had carried, and was confronted by six warriors, Konapiliahi at their lead.

"Muapo summons you," he said. "He has a request."

I looked back at Owen Bew and the Seager brothers, only one of them armed. Their doubtful expressions let me know that they were not going to die defending me. Muapo had reasoned out who I was, apparently, and now might exact the revenge he had waited for so long.

I had no other option but to go with them. "Must I go now?" I asked.

Konapiliahi smiled. "Pono," he said, "it is a matter of the future, not the past."

"Will Laka be there?"

"She will not," he said. "She is helping a friend to the east, a woman who had borne twins." He turned so that his blue side was toward me. "Muapo has requested your presence for reasons I am not aware of." He thought a moment. "Apparently he wants this meeting with you alone. Tell your men that you are visiting Muapo."

I told them, and their doubtful expressions remained. "Muapo is thinking of something other than vengeance," I said. "I shall go with them now. If you would, please tell Ka'awela that I have gone."

Bew looked with a somewhat fearful expression at the warriors, especially the cut-in-half Konapiliahi, while the Seager brothers stood back, the armed one holding his musket in both hands.

Konapiliahi looked at the path. "He requests your presence now," he said.

We walked. When we got to the place where years earlier we rock carriers had piled up our rocks, I paused and looked back, and then followed Konapiliahi, looking around at the landscape which was more temperate and less parched and windblown. It took us perhaps a half an hour to make our way to the path leading up to Muapo's kauhale. It was nestled between two ridges, the heiau to the left against the steep flank. I had not seen it from this perspective before. It was large in terms of his height from the bottom to the flat top. Over that lip I could see the shapes of god-images, and imagined the sacrifices that had taken place on the great, flat stone.

The path led us upward, climbing behind the now sweating Konapiliahi, his blue side glistening in the sunlight. At length we rose to a large, flat shelf toward the rear and against the ravine of the mountain ridges, in the center of which stood Muapo's house, a lofty structure with a perfectly arranged grass roof.

I was unsure of how I should approach that house. Too much experience with the white men had made me reluctant to crawl as I was supposed to. But I shook that off as we approached the low doorway. Konapiliahi stood aside, and I made to lower myself to my knees. "No," he said. "He wishes that you approach as the haoles do."

Muapo was not inside. The large space, impressive particularly because of the great height of the roof poles and dense thatch, seemed to me fitting for ali'i. Konapiliahi indicated a lauhala mat, and I sat down on it. He then went out a low, back doorway. No one else was inside the great house. I waited there some time, until I saw shadows appear at the back opening, at which I rose to my feet.

Muapo came in, and put out his hand. It was the haole greeting, and as we shook hands, Muapo's very soft in mine. Konapiliahi, who had followed him inside, nodded enthusiastically. "Please, sit," Muapo said, lowering himself somewhat gingerly onto a mat identical to mine. "Pono is your name," he said. "I know you, and I know of your hand in Kahimoku's death." He paused, thinking. At length he looked at me, and said, "I will tell you a story. Have you the time for one?"

"Yes," I said.

"Excellent," he said. He rearranged himself on his mat. "My forebears are ali'i. My great-grandfather lived in a hale on the very place we sit. It was smaller than this, and he needed little for himself and helped all people, even the common people of the mountains. He was a small chief, compared to others, but his spirit was great and he was respected by all. Another chief envied my great-grandfather for the love he wore about him like the greatest of all cloaks, and sought to allay the jealousy in his heart by killing that reminder of his own flaws, and thus did he invent a pretense for luring the well-loved man and his family to the very grassy hills you labored over, and there did slaughter my great-grandfather and his family, by placing them upon the ground and crushing their skulls with rocks. Yes, the very rocks you carried, dropped by gleeful warriors upon the faces of men and women and children, while at my great-grandfather's hale, warriors murdered all who stayed there. One child survived, an orphan seen by the murderer as a token of his victory and a living representative of that family that he could own as a satisfying memento of that victory. But that child, my father, learned of his own origins, and as a young man did plan revenge against his artificial father. It is not relevant how it was that he rose up and bested that murderer. It is sufficient for you to know only that he put upon me the task of erecting the heiau that changes the face of the mountain out there, and that he put upon me, his son, the task of exacting in reverse a vengeance that would match the magnitude of the slaughter that he survived, for the issue of that jealous ali'i and all who helped him in his treachery, would suffer as did my forebears, into a future that would mirror the horror of the past tenfold, and that the heiau would be built with the stones whose mana was tainted, or blessed, by my blood. Thus did I assign to Kahimoku the task of overseeing this enterprise, and until it was completed the very marrow of my bones would remain tainted by a long and deep-seated dissatisfaction, until my father's spirit could rise in peace into the land of Milu." Muapo went silent there, and I sat and waited. I drew breath to speak, but Konapiliahi held up his hand.

"That task is completed," Muapo said. "And now we live in peace. One chief becomes jealous of another, and strife blooms like flowers, but we live most of the time in peace. As we speak, a storm is on the horizon, a black storm rising above the calm water. Two men argue over a trifle, not seeing this storm. It rises high into the sky and its first light breezes cross the faces of these men, but they do not feel it. Then they settle their differences and play in the water, and watch their children. They do this as the sky blackens with the storm, and are blind to it."

Muapo paused, one hand in the air. I waited. He looked off to his side, thinking. "Some years ago I would not have grasped your hand," he said. "I would have seen it as a defilement. But the haoles have taught us much. I have dug a hole and I have placed my need for vengeance against you in it and covered it with dirt. Kahimoku was my son." At my expression he raised his hand. "He was not a sacred son but a son nevertheless, he who studied the faces of all to find evidence of that old, hated blood it was my task of ridding from the earth. He did not see that blood in your face, or he would have killed you. Whatever awful magic came to your aid that day I shall not know, but you are here and he is not."

Muapo looked at me, and I saw emotion on his face, but he was at the same time thinking of something else. I looked at Konapiliahi, who nodded.

"I feel the wind on my face and I hear the thunder in the distance," Muapo said. "I look at my house and I see that wind stripping it to its bones. That storm is moving toward us in the form of a warrior, and the storm bears the name Kamehameha. It is true that I am a chief, but I am as manini is to manō. If I am to remain a chief I must cultivate favor from greater chiefs. Kahekili grows old as I grow old. He is blind to the storm, but I am not." Muapo repositioned himself, looking intently at me.

"You are as no other I know," he said, "because you speak both languages. The haole Beck-wit told me this. The haole Beck-wit is a wise man, and a generous one. He gave us three of the Muss-kit, and the black sand that explodes. He said that you speak the haole language as well as the haole. Can you read a lie in the haole language?"

"I do not know," I said.

"Are the languages alike?"

"They are alike in that both use one thing to mean another, as in our language a storm is a man, in theirs a ship is a woman."

"Ah," he said. "You shall go to Maui as my representative. You must go without the haoles, and you must not reveal that you speak their language." He looked down at my legs, and then reached over and touched my knee. "This thing you wear. What is it called?"

"It is called 'trousers,'" I said.

"Tra-osers," he said. "That is amusing. You are not to wear these. You are to wear a malo, and as the crossing of the channel might be cold, you will be given a fine kihei." He nodded gravely. "Yes, you shall be my eyes and ears in this, and you will find Kamehameha and tell him that Muapo awaits him as a friend. Or if you can, you will kill Kamehameha in my name and Kahekili's name. I know that the former of these two is more probable, because Kamehameha is a great warrior and will not allow himself to be killed. If it is not possible to see him, then you are to see what the Maui chiefs are doing about the coming storm—they are Kapakahili and Kalanikupule. I wish to know if the warrior can be stopped." Muapo paused there, staring at me. He seemed to be assessing my honesty. "You are to tell Kamehameha that when he comes to conquer Oʻahu, his friend Muapo shall be prepared to welcome him and fight by his side. If you need, speak to his haoles of this. If any man learns that you have been asked to kill Kamehameha, by me, I will deny that I ever said that and call you a liar. Do you understand?"

"Yes," I said.

"If any man claims that you were told by me to go and offer Kamehameha my allegiance, I will deny that and call you a liar. Do you understand?"

"Yes."

"If in the process you tell anyone but those who know my intent in this, I shall devote the remainder of my life to finding you and putting out your eyes." He paused, thinking. "It is merely a warning to you, that this we attempt is but a space between the intent of Kahimoku to collect your eyes and the fulfillment of that intent, should you stray from your promise to keep this secret. If you do only that, then I will leave my desire for vengeance in the ground. I am not asking that you succeed, only that you honor my request."

"I shall," I said.

"And besides," he said, "you may be able to find your woman of the mountains, is that not so?"

I was left somewhat surprised at what Muapo knew. He summoned attendants to bring us food, and although I had thought that I now knew all Muapo did, I had it proven later that he knew more: warriors were to go with me in a canoe upon these calm waters, led by Mo'omake, and as Muapo added, "your brother."

The prospect of this journey frightened me, for I was willingly separating myself from my haole benefactors, and they were not to know of this journey. I was simply ordered to vanish from them without any explanation. As I ate, Muapo pointing at various bowls and suggesting I try this or that, I was aware that I was getting what I wanted, to go to Maui, but what then? I knew nothing of the place. The warriors accompanying me, however, did. How their knowledge might help remained doubtful, for it might require months, or years, to find her.

At length I settled my mind on these questions and asked Muapo one more: "How long shall I stay on Maui?"

He paused, poi on two of his fingers, a tail swaying below, and said, "As many days as it requires for you to do these things for me." He ate the poi off his fingers. "Perhaps the turn of a month, perhaps two." He studied the food bowls. "Mo'omake was with Kahekili, until he fell ill. He remains a great warrior, but he remains ill nonetheless. I would like to see him return."

Konapiliahi sat back, sated. "Well," he said, "we must prepare for your journey."

"And I am not to inform my chief that I shall be absent?" I asked.

"I will inform him," Muapo said. "Here, this is halalu—excellent." He pushed the fish platter to me.

At dawn the following day, Konapiliahi accompanied me across the narrow plain at the end of the island to a sandy shore, at which waited two warriors and a war canoe. He went to it and showed me a kihei wrapped in a long tube, and opened it to reveal weapons, two ihe and a war-axe. The warriors did not know of my haole language, but Mo'omake did. So I was to act as Mo'omake's associate. The sun had not yet risen over the mountain, and I was chilled as we walked. From time to time I asked Konapiliahi about his family, his children, and the many events that had occurred during the time of my absence.

Much of this information was lost on me because I felt an increasing discomfort at the thought of meeting 'Iolana again, and recalled the last time I had seen him, at the end of that horrible slaughter on the plain of Ewa. In my mind he existed as a monster, half man and half evil spirit. Konapiliahi spoke to the two warriors, who remained by the canoe, and did not come to talk to me. They acknowledged me with brief looks, and then went back to waiting by the canoe.

After the sun rose over the mountain, I saw three figures approaching, walking on the wet sand just above the water. Konapiliahi moved to me and said, "It is your brother and four other paddlers. They are strong, and will get you and Mo'omake to Moloka'i before the end of the day. You will rest there and go on to Maui on the following day."

The figures approached. When their color changed from being dark silhouettes to men, I saw that the one leading was 'Iolana, bedecked with that riot of tattoos, barely recognizable because I could not separate his features away from the circles and writhing lines on his cheeks and forehead. He carried a leiomano, the chosen weapon of his youth. The two other warriors went to the canoe where the others waited, and 'Iolana walked to me. He stopped a few feet away, staring, and as he was closer now, I could make out his features. "Brother," he said. "We meet again." He moved closer, and then did greet me in the way of Hawaiians, by pressing his face to mine, after which he backed up a step to look at me. "You have done many things," he said. "You have turned out a man."

"As you have," I said. Konapiliahi stood by, watching this exchange, and then 'Iolana saw him and repeated the greeting.

'Iolana returned to me, and said, "We have much to talk of, but first we must make our way across the water. It is fortunate that it is so calm."

"Yes," I said.

Then, with little in the way of preparation, we placed ourselves in the canoe, which was large enough that we could each sit on a plank-seat, facing one another, while the four warriors paddled. Apparently we were not to exert ourselves in this journey, and so we were able to talk as the canoe surged softly with each dip of the four paddles. The weather was warm enough that we did not need our kihei, which sat gradually soaking up the water that sloshed in the bottom of the canoe.

I studied him as he sat there, and noted that he did not look well, that he had lost some of the powerful bulk of but a few years ago, that the whites of his eyes were reddened, and there were sores on his legs, especially around his malo. It is sufficient to summarize some of our conversation, his descriptions to me of Laka and her children, his account of being spared by an ali'i impressed by his ferocity in that early battle at the stream, his descriptions of his experience in Kahekili's and Muapo's courts, and the story of his body's decoration. A kahuna had seen Mo'omake in a dream, and was so frightened that he decided to create the very image he had dreamed so that the fantastic warrior would be at his command rather than someone else's, and so chose 'Iolana to be the bearer of the images from that dream. And toward the end of his description of these things, he said, "And brother, I am dying." When I looked at him questioningly, he told me that he had the affliction of the dripping ule, that he could barely urinate, that his ule was swollen, that horrible sores which he would not show me ate at his skin. His back ached constantly so that he could not sleep, and this had made him so wretched that he needed now only to find an honorable way to die, and he hoped that this trip to Maui might provide that opportunity.

"This saddens me," I said. "This affliction. Where does it come from?" I believe that even then I knew, for I had heard of the clap, as sailors called it, before, a horrible veneral affliction that did just what he had described but refused to show me.

"The haoles brought it," he said. "This is what the kahuna makani tells me." The term 'kahuna makani' in this context means a physician-priest, whose function is to treat illness through a connection to the spirit-world. "Others have this too," he said, "and they are worse. Their sores become leaking holes, and they get weak and die."

He turned and looked at the laboring paddlers. "There is more we must talk about," he said. "But not until we are alone." With that, he rested his forearms on his knees and his head on his forearms, and tried to sleep. I kept patience with the surges of the canoe, which the warriors had taken south, apparently so as not to be seen from the more populous shores of the island. Then, as my island receded into a salt mist, they turned the canoe toward Moloka'i, which rose from that mist as they paddled.

We reached the shore of that island in the middle afternoon, near a small harbor called Hale O Lono, where the population was sparse, because we were in a drier part of the island. The paddlers went off on their own, setting up places where they could rest, leaving 'Iolana and myself alone. I was stiff, my back and arms sore from remaining braced in that canoe so long, and 'Iolana seemed almost decrepit as we walked up on the shore. I asked him why the warriors were not inclined to converse with us, and he told me that they were ordered not to. Muapo wanted the secrecy of this journey well protected, and while I regretted being somewhat aloof with these men, I understood.

Thus did 'Iolana and I sit and talk. Again, the exact substance of this conversation is dim in my memory, but certain things 'Iolana knew were of considerable interest to me, and I waited for the time to address them. 'Iolana, however, wanted information from me, of a different kind. "You have seen the world of the haoles," he said. "The land of mists and fog. Tell me what it is like."

I described for him first the size of the world, and the size of the islands in the world, the distances. He listened to this intently, and then asked me what the haoles were like, how their world was different from ours. "It is very different," I said, "and in ways very similar. The world of the haoles is made up like our own in this way: there are two kinds of people—ali'i and common people, and the common people do the bidding of the haole ali'i. Those haoles I know were all, at one time or another, victims of these ali'i, and in various ways escaped them as I escaped Kahimoku." I went on to try to make clear to him why so many heads were chopped off in China, and why two boys were burned to death in King Philip's Land. As I described these things, I thought of Muapo's story, and understood how this pattern seemed to repeat itself, both in the things I had seen and in the stories I had heard. The world, it seemed, was made this way.

One of the warriors brought us food wrapped in ti leaves, dried he'e, sweet potato and poi, and we ate. Then 'Iolana sat silently for some time while the sun began to sink toward the ocean. Finally he said, "There are things you wish to know, and I will tell you. I will tell you all I know."

"I will listen," I said.

"The decoration of my skin took days. When it was done I was no longer myself. I was Mo'omake, the lizard of death. I was told to kill and I killed. The pono was taken by the lizard." The word 'pono' here refers to his own personal goodness and balance, and he was made pono 'ole, or without personal goodness and balance. "I did these things without thinking," he went on, "for the lizard was in my soul. I made my father's curse real and did not think as I stood above him, as he lay there with his face in the mud. And when you killed Kahimoku I was told to kill all those close to you to satisfy Muapo's anger, and so I gathered warriors and went to kill them. And I did not think. We went to the rock-gathering place, and then up the mountain, and they ran up the mountain. I remember climbing those rocks, cursing you and cursing them, my leiomano in my fist and death in my eyes, and then the stones came down the mountain. They struck some of the warriors, but I continued up the mountain, and onto one of those flat shelves created by the water, and there she stood, the little woman with the hair, a stone in her hand, and she did not cower. She did not move her eyes over these decorations on my skin. She stood with the rock in her hand and waited for me, and there, the mist of that mountain sweeping by, I let the leiomano down to my side, turned, and went back down the mountain. The warriors had reached another shelf and had found two old people and killed them, and when I passed their bodies I saw that they were our parents, their skulls split open."

'Iolana went silent for a moment, staring at his own hands. "My mind returned to me that day. I would no longer kill women and children. These decorations on my skin are no more than a kahuna's nightmare. And besides, my sickness came to me at that time, the decorations rotting on my skin. I will die before we return."

"I know haole medicine," I said. "You have what is called virulent gonorrhea."

His mouth moved in a soft imitation of these words. "This is the haole language."

"Yes. These words are in what is called a book."

"I have seen these. And you know these?"

"Yes. In one are described afflictions of the body, and yours is virulent gonorrhea. The book says that you should not eat fish, and should not dream of women, and should drink much water and eat things such as 'uala and kalo tops."

He laughed. "Not dream of women? It is true that when I dream of women the pain is horrible. But I cannot avoid dreaming of women. How do you prevent a dream?"

He seemed much interested in my knowledge of books and the haole language. As we talked, my mind reconstructed that image of Pekau holding a stone, and 'Iolana deciding not to kill her, and I pictured his warriors killing our parents, that bone and skull I found probably of my father or mother. He whom I had so hated and feared was, after all, a human being who had made his own tortured journey to end up the man he was as we sat there. These revelations confused me, and when he had finally exhausted our conversation and went to wrap himself in a kihei and sleep, I sat there on the sand and stared at the black ocean. Every man I had hated and feared had turned out, finally, to be a human being who had made some tortured journey—Kahimoku, Muapo, 'Iolana, even the one-eared man who killed my sister. And that soldier in China who had made such bluster and show over beheading old men, was he, too, a human being? Did he, at some time, experience the pain of the loss of someone? The learning of the world, as Beckwith put it, was a process that resulted in more confusion than certainty, it seemed.

But we were to travel on in the morning, and so I took a kihei, still a little wet from the canoe, and wrapped myself in it and slept in the sand, next to my dying brother.

§

Upon being informed of the continued spread of the affliction of the people at the far end of the slum, MacFarlane looked up from his ledger book, thought a few seconds, and then said, "That's quite far from me. But thank you again for the warning."

We were sitting in the shed, the little points of light coming through the thatch wall playing over the pages of the fourth ledger book. Pono had not yet arrived, and the heat was beginning to discomfort me. I had spent a bad night on the ship, my nightshirt soggy with my own perspiration, and moving up on the deck did nothing to help.

"And how long does this period of windless humidity last?" I asked.

"Maybe October," MacFarlane said.

"It's so hot that even the sailors remain in a funk. They've even lost their interest in women and fighting."

"Oh, they'll carry on with that at night," MacFarlane said. He sighed and looked at the opening into the thatched hut. "Where d'ye suppose he lives?"

"I don't know. When he leaves, he goes in the direction of your place."

"There's an area called Makiki," MacFarlane said. "Just up the mountain flank a bit. I suspect he's camping up there somewhere. People lived up there, but what with the diseases killing them off, there's more space."

"And there is nothing to be done? I went with Mrs. Searle the other day to one of those hovels, and children were dying. One was dead, in fact."

"Some of the mission ladies try to help, but the majority of the time, they're let alone to die," MacFarlane said. "I don't know that anyone knows what to do. They wait for the people to develop a resistance to whatever we bring, but that process might kill them all before any resistance is developed. The native doctors have their remedies, of course, but they don't work."

"Outside of your wife and your adopted child," I said, "does that concern you?"

MacFarlane looked at me, the morose expression its own response.

"Very well," I said. "I understand."

"One would have thought that our being here could be somehow made humane, and some have tried to make it that way, but the inclusion of disease into this process has created a—" he paused there, staring into a space next to my head. "—a catastrophe," he said. "It is a melancholy thing, seeing those thatched houses empty and falling."

There was an argument outside, two men apparently, and MacFarlane and I stepped out of the little room. Two men were standing not twenty feet from us, face to face, arguing: "I saw her first, you bloody bastard," and the other, "Who offered her more, mate? You?" at which the man smiled and held out his hands. Beyond them was the rigging of ships baking in the windless heat. The less well-off of the sailors folded his arms across his chest. "So what do you propose then?" he asked, to which the other replied, "I'll go first, and after she cleans up a bit, she'll be yours." The other considered this. "Aye, it's too hot to muck around with this. Go on." And they turned to go back down the lane, both satisfied, and nearly ran Mrs. Searle over. She stepped aside of them, swinging a rather heavy valise as she walked, and continued toward us, drawing the eyes of both men, who then went on their way.

Just as Mrs. Searle approached us and bid us good day, I saw Pono coming from the other direction. "Ah," I said to her, "here comes our storyteller."

"I'd be delighted to meet the man," she said, staring at the approaching form. She set her bag down.

Pono walked to us, and then looked at Mrs. Searle.

I introduced him to her, and she smiled and said, "It is a most interesting tale." But some expression had come across her face now, as if she were distracted by some thought. She stared at him as if she recognized him, then down at the dirt, and then she looked up once again. "I've been able to read but one of the volumes so far," she said. "It's very—" And again, that distracted expression, her eyes studying Pono's face. She seemed to think carefully before saying more. At length she said, "Are you continuing today?"

"Yes," he said. "I fear Mr. Davis feels the story has become too detailed."

"Oh no," she said, somewhat vaguely. "I found it very interesting. I wish I could attend, but I have to go to the houses over by the marsh. More people are sick."

"Gentlemen," I said, "I'll accompany Mrs. Searle part way to her destination, and come back. Perhaps five minutes?"

"Of course," Pono said. "It has been pleasant talking to you," he said to her. "What sickness is this?"

"A fever of some sort," she said, reaching down to pick up her bag. "I've the only remedies that seem to help—clean water, a few herbs and the like."

"Do you need help?" he asked.

"We always need help," she said. She thought a moment. "I'll come back this way a little later in the day. If you're not here, then I might stop tomorrow."

"Very well," Pono said. "I've had some experience with these things. Perhaps I can help in some way, if you wish. As I said, it has been pleasant talking to you."

"Pleasant indeed for me," she said, and stepped around us to continue on her way.

I followed her. "He'll talk for the next two hours or more," I said, "and MacFarlane takes some time to do his recording."

She stopped, and again put down the bag. "Five people have now died," she said. "I can do nothing about it, but I feel that I must try. But—" She looked back in the direction of the anteroom MacFarlane and Pono had gone into to escape the sun. "Something about that man," she said. "I have seen him before, I believe, but I can't remember where or when."

"Seen him? Perhaps you saw him while you walked by one day?"

"No," she said. "Oh, but this is frustrating." She shook her head, the perplexity plain on her face. "I know I have seen this man, and not just walking by."

"I notice that they all bear a strong resemblance to each other. Perhaps you've seen someone who merely resembles him."

"Perhaps," she said, but appeared unconvinced.

16.

I shall summarize our journey to Maui as succinctly as the narrative merits. We made our way across that channel to a coastline that was rugged, reddish stone dropping to boulders in the water over which large waves blasted. Atop these bluffs stood waving grass, but the warrior-paddlers apparently knew where they were going, for they labored over their paddles along this coastline until those bluffs dropped, and pale beaches appeared. And offshore, near a village of some sort, sat a haole ship with its rigging bare. 'Iolana was in pain much of the way, moaning, and doubled over, his back and groin torturing him. I was behind him holding onto the rails of the canoe as it rose and settled in the waves, my eyes going from the bluffs, and then to his back, upon which those nightmare swirls and circles changed shape as he tensed himself with the pitching of the canoe. My brother, the result of a kahuna's bad dream, had experienced much, as I had experienced much, but I wondered, my eyes locked in on that riot of illustrations on his skin, if all of these experiences had brought us to a place wherein those experiences would be of no use to us. The sense of a horrible foreboding overcame me, because somewhere up in those mountains I would look for Pekau, and I had by now convinced myself that I would not find her and never would.

The beach we finally did approach, called Oluwalu, was occupied by a group of warriors and ali'i, and I asked 'Iolana about them. "They know who I am," he said. "They know I come from Kahekili. Do not prostrate yourself before them. They are awaiting any message I might bring them, but will be disappointed, I think."

A quick greeting did take place on the beach, I not a part of it. The warrior Mo'omake appeared respected by all, but as I watched, standing next to the canoe and shaking the stiffness from my body from the crossing, I saw that there was considerable agitation amongst the men who talked with 'Iolana. I was impressed, at the same time, by the beauty of this island, for up the bluffs not a great distance from the shore stood a beautiful, dark mountain range, and to the right of that, a plain, and on the other side of that plain, what I understood to be Haleakala, the great mountain that at times became frozen on the top. On this day it was shrouded in clouds, however.

At length 'Iolana returned to me, a rather gleeful and agitated look on his face. "I believe we've arrived here late," he said. "The warrior Kamehameha has sacked Hana, on the other side and to the south. He is on his way, now, to take Kahului, which is over the plain there. We're going to join the army of Kapakahili to fight him off."

"And what of my promise to Muapo?" I asked.

'Iolana laughed. "You've still got your ears, have you not? Come, we shall spend the day fighting."

"I am not interested in fighting," I said. "I should remain here."

"Then what of your promise?" 'Iolana asked.

I considered this. My promise was to do as Muapo bade me to do, and failure would be both humiliating for me and dangerous for those I wished to protect—if Muapo were to find Pekau and my children, then that vengeance he claimed to have left in the ground would grow out of it like a weed. "Very well," I said.

"Then select your weapons," he said. From the canoe I drew two ihe, and studied them. The hard kauila wood shone in the light, and the barbs on both spears were sharp.

The group we marched with numbered around forty. We made our way up onto a broad and verdant plain separating two mountain ranges. 'Iolana told me that we were going to join a chief named Kalanikupule, the son of Kahekili, whose army was being readied to repel Kamehameha. Kalanikupule's army was located in a better-fortified position in a place called Wailuku, which was hilly, while Kahului was a flat area at the water's edge. The weather this day was hot and still, and I became only half-conscious of my surroundings as I walked behind 'Iolana, whose bearing had taken on a lusty energy as he talked with the warriors in front of him.

At length we traversed a low rise and approached the other side of the island. The warriors at the lead stopped and pointed to their right where, far up on the flank of the larger mountain, smoke moved slowly in the breeze. The presence of that smoke woke me. The supposition was that it was the invading warrior's army, now closer to Wailuku. Hana, 'Iolana told me, was far down the island.

As we neared the waters of Kahului, a warrior running toward us halted the procession. The message he brought was that Kamehameha had killed Kapakahili by himself in a battle, in an area called Kokomo, which was, I was told, right where that smoke drifted up the mountainside. We were to hasten to Wailuku and join Kalanikupule's army, for Kamehameha had already returned to the ocean and was making his way north toward Kahului leading an army paddling hundreds of canoes.

As we approached the ocean, the lead warrior led us up some bluffs to the area called Wailuku, and there Kalanikupule had gathered many hundreds of warriors, all armed, and lesser chiefs wearing red and yellow feather helmets. The chiefs were gathered together with their kahunas, and ʻIolana discussed the situation with one of the warriors close to the aliʻi.

I waited, sitting on a rock. Behind me, farther up those bluffs, there was a valley, into which people were moving, women and children and old people. I saw from my position the thread of a stream coming down out of that valley, and beyond, greenish-black mountains shrouded at the tops in clouds. The people were seeking refuge from the oncoming army by hiding somewhere up there. When I looked back at the men gathered around the chiefs, I saw muskets, not many, but it was reassuring to see them. In addition, to my surprise, I saw two haoles, seamen who, like Muapo's haoles, had attached themselves to the chiefs.

Our position was to protect this area called Wailuku, and when ʻIolana came back, I saw through the tattoos on his face an expression of a gleeful cynicism.

"Brother," he said, approaching, "we are small in number compared to the other army. This shall be difficult."

"They have muskets," I said.

"Six of them," ʻIolana said. "The haoles are here to show the warriors how to use them."

"Does Kamehameha have muskets?" I asked.

"Many more, I am told," he said. "The haoles are explaining to the men how to move so as not to present a target for them. Tell me, brother, if one uses a musket, how long does it take before he can use it a second time?"

I thought a moment, and then imitated reloading a musket: flip the frizzen, deposit powder, close the frizzen, powder the muzzle, put the wad and ball in, and tamp it with the rod. "Perhaps that long," I said. ʻIolana seemed puzzled as I had done this.

"And the man can do nothing during that time?"

"He cannot, unless he wishes to use his musket as a club," I said.

"If one were to point one at me, and the smoke came out but I was unhurt, would I have time to reach him with my leiomano?"

"Perhaps," I said. He nodded, and turned to look at the men grouped around the aliʻi. "But a musket is a great weapon," I said. I was about to say that I had killed with a musket, but it was not something I felt boastful about. I held my tongue.

Kamehameha was not quick to attack. He himself needed time for preparation, as did the army of Kalanikupule. This allowed me time to consult with 'Iolana about approaching Kalanikupule with greetings from Muapo, and 'Iolana drew me down to the circle of chiefs. Once there, I told Kalanikupule where I had come from, and offered greetings from Muapo, which he accepted, although with some doubt, I suppose, as to the use of this greeting at this moment. Kalanikupule was a handsome man, quite regal in his bearing and well loved by his people.

It should be said that warfare in my land, in those days before it became what it is now, was an elaborate business, not unlike feudal warfare of the sort I had read about and heard about from the men on the ship. Chiefs waited for kahunas to dream, or to have visions favorable for making war. Sometimes pigs or fowl were sacrificed before the chief's war-god, and in the case of Kamehameha, the war-god Kukailimoku was in his possession, and traveled with him. This carved and feather-decorated statue was priceless to him, and was carried above him as he went into battle.

All who were preparing knew how it would begin: the two armies would face each other, arranged so that the chief was protected inside the mass of warriors. The kahunas would make loud sounds announcing the war-god's presence, and as the two armies prepared to meet, small skirmishes would begin: slings would loft rocks, single warriors would advance and challenge single warriors from the other side. When it came time for the armies to fight in earnest, all would attack, but according to various strategies. Flank attacks, launching of spears, and so on.

But Kalanikupule's army had to wait, in the case of this engagement, for two days. Kamehameha was allowing both armies to prepare. We spent our time eating the food that had been prepared, and talking, and resting, but the tension was great, for many knew that on the day of the battle, they would probably be killed. To my knowledge, none of the warriors in Kalanikupule's army tried to run away or beg their way out of the conflict.

Some of the time during these days I left the waiting men to talk with the people who were slowly fleeing into the valley behind us. These were the women and children, and the old. I asked all I talked to if they knew of a woman named Pekau and her children, but none did. I asked if they had heard of a Manomano, but none had heard of him. They were, in any case, anxious to move on into the mountains or up what I learned was 'Iao stream, which wound its way up through the bluffs into the valley.

I had experienced that strange, morbid and melancholy emptiness before, that airy distance from reality that went with waiting to die. My promise to Muapo seemed to recede into the back of my mind, for what use was information if I would have my skull split open before being able to relate it? Why was it that I stayed and accepted the validity of my involvement in this, when I had in truth no real connection with the conflict, and I had been gone from my land for years? Perhaps it was 'Iolana, and some faint spark of a solidarity with him made me accept it. So stay I did.

On the second day of our waiting, I saw the two haole advisors standing away from the group of ali'i and priests, and made my way over to within hearing distance of their conversation. It would be of little use to Muapo, I thought, but I felt that I should at the least use the talent he had summoned me for. They sat on a flat rock near brush that ran into a small ravine, and they were talking in what sounded to me like the heavier British accent of Will Kelsey or Owen Bew. "—bloody fools. 'ave ye got the cape then?" followed by, "Hang the cape. I don't know what the 'ell I'd do with it anyway. Bloody shilling's what it's worth," followed by, "All right then mate, we'll watch the rotters get their 'eads caved in and leave," followed by a rough laugh. "And you've got the fella set up?" followed by, "Aye, 'e'll take us on that trail I mentioned, right over to the other side." The men looked out over the warriors, grouped in various places, many in the shade of trees. "Kam-ee-whatever his name is 'as got twice the number I'd say and an 'ell of a lot more of muskets," and then they remained silent for a few moments. They watched the earnest talking amongst the chiefs, and then one poked the other with his elbow. "I think the bloody monkeys are daft as one-eyed chickens. Look at the stupid witch-doctors, hairy bastards they be. This'd be more amusement if there was booty involved, but these animals don't 'ave the brains to keep booty. And they 'and their women out like crumpets," followed by, "Aye, my tool's in need of a rest." Then the other said, "Say, you'd consider a wager on the outcome here?" followed by, "Mate, you're as stupid as these monkeys if you think I'd do that."

I moved away. I let their insults pass, and focused my attention on the problem of what they appeared to know about Kamehameha's army, that it was larger than ours. And if I were to survive and speak again to Muapo, I would be able to tell him only that what I heard from the whites was no more than a joking conviction that we were all fools.

As if it were somehow ordained to be, the sun rose the next morning and illuminated beautiful cumulous clouds, the sky a deep blue. I had either forgotten to appreciate days like this since my return, or had not seen any quite as splendid. And word came, mid-morning, that Kamehameha's army was readying to move toward us.

Our position put us on the hills on either side of the stream, and Kalanikupule, having received the information that the opposing army was on its way, began arranging his warriors in a large arc, as if anticipating circling those who would come up the stream. 'Iolana had by now established himself as one of the warriors who would be at the front, and he had his leiomano, and on his malo cord he had hung a sling, with which he would cast stones. The ali'i and the priests remained at the center of this arc, and behind the warriors, all of whom were now armed and grouped according to their weapons, the ihe throwers toward the front, the pololū bearers behind them, and those with slings at the outer edges so that the flight of their rocks would be at angles.

The center of the cluster of warriors had many with war-axes and clubs and strangling cords. And with them, but just away from the very front, stood the warriors with muskets. There were perhaps six or seven of them. It is difficult to estimate the number of warriors there were in all, but I would estimate that there were over a thousand. One reason for this uncertainty is that I was in that state of a rueful equanimity. The heat of the sun and that multitude of voices and the rich color of the warriors with oil on their skin, the sumptuous clouds and clear air, all made this feel like a bright dream, and any thought of escape had long fled. That mass of warriors seethed with sound and movement and seemed to melt into one another to become one, a thick, brown coating of flesh upon the landscape, a living membrane upon it. I did not want to participate, but I would, and for reasons which even at the time I was unsure of: a vague promise, a feeling of allegiance with my brother 'Iolana, who seemed so eager to die that day.

I stood somewhat above the mass of warriors, and saw, first, the red and yellow colors in the far distance out over the plain of Kahului. Warriors came to inform Kalanikupule of the approach, and then 'Iolana came back through the crowd of warriors to me. "Brother," he said, "you are bound by your promise to Muapo, and must return to him. The paddlers wait on the other side. Fight if you wish, but you must escape if we are beaten. He expects you to tell him of this."

"I will remain with you," I said. "For as long as possible."

He looked out over the plain, at the feather standards bobbing above the amorphous mass of bodies. "Our position is good," he said. "They must come up to us, and the fighters at the front are a strong lot. We shall beat them back."

As the army approached, the horrible dread I felt intensified, the nausea gathering in my chest, and the longer we waited, the more I looked at the two white sailors sitting there on that rock waiting for their entertainment. And when the feather standards appeared now bobbing not three hundred paces from us, I saw that the men had moved a bit toward the valley, anticipating their escape. What possessed me to walk over to them I do not know, but that dread I felt was mixed more and more with an irritation about these men. When I was near them, they looked at me as if wondering what I might want.

"My suggestion is that you leave now," I said. "You'll miss your entertainment, I'm afraid, but I'd prefer that you weren't here to watch."

Both of their faces showed shock and a defensive contrition. "Why, we're advisors to the chief," one said, his hands out.

"Leave now," I said. "Or there shall be monkeys following you. Go and find your guide."

They did not remain to think this over. They backed away, hands raised apologetically, and then turned and ran. The last I saw of them, they were making their way into the valley, stopping from time to time to see me standing there with my ihe, at which they turned and continued on their way.

When I turned back, the two armies were facing each other, a space of perhaps twenty paces between them, and warriors were stamping their feet and yelling and gesturing with their weapons. I returned to the group of warriors, and looked for 'Iolana. He was one of the ones in that space between the gathered armies.

I shouldered my way through the warriors, and the awful fact of what was happening suffused me with its tangible reality—my hands holding the smooth shaft of the ihe, the shifting, bright panorama of dark heads, and the glistening, oiled shoulders sliding against mine, the clatter of weapons and the mix of those voices shouting at the gap between the armies, the smells of coconut oil and perspiration and fear, and in my mouth the dry and astringent taste of dread. 'Iolana stood just inside that gap, his leiomano by his side, along with three other warriors who taunted the opposing army. When he stepped away from them, all on the other side looked at him, and their yelling paused, for they were looking now at Mo'omake, the Death Lizard, whose riot of tattoos had now sharpened in definition on his body because of the coating of oil on his skin. Behind them I saw the great chief move outside the tight circle of his protecting warriors, a large man a full head taller than those surrounding him. He was at the moment removing a feather cloak, and when that cloak was removed, I heard the sounds of the voices on our side die off, for everyone looked now at this giant, made taller even than his great height by the feathered helmet he wore.

At the outer flanks of the gathering of his army I saw men with both hands crooked up at their shoulders. These were rock-slingers, and they were holding the rocks in their bags in place behind one shoulder, preparing to snap the sling forward with the opposing hand. One of the warriors with 'Iolana walked out ahead of him, and threatened with a spear, causing those at the front of the other army to jeer and shake their weapons. I tried to perceive our strategy against theirs, but my mind was sapped of reason or logic. The seething mass of warriors we faced was larger than ours, draped over the rises in the land, and moving in places like a thick, slowly flowing brown liquid.

As 'Iolana stood taunting the warriors on the other side, I recalled that I had not yet seen any muskets, where ours were visible to those across that gap. Standing there in that dreamlike state, my hearing dulled from the sustained cacophony of sounds coming from all directions, I scanned the mass of the opposing army, and then saw the muskets. The warriors carrying them were spread out in a line just behind the ones at the opening, who went on with their threatening gestures. I could not make a count on them, but there were more than we had. I stumbled into a depression past warriors, and heard the first clash of weapons to my left, and then a stone sailed over our heads, causing warriors to jump out of the way. As I rose out of that depression I saw 'Iolana, standing there facing the warriors who had hurled those stones.

The wall of spear-bearing warriors now moved toward us, crouched, and behind them stood the musketeers, setting their weapons in the crooks of their shoulders. I tried to make my way closer to yell to 'Iolana to step back, and then saw the gouts of smoke coming from the muzzles of three of the muskets, the reports drowned out by yells from our warriors, at which 'Iolana stumbled back a bit, and then put his hand up to his left shoulder, coming away with blood. A warrior behind him fell, and then crawled away past the legs of his brothers. 'Iolana then stepped toward the warriors with his leiomano raised, while the three who had been in the gap with him moved back into the crowd, which had pressed backward in response to the sound and smoke of the muskets.

I got to the opening, and went to pull 'Iolana back, but just as I approached him from behind, rocks bounced along the ground and warriors from the other side advanced, causing 'Iolana to advance toward them, and in this way the battle began. In the din of shouting voices I was knocked forward by one of our warriors and fell on my fists and knees, my hands still holding the ihe, and through the many tensed legs of those in front of me saw 'Iolana swinging his leiomano and then being sent backwards by a blow. Just as I rose, a warrior running at me with an axe raised tripped and fell, and before I could turn the ihe, another warrior brought an axe down on his head, and I stepped into a thick puddle of dark blood that had rushed from the large gash crossed by tangled hair, the warm blood sticky on my foot, and I pointed the ihe ahead. There were more musket reports, and I breathed the acrid, salty smell of spent gunpowder. I tried to advance, but those in front of me were backing my way, and then one sat down against my knees holding the shaft of a pololū that raced out of his chest and slick with his blood slipped from his hands. The bearer of that long spear was not visible because the shaft came between two of our warriors, who were swinging their axes. The clash of wood on wood and the screams were still ahead, and I pressed forward, my ihe up so as not to spear my own warriors, and was then able to see the enemy because two of our warriors fell back, one speared in the chest and one with a fan of blood spraying out of his head. Beyond them I saw the faces, tensed with anger and exhilaration, their bloody weapons before them, not yet seeing me because they were further addressing the job of killing the two who had fallen back. Then at my side a warrior swung an axe and before the arc of that swing ended at my head, I rammed the back end of the ihe in his face, at which the axe spun out of his hand and hit someone behind me.

We were being driven back, and I backed away with our warriors, feeling that sticky blood between my toes and my foot pasted with dirt from it. Kalanikupule's army moved back a hundred paces while the musket reports continued, some men falling and holding their wounds. Kamehameha's army did not follow us. Rather they regrouped, and regarded the forty or so bodies we had left in that gap, one of which was 'Iolana, a short spear through his back, broken off, so that the barbed front end of it jutted out of his chest by the length of a man's forearm. He was still alive, trying to roll himself up into a sitting position. A warrior aimed a musket at him and fired, and he rolled back down.

In that space of time after the first engagement, warriors moved out from the opposing army to look at the corpses. It was a tradition of warfare in my world that the 'first fruit' of a battle, or the first man killed, should be offered in sacrifice, in this case by the opposing army, whose superiority had now become apparent. The rest would be left to rot on the ground, or perhaps covered with stones as a memorial to victory. One warrior was dragged off into the crowd, assumed to be the first to die. Warriors were also interested in dragging 'Iolana off, perhaps also to sacrifice, because of the wondrous decoration on his skin, and so one warrior walked over and kicked 'Iolana's body over so that he lay on his back, that broken ihe jutting from his chest. Not many watched this, for in the process of regrouping, the chiefs inside their walls of protection conferred with warriors and priests, and others were studying their wounds, but I kept my eyes on my brother. Others near him on the other side watched. The warrior who had singled out 'Iolana walked around him once, and then leaned down to drag him off, but 'Iolana reached up suddenly and pulled him down by his malo cord, turned him, and pulled his body down on the spear to the sounds of yells of surprise from those near, and the scream of the warrior who had thought him dead. That man was pinned down on 'Iolana, chest to chest, and in a horrific embrace, he squirmed like a crab, the point of the ihe emerging from his back. Other warriors ran to them, and with their clubs hammered at 'Iolana's head until he was still, but could do little for the warrior joined to him by that spear.

This brought up yells of exultation from our side, and energized their spirits, for Mo'omake had truly lived up to his exalted name, the Death Lizard, and had struck this last time in his life. That exultation was short lived, for the opposing army once again readied itself and advanced, walking with the pololū bearers shoulder to shoulder with the ihe bearers, and behind them those with muskets, axes and clubs. I was among the front line waiting to engage the oncoming warriors. Again, my mind remained muddled as to the severity of this situation, and I was distracted by the bloody mud on my foot, the sensation of my toes pasted together by the gluey thickness of it. A line of expanding globes of smoke followed by the reports caused me to flinch, and two warriors nearby fell backwards with shouts of pain. As the musketeers addressed their weapons, I heard ours go off, perhaps three of them, but no one fell on the other side.

Then the front line of that army came at us at a run, their spears ahead of them and fierce screams coming from their mouths. I was placed on the right side of our arc of warriors, and saw the attackers running into the middle of it while we at the edge readied ourselves for the clash, warriors with axes and clubs sprinting between the spear bearers. I lowered myself into a crouch with the ihe pointed at an upward angle, and the first man to come at me saw it and slipped to the side while raising a war club, at which a pololū ran into his belly and he fell sideways, the long spear banging into my side. I went down on my side and another warrior stepped on me and then vaulted off my ribcage to continue on, and then I struggled up to my feet and raised the ihe. Just as I turned the spear another warrior swung a war-axe but beyond my head so that his forearm hit my shoulder and the axe dropped behind me as I rammed the ihe up and felt it slide into his trunk, at which he fell back, but I jerked the spear out of him, pulling flesh with it, and swung the back end around into the face of another who was running past me. He went down on his back, and before he rose up again two warriors beat his face in with clubs, the shots powerful pops which then became liquid in their sound, and I felt his blood spraying my lower legs.

More fighting was occurring in the middle of the arc, and at the edges on my side, and on the other side a little higher on a bluff, pressed in toward the center to help those who were fighting the largest group. Then more warriors attacked, apparently having deliberately waited until now, and upon seeing this, our army ran farther into the valley, this time three hundred paces to a place where the flanks of the ridges on each side had pressed in, and where the stream had cut deeper. We were now climbing over boulders and walking in the water, and I remember feeling a relief at having that muck washed off my foot, and I put my ihe point in the water to wash the sticky bits of flesh torn from that warrior, but it would not come off. I picked at it, and then looked up. Where we were now, we had an audience, those women and children and old people who had climbed up the flanks of the valley. Some were crying out, because their husbands and brothers and sons were down in the stream bed trying to regroup for the next attack, or were farther down the valley bleeding their last.

Beyond, up the stream, I saw a mountain in the middle between the flanks of higher mountains. It was narrow and sharp and tall, and beautiful in its greenness. I stopped picking at the sticky bits of flesh tangled in the spear barbs and turned back to see the opposing army making its way toward us. The musketeers were now in front. I turned to see Kalanikupule surrounded by his warriors, but he was farther up the stream. Our musketeers were in the middle of the main group, most of whom were either holding their own wounds or helping those who were. I made my way over some rocks to those musketeers. "Come to the front," I said to them. "We shall knock a couple of them down."

"We have no powder," one said. He held up his horn and shook it.

"How much did they give you?"

"Little, and three balls for each of us."

"Do you have any left?"

One held the musket out to me. I looked under the frizzen, but it was empty. "Is there a wad and ball inside?"

"Yes," he said. "But there is no powder." I took one of the horns and tapped it against a rock, pulled the plug and shook out what powder there was.

"May I use this?" I asked.

He raised his shoulders. The fright on his face told me that he would not protest. He was shaking, and turned to make his way farther up the streambed. The four other musketeers stared down at their weapons, and then followed him. I picked up my ihe and carrying that and the musket, made my way toward the front to where the braver warriors were now yelling down at those advancing upon us, and settled myself into a crouch. I drew back the hammer, and aimed, but could see no ali'i to shoot at. The chiefs were farther down the stream. So I chose one of the musketeers, and aimed very carefully, and pulled the trigger. The musket did not fire. I pulled the hammer back a second time, aimed, and this time the musket fired, dropping one of the musketeers. Another warrior picked up his musket, and the entire mass of them continued their approach.

With no powder, the musket was useless, but I did not want any of the opposing army to have it, so I threw it in the stream. Just as I turned back, there was another line of gouts of smoke from the muskets, and more of our warriors fell, or grabbed their wounds and ran back through the crowd of warriors. Before that smoke drifted away, those with clubs and axes and leiomano came sprinting around the musketeers, and ran shouting into the center of our group, but this time, because the valley had narrowed, the engagement was confined to a smaller space, and other warriors advanced by climbing up over the bluffs to come down at us on the sides. While those with clubs and axes were struggling in the center of our group, spear bearers advanced and worked their long spears between the warriors to pierce the bodies of ours. I saw one shoot past my side, and grabbed it and pushed it down to the ground, and upon bracing myself for the first warrior to meet me, I was knocked off my feet by one of my own, who had apparently been shot, for blood leaked from a hole in his face. I scuttled backward and turned the ihe, but again our warriors were backing away, and so I moved back up the stream with them, leaving the jeering warriors to ready themselves for the next charge.

By then I was afflicted with a strange, rumbling deafness, because I barely heard the screams from the mountainsides or the reports of muskets or the yells of pain nearby, and the strange dream this had all become kept me from thinking clearly: that I should run, make my way right up that mountain. I found myself picking again at the bits of flesh in the barbs of the ihe, and looking again at that single, beautiful mountain. But that pause was short lived, for more musket fire came at us, and again, a crowd of warriors ran up the ravine at us. The fighting, this time, took place around large boulders and in the water. The opposing warriors hacked and thrust their spears, the musketeers fired and loaded, and fired again, and because I was on the fringe of the largest group, I could see that the warriors had fought their way into the center of that group. Finally those on the edge were engaged, again with spears, clubs and axes. I threw rocks at them, and when that failed, readied the ihe, and made to retreat. As I turned to run, I felt the sudden whipping of cord around my legs ending with stones banging my shin, and they were trussed together so that I fell into the edge of the stream, still holding the ihe. I tried to engage the cord, to unwrap it, but a warrior was running toward me with a club. I picked up the ihe and made to launch it at him, and he stopped and looked at me with a goading insolence. He was going to kill me and enjoy doing it. I lowered the ihe to continue unwrapping the cord, and discovered that it was loose enough for me to slide one leg out, and just as I was about to pull the other leg out, he attacked with his club over his head. In one motion I swung the tripping cord that was loose and whipped the stone down on his foot, at which he fell on me, his club still in his hand. He came out with an infuriated yell and tried hitting me with the club, but the blows landed on my back, and I got my hands on his neck and drove my thumbs into his windpipe as he tried running his fingers into my left eye, but then he gagged and began scratching at my wrists, and when I had the advantage, I slammed his head against a rock three times, until he was unconscious. I unwrapped the cord and turned to escape up the valley.

The water in the stream was red, and the stream's volume had lessened. I grabbed the ihe and crawled around the boulder to see a heap of bodies, their huge wounds and crushed heads leaking blood into the stream, and the stream above them swelling as of being dammed, and the smell of spent powder and blood and human waste was thick in the air. The fighting was farther up the stream now, the screams and the sounds of clacking wood and shattering skulls, and above, those observers continued crying out. When I looked back down the stream, I saw the aliʻis' standards bobbing above a procession, and realized that I had been left between the two armies, or the one army and what was left of the other. I stood up into a crouch and thought to run up the stream, but saw that I would be running at the glistening backs of warriors raising and swinging their clubs, and ramming their spears, for Kalanikupule's army was being slaughtered. Warriors crouched over others on the ground and clubbed their faces into themselves, and prodded in their trunks with spears, and cut great gashes in their flesh with their leiomano. Those crawling away were first laughed at and jeered, and then overtaken and killed by various means. Warriors behind flipped bodies over, looking for the living, and finding them, clubbed them to death or slid their spears up under their rib cages.

Far up the stream, laboring over the boulders and running up the steep sides of the valley, were the aliʻi and warrior protectors and priests, while the remainder of the army stayed below and continued fighting. I remained where I was, trying to see some means of escape that did not involve having to fight with anyone, and the only option seemed to be to climb the steep, grassy side of the valley, up toward that audience who moved along the ridge as the armies moved. I waited a few seconds, and behind me I heard the grunts of the man I had made unconscious. He was sitting up and holding his head. Then I bolted for the steep incline, and was a fifth of the way up when something struck me in the shoulder, a rock, I thought, and, holding onto the grass to keep from sliding back, I laid down the ihe and used my free hand to reach up, and found that I could not raise my arm. I looked at my forearm there grasping a fistful of grass, the scratches on my wrist. I was confused as to how it was that one could have thrown the rock, but then felt the warm flow of blood down the left side of my back, and felt it sticking in my arm pit.

I looked down, and two warriors were climbing after me while a third down at the base of the incline worked at reloading his musket. I had been shot. The warriors' climb toward me was rapid, their clubs in one hand while they pulled themselves up by grabbing the grass with the other. I continued upward, and just above me, there was an explosion of dirt, some of which got into my eyes. I shook the dirt away and looked up and realized that it was too far to the top, and that those warriors would reach me before I got there. Three women at the top were looking down, and calling to me, although the noise below, the shouts and the hoarse, jubilant laughter, drowned them out.

I could no longer carry the ihe and turned and flung it down at the warriors, but it danced over them and clattered down toward the streambed. So, using one hand while holding the other arm against my side, I continued the climb, and now heard the calls from above me. The women were sweeping their hands to their left, and at first I did not understand what that meant, and then did. When the right time came, and that was when the men were not twenty paces behind me, laughing and looking gleefully in my direction, I moved sideways, at which two large rocks came rolling down through the grass. The warriors paused, seemed to consider continuing, but more rocks, larger this time, rolled past me and toward them. They moved out of the way as the rocks rolled on down toward the streambed, and then discussed the matter, and turned and made their way back, I assumed because chasing me was taking them away from participating in the rest of the killing down near the stream.

I looked once again at the valley floor, where Kamehameha's army moved over the landscape collecting the weapons of the dead and killing the remainder of the army farther up the stream. On the valley floor lay a heap of bodies, perhaps hundreds, and behind them a pond had formed, a reddish-black body of water, halted by the dam of human flesh, so that red rivulets swept around the bodies and rejoined the stream below. Because the streambed and the ravine curved out of my sight, I could not see what was happening there, but heard, still, the clash of wood on wood, the shouts of exultation and screams of pain, and musket fire.

When I reached the top, I pulled myself over, and then found that I could not rise because of the pain, which shot down my side and over into my neck, a kind of chafed numbness where the ball had struck me. I did not see the women. I sat up, and after a short while they moved out from behind some brush, warily staring at me. One of them, an older woman who was quite thin, approached. The other, who was perhaps her daughter, stayed by a bush, staring at me with a shy wonder. The older woman then went behind me to study the wound.

"It is severe," she said, and I felt her touching it. "You must come with us."

"I must go back to a place called Oluwalu."

"You'll not get there," she said. "You are bleeding. Is this the smoke-stick?"

"It is called 'musket,'" I said.

"And is there a stone inside here?"

"There is a metal ball. You may have it if you can take it out."

"Then I shall have the metal ball," she said. "But I will not take your life from you to get it. I will summon the Kahuna lapa'au. Come."

§

While it is true that the battle Pono described is well known in history, I still held that secret, albeit fading, skepticism about him, and about the validity or truth of the story being told. When he had finished that day, he must have seen the look on my face, for he turned and pulled his shirt collar away to reveal, on the back of his left shoulder, a shiny scar that was, he said, where the ball had hit that day so many years ago. True it is that scars create a peculiar map of our experience, and offer even us who are forgetful a clue to an injury no matter how old, and it is true that memory connected with scars is sharper and perhaps more lucid than other forms of memory.

Pono bade us good day and went outside to the lane. There he stopped, and spoke in the Hawaiian language to an old kanaka, I imagined asking about his family. "Well, he's still asking, I see," I said, and MacFarlane paused, his quill in hand.

"I suppose he will until the day he dies," he said.

"Mrs. Searle believes she's seen him somewhere," I said.

MacFarlane considered this. "Of course he resembles those men of his race, but at the same time, his features are distinct. But I can't believe she'd have seen him." He thought a moment. "My wife thought she had, too," he said. "Then she said that perhaps she hadn't. So he's one of those men we've all seen before."

"Yes," I said. "Still, I wonder." Pono continued talking to the old kanaka. "Well then, I shall go back to the ship. Repairs are underway."

"So, tomorrow then?"

"Tomorrow it is," I said.

But there were, this day, no repairs being done on the ship. In fact, the little crew it still held were baked in the heat by day and slept their fitful sleep by night, languid and irritable. I had back there in the shed hatched a mischievous plan, that of following our storyteller, just to see where it was that he lived. I needed the exercise, and the thought of languishing another afternoon on the ship was so hateful that I resolved to carry through with this plan, just for the amusement.

I left the shed and walked up the path toward the mountains, and then turned to my right and made my way to that path that led to MacFarlane's house and to the slum beyond it where, I imagined, Mrs. Searle was at the moment trying to prevent the deaths which seemed inevitable amongst these people. I made my way to the mountain side of that slum, which was a series of bluffs rising toward a mountain fairly close to the waterfront, perhaps two or three miles, those bluffs crisscrossed by a series of paths and huts, and fenced-off areas wherein kalo was being grown, that root vegetable that made their poi. There were many dogs, chickens and children up there, although this day I think the heat had kept most of the children inside, and the chickens were ruffling their feathers in holes they had scratched into the dry dirt, and the dogs slept away the hot hours of the day.

Actually, out away from the port, the air was quite fresh, and a breeze did blow down the mountain. It was a pleasant walk, although a long one. When I found a rocky area with some emaciated looking trees providing a bit of shade, I sat down. It was not five minutes before I saw the figure advancing up one of those paths. Pono marched along with a resolute stride, from time to time stopping to talk with a child, or to talk to a barking dog. I felt some embarrassment about what I was doing, and there decided not to pursue him farther up. I suppose the pleasantness of the air at this slight elevation made it such that I could pack my curiosity about him away for another time.

But I did see him advance farther up a trail to the base of that cloud-shrouded mountain, which, like the others in that range, seemed to have brief, refreshing showers each morning, few of which ever reached the port which baked away in the dry heat. I could see him appear and then vanish, around patches of brush, and then, after a time, see him farther up, after which he went into some low wooded area and out of my sight.

I sat there for some time, my eyes sweeping across the panorama of the port, and the little housetops, and off to the left, the marshy, flat area behind the long arc of beach I had walked many days ago. I felt a strange feeling of both sympathy and distance, for I knew that I would very likely leave this place, and perhaps never return, and this meant leaving behind this place's problems, which Mrs. Searle felt merited her presence, I suppose for the rest of her life. I do not think myself a small-minded man, but realized while I was sitting there that I had been temporarily afflicted with a bout of small-mindedness, about both Pono and Mrs. Searle. The former, I suppose, did not deserve my skepticism. And the latter, toiling away with the sick and the dying, had for me been a bafflement. Was I, the visitor, supposed to throw in with her and try and do something for these people? If their deaths were inevitable, then would I be exerting all that energy for little but a bit of self- congratulation?

In any case that walk up those bluffs convinced me that I should not leave this place without at least trying to do something useful. To what effect, I did not know. But it was perhaps the thought of the favor of Mrs. Searle that caused me to think this way.

17.

The earlier-referred-to phrase 'I ke aha' would, that night, sit in the center of tortured dreams, for the question of 'why?' was one not a single person I had associated with stopped to consider during the journey here and then during the battle. I thought this even as I followed the woman through the woods, farther up a series of ravines, my left arm numb against my trunk. The younger of the two, her daughter I supposed, walked ahead of her, from time to time stopping to look back at me, that odd, wary and fascinated expression on her face. At length we arrived at one of those mountain shelves not unlike the ones on my island, where there was room enough to establish a house, and theirs was small, with a grass roof, and was fronted by a fire-pit. The rock face at the back of the shelf glistened with oozing water, and on one side were lines of 'uala plants.

I was so exhausted that I found it difficult to stand, and then felt a powerful nausea creep up my trunk, at which I made my way to a brushy area on the opposite side from the 'uala and vomited into the dead leaves. The old woman did then bring a gourd of water, which I drank, gasping with the pain and the nausea. She pulled me toward the house, but stopped in a patch of sunlight and told me to sit, which I did. All the while this was happening, the daughter stood off by the 'uala plants and watched with that same odd curiosity and shyness.

I do not know what affliction it was that attacked me, but I began to shiver, and then my mind went into a dreamlike swoon, so that the talking I heard was both sharp and distant, where I was conscious but not conscious, and in this timeless dream I was aware of an old man instructing the old woman how to hold me as he dug into my shoulder with some wooden instrument and removed the ball. With foggy eyes I saw the woman holding the sticky ball in her hand, bobbing her hand up and down to test its weight. Then I was lying on my back, my shoulder trussed in matting and pressed down on a soft but firm surface. I allowed my eyes to drift shut, and slept.

In silence I saw men grinning and swinging their clubs and axes at children, and I saw the mutilitated bodies of men whose expressions bespoke the 'I ke aha' even in death, their teeth bared and their eyes open to the sun and their wounds festering and turning to rot, and I saw men rot, their bodies first swelling and then settling amidst a bursting of worms out of wounds and their swollen faces bespoke the same 'why?' and remained on those faces as their skin darkened and turned black and settled upon those bones, and even after the sun had seared off the last bits of dried flesh, the skulls still bespoke the *why?* with their dark sockets and their angular jawbones clenched as if still in pain, lizards crawling inside the empty spaces of their skulls. I saw babies born and asked why this baby was born and the answer was that he was born to kill, and I saw other babies born and asked why those babies were born and the answer was that he was born to be killed. Behind many of these dream thoughts was a voice speaking, and it may have been the voice of Manomano, but I could not discern any of the words this voice spoke.

But amid these dreams were pleasant ones wherein I and Pekau made children, the pleasure and release such that I could not put those dreams side by side with the dreams of strife and universal death. I smelled her body and her breath and felt her hair settle upon my chest, felt the hot constriction down there and the heat of our bodies pressed together, the warmth of her stomach on mine, and then again saw gleeful warriors hacking at flesh and smashing bones and driving their spears through children, of men in red and yellow feathers watching while men who did not understand why had cords wrapped around their necks, while the dead stared at the sun in wonder as flesh was stripped from their bodies so that their bones could become someone's prize.

So vivid were these dreams that there was no time, only a richness of color, of blood and slashed skin and splintered bone, as if seen under powerful sunlight, and so vivid was the sensation of myself and Pekau making children that I could not separate it from that lost reality, so tangible was the sense of her touch.

One night I awoke from this strange state, from another of those pleasant dreams of Pekau, aware of movement, and opened my eyes to see, first, moonlight slanting in the low doorway faintly illuminating the edge of the mat upon which I lay, and then above me the form of a person, and felt thighs against my sides and felt myself hardened and all the way inside that unmistakable heat. The pain in my shoulder was evident, but lessened, and the form above me moved against me, hair scratching my lower belly, the hair swinging below her head moving on my chest, and then she moaned softly. I looked up and perceived the shape of her neck and chin, and saw that it was the younger woman who had watched me with such fascination.

I lay there silently while she moved, and then it was over, after which she slowly moved off me and then carefully arranged a kihei over me, and very furtively left the little house. Then I was fully awake. Had she caused those dreams of Pekau? And did she not have a husband who could do for her what she had clearly decided I might give her? The answer came easily on the tail of the question: her husband was most likely rotting in the grass at the bottom of the ravine. All husbands were rotting down there, unless they were rotting on the great chief's sacrificial stone.

I drifted into a half-sleep, and came awake next to sunlight illuminating that piece of mat. I tried moving, and discovered that I was quite weak, but I could form a fist with my left hand, and the wound on my shoulder did not hurt me as much. My shoulder was wrapped, somewhat tightly, by fine matting and cord, and I was otherwise naked.

I heard activity outside, the crackling of a fire and soft speech, apparently between the old woman and the young woman. I attempted to sit up, and found that I could. I looked around in the half darkness of the little house for my malo, found it and put it on, and then made to move out of the house. Apparently they heard me doing this, for their conversation stopped, and as I made my way out into bright sunlight that hurt my eyes, I saw the old woman sitting by the fire, but the young woman was gone.

"Aloha," she said.

"Aloha," I said. "I wish to thank you for helping me. I feel a good deal better."

"Sit here and eat," she said. She had, spread out by the fire, warm 'uala, banana, and some dried meat, dog perhaps. I sat down gingerly, and ate.

At length I paused. "And where is your daughter?"

"You will not see her," she said. "She is my granddaughter. She is very shy. She runs whenever someone comes here. She is up the mountain."

I ate more, and the expression on my face must have communicated to the old woman what I knew, for she reached over and slapped my knee. "Come now," she said, "do you begrudge the poor girl your keakea?" The word 'keakea' means semen. She laughed, and I held up my hands doubtfully.

"No, I do not," I said. "I was unaware that I was making that gift to her. What of her husband?"

"Dead," she said.

"Then I am happy to have given her that gift."

"She has no children but wants them," she said. "There are few young men left. There are few left anywhere who do not carry spears and look for others to kill."

"And the great chief," I said. "What of him?"

"He has left," she said. "It is said that he is in Kahului."

"How long have I been asleep?" I asked.

"Three days," she said. "There was some fever, and you were weak and mumbling in your dreams, but the kahuna lapa-au has said that your wound should heal, for it is not red or swollen."

"And your granddaughter?" I asked. "How many times did she visit me?"

She laughed with a fresh intimacy, and slapped my knee again. "Judging by how long she slept during the day, I think she must have been visiting you many times."

"I must get to a place called Oluwalu, across these mountains. Is it difficult?"

"There is a trail," she said. "I know that you are a warrior and must go to do your fighting, but there are other women in these mountains like my granddaughter. You would be able to make the keakea gift to many of them." She thought a moment. "After all," she went on, "when the men kill each other, and I am glad that the wind carries the smell of rot elsewhere, we women must conspire to create more, is that not so?"

"Many died down there," I said.

"And what we have left are boys and crooked old men. We women wield the digging stick now. There is no kapu, for there are no men to honor it. You sit and eat with me, and think nothing of it."

"I have been away from our world a number of years," I said. "I have seen much, and the kapu is honored as if you were my mother and I a boy. I think of it this way."

She asked me about the world I had seen, and I spent some time describing it. I told her my name, and she told me hers: Nahakea, her granddaughter, Po'iao.

She repeated the invitation to stay, to attempt living without a spear, as she put it, but I stressed once again that I had to find my way to a place called Oluwalu, and that I should leave as soon as possible. I felt well enough, if walking were all I would need to do.

She prepared food for me, and while she did that, it occurred to me to ask more questions. "Do you know of a man called Manomano?" I asked. "And a woman who has three children, a woman named Pekau?"

This she thought about, and said, "No."

And so I bade her goodbye. I made my way down a steep path, but one which ran along the ridge above the valley and the stream below. There was furtive movement above me, and I looked up to see Po'iao moving through the brush parallel to my movement. I stopped and looked up to wave, but upon seeing me looking in her direction, she vanished.

Going by the instructions given me by Nahakea, I made my way along this path, which remained quite far above the narrow valley. Down near the stream I could see the remains of the battle, bloated bodies, some being fed upon by dogs and pigs, but the smell of them did not reach me at that height. I passed the sharp mountain called 'Iao, and continued between the high mountains, their tops shrouded in clouds.

The occasional vibrations that ran into my shoulder from my foot slipping shot a powerful pain into my shoulder and side, but this pain was bearable. Another kind of pain assailed my thought: Pekau and the children, Manomano. No one had heard of them. I knew the island was large, and knew that the assumption that everyone might know everyone else was incorrect, but my hopes of ever finding them were fading, and this caused in me a feeling of a remoteness from all in my life that was worth living for. I was now merely an ambulatory mass of flesh and bone, passing above masses of flesh and bone that were rotting and being fed upon by dogs and pigs. What use would it be to me to make my way back to the ship, if even this were possible? I did not know.

I walked much of the day, and encountered only children, old women and old men. They greeted me warily, for they all knew of the slaughter and knew that Kamehameha's warriors were still on the island. I asked that question of each of them: do you know of a Pekau, a Manomano? And each said they did not. At length the valley I widened and I saw the land open up before me, sloping down toward water, another smaller island, called Kaho'olawe, not far across it. And at the end of the day I stood upon that sand, trying to decide which way Oluwalu might lay. Judging by the rise of the mountains to the north, I assumed that it was south, and so I began walking on the beach. I saw no one. It was apparent that word of the slaughter of the Maui army had made its way to all the corners of the island, and the people were in hiding, fearing the appearance of warriors intent on continuing their slaughter.

Then I saw ahead of me the manu of a canoe sticking out from some bushes. When I was abreast of that manu, a warrior rose from the brush, one of the paddlers. I stopped, turned, and made my way through the heavy sand to him. Two other of the paddlers rose from the brush. "Are you missing one?" I asked.

"He ran," one of the paddlers said, studying my kapa wrapped shoulder. "You have been wounded."

"A musket wound," I said.

"You were in the battle," he said. The other two looked, one with his hand on his chin.

"Yes," I said, and went on to describe it briefly. The men listened intently, from time to time looking over their shoulders toward the valley I had traversed. I finished by saying, "I believe Kalanikupule and other chiefs escaped, but I do not know where they have gone. The warrior Kamehameha has many guns, and will do what he pleases. If he wishes to take Oʻahu, then he will do that. This is what I must tell Muapo."

"We do not wish to go back to Muapo," the paddler said. "Muapo does not like displeasing information."

"Muapo may blame you, or us," another said.

"I must get back to Oʻahu," I said. "Perhaps you will take me back and then take the canoe where you wish."

"Here it is dangerous," the paddler said, sweeping his hand about him. "Our island is also dangerous. Would you take us on your ship?"

"What ship?" I asked.

"We know who you are, Pono the Needle-Fish. You talked in your sleep, and you talkled in the haole language. You have been to the land of mists and fog."

I looked around, thinking. Of course I could not help talking in my sleep. But this violated my promise to Muapo. "Have you told anyone this?"

The man looked around. "Who shall we tell?"

"Yes," I said. "I shall talk to my chief, the haole Beckwith."

"Beck-wit," he said. "The chief of the great canoe. Will you tell us about the land of mists and fog?"

"Yes, for we cannot sail now," I said. "We shall go in the morning, and between now and then I shall tell you of the land of mists and fog."

"We know of the incident with the priest Kahimoku, for it is told in different ways by many," he said, looking at the other two. "We believe that you are a warrior with great mana, and days ago as we paddled, we were afraid to speak because of the presence of Moʻomake. Did he die in the battle?"

"Yes, but he took many warriors with him."

"He shall now bring terror to people's dreams," the paddler said.

Settled in that brush with these men, I told them the story of the land of mists and fog while they fed me, and asked more than once if I was in pain. These men were young, and I suppose not unlike me. They had good intentions and an insatiable curiosity about the world, for their rapt attention seemed inexhaustible, and as warrior-paddlers attached to Muapo, they struck me as ensnared in his machinations rather than his willing minions. They were named Kua'i, Makili, and Koikoi, the leader and oldest Kua'i. And as I told the story, I found myself repeating to them the principle I understood to be the rule of this strange greater world they were so eager to learn about: that everywhere there were two kinds of people, ali'i and all others, and that the world's ali'i did in the land of mists and fog what they did in our world. While it was true that boys could be burned to death over a couple of leaves of a plant, or that men and boys could have their heads chopped off over the question of how they grew their hair, the various causes for this behavior drew themselves back always to the first rule, that once the title of ali'i was inherited and then bestowed upon a man, that man began to shut off certain portions of his mind's logic, and other less logical principles took hold and drove his behavior.

I described to them the maps I had seen, and most fascinating to them was a picture I drew in the sand, of the continents and the oceans, and in the center of one part of this picture in the sand I placed a line of tiny shell pieces and told them that these pieces represented our world, and that these other areas here represented King Philip's Land, and here, China, and here, a place called The Americas, which I had not yet visited.

My recollection of the place called Europe from the maps was somewhat vague, but I created a line indicating a mass that took three steps to walk across in the sand to indicate the size of this place compared to our world.

Kua'i asked me to speak the haole language, and I said, "'ow do ye do, mate?" and "Would ye like to give a scrap of this to Madame Churchill?" To each statement, all three said, "Ae," and then formed some of the words with their mouths, tried to speak them, and laughed. And more difficult words: "Encyclopedia Britannica," and "advanced rigor mortis," and "Will you 'ave sugar in your tea?" Kua'i said that he would like to know this language so as to be able to speak to all people, and I corrected that wish by pointing out that there were many languages, perhaps hundreds, in the great world. This they thought over in a quiet amazement.

This conversation went on for some time, until their questions were exhausted, not by the lack of curiosity but rather by fatigue, for we had to leave soon.

Our return voyage, they told me, would commence before dawn, and we would make our way north along the island and from there see Moloka'i, and would paddle to the western end of that island and thence to our home. And so we did that, again in quite calm waters, I offering from time to time to help with the paddling, which they declined and advised me to rest.

One curious feature of this trip was that as we left Maui and aimed the canoe for the western end of the next island, we saw in the far distance to our right a large grouping of canoes laboring across the channel toward Moloka'i. I thought it must be the great warrior giving chase to Kalanikupule, and upon seeing those canoes, my paddlers stopped speaking to each other in English sayings – 'ow do ye do, mate? – and focused more energy on creating as much distance from those canoes as possible. When we were safely off the western end of that island, O'ahu came into view, and they returned to their chatter, frequently asking me for correct pronunciations: turn 'er to port, mate, I'm delighted to meet you, sir, got any backy for my pipe? You bloody fool.

Our crossing went smoothly, those three warrior-paddlers very skilled in their handling of the swells and waves, and they did not turn the canoe over once, which I appreciated because I feared the consequences of getting the wound on my shoulder wet. As we crossed before the broad expanse of the leeward side of our island, I studied the shape of it from that distance of an hour's paddle out into the ocean. Cooking fires were visible in the lowlands, and the sky above it was fair. The one thought I could now not escape was that no one I had spoken to had ever heard of Pekau or Manomano, and as I sat there, one hand gripping the gunnel of the canoe, that sensation of a peculiar, lifeless isolation came to me once again. Pekau and my children were dead, and had been for some time. Very likely they had drowned on their way, or drifted in the currents and died of thirst. This dream of mine, to find them safe and to continue my life with them, had been but a cruel illusion, but one that had sustained me through the past few years, and now I had nothing to sustain me. This new state of being for me felt like death.

As we crossed before the broad expanse of my island, I became aware that this ill feeling of mine concerning the likelihood of the deaths of all close to me save Laka was accompanied by another ill feeling, this one physical. That caustic pain in my shoulder had by the time we were off the great plain of Ewa spread down my back and into my neck, and I felt myself becoming feverish and dizzy. I told my new acquaintances of this, and one of them, Kua'i, turned in the seat and asked me to turn so that he might look at it. He told me that the wound was leaking a yellow fluid into the covering, and that redness in the skin had spread away from it. He then turned back to his paddling. So I sat there hunched over, my eyes closed, and rocked with the motions of the canoe.

By the time we had reached the end of the island, I was hot and dizzy and sick to my stomach. And when the canoe slid up into sand, I felt weak, and I trembled with chills, although I was perspiring heavily. I was dimly aware of the paddlers talking near me, and did not want to get up from the plank.

They were wondering, it seemed, why the great canoe was no longer there. They were wondering if the haole Beck-wit had left.

At length I did struggle out of the canoe, and stumbled up on that beach amid a gabble of voices, not those of the paddlers. I looked up at the face of Will Kelsey, who was holding a musket and leaning down to look at me. "I must go to see Muapo," I said.

"We've seen enough of him, mate," he said, and then behind me I heard the report of a musket.

"What is happening?"

"Muapo held Jack Audrey as an 'ostage, mate, and we've just liberated the blighter, much to that pudgy little chief's displeasure."

"Why did he hold him?"

"I'll tell ye later, lad," he said, and disappeared.

I heard one more musket report, but it sounded flat and distant, as if coming from some dream. I lost consciousness.

Indeed I lived then in the land of horrible dreams. Sounds sharp and soft, distant and close, raged on in a senseless babbling, disembodied voices, words sliced through the middle and their parts separated off so that no sense could be made of them. I saw Pekau and my children and Manomano working their way through high seas, saw the canoe flip over and saw her desperately trying to hold her children above those waves until they all sank, the last visible part of her hair which spread out upon the water and then drew quickly down into it, all their hair following them down slowly in a dreamlike curling through that darkening water. And so long ago, I knew, so that their bones were now littering some bleak patch of sand no man had ever or would ever see.

At times this dreamlike state remained silent and nearly comfortable. I watched, laughing, as men beat other men to death, men in strange uniforms hacked the heads off children, as stump-eared boys drove spears into the bodies of young girls, as men struggled under the rocks that stole their breath from them. At times I felt myself urinating, and held my breath as I did so in a watchful and fascinated silence, a me observing myself with an amiable curiosity and without shame or wonderment at what it was I was doing. It felt to me as if I remained in this state for years, for the image of Pekau and my children slipping into the void returned so many times that I began to tire of the irritating repetition, and each time I saw this happen I watched in a mute and fascinated silence, but each time I thought I might reach for them, my hand would not obey my mind's command, and they slipped out of sight. And now they were in the underworld, the land of Milu, wherein dwelt the dead.

At length these dreams took on a strange pulse, an odd snapping and groaning sound that did not make me wonder, for I was as if reduced to a sentient vapor, and that repetitive imagery became my life in this world. After a time the snapping and groaning sounds, the strange sweeping, dizzy oblivion I as that vapor occupied, began to match my slow heartbeat, that rhythmic sensation of little shocks of increased pressure at regular intervals I felt in my face, my lips, and which sounded in low squirts in my ears. And one day in this dream I felt pain, almost as if I had been feeling it all along, but now was aware enough to remember that I had felt it, along with other things: a stiffness, a series of sounds, the sensation of a rocking movement, a strange sliding through space along with odd reports of sound. I tried to move to relieve stiffness and opened my eyes to a humid darkness and a smell: that of the bilge from the low interior of *The Tiburon*.

I felt a familiar rising and then sinking, a slow curl through space that was caused by the ship's tipping as it breached a wave and then settled into the recession of a swell. I wondered why we were moving, and where we were going. But I was too fatigued to move, and even those very light attempts at changing my position caused the shock of a tangible pain in my shoulder, but it was in the wound only, and not the pain I dimly remembered as radiating into my neck and down my back and arm.

There was a foul taste in my mouth, the remnant of which was familiar and not familiar at the same time. I knew this odor but this odor had never been in my mouth, and I lay there for some time wondering what it was, my memory laboring over why I was where I was. While it seems as if one should instantly recall the origin of a pain, I should say that it took me some time to recall the battle in the valley, my climbing that steep valley wall and my being hit by the musket ball. I then recalled the journey back to my island, and all after that seemed vague. I had seen Will Kelsey, I had talked with the paddlers, I had gone to see Muapo and Konapiliahi. Then I realized that I was recalling seeing Muapo and Konapiliahi before leaving.

As that time of confusion went on, so did my eyes adjust to a faint light making barely clear the heavy beams of the creaking ship. I heard thumps above me, the sounds of shoes hitting the planking, and I heard voices. I could not determine if we were asail, or sitting in the swells. At length a yellow, shifting light opened up, and a form bearing a candle made its way toward me. I squinted my eyes, and made out Will Kelsey.

"Morning, mate," I said.

The face on the other side of the flame registered a mute shock, and then he turned and yelled, "Roger! Dick! 'e's come to!"

"What's the matter?" I asked. "'ave I overslept?"

"Overslept?" he said. "Mate, you've been asleep for a week. We took you for dead, man. We were ready to cast you over the side, we were. Owen said it was a poisoning of the blood. Septicemia I think he said. He said you'd not make it."

"I must go and talk to Muapo," I said.

"Lad," he said. "We've left old Muapo behind a hundred fifty mile. We're going to the Americas."

Suffice it to say that I had much catching up to do. Will Kelsey told me that Muapo's messengers had learned about the battle on Maui, and Muapo sunk into an attitude of panic and doom, considering the inevitability of the great warrior's coming to take Oʻahu. So he took Jack Audrey as a hostage, and then sent his haoles to confer with Beckwith to the effect that Muapo would require Beckwith's cannons and more muskets. It would be a simple matter, these haoles told Beckwith, to send a large double-hulled canoe out to the ship and bring those cannons in one by one, until Muapo could mount them at the fringes of his great hale, all looking down at the plain from which he was sure the invading army would approach. Mr. Audrey would be kept safe if this was done. If it was not done, then poor Mr. Audrey would be killed upon the great flat stone, and any other men Muapo's warriors could catch would also be thus executed.

"While it seemed unlikely that Mr. Beckwith would trade all his cannons for one sailor," Will Kelsey said, "a feature of this bargain Muapo did not seem to appreciate, it was ironically true that Mr. Beckwith was not inclined to trade that sailor, and so went with twelve men up to Muapo's hale bearing muskets, to claim Mr. Audrey and prepare to sail. Muapo's haoles were baffled by this loyalty, the lowly blighters they were, and in the ensuing clash between Beckwith's men and Muapo's warriors, a few men fell, but Mr. Audrey was rescued. That big man with all the tattoos on one side of his body took a ball in the leg, but seemed unaffected by it as the sailors, loading their muskets and walking backwards down the hill toward the beach, made their escape. The three paddlers who had brought you back Pono were confused by all this, and watched from below, raising the ire of Muapo, who ordered that they be taken and killed. One did, however, escape, a man named Koo-aye or something like that, who ended up wet and shaking and frightened on the ship, looking around him with the largest and most amazed of eyes as the last of the islands receded into the pale, misty horizon.

"And so," Will Kelsey said, "here we are again having made ourselves unwelcome in another part of the world, to add to all those parts of the world where lengths of rope awaited. It's Roger's way," he said. "Show me a port we can go to, and give us a chance to go, and like magic, we can never return.

He finds an excuse to make this ship famous, he does. I look at a map o' the world, and now put little X's on ports that might welcome us, where before I might have put the X where we'd made ourselves famous. The world's covered with those latter X's, Pono."

"The world is big, however," I said.

"Getting smaller by the day, mate," he said.

I made a move to sit up, and was shocked by the force of the pain in my shoulder. Will Kelsey urged me back with the flat of his hand. "Ye can't move yet, Pono." He moved away, and I heard the soft, grating sound of a jug on one of the tin cups Owen Bew kept in the kitchen. Kelsey came back. "Drink this," he said. "It'll 'elp you with the pain." He held the cup to my lips, and I drank. It was, I believed, whiskey, that same smell I had the remnant of inside my mouth. It burned going down my throat, and I relaxed back. "Yer friend Koo-aye, or whatever it is, now there's a jumpy fellow for you. We're teachin' him the language now. Know what 'e said to us first?" He laughed. "Said, ''ow de do, bloody mate.'"

"I will talk to him," I said, beginning then to feel a strange, swooning sensation, a slipping away into dreams and a bodily heaviness. "I will."

And in those dreams Manomano did speak to me: I call you from the land of death, he said. I have been here years in the underworld peopled by all the dead before you and before me. You have gone far, out into the land of mists and fog, and you live yet, and you shall live long, but I cannot say that you shall ever see the fruits of my flesh again, because this knowledge is denied me. She is not here in the land of death, is not in the land of her birth. What land she is in I cannot say. 'Iolana is here, and as he came so did the lizard decorations slip like blue liquid from his body.

When I awoke the pain was as before. This time I made no attempt to move. I lay there feeling the slow roll of the ship, and listened to its creaking and groaning as we made our way to another land.

A few minutes after a series of cannon reports from the ramparts of the old fort heralded in another shipload of thirsty and lustful sailors, I made my way along the grog shop lane, as I had begun to think of it, and saw Mrs. Searle hastening toward the slum wherein, I understood, more of the native people were dying of this apparent epidemic that seemed to raise so little ire or concern from the whites who occupied the port area. I was due at the little copying room, and did see Pono at the thatched doorway looking after Mrs. Searle, his hand to his chin. When I arrived at the doorway, Pono turned to me. "Aloha," he said. "That was your friend Mrs. Searle who went by just now. She seems in a hurry."

"It's this sickness," I said. "I believe she has been working helping the people."

"But she seemed in some distress. I wonder if we could be of some help."

"As you wish," I said. "Let's talk to MacFarlane."

"I heard," MacFarlane said from inside the room. He emerged at the doorway. "I shant be able to go with you."

"No," Pono said. "You'll end up sick yourself and so will your wife."

"What of you, though?" MacFarlane asked.

"I've seen this before," Pono said. "I learned over the years that those who travel much develop resistances to these afflictions. But you've been here some time. If I were you, I'd stay away from the area."

"And I," I said, "have traveled much. So, Pono, shall we go?"

He nodded. We arranged with MacFarlane to meet later in the afternoon, and if the drunken sailors might permit, we would advance the narrative then, with the sun slanting in little coin-sized circles of light on his pages from the other side of the room.

Thus did Pono and I make our way up that lane, and thence to the east, where the path led first past the better looking huts, MacFarlane's included, into the area of the slum, where suspicious chickens watched us pass, and dogs tied to saplings barked at us. For reasons which escape me even to this day, those huts were located in an area whose air seemed far more heavy and humid than did the air at the port. This time, there were fewer cooking smells, and as we walked, I behind Pono, I wondered why it was that this place had been chosen by those people, for the humidity made that air seem foul, tinged by the smells of waste and mud and rotting fruit.

But as we walked, that smell I had thought of as generated by unclean habits changed into a more definite odor, that of carrion. Pono stopped and studied the huts, inside of which we could see the movement of human forms, some huts with children sitting in wan subjection to the heat outside. Here the dogs did not seem to have the energy to bark, and the chickens were in the shade, many of them ruffling their feathers in dust pits they had scratched into the dry earth. The sun was merciless in its force, and I was perspiring, the odor of my clothes wafting up across my face.

At length we neared the line of huts I had visited before with Mrs. Searle, behind which we could see the profile of Diamond Hill, or Leahi, as Pono called it. The smell apparently came from this area, a dead dog or pig perhaps.

Pono stopped and looked around. "She is in one of these huts," he said, approaching one. He called in his own language, and waited, then turned to me. "Empty," he said. We looked around for human movement. Finally I saw something, somewhat up a bluff from where we stood, a patch of white moving.

"She is up there," I said, pointing. This time I led the way, between two huts, to a rocky area we had to climb up, above which was a grassy area where there were no huts. I walked between thick tufts of grass to a place where we could see her clearly. She was digging with what appeared to be crude shovel made of wood, and she was weeping. Her dress was muddy down around the hem.

"Something is amiss," I said to Pono. "I shall go talk to her."

I approached, and she saw me, but continued with her digging. Her face, I saw, was crossed with a look of a kind of determined bereavement, a combination of sadness and anger, and she drove the wooden shovel into the hard dirt again and again.

"May we help?" I asked.

She stopped, sighed, and stood up straight. "You needn't," she said. "There's nothing to be done but to bury them, and I can do that." She swept her hand around, indicating the areas near her. "I've buried a few here," she said. "It's interesting to me how an event like this seems not to make any impressions down the hill there."

Pono came up by my side. He looked at the hole Mrs. Searle was digging, and then walked to her. "Please," he said. "Might I do this?"

"Oh, well, yes. I suppose it would be something of a relief," she said.

"And may we help with the rest?" he asked. He took the shovel from her, and looked in the hole. He seemed to be thinking about something, and then looked up past us, toward Diamond Hill. He was remembering something, I was sure, but I decided not to ask. Then he turned the shovel upside down and jammed the pole handle into the dirt, and levered it up. Once some of the dirt was loosened, he turned the shovel over and spaded it out to the fringe. I moved up toward Mrs. Searle, who watched him with that expression of inward turning perplexity, after which she stared at some middle distance toward the mountains.

To her, I said, "I've noticed that a number of the huts are empty."

Watching, she had apparently not heard, and then she seemed to have heard as if absorbing what I had said in a slow recognition, for she turned away from the mountains and stared rather blankly at me, and then said, "Oh, yes. I've convinced some of them to leave the area temporarily."

"And do you think this has run its course?" I asked.

She turned back to watch Pono at work flinging spadefuls of dirt up out of the hole. "Well, I hope so," she said. "There's no way of knowing."

At length Pono paused and looked at Mrs. Searle, who looked at the hole and said, "That is quite good. Now if you gentlemen will help me with the body?"

"Certainly," he said.

She led us back down the same path we had taken up, and thence to the line of huts, and then to one that I had identified as empty. Behind it, there was a piece of filthy bark cloth spread out, and I could see the shape of the body causing it to rise in the middle. She paused, and then reached down to pull the cloth away.

A cloud of flies came up around the fringes, and there the body lay, a young woman who was beginning to bloat, and the stench that rose with those flies was such that I had to fight to control the impulse to retch. Her skin had blackened in places, and liquid glinted in the small folds in her skin, her eyes and mouth distorted by the swelling and clotted with dried mucous. Next to her head lay a long black braid, perfectly woven and thick, seeming to me the hair of a living person. I had my hand to my mouth, and looked up at Mrs. Searle and Pono, the latter of whom stared down at the woman. "She was seventeen," Mrs. Searle whispered. Then she looked at Pono, who stared down at the body, his eyes lost in some rueful speculation.

"So," Mrs. Searle said, "we shall roll her over onto the mat, and carry her up." She thought a second. "No, we shall put the mat on her and then roll her so that—" Pono nodded. He stooped down and pulled the mat over the body. Then Pono and I went to one side, and, pressing the mat down, he on her shoulder and myself pressing it to her thigh, we lifted and rolled her, but as I pushed, I felt the skin underneath rip and then separate, and as it did so, so did fluid soak into the mat and reach my hands. I pushed her over and then rubbed my hands on a tuft of grass nearby. The stench of that fluid rose from my hands and again, I had to resist the urge to retch.

We carried her up the path in the filthy bark cloth mat, I in the rear, the stench thick across my face. Mrs. Searle followed us, and behind me I heard her praying. When we had put the woman in the hole and pushed the dirt over her, I doing so vigorously so as to remove the remnants of that foul fluid from the palms of my hands. Mrs. Searle did then pray over the grave while Pono walked around looking for a rock to mark it.

I had assumed that this would be the work for this day, but Mrs. Searle was not finished. After she was satisfied that the grave was properly marked, with a pale stone the size of a man's head for that purpose, she said, "Well, now I shall go visit the sick."

"Are there more?" Pono asked. "Perhaps we can help with that."

"I would appreciate it," she said, lifting her hand to her bonnet as a gust of wind came down the mountain. "The affliction seems to be moving west along the huts. The symptoms begin with coughing and fever, and then with congestion in the lungs. It's the congestion that causes the death."

"And their kahuna lapa au?"

"He is right here," she said, looking around. "I should say over there." She pointed at another rock. Now I perceived that there were a number of these rocks set about, and realized that we were standing in a graveyard, albeit one of her own devising. "Some of the men helped me bury him before they left. They took their wives and children over the pass," she said, "to the other side of the island. It reminds me of people escaping the plague in Europe by going to the mountains. In any case, the huts at the end of the line near the marsh are now all empty, their inhabitants either dead or gone."

"What do you prescribe for this?" he asked.

"Camphor, vinegar to induce sweating, and clean water," she said. "It's not the scarlet fever or the pox or measles. I don't know what it is, some catarrhal fever, and our only chance to help them is to deal with the congestion. The camphor comes from some tree in China, It has a most pleasant smell, and helps clear the breathing passages."

Thus did we make our way back down toward the huts. Mrs. Searle emerged first into that area where the last four were, and stopped. Then she turned to us, looking for the most part at Pono. "Excuse me," she said, "but how long have you been here?"

"This voyage?" he said. "I would say a month."

"And you were here in recent years?"

"Yes, from time to time," he said. "For periods of years in the last couple of decades, however, I was in the far west of your continent, in China and other places."

"So I could have seen you then," she said.

"Could have?"

"I have this irritating inability to remember how or where, but I am convinced I have seen you. And it's not merely your appearance. It is your speech and bearing. I don't know, I—" She sighed. "Now I think I must be mistaken."

"Well, perhaps it'll occur to you," he said. "In the meantime, I must ask where these other sick people are."

"Oh, yes," she said. "I've already set them up with some of the remedies. Come this way."

I will summarize the remainder of this day. Pono turned out to be quite the skilled physician in that he helped her tend to the needs of two families, in huts side by side along that row. The first family was made up of two old people, and three little children, and again I assumed that the children's parents were off wallowing in the various iniquities of the port. All were sick, but apparently on the mend enough that we could assume they would survive. The other hut, however, had but two people in it, a woman and her mother, both of whom coughed harshly and rolled around on their mats in a high fever. By the end of the day the older woman died, and the daughter continued bearing up under her illness. And so once again we hauled a body up through that grass to Mrs. Searle's makeshift cemetery, and labored in the waning sunlight to dig a grave, and when this was done, Mrs. Searle did again pray over the deceased. I thought then that we might all go on our way, but Mrs. Searle decided to remain in the hut of the surviving woman, to help her through the night. Pono volunteered to do the same, but she convinced him that his assistance would be more practical and more welcome if he were to remain available by day. He agreed to this, and bade me goodbye on the path fronting those huts, with arrangements to meet the following day.

That night, and nights following, I was aware of the hint of that stench of death on the palms of my hands. As one sleeps, one's hands remain close to the face, and so did that faint smell accost me, no matter how many times I rose in frustration from my bunk to go to the bucket and wash my hands with soap. Sometimes after that, I mean weeks, even months, I would pause, aware of the hint of the smell of rot in the air, and then lift and smell my hands, convinced that somehow it had remained there, perhaps residing under my nails, which I cleaned until they were sore, and clipped until they were near the quick. It was perhaps a trick of the mind, but it did bother me for quite some time.

18.

So, as I made my slow recovery from what Owen Bew described as a poisoning of the blood, *The Tiburon* cut its way through the swells of the great ocean. Each day Owen Bew came down with a candle and a clean dressing, and changed the dressing on my shoulder, saying, "Aye, ye knit well, me boy. In a bit you'll be as good as new." I will admit here that I enjoyed the carefully paced administration of the only medicine I took for that recovery, whiskey, because it caused in me that strange swooning and painless lapse into dreams, many of which involved the lost Pekau, and some of which were horrific and inexplicable.

My shipmates did come down to speak with me during the days. Beckwith particularly, who seemed quite concerned about my health, would sit and ask me questions, and would question me about the practices of my world where military matters were concerned: "There is no quarter then? When one army beats another in a battle, do all in the losing army die?" I nodded in confirmation. He had heard of this, he said, concerning the Indians of the great continent to the south of the one we were sailing to, where a battle would result in an entire army being sacrificed before a stone god by having their hearts cut out. "Indeed," he said, "it is a miracle that there are people left yet to populate this injured world, for so barbaric are our practices that one would think all would eventually die."

I told him about my dreams, told him that Manomano had spoken to me from the land of death. "Is this the father of your wife? Yes, I recall your describing him to us."

"He told me that Pekau is not in the land of death," I said.

"Pono, do you know where your dreams come from? They come from you. You fear that Manomano is dead, and so you dream that he is. You hope that your Pekau is alive, and so you dream a dream in which Manomano tells you that she is."

"This is logical," I said. "The dreamer is the author of his own dreams."

Beckwith laughed. "Pono, you've become quite the English speaker. And your Koo-aye," he said. "He's become quite the British sailor, although he's caught 'imself a cold, he has. I hope it isn't serious."

And Dick Burrows was a frequent visitor. He was less articulate than most of the men. He would sit down by my bunk, and say, "How you doin'?" to which I would say, "I am feeling well." He would be silent for some time, and then launch off into speculating on what we would do when we reached the continent. "Bear," he said. "Now there's huntin' for you. You an' me, we'll go after some bear. If not that, then deer." Another time, he sat for an oddly long time before clearing his throat. "You know, Pono, there's a girl back in your place I hated leavin'. Lana's her name. Probably too young, but—" He stopped there. "Well," he said, "I ever get back there, I'm likin' to find her and stay. Just so's you know. We'd be neighbors maybe, huh?"

"It is my hope to go back someday," I said. "I have been thinking about this. I have been dreaming about my wife, and I am not convinced that she is dead."

"You got to stick with that," he said. "Hope's a good thing, you know. You ain't seen her dead, so you don't know."

And so these conversations went. While I was recovering, I did from time to time need to relieve myself, and this was achieved with a chamber pot, provided by Owen Bew, that I was able to squat over whilst holding onto the bunk with my good arm. After a few days of feeling somewhat soiled by this arrangement, I became determined to make my way to the deck, for I had become quite bored lying there.

I stood up, feeling my balance, and then made my way to the light coming in from above. I negotiated the narrow staircase by pulling myself up with my good hand. And when I emerged into that light, so bright that it drove my eyes shut, I heard a lusty cheering from the men. "Aye, 'e's come round!" and "Ahoy mate," this latter from none other than Kuaʻi, dressed in sailor's pantaloons and one of Owen Bew's oily old caps. He then sneezed. As my eyes adjusted, I looked around at a beautiful day, the immense cumulous clouds blazing white on the horizon.

During that crossing to the great continent, my sense of my own life had somewhat changed, perhaps because of the effects of my 'medicine' in the form of that hot liquid, or perhaps because of what seemed to me a failure of fate, that I had not come any closer to finding Pekau than if I had never returned to my land. What did this mean? Was I to abandon any hope now, and carry out my life according to whatever plan chance and probability had for me? I counted the years since I had last seen her, nearly five, and thought then of what other events had taken place in my land. Wars, death, and now the problem of the various afflictions my people had begun to suffer, my brother included, that no one from my land had ever heard of. Much had changed because of the meshing of my world with such worlds as the land of mists and fog, and the other lands far to the west of mine. The whiskey so freely offered me, to ease my pain, eased also, I believe, any hopeful thinking on my part, to the point that I saw my future as one lived alone.

In the succeeding days I moved about the ship, but the recovery was so long that I tired easily, while around me the men played their games, smoked their pipes, and amused themselves teaching Kua'i their language and the various duties expected of a sailor, the first the use of the holystone. When I became frustrated at having nothing to do, I would extract a chicken from the cage and make my way to the hold, and watch as she ran around in the dim light of a candle pecking at insects. The ship cut through the gentle swells under fair skies, and at times, feeling enfeebled by my weakness, I stole down to Beckwith's cabin and picked material off his shelves to read. I had not exhausted the Encyclopedia, but experimented by reading things that were not information in the basic sense. I thought that perhaps I should amplify my knowledge of where the majority of these men had come from, England, and asked Beckwith if he might recommend something to me. The result was what he called a 'pamphlet,' or a small book without hard covers, by a Mr. Swift, in which he proposes that the inhabitants of part of that country suffering from a famine offer their own children for sale as food for the tables of the more affluent. I had at first suspected some joke in Beckwith's offering me this pamphlet, and he later explained that the author was using an irony in his proposal. But I asked beyond that: was it true that in his country as in other countries, aside for the unfairness of being hanged for the theft of a cane, there were conditions in which some starved while others lived in luxury? Yes, he said, it is the law of the world.

Such reading made me somewhat melancholy, and in order to stave off that melancholy I drank more of Beckwith's whiskey, which had the effect of making me even sadder. In my world men became the victims of an overindulgence in 'awa, and in the world of these men, whiskey, grog, and other such drinks tended to do the same. I shall admit that I depended much on Beckwith's whiskey, without knowing the damage it was doing to my spirit. I saw all things clouded with skepticism and a kind of philosophical weariness. There seemed no use for me now that I could safely assume that I was alone in the world. When we were some weeks into that crossing, the men began to manifest an excitement at the idea that one day we would sight land, and Beckwith began drawing the men together to instruct them, once again, on the rules of our approach, that we avoid being seen by other ships.

We would avoid what he called King George's Sound, or Newt-ka, which was a bay far to the north in the rainy part of this land mass. We would also avoid the Spanish Main, which lay to the south.

The reason for avoiding both was that Beckwith was known by those trading on the coast, particularly a company called The Associated Merchants of London and India, and The Kind George's Sound Company, both of whom, he said, were well endowed with cannons and men willing to see *The Tiburon* sink, and as for the Spanish, Beckwith did not want to be seen by them either. The southern part of the coast we were approaching belonged to them. We were to trade with the Indians of the area between the two groups of seafaring people. If we were to encounter villages, he said, it would be likely that they would be what he called 'pueblos,' or clusters of buildings dominated by a Spanish church.

The story was familiar: there were native peoples all throughout this continent, and there were people who endeavored to convert them into the Christian religion. And true it was, Beckwith said, that those who refused to be converted were at times burned to death, or murdered in various other ways. The rengades who refused conversion sometimes retaliated in kind, and murdered either those who had been converted or more to their liking, those who wished to impose that conversion.

"A stew pot of murder," Will Kelsey said. "Ah, what a joy it is, Roger, to follow you about the world. Did you ever enjoy yourself when you were a child?"

"Indeed I did," Beckwith said.

"Ar. You wouldn't know it now, would you boys?" Kelsey said, looking at the other men.

"Pueblos ain't the problem, and Spaniards ain't either," Dick Burrows said. "Problem is mongrel Spaniards. They'd as soon slit your throat as say hello."

"What is a mongrel Spaniard?" I asked.

"Half injin and half Spaniard," Dick Burrows said. "Them's the true renegades. Them's the ones that feast on killin'."

And why were we going to this continent? The answer was pelts, seal skins, bear skins, the skins of what they called deer, and the hides of other animals, which, when we filled the belly of the ship with them, would take us back to bloody China.

Kuaʻi moved along the rail to where I stood. In our language, he asked, "What are they saying?" I explained to him the essence of what we were doing, and then looked back at Beckwith, whose expression had now taken on an oddly philosophical look. He was thinking. I turned to Kuaʻi, and said, "We are going to the land of mists and fog." At this, his eyes widened in wonder.

"Gents," Beckwith said, "the century's tirin' itself out. I want ye to listen now."

"Speak up!" Ben Fowles called from the wheel. Beckwith turned.

"Very well," he said, louder. He went up the three steps to the quarter-deck, closer to Ben Fowles, and turned back to us. "All the oceans have shrunk, lads, to the point that we're findin' it harder and harder to move without being seen. We've done well, and each of you lads 'as got his share down in the cabin, and your shares are enough for you to live in comfort the rest of your lives. I want all you lads to think over where you'd like to be once that time comes, that time when you decide to give this up."

"Bah!" Owen Bew said. "I shan't give this up. My 'ome's in the galley and I plan to finish out my days with my pots."

"Aye," Beckwith said. "I know that, Owen. Perhaps when the time comes I can turn this home of ours over to some enterprising person such as Will, here, or perhaps Ben, for like you, they've been with this vessel the longest. But I've come to regard our business on the ocean as coming to an end."

There was a murmur of disagreement from the men. Will Kelsey looked at Beckwith and said, "Roger, there're depredations all over the place for you to study. Come now, soon we'll be sniffing evidence of some new catastrophe, and you'll feel better."

"When the scientist studies his experiments and comes up again and again with the same conclusion, the scientist gets a bit weary," Beckwith said. He looked toward the east, at the ocean and the huge clouds. "P'raps I think on these matters too much, lads. The one place I think of as a safe place is this ship. And then Pono's land, that was pleasant, and I thought that p'raps we'd found a place off this ship where there was peace, but I'll admit that I was wrong."

"I ain't finished with Pono's land," Dick Burrows said.

Beckwith looked at him. "Aye, Dick, I can understand that. You're young. P'raps that's the place for you, eventually. I want to ask you lads, this one question: would ye like to make one more cross after we collect our shipment? We're talking here about two years, maybe three. I'm thinking that—"

"Ar! One more!" Ben Fowles called from the wheel.

"Agreed," Will Kelsey said.

"Without question," Tong Guan said.

Owen Bew stepped to the quarter-deck stair. "Now dammit, Roger," he said. "What the bloody 'ell are you contemplating?" Beckwith appeared ready to speak, but Owen went on, his face becoming somewhat florid. "Hold your tongue a moment. If you think you're going back to England then you're daft. Do you want to end up like Billy Kid with a rope around your neck? Well, I'll not allow it, damn your soul! Ohh, I know that look, that bloody *I want to go 'ome* look you've got on your face, and damnit, I won't allow that, do you understand? Why, I'll truss you up like—Oh the 'ell with it! Just be warned that I'll not allow you to do that, do you understand?"

"Owen, I wasn't thinking that far ahead, really," Beckwith said. "But it did occur to me that—"

"God-damnit! I will not allow it!"

"Very well," Beckwith said. "For the present, we've got plans for one more crossing to China then. Does that satisfy you?"

"Only if you pump that bilge from your head, boy," Owen Bew said.

"Indeed," Beckwith said. "I shall pump that bilge from my head then."

"I'm not in the business of cooking for the daft," Owen Bew said. Then he turned to the others. "I have been on this ship longer than he has, mates, and sometimes I must assert myself. So don't pay any attention to this little disagreement."

Thus did our journey to the land of mists and fog continue under fair skies.

During that crossing, I showed Kua'i the marvels of this new world: the candle on the wall outside Beckwith's door, the telescope, the mysteries of the musket, and the Encyclopedia. He spent much time with these volumes, studying the letters and words and the illustrations of elephants, foxes, the innards of human beings, and so on. During the bright days we stood at the stern, watching that water fold silently in a widening wake, and I showed him what I knew about the ship's complicated rigging, the pulleys and booms, the metal fastenings, and the intricacies of the wheel's operation of the rudder. He was a bright young man, quick to learn and eager to see the world.

His sleeping arrangements were similar to mine in that he preferred being out on the deck. The bowels of the ship held the bilge smell that the men did not seem to mind, but that bothered me, and him. So he arranged a hammock not unlike mine, and rigged it a few feet away from mine.

During this time my shoulder healed, and I will admit that I began finding excuses to allay a pain that was not really there, because I did like the feeling that came over me when I drank the whiskey, a sensation that sometimes settled on me like a pleasant fog.

But nature's unpredictability intervened in this voyage. Each day held for us an increase in the speed and the vagaries of the winds, and the swells began to amplify. During the nights I would be forced to get myself out of the hammock and then sit against the wall with my feet braced on the planks, for the pitching of the ship made sleeping impossible. And during the day, when the wind became nearly violent, the men would be forced to furl some of the sails, and then that blue sky which had been so beautiful was blocked out by a gray cloud-ceiling, and the ocean's horizon became vague under the roiling showers in the distance. Will Kelsey explained it to me: isn't it true that in your world one can see fair skies all around, but for your island, which seems always capped by clouds? We are approaching the continent, and if you imagine its vastness, a thousand times the size of your island, then you can imagine the vastness of the clouds hovering above it, and the distance out into the ocean that those clouds reach.

As had happened before, the men now began to manifest a tension, and a shortness with each other, for standing there on the deck in stinging rain, your hands gripping the rail, becomes aggravating after a while. Kuaʻiʻs expression had taken on a strange, drawn look, as if he were locked in the state of trying to comprehend the magnitude of the ocean we had crossed and the supposed magnitude of the landmass we approached, its weather's magnitude a frightening portent.

By night we moved with extreme caution, half of the sails reefed, and as each day dawned, the men kept watch off the starboard rail for land. We were slowly moving north, but it was difficult to tell because the heavy, gray sky above blocked out the sun. And from time to time the horizon vanished in lashing rains, the men leaning on the rail looking for land, Jack Crabbe with his face locked in a perpetual leer, Will Kelsey or Ben Fowles at the wheel wiping the rainwater from their eyes as they studied the severly limited plane of vision all around the ship. The wind pushed against the ship, tipping it so that from time to time we heard pots hitting floors below, followed by a string of oaths from Owen Bew. But that storm waned slightly, and amongst the men the expressions took on a hopeful aspect, but for Jack Crabbe, whose leer seemed to have affixed itself permanently on his face.

Then *The Tiburon* swept through a thick fog. This made the men more anxious, so that now in twos and threes they hung over the prow looking down into the water for shoals, and Dick Burrows stood at the starboard rail with a pot and a wooden spoon banging it slowly, like a drum, waiting for the report of an echo off some rock outcropping. He claimed he smelled pines, at which Roger Beckwith sniffed the air, claiming that he smelled nothing at all. Dick Burrows said, "No, it's pines, and dirt."

Beckwith studied his compass and periodically told either Ben Fowles or Will Kelsey to bring her more to port. We had left the storm and entered the fog, the lack of any sight distance in ways worse, because we could find

ourselves headed toward an obstacle without any chance to turn the ship
once we saw it. And then, with a frightening suddenness, we all smelled
carrion, so horrifically rich that some of the men gagged and gripped their
mouths. Kau'i stared at me, frightened, and said, "What is happening?"

I did not know. The carrion smell was so strong that it seemed to sweep
up across our faces from something in the water, but that water was a leaden
gray, nothing in it. I was about to turn to make my way to Roger Beckwith
when the ship rose up and tipped, and then settled again, just slightly enough
that Beckwith, turning, stared into the fog with a strange, thoughtful look
on his face.

"Will! Port!" he called. "Lads, open them." The men rushed to unfurl
sails and pull reefing lines off, but there was not enough wind. Beckwith
looked at the cutter. "Can we tow her?"

"Let's lower the cutter," Will Kelsey said. The men ran to the capstan.
Again we felt the ship rise and settle, and this time off the starboard bow
we saw that lump in the water rise to a crest and then vanish into the fog.
Beckwith made his way along the rail to look, and said, "Oh lord."

The swells breaking meant we were very close to land. All the men
knew full well what was happening, and tugged at ropes to turn the sails,
addressed the capstan. But these efforts were in vain, for the ship rose again
and listed, and we felt movement, and then a settling, the ship righting
itself, but only for the time it took the next swell to rise, at which the ship
again moved, tipped sideways so far that the chickens' cage came sliding
down the deck at me amid squawking and the flapping of wings. I stopped
it with my foot and turned, and as I turned I saw sweeping past us a large,
black rock outcropping with one plume of white water crashing up its side.
We were sweeping toward the shore and could do nothing about it.

"Get a grip on something, lads!" Beckwith yelled. "Will, turn her in if
you can!"

"Aye!" he yelled. Kelsey was up there at the wheel spinning it, trying to
put the swells behind the ship, but each time it began to turn toward shore,
the next swell turned it sideways so that it tipped again. As yet we could not
see any shore.

"Pono," Roger Beckwith called. "Can ye poke yer 'ead down and call
Owen out? And anyone else down there?"

I made my way to the opening to the stairs and called Owen's name.
Above me I heard Will Kelsey yell, "There it is! It's there!" When I heard no
response from Owen, I made my way down, on shaky legs, and found him in
the galley holding onto his stationary table, blood on his forehead. "Owen,"
I said, "it's time to come up."

"Leave me be," he said.

"Owen, Roger told me to bring you up," I said. I took his arm.

We both saw an angular black stone the size of a man's torso pass along the wall snapping pots and pewter plates and mugs to the floor, the stone seeming suspended on some shelf, moving not with great speed but with a strange, almost stately progress, separating two great planks of the ship as it went and breaking in two the vertical beams called futtocks, in an almost deafening sound of splintering wood, a strange screeching at the point where the stone separated the planks, this followed by a rush of water into the galley. At once we were up past our knees in very cold water, and watched as the stone receded, grew smaller, and then vanished just as it softly hit a hanging frying pan that swung back and forth on its nail.

I took Owen's arm and pulled him toward the stairs, and just as I was about to grab the rail and pull him behind me, we heard the explosion of impact and were hurled backwards into the water which then rushed past us into the hold as the fore of the ship rose. Then all was still. It was perhaps fortunate that the water was there, for were it not, we would have hit the galley wall with enough force to injure ourselves. The ship was now on its side, at an angle to the left of the fore. From above I heard shouts, the squawking of the chickens, and the sound of surf hitting rocks. "Owen," I said.

"Aye, lad," he said.

We negotiated the stairs, I pulling Owen behind me, and when we emerged, I saw that the ship had been thrown up on boulders, the men either hanging on the high rail or wedged against the gunnels on the lower side. Some of the men were crawling over the boulders toward land, this being a line of high trees, a forest. Jack Audrey was using a gaff hook to pull his yarn winch out of the water. Upon emerging from the doorway Owen and I both slid down so that our feet were braced where the hull met the deck. The ship had entered a very narrow rock cove, and then had been deposited by a great wave on the boulders. And the next wave that came in the cove sloshed powerfully against the half-submerged belly of the *Tiburon* and rocked it, but only slightly. The mast-pole was split, and much of the rigging was draped down on the deck. Roger Beckwith stood upon a boulder above the ruined ship, his arms around himself, and shivering. Above him stood Madame Churchill, ruffling her feathers and clucking. "Tong Guan!" Beckwith yelled.

"Aye sir!"

"You Seager boys!"

"Present!"

"Well thank the almighty for that!" he yelled. "Will!"

"Sir!"

"What do ye make of the tide?"

"On the way down, sir!"

By my reckoning it was late morning. Owen stood next to me with his hand to his forehead, and I moved my left arm, which felt as it had before, although I was very cold.

It seemed a miracle that, badly damaged as the ship was, it rested there upon those boulders appearing whole. The great, gaping hole in the side was not visible to me from where I stood, and I saw the prow, which was misshapen.

"Lads!" Beckwith yelled. "Listen to me. We've got to get the powder from the 'old, the muskets, and we've got to remove the booty from my cabin."

"What is he saying?" Kuaʻi asked from behind me.

We salvaged what we could from the ship, and the men worked with considerable speed doing this, scrambling with powder kegs and muskets up over the rocks to the beginning of that forest. I did what I could, but was cautioned by Roger Beckwith not to overexert myself. He believed that the ship was a total loss, and wanted everything out of it before the next tide came and reduced it to flotsam.

I watched this activity from a boulder. I studied the strange, narrow inlet that the ship had passed through, one side of it the rock that had split the side of the hull. An idea came to me, and it was based more or less on my world's use of fishponds in the near-shore waters of my island. Something could be done to prevent further damage to the ship, so I went to Beckwith, who was receiving things from the hold doorway.

"Sir," I said. "I've an idea."

"Indeed," he said, studying a powder keg. "Ah, this one's dry. And what of that smell? Something was dead around here, and now I don't smell it."

"P'raps Will should be here to listen," I said. "And the wind is coming south. Whatever died might be to the south of us."

"Aye. Will!"

And so Will Kelsey came to us, making his way along the V shaped trench formed by the hull wall and the deck.

"Very well, Pono, what's your idea?" Beckwith asked. Dick Burrows came out of the hold dripping, and wiping water from his eyes. "Dick," Roger Beckwith said. "Listen in."

"The opening the ship came through is narrow," I said. "If the next high tide is twelve hours from now, we can close the opening by putting rocks in it. This will help control the waves somewhat."

"Aye, and what use is that?" Will Kelsey asked.

"The wave that lifted the ship here raised it before it hit the rocks. If the barrier were to prevent a wave from breaking with all its force, then the ship will not move from its position."

"Hold up," Dick Burrows said. "He's got a point, Roger."

"Sir, we've got wood up there, and we've got rope, a lot of it. If the opening is not deep, we can shut off part of it with rocks today, p'raps the rest tomorrow."

"As yet, I do not get the point," Beckwith said.

"Sir, it is a principle of physics. It could have been Will or Ben Fowles who told me, but he said that with a fulcrum, you can move almost anything. If we protect the ship by blocking off the waves, then we can address the problem of repairing it."

"Do you know how many ton she weighs?" Will Kelsey asked. "And how do ye suppose ye'll get 'er out once she's repaired?"

"We go in the water and remove the rocks."

"*You* go in the water and remove the rocks," Will Kelsey said.

"Yes," I said. "It can be done. I would ask you this, for the sake of argument: if we don't, then what do we do, build another ship?"

Will Kelsey stared at me, and then uttered a "hmmph".

"I'm for doin' what he says," Dick Burrows said. "I'm for fixin' 'er and doin' what you said, another crossin'."

"Will, let's get a length of rope and a stone," Roger Beckwith said. "Let's find out just how deep this inlet is. And I know what makes you want another crossing, my transparent American friend: a woman."

We gauged the depth of the inlet at seventeen feet. The draft of the ship was less than that. Roger Beckwith stared at that opening for five minutes, after which he yelled out to the men to gather round. When they were all present, still shivering and confused about where they had found themselves, Beckwith described my idea to them, and set them to carrying stones to throw into the water at the narrowest part of that inlet. The Gentlemen of Leisure, considering the problem, came up with the idea of going to the trees and hauling back down a section of trunk from a dead tree the thickness of a man's thigh, and worked at undermining some of the larger boulders at the edge of the inlet. The first one that fell into the water was a round stone more than three feet in diameter, and it rolled off the outcropping and dropped into the water with a deep *ploosh*, creating a plume of water that rose fifteen feet into the air, bringing out a cheer from the men.

I worked with the men until my shoulder began to ache. I noticed also that Dick Burrows stopped from time to time to study the line of trees above us, and then went to speak with Roger Beckwith, who then called me over to them. "Pono," he said, "you go with Dick up into those woods and look around. Dick here's seeing things, I believe."

"I ain't seein' nothin' that isn't there," Dick Burrows said.

"Very well. This seems to me as remote a place as you can find, however," Roger Beckwith said.

"Don't mean there ain't people here, Roger," Dick Burrows said. "And takes just one person to see this ship, then you'll have every murderer in five thousand square miles comin' this way."

"Very well," Roger Beckwith said. "You and Pono go do your looking around then. And let us suppose that you encounter some source of materials that might help us. Before you, as we say, render him minus his brains, would you remember to negotiate to this effect? Take some coin with you and perhaps do the civilized thing and spend it?"

"If there's a chance to do dickerin', then I'll dicker."

"Ben says that he's got tools, he's got glue, but he needs nails, bolts, screws of any kind, hasps, any chunk of metal you can find. He can strip other parts of her but that only goes so far. He's going to have to make ribs for her, and there's plenty of cured wood here, but no way to fasten them. Can you keep that in mind?"

"We'll keep it in mind," Dick Burrows said.

We made our way up the rocks toward the first trees. From the pile in which the men had deposited the articles from the ship, Dick Burrows pulled out my musket and his, and two powder horns and the small satchels that held the balls and wads. He then studied the muskets, blowing under the frizzen and running the rods into the barrels with wads, and satisfied himself that they were dry enough to use. The air was heavy with moisture, and the fog still hung in the trees. Owen Bew had set up the chicken cage once again, and was walking around in the area clucking and holding out a handful of bread crumbs.

"We'll walk a bit," he said, "see what's out there."

"Yes," I said. Dry though my musket was, it still felt wet, like objects in my world during the wet season. The metal of the barrel and hammer seemed to sweat tiny beads of water, but the powder still shook inside the horn.

There was a strange silence in those trees, 'pines' Dick Burrows called them: tall with brittle branches down lower, and under our feet was a pleasantly soft bed of needles. The air had a pleasant smell. We moved along the right side of the ridge the pines were on for three or four hundred paces, and again smelled that carrion odor. Dick stopped, looked around, and then moved back toward the bluff overlooking the water. When we got there, the smell was strong, an updraft from the breaking waves, and we looked down the bluff over the boulders to a sandy patch in amongst black rocks. There, moving about in the wash of smaller waves that raced up the sand, lay a very large blob of whitish material, half the size of *The Tiburon* it appeared. It rolled up in the sand, and then settled flaccidly back, parts of it flopping over in the water.

"That's a whale carcass," Dick Burrows said. "So it ain't another China coast." He looked around, thinking. "That kind of thing attracts bear," he said. "Not now, but maybe a couple days ago before it went sour."

I had seen illustrations of bears in the encyclopedia, and was a bit hesitant about the idea of seeing one alive. But Dick Burrows seemed unconcerned about it. He jerked his head and I followed him back up the bluff. Apparently he was looking for some place where he could see at a distance, and it took us some time, perhaps an hour, to find that place. We worked our way through the semi-darkness of those pines up until we again encountered the black rocks, which interrupted the pines' growth in places. And then beyond those rocks we climbed up until the land opened up before us: first, huge mountains in the far distance capped with snow, above grasslands bisected halfway by a river, and on our side of the river, more waving grass sweeping up toward us in an increasing density of shrubs and smaller pine trees. To the far right, that river glinted under the flat light, and in the distance to the south, sunlight bathed low mountains. I thought it beautiful, both stark and rugged but also verdant and inviting. Perhaps it was the river, the promise of fresh water, and the greenness of the grasslands. Far to the south, the faint suggestion of a widening of the valley held, still, the silver thread of that river.

"Don't see a soul," Dick Burrows said, and just as he said that, we both heard a thump behind us, and turned. I had thought a person was there, but Dick remained unconcerned. Presently a beautiful, reddish brown creature on spindly legs pranced past us, its head thrown up so that what looked like dividing tan branches sprouted out of its head. It was a deer. It pranced past us, its short tail up and revealing white fur underneath.

"We ain't goin' hungry here," he said.

By the time we had returned to the bluffs overlooking the ruined ship lying on the rocks, the men had been carrying rocks for hours, but they were not yet visible under the water. They had, however, anticipated the problem of the incoming tide, and had lashed the hull of the ship with ropes and then played those ropes over the boulders to places where they could tie them off using dead wood from above braced in the boulders, assuming that if the tide were to move the hull, the ropes would prevent her from rolling back into the water and being destroyed altogether.

Up at the very edge of the pines, Owen Bew had established an area wherein he could light a fire, and attend to the salvaging of what foodstuffs the men had rescued. The majority of these stores were left inside the ship, once the men were convinced that *The Tiburon* could be saved. The fresh water was safe, as were some of the materials Owen used in his cooking: flour, dried and salted meats, salt, and so on. I was concerned also about the chickens, but because they were our chickens and perhaps as confused as we, I saw them scratching the earth on the perimeter of Owen's cooking area.

Thus did we wait for the high tide. What water was in the hull was left there for a ballast to steady the ship, although it was likely that it destroyed some of the booty Beckwith had stored there, things from China and Macau. It was difficult to determine how far we were from the sun's dropping into the ocean, because our visibility out into it remained at less than a quarter of a mile. And so did those waves rise, and blast in through the inlet, but with less force because of the interruption of those rocks under the surface. And as the light waned, we watched and listened as the waves, creating plumes of white mist that drifted off in the soft breeze, hit against the side of *The Tiburon* and rocked it slightly so that we could hear the grating of wood on stone. At length the men began to move back toward the pines to establish sleeping places for themselves, but Dick Burrows, Will Kelsey, Roger Beckwith, Kuaʻi and I stayed out above those rocks and watched, until, hours later in complete darkness, we satisfied ourselves that the ship was still there and would be by morning.

Kuaʻi chose to sleep near me. He asked me as he lay there under dirty clothes on those pine needles if we would ever return home, and if we would die here. I told him that I did not know, for the world was immense, and if we were unable to save the ship, we might remain here on this vast continent forever. This did not concern him in a way you might expect, that, alienated from his homeland, he might lose his spirit and therefore his life, but rather in that he wondered if he would be able to learn all that one must learn in order to exist in a place like this, in the land of mists and fog.

I awoke to a blue sky, with a line of bright clouds out over the water. I had slept longer than the rest of the men, probably because of fatigue associated with my illness, evidence of which I could no longer feel. "Aye boy," Owen Bew said, poking a stick into a fire, "you slept like the dead. They're throwing more stones into the water."

"Is she still on the rocks?" I asked.

"She is," he said. "I am beginning to believe it's possible to repair 'er."

I felt somewhat proud for having conceived of the idea. But the repair of a ship is a long and complicated matter. I rose from the pine needles and made my way to the edge of the bluff, from which I saw *The Tiburon* lying on the rocks and the men hauling stones to the water, and heard them being thrown in. With the sun out, the men appeared to be in better spirits than the previous day.

When Dick Burrows saw me he made his way up the bluff. When he got to me, breathing rather heavily from the climb, he looked out over the ocean. "There ain't no way we won't be seen, if not by injins, then another ship. I don't like this."

"What should we do?" I asked.

"I'm for buryin' the valuables, and settin' up some kind of protection for ourselves, or at least figurin' out who's around here so's we know if we should. You an' me, we go out again, all the way to that river, then down it. We stay out two, three days, find out what's out there, if there's anything we need to worry about. I talked to Roger about it, and he's for it. He says look for those screws an' nails and all."

"When shall we leave?" I asked.

"Today. We take blankets, a coupla tarp pieces, an' we'll take a little grub with us too," he said. "We can hunt out there. Rabbit, deer, whatnot."

Kau'i wanted to go with us, but I convinced him not to. Unfamiliar with this new world, I explained to him, he would have difficulty with the coldness of the nights, and with the walking on his bare feet. I had sandals with thick soles, and warmer clothes. He was unsure of being left back with those other men, and I told him that they would help him learn their language. This promise satisfied him.

Thus did Dick Burrows and myself set out. Each of us carried a pack with our needs, wrapped up in rolls tied at each end with rope so that we could sling the packs over our shoulders. We made our way to the bluff, and then walked south along the base of a long mountain range. The trees we walked along were immense, their trunks as big around as the houses from my land, and in those groves shafts of yellow light held suspensions of dust that blinked tiny, bright points of light. The silence of these forests seemed to me strange and haunting, as if no human had ever disturbed the damp ground beneath the trees. When I talked to Dick Burrows, I whispered.

But Dick Burrows remained cautious and thoughtful, wanting to know, mile by mile, where we were in terms of where we had been hours before, because as he told me, he wasn't itchin' to wander off without the means of gettin' back. We camped in a place near those trees, and he decided that we wouldn't light a fire. We would eat biscuits and dried meat, look around for a berry or two, as he put it, and set out the next morning.

So our journey went, into the following day. That valley to our east widened as we went, and then became so vast that the distance to the other side revealed the silhouette of a mountain range, with no visual definition, the land between a bright green. We traversed hills that dropped into dry ravines and then led up other hills. Late that second day, Dick Burrows began looking in one direction, ahead of us and to our east, and then he stopped. "Ten miles," he said. "Injins maybe."

I looked out over that vast plain. I could see nothing.

"They're ahorseback," he said. I continued looking, waiting for something in that vast plane of vision to move, and then saw, so far away that I was amazed that he had been able to make it out at all, a tiny line that moved toward the north over some rocky terrain, appearing as a minuscule filament creeping close against an irregular surface. "Tell you what," Dick Burrows said, "we'll wait here and see who these folks is."

So we waited. Sitting in the shade of one of the great trees, we watched that filament appear and then disappear according to the landscape. "They ain't goin' north," Dick Burrows said. "Some reason they're comin' our way." He thought. "Got it. They're comin' up to the shade, and maybe wantin' water in that crick down there."

"Should we wait and talk to them?" I asked.

"Nope," he said. "Something ain't right. Bet you we're way south a where we wannadabe. Roger wasn't too interested in messin' with his octant once the ship went on the rocks. But if we're where I think we are, were down in New Spain."

"King Philip's Land?"

"'Nother of his lands, I think. I don't like messin' with them Spanish soldiers," he said. "Way I understand it, they set up these forts and missions and then they haul in the injins and make them work and then convert them, like where we was on your first cross where the people were under the guns of them soldiers. Roger told me last time we were here, up north more where the Russians are, that the south along the coast was no place for the ship because of them Spanish."

We watched the line. In time I was able to see it not as a filament but as a series of brown dots moving, men on horses, for the shapes of these blotches showed something small atop something larger and round. Then Dick Burrows shaded his eyes into a squint, and said, "Trackers in front, that's what it is."

"Trackers," I said.

"That's why they turned. They're trackin' somebody. There's a couple injin trackers up front, going toward one of these ravines up here, maybe four, five miles to the south. We'll wait until they go into that draw and then set on over to see what's doing."

We waited, that line of men on horseback coming close enough that Dick Burrows cautioned me against moving or showing any shiny part of my musket. The men on horseback seemed to be wearing uniforms, longer brownish jackets with decoration on the front, and plain, flat-topped hats. They all had muskets. I counted sixteen of them, and Dick Burrows guessed that the trackers numbered three.

A few minutes after the last of the soldiers went into a ravine about a half a mile away, we made our way over the ridges toward the one they had entered.

After about twenty minutes of climbing and working our way around brush, and low shrubs, we came upon the lip of the ridge overlooking the ravine. The soldiers were there, in the shade, and nearby sat the injin trackers, one holding a rope that went out of sight under the base of the ridge. Then the tracker pulled on the rope, and two men wearing pantaloons and naked to the waist, stumbled toward them, one with an injured leg. They were tied together, side by side, the rope dividing just in front of them so that the men had sections of rope around their necks. They went down to their knees, and sat listlessly while the soldiers looked without much interest at them.

"Don't move a muscle," Dick Burrows whispered. "Them's what they were trackin', and now they got 'em."

The two men were dark-skinned, and had black hair. I assumed that they were the same race as the trackers. Injins, Dick Burrows called them. We waited on that ridge for perhaps two hours. The soldiers and trackers took food from bags hung over the horses' backs and ate, not offering any to their prisoners. Then the soldiers rose from the shade and prepared to mount their horses. The trackers rose also, and one of them jerked on the rope, at which the men stumbled after the horses who now moved down the ravine toward the great plain. But one of the prisoners, the one with the injured leg, fell down, and apparently protested that he could not walk. The soldiers discussed this for a few minutes. Then a tracker drew a knife from his waist, the blade glinting once at us, and cut the rope from the injured man's neck.

A soldier addressed the tracker, who looked to his side at him, and then in one quick motion drove the blade of the knife into the injured man's chest, rapidly pivoted it back and forth, and then withdrew it, after which the injured man fell limply to the ground. The tracker carefully wiped the blood off his knife on the man's pantaloons, and the soldiers, trackers, and remaining prisoner made their way out of the ravine in a strange, languid procession. I stared down at the dead man, and then turned to Dick Burrows. "Because he could not walk, it became expeditious for them to kill him."

"Call it what you want," he said. "But we wanta make sure they don't put a rope on us. We wait a bit, then follow them. They're takin' that fella somewheres. We'll find our screws and nails there, I spect."

We waited there until the procession had moved away a half a mile. By this time, two large dogs had appeared farther up the ravine in which the dead body lay. Coyotes, Dick Burrows called them. He told me that we didn't need to wait around to watch them feed on the corpse.

§

Mrs. Searle felt that the spreading of this affliction was moving too close to MacFarlane's house. She stopped at our meeting place one morning to inform him of this, but he had not yet arrived, nor had Pono. I had risen early, and having stepped off the cutter onto what was supposed to be a wharf, merely some jury-rigged boards and posts vanishing into filthy water, I stopped to watch a fight between some sailors, angry at each other apparently because of a debt, and the fisticuffs were quite interesting to behold, quick and vicious. Fights of this sort happened often, so other sailors, kanakas, shopkeepers, all stopped to watch without offering to intervene. The fight went on for five minutes, the men kicking at each other, punching, trying to get hand-holds on limbs so that they might bite, and it finally ended in mutual exhaustion, curses, and a parting, each going off spitting bloody saliva and touching facial wounds.

"Did you see the row down by the wharf just a bit ago?" I asked her.

"I saw it at a distance and decided to mind my business," she said, reaching up to hold her bonnet while a dusty wind swept down the lane. Apparently something else was on her mind. "Matthew," she said. "I have a request. I do not want to make anyone become the least bit excited about this, but I need to read more of Mr. MacFarlane's ledgers. Something odd has occurred to me, and I thought that perhaps it might help."

"I shall ask him," I said. "What has occurred to you?"

"I would rather not say," she said. "Please," she added, her expression becoming somewhat sad, "don't take this as a woman being arbitrarily mysterious. Would you do this for me without saying anything? Just tell him that I am interested in the story?"

"Of course," I said. "And today, are we to help you?"

"If you have time, after your session, might you come to the huts? I've got more bodies to dispose of." She appeared sad and thoughtful, as if consulting her mind over the question of how the inevitable might be countered.

"I am sorry," I said. "This is a terrible thing."

"It is. We can do nothing. We brought it, and we cannot stop it."

That statement, which she had made before, made me momentarily conceive of the world as immense and varied but at the same time shrinking because of all the great explorations. Cook, La Perousse, and others had connected its peoples much to the advance of Western science and geography, but at the same time much to the misery of those isolated peoples whose inability to resist diseases left them so vulnerable.

"Well," she said, turning her gaze toward the mountains, "here comes Mr. MacFarlane."

He walked briskly toward us, acknowledging us with a nod and a vague wave.

When he reached us, I saw that he carried all four of the ledgers. "Ethan," I said, "Mrs. Searle is ready to read more."

"Very well," he said. "You want the second ledger?"

"That would be kind of you," she said. "By the way, you've very fine penmanship." He had not yet handed it to her. She saw the worried expression on his face and said, "I promise you, I shall not lose it."

"I've been making a copy," he said. "I've got most of the first ledger done."

"Good idea," I said. "MacFarlane, you're quite enterprising."

"Would you rather I waited?" Mrs. Searle asked, "until after you've done a copy of this one?"

MacFarlane considered this, and then turned to see Pono making his way toward us. "No ma'am, I trust you," he said.

19.

*D*ick *Burrows and I followed* those soldiers' tracks throughout an entire day, walking along that magnificent valley and encountering more deer, rabbits, and large birds that floated in the bright blue sky. His attention to our location was very acute, and he tried memorizing various reference points in the terrain. He said that following these tracks was not difficult, but if rain fell behind us, we might lose our sense of where we were.

Our journey took us into land that appeared drier than the land to the north of us, and late one day, we made our way up one of those ridges to look out over that plain toward some body of water in the far distance, thirty or forty miles away, he said. It was either a large lake or a bay. The other feature of this landscape was a grouping of buildings some twenty miles inland from where we stood on the ridge, a village of some sort, he said. "Don't see smoke," he said. "Means it's mostly vacant, because you'd see smoke." He looked around, then kicked at the dirt under us with the toe of his boot. "We'll stay here tonight, go over there in the mornin'."

"We'll be out in the open," I said.

"We'll go 'fore dawn maybe," he said. "How you holdin' up?"

"My feet hurt," I said. "Aside from that, I am as you say, topping."

"As the Brits say," he said.

We sat and ate, drank water, and then arranged our pieces of sailcloth so that we could sleep. Later Dick Burrows shook me awake and told me we were moving on, and I sat up in a flat, silver moonlight, the sky lit with millions of stars. While we ate more, I saw the gradual lightening of the sky to the east, so that the mountain range on the other side of the immense valley faintly showed its profile.

We made our way down to the plain before dawn, and walked in the morning sun through windblown grasses and around muddy lowlands flanking small streams. At length we came upon a place where we could see the buildings, now no more than a mile away, and Dick Burrows studied it for some time. "Smoke," he said, finally. "Little bit, maybe one fire." He looked back at the mountains we had left, then to his left and right, and said, "Quiet, it is. Like there should be people around, with good growin' soil like this." He studied his musket, lifted the hammer and let it back down, and wiped his thumb over the little brass ball atop the muzzle. "Let's take a look."

The village was surrounded by a low wall with openings through which we could see small houses, but no people. We approached that wall, and then stood looking over it. "Goat," Dick Burrows whispered, waving flies away from his face. He nodded his head in the direction of a four-footed animal tethered to a pole. It had two horns and a round belly with a pink bag hanging between the back legs. From the encyclopedia I recalled seeing animals like this. I thought this briefly because I was alert and a bit frightened at how out in the open we were, but Dick Burrows seemed unconcerned. The village smelled of dung and rotting food, and it struck me as oddly decrepit considering the beauty of the surrounding countryside.

"Hold," he said. An old woman emerged from a small house pulling a man behind her by a rope. She carried a bucket in one hand, and jerked the rope so that the man would follow, in an awkward, loping gait, hands out before him but limply hanging down, and the rear of his trousers was soiled with fecal matter. She pulled him to the skeleton of a tree and tied the rope to one of the branch stumps, and went to the other side of the village carrying the bucket. Then the man, tethered to the tree, sat down and began rocking, bobbing his head with a furious energy, his hands out before him.

"An idiot," Dick Burrows said. "Don't figure this yet. They the only residents?"

I watched the man rock. He was thin but muscular, his neck very thick, and his bobbing continued, a small gathering of flies moving about his head.

"Wellp," Dick Burrows said, "I guess we'll just go introduce ourselves."

We went through one of the openings in the wall. Inside, we scanned the small buildings, and saw one slightly larger one with the front door open, and Dick Burrows led the way toward that door. He motioned me to move toward it from the left side so that our shadows would not show on the ground. When we got there, standing against the coarse stucco wall, he looked once again at the works of his musket, and then turned from the wall and looked inside. "Easy," he said. "Easy fella."

I looked inside. A man sat at a table with a flintlock pistol that he pointed at his own head. "Anglais?" he asked.

"That's right," Dick Burrows said. "Fella, you can put that down. We ain't gonna hurtcha." The man sat there, staring, the pistol to his head. He was large and somewhat fat, his clothes dirty, his beard tangled and skin mottled and creased, and the pistol shook as he held it to his head.

The man considered what he had heard, and then lowered the pistol and laid it on the table. "Ah," he said. "Yes. If you were one of the renegade natives of the area, I would have pulled my trigger rather than go ahead and endure their torture. But English, yes. I haven't spoken it in years, Spanish being the lingo here."

"Where's everybody?" Dick Burrows asked. The man was staring at me.

"If your friend here is not an Indian, then what is he?" he asked.

"I am kanaka maoli," I said.

"That's O-why-a," Dick Burrows said. "From way out in the ocean there. Where's everybody?"

"So how'd you git here? You walk?" the man asked.

"Naw," Dick Burrows said, "we're from a ship, tied off down south fifty miles or so. We're out lookin' for fittins, screws and bolts and the like. You got any you could sell us? I mean once you tell us where everybody went?"

"Ah, and my ship is down south fifty mile or so, too. But it's in a thousand pieces," the man said. "Fittings, yes."

"I got coin here, so we'd like to buy," Dick Burrows said.

"Meaning of course that your ship is to the north," the man said. "It couldn't be to the south. The Presidio's to the south. She damaged?"

"Presidio? What's that?"

"Like a town, but run by the friars and their soldiers," the man said. He shifted in his chair, pushed the pistol away and put his elbows on the table, his hands supporting his chin. He sucked at his teeth, and nodded. "Fittings," he said.

"Up a ways we seen soldiers catch a couple injins, and the trackers, one of 'em I mean, knifed one who couldn't walk, and they dragged the other off. What was that?"

"They're apostates," the man said. "The one they killed couldn't work."

"Apostates? What's that?"

"Ah," he said. "Well, I shall tell you then. You fellas like a drink?"

Dick Burrows looked at his musket. "Any soldiers around here?" he asked.

"Occasionally," he said. "But we are of no concern to them."

"So where's everybody?" Dick Burrows asked. The man turned in his chair and prepared to rise, then stopped, his hands on his knees.

"Why, dead of course," he said. He rose from the chair and went to the back of the room to a hanging blanket, which he pulled aside, and went behind. Then he came back out with an earthenware jug and three tin cups. He placed the cups on the table, and poured an amber liquid into each.

"Made out of cactus juice," he said. "It's not the best, but it'll do for occasions such as this. I mix in corn whiskey, so you'll get a hint of that."

"So why're they dead?" Dick Burrows asked.

"Don't know what it is, some fever or another, comes through here once a year, and the poor folks in these pueblos get it and die. There isn't anything big in this place but the graveyard, and that's where most of them are."

"So who's the old woman we saw?"

"Elisenda, and her son. Name's Juan," the man said. "She's a half breed Indian, and a few years ago there were as many as fifty people here along with a few soldiers. All the folks in the area've been Romanized, you see."

"Romanized," Dick Burrows said.

"Made into Romanists. The Spaniards from the south have come up and established their missions here, and brought up their army." He looked at the cups. "Will you have a drink?"

"Sure," Dick Burrows said. He picked up one of the cups and handed it to me, then another for himself. I sipped at the drink. It was vaguely sweet, but very strong, burning its way down. "Ooee," Dick Burrows said. "Packs a whallop that does."

The man laughed. "Helps a fellow to make it through the day, you see. So as I said, the Indians here aren't what you'd call hostile. In fact they were always quite peaceful. So the soldiers come up and say, 'Now it's time for you heathens to accept God and the church.' The Indians might say, 'I'd rather not,' but when the soldiers run them through with their pikes or shoot them or string them up or in their nastier moods chop off limbs, they say, 'Ah, yes, I'd be delighted.' Then the soldiers put them to work building their pueblos or herd them down to work at the bigger places like the Presidio on the bay."

"What bay is that?" Dick Burrows asked.

"Got various names, but it's a big one, and I'd put it at fifty miles from here."

I found myself becoming dizzy from the power of that drink. I recalled a question that Dick Burrows had asked. "So wha'—" My mouth was having difficulty forming the question. "What is that word, 'apos—"

"Apostate," the man said. "Those two Indians were probably apostates, or people who woke up one morning and decided that they weren't born to be Romanists, and so they decided to grab a few things, maybe stuff to barter like a silver candelabra or a little of the friars' money, and leave. The soldiers track them down and bring them back."

"So where you from?" Dick Burrows asked the man.

"I was a shopkeeper in Boston once," he said. "Married to a woman who made me life miserable, so I shipped out." He paused, took a sip of his drink.

Then he wiped his mouth on the dirty sleeve of his shirt. "Run aground down by that bay, so I made my way up here, thought to keep going north to join those trappers up there, but they've got everything locked up, those Russians, and then the Brits. I drifted a bit and ended up here. Probably a bit of a weakness in me, but I thought to help the Indians a bit, you know, teach them and so forth, but they'd just be getting the hang of, say, writing words on paper, and get sick and start coughing and then die." He drank again, wiped his mouth. "Got to the point that I thought my teaching was killing them somehow, you know, so I tried backing away, hiding in here, watching them, but they'd get sick and die anyway. Oh look, my little boy's learned to write his name. Oh look, my little boy is coughing." The man then opened a drawer in his table and drew out a ledger book, and set upon the desk a quill and a bottle of ink. Then he sighed. "May I ask you one question?" he said.

"Sure," Dick Burrows said.

"I'll not ask yer names, only this question. First, you," he said, indicating Dick Burrows. "Might you tell me how many men you have killed?"

Dick Burrows thought this over, began tapping his thumb on the fingers of one hand, thought again. "Don't know for sure," he said. "Twelve maybe."

The man dipped his quill in the ink bottle. Then he cleared his throat and wrote something there. "And you, sir, how many men have you killed?"

"I would estimate that the number is five," I said, "but I cannot verify with any degree of accuracy that this is correct."

The man stared at me for some time, and wrote in his ledger. "Ah," he said.

Dick Burrows looked at me, then at the man. "Well," he said. "That's some interestin' record keepin' there, that is."

"Yes, it is," the man said. "I have been for some time fascinated by this, and have studied in my mind the mathematical balances of things, you know, births and deaths, and the like. I remain fascinated by the idea that there are yet people here, there are yet people almost everywhere, despite my record keeping. But let us not dwell on such morbid subjects. Let us have another drink. Where you from?"

"Well . . ." Dick Burrows said.

I found myself nearly dizzy, and told them that I would wait outside, perhaps sit down in the shade a bit. So as the two men continued talking, I went outside. The man called Juan, tied to the tree, sat there rocking, his hands out and hanging limply. I moved past him to the stucco wall and sat down in a meager strip of shade, and leaned my musket against the wall. Fatigued as I was, I closed my eyes, but realized that I should remain alert should anyone come along. So Juan continued rocking, the vigorous tension in his body causing his thick neck muscles to flex. His face was misshapen, and some of his teeth were missing, and in his deep-set eyes there was an alert, ferocious look. I was aware of a stench emanating from him, of feces and urine and perspiration. Juan continued rocking, his head bobbing almost furiously, and then he paused, a sudden tension in his wrists and hands, and punched himself on the right side of his head, after which he turned and looked in my direction, but past me at some point on the wall near my right shoulder, his face suddenly composed, intelligent, wistful and contemplative, as if something both fascinating and perplexing had occurred to him. Then he continued his vigorous rocking, which went on for perhaps a minute, after which he paused suddenly, punched himself on the side of the head, and then stared again at the same spot on the wall near my shoulder, again with that expression of thoughtful wonder.

I slept then, for perhaps twenty minutes, for when I again was aware of my surroundings, the thin shadow I sat in had widened past my feet. Juan was rocking. He rocked until he paused, struck himself, and then stared at the wall by my shoulder. I began to wonder about the condition of his head. I watched him repeat this pattern perhaps fifteen more times, and perhaps the most fascinating thing about Juan was that there was no variation in the pattern of his rocking, pausing, punching himself in the head and then staring, always at the same spot on the wall near my shoulder. Perhaps he was aware of my presence, but I saw nothing on his face that indicated any acknowledgement of it.

The shadow had moved out another foot when the old woman walked through one of the openings in the wall carrying a bucket of water. She saw me and stopped, her mouth open, and then hastened to Juan, the water sloshing out of the bucket into the dirt she crossed, creating little puffs of dust. Then did the woman lower the bucket to the ground and speak to me rapidly in a language I did not understand, her voice a mixture of anger and pleading, and then she looked at Juan as if to inspect him for evidence of some violence committed against him, after which she sighed and gently caressed his face with the tenderness one would use in caressing a baby, but all of this was something Juan seemed unaware of. He continued rocking, paused, and then punched himself on the side of the head.

The woman placed her hand on his shoulder and then looked at me, briefly, with an expression of calm sorrow, and then whispered some order at Juan in a soft, pleading tone. Then, her eyes on me, she untied the rope from the tree and pulled Juan up, picked up the bucket and led him off through one of the openings in the wall, Juan loping awkwardly behind her, leaving me staring at the patch of dirt he had occupied, that dirt now of interest to a small cloud of black flies.

I sat there, staring at the patch of dirt. I began to moan softly. This, I thought, was one of the most fascinating things I had ever seen in this new, vast world Roger Beckwith was showing me. I believe it must have been the whiskey that put me in this dark mood, but I stared at those black flies for some time, thinking, this is what I have come to see, this is the fruit of my long journey. Great ships, magnificent buildings, astonishing achievements in science, all paled before this. This was the essence of what Roger Beckwith had been leading me toward. This was the final secret.

I see Juan, to this day, with the same awful, lucid clarity as the day I first beheld him. He is burned into my memory, and since that day I have often thought of Juan, and to this day cling to the hope that he is still alive, that his mother may still be alive, although I know it is perhaps unrealistic to hope the latter. In that recollection lies some mystery, I suppose, and I have contemplated the various possible truths it represents for me, and to this day remain undecided. Perhaps it is many truths.

At length Dick Burrows and the strange gentleman emerged from the low hut, the gentleman jovially explaining something to Dick, who nodded and fumbled in his trousers for something, the musket cradled in the crook of his elbow. He drew his hand out, and showed the man the contents, the coins he brought I assumed, and then did they walk past me toward another low building on the other side of the open area. I rose and picked up my musket and followed, a bit wobbly on my legs because of the liquor. The building they entered was apparently a smithy's shop, for dusted tools hung on walls, and an enormous anvil sat in the center next to an old firepit. While they discussed the objects in the decrepit structure, I stood outside and looked around at the little huts, none of which seemed occupied. All dead, the man had told us, and I wondered why it was that, like the recent developments in my world, wherein men became afflicted with illnesses I had never before heard of, here, too, people were dying from illnesses that were apparently recent in their world.

Then I heard the clanking of metal, the two men studying various bolts, lengths of iron, nails and the like, those they selected thrown into a pile in the dirt by the firepit. The man recommended several iron rods that could be hammered to any shape the ship's carpenter wished. As the pile grew, I found myself recalling my days as a rock-carrier, and went to the pile to lift some of these objects so as to appreciate their weight.

"Hundred pounds maybe," Dick Burrows said to me. "We're to be pack animals now, Pono."

"I have done it before," I said.

"You speak well," the strange man said. "You learned all this in what? A few years?"

"Yes," I said. "My shipmates taught me the language."

"Reads too," Dick Burrows said.

"That so?" the man said, holding a large door hinge. "This you can hammer."

"Yeah, we'll take that," Dick Burrows said.

So this conversation went, until we had our hundred pounds of bars, hinges, screws, bolts, rods, and the like. Dick Burrows discussed with the man the possibility that we might come back, a month or two maybe, he said, and the man said that godwilling he'd still be here, if some roving band of berserkers didn't gut him and boil his eyes. Besides, there needed to be one man present to keep records.

We loaded the metals in our bedrolls, draped them over our shoulders, and so we bade the strange fellow goodbye and made our way through the brush toward the bluish, nearby mountains. While we walked, Dick Burrows always alert to whatever might be near us, I considered the idea of the troubling absence of people here, and the pestilence that had removed them from the land. Why, I wondered, had I not succumbed to the same pestilence? It was true that I had experienced that poisoning of the blood as Owen called it, but I had survived that. These ruminations accompanied my walk behind Dick Burrows, my eyes either on the ground before me, or on those beautiful, dark mountains all around us.

Our journey back took us six days. It was in part due to the weight we carried, made more difficult as we negotiated hills and steep creekbeds, and in part because Dick Burrows wanted to remain alert to our surroundings, to the point that we would stop for hours at a time while he sat and gazed out over the lowlands to our east. We did see, far off, men on horseback, Indians, he said.

Another time he spent an hour scanning the terrain behind us because in the far distance he saw a wagon, or what he thought was a wagon. And another time he seemed convinced that we were being watched from a high tree line to our west, and so because of that we went around an entire low mountain to remain out of sight of the place he was sure those eyes were.

I trusted him, yet I wondered as we walked if he was not imagining those eyes, if he was overly cautious. I had forgotten where it was that we had emerged from that forest the first time to see the vast lands to the east, but he had apparently committed to memory certain visual aspects of this landscape. He stopped, causing me to stumble nearly into his back, I having become sleepy and somewhat dullwitted.

"Don't like it," he said.

I looked ahead, and saw nothing unusual. "Did you see someone?"

"Got a whiff of somethin'," he said. "Like new rot, not that whale. It's fresher."

"Perhaps it's a dead animal," I said.

"Nope." He pulled the bag off his back, looked around, and found a flat rock in the shade of a gnarled shrub. There he dropped the pack on the ground, the metal inside clinking dully, and leaned his musket against the rock. He sat down, staring in the direction we had been going. I pulled the bag of metal off my shoulders and sat down.

It was perhaps an hour later that, far away, someone rode out of the woods with some bright object bouncing on the rear haunches of his horse. The rider went down a ravine, vanished for five minutes or so, and then appeared far below us cantering along.

"Now that's bad," Dick Burrows said. "That's an injin, and that's likely one of Owen's pots on that horse."

"The men have been attacked."

"Yup, and all's we can hope for is that they got away from whoever this is."

The sudden dread I felt at this opened up a vast confusion in my mind: were we then stranded here, perhaps forever? The two of us could not sail a ship. If any harm were done to the men, would we walk as we had been walking for the past few days, but now for years? I had heard about the vast size of this land, and knew how far we were from my home.

Dick Burrows showed no sign of moving. He scanned the trees carefully, waiting. I began to wonder as another hour passed, how long we would watch.

"Waitin' for the shadow to cross those trees," he said after some time. I understood then, what he meant: we were waiting until the sun went over the trees enough to provide shade, not for our comfort but rather for our being more difficult to see. When the shafts of light began to appear on our side of the line of tall trees, those shafts hazed into a yellowish-white by dust, Dick Burrows nodded, and we donned our packs of metal and made our way up one of the ravines toward the trees.

"Pono," he said, when we reached the trees, "I know you seen plenty. But hereabouts like everywhere else there're likely all kinds of castoff men, and they ain't got much in the way of kindness. So you an' me, we need to be ready to see plenty more."

"Yes," I said.

We pulled our heavy packs off and laid them by a tree. We made our way through the trees, Dick Burrows stopping frequently to listen, and to peer ahead at the dark spaces under the trees. Again he claimed to smell something, and I realized that I did too, although I could not identify what it was.

As we moved, I began to recall the surroundings, to the extent that I knew our rough encampment was not more than a hundred yards before us. The closer we got to it, the more Dick Burrows approached with a hunter's stealth, his musket at the ready. I imitated his movements, staying low, and trying not to crack twigs under my feet. We approached the fringe of an opening, beyond which was Owen's fire and some of the materials from the ship. The place had been disturbed: pots lay around, there was a broken musket by the dead fire-pit, and some of the men's clothes were strewn about.

"There was a fight," Dick Burrows said, "and I think it went inland that way." He pointed to the trees away from the shoreline. He stepped lightly to the bank and looked down. "Ship's still there. Fact, they've been working on the hull a bit, I see."

"What should we do?" I asked.

"We'll make our way inland, follow some tracks," he said.

We were perhaps fifty yards inland when Dick Burrows stopped. "All right," he said. "There's a man hangin' from a tree up ahead. Been gutted, and it isn't pretty."

He led the way around another small clearing. I hesitated to do so, but did look to my left, and there, flies buzzing around, a man hung upside-down, legs bound at the ankles, his stiff arms at an angle below his head and shoulders dripping a sludge of half dried blood, his intestines, blackening and dully glinting hanging down over his face and upper body. The skin that I could see was white. "Who is it?" I asked.

"One of the Seager boys," Dick Burrows said. "Don't know which, but those trousers belong to one of them. Strung high so's bear and coyote don't feed on him."

We made our way past the hanging body and past tall trees, Dick Burrows studying the ground. I wondered why they would worry about bears and coyotes, and concluded that, like some of the habits in my world, the killers wanted the evidence of their deed visible. We walked another hundred yards, moving closer to where the tall trees would give way to the open valley. Dick Burrows was following tracks, and then he stopped.

Ahead of us were the majority of the ship's men, and they were placed around behind boulders and trees, their muskets up. Some were apparently resting back farther from the men who were crouched by these boulders. "All right," Dick Burrows said, "they're not all dead. Fact, that there looks like twelve, thirteen men." It was also apparent that whomever they watched from those rocks were farther down a wide ravine, and the land was such that our men had an excellent position. "It's a standoff is what it is," Dick Burrows said. "Let's go find out."

He whistled, at which some of the men turned. Roger Beckwith moved away from a rock and signaled to Dick Burrows to stay down. "Can't see 'em!" he called. Apparently the contours of their position put the men they faced at a lower elevation, so Dick Burrows and I went ahead down the ravine. When we reached Roger Beckwith, I noticed that Owen Bew and Will Kelsey were standing above Tom Crabbe, who sat on a stone leering up at them, his face held in a look of furious displeasure.

"Some fifteen or twenty of them out there," Roger Beckwith explained. "The Seager boys went up north along the coast and found a river and a cove, a couple of old trappers and some of the natives of the area who they said're eager to help." He turned, shook his head. "But then these blighters came upon them, killed Don, the older of the two, and they've got Jack Audrey, the younger Seager boy and your friend Koo-awai over there, Pono. Can't understand them, what language. Russian we think. One's negotiating with us, 'ave been all the day now, and he speaks some English."

"What do they want?" Dick Burrows asked.

"Why, everything, mate," Roger Beckwith said. "They're preparin' to loft a head at us I suppose, just to back up their little demonstration with Don Seager."

"So that's why Jack's got his hackles up?"

"'ave to put a rope on him, I'd say. He's been marchin' off down that ravine with his musket up, and we've got to go grab him and drag him back. Can't reason with him."

"Jack Audrey's got a talent for bein' a hostage, don't he?" Dick Burrows asked.

"Yes, he does."

Dick Burrows looked about him. "How long you think this'll go on?"

"Until the three poor devils are dead, I suppose."

"And why don't they attack?"

"I believe they're trying to do this without getting any holes in them," Roger Beckwith said. "As one would expect, they feel negotiating is more practical."

"You think they seen us come down that draw?" Dick Burrows asked.

"It is doubtful," Roger Beckwith said. "Why do you ask?"

"Pono and me, we'll take each of us three muskets, light ones, and we'll go back up, go south a mile, and get behind them. They know how many you are?"

"I assume they do," Roger Beckwith said. "This is like a pair of lines in a war, I suppose, and as we counted, so did they."

Dick Burrows looked at Tom Crabbe. "You think you can spare one man?"

"Yes, we can spare him. He isn't being very agreeable about this."

Then we heard a voice, that called something out. "Gen'lman, you shall have your mens back! I give you time of two hour! We grow tiresome!"

"I'll agree with that," Roger Beckwith said.

"Tell them you'll go get your booty and do a trade," Dick Burrows said. "'fore an hour's out, we'll be behind them."

"Will!" Roger Beckwith called. Will Kelsey left Tom Crabbe and Owen Bew and joined us. "Call to them that we'll get the booty."

"Aye, I suspect Dick 'ere's got a plan, does he?" Will Kelsey asked.

"Indeed, he has a plan."

"Will," Dick Burrows said, "when you call this out, get everyone up there so their heads can be seen. I need six more muskets. Me, Pono and Tom over there are gonna circle and come up their backs."

"They've got horses," Will Kelsey said. "There are probably others out there trying to circle to the rear of us."

"Terrain's too rough right above this ravine," Dick Burrows said. "Put a man up top in the trees to watch. If any come through the trees up there, you can pick them off."

"You assume too much about our marksmanship, Dick."

"They don't know nothin' about your marksmanship," he said. "We'll start it up from the other side, but what with nine muskets, we'll need you to come on down the ravine. Make sense to you?" Will Kelsey nodded skeptically. Dick Burrows then turned to me. "Pono, we need some shirts or rags or somethin' to wrap the muskets in so's they won't clack while we're doin' this."

I hastened to this task, collecting vests from Ben Fowles and Owen Bew and a shirt from Tong Guan. By the time I had these, Dick Burrows had collected muskets. He verified for himself that they were all properly loaded, and then went to Tom Crabbe. "We got to do some runnin'," he said, "and we've got to be quiet. Can you do that?"

"Aye," Tom Crabbe said, "I can. Let's go then."

Dick Burrows handed him two muskets wrapped in a vest.

"The rotters killed 'im, didn't they?" Tom Crabbe asked, his face held in that sour leer. "Gutted him they did, the rotters."

"We aim to find out now," Dick Burrows said. "Best chance is us keepin' our heads."

"No, they gutted 'im," Tom Crabbe said. "I'll not—" He did not continue.

We made our way back up the ravine. A light musket weighs perhaps eight pounds, so I found myself becoming somewhat breathless carrying one in one hand and two clutched in the other in the crook of my elbow, wrapped so they would make no noise. When we reached the trees, Dick Burrows turned south, and we ran, Dick in the lead and stopping from time to time to listen, and to look ahead. At length Tom Crabbe stopped, looking with an angered leer at Dick Burrows. "Where the bloody 'ell are we going, Dick?" he asked, gasping for breath. "South America?"

"They got men on horseback," Dick Burrows told him. "We gotta make a bigger circle. Elsewise they see us."

We ran. Finally Dick Burrows found a ravine to his liking, and we went down it. The distance back to the men was nearly a mile. I was tempted to agree with Tom Crabbe that Dick's caution was excessive. But once we were in the open, making our way north toward where the men were positioned, I understood why the circle was so wide: we rose from some bushes to move toward another cluster of bushes and saw a man on horseback not a hundred yards from us. The man was white, wore a long coat and a strange hat that had a tail on the back, and he was looking through the brass tube of a telescope at an angle back up the bluffs toward the trees. We waited until he slid the device closed and put it in a sack on his horse's flank and turned the horse back toward where the men were positioned. As the horse clattered over some rocks, we continued on, moving from one cluster of brush to another. Above us toward the ocean the trees loomed, and we were clearly in plain sight of anyone who might be up there.

Dick Burrows stopped us and turned. "Listen," he whispered, "they're over there fifty yards or so. Tom, when it comes time to shoot, aim careful. Don't get riled and don't get shaky, just bead in on the one of your choice and hold a second before you pull."

"Aye," Tom Crabbe said. He was exhausted, breathing heavily and waiting for his hands to steady. I was gasping too, my heart thudding in my chest.

Dick Burrows moved through the brush, remaining low, until he found a spot from which we could aim. He turned and beckoned to us to join him. There were perhaps fifteen of them, most wearing long coats, and two Indians, one of whom wore a strange plate on his chest that resembled a dulled silver turtle's shell. The horses were out of sight, but to the left, I thought, because there was a thick area of brush there. We could not see the three hostages.

"Tom, you take the man on the far left," Dick Burrows said. "Pono, see the fella in the middle? You put your bead on him. I'll do the one on the right."

"'ow about the second?" Tom Crabbe whispered.

"Your second is the second from the left. Pono's second is to the right of his first. My second is next in from the right." He looked around him, thinking. "After the first shot, if there ain't anyone to bead on, then you fellas turn out and wait to see who shows up by our sides. I'll keep aimin' straight at them. We gotta hope the boys'll come down to help."

"Well let's do this now," Tom Crabbe said, laying his two extra muskets on the ground.

"Wait a bit," Dick Burrows said. "They ain't doin' much right now."

"I shan't wait till they gut him, if they 'aven't already," Tom Crabbe said.

Dick Burrows looked at him and nodded. "All right," he said. "I'll shoot first, and you shoot when you hear the hammer snap. Then pick up the next musket and wait. Don't shoot until you're sure you got somethin' to shoot."

Because of my fatigue, I found that I was not, this time, a victim of the vagaries of my own nerves. In fact, that these men had done what they had done to Don Seager justified what we were doing, although in my long experience with such violence, I had never been able to summon up the fervor associated with the vengeful impulse. I waited while the others raised their muskets and carefully aimed, and aimed myself, the bead planted on the back of one of the men wearing their long coats, as instructed, the man in the middle. I waited.

At the click of Dick Burrows' musket I pulled, and saw after the musket bucked the man I shot hunched over and running to his left, and then all were running to their left, leaving two sitting down. I picked up the second musket, but saw no one, and turned to my side, at which I heard the screams of horses and the clatter of hooves on stones. Tom Crabbe ran straight at the position the men had occupied, and while men came down the ravine from the other side, horses came through the brush. Dick Burrows rose from the brush and made his way after Tom Crabbe, and I followed, but a horse came out of the brush and came straight at me, and I dove to the ground as it swept over, one hoof knocking the musket out of my hand. I rose and retrieved it and went on toward the others. Tom Crabbe had his musket by the muzzle and swung it at a horse that had erupted out of the brush at him, hitting it in the neck. The man on the horse drew it to the side and rode back into the brush, Tom Crabbe running after him with the musket over his head. Then one of the Indians, the one with the strange turtle-shell on his chest, rode partway up the ravine, stopping on the bluff. He turned and looked down at us, and then kicked his horse so that it ran down the bluff out of sight.

When I got to the position, I saw Tom Crabbe untying ropes from Jack Audrey. He was apparently unhurt, as were the younger Seager boy and Kua'i, who stared up at me, still trussed in his rope, his eyes wide with astonishment. Dick Burrows looked down at the two men who had been shot. Both appeared to be alive.

"This one ain't gonna die," Dick Burrows said. "Let's keep our eyes out. They ain't done."

The one who would not die was no more than a boy. His expression showed a kind of awestruck fatalism, as if waiting to be chastised for some trivial indiscretion. The other man lying on the ground stared at the dirt before his eyes, appearing fascinated by what he saw, but this expression, I thought, was an indication that he was dying.

The men from above arrived, Roger Beckwith at the lead.

"Who else's up there?" Dick Burrows asked.

"No one, Dick," he said. "We drove them off."

"They ain't done. Put four or five back up there."

Roger Beckwith turned and spoke to the others. Then he looked around at the men being released from their ropes, and at the dying man, and finally at the boy, sitting there waiting for his punishment, his eyes wide with curiosity.

"Owen," Roger Beckwith called out. "Come check this rascal."

Owen Bew went to the boy, got down on his knees, and looked at his chest, his legs, his head. The boy submitted to this with the same expression he had earlier. "'e's got blood in his hair, Roger, but not much in the way of a wound. He's been grazed."

Roger Beckwith went and lowered himself to one knee. "English?" he said.

"You majesty?" the boy said.

"Ah," Roger Beckwith said. "We've got something to go on here."

§

Our uninterrupted string of scheduled days of Pono's storytelling was compromised by a problem: MacFarlane's wife's little sister had taken ill with a fever and a cough. He came to the little thatched room one morning without his ledger book, and sat down at the table. "I don't know what to do," he said. "She's a frail child, and I can't—" He paused, looking at the watery, coin-sized spots of light moving on the wood. "I must do something, but I don't know what."

Pono thought a moment. "Matthew, do you have a suggestion?" he asked.

"I can ask at the ship," I said. "Perhaps there's something we haven't thought of."

"It won't work," MacFarlane said. "She's a child of this island. It won't work."

"Do you know a kahuna lapa'au?" Pono asked.

"The one I knew of near my place is dead," MacFarlane said.

"Old Manomano knew the medicines," Pono said. "For this I think he would have prescribed 'awa and a potion made of the bark of 'ōhi'a 'ai, and then collected ti and dipped it in spring water and then wrapped the patient in it."

"What is the bark for?" I asked. "I do not recall this being in your narrative."

"The cough," Pono said. "And as I said, the narrative leaves much out. He looked at MacFarlane, thinking. "Is your wife well?"

"Yes, she is. She's trying to keep the girl comfortable, and shows no signs of any illness. I don't know what—" He looked up at Pono, a fatigued, contemplative anguish on his face.

Pono pulled the chair he usually sat in to the table and sat down. He put his hands on the table, and stared at them. Then he looked at MacFarlane. "I can go up to Makiki and get these things," he said, "in a matter of hours, I think. Do you have ti at your house?"

"Yes, for wrapping meats that we cook in the pit," MacFarlane said.

"Do you have cold water?" Pono asked.

"Got a good cask," MacFarlane said. "Surrounded by stones it is, so it cools at night and stays cool during the day."

"I suggest you strip the spines from ti leaves and try to attach ends together so that they form a line," Pono said. "Enough to wrap around her perhaps twice. Make four of these lines, and dip two in the cool water and wrap her around her chest and her abdomen. After an hour or so, take the leaves off, and put the other leaves on, first dipping them in the water. Keep at this while I go up the mountain for some 'awa and bark from the tree I mentioned. I assume you have the means to boil water, so I'll bring the bark down and pound it at your place. When did she first show signs of this?"

"Early yesterday, I think," MacFarlane said. "But I'll go and do this."

"Very well," Pono said. "I'll be back in perhaps three hours."

I volunteered to go with Pono, but he told me that it wouldn't be necessary. It was as if he wished to keep secret where he would find these things, or keep secret something else, I was not sure.

After he left, I wondered again about Pono, about where he stayed, and why so far from the port. It was true that the port was a filthy place, the water befouled by human waste and garbage with clouds of flies hovering above it, effectively the essential character of the place, but one would have expected that he might choose to stay closer. It did make me wonder.

"Think you can help me with this?" MacFarlane asked.

"Of course," I said. It was not that he needed this help, but rather that he needed the company, I think.

We spent the late morning at his place, his wife sitting near the child staring sadly at her while MacFarlane carried out Pono's prescription, using the shiny ti leaves dipped in the water. The child was hot, wan and passive, and fell into fits of a deep, liquid coughing every forty-five seconds or so. I did not think she would survive, and indeed the child's sister seemed resigned to it. She sat there and stared at the child, moaning to herself, and there was one moment after we had been there two hours that I had to go outside and stand on that bleak, barren path looking toward the other hovels in the distance, and I had one of those moments of a sad recognition, in which one sees some truth that had been denied because of self-interest or perhaps a crass ignorance: this was all happening, and there were people at the port and in the town, such as it was, who ignored it. They rose each morning to their tasks, whether refitting ships or converting heathens or opening their shops so that they might make a wage, and not a mile from where they were doing this children such as the child inside the thatch house were lying coughing themselves to death, burning themselves away with fever.

What was their excuse? We can pity these poor devils only so much, and because there is little we can do, we must turn our backs upon them. Do your work for the living, and do not waste your time on those whose prospects are dim. And perhaps this affliction had visited those of the mission, which would make extending their help impractical. I sighed and turned to go back inside, and just before doing so, saw something white in the distance moving through the heat which seemed to boil up off the dirt, just a brief glimpse of someone moving from one of the huts to another. I reasoned that it was Rebecca Searle, and thought it interesting that I should see her just as I had conceived that awful thought.

Pono returned less than an hour after that. He had with him a stone jug of 'awa and strips of bark he had peeled from a tree, what he called 'ōhi'a ai.

MacFarlane's wife, Henrietta, immediately rose to greet him, and they talked in their language for a few moments before Pono went to look at the child.

"You've done a good job here," he whispered to MacFarlane, touching the wrappings on the small body. The girl, upon hearing Pono's voice, shifted her eyes to him, and then coughed. Pono turned and spoke to MacFarlane's wife in their language, and she went and got him a small cup, into which he poured the tan liquid, that looked to me like very muddy water. This he held to the girl's lips, and she drank the entire cup, stared at the middle distance for a moment, and then once again moaned.

It shall be sufficient here to summarize the rest, and I preface this summary with one observation: there are mysteries in life that we shall never be able to explain. Pono did sit the night in that house, as did I, refusing to abandon this apparently fruitless enterprise out of a sense of duty, or perhaps competition. When he felt it right to do so, he administered a tea made of this bark, and then had the child drink more of the 'awa. MacFarlane and his wife continued to change the ti wrappings. I recall watching MacFarlane and his wife and the tenderness with which they treated the child, and in particular MacFarlane's wife, her bearing and her beauty, something I had had to learn to appreciate in these people, for at first I had thought her, and them, unappealing physically.

Long into the night as I sat with them, I fell off into a fitful sleep, and then awakened to go outside to relieve myself. There, standing in the darkness and seeing on the eastern horizon the first emanations of a pink light, with bright stars above me, I thought how beautiful and how doomed this place was, how beautiful and doomed its people. This thought shamed me, for I had but months ago thought myself part of a great process engendered by explorers and men of science from my world, and now wondered seriously if all of our sweet intentions were turning to gall on the tongue. But in a remarkable counterbalance to these thoughts, I became aware that the whispered exchanges among the others carried in them the sound of a growing surprise, even a hope that Pono's efforts were after all not going to be in vain.

The child slept soundly, her fever abated somewhat, and by midday she coughed far less than originally. Henrietta provided food for us, in this case cooked sweet potato, dried fish and poi. By late in the day the child had begun to eat. I had of course seen illnesses like this before, and concluded that indeed she had passed the worst point of danger, for her chest seemed to have cleared, her fever seemed gone, and I believe that I was finally convinced when she asked her sister if she might be able to read one of her books.

We decided that it was safe for us to leave, Pono to go to his place, wherever that was, and I to the ship for some much needed sleep. There was one moment I shall never forget: we stood near the little doorway to his house, and MacFarlane shook both of our hands and then went to sit down at his little table, and there seemed to lose himself, for he put his face down in his hands and I think he wept, which caused his wife to move to his side and place her arm over his shoulder, and then to whisper to him softly. Pono nudged me with his elbow and whispered, "We shall let them rest. Indeed they both need it."

And the following day MacFarlane showed up in a chipper mood, and told us that the child was better even than she was the previous day, and had apparently beaten the affliction. He said also that he had seen Mrs. Searle on her way to the houses farther away, and she told him that the worst phase of this affliction had passed. One matter remained of concern to her, and she told him that she would address that with us after she finished her day's work. Our assistance, she told him, would not be necessary this day. A matter of concern with us? I thought. She was being mysterious again, but I had become used to it. So, once again, MacFarlane sat down at the little table and arranged his quills and bottle, and opened his ledger book.

20.

*R*o*ger Beckwith ascertained* that the boy, who called himself Tadeusz, was a Pole. I recalled a place called Poland from the Encyclopedia, somewhere in the center of that angular blotch depicted on the page. As we discussed what to do next, ten of us standing there while the others remained up in the trees and on either side of the ravine to watch for their return, we decided to bury the dead man, and to take the strange boy Tadeusz with us. Roger Beckwith said that first he would need to consult with Joseph Seager on this matter, for the boy was a part of the band who'd killed his brother.

We found a depression in the nearby terrain and pulled rocks and some soil out of it, and I and Dick Burrows carried the man to that depression, his head bobbing loosely just ahead of my shins, laid him in it, and covered him as best we could with dirt and rocks. "He ain't worth prayin' over," Dick Burrows said, "but Roger'll do it anyways, since we're all going this direction eventually."

Thus did Roger Beckwith recite a prayer over the man, in this case *The Lord's Prayer,* while those of us in attendance stood around the grave. The boy went to his knees, somewhat to the wonder of the men. When we were done, we gathered our muskets and made our way up the ravine to the trees. Joseph Seager was there, on watch, and saw the boy approaching with us. When we reached the place where he sat, upon a rock, his musket across his knees, Roger Beckwith paused. "Well, Joe," he said, "this is one of the bandits. What do you think we ought to do with him?"

Joe Seager looked at the boy. "He hasn't got the brains yet to be evil, Roger. I'll allow that I'm not in the mood to be chummy, but it goes no farther than that. I'm thinking now that I'd like to get my brother down and bury him. That ends it."

"Now's not the time to go over this," Roger Beckwith said, "but you told us about this place up the coast that has calm water and friendly people. D'ye think we can get *The Tiburon* up there somehow so that we can refit her?"

"The old trapper told me that if you can get her out in the water for a series of calm days, you can tow her up there."

"What about ruffians?" Will Kelsey asked.

"The gents up there, Indians included, have got a sort of garrison, a small one. They've got good protection, he said."

The reclaiming of Don Seager's body was achieved by Tong Guan's hoisting himself up the tree from which the man hung, working his way out a branch the way sailors work themselves along crosspoles, and then cutting the rope which suspended him so that Joe Seager and Will Kelsey could catch the body and lower it to the ground. The entrails flapped heavily, stirring a cloud of blue flies, and Joe Seager then quickly covered his brother with a piece of dunnage from the hold. Again Roger Beckwith led the prayer, and we buried him there near the camp area, Joe Seager placing a large rock at the grave and then spending half a day with a hammer and chisel knocking crude letters into the rock, so that a memorial might remain to his brother. The young Pole named Tadeusz did not want to watch this procedure, and sat down facing away until the man was lowered into his grave, at which he joined the prayer, his eyes wide with wonder and doubt as to his fortunes. But he made no attempt to run. Where, after all, would he run? After that, the boy took to following Tong Guan around, the two of them trading English phrases and gesturing to each other and speaking in their respective languages.

The problem with the ship was now to be addressed in earnest. Ben Fowles discussed with Roger Beckwith the problem of restoring the frame, particularly what he called the fifth, sixth and seventh futtocks, which had been broken in half by that protrusion of rock that Owen Bew and I had seen as if floating along the wall. The larger part of the metal we had secured would have to be used for the repair, but he calculated that what we had brought, the hundred pounds or so, might be enough to float the ship again, and the stripping of other metals off her might suffice to make her worthy enough to catch wind. If not, we'd have to warp her. This terminology he used confused me, and Will Kelsey explained: we might have to move the ship, part of the journey anyway, by moving over land with ropes attached to her while on the ocean the cutter acted as a counter-pull and towed the hull.

Day by day the men studied the ocean, gauging high and low tides, gauging the activity, trying to calculate whether or not a badly wounded hull under a little sail might be able to limp up the coast. If it ran into any kind of unexpected conditions, it would most likely be blasted to pieces against the rocks. And was there any way that she could be camouflaged so that the inevitable Spanish ship going by would not see her? The men argued this point for days while Ben Fowles labored over the problem, Dick

Burrows and I helping him shape a part of a tree trunk into a section of rib
for the ship's frame. My hands grew blisters from days of hacking carefully
with a small hand adze under Ben's watchful eye. He would interrupt me to
make measurements, to study pictures he had drawn with measurements and
angles and points at which holes would be drilled.

And in the background the argument went on: "Are ye daft, Roger? We're
looking at fifty mile!" followed by, "Mate, we're looking at residing the rest of
our bloody lives here if we don't." And Owen: "Lads, we're putting 'er back
together or nobody eats, ye hear? I'm not in the mood to feed the lot of you
for the next twenty years without a proper stove, so you mix that into your
considerations, and if you don't, I consider putting a stop to mixing anything
in these pots. That is, those I've got left."

To hide the ship, Tong Guan and Tadeusz collected pine branches and
went down to the hull, climbed it, and began decorating the parts of the ship
that were most visible at a distance, so that the bowsprit became a small grove,
the clew lines became anchors for collections of brush, and the mast poles
were transformed into tall pine trees. Roger Beckwith, Don Bentley, Will
Kelsey and myself went out on the cutter and rowed along the shore, perhaps
two hundred paces out, and looked at the boys' work. "Aye," Beckwith said,
"can ye believe it? Two boys, a Pole and a Chinee, and they've created a right
little grove there in the rocks."

"Think a Spaniard can tell it's a ship?" Will Kelsey asked.

"I'm looking at a little grove of trees," Beckwith said. "Tell me that's a
ship."

"It's a ship, Roger," Dick Burrows said. "If I had my rathers, I'd as soon
them Spaniards passed three mile out."

"They'll be wary of the swells, and pass three miles out," Beckwith said.

Ben Fowles built a 'kiln' up the bluff near the woods. The object was to
collect sap from the trees, to cut some down and dig up the roots of others, to
make a source for this sap, with which we would make oakum. He explained
to me how it was done, but the complicated process was confusing enough
that I satisfied myself with doing what he ordered. I formed a small force
made up of Tadeusz, Kua'i and myself to do this work, so that during those
times I was not helping Ben Fowles in the hold, I sat with the two of them
and showed them how to pick oakum, or the three of us collected roots and
pieces of tree trunk to put in the kiln. I asked Will Kelsey how much oakum
they thought they would need to seal the ship tight, and he said, "Oh, a ton
or so."

And so a considerable number of days, then weeks, passed. Once, while
we worked on futtocks and planks, we did see a ship pass, perhaps two miles

out. Because we knew they'd have telescopes, we hid while it did. But these weeks were tolerable, even pleasant, so much so that the chickens, settling into their routine of being staked outside during the day with strings attached to one leg while they scratched for insects, and settling down by night in their pen, began again to lay eggs, and their attitudes of eagerness during the day and ruffling irritation at being disturbed at night, made me feel oddly secure. Chickens are very astute, and can be alarmed at the slightest noise, at which a frightful display of panic manifests itself in a cacophonous squawking, which happened more than once when our camp was disturbed by first, a bear, which lumbered off when confronted by Owen Bew banging a pot with a wooden spoon, and then by a coyote that sneaked into the camp during the day to assess his chances at eating some chickens.

Dick Burrows and I went hunting, and on our first trip, he shot a deer. The first thing he did with the carcass was castrate it and remove glands from under its tail, because, he said, the taste of the meat would become somewhat sharp if he left these glands in place. The meat of this creature was quite good, and fed the men for days. Owen Bew dried some of it with salt, and lectured us more than once about eating certain berries he spent much of the day collecting, along with various plants he knew to be nutritious. I obeyed his commands where food was concerned, for I remembered the tale he had once told me about the boy named James Smith, whose affliction, he said, was caused by improper nutrition.

The men's study of the ocean resulted in a series of observations. Its tendency to be calm increased, particularly between tidal changes. This was summer, and the ocean remained calm providing no storms occurred. As fortune would have it, we had crashed her on those rocks at the beginning of the summer season and if all were to go as planned, we might be able to float her providing Ben Fowles had the hull secure in time, and providing that a period of higher tides might arrive while the sea remained in its calm phase. The damage could be temporarily secured so that she would float, but once we had her in a more appropriate location, the hull would have to be further repaired.

We were there at that camp for more than two months. Suffice to say that what I recall about this place was that it was pleasant, cool at night, fogged in during the mornings, but quiet and sweet smelling. I often walked in the great forest, feeling the strange, vast hush of that silence. But most of the time I helped Ben Fowles, sweating in the stinking heat of the hull and helping him to fit great pieces of lumber into place, hammering pegs into holes, holding boards together while he slathered glue in place and screwed clamps on the seams, and lying in one uncomfortable position or another running a saw blade into awkward places and raining the dust onto my moist forearms so that splintered beam ends might be cut off, and then notched so that other pieces of wood might be hammered into place and pegged, or fitted with odd pieces of rusty metal with bright drill holes he had put there. Ben Fowles was a peculiarly calm man when working with wood. He would lose himself in his work, so that two hours might pass while he made a piece of wood fit, muttering not to me but to the wood itself: "There, you bloody little rascal, you thought you'd fit and now you don't, and why? Because you're too fat right here, and now we've got to pull you out again and scrape more of your little belly off now, don't we? Don't concern yourself. It won't hurt at all, and you'll not have to undergo the shame of not fitting. Ah, I knew when I birthed you from that log that you'd be a rascal. Ah, Pono's laughing. Now don't you pay him any mind. I'll send him off to do his picking."

When it came time to attempt to float the hull, we began discussing the exact means by which to do so. It had been buttressed all this time by logs braced against boulders, by ropes holding it up that were attached up to tree trunks, and so on. The decoration put on by the two boys had to be replaced every few days because it turned brown, and this the boys took a particular pride in maintaining.

We chose a day when high tide would occur in the late morning. The men had made careful calculations, studied the buttresses and boulders and logs, and had decided that if we were to cut the ropes just so, the hull would slide on the logs perhaps ten feet and then be afloat in the little cove. Prior to this we would have to go into the water and try to move rocks so that the hull might slide over. I volunteered to begin this work, and knew that, under the water, even man-sized stones could be moved because they weighed less in that medium, and because many of them were round, I would be able to roll the larger ones. Some of the men seemed unconvinced that I could do this, and when I stepped into the water wearing only my malo, I experienced a doubt as to whether or not I could because the water was very cold.

In addition, the water was greenish and somewhat murky, because of plankton, Will Kelsey told me, so when I made my way over the slippery stones, and then immersed myself in the water, I worked by feeling with my hands, the cold water on my open eyes making all I saw indistinct and yellowish. Each rock I rolled away from the top of the little barrier bounced down over other rocks making sharp clacking sounds as they went. I worked thus for two hours, and had to use long pieces of wood to lever some of the rocks up so that they might roll off. The depth of the opening in the middle of this barrier got to twelve feet, and reasoning that we could aim the ship through the depression I had created, Beckwith told me to come out.

So it was that *The Tiburon* floated once again. I recall shivering on the bluff above the cove watching as the men positioned themselves, and began levering stones out from under the hull, after which they saw the hull begin to slide on the large logs placed under her keel. Then they cut the ropes all at the same time, and she slid down into the water, her mast pole and mizzen swinging over nearly into the water, and then waving back and forth like an inverted, decreasing pendulum. This was followed by cheers.

Once the ship was afloat, everyone became anxious to reload her with the muskets, food, booty and personal effects, and to work on the undamaged rigging so that she might catch wind. There was none this day, so we hitched the cutter to her stem, and eight men in the cutter pulled furiously for some time before she began to inch toward the low spot in the barrier. She swept over it without touching.

Beckwith reasoned that it would be wise for a number of us to arm ourselves and follow the ship from land, working our way over the bluffs as she was towed along, perhaps a half a mile out in the water. Joe Seager led Dick Burrows, Tom Crabbe, Jack Audrey and myself along the bluffs, and when we were a mile north of the cove, Dick Burrows reasoned that he should parallel us from a hundred yards or so and keep an eye out for Indians or Russians or whatever other type of fellow there might be out there. Then when the shift in the tide was due, the men in the cutter towed her farther out so that she would not be caught in the swells. So went the journey, and at night, while we rested on the bluffs, we could see the faint light of lanterns out on the water.

We arrived at the little harbor Joe Seager had described the next day, the ship behind us by perhaps two hours. A small river ran down from the bluffs and created a pond that then emptied into the ocean, and for the most part the area around this pond was muddy and rank, the camp on the south side on land elevated somewhat above this mud. From a bluff above, we watched as Indians moved about and plumes of smoke from cooking fires rose up and vanished over the ocean. "The old trappers live in the hut there," Joe Seager said. "They trap bear and sell the hides to the Russians from the north. They come down from a large bay up there with a strange name that I've forgotten. He said that there are Englishmen up there too from time to time, buying hides for China."

"These merchants or navy?" Dick Burrows asked.

"I think merchants," Joe Seager said. "This doesn't mean you'll not see a seventy-four, however. So I suspect Roger won't want to go north."

Seager went first to the camp to talk with the trappers. After a few minutes he emerged from the main hut and signaled to us to come down, which we did. Dick Burrows went with his musket at the ready. When we got down under the bluff, we were greeted by the Indians, who seemed cheerful and curious about us. Some of them looked at me particularly, I assumed wondering if I was one of their own in different clothes. They all wore short pants of leather and vests decorated with beads and pieces of bone, but their arms and legs were bare, their hair long and black and tied behind their heads. One man, thin and dark, older than the others, approached me, stopped quite close, and stared at my face, and then turned and spoke to others. Then he looked back at me and nodded, smiling. I felt a familiarity with them, for they did resemble the people of my world, although there was no similarity in language. But this little gathering of people could not have been particularly popular with merchants because the little bay was small, and just inland of it the air smelt foul, with flies buzzing over the mud. For men such as those who had attacked our group, this camp was no prize.

The two old trappers were Emil DeGroot, a man from Holland, and a Frenchman named Pierre Renay, who spoke excellent English. Both sat at a table made of split logs, the wood stained with grease, and they were rather disheveled, wearing filthy clothes and sporting beards stained with oil, their hands dirty, with grime-packed fingernails. The four of us stood inside the hut before this table, waving flies away from our faces, while the better English speaker Renay described to us the situation of this tiny port.

Behind us, at the opening, the Indians peeked in, whispering amongst themselves. This made Dick Burrows somewhat wary, so that rather than face the two men, he stood facing the doorway. Renay pointed out to us that we needn't fear the Indians whom they worked with. "These are amiable folks, and you see what fine people they are in their physical presence."

I turned to look at the doorway, and the dark silhouettes of the three heads blocking the light showed white teeth. I smiled back and put my hand up, and then turned back to the discussion. "Now the arrangement we can make," Renay went on, "shall be that we shall expect compensation for help we give you, and for quarters we provide."

"Aye," Tom Crabbe said. "We'd expect to pay. I'll talk to the captain of *The Tyburn* about it, but we'll compensate you well enough."

"Life here is not always this pleasant," Renay went on. "Our Indians are Wintu, and a few of what we call Nomo Lacke, and they have their enemies, the Yukans, who like marauding and killing, especially the Nomo Lacke."

"Ja, excellent folk, dees Wintu," DeGroot said. "Bad the Yukans."

Renay laughed, and then said something apparently in DeGroot's language, at which DeGroot looked at us. "My English very bad," he said. "My excuses."

Renay laughed again. "Excuses, yes," he said. "We can be of help in the repair of your ship. You fellas are likely well armed, so you needn't fear anything from us beyond what we'd ask for that help. Do we have an acceptable arrangement?"

"Aye, we do," Tom Crabbe said.

"What we do," Dick Burrows said, "is position the ship with the cannons—"

Crabbe elbowed him.

"Please, go on," Renay said. "I know what you were saying, and I do not reproach you. You position the ship so that cannons aim at our house here, do you not?"

"That's right," Dick Burrows said.

Renay stared at him a moment. "I do not reproach you for that," he said. "You must feel secure that you have some control, do you not? We shall prove our good intentions then."

"We sh'll prove ours in return," Tom Crabbe said.

Suffice to say that our arrangement benefited all concerned. Our stay there lasted far more than the few months we assumed we would need, for we learned upon the appearance of *The Tiburon* that in the process of being towed she had taken on water, which proved the damage to be more severe than we had earlier assumed. The supposed two or three months turned out to be nearly two years.

§

The humidity began to increase, and MacFarlane told me that because it was September, we were in the time of the light winds, and this period would last as much as two months. I had already become used to waking up in the middle of the night with beads of perspiration running down my temples and cheeks. But now, one could hold a bird feather up and drop it so that it floated straight to the ground. In addition, poking around in the ship discussing repairs with various men I'd hired to do the work had become irritating, and I wished to abandon concern for that and go someplace where it was cool. But there seemed no place that was comfortable, unless there came a surprise breeze from the mountains, and the relief from those breezes lasted only a short time.

We were waiting for Pono to appear, and while we did this, I asked MacFarlane what he did to ease the discomfort.

"Not much you can do," said he. "You try to get accustomed to it."

"I fear I won't be able to," I said.

MacFarlane looked at me. By now I had become familiar with the peculiar way he looked at me, with a sort of thoughtful assessment.

"Is something on your mind?" I asked.

"Y'know," he said, "Pono I understand, because he's been telling his story, but I have to admit that at first I wasn't too fond of you."

"Understandable," I said. "Our nations are always at odds."

"It doesn't have much to do with nations," he said. "It has to do with what a man like you shows, and at first, I thought you showed little in the way of amiability or kindness." I opened my mouth to react to this, but he held up his hand. "Forgive me," he said, "but I was a bit surprised at how you showed yourself with the sickness over there, with burying the bodies and with helping out with my little girl."

"I'll admit I'm surprised at how well the native remedy worked," I said.

"You're dodging the point quite well," he said. "I know, and that's all right. I notice also that you stay on the ship, and don't take to being entertained by some of the more well-heeled folks here. Why don't you?"

"I am not sure," I said. "I need to be on the ship to make sure of the repairs and the other business."

"That isn't quite enough," he said.

"And yes, I do feel somewhat out of place in their presence," I said. "I did meet some of them, even told them what we were doing here, but it fell on deaf ears."

"Well, I like what we're doing here," he said. "You pay well, and I suppose I've taken a liking to you."

"And I you, I'll admit," I said. "Struck me as strange that Americans could be just as chummy as Brits."

MacFarlane laughed, got up from the table and went out into the sunlight, shielded his eyes with his hand, and came back in. "Here he comes," he said.

Pono was about to enter the little anteroom, but stopped. He looked in the direction of the port, waved, and then came inside. "Mrs. Searle is coming," he said. "She has your ledger under her arm."

"She's been reading it," MacFarlane said.

Rebecca Searle came to the doorway. "May I come in?" she asked.

"Of course," Pono said. "How are you today?"

There was a short conversation then, about the condition of the people in the huts to the east, holding their own, she told us. Some were still taking ill, and she was doing what she could. Pono volunteered to help, which she accepted, but after we had finished our business here, she said. She had come about another matter.

"Please," I said, "sit here at the table."

She did so, arranged herself, and then stared with a perplexed expression at Pono. "I have some information that might be of interest to you," she said. "I have read, now, two of the ledgers, the narrative to the point of your living at the place where the rock-carriers worked." Whatever information she had seemed to pain her, for she stopped, and folded her hands on the table. "This past year there was, among other such journeys, a trip taken by some missionaries around the islands, including some from the mission here, Thurston and Bishop, and a man who'd come later, named William Ellis. They traveled around the islands carrying God's word to the people, and while I now have my doubts about the use of this, and about the eventual outcome considering what our presence here has meant so far. . ." She stared off at the thatched wall then, and shook her head sadly. "Pardon me," she said. "My feelings are another matter. These men encountered all sorts of people in their travels, and on the largest island, Hawai'i, they met a man who, as they said, 'needed no converting,' for the man was already a self-styled missionary, having learned about God and Jesus the previous year, and having taken our religion so firmly into his heart that, well, he became something of an embarrassment, I suppose. This is not uncommon, for some adopt the new religion with a peculiar fervor, especially after they abandoned their own traditional beliefs. But to continue, he had gone around lecturing to his people about God and Christ, but much to their amusement and sometimes their irritation, for he became involved in a number of fights as a result. After the visit by Ellis and Thurston and the rest, he made his way up here for a trip that lasted a month. He wanted to speak further with the mission people, but again, he made rather a show of himself at the port, proselytizing sailors who threw garbage at him, blaming his own people for their iniquitous behavior, and so on. He speaks decent English, but when it comes to his bombast, he misuses words in a rather embarrassing way."

"I haven't heard of this man," MacFarlane said. "I missed him, I suppose."

"Yes, perhaps," she said. "He was gone within a few days, walking around in remoter parts of this island lecturing his people, and if they were sick, he blamed their sickness on their failure to have taken God into their hearts." She looked once again at Pono. "The man is renowned somewhat for being a buffoon, I am afraid. Finally he left, to go back to his island to continue his work there, and as I understand it, he's continued his work, tending to find groups of people who have taken ill with one kind of sickness or another. He blames their sickness on their failure to take God into their hearts, even those who have never heard of our God. It is as if he does not accept this as an excuse. Now he has traveled to other islands, Maui and Moloka'i, advancing his cause, but alienating people as he goes." She raised her hands from the table and placed them on the sides of her face. "I hope I am not bringing up trouble with you, but I mentioned that I had seen you somewhere. That is not true, I recall now. It took me days to remember this, for it was a year ago, but the man I saw bears so strong a resemblance to you that I cannot remove the image from my mind."

"How old is this man?" Pono asked.

"I would say he is in his late forties, and stout, well proportioned as you are. And this last point makes me wonder all the more, now. He calls himself God's Hawk."

Pono's face underwent the look of such wonder and surprise that he seemed not to breathe. He thought, staring at the doorway. Then he whispered something, and MacFarlane stood up from the table.

"Pono?" he said. "That name?"

"'Iolana," Pono said. "The name 'Iolana means 'soaring hawk' in our language. This man—" He shook his head. "This man may be my son."

"Pono," Rebecca said, "the other thing I should mention is that as I understand it, he is likely to be here within a week. The people at the mission were having a somewhat joking discussion about this yesterday." There she looked at him with an expression of deep sympathy. "Oh my, I am so sorry for having told you this, in a way. I don't know if I've done the right thing."

"You have done the right thing," Pono said. "And I thank you for that."

Pono looked at the doorway. I saw the look in his eyes, as if he wanted at that moment to go to the harbor and ask when the next ship might leave for another island.

"What will you do?" MacFarlane asked.

Pono turned back to us, a look of confusion on his face. "I don't know," he said. "It is possible that this is a coincidence, but I think it is not. It has been so long." He looked out through the doorway. "So long," he said. "I buried my hope years ago."

"Is there any surer way of knowing when this man will arrive?" I asked Mrs. Searle. "A week or so, you said."

"That is as close as I can come to a firm date," she said. "Bigger ships come and go, as you know, but the smaller ones, the yachts or small sloops, might come any time. It may take no more than a few hours to get from Moloka'i to here."

"I shall wait here then," Pono said. "Perhaps remain during the day at the port, assuming that this ship will come into this port."

"That depends upon weather," MacFarlane said. "They might go to the windward side. The weather's after all very calm now."

"Pono," I said, "We should take a break from your storytelling, if you wish. I think this information must distract you considerably."

He looked at me, nodding. "Sir, how else might one wait?" he asked.

"I hope this information hasn't ruined this process," Mrs. Searle said. "Perhaps I should have waited."

"The bulk of this story has been told," Pono said. "Those earlier years required much in the way of explanation of the customs of my world, and I have always felt that one's earlier experiences rest in the mind with greater clarity than later ones."

I considered this, and nodded. "This is true, I think," I said.

"And I must accept the possibility that this remains some coincidence," he said.

Mrs. Searle rose from the table. "I must go," she said. "I'm sorry that I had to tell you of this, in a way."

"No," Pono said. "I appreciate what you've done."

21.

*T*hat *muddy area* and its immediate environs, part of a small plane of land under the bluffs, became our home for nearly two years, as I have said. The repair of a ship is a complicated business, interrupted frequently by heavy rain, or cold weather. We set up our billets in the woods partway up the bluff, all of us fascinated, in a way, by DeGroot's and Renay's preference for flies, for the odor of the mud, for the discomfort of having to slog your way around. We chose to imitate the method of living of the Wintu, who preferred conical huts made of poles and covered with heavy bark. They taught us how to build them. Ordinarily they kept to themselves, or were gone for weeks at a time, hunting or checking on their bear traps, which were enormous devices, the length of a musket, which were opened on the ground so that the two halves resembling the jaws of a great fish were spread all the way out, and secured with a lever that was attached to a round plate in the middle upon which the bear was to step, thus snapping the trap closed.

DeGroot and Renay did not go out on hunts with them. They remained in their hut, prepared to barter with any ship that came past. Our ship lay in shore, around the edge of a spit of land, in shallow water that caused it to rest in the muck at low tide. We were all instructed by Beckwith to be prepared to announce that we were traders having come around the Horn some years ago, from England. The logic of this bit of acting on our part was that it would take any ship years to discover that there was no such ship, perhaps to discover that the meddling with the dull gold letters was a change from *Tiburon* to *Tyburn*. The passing of years, Beckwith reasoned, made it such that whatever ropes were waiting for everyone on the ship were gathering dust, the reason for keeping them beginning to be lost upon those intent on justice. Yet should any be identified by officers of any ship, a rope would be produced, so everyone was to remain on guard.

The house I lived in, at least in our earlier months there, was large enough to include Kua'i, Dick Burrows, Ben Fowles and Joe Seager. Other houses had their groups: the Gentlemen of Leisure in one, Tong Guan and Tadeusz in a small one they built, and Roger Beckwith, Will Kelsey, and Owen Bew in one, much of that house with Owen's cooking implements and some of the more valuable things from the ship, like the octant, some powder, and so on.

Thus did we set to gathering cured hides of bear, deer, and smaller creatures such as the raccoon, beaver, and from time to time, when the Wintu went up the coast, the dark, glossy hides of seals they carried back.

During the earlier part of our sojoun there, while I was not helping Ben Fowles with the ship repairs or needed rest for my hands which were made sore by picking oakum, I wandered those woods in a melancholy contemplation, for the hushed silence of that vast forest was both comfortable and at the same time an appropriate setting for such thoughts. I carried my musket without ever using it. One day I came across a Wintu hut, somewhat set off from the rest, and saw two children playing in the shade at its base. They wore only loincloths, one a boy and one a girl as far as I could tell. I made a move to approach the little hut, and the children vanished into it. Then did a woman emerge holding a musket. She stood at the opening and stared at me flatly, as if waiting for me to move. I raised my hand and waved to her.

This gesture apparently reassured her, for she lowered the musket, and the children came back out of the hut. They stood there next to their mother, staring at me with their dark eyes. I went away. I asked Renay a day or so later about her, and he told me a story, first inviting me to try one of his alcoholic concoctions, which I did: she had one husband, who lived in that same dwelling with her for two years, at the end of which there was a raid by the Yukans, and the poor man was killed. She then had one child. Some time later another young buck took a liking to her and moved into her dwelling, and he lived with her two years, at the end of which was a raid by the Yukans, and lo, the man was killed. But she now had two children. At the moment he spoke, he said, she was awaiting another hapless buck to come along, to give his life to the Yukans and another child to her. No Indian in the area wanted to test out this seeming inevitability, regardless of the comeliness of the woman or the comfort of her dwelling.

Was I perhaps the very buck she waited for? I told him I did not know, I was merely curious. Meanwhile, the drink he had given me had made my head somewhat dull.

"Yes," he said, waving flies away from his face. "Soon we will be in the season of the good salmon. Think of that and not the woman."

"Has anyone thought of living with this woman for perhaps a year?"

"The Wintu are superstitious. And I should add that they are not unintelligent."

"And what is the season of the good salmon?"

"The fall. It is an oily fish, and its taste is to be preferred over the spring salmon."

"I see." I left his house, stumbling somewhat because of the drink.

So I resolved to avoid the woman with her two children taken in trade for the lives of her former husbands. But on my walks, especially when I meandered near her dwelling, I was aware of highpitched, soft laughter from the brush around me, and knew that her children were making a game of following me.

Each day as I walked in those woods, followed by these two little laughing shadows, I thought of the woman, thought of Pekau whom I had lost forever, my children whom I had lost forever. Was I to live the rest of my life in solitude, including denying myself any connection with women? While it was true that the young woman on Maui who had stolen my keakea, Po'iao, was not the recipient of that keakea by my choice, I still recalled her with pleasure, as I recalled the lost Pekau both with pleasure in far more magnified intensity and with a sense of a kind of tragic sorrow that had settled itself into my being like some permanent affliction.

I assisted in the repair of the ship any way that I could, so these sojourns into the woods were not daily, nor were some of them very long. There would be delays as glue dried, and as work continued carried out by Ben Fowles only. I would return to those walks to be joined by my little shadows. At length they began to show themselves, as if testing their own bravery, and I began a tentative kind of play with them, for example, carrying with me pebbles that I would loft at them as they hid in the bushes.

The ship's men knew of my interest in her, and so they began referring to me in the evenings as he with two years to live. "Ar, Pono, 'ave some of this salmon. You might just as well eat heartily whilst you're with us, and lad, we'll miss ye."

"I haven't yet talked to the woman," I said, poking a stick into the fire.

"Aye, but you will. And that's the beginning of the end for you."

"I do not believe this story makes my demise inevitable, gentlemen. You're men of science, are you not?"

"We're men of science until we encounter stories such as this one."

"This is but a story. A coincidence," I said.

"Aye, Will, would ye like to test the story out with that one?"

"I sh'll decline, mates. I've got plans for my future."

One day I made my way through that brush, followed by the children from their secret distance, and approached the conical hut. This act brought the two children out, and they ran and stood at the doorway, facing me. Then did the woman appear, this time without her musket. I remember staring at her trying to think of what to say. She reminded me of the women of my world. Her hair was black and tied in a braid that fell down her back, and she had dark eyes and full lips, her body strong and stout, her bearing carrying with it an undercurrent of mysterious sultriness.

I walked to within a few feet of her and introduced myself in English, and she understood the name Pono. She placed her hand on her chest and announced herself as Ol-tuh-epumsas, or Ol-then the sound of 't' and then 'epumsas'. The pronunciations in this language are difficult to describe. But in time I would find that the name meant 'spring moon,' or the month April. She invited me into her dwelling, where we sat and ate dried fish and berries, the two children somewhat grave and proper as we did so. The fish was 'xonos nur', or dried salmon. Because I spoke to her briefly in English and she to me in her language, I cannot say that much was communicated. She did, at one point, adopt a somewhat saucy expression, leaned over and slapped my knee, and said, "Kuresa," at which the children went into a flurry of laughing and talking, and left the hut. This word was simple enough that I was able to recall it when I got back to the camp, and repeated the word to the men, who of course did not know what it was. The next day, while we worked on the ship, I saw Renay and asked him what the word meant, and he laughed and said, "It means that she would like to bed with you."

"Was it then a request?"

"No," he said. "An observation. She was saying that you are a wita who is, shall we say, attractive to her. Wita is man. P-oqta is woman. Wita and P-oqta. Man and woman. You and she hayhay pura, which means that you like each other, or enjoy each other's company. She wants elwine p-ure suke, which means 'to stay together.'"

So it was that I adoped this small family, the process a series of visits during which I made attempts to communicate with her. She seemed more interested in learning English, so for some time, early in this arrangement, I taught her English words, which the children picked up quickly. They were Bolboloq, the eleven or so year-old girl, the name meaning 'butterfly' in their language, and the younger boy Tl-uk Witil, which means 'fast eagle'. They quickly accepted being addressed in short form: Bo, and Tl-uk. I thought it appropriate that I learn to converse with them in their language, but the three of them would have none of it. It was the same in my world: visitors brought a language with them, and the residents wanted that language, rather than the reverse.

And as she had said, I was 'kuresa' for her. One day as the children drifted off to play by a nearby stream, she communicated her desires to me very directly, by removing her leather garb and then pulling at mine. I recall particularly how the sunlight coming through fissures and little holes in the bark shell of the hut danced on her flesh. This consummation was carried out with laughter and whispering on her part, and then by sounds I was much afraid the children would hear. Suffice to say that she was not difficult to please, and quite unabashed about the act.

The work on the ship continued into the late summer, and during this time, Sas, as I had begun to call her, showed me long, barbed spears and went through a combination of mime and various English words I had taught her. The salmon were apparently coming in from the ocean and making their way up various streams to spawn, in fact, had been since the early summer, but now were coming in greater numbers. Tl-uk also went into a dramatic pantomime of an animal, producing growls and waving his arms around, and then laughing. This was a warning that we needed to be wary of bears.

The fishing itself was not a complicated matter. With our spears, we waited on the banks of a stream for them to come up from the ocean. The stream was small, and I understood that this same migration was taking place in greater numbers elsewhere, so that one could spear, or trap, hundreds if not thousands of these large fish. For us, it was a matter of waiting, the children acting as sentinels upstream should anyone we did not know approach us. Sas speared the first one, a dull silver fish two feet long, and quite fat, with a strange snout, upper and lower sets of teeth appearing almost canine set in the rather thin jaws. She flipped the fish out into the dead leaves and then, with a stone, pounded its head until it was still.

We did this a number of days, Sas dealing with the fish in and around the hut, drying it in the sun, putting ocean salt on it that she and the children had scraped from stones and depressions in rocks at the water's edge, sometimes cooking and drying it so that it became hard and dark, but tasted quite palatable to me. We were in preparation for the coming of winter, and there was a good deal of tramping through the brush and woods looking for certain kinds of berries, setting traps for rabbits, and so on.

This new domestic arrangement did not take me away from my duties concerning *The Tiburon*, for each day I went down the bluff to the stinking bottomland around that small bay, and made my way to the ship with other men carrying various pieces of metal to set in place, measure, and to take back to pound with hammers on boulders, to fashion so that they might be used as futtock braces, or as splices for broken boards. It was frustrating work for the men, some of whom became irritated and petulant with the process: "Aye, the damned thing can sail right this moment, Will, and I'll go berserk if we do this another day," followed by, "Then you'll go berserk, Don, because we're still doing this," and Roger: "Gents, I'd appreciate it if you'd belay imbibing of that filthy piss Renay makes until sundown," followed by, "It's the only way to make it through the day, Roger," at which Roger looked over his shoulder and said, "Well then, I think I'll go 'ave a bit right now, then," at which Don Bentley said, "If you're 'aving some now, then I am too, Roger, and you can't prevent me from doing that because right now you're not captain of much I can see," at which Dick Burrows said, "If you're not hammerin' that metal right now, Don, give her to me," at which Don Bentley said, "I am hammering this now, Dick," at which Roger said, "I don't hear the sound of hammering. Tell me, Dick, do you hear the sound of hammering?" at which Dick Burrows listened carefully and said, "Can't say as I do."

These conversations sometimes went on for minutes while the men tried to control their tempers. Ben Fowles would emerge from the hold pale with sawdust glued to his skin by sweat, and look at us, make a sound—hmmph—and vanish down into the hold. When one or other of the men asked him why we weren't floating her right then, he went into a fusillade of invectives: "Are ye daft? You sail her now and you drown, you idiot. I can take you down and explain to you what the problem is, but the real problem is that you won't listen, now isn't it?" Dick Burrows and I went out after more metal, but not as far as we had gone that first time. Renay told us of ruined camps to the south where we might find pieces we could fashion into parts for the repair. He himself had various pieces he donated to the enterprise. I believe he appreciated Roger Beckwith's generosity in compensating him for his help, for he offered the aforementioned filthy piss to us every day. Disciplined as the men were, I believe all of them dreaming of the day we might again sail, they did not misuse that privilege. This was perhaps due as much to the quality of the offering as to their scruples.

As winter drew near, each day began and ended in rain. At first it was welcomed, for we were able to store up large quantities of clean water, and the very freshness of it felt pleasant. But as the weeks passed, it became clear to the men that it would not abate, and within a month most of them seemed pulled into themselves in a kind of melancholy funk. One or another would emerge from a hut, look up with a sigh or make a growling sound, and return to the hut. So it went on, week after week, and then month after month. The men somewhat adjusted to this, especially when the weather turned colder, for keeping warm required work of sorts, and the business of keeping fires going, of maintaining and tending huts, kept them busy.

Ben Fowles told us that he would not fit new pieces, nor would he glue or cut wood while it was swollen with moisture. The business of repairing the ship had to wait until fairer weather, because he was not sailing on a ship whose innards would shrink and begin to rattle the first day the air dried. "H'm, I think about that excuse and I wonder," Will Kelsey said, and Ben Fowles said, "It's not an excuse, Will, it's carpentry."

"Wood is wood, is it not?"

"I sh'll leave the repair to you then, Will."

"You will not," Roger Beckwith said.

"Then tell him not to insult wood that way, or insult me."

"Will, p'raps you shouldn't insult Ben or his wood."

"I'll not insult the wood then. Ben on the other hand, well, I just can't give it up."

"Ar, now there's a compromise."

At length the frigid dampness did also dampen the tempers of the men, so that we passed our days as if waiting, each lost in his own contemplative solitude, the gentlemen of leisure playing games day after day, Roger Beckwith reading, others finding activities to help pass the time. The winter passed in this manner, the rain a reality of nature the men were able finally to accommodate into their lives. At Sas's hut, I spent most of that time teaching the English language to my three pupils, who were inexhaustible in their interest. By late winter, when we had begun to see more of the sun during the days, our communications had become quite sophisticated.

The long period of drying out, in the spring, carried with it rumors of the likelihood of raids by the Indians called the Yukans. Renay and DeGroot were the bearers of the rumor. They claimed that it was simply a means of welcoming the spring for them, this marauding, and our Indians, as they referred to them, would for some time be difficult to see, because they would take to hiding, and being extremely watchful. Sas told me that the two white men were speaking the truth, that the Yukans tended to do this, and it was more "the chance" that they would happen upon this camp and do their marauding. She tended to put the word "the" before other words in a not altogether grammatically proper manner: "The you and the I sh'll eat now."

My concern at this time was that our hut was up the bluff, and in plain sight. What would that mean? If I were to have to remain watchful, what of the times I was down the bluff working on the ship? Sas showed me a tree they could climb if they needed, a huge fir tree, with a rope she had tied to one of the lower branches, and far in the upper reaches of the tree, she had built a small enclosure, not visible from the ground. I climbed it once, made my way up those branches to within perhaps twenty feet of her 'house' as she called it. This did not relieve me, however, for what would she do during a surprise raid? She responded to this unease of mine by telling me that most likely the Yukans would ignore us this year, as they had in past years. "Not as the many," she said. "Old time, the many, but now the many die."

And so did that spring pass, into the beginning of the salmon fishing season, and the work on *The Tiburon* resumed in that drier air. This gave considerable encouragement to the men, for it became clear that the ship would sail, perhaps before the bad weather and rain. The beauty of that high forest, the coast, and the open land over the bluffs from the ocean, was such that one could pass the time simply walking around and looking at various scenes. I did this with the children on occasion, the two of them darting in and out of ravines and running across open spaces. They were healthy children, good-natured and intelligent.

On one of these walks I took, alone this time, having finished helping Ben Fowles fit boards across elaborate repairs on the hull, I was standing upon a bluff scanning a long view for animals, deer or bear, and caught movement far off in the brush. I turned and waited, watching the spot where I had seen this movement, and then saw more, distant, watery shapes moving in the brush, and what appeared to be wisps of smoke trailing behind some of them. It was a hot day, so the air just above the land seemed to boil and undulate with the heat, and I thought I must be mistaken. When I concentrated and this clarified in my vision, I saw that they were men, dark men moving through the brush toward the encampment.

I ran. The distance to the encampment was perhaps two thirds of a mile, and my intent was to get there before these men did. I had my musket, slippery from perspiration. But by the time I had gone halfway, I began to hear musket reports, and shortly after that, plumes of smoke rising above the trees. I ran toward Sas's hut, and when I got to the clearing it occupied, I saw that it was lying over, a pile of poles and bark, one end of the pile burning. I ran then toward the tree where they said they would hide, and the rope that she had hung from a branch was there. They were not in the tree.

Now the musket fire was down the bluff toward the ship, and I ran into the woods toward the sounds, hoping that Sas and the children had made their way to the safety of the other huts and the ship's men, but those huts had also been knocked over. The musket fire was down the bluff from me, but I could not see the Yukans, if those were the attackers. Then I did. They were moving in the brush, firing at the house on the flats, and the return fire came from the house.

I understood at that moment why DeGroot and Renay preferred the stinking, muddy setting for their house, for the Indians, were they to attack, would have to slog through it. At length the firing abated. I did not raise my musket, nor did anyone firing on the house see me, apparently, for they vanished into the brush below me, climbing the bluff somewhat to the north of the house.

After some time, I saw men emerge from the house, others make their way down the ropes from the deck of *The Tiburon*. It appeared that the attack had not been successful. I went down the bluff carefully, making sure that the men saw and identified me, and that there were none of the marauders left.

As the men spread out, walking along the edge of the mud, I looked for Sas and the children. I could not see them, so went to Will Kelsey, who was closest to me. "Have you seen Sas and the children?" I asked.

"I 'aven't, Pono. I think they're hiding."

One of the Wintus saw me and the look on his face suggested otherwise. I went to him, and asked if he had seen Sas, but he shook his head, and indicated that I should follow him to Degroot and Renay's house, which I did. Inside the house were the two owners, and four Wintu positioned at the windows and looking up the bluffs. The Wintu with me spoke to Renay, who nodded, listened, nodded again. Then, as others came into the house, he turned to me.

"He thinks they've been taken away by the Yukans," he said. "He thinks that she and the children are prizes for them because of the sickness among their own."

"Where would they go?" I asked. "In what direction?"

He spoke to the Wintu, who answered. "They will go north, and inland."

"Then I shall try to get them back," I said. "Ask him what they will do with Sas."

He spoke. The Wintu listened, spoke. "He does not know. He believes that it is possible that because she is a strong woman, they may take her as one of their own. The children are strong, and the Yukans will take them as their own."

Roger Beckwith and Dick Burrows came inside, also listening to this exchange.

"I shall try to get them back," I said.

"Pono," Roger Beckwith said, "they'd be far away by the time you found them, and what would you do? A one-man attack?"

Dick Burrows looked away, then at Beckwith, then at me. "Pono an' me, we'll go look for them."

"And 'ow long will ye look then?" Roger Beckwith asked.

"We'll track a little, and see," Dick Burrows said.

"I appreciate this," I said.

Beckwith stared at us. "A two-man attack then," he said. "What makes you think you can get them back?"

"We'll figure somethin'," Dick Burrows said.

"Very well," Beckwith said. "But when the ship is ready, she sails. I don't know how close Ben is with the work, but when she's ready, she sails."

Thus did Dick Burrows and myself pull together dried fish, powder and balls, and other things we might need, including rolled up sleeping mats, and made our way inland. Burrows was easily able to find the markings left by the Yukans out at the edge of the camp, and we made our way during daylight through the woods, and out into openings where we could see at some distance. When we came to these areas where we could see, we realized that much of what we saw was more forest, so the only way we might actually see any movment would be in riverbeds or in those rare areas where bare rock prevented the growth of any more than brush.

But the sign they left, he said, was clear enough that we would not lose them. He also pointed out that abducted families, if they were to be blended into the tribe, would not have to be put in irons, because if they were to run, there was nowhere to run to. "This is how I figure we'll take them back, if we get the chance," he said.

In the evenings we stopped, and found places to lay out our sleeping mats away from places that might harbor snakes, which I had seen by this time, particularly the rattlesnake, which would lie coiled with its tail up and vibrating rapidly, creating that strange sound. Lying staring up at the dome of stars, a sight that reminded me of my world and my youth, I wondered how many families I would have to lose in my lifetime, if it were somehow destined that I experience this.

I wondered also if Dick Burrows felt the same way, for he had lost one too, under circumstances that were perhaps worse than mine, for I did not know what the circumstances of my losses were. I could only speculate. In both cases the families had simply vanished, creating in my mind a situation wherein a multitude of different visions assailed my nighttime efforts to sleep: of them being slaughtered by warriors, of them drowning while making their escape to another island, of them being abducted and put on the sacrificial stone, or otherwise abused by those in power.

We followed the tracks for days. I had assumed that a group of marauders now burdened by their new charges would move slowly, but this was not the case. Dick Burrows began also to suspect that the information provided by their signs had meant a change, that footprints and overturned stones, broken twigs and the like, suggested a smaller group than the one we had been following. At one point he stopped, kicked at a stone on the ground, and said, "I ain't gettin' this now," he said. "This looks like no more'n fifteen, while before it was twice that." He looked around. "Means they split up, and Pono, I don't know if we're followin' the group with your Sas or not anymore."

"We shall see," I said.

We climbed higher hills, from which the long view became more open. In the far distance lay the beautiful, peaceful and green landscape, one view upwards of a hundred or more miles, Dick told me. We looked out over this view, and saw no evidence of human presence. I wondered then about this vast landmass, if one could walk for a year without seeing another person. I asked him about this, and he said, "They're around. They're in low lyin' areas, in places you'd expect them to find safety and shelter."

The next day, upon making our way up to another bluff, we saw perhaps ten or fifteen miles away plumes of smoke, apparently cooking fires. "That could be them," Dick said. "We'll make our way there and see."

The ten or fifteen miles took four or five hours to traverse, and the closer we got to the source of that smoke, the more Dick Burrows became skeptical about it being a camp. It was not a camp. It was the remains of one, smoldering huts, bits of fabric flapping off the edges of ruined pole-houses, and in the middle, two coyotes feeding upon the corpse of a man. We stood there and studied this scene for some time. "There isn't anything there for us," Dick said. "That's probably what the fellas in the mud-house call a Wintu village, or that other kinda Injin, Nomo Lacke. Looks like the Yukans were here, too, I guess, if they were Yukans in the first place."

"The Wintu believe it is the Yukan."

"Well, whatever they were, they put this camp to waste, I'd say."

We ventured forth toward the ruined village. Oddly, there were few corpses, and all men, no women or children. The aforementioned coyotes saw us and loped off into the brush at the fringe of the village site, and waited while we looked around. We counted but six dead men. All had been killed by either spears or clubs, not unlike the battlefield dead from my world. By the look of them, the evidence of their having been fed upon by coyotes and perhaps other creatures, and the presence of so many flies, it was apparent that this raid had taken place many hours before, and that the the huts had been smoldering a long time, perhaps since the previous day.

The business of finding the trail of the marauders became more difficult then, because much of the surrounding area was rock. Dick Burrows used various strategies for finding the trail, particularly the trick of a spiral away from the ruined camp, which he worked at for half a day, circling it in a widening spiral looking for that trail, but he confessed that he was unable to locate it. On one circling he came upon a stream, which then divided at another part of a circle. He crossed the stream at both locations and studied the ground. I did what I could, studied the ground, but without the skill and experience in this talent he had, I was of little use.

Suffice to say that we were forced to abandon the search. Dick Burrows did not want to, but he explained, tipping his head toward a vast scene of mountains, forests, and intermittent patches of brushland, that they could be anywhere out there, and because we had lost their trail, we had nothing to go on. I agreed that we should go back. Roger Beckwith had said that when the ship was ready to sail, it would sail, and I reasoned that even if this family of mine had not disappeared, I would very likely have gone with my shipmates anyway, for they were a family of seven years.

And indeed, upon our return, we saw much activity around the ship, and saw that our encampment was nearly abandoned but for Tong Guan and Tadeusz wandering around kicking in the leaves, apparently looking for small items people had dropped. Men were up working in the rigging, and I saw, from a distance, the glint of pots being handed down into the hold. It was someone passing them down to Owen Bew, which meant that our next meal would be out at sea.

As *The Tiburon* leaned and cut through that water leaving the great continent behind us, I was aware of how much time had passed since I had been rescued by these men from the war axe. The year 1794 was approaching, and one signal of this passage of time was the death of two of our chickens, from old age, Owen Bew told me. They had become "broody and petulant, declining food offered them and remaining ruffled inside their feathers, incommunicative and sour." And as he told me this, on a fair day while the ship carved its way southwest, I was aware of how Owen himself had aged in the years I had known him, and indeed how some of the other, older sailors had: Will Kelsey, whose hair had gone gray, Ben Fowles, whose long labors over the repair of the ship had caused him to thin out considerably, so that his body was lean and bony.

I was given to understand, too, that we were beating our way south in order to leave a winter in the northern hemisphere, to find summer in the southern, for the months that it would require for us to get to the China seas. The hold was laden with pelts, seal procured through DeGroot and Renay, bear, the hides of deer, and so on.

As for returning to my world, it appeared that if we were to do that, it would be after we bartered away our shipload in Macau or some other friendly port. So to pass the time when I was not engaged in the ship's work, I showed Kua'i the various intricacies of the encyclopedia, and worked at teaching him to read.

The conviction amongst the men was that, the century moving toward its end, the great ocean was now crowded with ships of many different nations, and we had become a vulnerable anomaly, with fewer and fewer places to hide. Sailing folk, Will Kelsey told me, have long memories, and it didn't matter that Roger Beckwith's depredations had occurred many years earlier. The rope still sat there having gathered dust all these years, but in the minds of the men of the sea, the supposed crimes were as fresh as yesterday.

Then another, more threatening development began to occupy the men's minds. One day while I was below helping the gentlemen of leisure work on the cannon mounts, which had loosened once we were out on the water, Ben Fowles, Beckwith, and Will Kelsey came down to study the futtocks Fowles had installed, those made with dried wood from the forest. The beams, Ben said, were stout enough, but various causes had made them unstable. "Wood of different sorts swells and shrinks according to their type," he said, "and these beams are working themselves loose. We can pound oakum all day, but it won't help." He put his ear to one of them, and said, "There's a groan in there I don't like. The beams are moving and the bolts are widening their bores as we speak."

"And what does this mean?" Beckwith asked.

"It means that every day on the water makes her weaker," Ben Fowles said. "When we're in port, we've got to do a proper repair."

"I believe you've already repaired 'er, Ben."

"As well as I could, yes, but no builder would use this wood for a futtock."

"Very well," Beckwith said. "And what port would you recommend?"

"Bristol?" Will Kelsey asked.

"Aye, Bristol," Ben said, and laughed. "She'll be seaworthy and we'll be swingin' from our ropes."

From then on all of us began hearing the popping and groaning from the starboard side of the ship, and in their dreams, I imagine that the men saw bolts widening bores, saw wood splitting and glue breaking loose. Were we to find ourselves in a storm, we could be floating with our hands clutching debris.

Beckwith's charts showed us moving along another great continent, one I understood was peopled by either descendants of Spanish seamen or 'injins' as Dick Burrows called them. We would not go there. We would make our way to the bottom of the world and then cross into the China seas. We would avoid clusters of islands in the southern part of the great ocean, because those islands were well known by the British and French.

There were periods of many days when the wind did not blow, and we were forced to wait for the sails to round out with it. Roger Beckwith, hovering over his charts, told me that we were north of the Equinoctial Line, a term describing midway between the top and bottom of the earth. For this reason, he said, we were in a doldrums area. And then he claimed that we had crossed the Equinoctial Line, and were now certainly in the bottom half of the world, farther south than we had been since I had come to the ship. I studied the maps in the encyclopedia, and saw the China we had visited, and King Philip's land, and indeed that line fell below both. At night I dreamed that this bottom half of the world might be somehow different from the top in that perhaps there were ali'i who did not behave as the top half of the world's ali'i behaved.

The sighting of land is ordinarily an occasion for excitement, but for us, it was an occasion for caution, of whispers and eyes jammed into the telescope to determine if that dot upon the horizon might be a seventy-four. The first such sighting took place just after dawn one morning as we were in the area where Beckwith expected the sighting of islands, "like yours, with people like yours," he told me. But this sighting was first of a cloud-topped mountain, and then of the top rigging of two ships, British, Beckwith surmised, and we turned the ship away from this sighting. We continued sailing in a westward direction.

One more such sighting took place a week later, and again we fled, because of the top rigging of another ship. I began to wonder if the men had been right, that the great ocean was crowded with ships. But at length we sighted what appeared to be a high island, the entire horizon off the port transversed by a huge line of clouds.

At first it appeared as a phantom shape in the sky, around which we blinked our eyes, for its height suggested some curtain of mists between us and it, and if we but sailed for a few minutes in the direction of this shape, we would find ourselves staring at a shoreline. We did so, and that shape in the sky remained where it had when we first sighted it. Beckwith went to his cabin to study his charts, and came back on deck to stare at this strange apparition. "We're farther south than I'd thought," he said. "I believe this is what is called Staten Landt, or in the encyclopedia New Holland, or what Cook called New Zealand."

"If it is," Will Kelsey said, "I'll give Tadeusz the octant and see if he can do better."

"He might do better," Beckwith said, staring at it. "A Dutch explorer named Abel Tasman sighted this place more than a hundred years ago, but I believe from the west side of it. Gents, this is a large land mass, peopled by some bellicose folk."

"Just what yer lookin' for then, eh mate?" Will Kelsey said.

"We must go somewhere," Roger Beckwith said. "But on the charts, this landmass is made up of two very large islands, and we've got to make our way around them if we're going to the China seas."

"Right then," Will Kelsey said. "Then I'd say let's go around them."

"We sh'll take a look though," Roger Beckwith said. "No point in coming to this place without taking a look at it."

"This means that we're at the bottom of the bloody world, Roger," Kelsey went on. "We can turn ourselves the other way and take on the 'orn."

"I shall live my life without ever taking on the 'orn again," Beckwith said. "That world no longer exists for you, me, and every man on this ship."

We sailed toward that strange, high apparition of mountains. I asked Beckwith who the 'bellicose folk' of this place were, and he said that they were called 'aborigines' by earlier explorers, and Indians by others. He knew little of the area and its people, but bits of information he had received over the years told him of a very large pair of islands, beyond which was another vast, dry continent called New Holland, a place not very much explored. We were to sail to the north of this continent to find the China seas. Whatever the mistake was in the plotting of our course that had led us this far south, he couldn't say, but once we were beyond these islands and north of New Holland, we would find our way to ports where we could unload our cargo.

I realized, by this time, that the very nature of our furtive movement over this world made it such that we did not know what developments in exploration and shipping there were. It took meeting people like DeGroot and Renay for us to find these things out.

By the time that line of mountains had clarified in our vision, we understood the magnitude of the landmass we approached. Beckwith decided to fly what he called St. George's Cross, the ensign of England, assuming that the ships that might be present in these waters would be British. We sailed along the coast for two days, moving north, and always off the port rail there was that high profile with the white clouds on top. We remained perhaps five miles out, and reports called down from the mast told us of white sand beaches, of rivers that flowed into the ocean, of green bluffs gracing the shoreline.

Will Kelsey's conviction was that Roger Beckwith would need bait of some kind to make his way closer to shore, and that bait came the third day, in the form of a flashing light from one section of rocky shoreline. At first we surmised that it was some object that reflected the morning sunlight, but as we sailed north, the flashing of that light followed us, so that we conjectured that someone on the shore was the source, turning a piece of mirror, perhaps, to signal us. Beckwith thought this over, studied the flashing light. Indeed it flashed in a rhythm, stopped for a few seconds, then flashed once again. Someone in distress was on that shore.

Beckwith ordered the ship turned, ordered also that we ready the muskets, and that the gentlemen of leisure prepare to man the port cannons. We would move to within a mile of that shore and wait, perhaps get a closer look at the source of that signal. This we did. If all looked safe on shore, we would take the cutter in to look around. The closer we got to that shore, the more pleasing the land looked, with green bluffs interspersed with black rock formations, fronted in places by white sand beaches. Then we sighted a shipwreck, the remains draped over those black rocks, a tail of sailcloth lying on the water and rising and falling in the swells. From what evidence was visible, Beckwith and Kelsey thought that the ship was a whaler, although they could not be sure.

After we waited for some time, again seeing that flashing of light from a darker area in the rocky part of the shoreline, we lowered the cutter and eight of us rowed toward the shore, myself, Roger Beckwith, Dick Burrows, Will Kelsey, Crabbe and Audrey, Joe Seager and Don Bentley, all of us armed. Rather then aim the cutter at that flashing light, we chose to go toward a somewhat calm-looking stretch of sandy shoreline to the left of the light. As we rowed, we saw two men emerge from brush at the right end of that beach, and then another who climbed the rocky bluffs rather rapidly. "Keep an eye on that one," Dick Burrows said.

The men on shore were Will Pitt and Richard Johnson, sailors from the whaler there on the rocks. Their clothes were dirty, they were bearded and somewhat gaunt, and were missing teeth, and were unarmed. They were waiting to be picked up by another ship, and were bartering with the locals for some very interesting goods, those locals being "a bunch of filthy, bloodthirsty monkeys who want nothing but muskets, so you fellas'd better keep a close eye on yours." Then the speaker, Mr. Pitt, saw me standing there in the sand, and stopped talking.

"And the ship is due when?" Beckwith asked.

"Who's that fella there?" Pitt asked.

"Pono's his name, a better sailor there rarely shall be," Beckwith said.

"Where's he from?" Pitt asked.

"The Sandwich Islands," Beckwith said. "'e's been with us eight years."

"He speak English?"

"I do," I said. "Quite well, I believe."

The man's bearing changed somewhat. Perhaps he was aware of his aforementioned "filthy, bloodthirsty monkeys" reference to the people of this area. He thought for a few moments, and then said, "All right then, let us show you our discovery here. It's but a short walk."

"What's the fella on the rocks doin'?" Dick Burrows asked.

Pitt stared at him. "An American?"

"Yep," Dick Burrows said.

"He's standing watch," Pitt said, staring somewhat skeptically at Dick Burrows. "Your ship's been seen, no doubt, by some of the, ah, residents of the area. It is likely they're on their way here now." As if his having mentioned this brought the thought of it forward in his mind, he suddenly looked wary and afraid.

"Speaking of the ship," Pitt said to Beckwith as we walked along the shoreline, "it's due in two weeks or so, and we're doing our best to 'old out."

His partner, who had not yet spoken, ran ahead and held the branches of a bush aside so that we could pass through. Crabbe and Audrey declined, choosing instead to stay with the cutter, and Dick Burrows stopped at the opening of the cave and told Beckwith that he would stand watch there.

The men lived in a cave the size of a small house, with a high ceiling. At the front of it they had a fire-pit with red coals in the base, the faint smoke drifting toward the water. I noticed no muskets. In the cave were sleeping-mats, food stores, three water casks and two large trunks, possibly salvaged from the wreck. It was cool, quite comfortable inside this cave, although coming from the north of it I could smell a fecal stench, perhaps their toilet, which someone had failed to cover with sand. In any case, Mr. Pitt seemed somewhat gleeful and conspiratorial as he prepared to show us the fruits of his barter. "Now first I should say this," Pitt said. "We've hidden our muskets, and the people here know that, so they let us alone until they've got something to trade. We trade our muskets, and for the present we're engaged in a kind of truce, because they want the muskets and won't kill us if they think they'll not find them. So they won't hurt us, although they appear quite ferocious when you first see them."

He turned to one of the trunks, and slowly opened it. Inside were wrapped objects, the wrapping in this case torn sailcloth and clothing. Pitt lifted one object out, and very carefully pulled the sailcloth away from it. He then held up before us a dark brown human head, its face held in a toothy leer, the skin bedecked with tattoos in circular patterns around the mouth and on the forehead. The hair was drawn back and tied at the back of the skull. In the eye-sockets were shell pieces, and the skin appeared as smooth as leather, the lips somewhat shrunken and the nose perfectly normal. I stared at it, amazed, for the head reminded me of 'Iolana.

"Indeed, what is this?" Beckwith asked.

"A dried 'ead, sir," Pitt said. "It's light. It's been emptied and baked, you see."

"And what do you plan to do with it?" Beckwith asked.

Pitt came out with a rueful, amazed laugh. "D'ye think we'd put these in our 'ouses, sir? These are for collectors in England. There was a Mister Banks who sailed with Cook, y' see. He got one, maybe twenty, twenty five year ago." He bounced it a little in his hand, the hair shaking behind the leering face. "Got twelve of these beauties, plan to sell 'em back 'ome."

In the breeze, now, I became aware of a slight hint of decomposition from that head, but faint and soily. The tattoos on the face were very elaborate. "Who cut the man's head off?" I asked.

Pitt looked at me. It was as if he did not expect me to ask any questions. He looked instead at Beckwith. "If you take us with you, we'll arrange a bit of sharing of the proceeds here," he said.

"Who cut the head off?" I asked.

Pitt appeared confused. "What d'ye think, sir?"

"Pono's question interests me," he said. "Who cut the head off?"

"They cut the 'eads off their own dead. It's called mokomokai. A man dies, and there's a process where they cut off the 'ead and dry it, and then keep it. All very primitive and done with the savage rituals and the like."

I turned the word 'mokomokai' around in my head. "What do the natives of this place call it? What do they call themselves?"

Again Pitt seemed to want to ignore me. He thought, but then turned to his as yet silent partner and said, "That word. What is is?"

"They call this place 'Aotearoa,'" he said.

I watched the man pronounce the word, and then heard its echoes. Ao. Day, or cloud. Tea. Kea, white. Roa. Loa, long. "Cloud, white, long," I said. "This is my language, or similar to my language. This is the land of the long white cloud. These people are of my race."

"Maori," the man said.

"Maoli. Kanaka maoli," I said. "I know of no such practice in my world, that of removing heads and preserving them. But I can surmise that these keepsakes are the preservation of the dead person's mana, or spirit. Who gave these to you?"

"We traded for them," Pitt said. "First one was two muskets, and then we realized our mistake. These blighters'd take a bloody belt-buckle for their daughters."

He seemed, again, to have understood what he had said. "Sir," he said to Beckwith, "could we talk without him present?"

"No, we could not," Beckwith said.

"Please go on," I said. "I'll not take offense."

Pitt sighed, almost as if exasperated at our lack of enthusiasm. "These people spend most of their time killing each other," he said. "When they understood what a bloody musket was, they wanted every musket they could find. There are chiefs here who raise their armies and raid the other chiefs and they kill them, take their 'eads and dry them like this beauty here." And again he bounced the head in his hand. "I sh'll show you another," he said. He rewrapped the head he held and put it back in the trunk, and then addressed the second trunk. From that he withdrew another wrapped head, this one of a woman, with long hair and tattoos on her face, the leer less pronounced than on the first head. The hair hanging from the back of the skull was long and reddish, and braided. "Not as much decoration on this one," he said. "See the chin? They all 'ave that on their chins. This one was a chiefess, they said. Wanted three muskets for this one, but we said no, we don't need any bloody chiefess if she costs more."

"Interesting," Beckwith said. "I assume that the people here consider these heads as heirlooms then, if they take the trouble to save them. But a musket is worth more."

"A musket is worth more," Pitt said. "We saw a fight not a week ago. One chief took his fellows after another chief. They met in a battle right up the 'ill there, and because he had the muskets, he won. And I'll tell ye, the winner here doesn't show much in the way of mercy if you know what I mean. In fact, they kill everybody and, as you might assume, they remove their 'eads."

"We can also assume then," Beckwith said, "that the collection of the aforementioned heads is done with a goal in mind, to trade for more muskets."

"Aye sir, that's the truth."

Will Kelsey stepped toward the woman's head, and looked carefully at the skin, reached up as if to touch it, and then drew his hand back. "Aye," he said. "Strange it is."

"Dick," Pitt said over his shoulder, "tell them about Du Fresne."

"Aye," Richard Johnson said. "Now there's a tale. 'e was the first explorer here, back in seventy-two. Spent a couple months 'ere a cavortin' with the women, he and his fellows, and were treated like royalty. Then one day they were set upon by these Maori folk for no cause at all, killed, cooked and eaten. Aye, those bloody animals raised cooked liver and kidney in their 'ands, sliced huge chunks off thighs and cooked 'em up and ate them, cut out their tongues and sliced them up and ate them, likely roasted their balls too and ate them. Then Crozet, Du Fresne's second in command, up and slaughtered five hundred of those devils, women and children too, as a means of revenge, but the fourteen killed couldn't be equaled by any five hundred of them animals, so Crozet thought of maybe taking a thousand more, but killing's hard work you see, so he left, and not knowing it left behind him a gift for those savages, who started dying all over the place. Ague, you know, disease and the like. So there's some kind of justice after all, eh mates? Story goes that fully a third of the blighters got the ague and roasted in their own juices."

"Indeed," Beckwith said. "That's an interesting story. Did anyone see the people here eating Mr. Du Fresne?"

"No, but that's 'ow the story goes, sir."

"Pono," Beckwith said to me, "do you believe that the story is true?"

"No," I said. "One would assume that they would have cooked and dried the heads of the slain then, is that not so?"

"But that's the story," Pitt said. "About their 'eads I don't know."

Beckwith stared at him, thinking. Dick Burrows came into the cave and looked at the dried head, then around at the trunks, the clothing and food stores. Something appeared to concern him, but I had become used to this expression. I made my way to him and said, "You've seen something."

Pitt and Johnson continued talking with Roger Beckwith, and Dick Burrows looked around in the cave. "These are British whalers," he said. "We didn't change the letters on the ship."

"But she's a mile out," I said.

"Yep, an' I'm lookin' for a telescope," he said.

I understood. "I haven't seen one. Do you think they might know of our ship?"

"They all know," he said. "But I get a uneasy feeling here." He looked at the cave opening. "I'm goin' up that bluff, look around. If there's a man on watch I'll find him. If there ain't, then we need to figure out what to do. Get out of here maybe."

"Very well," I said. "When I get the opportunity, I'll tell Roger."

Dick Burrows left. It occurred to me that he may have been right. Why would these men be here, and how would they know that their ship was due in two weeks? If they were left here to barter with the native people, why did their captain allow this vulnerability? It didn't make proper sense, in ways. I looked around once again, and counted out the piles of sleeping mats and clothes, and thought that I was illogically convincing myself that there was more of that sort of thing than three men would require.

Pitt was still talking with Beckwith. "If I get these back 'ome, they'll bring a fortune, sir. You'd need only to belay the usual superstitions about things like this, and we could 'ave an agreement." He laughed, shaking his head in wonder. "The way I understand it, these 'eads are prized by these people, because the tattoo is a history-map of sorts, of the person. Because they keep slaves 'ere, I understand some of the chiefs are considering tattooing them and cutting off their 'eads for trade. Can you believe it?"

"As commerce," Beckwith said, "it's certainly curious."

"Aye," Pitt said. "A curious commerce it is."

I went out of the cave and looked up the bluffs. I looked down at the musket in my hands, verifying for myself that it was ready, and walked partway up, on the rise that lay above the cave. I was confused, I believe, by the idea that the people of this place spoke a language that so closely resembled mine, and that, as in my world, the order of this world seemed similar in that chiefs and their warriors went out and killed chiefs and warriors, apparently as a matter of course. I stopped above Crabbe and Audrey, and told them I would climb on up the bluffs to look around, as Dick Burrows had. "Aye, and come back soon," Crabbe said, leering at me and looking around. "I don't like this place. 'ow do we know what's up that coast?"

"That is what Dick wants to know," I said. "Tell Beckwith I'll be back." I turned and went up the bluff. And a fair land it appeared to be. The hills were verdant and pleasant, the air temperate. As fine a place as anyone would desire, but for the problem of chiefs and warriors. Up there as I looked around myself, I was aware that the man on watch was nowhere to be seen, perhaps farther up the bluff so as to have a better view of the surroundings. Nor could I see Dick Burrows.

I scanned the ocean from this higher vantage point. *The Tiburon* lay a mile offshore, and there was nothing on the far horizon. The coastline to the south was clear, but to the north it was blocked from sight by a large, stony outcropping topped with trees.

It first interested me that I could see no human or animal, except for seabirds. If the land were so inviting, why weren't there people around? Perhaps this was like the great continent we had just left. I made my way slowly and somewhat warily toward the high rock outcropping, thinking of finding something of interest on the other side.

Upon reaching a path winding over a grassy hill inland from that outcropping, I saw two figures, one large and one small, coming my way, the larger one Dick Burrows, running at a medium pace, his musket in his right hand, the smaller figure a boy with skin browner than mine, wearing a malo.

Burrows saw me and continued running until he reached me, the boy behind him.

"He don't talk," Burrows said breathlessly. "But he showed me our problem."

"Aloha," I said to the boy. Then I spoke in my language to him, asking him if he lived here, and if his people were kanaka maoli. He was breathless too, and appeared confused, apparently not understanding me. He pointed to his mouth and said, "Ahh."

"We've got to get back," Dick Burrows said. "Over that hill is a little bay with a British whaling bark and two brigs, and the brigs are being readied to sail. I don't know what a whaler would be doing way down here, but we been taken for fools."

The boy held something in his hand, a ball from Dick Burrows' sack, I assumed.

There was no time to try to communicate futher, although I wished I could, for the boy looked very much like my people. Dick Burrows and I made our way back toward the cave, the boy following. We got to the bluff over the cave, but there were no people in sight. Crabbe and Audrey were not with the cutter, and the oars were gone.

"Here's what we got," Dick Burrows said. The boy stood there listening, bouncing the lead ball in his hand. "The other six've maybe been taken prisoner. Shoulda known this would happen, but they saw the ship and set this up. The man on watch went to that bay over the hill to let them know this prize is here. They're British ships, and there isn't any doubt but that they want *The Tiburon* for all that's in it."

In the silence following, the boy looked at me. At this moment I realized how he resembled boys I had known in my world. Did he fish here? Were his parents like mine? But there was no time for this. "So what shall we do?" I asked.

"The oars are gone. They've got the fellas tied up most likely in that cave." He looked around, and spat. The boy turned and spat too. "Yeah, yer a good little fella," Dick Burrows said to him. "But you gotta go now." Then he stepped back quickly, and the boy did so in imitation. I was still out of sight of the beach, peeking through the leaves of a bush. One of the men, Pitt it was, walked out on the beach and looked up the bluff. He carried a musket.

"Mates!" he yelled. "Your ship's to be boarded soon! We've got your shipmates trussed up like swine. We're taking possession of your ship."

"Stay outta sight," Dick Burrows said. Then he pulled the boy farther to the side. He dropped his musket ball and picked it up, then crouched behind a rock.

"Mates!" Pitt called. "It's done with! But we'll spare you. It's a fine country 'ere you can vanish into!"

"A lie if I ever seen one," Dick Burrows said. "He knows who we are." He turned and stared up the hill. "It come to this, then."

"To what?" I asked.

"Beckwith has a policy. If we're captured, we're to shoot our way out. A ball's better'n a rope. That's what he always said."

Three more men came along the beach, Joe Seager, his hands and legs tied, Don Bentley the same, so that they could move only in small steps, and a man I did not recognize from before, a large man in a filthy military tunic, who carried another musket, and urged the tied men forward with the butt.

"Mates!" Pitt yelled. "Your Captain Beckwith is safe. Come down and hand over your weapons." Then, in something less than a yell, he continued: "What's he got to answer for? The slaughter of two dozen British soldiers? Sinking a ship or two? That won't wash down here at the bloody bottom of the world. Come, we've all done things that don't wash way down 'ere, now 'aven't we?"

"We gotta drop the both of them and get to the ship," Dick Burrows said.

"The others will die then," I said.

"I know, but that's our orders, Pono. I don't like it none, but those ships are about a hour and a half away. We gotta do this now."

Pitt talked with the large man, then looked once again up the mountain.

"We don't know how many men they got in that cave," Dick Burrows said. "But we gotta drop these two, load and go down there." He looked around. "Got a idea," he said. "Far as you remember, is the bluff on top of that cave just straight up from it?"

"Yes," I said.

"Can you drop Pitt and load, and then climb on there and aim straight down? I'll go down and move in from the beach. If there's anybody by that bush we passed around, you drop him next."

I felt myself now shaking with fear, which Dick Burrows seemed to see. "Yeah, this don't feel right to me neither," he said, and spat again. "But we gotta do this now. Those brigs are pullin' outta that bay right now. Only good thing's that the wind's north, so they'll have to tack to get to the ship." He looked down at the works of his musket. "You take Pitt. I'll take the big fella. Aim for the chest. We can't miss."

"Very well," I said.

"Remember how I showed you this. You're shootin' down, so aim just a little low, base of the ribs maybe. We're not that far, so there ain't much in the way of trajectory, so just a little low."

When he raised his musket and set himself to aim, the boy vanished into the brush. I aimed very carefully, at Pitt, who at the moment presented a profile, and Dick Burrows saw that. "Wait," he said. Then Pitt turned to the larger man, who was apparently going to drag Don Bentley and Joe Seager back toward the cave.

I pulled when I heard the snap of Dick Burrows' hammer, and the large man fell. Pitt grabbed his shoulder and ran toward the cave. Dick Burrows quickly reloaded his musket, while Don Bentley and Joe Seager fought their ropes, hopping toward the cutter. I worked at reloading my musket, hearing reports from below, and then Dick Burrows was hopping over rocks and sliding down toward the beach. When I had the musket loaded I ran along the bluff toward the roof of the cave, and then went down on my belly to look over the edge. I heard one more report from below. Burrows had been right. There was a man standing behind the bush, reloading his musket, and I rolled myself into position and aimed down at him. Just as he raised his musket to shoot, I pulled and he fell, then crawled back toward the cave. I worked again at reloading, and heard shouting from below. I was too high up to jump down to the sand.

I got up and ran around to the bluff overlooking the beach. Don Bentley lay in the sand bleeding from his head and Joe Seager worked on his ropes, blood dripping from his mouth. I thought to go to their aid, but hearing another report from the cave, I ran down over the grasses and rocks to the beach and turned toward it. Past the bush, I saw men hopping out of the cave, Dick Burrows at the edge aiming the musket inside.

Dick Burrows signaled me forward. I ran there, past Beckwith and Kelsey, Crabbe and Audrey, who appeared safe, working at their ropes.

"Two got away," Dick Burrows said. "Went over those rocks." He pointed in the direction opposite from the beach. I helped the four men with their ropes.

"Dick explained our problem," Beckwith said. "Pono, take some embers from that fire and burn those bloody trunks in there, will you please?"

"Yes sir," I said. "Joe and Don are wounded," I added. Crabbe and Audrey, free of their ropes, ran out toward the beach, while Will Kelsey, gasping for breath, got the ropes off his legs and went into the cave for the oars. Beckwith helped him while I ran out, found a flat stone, and carried a red ember into the cave. There, surrounding the trunks with their sleeping mats, I rested the ember in the fabric and blew on it until a fire started, and licked lazily at the wall of one of the trunks.

"Let's go," Dick Burrows said. I followed him out to the beach, where the men worked at pulling the cutter to the water.

We pulled the oars, the land receding, billows of black smoke coming from the brush fronting that cave. Don Bentley lay face down on the floor of the cutter, the water sloshing back and forth and rocking his body. I felt an irrational impulse to turn him over so that he might breathe. Joe Seager sat on the stern plank leaning over his thighs, blood dripping from his mouth from a wound in his chest. He rolled off the plank before we got to *The Tiburon*.

Those on the ship had heard the musket reports and seen the fire, and had the ship readied to sail when we got to her and climbed over the ropes to the deck, and hoisted the bodies of Joe Seager and Don Bentley, and then the cutter, up. As the ship leaned, the wind from the south popping her sails full, we saw the top rigging of the two brigs pass into sight around the outcropping of land. The men expert in managing the sails rushed around the deck, including Kua'i and Tadeusz.

Will Kelsey was at the wheel, the men working about the booms. "Ready about!" Kelsey yelled, and Beckwith pulled me down toward the rail. The boom swung about.

"Hard a-lee!" Beckwith called. Then he turned to me. "Go down to the cannons."

I did so while Kelsey and the men worked at tacking, trying to beat their way into windward while the brigs swept out from those rocks, as if to pin us against the land. I stood by the cannons, Bob Olney overseeing while Tong Guan, Crabbe and Audrey, and Tadeusz, worked at positioning them against the tipping of the ship. Pots fell on the floor below. Above, Beckwith shouted out the orders: "Helm's a-lee!" followed by "Coming about!" to the sound of pinioning booms and the sails slapping taught as they caught the wind. Beckwith leaned down to us. "Bob, what's the bilge-level?"

"Low, sir."

"Aye, now there's a proper development," Beckwith said, and went up.

"Brigs are fast," Bob Olney said. "Corvettes are too, but we'll not outrun these vessels. Only good thing's we're running light." He leaned out to look at them as they, too, worked against the wind, their booms swinging and sails popping with wind. "They've got swivel guns," he said. "So they'll get a little closer and start peppering us." His eyes narrowed. "Pono, you get three or four muskets."

"Yes sir," I said.

"You move across as we tack, throw a couple balls each time, at anything, man, sail, anything. Dick Burrows taught you to shoot, and he says you're good. So when those ships get close enough, pester those ships, eh?"

"Yes," I said.

I collected the muskets belonging to Joe Seager and Don Bentley, and one other along with my own. As I set myself up, first on the port side because the two brigs were sailing outside of our line, gaining on us, not coming directly at us either, but making their way as if to pass us on the outside of the shore. I could see the figures of men moving on these ships, both of them with far larger crews than ours. I swallowed over a dry throat, for they were both beautiful with their sails curved in that voluptuous shape duplicated again and again on the smaller sails, all the way to the topgallants. As *The Tiburon* tipped and its booms swung, so did theirs in an almost perfect imitation.

As this pursuit continued, the ships out of range of any musket shot, it appeared that one of them had begun to lag back somewhat, perhaps because it was closer to the shore. I went up to the deck to see what the men were doing. Kelsey's tack had lengthened, as if, farther out from the shore now, the wind had strengthened somewhat. Owen Bew stood holding the rail and calling up to Roger Beckwith, who stood with Kelsey at the wheel. "I say do it!" he called.

"Aye, it's that or the rope," Beckwith said.

Will Kelsey worked the wheel while the booms swung, and then *The Tiburon* leaned and angled out on a starboard tack. The sails filled and I felt the subtle surge in movement as she cut outward toward the line of the other two ships, one of which was now almost abreast of us and nearly within musket range. I made my way around to Dick Burrows, who worked the ropes for the next tack. "What are they planning?" I asked.

Dick Burrows worked at opening and closing his hands, sore from hauling ropes. He was breathing heavily. He had a somewhat excited, if not amazed look on his face. "They're going to cut between them and run north."

I looked at the two ships. It would not be possible, I thought, for if we missed the stern of the first, we would be rammed by the second, assuming that those two brigs planned to tighten their positions against us and the shore. I understood then what Beckwith was contemplating: if we slid between the two ships, we would be perpendicular in position to them, both our banks of cannons operating while their ships would have only their swivel guns. This would last about fifteen seconds, however, after which they would take advantage of our closeness and blast our hull.

Beckwith, standing behind Kelsey at the wheel, seemed calm about the prospect, for he turned his head from one brig to the other, apparently waiting for the ships to close upon us. And then they were closing upon us, for on the forward ship's next port tack, matching ours, their line brought them closer than they had yet been, and I went below to my muskets. Bob Olney had seen their maneuver, and he had the men prepared at the port cannons. I picked up one musket, and set myself to aim. The first target was a man behind a swivel gun. I pulled the trigger, producing a flat report. The man continued working at the swivel gun. Other men on the deck moved around without pause. Then Bob Olney and Tong Guan came to the starboard side and readied two cannons. "Get ready, Pono," he said.

It struck me then how extraordinarily silent it was, considering what was about to happen. The calls of one or another of the men, announcing swinging booms or the other ships' maneuvers, were interspersed by nothing but the sound of *The Tiburon* cutting the water, a soft hiss that I had become so familiar with.

"Closing!" Bob Olney yelled. They were. The crews of the other ships were preparing to board us, for many of them stood at the rails, and I could see the glint of weapons, muskets and swords.

Will Kelsey and Roger Beckwith had seen this maneuver, because I now felt the ship tipping on the starboard side, the maneuver bringing her so hard by the lee that I thought she might upset, and then we were sailing straight away from the shore. There was no doubt now about range, for it appeared that we intended to ram the second ship in line while the first, seeing our maneuver, began its turn. I readied the musket and waited, watching the lines of the two ships, and then a cannon went off, the billow of smoke crossing my face, at which a sail on that second ship snapped and tore in the middle. A cannon went off on the port side, then another, but I could not see the results of that. I aimed the musket, waiting for a figure to appear, but the men on that ship were moving too fast, one rising up to the swivel gun and charging it, at which a rain of metal hit *The Tiburon*. The ship was huge now, a hundred feet from us, the faces of the men I could see clear in my vision, the slick sides of the hull streaming water. The gap between the two ships had narrowed so rapidly that it seemed as if men from that other ship would be jumping off the rails onto *The Tiburon*, but the speed she picked up at that moment pulled her broadside of their bow, and another cannon report followed by the smoke resulted in splinters of wood raining away from the starboard side of the bow. I saw two men working at the swivel gun and fired, and then I picked up the other musket and fired, at which both men lowered themselves, and another cannon report sent that salty, acrid smoke across my face, and then one of our sails settled from above, a boom slamming on top of it, and the powerful shock of a cannonball hitting the starboard hull shook the floor I stood upon. I reloaded the muskets, my hands shaking, and another rain of metal hit the hull behind me, followed by a yell, but now we were past the bow of the second ship and tipping again to race north while the front ship did the same. I heard flying metal popping our sails. The cannons on the starboard side went off, four reports, and I climbed up and over to that side. Bob Olney and the others were working at reloading, and then three gouts of smoke belched from the side of the turning ship, at which a hole appeared just below the rail not six feet from where I stood, and blew a hole in Beckwith's cabin wall.

Bob Olney ignored the damage as he hovered over the cannon and pulled at its rear wheels. Tong Guan put in a powder canister and a ball, followed by a wad, which he pounded in with the ramrod. "Run 'er out," Bob Olney said, and they pushed the cannon into firing position. He carefully set the cannon, stood back and waved the others back, and then touched the powder-hole, at which it fired and jumped back in its recoil, causing the floor to shudder. The ball hit the hull of the ship's stern, low near the water, and Olney said, "Aye, we got 'er." Tong Guan quickly sponged the bore and set to load another canister in.

We fled north. The engagement seemed to have ended with us more intact than the two ships after us. From the starboard rail, leaning outward, I could see the first ship with its stern low in the water, and the second lacking enough sail to chase us. I went up to the deck. Will Kelsey was there at the wheel, Roger Beckwith below him studying the two damaged ships left behind, and far ahead, on the shore, I could see wisps of smoke coming from bushes lining the shore. It took me some time to recall that the smoke was from the remains of the fire I had set in the cave. Then when I looked once again at Beckwith, I saw something in his expression, a melancholy wonder, and Will Kelsey looked the same, and I turned to find out who it was that had been killed.

We committed the remains of five men to the sea later that day. Joe Seager and Don Bentley, wrapped in sailcloth, and lined up in sailcloth on the deck next to them, Kua'i, Tadeusz, and Ben Fowles. Kua'i had received a hunk of metal to the forehead, leaving a triangular hole in the center, the back of his head open, yellowish tissue at the edges. Tadeusz had his neck broken by the falling boom, and Ben Fowles, our carpenter, was too close to an explosion of a ball that sent a thick sliver of the hull through his heart.

I learned that in the ship's long history, spanning back to early in the century, she had never experienced a tragedy this severe. The men were numbed by it, standing there while Owen Bew read from the Bible, and then Dick Burrows and I lifted the bodies and one by one cast them into the water. We were left with a crew of but fifteen, laboring north with damaged rigging, the hull badly damaged but fortunately, far enough above the water line that she remained seaworthy.

Another indication of the hazards of our travel occurred the same day we cast the bodies into the water. Far out on the horizon, we saw the faint shape of the rigging of an immense ship, what Will Kelsey called a capital ship, loaded with fifty or more cannon, and her mast taller than any ship we had yet seen except for that on the seventy-four we saw off the China coast. He speculated that, our being against the rocky shoreline, she would not see us. It seemed an omen of the future, that no matter how remote the ocean we visited, there would also be seventy-fours, whalers, brigs, all manner of vessels, each carrying the colors of their nations and the right to sink us.

We made our way along that coast, passing the inlet from which the two brigs had come, the men talking softly amongst themselves, others scanning the horizon with rueful, contemplative expressions on their faces. I leaned on the rail near my hammock, staring at Kua'i's hammock, and then saw Crabbe and Audrey at the rail near the stern. Crabbe whispered something to him, and then placed his hand low upon his back, at which he turned and looked at the former with a melancholy wonder, and then sighed.

Later the same day I asked Will Kelsey where we were going.

"Pono," he said, "we're going nowhere, and there's nowhere to hide."

"Shall I ask Roger?" I asked.

"He's sulking," Will Kelsey said. "Feels responsible for all this. How much work did you do with Ben in the repairs?"

"Enough, I believe," I said, "to know the use of his tools."

"We've got much work now with this old girl," he said. "But I think someone must venture into his cabin and repair that wall. He sits there staring at it. But give him a couple of days to think these matters over."

"I shall," I said. "I'll wait two days and then do the repair."

"In the meantime, I shall hold to a northerly line until we leave this place."

It occurred to me there that in a way the death of Kua'i was my responsibility. I had told him of this world, and my telling had made him want to see it. Despite the dim prospects he might have had, he might at least be alive back in my world.

Our slow movement north along that coast was paced by the men laboring over the creation of a jury-mast to replace the top half of the mizzen that killed Tadeusz. The lack of this aft rigging made for awkward sailing, and the men kept a careful watch on the horizon for the appearance of more of those large ships that they were now convinced crowded this great ocean. Will Kelsey told me that we were making our way to the South China Sea, perhaps Macau, although he was no longer sure if that was Beckwith's intent.

I went the next day to Beckwith's cabin and knocked on the door. When he did not answer I opened it slowly, and there he sat at his table, staring at the hole in the wall, a quill in one hand and an open ledger on the table.

"Come in, Pono," he said.

I went in and stood there looking at the hole, then at the ledger, whose page was blank. "I shall repair this," I said.

"Aye, I would appreciate it," he said, and placed the quill on the table. Then he looked up at me. "I keep a sort of account, you see. You are on the right side of my account because you are still alive. Will, Owen, the rest, are all still alive. My plan was to see all of you live out your lives. Of course I will not be around to see all finish those lives. But I think of Will, whose life I consider a decent achievement. Was to be 'anged you know, and we stole him from a jail in a place called St. Augustine, a hot place near the old Spanish Main."

"This is on the great continent," I said.

"Yes, on the far side from where we were," he said. He looked at the blank page, and picked up the quill, held it in the air above the ledger, and then put it down again. "Five people have died now, all in a day. My account is in danger of going into a debit. I can't 'ave that, Pono. My life will have meant nothing."

"Your life has meant much to me," I said.

"We must terminate our journey," he said. "There is a place called Batavia, and we shall go there. It is run by the Dutch East India Company, the wealthiest of such companies in the world. There we can safely trade what we have for some comfort. There are hundreds of islands there, places where we can live, I believe, if we can tolerate the heat at certain times each year. It is on the equinoctial line."

"Yes," I said. "The middle of the earth."

"This means that we will not, at this time, be sailing to your world, for the old girl probably won't be able to take it. The hull is no longer strong enough for high seas."

"I understood that, yes," I said.

"I will not sell her," he said. "There are two possibilities: one is to take her to Batavia and dismantle her, I thought to make mantelpieces, tables, beds and whatnot, as mementoes of our adventures. The other is to repair her and ask the mates which of them might be interested in sailing her out, and this way you might go back to your world."

"I do wish to go back to my world," I said. "I have learned much, and I thank you for that, and now it makes me want to return to my world."

"We have all learned much," he said. "We have learned that we humans have much to learn, and that learning itself does not shield us from ourselves. On the face of every man I have ever seen commit an act of cruelty upon another man, I have seen in the tightness of his jaw an expression of conviction of his justification and the rightness of what he was doing, regardless of the inconvenience of the obvious, whether it's a hangman putting a rope around the neck of a boy, or a man raising an axe over the head of another man, or a man setting fire to a boy because he stole a leaf. And I see the other side of it, thinking of Pitt and his dried heads. Does it interest you that these objects would be so valued in an advanced society such as England, or France?"

"I wonder how one would eat his dinner while one of them watched from a shelf."

Beckwith laughed. "Ah Pono," he said, and sighed. "You've been somewhat of a surprise to all of us, I should say. You learn so fast."

"I have much yet to learn," I said.

"We all do," he said.

§

At the time I had arranged to have Pono's narrative recorded, I believe I was in pursuit of a tale of adventure, and adventure there was, but tainted by things one ordinarily would prefer to ignore. Perhaps it was the maddening humidity, that September inevitability MacFarlane had warned me of, but I must say that I saw in myself something unexpected, perhaps even alarming for a man of the age I was. I had come to this place with dreams, expectations of the benefits of the legendary willingness of these women, but the closer I came to understanding the truth of this place, the more repulsed by the idea I became. And it was not due to any disappointment as to their comeliness. It was due more to the understanding that any one of them, no matter the age or the degree of attractiveness, might a month after I, say, offered a coin or two for the pleasure of that company, end up rotting in the grass behind a thatch hut, that beauty gone the way of all human beauty, and far too soon to ignore. What of that girl with the sailor, whom I had seen that first day? Was she yet alive, or had she succumbed to some fever?

It was Pope who said, "Know then thyself, presume not God to scan," and I believe I was discovering in myself a tiny flame of some philosophical recognition that in ways shamed me, for men of my age were supposed to, nay were just yards away from our little hut, indulging in whatever iniquity they desired, lustily cavorting with these women without a thought of their prospects, or the prospects of the people here in general. "Born but to die, and reas'ning but to err," another point made by the poet, "alike in ignorance, his reason such, whether he thinks too little, or too much." Indeed I suppose I was thinking too much. And I was faced now with conditions I could not ignore, and felt the greatest respect for Mrs. Searle, who'd acted upon these recognitions long before I thought of them.

And Pono: was there not something, anything for him, some redeeming event in his life that might rescue something for his later years? It seemed not. This confusion, for me, was I suppose my own facing of the poet's riddle of the world. But his story went on, he sitting in his usual place, with a line of sight out the door toward the harbor, telling this narrative with his eyes drifting to that brighter patch where the line of sight was, his face held both in recollection of the events he described, and in a strange, rueful expectation at what he might see on the dirt path outside. I had speculated, too, about this 'Iolana, or God's Hawk, and quickly concluded that, given Pono's luck, it was probably a coincidence, one of those possibilities that seems at first a certainty, until one thought over the likelihood of the survival of a child in that world he described.

Mrs. Searle, meanwhile, had been venturing farther out into the slums to the east, doing what she could for those who came down with the ague, but she told us one morning that the seeming abatement of the epidemic, if it could be called that, had continued to the point that she had hopes if seeing it extinguished.

One morning as I made my way past the grog shops and other buildings toward our room, I saw Pono speaking with a large, bearded man, apparently a ship's captain recently arrived. I had seen two ships come in during the past two days. I approached the two, who were standing in a bit of shade on the lee side of a building. "Ah," Pono said as I approached, "this is Matthew Davis of *The Clarel*." The man looked at me with a kind of grave propriety, and put out his hand.

"MacBriar," he said. "Of *The Widmere*." He then turned back to Pono and said, "Yes, a somewhat portly gentleman in an ill-fitting suit."

"Lahaina, you said?" Pono said. "And did he indicate when he might be here?"

"A week perhaps," MacBriar said. He cleared his throat and adjusted his tunic, apparently irritated with the humidity. "A bit of entertainment, I suppose," he went on. "You'd think he might add the idea of charity to his bombast, but not the case. But as I said, we had a good time of it watching him."

The man then harrumphed and pulled out a pocket watch. "I've got to be off," he said. "Matters to attend to. It has been a pleasure to talk with you."

"And you," Pono said.

The man left, making his way toward the water.

"Is it 'Iolana?" I asked.

"He's been preaching on Maui," he said. "MacBriar said nothing about resembling me physically. I wonder now, if this isn't a coincidence."

"Well then," I said, "you've a week to wait. At the very least it's better than expecting him each day."

"Yes, it's a relief," he said. Then he looked in the direction of our room, thinking. "We shall continue then. I'll do my best to stay the course."

"Very well then," I said. "I believe MacFarlane will be waiting."

22.

*I*t *required three months* for us to make our way to Batavia under the British flag, our ship again named *The Tyburn*. The men felt that this was a great risk to us, for many ships went to Batavia to do business with the Dutch East India Company, and any one of them could suspect the ploy and engage in an assessment of facts and records to determine if there was such a ship, but Beckwith reasoned that, Batavia being composed of many islands, smaller and less populated by whites the farther you got from the port, we might be able to hide until the very memory of our supposed crimes entered the realm of drunken sailors' lore. One and a half of those months were spent on a small island that sported a shipwreck, whose remains we used to do repairs on *The Tiburon*.

I shall forego an extended description of our efforts to repair the ship, but to say that the duties of carpenter fell largely to myself and Will Kelsey, whom Beckwith thought needed activity to keep him from becoming petulant and difficult to live with. Aye, Kelsey agreed, as long as the spirits hold up. He was referring here to grog, and to the other more refined strong liquids Owen Bew so jealously guarded down in his galley.

When, upon studying the hull of *The Tiburon*, we discovered that some of the planking had thinned out considerably, Beckwith concluded that he had been right, it was time to retire the old girl. Thus, with the ship repaired, we made our way northwest into the zone of that tropical humidity that so maddened the men a few years before.

Batavia. It was a name given to the place by the Dutch, formerly called Jocarta, according to Beckwith. Because the British had been at war with the Dutch, and won a treaty in 1784 that gave them the trade advantage, Brits would not be the most welcome of visitors to Batavia. It didn't matter, Beckwith said, because the British had engaged in piracy for many years, and although the VOC, as he called the Dutch East India Company, was around two hundred years old and very wealthy, the British owned the oceans, and therefore regarded any VOC ship as no more than booty to be collected in England's name.

"So why do we pick Batavia?" Will Kelsey asked. We were moving very slowly to the northwest in a nearly flat sea, into that windless heat.

"It is a place of many peoples," Beckwith said. "There are many islands outside the port, and the port is large, such that a Brit with a little money will be ignored." He thought a moment, and then went on. "We're privateers, an armed merchant out of Halifax, called *The Tyburn*. And this is the Halifax in the Americas. I've got an old Letter of Marque issued in 1779 that should pass. There's just enough confusion what with the French, Brits, and Dutch and peace treaties and so on that we'll be able to sail into that harbor, and nobody'll know what to do with us except to ask what our cargo might be."

"Aye, and we'll live in huts then," Kelsey went on.

"No, you shall live in a house," Beckwith said. "You shall be a rather wealthy gentleman, if you prefer. My name, by the way, is Brown. Captain Brown of Halifax."

This the men considered, weighing it against the thought of the climate of the place. Perhaps they had visions of being fanned by tropical leaves held in the hands of dusky maidens, but the explanation seemed enough for them to press on. Only Owen Bew seemed somewhat petulant about the prospect. He banged his pots down in the galley, muttered to himself, and came up on deck to stare ahead toward the hot, misty horizon, as if he were being taken to the most hated of all places. I believe that for Owen, no land was acceptable, and he had probably envisioned sailing in the bowels of *The Tiburon* forever, no matter her condition.

The region called Batavia was a series of islands spanning many hundreds of miles from east to west, the central port on the north side of one of the largest islands. Beckwith's strategy was to approach as merchants, but not to sail into the harbor. He said he'd studied the charts, and saw islands between Batavia and disputed territory held by the Portugese where we might find a place to stay.

The year of our approach was 1795, nine years after my abduction from my land. I had seen much in that time, and wondered, now, what the future held, for if the ship were to be retired, then all of us would be stuck in this place and would disperse outward into various hiding places, and perhaps never see each other again. Should any of us desire, ships leaving Batavia went in all directions, so we were not marooned here. We were simply to be let loose here to deal with our futures as we saw fit.

Weeks after we went through a strait from which we could see land on each side, with the land to the south, I was told, being that of a huge continent that was essentially unexplored, we sailed into the calm, humid waters of our destination. A number of days into that sail, we beheld land, islands, one after another, low and under the seeming perpetual haze of the area. The island Beckwith selected, after muttering over his charts in his cabin, and after studying various papers that named and described businesses connected with the area's shipping industry, was one that was a one-day sail from Batavia itself, and populated by traders, merchants, gentlemen of wealth, native people who served them. All depended upon how the residents of that island might judge the value of our cargo. It was called New Tilburg, after a city in Holland, and was off the coast of a larger island. Its name meant that it was under the control of the Dutch, but it was in effect remote enough from the Trading Company's center to afford a kind of anonymity.

It had no proper port, although it had a deep-draft cove, one which *The Tyburn*, as she was now called, could enter without danger. The men, though, were suspicious of the presence of reefs and shoals, so because the seas were calm, we towed her in using the cutter, passing dense foliage that hovered out over the still water, with flies and other insects buzzing above it, the smells from the shore somewhat putrid, muddy and rich. The sunlight had an orange quality, rich as of the reflection of firelight at night, the haze in the sky rendering that orb into a dull yellow ball that resembled the yolk of an egg. People of the area stood on rocky ledges watching, Malays the men said, and some Chinese. They wore either long pale smocks or white loincloths.

The other men on shore, two whites who appeared later, seemed not to see our approach as anything unusual, which reassured us. Two of the natives and the two whites got into a small cutter and rowed out to greet us. Beckwith briefly addressed us, saying that we must behave like merchants, and cautioned Dick Burrows particularly against greeting them over the muzzle of his musket.

I will forego our introductions in favor of an announcement made by Mr. Rennie, surprisingly a British gentleman in the shipping business, that the VOC, or the Dutch East India Trading Company, was bankrupt, as of just weeks prior to our arrival. Sitting in the cutter aligned with ours, and holding on to her rail so that the two boats would not separate, he said, "What this means for the future we don't know, sirs, but I will tell you that we are an island of empty houses and natives eager to work." The other white man was French, a Mr. Michel, and quite old, but he looked at all of us with the appearance of pleasure and relief that we had indeed towed our ship into his small harbor. He was a business partner to Rennie, and had been living in the area twenty years.

"We shall provide opportunities for work," Beckwith, now Captain Brown, said. "We've a hold full of pelts from the Americas, and just enough in the way of wealth to stay here a bit. What do you recommend?"

"Aye," Mr. Rennie said, "it's a right good bit of luck for us, for the place is becoming a bore. Half of the whites 'ave left, and the houses are growing mold."

"We sh'll occupy them, then," Brown said. I detected something of a foreign sound to his speech. He was trying somewhat unsuccessfully to imitate Dick Burrows' patterns of speech, and to present himself as an American.

"We've much to talk about then," Rennie said. "Much. We shall outfit your ship with native guards and invite you to a repast here."

"We'll leave a few men on board," Brown said. "Of course your native guards are welcome. We'll have our men relieve each other at half days then."

"Aye, excellent," Rennie said. "Our boys speak a bit of English, Dutch, a little German and some French."

What, then, would the consequences of the reported bankruptcy of the VOC mean to us? I asked Will Kelsey about this while the men talked, and he said he had little knowledge of the processes. Perhaps the VOC would be taken over by others, and in any case, bankruptcy did not mean the immediate cessation of shipping. That, he believed, would go on. Thus did we continue rowing toward a black, dripping jetty that opened into a green lawn, and upon approaching this jetty, I saw a large, very elaborate white house, an imitation, Will Kelsey said, of an English country estate.

The house of Mr. Rennie was in many ways a fascinating place, for I had never seen a house of the sort the men had casually referred to over the years. The furniture was of ornately carved wood, there were rooms separated by doorways, a large kitchen in which some quite merry Malays worked at preparing food, and there were mirrors hanging on walls, and oil paintings of horses and ships. Rennie had many books, some of which I looked at while he talked with Captain Brown. I pulled one out, and its leather ended up on my fingers, and the pages felt wet, almost soggy, and inside the cover along the place where the pages joined were small white worms, and the dust of their work fell out on the floor. I paused there, looking around me. So the marvelous world of these people was subject to decay, to a strange bankruptcy of its own. So humid was the atmosphere that the glass on some of the pictures hanging on the wall had water dotting the inside, the pictures themselves stained with moisture. The gathering place for our repast was a large room with a long, shining wooden table, circled by a series of identical chairs, each with fabric cushions built into them, and there we sat as the Malay cooks brought out fish, duck that tasted to me like bitter chicken, odd fruits, bread, and a drink called arrack, which was a rather strong whisky-like liquid popular in the area. While I studied the plates and glasses we ate from, and the metal implements, Rennie and our Captain Brown discussed matters of European politics, developments in trade, the VOC and an uncertain future in the shipping business, especially, Rennie said, when the most successful pirates in history, the British, seemed so unabashed about making prizes of any and all ships they encountered on the water.

The merriment of the cooks had an explanation. They felt saved, Rennie said, by the sudden appearance of gentlemen of wealth. Because other wealthy whites had left, they were afraid that they would not be able to feed their families, and upon learning of our intent to stay, experienced a fit of industriousness and vigor that seemed out of place in the hot, still air.

At length Rennie invited us to take a walk. He wished to show us two houses farther toward the center of the small island, vacated a year earlier by some wealthy white men, in this case Frenchmen who had labored here many years to build their fortunes. Rennie and two Malay servants led the seven of us who had come to dinner down a somewhat overgrown lane that once, he said, sported fine carriages. Perhaps a quarter of a mile in, the lane going straight through some quite dense overgrowths of plants I was unfamiliar with, and others I knew, such as breadfruit trees and banana trees, we emerged in a clearing centered by another white house that resembled Rennie's. It was surrounded by high grasses, and when Mr. Rennie took us inside, he explained that the house was 'a hotel of sorts,' fitted out with many rooms with a common area near the front door. Unfortunately, with the dissolution of the VOC, there were few people left on smaller islands such as this one. Here we could stay, he said, for two rix-dollars, which would be about two bob, per sailor per day, or if Captain Brown would wish to make an arrangement for a longer stay, the price of course could be lowered.

"What is a 'bob'?" I asked Will Kelsey, now somewhat unsteady on my feet because of the arrack.

"A shilling," he said. "I'd bet that Beckwith'll have to do some mathematics on how escudos, bobs, and rix-dollars figure together."

Rather than pester him as to what a rix-dollar or an escudo was, I followed Rennie and Captain Brown and the others around in this house. Each room had a 'bed' as it was called, but somewhat smelly, the large cushions stained and moldy, the floors under them dusty, the walls sporting small lizards and insects. These mattresses, Rennie told us, could easily be replaced by some fine work by the natives, or bought from the Chinese, who were the merchants of the area.

So the arrangement, despite the negatives, which were that the climate was simply not what Kelsey called "a white man's climate," and the remoteness from anything approximating what the men might have thought of as home, had its positives, namely that the Malays and many others here were fairly "addicted to gaming," as Kelsey put it, which brightened the spirits of the gentlemen of leisure, and that the booty that Beckwith had collected over the years could easily be converted into 'good coin' as the men put it. It meant that the shares the men were to receive, and they were large, were in effect protected by a system used for many years in the VOC's business. There would be no loss of that, and there would be no question as to conversion rates between rix-dollars and pounds and the like. The men could remain here as long as they pleased, and perhaps when the right times came, ship out to return to whatever home they felt was safe for them. Dick Burrows would go one of two places: his home on the great continent, or to my world, a place he had not been able to remove from his mind.

And what of women? There were many Chinese in the area, the merchants, traders, and the like, but there were no Chinese women, because they were not permitted in this place. Men took Malay wives when they felt that need. If one were to remain here some time, Rennie told us, one best learned how to speak the common Malay language. You could of course do quite well without that, because so many of the Malays and Chinese spoke a sort of broken English that had over the years formed itself into a second language familiar to all, as they spoke broken French, broken Dutch, broken German, and so on.

In any case, Beckwith was satisfied that this place, this humid, moldy island with its smells of mud and rotted fruit, would do quite well for us. The men, I thought, were unsure, because they'd been in this climate before, and could barely stand it.

As for myself, my aim was to return some day to my world, but I was so far from it, and so many years had passed since I had last set foot there, that I did not know if it would ever be possible. The dreams I had had all those years of Pekau and the children were now old dreams, expectations that had eroded into fantasies, and I had long accepted the reality of my time on this earth, that I could never replicate that life, hard as it was on that mountainside, with its struggles and joys. The thought of a Malay wife, therefore, did not excite me, as having a room to sleep in with a new mat for the strange, wooden frame did not excite me.

Standing there back at Rennie's house, I looked out over the dark water of the cove at *The Tiburon*, thinking that I would prefer to remain in my hammock. If there were anything left for me, I suppose I recognized even then, Mr. Rennie had a house full of books, and as I saw them and thought of them later that same day of our arrival, I decided that my aim for the period of time I was marooned here was to read each one of them.

I do not wish to deny you the details of this narrative, and suspect that you might become suspicious at what I say next: the seven years I spent there seemed interchangeable, dry seasons bleeding into a rainy seasons that seemed always to take up half the year, and to make everything moist, the page of a book feeling like some thin skin removed from an animal, so soggy and limp they became. Of course there were events, developments that interrupted the seemingly predictable nature of this life. A man came to dinner at Rennie's, and this dinner included myself, Will Kelsey, Crabbe and Audrey, Owen Bew and Captain Brown, as we had become used to calling Roger Beckwith. That man told a story of the great warrior Kamehameha, who had advanced with his army upon the island of O'ahu, and engaged a rival chief in a battle that spread up a valley, the top of which was a cliff on some five hundred feet. The losing army fought valiantly, but upon being pushed backward to that precipice, either jumped, or were thrown over, thus sealing for this warrior the kingship of the entire chain of islands but the most northwesterly, Kaua'i. The story fascinated me, and the teller, once he understood where I was from, listened to me as I told the story of the battle on Maui that I participated in. I wondered, too, if Konapiliahi might have been one of those doomed warriors, or if Muapo had forged some friendship with the great warrior that meant Konapiliahi's rescue from that fate.

Tong Guan became a Batavia merchant, hiring on with a rather wealthy China man who had booths at the Batavia market. He moved to that city a day's sail away, and as I was told later, made his way back to China, presumably to marry into the family of his employer and continue in the business.

A typhoon blew *The Tiburon* across the cove and left it leaning against a dense stand of mangrove, lodged in mud with its prow pointing in the direction of Rennie's dock. It was otherwise whole, but rotting there, held up by the branches, and became a house occupied by Malays who put chickens in the little coop on the deck to replace ours who died one by one, leaving the surly and petulant Madame Churchill, who avoided the typhoon by dying a day before it arrived.

From time to time I, Owen Bew and Will Kelsey and Dick Burrows had gone out to it, thinking of keeping her seaworthy in case we wanted to raise a crew and sail away, but the heat and moisture had worked at reducing her into a stinking hulk, the wood softening and becoming putrid so that one could run a fingernail along a plank and come away with a dark sludge that looked like mud, but was in fact the rotting wood itself. The cannons became fouled with sludge, the dripping metal seeming to swell, the bores growing moss. The bilge became a sloshing pond growing the larvae of mosquitoes, the newly hatched buzzing above the stinking water and rising from the hold. Another creature the hold provided billets for was the red-headed centipede, a frightening segmented thing eight inches long that snaked rapidly around corners and hid under wet leaves, or between planks. These might have been more plentiful but for their apparent value to the Chinese, who used them for medicinal purposes. As for these centipedes on the island, the Malays kept them out of their houses by putting chickens to work around the outside, scratching and pecking all day, and occasionally unearthing one of them and, after flurries of squawking surprise and excitement, pecking them to death and eating them.

A large veranda at the back of the house became a gaming room where the gentlemen of leisure spent their days, now accompanied by Malays who loved playing cards and other games with them. Money seemed not to be a factor there, so as Mr. Rennie put it, there was little chance that one of them might feel cheated and go after one of the white men with a keris, which was a heavy and somewhat impressive knife the Malays kept in their houses. The gentlemen did not distinguish according to rank, so a servant played a game as an equal. I would see them late in the day, finishing their games, rising from the table with stunned, distant looks, as if they had exhausted themselves. They would stumble to their dinners and go to bed just as the air began to cool somewhat, and rise the next morning and make their way to their table. I should say that the Malays were a fine people, and resembled my people somewhat, although they appeared to me smaller in stature. Their language bore similarities to my own, but I did not go into any deep consideration of this because I had immersed myself so deeply in the English language.

Our adaptation to the heat took the form of imitating Mr. Rennie and Mr. Michel, in that their habit was to rise with the sun, do whatever business they needed to do in connection with their trade, which was little, eat, and then sleep through the hot hours of the afternoon, get up and wear naught but a pair of cut off sailor's pantaloons, eat again in the evening and go to bed sometime around midnight. Sleep was always difficult, because one woke up in the dark with beads of perspiration on the chest and face, and the discomfort of this was simply a condition of life here. But it was a life of the sort of luxury the men might have imagined, but for the location and the climate.

Dick Burrows and I fell into the activity of fishing around the reefs surrounding the island. We would go out on a small boat with Malay fishermen and spend much of the middle part of the day in the water, fishing with spears. I tried to teach Dick Burrows the technique of trapping water so that he could see as I had seen and could again, now, with practice, but he claimed that the shape of his face did not allow that.

The Malays, who tolerated us with jovial whispers, fished very successfully with nets, while we would spend hours in the pursuit of one, but the activity kept us busy. Dick Burrows became an expert at the use of a spear, and he told me that his learning of this art was in preparation for his eventual return to my world. I believed this was, for him, one of those fantasies of the sort that I was assailed by, and understood just how forlorn we had all become out there in so alien a land.

And what shall I say about myself during those years? There were of course activities of interest, fishing, occasional trips to the main port of the huge and colorful city of Batavia, concern about the developments with the VOC and our futures here. As for the Batavia markets, the first time I went there I witnessed an execution. It was a Malay man who had run amock, as Rennie put it, and was to be "broken upon the Catherine wheel." The means of execution was to tie the man to a large wagon wheel, and then turn it and break all his bones with a metal club, the beginning of which I observed, and then shouldered my way through an excited crowd of Chinese, Malays, whites, and went away. The man had felt cheated in a game of some kind, and in revenge he had gone and murdered four people with a keris. It was called the Catherine wheel because far back in history a woman named Catherine of Alexandria who was to be executed on this wheel was pardoned and beheaded instead. The explanation seemed to me dubious, but that is what I was told.

The dissolution of the VOC began with the dismissal of the "gentlemen seventeen," men who oversaw the company, and in the years following that, the company was nationalized, or taken over by its owners' government, but it was in debt, and according to Rennie, all of its shipping was vulnerable to the English pirates who, as he said, "regard all ships as prizes." Fortunate, he claimed, that we were all wealthy, and whatever happened could happen whilst we sat and dined and drank fine wine.

Some of the men took Malay wives, as advised by Mr. Rennie. Others engaged in 'cavorting' as they could, although the strictures of the Mahometan faith made this difficult. Beckwith tended to sit in his room, which now resembled his cabin on the ship, and read, or think, most of the time lost in his deep philosophical ruminations. I managed finally to settle into my room, which was one room away from the one occupied by Crabbe and Audrey, whose nighttime sounds sometimes came through the wall to me. But when

I was able to sleep, my mind tumid with the words I had read from Tacitus, or Plutarch, or Homer, those words would stretch out in my vision and turn into a gray smoke out of which the ghost of Pekau would emerge, and we engaged in that activity as we had, and I began to anticipate this when the desire for such relief came upon me.

In the year 1802 a development took place that woke me from years of a strange slumber paced by book pages and fish wriggling on spears, and perspiration. A man visiting Mr. Rennie told a story of a special wood grown in abundance in the Sandwich Islands, called Sandalwood. A picul of this material, which is about one hundred thirty-three pounds, was worth much to the Chinese, and a shipload would bring a fortune. There was a good deal of it in the islands, the man said, and he was considering fitting out a ship to collect it.

I did not know what tree he referred to, unless it was the tree of the fragrant wood we called 'iliahi. If it were true that this wood was valuable to the Chinese, then I could assume that ships would be going in that direction to collect it. The man described its uses to the Chinese: incense, perfume, boxes, combs and the like.

I discussed this with Dick Burrows, who said he was ready to leave. Batavia was not his country, and he felt as if he was constantly and subtly rotting, unable, he said, to sit and discuss whatnot all day and then eat and sleep. "I don't read much of anything, and I don't talk much," he said, "so when you're ready, I'm ready."

And when it became known to Beckwith and the others that we planned this journey, he and the rest began treating us with a peculiar deference, as if once we left, we would never be seen again. I felt saddened by this, for those men were my benefactors, and the prospect of never seeing them again kept me awake at night. But Owen Bew was helpful in that, one day as I sat at the edge of the still water, he approached and sat down next to me. "My boy," he said, "it is appropriate that you intend to return to your world, as it is appropriate for Dick, too. You've a place to go. We don't." He leaned back, looked ruefully at *The Tiburon* that now sported drying clothes belonging to the Malays. "Our sailing days are over it appears, because we can't raise 'er from the dead, now can we?" He laughed. "Well, me kitchen's in the 'ouse now, and it's a right proper one too, and the Malays are good folks. Roger's done a capital job of overseeing our shares, to the point that we sh'll never want for anything again." He patted me on the shoulder. "But we'll miss ye." He thought a moment. "And it'll be safe now, because of the treaty between England and France. Likely you'll go on an English ship."

"So you'll keep an eye on Roger for us, eh?" I said. "Keep him from taking any bait?"

"Aye, we'll do that," he said.

Rennie identified the ship as *The Ramsgate*, docked at Batavia and fitting out to go to the Sandwich Islands. Burrows and I would become mere passengers, our ways paid in full, but we would also be asked to participate in some of the work should we be needed. We had only to make our way to the Batavia port to get on the ship on the appointed day. As for our shares, we were warned that were we to carry any coin that made enough noise to attract attention, we might end up dead. For myself, I did not at the time have much of a sense of money, and so I said that I would not need my share, that Beckwith, or rather Captain Brown, could hold it for me should I return. The sandalwood, after all, would be coming back this way, and I had no clear idea of how things would be in my world. Dick Burrows slid gold coins into a vest he wore, and sewed them in place, and also informed Brown that the rest could be held for him should he return.

And so came that day when Dick Burrows and myself, standing on the shore and waiting for a small Malay skiff to take us out to a sailing junk that would make its way to Batavia port, bade goodbye to the men. There is little to say about this parting except for the odd atmosphere of things as the little boat made its way toward us. Will Kelsey, Crabbe and Audrey, Owen Bew, Beckwith, and behind him the gentlement of leisure, stood and regarded us with thoughtful nods, level stares that signified perhaps committing our visages into memory, the clearing of a few throats and finally a hesitant handshake from each. Beckwith seemed thoughtful and sad, as if imagining our fates out there upon the water, and finally said, "We sh'll be here, lads, should you wish to return. And Pono, I'm afraid that the only gift I could give you will be too heavy to carry."

"I have committed the majority of the encyclopedia to memory, sir," I said. "All the way to Zygophyllum, which has a corolla of five leaves."

"Ar," Will Kelsey said, and laughed.

"And there are eight species," I said, "none of them natives of Britain."

"Aye, so we shan't go there to find them then, lads," Beckwith said.

I remember sitting in the skiff looking back, now at three figures, Will Kelsey, Owen Bew and Roger Beckwith, the latter holding his hand up in a hesitant wave just as the skiff made a turn and the mangrove along the shore blocked them from view.

There is little else to say about the voyage itself. I felt somewhat stunned by the parting, wondering how it was that friendships are forged and then for different reasons broken forever. Dick Burrows was quiet, too, and when I looked at him, still hale and quite vigorous appearing, I detected the same brooding sadness. He had spent more years with the crew than I had, and I am sure that he was thinking about this parting with the same sort of melancholy doubt that I felt. But we were to sail, and not twenty four hours after we left the men, we stood on the deck of a large, recently built merchant called *The Ramsgate*, and looked up as the sails shuddered and then popped, filling with wind.

§

Mrs. Searle's forays into the slum had extended themselves farther toward the east, where there were, she said, a less dense collection of huts and some adobe houses, lived in by some natives and also by families made up of sailors and their native wives and half-caste children. Usually the women were alone because their husbands were at sea, or unfortunately dissipating at the harbor. These houses dotted hillsides, some of them up mountain flanks and hidden in amongst brush and trees. Half of her labor was walking, she said. I volunteered to accompany her, but she declined, saying that I had the project of recording Pono's tale, and she would not want to be responsible for any interruption in that. This made me wonder, for she was advancing inland toward the very area Pono seemed to return to each evening after our recording of his narrative was done.

Indeed my curiosity about Pono had seasoned, because of the melancholy nature of much of the latter part of his narrative. Earlier I had wondered where he lived, and if the somewhat lusty nature of his youth remained with him in his older age, for as I have said, he was well-proportioned and youthful for a man his age. Now I beheld a man who seemed baffled by the turns of his life, and I suppose my curiosity about his current personal life had abated. The poor man, to have lost so much. But he had told us that the end of his narrative was nearing, and we were at the year 1804, the year of his return.

MacFarlane and I had some time before Pono's arrival, so we went to one of the stores in the port town, this one operated by the Marshall and Wildes Company. MacFarlane needed more ledger-books. Other ships had come in during the past few days, and so the lingering smell of mass inebriation hung in the air about the dirty grog shops. In the very alleyway where I had seen that old sailor and the young girl the first day I was there, we saw two sailors sleeping in filth, one of them having wet his pantaloons like a child. We went on.

"Well," MacFarlane said, "this is the way it is here, and I feel fortunate that I live some distance away."

"Your girl is well then?" I asked. "She has recovered altogether?"

"Yes," he said. "I don't know what I'd have done if she had died." We continued walking, noting activity at the water, cutters coming in with sailors sitting on the planks, small barges being unloaded onto the dirt fronting low warehouses. This time of the morning was usually somewhat quiet but for the sounds of port activity, almost pleasant but for the red dust raised by the wind and the dry, arid appearance of the place. The brothels were quiet, the grog shops open but containing little more than men slumped over tables and operators moving behind the planks that separated them from the rabble of drinkers by night, and provided them something to lean on by day.

"Look there," MacFarlane said, pointing. We saw Pono, standing on the shore watching the cutters come in. "He's early," MacFarlane went on. "Asking about this 'Iolana, I suppose."

"Yes," I said. "I suppose he'll do that the rest of his life, poor man."

"Well, let's just go buy those ledgers," MacFarlane said.

"If you would," I said, "I'd like to stay and watch, wait for him in case he misses us. I'll wait here."

"Yes," MacFarlane said. "I'll be but a minute or two."

MacFarlane went on toward the store. I stood back a bit, finding shadow in a hut overhang, and waited. Pono stood there watching the cutter come in, and when it did, he helped pull it to the wooden platform that allowed the men to step up on land, the cutter sitting in calm, filthy water with all manner of garbage floating on top. The men jumped up onto land, other men throwing sacks after them, which they caught, and after brief thanks, goodbyes and the like, they dispersed one by one into the port town. One of the last climbed out, an older man, and Pono stopped to talk to him. I imagined that he was asking where the man's ship had been, was there ever in his recollection a Pekau mentioned? I wondered how many times he had asked strangers this question, and then realized that he was probably also asking about a man named 'Iolana. In any case the two men talked for some time, in fact until MacFarlane returned with his ledgers.

"I wonder," he said, looking at them. "D'you think the man has information of interest to him?"

"I don't know," I said, "but here he comes." Pono had finished talking to the man, and they parted, the man making his way in a rather fast march straight inland, while Pono watched. Then Pono turned to make his way toward our meeting place, saw us and waved, and then approached. "Ah, you've bought more ledgers," he said. "So, we shall continue." He appeared in good spirits.

"Did the man have information for you?" I asked.

He seemed momentarily distracted. "Information?" he said. "Why, no."

"Oh," I said. "I had thought you'd been asking about this 'Iolana."

"Yes, well, I suppose I should have," he said, his formerly chipper mood now darkening somewhat. "Although I'm not certain that I'll appreciate the results." He nodded gravely. "Well then, shall we go?" he said.

23.

*O*ur return voyage was uneventful, the captain and crew well experienced in crossings of the Great Ocean. In my nighttime ruminations, I began again to conceive of that mountainside that was once my home, and increasingly, I convinced myself that I should go there first, to see if anyone might have heard of a Pekau or a Manomano. People went from island to island, traveled and went home again. What if someone had traveled to another island and found Pekau, then returned to that mountain? In addition, my sister and Konapiliahi, and their children, were still there, and I hoped, still alive.

I discussed this with Dick Burrows, and because he had always been amiable and helpful, in fact my closest friend, he agreed that if I wished, he would like to accompany me, to return to that place that he had once enjoyed so much. He was a realist, however, and speculated that given the long period of time that had passed, the girl Lana would not be there, was dead perhaps, but as he put it, "Got to make up a reason for doing anything, I reckon."

The captain was going to Molokaʻi, he told us. The problem with this new sandalwood trade was that the Americans had made a place for themselves on the northwesternmost island, Kauaʻi, and others claimed the island of the seat of government, Oʻahu, and the other two larger islands were likely now occupied, agreements already made between the natives and the merchants. His information was that this smaller island, which was lush and high, would have an abundance of sandalwood, and the plan was to try to establish a base there, and fill the Ramsgate's hold with this wood. And yes, he had men familiar with the islands, men capable of forging agreements with chiefs. He had already sent them six months earlier, two sailors and a Sandwicher. The Sandwicher, he said, was a native of the islands who had sailed with his crew for years.

We approached the captain about the question of our being allowed to get off the ship on Oʻahu's western shore, and businessman that he was, he asked that we compensate his company for the time necessary to do this, for according to his charts, this would require diverting the ship from its route. Dick Burrows settled the matter with a few gold coins called escudos.

And so it was that we passed the high island of Kauaʻi, and under fair skies, made our way toward my island. Not two hours after passing the first island, so that behind us it had begun to recede into a salt mist, the broad shape of Oʻahu emerged likewise. By the charts I knew we were approaching the very point, and mountain flank, that was once my home, and I understood the risk this involved, for Muapo was the chief of the area. The last time I had seen him was more than thirteen years earlier, when he sent me to Maui with ʻIolana, Kuaʻi, and the others. It seemed to me a lifetime, those years, and I began wondering about Laka, Konapiliahi, and those mountain people who had taken us in. Was Kaʻawela still alive? I doubted this, for he had been quite old when we had last been here.

Dick Burrows and I, both of us heavily laden with all our possessions, stepped off the cutter onto rocks below the very shelf Beckwith had rescued me from eighteen years earlier. It was late in the day, the sun a couple hours above the horizon. We bade goodbye to the temporary acquaintances we had made on the ship, and made our way up toward the path that ran along the shoreline. There was, however, no path. Because it was late spring, the mountainside was verdant, the rocks above shining with water in places, the stream whose water we had drunk hiding somewhere under hardy grasses. "Not a soul around," Dick Burrows said, adjusting his pack and staring up the mountain. He slid his musket out of straps on his pack, and looked back at the cutter making its way back to *The Ramsgate*. "You suppose there's anybody about? Don't look at all like country crossed by many."

"We have been seen," I said.

"Well, then I'll just keep my musket at the ready then," he said.

"I would have thought canoes would come once the ship was seen," I said. It seemed odd then, as if there were no people on the island. "But we can wait here."

An hour passed as we looked left and right, and up the mountain. A soft rain blew off the mountaintop and made the leaves of the bushes and grasses slick and bright. As usual, Dick Burrows said little, perhaps three sentences: "Well, now this is weather I like," and ten minutes later, "Was all right, us fishing there in Batavia, and I'm gonna fish here," and perhaps a half an hour later, "You suppose they still have their little huts up there in them ravines?"

"I hope so," I said

Then, far to the north, on the opposite side from the point at which we had piled our rocks, we saw moving figures, children, and then, following them, slow moving men, three of them. The children ran toward us and then stopped and ran back, then ran toward us. "H'm," Dick Burrows said. "Don't see much in the way of a threat there."

One of the old men ordered the children back. He was thin and wizened, and it took me some time to recognize him: Kaʻawela, using a long stick to support himself. I stood up and approached him, and when he saw me, he smiled and nodded.

"So you have returned, Pono," he said.

"Yes. Tell me of the past years," I said.

"Is that Kiko?" he asked. Kiko was very likely the name they had given Dick Burrows, although under the circumstances of our departure the last time we were here, I would not have known.

"Yes, it is," I said.

"You both look well," he said, and then thought, turning the stick in the earth. "You do not appear ill. Are you?"

"No," I said. "We are both in good health."

"Very well," he said. "You shall come with us. We are very much afraid of the sicknesses. We remain here and avoid them."

And so Dick Burrows and I were led by the old man up a ravine, through lush growths of grasses and bushes, and higher up, kalo and ʻuala patches. The children ran ahead, apparently announcing to those up on the mountain shelves, that we were on our way. At length we arrived at one of those shelves, perhaps fifty feet by fifty feet, and those waiting were younger women, old women, and more children.

Where, I wondered, were the men? Those who greeted us knew who we were, for the older women seemed amiable and not the least bit afraid or shy about us. I did not recognize any of them. We were commanded to sit by a small fire, and the few younger women there set about preparing food, while Kaʻawela watched, and spoke to some of them. Then he sat across the fire from us.

"Pono," he said, "these are troubled times. I see by the expression on your face that you wonder where the men are."

"Yes," I said.

"Please inform Kiko that I am sorry I cannot speak your haole language."

I did so, but Dick Burrows had a strange expression on his face. He was not listening. He was staring across the space at the women preparing the food, his mouth open, his face crossed with a look of amazed wonder.

"Is something wrong?" I asked him.

"I— No, nothin'," he said. But he still looked away.

I turned back to Kaʻawela. "Where are the men?"

"Either at sea or in Waikīkī," he said. "Many of our young men have gone away on the haole ships. They do not come back. The other men have gone to wait for the command to attack Kauaʻi."

Kaʻawela leaned back in thought. He picked up a stick and stirred the fire, then looked toward the ocean, above which hung the sun. "The great warrior is not satisfied," he said. "Kamehameha took all the islands but that last one, whose chief was a boy but sixteen years of age, Kaumualiʻi. Years ago he raised a great army and in a fleet of a thousand canoes went off toward Kauaʻi, that thorn in his foot that reminded him every step he took that it was there and did not belong to him, that thorn assailing him even as he rose in the middle of the night to relieve himself in the echoes of a laughing boy chief, and he vowed to go there and pull the thorn by slaughtering those who refused to give themselves to his rule, but a great storm blew across the ocean and overturned many of his war canoes, and drove him and his army back to Oʻahu. He was shamed by the gods. It was as if all the powers he did not own were laughing, the powers of chance, death, nature's whimsical ridicule. All of them, and he returned with the thorn buried in his foot, and so it has remained there these years, festering and reminding him that he was not the ruler of this world." Kaʻawela did then turn and look at the women, as if wondering what was taking them so long. I turned to Dick Burrows, who had moved back, almost as if afraid of what he was seeing.

"Dick, are you well?" I asked.

"I'm fine," he said. "Pono, ask him—"

"He shall return," Kaʻawela went on. "He has raised another army, greater even than the one the gods ridiculed. There are more than a thousand canoes in Waikīkī. Every man capable has gone to join him in this. Muapo and his warriors have gone. They wait for the right signs, for fair weather and good dreams. They have been encamped there on the beach for two weeks now, engaged in games and revelry, in preparation and in waiting for the last of the warriors to arrive. I believe they will make their way over the water within a week."

In the silence following this, I looked once again at Dick Burrows, and he remained staring. "Dick?" I said. "A moment ago you had a request."

"Request," he said. "Pono, ask him about that girl over there. The one with the bowl." I looked. At first I thought she was a child, but upon closer study, I saw that she was a smaller woman. She was softening poi with her hand, the bowl braced against her hip, the orange light of a slowly dropping sun illuminating her skin.

"Kaʻawela," I said. "Kiko would like to know who the small woman with the bowl is."

"Ah," he said. "She is my granddaughter. Her husband is dead, and she is now twenty-four. She is shy."

I turned to Dick Burrows, to see that he was not there. He had risen, and was standing off from the fire, apparently to prevent it from intruding upon his view of the woman. He placed his hand upon his head, and then looked at me. "Kuchik," he said.

"Her name is Haulani," Ka'awela said. "What word did Kiko use?"

"I do not know," I said. I rose from the fire, but Dick had made his way around it toward the women. When the little woman with the bowl saw him approaching she came out with a small gasp and moved away toward some bushes, her hand still working the poi. Dick was left there, staring at her as she kept her distance from him, her hand still vigorously working the poi, animating her upper body somewhat pleasingly.

I made my way to Dick, who stood there with the most befuddled look I had ever seen him bear. "What was the word you used?" I asked.

"Kuchik," he said. "It's part of a Tuscarora word that means bluebird." He looked at the woman, who was now in the shadows by the bushes. "My girl was Kuchik. She looks so much like Kuchik that—" He did not continue.

"Shall I ask Ka'awela if he would consent to your meeting her?" I asked. He looked at me, considering this.

"If you could," he said.

So as we ate, the women watching from a distance in deference to the old kapu, Dick seemed unable to take his eyes off her, and did not eat with his usual vigor. Ka'awela was amused. "He is smitten," he whispered to me. "I recall him with a girl named Lana, who is now dead. But apparently he has forgotten her."

"It appears so," I said.

"And the poor girl," he went on. "She hides and remains shy. When we are finished I shall call her over."

And so my friend Dick Burrows had his attention consumed by this little woman, and I turned again to Ka'awela. "If Muapo went to join the army, I assume his warriors went too, including a man named Konapiliahi."

"We know him," he said. "We have known Konapiliahi from the rock-carrying days. He is a great warrior and frightening to behold, but he is a kind man. He has been good to us. If Muapo went, Konapiliahi went with him."

"He is my sister's husband," I said.

"Ah," Ka'awela said. "And you would like to know of your sister. Do you know where she is?"

"No," I said. "It has been many years. I know she had four children, but they would all be grown now."

"If they are boys, they are with Konapiliahi," he said. He stared into the fire, thinking. "This is a troubling thing," he said. "Kamehameha will not be satisfied until he wins Kaua'i. There is much strife ahead of us."

"I must go to Konapiliahi," I said. "What is left of my family is with him. Dick shall not go with me." I turned to look at him. The woman named Haulani sat facing him, her hands hidden in the folds of her pa'u. Dick appeared very shy too, looking at her and then looking away. It appeared quite awkward, and I smiled, glad that he had found something worth living for in my world. The sun had begun to set, the sky above the horizon orange.

So it was that on the following morning, I stripped myself of my haole clothes, and borrowed an 'ihe from old Ka'awela, and set out for Waikīkī. I left my musket with Dick Burrows, because it would be too much a prize for others to ignore. Ka'awela told me that I would not be molested on the way, for all people knew that if a warrior should be seen walking, that warrior was on his way to join the great army. He told me that I would have no difficulty seeing the shoreline, even from a great distance, for the thousands of war canoes would darken the beaches. These would be a fleet of peleleu canoes, or canoes that have double hulls, or are larger and wider than fishing canoes. The great warrior had spent some time having them built, and even as I stood there bidding goodbye to Ka'awela and Dick Burrows, they were amassing more.

Because I was well rested, and had eaten well, the walk was in ways pleasant. I passed our rock depositing area, and from there made my way across the hot, dry plains of Ewa, and stopped from time to time to rest, and to stand in the water to cool my feet. The 'ihe in my hand was old, the barbs dulled and the wood smooth with the oil of the hands of men now long gone. The possession of this weapon made me remember much of the old times, and I wondered how it was, with all the things I had seen, that it still was with me, after all these years. I also had a large water-gourd, unnecessary I thought, but Ka'awela had warned me of the heat on the great plain of Ewa. Those I saw along the way were women and children and old people, all of whom called out 'Aloha' and waved. By just after mid-day, I made my way inland to pass around the great marshes to the place that would later become this port town. In fact, when I walked up on one bluff, I had a view of the area and saw a cluster of buildings, and in the harbor, a haole ship. I made my way around that area, and from there, waded across streams and climbed bluffs until in the distance I could see the beach in the waning sun darkened by many canoes, and the undulating, baking mass of bodies of men.

So I continued walking, thinking that once again, men were to fight because a warrior chief was not satisfied with what he had. If I were to go to Kaua'i with Konapiliahi, would we engage in a battle such as the one I had experienced on Maui and end up routed and running for our lives? I did not know. And did it matter? That I didn't know either. Perhaps I was cursed from birth to be a witness to all the horrors of our world, and would once again be a witness. Perhaps this was my last journey, for in the battle I might be killed. But I kept walking, for it seemed to me that there was no other way for me to live but to accept what was before me.

The first warriors I encountered were swimming in the shallow water, talking amongst themselves, and were gleeful and did not remark my passing except to ask whom I was associated with. "I am going to find my brother Konapiliahi," I said. None of them knew of a Konapiliahi, so I continued walking, now along a long stretch of beach sparsely dotted with the encampments of warriors, none of whom manifested any suspicion of me. They were eating, sleeping, they were relieving themselves in the sand high up from the beach. Women and children were there, tenders of the food, and attached in one way or another with the warriors.

In the waning light, I became fatigued, my legs sore from walking through the sand. I thought it best to stop, perhaps sleep and try to find Konapiliahi in the morning, but I was afraid also that the great warrior might launch his army before I could find him. I pressed on, now along a beach that curved inland somewhat, to a stream that went into the ocean, across which I waded. I was now in an area more crowded with warriors, their dark, slick bodies illuminated by the fading sun, the smells of food and excrement and smoke strong, the sounds of wood clacking on wood coming from before me and behind as those men practiced their fighting.

But upon approaching the area called Waikīkī, I was amazed at the number of warriors gathered. Far in the distance I saw the kahili of the ali'i, and before me, the crowd of men was so dense that I could see no sand but that over which water swept. There were many women and children there, old men, and on the sand beyond the warriors I saw hundreds upon hundreds of large canoes. I believe that there were more than ten thousand warriors on that beach, and perhaps thousands of others serving them, children running around as if all of the gathering were a great Makahiki celebration. Sounds blended, the surf hissing on the shore and the gabble of a thousand voices, the fading orange light playing over those bodies, the rich odor of human flesh, all of it reducing my perception into the sensation of a strange dream.

I pressed on, toward the distant kahili hovering above this mass of flesh. I believe I would never have found Konapiliahi if he had not found me, but

I heard my name called from high up on the beach, turned to look, and saw him standing there with a small group of warriors, separated somewhat from the rest. I went up the sand and greeted him in the old way, face-to-face, and said, "It has been long. I am glad I found you."

"Come with me," Konapiliahi said. I was startled at how old he looked, shriveled, so that he seemed shorter, his blue side now faded somewhat into a great bruise, his hair gray and his skin mottled and flaccid.

He drew me to a fire, one of many, for the sky had darkened. There he told me to sit, and he sat on the other side. He leaned back and looked around, somewhat gleefully. "Ah," he said. "One last battle perhaps. The chiefs are over there." He pointed toward the kahili. "Their haole advisors are with them."

"Tell me of Laka," I said.

"Laka died three years ago," he said, shaking his head. He stared at the ocean, and sighed. "And I thought you had, too," he said. "You have been gone so long."

"And her children?"

He turned, and looked down toward the water. "There," he said, smiling. Two very large warriors were at the moment wrestling, laughing as they did so, watched by boys and young women. "They are Kiamo and Maunanui," Konapiliahi said. "My sons. The girls remain at home with the children."

"Ah, you have grandchildren then," I said.

"Yes," he said. "If those two louts down there knew their uncle was here, they would come. But look," he said, gazing proudly at them, "are they not fine young men?"

"Indeed," I said.

"They have no time for us," he went on. "They have time for young women and for fighting only."

I watched them for a few moments. It struck me how strong and clean they appeared, and it reminded me of the loss of my own children, and I wondered, why was it that this enterprise was conceived? Barring some unforeseen disaster, they might go on to father many like themselves. All that stood in the way was an event such as this, wherein they would gleefully take their weapons and face other young men who were strong and clean. Konapiliahi then seemed irritated by their play, and called them over. "They will want to hear of your travels," he said, and put his hand on his stomach. "Ah, I have eaten too much," he said.

And so we spent much of the evening sitting at that fire, these strong young men suddenly deferential and seemingly awed by my presence, and then by the stories I told. They wanted particularly to know of the world outside of the one they knew, wanted to know about haoles and muskets and cannons and great ships. They offered me food, which I ate, and water, which I declined, holding up the large gourd I carried and telling them that I was intent upon lessening its weight. All along the grass line above the sand the women had suspended water gourds for the warriors, who went and cupped it out of these gourds to their mouths. There was food in such abundance that I thought it unlikely that these men could eat it all, but eat it they did. The night wore on, and these sturdy boys did not want me to stop talking, and so I talked. They were my nephews, my blood, and I thought while I talked that after all there was a family for me to come home to, although I had not met my nephews until this evening.

At length even these boys grew tired, and Konapiliahi, who had complained of a fit in his stomach, had retired and was already snoring on a mat on the sand. I was so fatigued that I found it easy to sleep there next to him, lying in the sand, and I remember hearing the moaning later in the night, some warriors toward the east of us apparently ill, and thought nothing of it. I was awakened a little later, for the moans had increased, and I sat up and looked in that pale moonlight, and saw men bent over and holding their bellies, others going down to the water moaning and cursing, others yet squatting in the sand and running out watery, stinking waste. I lay back down, thinking that these men simply were experiencing fits in their bowels.

But by the first faint light of the dawning of a beautiful day, the illumination of the clouds wondrous in their hues, I saw that more were thus afflicted, and turned to see Konapiliahi moaning, his sons farther back in the bushes retching and moaning, and all along the beach men were hunched down and gripping their knees and rocking back and forth with some terrible pain. Konapiliahi lay down on his side, and I reached out to touch him, comfort him perhaps, and his skin was hot, perspiration making it glisten, and his face was drawn with pain. "Can I help?" I said, sitting up. He did not respond. I got up and went to his sons, but they were lost in their misery, so I made my way farther toward the women, and as the light intensified, I saw them, too, hunched over and holding their knees to their chests, and little children vomiting and crying out in pain. I turned and went down to the sand, toward the water, where men were floating there and moaning and crying out.

Others who were not ill wandered through those lying in pain on the sand talking to one another and gesturing, and I went to a warrior and said, "What is it? Are there sick ones behind you, too?"

"Many," he said. "What has happened?"

"Something in the food?" I asked. "Perhaps we should not eat the food. Or the water. Perhaps it is the water."

"I have water," he said. "I brought it from Makiki."

It occurred to me that I had my own water too. Was there some poison in the water gourds? Then I thought of the great chief, and could see, in the distance, that kahili marking his place. I returned to Konapiliahi. Perhaps this affliction would pass, that all the men would feel well later. But as the morning wore on, the sun coming up and bathing all the sick men in a bright light, I saw that indeed their conditions were worsening. Konapiliahi experienced first a fever that made him frightfully hot, and then would lapse into chills, and from time to time I tried to comfort him by rubbing water on his forehead, but he continued moaning, and then coughing and retching, and waved me away as if my ministrations were hurting him. His sons had gone inland to be watched over by women who were not ill, and I went up the sand to ask after them. They were lying on mats and moaning, the women fanning them.

I went back to Konapiliahi. I sat with him through the late morning as he went through his fever and then his chills and his moaning. As the sun went over and sent its heat down on him, I pulled him farther up the sand into the shade of a palm tree, and he seemed to feel better there, for he seemed then to sleep.

On the beach the men who were not sick tended to those who were, trying to cover them with mats from the burning sun, and pouring gourds of ocean water on them. Other men erected a series of small tents using sleeping mats and had dragged the sick into their shade. I helped these men, and tried also to help the women inland, but those who were not sick sent me back to help on the beach. Konapiliahi's sickness worsened. By late afternoon the skin on the brown side of his body began to bloom with reddish blotches that darkened, as if eruptions of blood had made their way to the surface, and his breathing became labored, and then light. I thought he was becoming cold again, although the dreadful dark hue of his skin seemed to suggest that he was cooking from the inside.

I thought that perhaps the decline of the day's heat would help, and as the sun dropped behind clouds to the west and the breeze cooled, I put my hand once again on Konapiliahi's head, and it was not as hot as before. This, I thought, was a good sign, and before that day ended, I got up from the sand to walk in the direction of the great chief's kahili, to see if a kahuna lapaʻau might suggest a remedy for this. I went perhaps two hundred paces along the beach, and saw an old man walking amongst men lying in the sand, and he was moaning, but not from the sickness. Rather it was from what he saw: that some of the men in the sand were dead, their bodies blackened. "Auwē!" he called out. "It has come true."

I approached the man. "Makua," I said, "what is happening?"

He looked at me. "Not sick?" he asked.

"No, I am not sick," I said.

"A seer warned him of this. The seer said pestilence awaited him if he gathered this army."

"Awaited whom, might I ask?" I said.

"Kamehameha," he said. "Lonohelemoa warned him."

He went on, looking down at the prone warriors. I did not know who Lonohelemoa was, but I was left standing there in the faint light of dusk before a man lying on his back in the sand, his skin almost black, his eyes dulled and his teeth bared. Flies sat on his eyes and mouth, and his malo was wet and stinking.

I thought I should drag the body somewhere, but where? It seemed horrible that the poor man should lie there at the mercy of flies. I looked around, and noted that there were others lying dead in the sand. I pressed on toward the yellow and red kahili, thinking that perhaps this affliction was limited to the area I was in, but the farther I went, the more I recognized that the affliction was the same, in fact, possibly even worse than where I was, somewhat at the fringes of this great gathering of men. Everywhere there was moaning, there were men hunched down in the sand, others tending to them, and when I got closer to the kahili, warriors with spears held them up, indicating that I should not proceed. I wanted to ask them about the great chief, but decided not to, and turned back. Darkness would be upon us soon, and I thought that with the cooler air, there might be some hope for Konapiliahi and my nephews. I went back and sat with him.

In the middle of the night I was aware of being hungry and thirsty, and slaked my thirst with my gourd, but decided against eating anything. I felt Konapiliahi's shoulder, and once again it was hot, but he seemed more comfortable than before. Then sometime shortly before dawn, he began retching and coughing, and writhing as if he could not get his breath. He was able to look at me, his eyes both dull and at the same time thoughtful and wondering. "Pono," he whispered, gasping and then getting his breath. "It has come." Then he began again to cough, and to retch as if unable to purge something from his throat. This movement changed into a long shudder followed by a wheezing sigh, and then he was still. I rolled him over to see if I could help, but he had died.

I sat in the moonlight. I thought of his sons back there in the darkness, tended by the women, and wondered how they were. I thought of the gods that looked down over our doings, I thought of our mythic protectors, and remembered also the haoles and their god, and their prayers to that god. I believe I was too benumbed by what had happened in such a short time that I did not know what to do. All I could think was that I should not eat any food here, and I should not drink any water but that I had brought with me. This would have been Owen Bew's warning.

I think it was caused by the fatigue, but not knowing what to do, and sitting there next to my dead brother, I lay back and drifted once again into a troubled sleep. And in that sleep I heard the voice I had waited to hear for eighteen years, and if it was a dream, I was in that dream like an awed and captivated child as the voice said to me, "You the father of my blood have lived these years to witness my troubled visions. I told you that I saw the shape of your future, long ago. You have seen much and you are seeing more as I speak. I come to you from the mouth of your dead brother lying next to you, I come out of the land of Milu to whisper to you through his dead lips. You are witnessing the sliding way of death, of the people of our world dying away. This has been your burden and shall remain your burden. I cannot lessen this burden, for I am without power in the land of Milu. I have watched you in silence all these years and continue to watch, you the father of my blood. I can say nothing more but for one thing: she is not here."

I woke to the coming of dawn, and the sounds of moaning. I found myself laughing just a bit, not out of any feeling of jocularity but rather because of what I saw just then as the hopeful workings of my mind. Will Kelsey would call it 'a figment'. I had manufactured for myself an explanation, and at the end, in the voice I had created in my dream, for Roger Beckwith had told me this too, I had held open for myself some small hope that the dead Pekau was alive, and that, because of this 'figment' I had a reason to go on with my existence. Was there, finally, any point in my being a witness to all this? I didn't know. I had been spared so many times that it seemed as if this forceful evidence of some providential reasoning behind fate's exercise of my life had indeed endowed it with a reason. I looked at the lightening sky, the pink and yellow dawn showing over the great crater of Leahi, and thought that if there was any reason now to move, it was to try to help those who were now producing the moaning that had awakened me.

I pulled Konapiliahi's mat from under him and covered his darkened and stiffening corpse. I paused, and put my hand on his cold cheek, and drew it away, leaving dents where my fingers had been. I drank water. I then walked out onto the beach to see it littered with corpses, the wind having piled small dunes of sand around them. The breeze was heavy with the odor of excrement and the faint smells of food. To the east the sunrise over Leahi was grand, the huge clouds' bellies illuminated to a nearly blinding white. In the distance I saw men walking amongst the bodies, others away from the sand in the grasses helping those still hunched over and moaning. There were many men there, and it was apparent that those still alive had been moved up into the brushy areas to keep them out of the wind. But for the moaning it was strangely quiet, the hissing of water on the sand as it had always been, and I saw that many of the men not sick had fled, had left the death behind them, and even the larger grouping of warriors under the kahili, which was still there in the darkness under the shadow of Leahi, had been reduced to but a few figures moving about.

I turned and went back past Konapiliahi's body and into the brush where his sons were lying the night before. I found one corpse, covered by a stained mat, beyond that corpse the corpse of a woman. One of the brothers had died, and the other may have been taken farther inland. I walked inland, over baking dunes and rocks, toward the marsh that lay between the ocean and the valleys beyond. There was nothing there, so I turned to go back, this time at an angle toward the kahili. Perhaps I could help, I thought, either with the living, or perhaps with the disposal of the dead. Those bodies on the beach would begin to rot, and it was so much an insult to the many spirits represented in them, their mana, that it had to be avoided, if possible. In the distance, as I walked over the dry and barren landscape toward the beach, I saw many men, apparently tending to those bodies. I started to go to them when I heard whimpering to my left. The sound was faint, perhaps someone dying, so I waited until I heard it again and then followed the sound, to find the darkened and swollen bodies of two women, and sitting in the meager shade of a bush, a naked girl of perhaps six years, staring up at me with large, stunned eyes. "Child," I said, "come with me."

She ignored the order. I leaned down to look at her, to see if perhaps she was sick and dying, but she was not. She looked slightly different from the children of my world. She was a half-caste child. Leaning over and looking at her, I was aware of the fecal stench coming from the two corpses, and held my hand out. "This is no place for you," I said. "Come with me."

At length she crawled out of that shade, and I took her hand. When I first held her hand, I began to tremble, and to hold my breath, and I looked down at her, at her eyes. I stared at her face for some time, captured in a mute wonder. I suppose this was because she was alive, and that she was alive seemed a strange dream. I thought it best to take her back to where I had slept, and so I did, and had her sit in the shade of a bush just a few paces from Konapiliahi's body. "Listen to me," I said. "I am going to help over there," and I pointed in the direction of the kahili. "I want you to remain here until I am finished." I picked up the water gourd. "Drink water," I said. "This water is from another place, so it will not sicken you." I pulled the plug, and awkwardly, she drank, and then looked up at me with that same look of stunned wonder I had first seen. "I shall take you to people who will take care of you, but you must remain here while I help the men over there. Can you do that?"

"Ae," she said.

I paused before leaving her. I found myself nearly breathless with wonder, seeing myself standing there staring at this child, born of my people's blood and the blood of others, sitting naked in this great wasteland of death. I found it difficult to force myself to move, to go on to the next voluntary act in my life. At length I took a breath, let it out, and turned away from her.

I made my way along the sand past the blackened bodies toward the kahili. This time, no warriors barred my way. They were pulling bodies inland, and I walked up over a dune and looked, and saw hundreds of bodies, all of them dark and baking in the morning heat, the smell of excrement and death strong in the breeze, and beyond, men rocking in their pain and lying on mats, others tending to them. Closer, I saw an old man sitting on his knees, who slammed the upper part of his body on the ground, his face into a stone, and then he looked up at me, his bloody mouth in an anguished, gasping misery. "My sons!" he said, the blood dripping from his lips. "Auwē! My sons!"

I could not comfort him in his grief. I went instead to talk to the men who were not sick. They were discussing digging pits for the disposal of the dead. One turned to me. "You are not sick," he said.

"I am not. I am here to help," I said. "I want to ask you first, about food and water."

"We will not drink it or eat it," he said. "Men have gone east to the reefs to fish, others have gone for niu, others for mai'a. We will not drink this water. It is poisoned."

"I shall help, then," I said.

I stayed there more than two weeks. I was able to secure mats, a kihei, and was able also to get food from the men who had gone to fish the reefs and others who went toward the mountains. We worked in groups of four, each holding an appendage, and carried the bodies to pits others were digging. The process was unceremonious and horrific, for day by day the bodies' conditions worsened, so that the subtle movement of maggots showed around malos and in eyes and mouths, and the odor of decomposition burst forth along with clouds of flies from some we raised from the sand.

My little charge, whom I called Ka'a, because she did not tell me her name and said little, stayed where I had left her and ate the food I brought. Perhaps it was the fatigue, but I was unable to get information from her about her family, or her name, merely vague responses, and the pointing of a finger toward the mountains, and as I said, because I was working all day at the burial of the bodies and the tending of the living, those men who managed to survive the sickness. Many of them lost their hair, and were so weakened by the affliction that it seemed a miracle that they survived. In those days following the affliction, groups came from inland to look for their relatives. We were told that the affliction had affected many in the areas they came from, but not to the extent that it had on the beach where the army had gathered.

As I slept, Ka'a pulled herself close to me to avoid the cold, and in the mornings before I awoke to continue our labors, I would be aware of her sitting wrapped in her kihei watching me. At the very least, I thought, walking along toward the bodies, there was one healthy being under my care who would not die of this.

During the two weeks I was there, other waves of the sickness afflicted some of the formerly healthy, and they, too, retched, rolled themselves up into balls, burned with fever and trembled with chills, and died, while others did the same and lived, losing their hair in the process. I learned that Kamehameha had been afflicted and survived the sickness, but that the greater part of his governing group died, his counselors, priests, many of the chiefs close to him, Muapo among those mentioned. And I thought of Muapo, that fastidious, careful chief, brooding over his alliances and his enemies. He, too, had succumbed to this, and I wondered then if the voice of Manomano in my dream were truly a voice from the dead, telling me that I was witnessing the sliding way of death. As the days passed and more men curled up and died, and we dug great pits to dispose of them before they rotted, we began to see a decline in the number of people coming down with the affliction. It was apparent that it had run its course, and I thought more and more of the likelihood that those who were healthy would remain healthy, Ka'a included. Our labors continued, and at the times we thought we were close to completing those labors, a few more men would fold themselves up, burn with fever, and die.

I recall particularly the nights during which I lay there on the sand high up on the beach, and listened to the sound of the waves breaking with their endless regularity, those waves having done so for thousands of years, through many generations. When it became cold, Ka'a would shift next to me and I would put my arm over her, or a piece of clean mat, and continue listening to those breaking waves, or sit up and watch the white lines of surf expanding and then breaking up as the waves died. The solitude of these nights was not comforting, for I feared that she, too, would sicken and die, but she did not. It was both a marvel and in ways a strange, timeless and sometimes cruel mystery, I thought, that, here under my arm was this small living being, her heart beating throughout the night, those waves sweeping up on the sand, the stars making their movement through the black sky, while within a few paces of where the two of us were lying, curled up against the cold, so many had died, strong, fully grown men. Why had she survived when they did not? Why had I survived? I did not know.

The name given to this affliction was 'the squatting sickness', the exact word in my language, 'Ōku'u. As for the loss of hair experienced by those who survived, that was called po'okole, or a combination of two words: po'o, meaning head, and okole, meaning buttocks. No person I talked to could remember hearing of anything so costly. I tried to estimate in my mind how many people had died, and learned later of deaths elsewhere, the process lingering over a period of a few weeks. Of those warriors waiting on the beach to go to Kaua'i to take it from its young chief, I believe half died, perhaps five or six thousand. From what I understood of the spread of this sickness during that time in other places, the estimate might reach fifteen thousand, perhaps more.

When, at last, our work was complete, I made my preparations to return home. I was able to find a pa'u for the little girl that I washed in the ocean and had her wear. I did not know if I should take her far from her home, which I assumed was nearby, so early one morning upon bidding farewell to the men I had worked with, I took her hand and we walked to the west. When I saw people in the distance, I took her to them to ask if they knew who she was. No one did. Because the dwellings of the people were either at the shore or near the mountains, the midway areas somewhat windswept and dry, I took her toward the mountains. I asked her again what her name was, where she had come from, but she did not respond. I believe she was in a way numbed to everything. The mountain flanks seemed safer considering the sickness, and indeed I saw a more normal-appearing setting as we walked. We came upon a hale with kalo patches behind it, chickens in the yard, and stopped. An older man and woman came out, kanaka maoli, and the woman's eyes fell on the girl with a look of such motherly concern, possessiveness even, that I could not get far in my explanation before they claimed her.

The couple took the girl into their house, and I walked west, past empty houses, and then to a place where I sat and rested, sitting on a rock. A hen emerged from a bush trailed by recently hatched chicks. She saw me and walked off, the chicks bouncing along in an awkward frenzy behind her. She then found a place to scratch, her brood in attendance. I remember thinking that I needed to sit, and to breathe, and feel the presence of myself, somehow understand how exactly I was situated in this world. I was fascinated, even, at my own pausing this way. Perhaps I had read too much. Perhaps I was given to an excess of thinking, as of many of the men whose words I had read.

I watched the hen and her chicks. Konapiliahi had said it: one last battle. They had gathered, had practiced, had anticipated the clash of wood and stone, the yells of battle, but had not known that the yells would be moans, the clashes of wood on stone the quieter sound of digging pits for their remains.

From there, I made my way home. And I recall particularly that the day was fair and beautiful, great billowing clouds lining the horizon to the southwest, and a pleasant breeze at my back. I looked back a number of times toward that place of death, and then turned away from it, allowing my eyes to search outward to the distant, verdant mountains.

§

The hot breeze came through the door opening. MacFarlane tapped the point of his pen upon a blotting paper, and sat up straight. Those little disks of light played over the open ledger book, and then a group of men walked past outside, discussing shipping: "—for the present. But some kind of an increased tarrif should be—" And then I heard no more. Pono sat there lost in some recollection, I suppose.

"And your age would have been forty-four," I said.

"Yes," he said.

"I have heard various things about your peoples' history, but I have not heard of this," I said. "I wonder why. It was but twenty years ago."

"Battles, the manipulations of chiefs, and that sort of thing, are of interest to people," Pono said. "An epidemic of a fever is not something men choose to discuss at gatherings. It would seem that as yet it does not attract much attention."

"Well, I shall say it attracted mine," I said.

"Sir," Pono said, "you've helped a good deal." He nodded thoughtfully. "I would have thought you'd spend more time with the shippers here."

"I've been fascinated by all this," I said. "And besides, I've had to do a few things overseeing our work with *The Clarel*. She'll be ready to sail in a week or two, and we'll take our silver and copper to China."

"Will you come back this way?" he asked.

"I don't know," I said. "The captain, a rather imperious gentleman who believes the advice of an idler like me is useless, may choose to return to England the other way. I don't believe he wants to endure the Horn again."

MacFarlane stared at the ledger book, and then, apparently perplexed about something, began flipping the pages over from the end of it. He came to a page and stared, and then looked up at Pono. "The little girl," he said. "You said she was around six years old, a half-caste child."

"Yes," Pono said.

"And you left her at a house at the base of the mountains."

"In the Makiki area," Pono said. "I suppose I was not as observant as I might have been, so I don't know with any certainty where the place would be today."

MacFarlane nodded. "Interesting," he said. "My wife is twenty-seven. She said she was an orphan, and believed that her father was a French sailor. She said she was raised by her grandparents."

"In this area?" Pono asked.

"Yes, just up there toward the mountains. I wonder if she could be the little girl."

"It would be fitting," I said. "That is, it would be fitting that something came out to the fulfillment of some good fortune, considering the rest."

"Yes," Pono said, and then laughed ruefully. "But I believe there are many stories like this. My guess is that this is a coincidence."

"If you don't mind," MacFarlane said, "I might consider it otherwise."

Pono laughed again. "Well then, sir, that is your choice." He then raised his hands and slapped his knees lightly. "I suppose it could be as you wish. I have at times thought of this collection of islands as vast, a universe of its own, and at other times have considered it tiny, a string of landmasses in the middle of a great ocean. It is both, I suppose, and considering the latter perception of it, that little girl might be the one who became your wife. But it was after all but a simple gesture of kindness. I didn't want her wandering around that place."

"Simple gestures of kindness are not simple," MacFarlane said. "She would have died. I'm sure of it, thinking of your description."

"Perhaps," Pono said.

"I shall ask her," MacFarlane said. "Perhaps she'll remember something."

"As Matthew said earlier," Pono said, "it would be fitting, wouldn't it?"

24.

The reader of this volume will now be informed that the last words of Pono's narrative are 'verdant mountains.' It is left to a man perhaps less skilled in the art of descriptive writing to finish this narrative, in effect, for him. I shall try.

I will say first that *The Clarel* did sail to China, generally under fair skies, and that our business was done there, and from there we returned to England via the route taken by European sailors for hundreds of years, *The Clarel* laden with silks and ornate dinnerware and other things, and therefore I left those fair islands, and their multitude of personal tragedies and sorrows, never to return. As for correspondence with the young Mr. MacFarlane, whom I considered a good friend, there was none, so when I left, I saw him, too, for the last time.

I shall return, then, to that day he described the horrible epidemic. I was sitting there picturing it, again wondering why such events required storytellers such as Pono to become known, while the details of a single death, even down to the trivial, of someone like, say, Cook, seemed known by all. Men could talk for hours about the fate of Cook's body, as if the body of one man rated such extended speculation, while Pono's story of that horror on the beach rated no more than, "Indeed. So five thousand died, then. Interesting."'The answer might be that it was not our concern, and I suppose that it had become a concern to me because of all that I had come to know of his people. Strange it is that, upon first appreciating the place, one ignored its tragedies in favor of partaking of its various opportunities, generally in the form of its willing women, and I suppose no sailor I was aware of thought beyond those opportunities to a deeper appreciation of the whole of its history, except perhaps for MacFarlane.

As the capricious little spots of light upon the table moved to illuminate in their dancing patterns the front of MacFarlane's shirt, and the dirt floor behind him, we sat in our brooding ruminations for a few minutes before Pono would bid us aloha and go to whatever place he stayed. I believe he was just getting ready to go, when something occurred to me, and when I thought of it, I thought I must have had some lapse of sensibility that kept this idea in the back of my mind until now. "Pono," I said, "something has been creeping about in my mind, and I thought I should ask."

"Yes?" he said. "Please, I'll try to answer."

"Your narrative has brought us forty-four years closer to this day. You've covered, I believe, most things of importance, and the story you just finished has put us at a mere twenty years from today." He nodded, his eyebrows raised in question. "You said that your friend Dick Burrows came with you here in the year 1804, and prior to the description of the epidemic, you left him sitting with a woman named Haulani."

"Yes. Interesting that you should recall her name," he said.

"Might I ask what became of Dick Burrows?" I asked.

"Matthew," he said. "You're asking me to move ahead with the narrative, then. I have but one small offering left, in which the fate of Dick Burrows will be addressed."

"Very well, then," I said.

"And as I said, it is a small offering because for my purposes the story is done, but for my more recent sailing days, which are not dramatic in the way other things were. So," and he slapped his knees again, "we shall finish tomorrow."

We sat there a few more minutes, MacFarlane checking his ledger, and sitting up straight and stretching himself after having remained hunched over that book so long.

I looked out through the doorway at the harsh mid-day light and saw Mrs. Searle hastening in our direction. There was a purpose to her walk, her skirt clutched in her left hand while she fought the wind with her right, which held a stained parasol. This time of the day in the port town was gruesome, I should say, the drying wind raising red dust, the people hiding themselves in whatever meager shade they could find. She approached our room and let the parasol down, and then looked inside. "Good day," she said.

"Come in out of the sun," I said and rose to offer her my chair. She nodded and sat, and then settled her eyes on Pono, a look of a distracted perplexity on her face. She leaned the folded parasol against the thatch wall, and then placed her hands in her lap.

"He is at the base of Leahi," she said. "He has a sloop, and it is anchored just offshore." She sighed. "I understand that he went there because the last time he came here the sailors threw rotten fruit at him. He apparently could not prevent himself from lecturing to them, and I understand that he managed to get away before he got worse from them."

Pono thought about this. "And how long do you think he will stay?"

"I don't know," she said. "But because he is known by the people here, I mean the Hawaiians, he will very likely gather a large crowd. The population beyond Leahi is quite large, and people will very likely come down from the valleys behind Leahi."

I could see Pono's expression: that gazing out the door opening to the east. Leahi was not visible from this room, but I know he was visualizing it.

"Pono," I said. "Would you like to go there?"

"Yes," he said. "I think I should go now."

"Would you like company?"

"Yes, I would," he said. "If you would be so kind, I would appreciate that."

"I would like to come, too," MacFarlane said. "But I must stop at my place and let my wife know."

"And you Mrs. Searle?" I asked. "Do you think the hike would do you good?"

"Yes," she said, "if I may be included. I must warn you, it will be hot on the path through Waikīkī."

"Please," Pono said. "Come along, if you will. We shall endure the heat."

Thus did we prepare for our three-mile walk to Leahi. MacFarlane ran off to deposit his ledger-book at his house and tell his wife that we would be out during the late afternoon, and when he returned, we made our way outside toward the path.

And the walk was indeed hot. Because the path was wide, angling in to the shoreline, we were able to walk four abreast, talking on the way, stepping on our sharp shadows in the sand, the sound of the surf breaking offshore, and from time to time a pleasant breeze coming from the east. I suppose the conversation would have been more amiable and pleasant had Pono not shown his apparent reluctance to carry on with his search. I believe he was worried, the expression on his face one of a contemplative sadness, as if he were anticipating information that would make him sad. But we did talk, and he did respond: "This is the place where the squatting sickness happened," he said, holding his hand out to the sparse brush up from the beach. "I can't identify the exact place where I slept, but here is where so many died."

"Still makes me wonder," MacFarlane said, "that it happened only twenty years ago. I had not heard of it."

"Yes," Mrs. Searle said. "Those who died just weeks or even days ago are forgotten, too. This also makes me wonder. But I have heard of this squatting sickness."

We walked on. It was indeed hot, but the breeze kept the heat from being intolerable. I recall hoping as we walked for some good result, considering the sumtotal of Pono's tale. And I became somewhat unsettled, noting that the clouds above the mountains were bright and sumptuous, the day beautiful as so many days of death he had described were beautiful. Would this repeat itself too? It was as if he were attended throughout his life by curses, by repetitions of one kind of horror or another, to the point that the good result I hoped for seemed remote.

At length we had made our way across the beautiful bay to the foot of Leahi, its flanks folded with deep crevices, the brush all the way up to its rim brown from lack of water. We saw no sloop anchored offshore. Mrs. Searle speculated that it would be anchored farther around the crater's oceanside curve. "There are two paths, one inland around the back of the crater, and one along the ocean. I suggest we take the inland one, because it is likely that the people would be gathered in some open area around the back side."

"Very well," Pono said. And so did we continue our stroll. Here it became hotter, for the breeze that had refreshed us along the ocean was cut off by the crater itself. I had considered the port town as dry and dusty, but this region was as parched as a desert, the dirt under our feet puffing dust up with our steps. But as we made our way up the flank to work our way around to the back side, that breeze did once again refresh us. Then, from a higher vantage point on the flank of the back side of the crater, we saw in the distance a gathering of people, perhaps fifty or sixty natives sitting in the shade of some trees, and darker, clothed figures standing with them.

"That would be the man 'Iolana," Mrs. Searle said. "And the others with him are his assistants, in this case, I might warn you, rather large men ready to do what they must to protect him."

"Guards, then," I said.

"Yes," she said. She appeared unruffled from our long walk. In fact, she showed no evidence of perspiration, which I, unfortunately, felt on my back and in my armpits.

We stood there and studied this gathering for a few moments more, and then Pono looked at us uncertainly, and said, "Well then, shall we go?"

We walked on toward the group. Here it was cooler, and the place selected for the man's sermon, if that was what he was doing, seemed pleasant. As we approached, I saw those in attendance, and somewhat to my surprise, I saw three men in sailor's clothes, sitting at the back of the gathering, younger women sitting with them.

Pono walked toward the gathering closely watching the man speaking, his mouth open in wonder, and when we were close enough to make out individual features, to wit the guards, two rather formidable looking men, I suppose warriors in English clothing, and then the speaker himself, a Bible in one hand. I knew when I saw him clearly that he was Pono's son. The man was shorter; otherwise, every feature seemed an exact replica, but for black hair where Pono's had gone gray.

Pono stopped, and turned to us. "It is my son," he said. The look of wonder on his face was a study in itself, for it was crossed also by a perplexity, I suppose manifesting his fear that he might learn finally of the details of the death of his wife, or his other children. I was struck by a recognition then: the man's life had now come nearly full circle, but the last attachment where that circle would complete itself was but thirty paces from us, and indeed it appeared that he was reluctant to close it. I understood. And as if to corroborate this understanding, he looked up at the mountains to the north, at those billowing cumulous clouds, so white and beautifully formed that they might have come from the brush of a dreaming artist.

Mrs. Searle turned to look at him, her face suddenly stricken with sadness. "I should not have done this," she said. "I fear I have destroyed the last of your dreams."

"Ah, no," Pono said, and stepped to her and patted her on her shoulder.

"It was a mistake," she said.

"No, it wasn't," he said. "It is not a mistake to produce the truth."

MacFarlane looked at me. On his face, too, was that appearance of an anxious dread. He started to speak, and did not. Rather, he looked at Pono and shook his head.

"Well," Pono said, "we shall go and introduce ourselves."

He walked rather resolutely toward the gathering, the three of us following. When the men helping 'Iolana saw us they turned and took a couple of steps in our direction, as if anticipating some confrontation, and then 'Iolana turned, looked, and then went back to speaking in his language to the gathering.

The sailors at the back had risen, too, as if driven by curiosity about our presence here, so far from the port. They made their way around the gathering toward us. Indeed they seemed inebriated, for their walk was unsteady, their facial expressions flaccidly amiable.

Pono stopped perhaps ten paces from 'Iolana, his access to him blocked by the two men. "Aloha," he said, and then spoke a sentence to them in their language, the unheeding minister behind them continuing on, his hand raised, his voice strong and apparently commanding of the attention of the group. The exchange between Pono and the guards continued, the expressions on the guards' faces unmoved by whatever it was Pono was saying.

Then 'Iolana turned and snapped his Bible shut. He stepped rather brusquely between the two men and looked at us. "You," he said to us. "I am engaged here in my work." He appeared not to see Pono, or the resemblance the two of them bore. "What is it you want here?"

"'Iolana," Pono said. "I—"

"You people are from the port," 'Iolana went on. "You would walk all this way to cast stones at me?"

"'Iolana," Pono said.

"For you shall not succeed," 'Iolana said. "I am here to minister to these people, to whom was visited a pestilence, his punishment for their ignorance." He slapped the Bible in his hand. "This word is the truth and that port is a place of lies. You have brought your lies out here then."

"His English has improved," Mrs. Searle whispered to me. The two sailors from the back of the gathering approached, and stood watching us.

"Woman, if you would speak, then speak out," 'Iolana said. Then he seemed to relax, a smile crossing his face. "Yes," he said, and laughed. "I know your kind. I damn your kind, for you live in darkness, as do these poor souls sitting here. I speak to them to inform them thus: they are blinded by light and do not understand why. They have lived in darkness all this time, useless labor in the time before the Lord's light bathed us all, and you, of all people, your kind, allow it."

"Aye," one of the inebriated sailors said.

"Be gone," 'Iolana said to them, waving his hand. "Go back and sit in the shade, gentlemen, for you are too drunk to see anything." The half irritated, half amused expression on his face was so much like Pono's own expression that I was amazed.

The sailors looked at each other, as if wondering what to do next, and then ambled away. 'Iolana watched, and then snorted with an irritated shake of the head. "Fools," he said. He turned back to us. "Go to your Sodom over there," he said. "Leave me to my work."

Pono stepped toward him, which caused the guards to step toward Pono. "No," 'Iolana said. "Let the old man speak."

"I am your father," Pono said.

'Iolana made the sound of a rude guffaw. "God is my father," he said, and then seemed to inflate himself somewhat, as if the pronouncement angered him. "I have no father but the Lord. Go back to your Sodom."

"Sir," Mrs. Searle said, "can't you see the resemblance?"

"I am not speaking to you," 'Iolana said. "Why you are here interrupting this labor in his service I don't know. We are wasting good time here while they wait for the word." He turned back toward the gathering.

"'Iolana," Pono said, "I have one question."

"You would ask me questions," 'Iolana said, turning back to him. "You belong on your knees before me. You shall have all questions answered when you fall to your knees, sir."

Pono stared at him, his mouth open. He did not seem to know what to say. 'Iolana turned once again, and then did Mrs. Searle step to him, reaching out as if to touch his arm. The guards moved toward her, one putting his hand out as if to block her advance, and she slapped it away.

"Answer him!" she snapped. 'Iolana turned. She folded her arms, glared at one of the guards, and then looked back at 'Iolana. "The man wants a question answered, and you will answer it."

"Indeed," 'Iolana said. "And what makes you think you can force answers from me, woman?"

"Excuse me," I said.

Mrs. Searle raised her hand to me. "Please," she said. She turned back to 'Iolana. "If you think this is what his word means, to hold back on a simple question, then you're still in darkness, sir. Answer him."

"Tell him to accept the Lord," he said. "For I do not spend my time with those who will not accept Him."

Mrs. Searle drew a breath, and then blew it out. "You need to show a bit of Christian kindness now, sir. You are looking at your father—" And with his indrawn breath in preparation for speech she said, "We heard that before. Please, I know you are speaking on some other representative level. We need the truth. Where is your mother? Do you have sisters and brothers?"

"Ah, yes," he said. "I will no longer speak with them, for they refuse the light."

"Who refuses the light?" Mrs. Searle asked. "Please, tell us."

"She who bore me is dead to me now," he said. "She will not see the Lord's light, and her other issue remains a harlot begetting harlots. I reject them as my kin."

Mrs. Searle now had her hand to her mouth, and Pono had taken a step back, appearing breathless, the wonderment on his face a marvel to behold.

"Where are they?" Mrs. Searle whispered. "Please, you must say."

"Hilo," 'Iolana said. "In that savage southern district of the island. The lot of them in the mire there."

"Oh my," Mrs. Searle said. "Please, what are their names?"

"To me they have no names," 'Iolana said.

"Please, what are their names?" she asked. "You must tell us. In the name of God, you need to finish this for him."

"The old woman is Pekau, my sister Kaʻahupāhau," he said. "They live alone with my sister's children, some distance up the mountain flank from the bay." He then turned, brushed past his guards, and went back to stand over the gathering of people.

"Please," Mrs. Searle called to him. "What mountain flank? Tell him the name."

He sighed and turned. "The bay. There is a river that empties into it. They live up the river. They are known there."

"And a younger sister," she said. "Another sister?"

"No," he said. He went back to his gathering.

Perhaps we all stood absorbing this information in our own ways. I turned to look at Pono, but he had gone back some distance, and now sat upon a rock. Mrs. Searle looked at me, her face still held in that expression of profound wonder, if not a kind of shock, at this conversation. MacFarlane looked at Pono, holding his chin and blinking.

At length Pono looked up, but not at us. By instinct, I believe, he was looking to the southeast, for there in the district called Hilo, on the biggest island in that chain of fair islands, was the seeming end of his long journey.

There is little else to write here, except for our bidding Pono goodbye at the port, which took place on a muddy bank not fifty paces from that area where he told me that first battle-story. As it turned out, a small ship was scheduled to sail to the largest island in the chain the morning after Pono spoke to ʻIolana, a bit of good fortune capitalized upon by Mrs. Searle, who seemed anxious to get him to the end of his story. As for the narrative, I was satisfied with the distance it had come, and felt that the final closing of the circle into the very day we bade him goodbye was not necessary for my purposes.

MacFarlane and I stood there watching sailors fussing with the rigging of a sloop, some hundred yards into the bay, and then did Mrs. Searle appear holding her stained parasol above her head. She waved to us and approached, a busy, distracted expression on her face. "It leaves in less than a half hour," she said. "Where is he?"

I turned and pointed toward the flank of the mountain to the right of the valley above the port town, and said, "He usually approaches from there."

She looked, and then turned to the sloop. "Well, it's a fair-looking boat at the least. Where is the cutter?"

Then she did see it, bobbing at the shore.

"The sailors are at the store," MacFarlane said. "They'll return soon."

"Ah," I said, seeing a group of men approach, four of them. "There he is."

Two of the men were young, rather formidable-looking, both of them half-castes, I thought, one of them carrying a large duffel. The other was an old sailor, whom I had seen recently, that man Pono had addressed only days ago. The group stopped perhaps a hundred paces from us and talked, one of the young men handing the duffel to Pono, who continued speaking with them, and then nodded, turned and came in our direction.

"Aloha, gentlemen," said he, and then to Mrs. Searle, "and you ma'am." He turned then to me, and let the duffel fall from his shoulder. He placed it on the dirt and then looked at the sloop. "Matthew," he said, "I feel a bit irresponsible about not finishing the narrative."

"For my purposes it is finished," I said. "I thank you for it."

"As do I," Mrs. Searle said. She looked at the sloop. "I believe they're nearly ready. Here come the sailors." Two men made their way across the dirt, paused when a bit of wind raised the red dust to their faces, and then continued toward the cutter.

"Very well then," Pono said, and picked up the duffel. "I hope some day to see you again."

"We'll look for you," MacFarlane said.

"Yes," Mrs. Searle said. "I do hope you find her, sir."

"Perhaps," he said.

"Pono," I said. "Thank you once again."

He nodded and made his way to the cutter.

We stood there and watched as the men rowed out. Mrs. Searle, I believe, was concealing her sorrow at seeing him leave. MacFarlane turned and looked back at the lane between the shops, and there stood the three men, also watching.

"Matthew," he said. Then he laughed, his hand upon his head.

"What is it?" I asked.

"Is it your plan to take this story back to England and put it between covers?" he asked.

"I would think it proper," Mrs. Searle said, "even despite its somewhat salacious parts." Another blast of that wind sent a rolling cloud of red dust into our faces, and Mrs. Searle lowered her parasol against it.

The three men in the lane had now turned and left. I understood MacFarlane's question at that moment. "Indeed," I said, "what with the memory of the law, it would be fitting if we ceased speculating. But how old do you make the fellow out to be?"

"Pono's age or a bit older," MacFarlane said. "What was her name? The daughter of Ka'awela?"

"Haulani," I said. "You know, I am convinced also of another thing: your wife looked rather strangely at Pono when she first saw him. I misinterpreted the expression, I believe. I will think of your wife as the girl he saved."

Mrs. Searle now looked in the direction of the spot the three men had vacated. "Oh my," she said. "I think I understand."

"MacFarlane," I said, "we shall go to the store and I shall buy a bottle of their best brandy. Perhaps Mrs. Searle will join us?"

"Yes, I shall," she said.

MacFarlane laughed once again. "Strange," he said. "But what do you think? About the narrative showing up between covers? Is it a door we should leave open?"

"Yes," I said. "Let us leave it to our imaginations."

ACKNOWLEDGMENTS

The publisher thanks the following people who assisted with the publication of this novel:

Susan Bates MacMillan
Alissa MacMillan
Julia MacMillan
Laura M. Crago
Mark Panek

ALSO BY LŌʻIHI PRESS

Freelove, by Sia Figiel

Hawaiʻi: A Novel, by Mark Panek

The Idea Man, by Josh Green

Hawaiʻi Smiles: Island Stories, by Robert Barclay

www.ingramcontent.com/pod-product-compliance
Lightning Source LLC
Chambersburg PA
CBHW030537260626
47157CB00006B/2079